ALSO BY DEAN KOONTZ

Mr. Murder

Dragon Tears

Hideaway

Cold Fire

The Bad Place

Midnight

Lightning

Watchers

Strangers

Twilight Eyes

Darkfall

Phantoms

Whispers

The Mask

The Vision

The Face of Fear

Night Chills

Shattered

The Voice of the Night

The Servants of Twilight

The House of Thunder

Shadowfires

Winter Moon

The Door to December

DARK RIVERS
OF THE HEART

DARK RIVERS OF THE HEART

A NOVEL

DEAN KOONTZ

 Alfred A. Knopf NEW YORK 1994

THIS IS A BORZOI BOOK
PUBLISHED BY ALFRED A. KNOPF, INC.

Copyright © 1994 by Dean R. Koontz
All rights reserved under International and Pan-American
Copyright Conventions. Published in the United States by Alfred A.
Knopf, Inc., New York, and simultaneously in Canada by
Random House of Canada Limited, Toronto. Distributed
by Random House, Inc., New York.

Library of Congress Cataloging-in-Publication Data
Koontz, Dean R. (Dean Ray), [date]
Dark rivers of the heart : a novel / by Dean Koontz. — 1st ed.
p.   cm.
ISBN 0-679-42524-1
I. Title.
PS3561.O55D28   1994
813'.54—dc20   94-12090
CIP

Manufactured in the United States of America

FIRST TRADE EDITION

A signed limited edition of this book
has been privately printed by Charnel House.

To Gary and Zov Karamardian
for their valued friendship,
for being the kind of people who
make life a joy for others,
and for giving us a home
away from home.
We've decided to move in permanently
next week!

PART ONE

ON A STRANGE SEA

All of us are travelers lost,
our tickets arranged at a cost
unknown but beyond our means.
This odd itinerary of scenes
—enigmatic, strange, unreal—
leaves us unsure how to feel.
No postmortem journey is rife
with more mystery than life.

—*The Book of Counted Sorrows*

Tremulous skeins of destiny
flutter so ethereally
around me—but then I feel
its embrace is that of steel.

—*The Book of Counted Sorrows*

1

WITH THE WOMAN on his mind and a deep uneasiness in his heart, Spencer Grant drove through the glistening night, searching for the red door. The vigilant dog sat silently beside him. Rain ticked on the roof of the truck.

Without thunder or lightning, without wind, the storm had come in from the Pacific at the end of a somber February twilight. More than a drizzle but less than a downpour, it sluiced all the energy out of the city. Los Angeles and environs became a metropolis without sharp edges, urgency, or spirit. Buildings blurred into one another, traffic flowed sluggishly, and streets deliquesced into gray mists.

In Santa Monica, with the beaches and the black ocean to his right, Spencer stopped at a traffic light.

Rocky, a mixed breed not quite as large as a Labrador, studied the road ahead with interest. When they were in the truck—a Ford Explorer—Rocky sometimes peered out the side windows at the passing scene, though he was more interested in what lay before them.

Even when he was riding in the cargo area behind the front seats, the mutt rarely glanced out the rear window. He was skittish about watching the scenery recede. Maybe the motion made him dizzy in a way that oncoming scenery did not.

Or perhaps Rocky associated the dwindling highway behind them with the past. He had good reason not to dwell on the past.

So did Spencer.

Waiting for the traffic signal, he raised one hand to his face. He had a habit of meditatively stroking his scar when troubled, as another man might finger a strand of worry beads. The feel of it soothed him, perhaps because it was a reminder that he'd survived the worst terror he would ever know, that life could have no more surprises dark enough to destroy him.

The scar defined Spencer. He was a damaged man.

Pale, slightly glossy, extending from his right ear to his chin, the mark varied between one quarter and one half an inch in width. Extremes of cold and heat bleached it whiter than usual. In wintry air, though the thin ribbon of connective tissue contained no nerve endings, it felt like a hot wire laid on his face. In summer sun, the scar was cold.

The traffic signal changed from red to green.

The dog stretched his furry head forward in anticipation.

Spencer drove slowly southward along the dark coast, both hands on the wheel again. He nervously searched for the red door on the eastern side of the street, among the many shops and restaurants.

Though no longer touching the fault line in his face, he remained conscious of it. He was never unaware that he was branded. If he smiled or frowned, he would feel the scar cinching one half of his countenance. If he laughed, his amusement would be tempered by the tension in that inelastic tissue.

The metronomic windshield wipers timed the rhythm of the rain.

Spencer's mouth was dry, but the palms of his hands were damp. The tightness in his chest arose as much from anxiety as from the pleasant anticipation of seeing Valerie again.

He was of half a mind to go home. The new hope he harbored was surely the emotional equivalent of fool's gold. He was alone, and he was always going to be alone, except for Rocky. He was ashamed of this fresh glimmer of optimism, of the naivete it revealed, the secret need, the quiet desperation. But he kept driving.

Rocky couldn't know what they were searching for, but he chuffed softly when the red landmark appeared. No doubt he was responding to a subtle change in Spencer's mood at the sight of the door.

The cocktail lounge was between a Thai restaurant with steam-streaked windows and an empty storefront that had once been an art gallery. The windows of the gallery were boarded over, and squares of travertine were missing from the once elegant facade, as if the enterprise had not merely failed but been bombed out of business. Through the silver rain, a downfall of light at the lounge entrance revealed the red door that he remembered from the previous night.

Spencer hadn't been able to recall the name of the place. That lapse of memory now seemed willful, considering the scarlet neon above the entrance: THE RED DOOR. A humorless laugh escaped him.

After haunting so many barrooms over the years, he had ceased to notice enough differences, one from another, to be able to attach names to them. In scores of towns, those countless taverns were, in their essence, the same church confessional; sitting on a barstool instead of kneeling on a prie-dieu, he murmured the same admissions to strangers who were not priests and could not give him absolution.

His confessors were drunkards, spiritual guides as lost as he was. They could never tell him the appropriate penance he must do to find peace. Discussing the meaning of life, they were incoherent.

Unlike those strangers to whom he often quietly revealed his soul, Spencer had never been drunk. Inebriation was as dreadful for him to contemplate as was suicide. To be drunk was to relinquish control. Intolerable. Control was the only thing he had.

At the end of the block, Spencer turned left and parked on the secondary street.

He went to bars not to drink but to avoid being alone—and to tell his story to someone who would not remember it in the morning. He often nursed a beer or two through a long evening. Later, in his bedroom, after staring toward the hidden heavens, he would finally close his eyes only when the patterns of shadows on the ceiling inevitably reminded him of things he preferred to forget.

When he switched off the engine, the rain drummed louder than before—a cold sound, as chilling as the voices of dead children that sometimes called to him with wordless urgency in his worst dreams.

The yellowish glow of a nearby streetlamp bathed the interior of the truck, so Rocky was clearly visible. His large and expressive eyes solemnly regarded Spencer.

"Maybe this is a bad idea," Spencer said.

The dog craned his head forward to lick his master's right hand, which was still clenched around the wheel. He seemed to be saying that Spencer should relax and just do what he had come there to do.

As Spencer moved his hand to pet the mutt, Rocky bowed his head, not to make the backs of his ears or his neck more accessible to stroking fingers, but to indicate that he was subservient and harmless.

"How long have we been together?" Spencer asked the dog.

Rocky kept his head down, huddling warily but not actually trembling under his master's gentle hand.

"Almost two years," Spencer said, answering his own question. "Two years of kindness, long walks, chasing Frisbees on the beach, regular meals . . . and still sometimes you think I'm going to hit you."

Rocky remained in a humble posture on the passenger seat.

Spencer slipped one hand under the dog's chin, forced his head up. After briefly trying to pull away, Rocky ceased all resistance.

When they were eye-to-eye, Spencer said, "Do you trust me?"

The dog self-consciously looked away, down and to the left.

Spencer shook the mutt gently by the muzzle, commanding his attention again. "We keep our heads up, okay? Always proud, okay? Confident. Keep our heads up, look people in the eye. You got that?"

Rocky slipped his tongue between his half-clenched teeth and licked the fingers with which Spencer was gripping his muzzle.

"I'll interpret that as 'yes.' " He let go of the dog. "This cocktail lounge isn't a place I can take you. No offense."

In certain taverns, though Rocky was not a guide dog, he could lie at Spencer's feet, even sit on a stool, and no one would object to the violation of health laws. Usually a dog was the least of the infractions for which the joint would be cited if a city inspector happened to visit. The Red Door, however, still had pretensions to class, and Rocky wouldn't be welcome.

Spencer got out of the truck, slammed the door. He engaged the locks and security system with the remote control on his key chain.

He could not count on Rocky to protect the Explorer. This was one dog who would never scare off a determined car thief—unless the would-be thief suffered an extreme phobic aversion to having his hand licked.

After sprinting through the cold rain to the shelter of an awning that skirted the corner building, Spencer paused to look back.

Having moved onto the driver's seat, the dog stared out, nose pressed to the side window, one ear pricked, one ear drooping. His breath was fogging the glass, but he wasn't barking. Rocky never barked. He just stared, waited. He was seventy pounds of pure love and patience.

Spencer turned away from the truck and the side street, rounded the corner, and hunched his shoulders against the chilly air.

Judging by the liquid sounds of the night, the coast and all the works of civilization that stood upon it might have been merely ramparts of ice melting into the black Pacific maw. Rain drizzled off the awning, gurgled in gutters, and splashed beneath the tires of passing cars. At the threshold of audibility, more sensed than heard, the ceaseless rumble of surf announced the steady erosion of beaches and bluffs.

As Spencer was passing the boarded-up art gallery, someone spoke from the shadows in the deeply recessed entrance. The voice was as dry as the night was damp, hoarse and grating: "I know what you are."

Halting, Spencer squinted into the gloom. A man sat in the entryway, legs splayed, back against the gallery door. Unwashed and unbarbered, he seemed less a man than a heap of black rags saturated with so much organic filth that malignant life had arisen in it by spontaneous generation.

"I know what you are," the vagrant repeated softly but clearly.

A miasma of body odor and urine and the fumes of cheap wine rose out of the doorway.

The number of shambling, drug-addicted, psychotic denizens of the streets had increased steadily since the late seventies, when most of the mentally ill had been freed from sanitariums in the name of civil liberties and compassion. They roamed America's cities, championed by politicians but untended, an army of the living dead.

The penetrating whisper was as desiccated and eerie as the voice of a reanimated mummy. "*I know what you are.*"

The prudent response was to keep moving.

The paleness of the vagrant's face, above the beard and below the tangled hair, became dimly visible in the gloom. His sunken eyes were as bottomless as abandoned wells. "*I know what you are.*"

"Nobody knows," Spencer said.

Sliding the fingertips of his right hand along his scar, he walked past the shuttered gallery and the ruined man.

"*Nobody knows,*" whispered the vagrant. Perhaps his commentary on passersby, which at first had seemed eerily perceptive, even portentous, was nothing more than mindless repetition of the last thing he had heard from the most recent scornful citizen to reply to him. "*Nobody knows.*"

Spencer stopped in front of the cocktail lounge. Was he making a dreadful mistake? He hesitated with his hand on the red door.

Once more the hobo spoke from the shadows. Through the sizzle of the rain, his admonition now had the haunting quality of a static-shredded voice on the radio, speaking from a distant station in some far corner of the world. "*Nobody knows. . . .*"

Spencer opened the red door and went inside.

On a Wednesday night, no host was at the reservations podium in the vestibule. Maybe there wasn't a front man on Fridays and Saturdays, either. The joint wasn't exactly jumping.

The warm air was stale and filigreed with blue cigarette smoke. In the far left corner of the rectangular main room, a piano player under a spotlight worked through a spiritless rendition of "Tangerine."

Decorated in black and gray and polished steel, with mirrored walls, with Art Deco fixtures that cast overlapping rings of moody sapphire-blue light on the ceiling, the lounge once had recaptured a lost age with style. Now the upholstery was scuffed, the mirrors streaked. The steel was dull under a residue of old smoke.

Most tables were empty. A few older couples sat near the piano.

Spencer went to the bar, which was to the right, and settled on the stool at the end, as far from the musician as he could get.

The bartender had thinning hair, a sallow complexion, and watery gray eyes. His practiced politeness and pale smile couldn't conceal his boredom. He functioned with robotic efficiency and detachment, discouraging conversation by never making eye contact.

Two fiftyish men in suits sat farther along the bar, each alone, each frowning at his drink. Their shirt collars were unbuttoned, ties askew. They looked dazed, glum, as if they were advertising-agency executives who had been pink-slipped ten years ago but still got up every morning and dressed for success because they didn't know what else to do; maybe they came to The Red Door because it had been where they'd unwound after work, in the days when they'd still had hope.

The only waitress serving the tables was strikingly beautiful, half Vietnamese and half black. She wore the costume that she—and Valerie—had worn the previous evening: black heels, short black skirt, short-sleeved black sweater. Valerie had called her Rosie.

After fifteen minutes, Spencer stopped Rosie when she passed nearby with a tray of drinks. "Is Valerie working tonight?"

"Supposed to be," she said.

He was relieved. Valerie hadn't lied. He had thought perhaps she'd misled him, as a gentle way of brushing him off.

"I'm kinda worried about her," Rosie said.

"Why's that?"

"Well, the shift started an hour ago." Her gaze kept straying to his scar. "She hasn't called in."

"She's not often late?"

"Val? Not her. She's *organized.*"

"How long has she worked here?"

"About two months. She . . ." The woman shifted her gaze from the scar to his eyes. "Are you a friend of hers or something?"

"I was here last night. This same stool. Things were slow, so Valerie and I talked awhile."

"Yeah, I remember you," Rosie said, and it was obvious that she couldn't understand why Valerie had spent time with him.

He didn't look like any woman's dream man. He wore running shoes, jeans, a work shirt, and a denim jacket purchased at Kmart—essentially the same outfit that he'd worn on his first visit. No jewelry. His watch was a Timex. And the scar, of course. Always the scar.

"Called her place," Rosie said. "No answer. I'm worried."

"An hour late, that's not so much. Could've had a flat tire."

"In this city," Rosie said, her face hardening with anger that aged her ten years in an instant, "she could've been gang-raped, stabbed by some twelve-year-old punk wrecked on crack, maybe even shot dead by a carjacker in her own driveway."

"You're a real optimist, huh?"

"I watch the news."

She carried the drinks to a table at which sat two older couples whose expressions were more sour than celebratory. Having missed the new Puritanism that had captured many Californians, they were puffing furiously on cigarettes. They appeared to be afraid that the recent total ban on smoking in restaurants might be extended tonight to barrooms and homes, and that each cigarette might be their last.

While the piano player clinked through "The Last Time I Saw Paris," Spencer took two small sips of beer.

Judging by the palpable melancholy of the patrons in the bar, it might actually have been June 1940, with German tanks rolling down the Champs-Élysées, and with omens of doom blazing in the night sky.

A few minutes later, the waitress approached Spencer again. "I guess I sounded a little paranoid," she said.

"Not at all. I watch the news too."

"It's just that Valerie is so . . ."

"Special," Spencer said, finishing her thought so accurately that she stared at him with a mixture of surprise and vague alarm, as if she suspected that he had actually read her mind.

"Yeah. Special. You can know her only a week, and . . . well, you want her to be happy. You want good things to happen to her."

It doesn't take a week, Spencer thought. One evening.

Rosie said, "Maybe because there's this hurt in her. She's been hurt a lot."

"How?" he asked. "Who?"

She shrugged. "It's nothing I know, nothing she ever said. You just feel it about her."

He also had sensed a vulnerability in Valerie.

"But she's tough too," Rosie said. "Gee, I don't know why I'm so jumpy about this. It's not like I'm her big sister. Anyway, everyone's got a right to be late now and then."

The waitress turned away, and Spencer sipped his warm beer.

The piano player launched into "It Was a Very Good Year," which Spencer disliked even when Sinatra sang it, though he was a Sinatra fan. He knew the song was intended to be reflective in tone, even mildly pensive; however, it seemed terribly sad to him, not the sweet wistfulness of an older man reminiscing about the women he had loved, but the grim ballad of someone at the bitter end of his days, looking back on a barren life devoid of deep relationships.

He supposed that his interpretation of the lyrics was an expression of his fear that decades hence, when his own life burned out, he would fade away in loneliness and remorse.

He checked his watch. Valerie was now an hour and a half late.

The waitress's uneasiness had infected him. An insistent image rose in his mind's eye: Valerie's face, half concealed by a spill of dark hair and a delicate scrollwork of blood, one cheek pressed against the floor, eyes wide and unblinking. He knew his concern was irrational. She was merely late for work. There was nothing ominous about that. Yet, minute by minute, his apprehension deepened.

He put his unfinished beer on the bar, got off the stool, and walked through the blue light to the red door and into the chilly night, where the sound of marching armies was only the rain beating on the canvas awnings.

As he passed the art gallery doorway, he heard the shadow-wrapped vagrant weeping softly. He paused, affected.

Between strangled sounds of grief, the half-seen stranger whispered the last thing Spencer had said to him earlier: *"Nobody knows . . . nobody knows. . . ."* That short declaration evidently had acquired a personal and profound meaning for him, because he spoke the two words not in the tone in which Spencer had spoken but with quiet, intense anguish. *"Nobody knows."*

Though Spencer knew that he was a fool for funding the wretch's further self-destruction, he fished a crisp ten-dollar bill from his wallet. He leaned into the gloomy entryway, into the fetid stink that the hobo exuded, and held out the money. "Here, take this."

The hand that rose to the offering was either clad in a dark glove or exceedingly filthy; it was barely discernible in the shadows. As the bill was plucked out of Spencer's fingers, the vagrant keened thinly: *"Nobody . . . nobody . . ."*

"You'll be all right," Spencer said sympathetically. "It's only life. We all get through it."

"It's only life, we all get through it," the vagrant whispered.

Plagued once more by the mental image of Valerie's dead face, Spencer hurried to the corner, into the rain, to the Explorer.

Through the side window, Rocky watched him approaching. As Spencer opened the door, the dog retreated to the passenger seat.

Spencer got in the truck and pulled the door shut, bringing with him the smell of damp denim and the ozone odor of the storm. "You miss me, killer?"

Rocky shifted his weight from side to side a couple of times, and he tried to wag his tail even while sitting on it.

As he started the engine, Spencer said, "You'll be pleased to hear that I didn't make an ass of myself in there."

The dog sneezed.

"But only because she didn't show up."

The dog cocked his head curiously.

Putting the car in gear, popping the hand brake, Spencer said, "So instead of quitting and going home while I'm ahead of the game, what do you think I'm going to do now? Hmmm?"

Apparently the dog didn't have a clue.

"I'm going to poke in where it's none of my business, give myself a second chance to screw up. Tell me straight, pal, do you think I've lost my mind?"

Rocky merely panted.

Pulling the truck away from the curb, Spencer said, "Yeah, you're right. I'm a basket case."

He headed directly for Valerie's house. She lived ten minutes from the bar.

The previous night, he had waited with Rocky in the Explorer, outside The Red Door, until two o'clock in the morning, and had followed Valerie when she drove home shortly after closing time. Because of his surveillance training, he knew how to tail a subject discreetly. He was confident that she hadn't spotted him.

He was not equally confident, however, about his ability to explain to her—or to himself—*why* he had followed her. After one evening of conversation with her, periodically interrupted by her attention to the few customers in the nearly deserted lounge, Spencer was overcome by the desire to know everything about her. Everything.

In fact, it was more than a desire. It was a need, and he was compelled to satisfy it.

Although his intentions were innocent, he was mildly ashamed of his budding obsession. The night before, he had sat in the Explorer, across the street from her house, staring at her lighted windows; all were covered with translucent drapes, and on one occasion her shadow played briefly across the folds of cloth, like a spirit glimpsed in candlelight at a séance. Shortly before three-thirty in the morning, the last light went out. While Rocky lay curled in sleep on the backseat, Spencer had remained on watch another hour, gazing at the dark house, wondering what books Valerie read, what she enjoyed doing on her days off, what her parents were like, where she had lived as a child, what she dreamed about when she was contented, and what shape her nightmares took when she was disturbed.

Now, less than twenty-four hours later, he headed to her place again, with a fine-grain anxiety abrading his nerves. She was late for work. Just late. His excessive concern told him more than he cared to know about the inappropriate intensity of his interest in this woman.

Traffic thinned as he drove farther from Ocean Avenue into residential neighborhoods. The languorous, liquid glimmer of wet blacktop fostered a false impression of movement, as if every street might be a lazy river easing toward its own far delta.

~

Valerie Keene lived in a quiet neighborhood of stucco and clapboard bungalows built in the late forties. Those two- and three-bedroom homes offered more charm than space: trellised front porches, from which hung great capes of bougainvillea; decorative shutters flanking windows; interestingly scalloped or molded or carved fascia boards under the eaves; fanciful rooflines; deeply recessed dormers.

Because Spencer didn't want to draw attention to himself, he drove past the woman's place without slowing. He glanced casually to the right, toward her dark bungalow on the south side of the block. Rocky mimicked him, but the dog seemed to find nothing more alarming about the house than did his master.

At the end of the block, Spencer turned right and drove south. The next few streets to the right were cul-de-sacs. He passed them by. He didn't want to park on a dead-end street. That was a trap. At the next main avenue, he hung a right again and parked at the curb in a neighborhood similar to the one in which Valerie lived. He turned off the thumping windshield wipers but not the engine.

He still hoped that he might regain his senses, put the truck in gear, and go home.

Rocky looked at him expectantly. One ear up. One ear down.

"I'm not in control," Spencer said, as much to himself as to the curious dog. "And I don't know why."

Rain sluiced down the windshield. Through the film of rippling water, the streetlights shimmered.

He sighed and switched off the engine.

When he'd left home, he'd forgotten an umbrella. The short dash to and from The Red Door had left him slightly damp, but the longer walk back to Valerie's house would leave him soaked.

He was not sure why he hadn't parked in front of her place. Training, perhaps. Instinct. Paranoia. Maybe all three.

Leaning past Rocky and enduring a warm, affectionate tongue in his ear, Spencer retrieved a flashlight from the glove compartment and tucked it in a pocket of his jacket.

"Anybody messes with the truck," he said to the dog, "you rip the bastard's guts out."

As Rocky yawned, Spencer got out of the Explorer. He locked it with the remote control as he walked away and turned north at the corner. He didn't bother running. Regardless of his pace, he would be soaked before he reached the bungalow.

The north–south street was lined with jacarandas. They would have provided little cover even when fully dressed with leaves and cascades of purple blossoms. Now, in winter, the branches were bare.

Spencer was sodden by the time he reached Valerie's street, where the jacarandas gave way to huge Indian laurels. The aggressive roots of the trees had cracked and canted the sidewalk; however, the canopy of branches and generous foliage held back the cold rain.

The big trees also prevented most of the yellowish light of the sodium-vapor streetlamps from reaching even the front lawns of the properties along that cloistered avenue. The trees and shrubs around the houses also were mature; some were overgrown. If any residents were looking out windows, they would most likely be unable to see him through the screen of greenery, on the deeply shadowed sidewalk.

As he walked, he scanned the vehicles parked along the street. As far as he could tell, no one was sitting in any of them.

A Mayflower moving van was parked across the street from Valerie's bungalow. That was convenient for Spencer, because the large truck blocked those neighbors' view. No men were working at the van; the move-in or move-out must be scheduled for the morning.

Spencer followed the front walkway and climbed three steps to the porch. The trellises at both ends supported not bougainvillea but night-blooming jasmine. Though it wasn't at its seasonal peak, the jasmine sweetened the air with its singular fragrance.

The shadows on the porch were deep. He doubted that he could even be seen from the street.

In the gloom, he had to feel along the door frame to find the button. He could hear the doorbell ringing softly inside the house.

He waited. No lights came on.

The flesh creped on the back of his neck, and he sensed that he was being watched.

Two windows flanked the front door and looked onto the porch. As far as he could discern, the dimly visible folds of the draperies on the other side of the glass were without any gaps through which an observer could have been studying him.

He looked back at the street. Sodium-yellow light transformed the downpour into glittering skeins of molten gold. At the far curb, the moving van stood half in shadows, half in the glow of the streetlamps. A late-model Honda and an older Pontiac were parked at the nearer curb. No pedestrians. No passing traffic. The night was silent except for the incessant rataplan of the rain.

He rang the bell once more.

The crawling feeling on the nape of his neck didn't subside. He put a hand back there, half convinced that he would find a spider negotiating his rain-slick skin. No spider.

As he turned to the street again, he thought that he saw furtive movement from the corner of his eye, near the back of the Mayflower van. He stared for half a minute, but nothing moved in the windless night except torrents of golden rain falling to the pavement as straight as if they were, in fact, heavy droplets of precious metal.

He knew why he was jumpy. He didn't belong here. Guilt was twisting his nerves.

Facing the door again, he slipped his wallet out of his right hip pocket and removed his MasterCard.

Though he could not have admitted it to himself until now, he would have been disappointed if he had found lights on and Valerie at home. He *was* concerned about her, but he doubted that she was lying, either injured or dead, in her darkened house. He was not psychic: The image of her bloodstained face, which he'd conjured in his mind's eye, was only an excuse to make the trip here from The Red Door.

His need to know everything about Valerie was perilously close to an adolescent longing. At the moment, his judgment was not sound.

He frightened himself. But he couldn't turn back.

By inserting the MasterCard between the door and jamb, he could pop the spring latch. He assumed there would be a deadbolt as well, because Santa Monica was as crime-ridden as any town in or around Los Angeles, but maybe he would get lucky.

He was luckier than he hoped: The front door was unlocked. Even the spring latch wasn't fully engaged. When he twisted the knob, the door clicked open.

Surprised, stricken by another tremor of guilt, he glanced back at the street again. The Indian laurels. The moving van. The cars. The rain, rain, rain.

He went inside. He closed the door and stood with his back against it, dripping on the carpet, shivering.

At first the room in front of him was unrelievedly black. After a while, his vision adjusted enough for him to make out a drapery-covered window—and then a second and a third—illuminated only by the faint gray ambient light of the night beyond.

For all that he could see, the blackness before him might have harbored a crowd, but he knew that he was alone. The house felt not merely unoccupied but deserted, abandoned.

Spencer took the flashlight from his jacket pocket. He hooded the beam with his left hand to ensure, as much as possible, that it would not be noticed by anyone outside.

The beam revealed an unfurnished living room, barren from wall to wall. The carpet was milk-chocolate brown. The unlined draperies were beige. The two-bulb light fixture in the ceiling could probably be operated by one of the three switches beside the front door, but he didn't try them.

His soaked athletic shoes and socks squished as he crossed the living room. He stepped through an archway into a small and equally empty dining room.

Spencer thought of the Mayflower van across the street, but he didn't believe that Valerie's belongings were in it or that she had moved out of the bungalow since four-thirty the previous morning, when he'd left his watch post in front of her house and returned to his own bed. Instead, he suspected that she had never actually moved *in*. The carpet was not marked by the pressure lines and foot indentations of furniture; no tables, chairs, cabinets, credenzas, or floor lamps had stood on it recently. If Valerie had lived in the bungalow during the two months that she had worked at The Red Door, she evidently hadn't furnished it and hadn't intended to call it home for any great length of time.

To the left of the dining room, through an archway half the size of the first, he found a small kitchen with knotty-pine cabinets and red Formica countertops. Unavoidably, he left wet shoe prints on the gray tile floor.

Stacked beside the two-basin sink were a single dinner plate, a bread plate, a soup bowl, a saucer, and a cup—all clean and ready for use. One drinking glass stood with the dinnerware. Next to the glass lay a dinner fork, a knife, and a spoon, which were also clean.

He shifted the flashlight in his right hand, splaying a couple of fingers across the lens to partly suppress the beam, thus freeing his left hand to touch the drinking glass. He traced the rim with his fingertips. Even if the glass had been washed since Valerie had taken a drink from it, her lips had once touched the rim.

He had never kissed her. Perhaps he never would.

That thought embarrassed him, made him feel foolish, and forced him to consider, yet again, the impropriety of his obsession with this woman. He didn't belong here. He was trespassing not merely in her home but in her life. Until now, he had lived an honest life, if not always with undeviating respect for the law. Upon entering her house, however, he had crossed a sharp line that had scaled away his innocence, and what he had lost couldn't be regained.

Nevertheless, he did not leave the bungalow.

When he opened kitchen drawers and cabinets, he found them empty except for a combination bottle-and-can opener. The woman owned no plates or utensils other than those stacked beside the sink.

Most of the shelves in the narrow pantry were bare. Her stock of food was limited to three cans of peaches, two cans of pears, two cans of pineapple rings, one box of a sugar substitute in small blue packets, two boxes of cereal, and a jar of instant coffee.

The refrigerator was nearly empty, but the freezer compartment was well stocked with gourmet microwave dinners.

By the refrigerator was a door with a mullioned window. The four panes were covered by a yellow curtain, which he pushed aside far enough to see a side porch and a dark yard hammered by rain.

He allowed the curtain to fall back into place. He wasn't interested in the outside world, only in the interior spaces where Valerie had breathed the air, taken her meals, and slept.

As Spencer left the kitchen, the rubber soles of his shoes squeaked on the wet tiles. Shadows retreated before him and huddled in the corners while darkness crowded his back again.

He could not stop shivering. The damp chill in the house was as penetrating as that of the February air outside. The heat must have been off all day, which meant that Valerie had left early.

On his cold face, the scar burned.

A closed door was centered in the back wall of the dining room. He opened it and discovered a narrow hallway that led about fifteen feet to the left and fifteen to the right. Directly across the hall, another door stood half open; beyond, he glimpsed a white tile floor and a bathroom sink.

As he was about to enter the hall, he heard sounds other than the monotonous and hollow drumming of the rain on the roof. A thump and a soft scrape.

He immediately switched off the flashlight. The darkness was as perfect as that in any carnival fun house just before flickering strobe lights revealed a leering, mechanical corpse.

At first the sounds had seemed stealthy, as if a prowler outside had slipped on the wet grass and bumped against the house. However, the longer Spencer listened, the more he became convinced that the source of noise might have been distant rather than nearby, and that he might have heard nothing more than a car door slamming shut, out on the street or in a neighbor's driveway.

He switched on the flashlight and continued his search in the bathroom. A bath towel, a hand towel, and a washcloth hung on the rack. A half-used bar of Ivory lay in the plastic soap dish, but the medicine cabinet was empty.

To the right of the bathroom was a small bedroom, as unfurnished as the rest of the house. The closet was empty.

The second bedroom, to the left of the bath, was larger than the first, and it was obviously where she had slept. An inflated air mattress lay on the floor. Atop the mattress were a tangle of sheets, a single wool blanket, and a pillow. The bifold closet doors stood open, revealing wire hangers dangling from an unpainted wooden pole.

Although the rest of the bungalow was unadorned by artwork or decoration, something was fixed to the center of the longest wall in that bedroom. Spencer approached it, directed the light at it, and saw a full-color, closeup photograph of a cockroach. It seemed to be a page from a book, perhaps an entomology text, because the caption under the photograph was in dry academic English. In closeup, the roach was about six inches long. It had been fixed to the wall with a single large nail that had been driven through the center of the beetle's carapace. On the floor, directly below the photograph, lay the hammer with which the spike had been pounded into the plaster.

The photograph had not been decoration. Surely, no one would hang a picture of a cockroach with the intention of beautifying a bedroom. Furthermore, the use of a nail—rather than pushpins or staples or Scotch tape—implied that the person wielding the hammer had done so in considerable anger.

Clearly, the roach was meant to be a symbol for something else.

Spencer wondered uneasily if Valerie had nailed it there. That seemed unlikely. The woman with whom he'd talked the previous evening at The Red Door had seemed uncommonly gentle, kind, and all but incapable of serious anger.

If not Valerie—who?

As Spencer moved the flashlight beam across the glossy paper, the roach's carapace glistened as if wet. The shadows of his fingers, which half blocked the lens, created the illusion that the beetle's spindly legs and antennae jittered briefly.

Sometimes, serial killers left behind signatures at the scenes of their crimes to identify their work. In Spencer's experience, that could be anything from a specific playing card, to a Satanic symbol carved in some part of the victim's anatomy, to a single word or a line of poetry scrawled in blood upon a wall. The nailed photo had the feeling of such a signature, although it was stranger than anything he had seen or about which he had read in the hundreds of case studies with which he was familiar.

A faint nausea rippled through him. He had encountered no signs of violence in the house, but he had not yet looked in the attached single-car garage. Perhaps he would find Valerie on that cold slab of concrete, as he had seen her earlier in his mind's eye: lying with one side of her face pressed to the floor, unblinking eyes open wide, a scrollwork of blood obscuring some of her features.

He knew that he was jumping to conclusions. These days, the average American routinely lived in anticipation of sudden, mindless violence, but Spencer was more sensitized to the dark possibilities of modern life than were most people. He had endured pain and terror that had marked him in many ways, and his tendency now was to expect savagery as surely as sunrises and sunsets.

As he turned away from the photograph of the roach, wondering if he dared to investigate the garage, the bedroom window shattered inward, and a small black object hurtled through the draperies. At a glimpse, tumbling and airborne, it resembled a grenade.

Reflexively, he switched off the flashlight even as broken glass was still falling. In the gloom, the grenade thumped softly against the carpet.

Before Spencer could turn away, he was hit by the explosion. No flash of light accompanied it, only ear-shattering sound—and hard shrapnel snapping into him from his shins to his forehead. He cried out. Fell. Twisted. Writhed. Pain in his legs, hands, face. His torso was protected by his denim jacket. But his hands, God, his hands. He wrung his burning hands. Hot pain. Pure torment. How many fingers lost, bones shattered? Jesus, Jesus, his hands were spastic with pain yet half numb, so he couldn't assess the damage.

The worst of it was the fiery agony in his forehead, cheeks, the left corner of his mouth. Excruciating. Desperate to quell the pain, he pressed his hands to his face. He was afraid of what he would find, of the damage he would feel, but his hands throbbed so fiercely that his sense of touch wasn't trustworthy.

How many new scars if he survived—how many pale and puckered cicatricial welts or red keloid monstrosities from hairline to chin?

Get out, get away, find help.

He kicked-crawled-clawed-twitched like a wounded crab through the darkness. Disoriented and terrified, he nevertheless scrambled in the right direction, across a floor now littered with what seemed to be small marbles, into the bedroom doorway. He clambered to his feet.

He figured he was caught in a gang war over disputed turf. Los Angeles in the nineties was more violent than Chicago during Prohibition. Modern youth gangs were more savage and better armed than the Mafia, pumped up with drugs and their own brand of racism, as cold-blooded and merciless as snakes.

Gasping for breath, feeling blindly with aching hands, he stumbled into the hall. Pain coruscated through his legs, weakening him and testing his balance. Staying on his feet was as difficult as it would have been in a revolving fun-house barrel.

Windows shattered in other rooms, followed by a few muffled explosions. The hallway was windowless, so he wasn't hit again.

In spite of his confusion and fear, Spencer realized he didn't smell blood. Didn't taste it. In fact, he wasn't bleeding.

Suddenly he understood what was happening. Not a gang war. The shrapnel hadn't cut him, so it wasn't actually shrapnel. Not marbles, either, littering the floor. Hard rubber pellets. From a sting grenade. Only law-enforcement agencies had sting grenades. He had used them himself. Seconds ago a SWAT team of some kind must have initiated an assault on the bungalow, launching the grenades to disable any occupants.

The moving van had no doubt been covert transport for the assault force. The movement he had seen at the back of it, out of the corner of his eye, hadn't been imaginary after all.

He should have been relieved. The assault was an action of the local police, the Drug Enforcement Administration, the FBI, or another law-enforcement organization. Apparently he had stumbled into one of their operations. He knew the drill. If he dropped to the floor, facedown, arms extended over his head, hands spread to prove they were empty, he would be fine; he wouldn't be shot; they would handcuff him, question him, but they wouldn't harm him further.

Except that he had a big problem: He didn't belong in that bungalow. He was a trespasser. From their point of view, he might even be a burglar. To them, his explanation for being there would seem lame at best. Hell, they would think it was crazy. He didn't really understand it himself—why he was so stricken with Valerie, why he had needed to know about her, why he had been bold enough and stupid enough to enter her house.

He didn't drop to the floor. On wobbly legs, he staggered through the tunnel-black hall, sliding one hand along the wall.

The woman was mixed up in something illegal, and at first the authorities would think that he was involved as well. He would be taken into custody, detained for questioning, maybe even booked on suspicion of aiding and abetting Valerie in whatever she had done.

They would find out who he was.

The news media would dredge up his past. His face would be on television, in newspapers and magazines. He had lived many years in blessed anonymity, his new name unknown, his appearance altered by time, no longer recognizable. But his privacy was about to be stolen. He would be center ring at the circus again, harassed by reporters, whispered about every time he went out in public.

No. Intolerable. He couldn't go through that again. He would rather die.

They were cops of some kind, and he was innocent of any serious offense; but they were not on his side right now. Without meaning to destroy him, they would do so simply by exposing him to the press.

More shattering glass. Two explosions.

The officers on the SWAT team were taking no chances, as if they thought they were up against people crazed on PCP or something worse.

Spencer had reached the midpoint of the hall, where he stood between two doorways. A dim grayness beyond the right-hand door: the dining room. On his left: the bathroom.

He stepped into the bathroom, closed the door, hoping to buy time to think.

The stinging in his face, hands, and legs was slowly subsiding. Rapidly, repeatedly, he clenched his hands, then relaxed them, trying to improve the circulation and work off the numbness.

From the far end of the house came a wood-splintering crash, hard enough to make the walls shudder. It was probably the front door slamming open or going down.

Another crash. The kitchen door.

They were in the house.

They were coming.

No time to think. He had to move, relying on instinct and on military training that was, he hoped, at least as extensive as that of the men who were hunting him.

In the back wall of the cramped room, above the bathtub, the blackness was broken by a rectangle of faint gray light. He stepped into the tub and, with both hands, quickly explored the frame of that small window. He wasn't convinced that it was big enough to provide a way out, but it was the only possible route of escape.

If it had been fixed or jalousied, he would have been trapped. Fortunately, it was a single pane that opened inward from the top on a heavy-duty piano hinge. Collapsible elbow braces on both sides clicked softly when fully extended, locking the window open.

He expected the faint squeak of the hinge and the click of the braces to elicit a shout from someone outside. But the unrelenting drone of the rain screened what sounds he made. No alarm was raised.

Spencer gripped the window ledge and levered himself into the opening. Cold rain spattered his face. The humid air was heavy with the fecund smells of saturated earth, jasmine, and grass.

The backyard was a tapestry of gloom, woven exclusively from shades of black and graveyard grays, washed by rain that blurred its details. At least one man—more likely two—from the SWAT team had to be covering the rear of the house. However, though Spencer's vision was keen, he could not force any of the interwoven shadows to resolve into a human form.

For a moment his upper body seemed wider than the frame, but he hunched his shoulders, twisted, wriggled, and scraped through the opening. The ground was a short drop from the window. He rolled once on the wet grass and then lay flat on his stomach, head raised, surveying the night, still unable to spot any adversaries.

In the planting beds and along the property line, the shrubbery was overgrown. Several old fig trees, long untrimmed, were mighty towers of foliage.

Glimpsed between the branches of those mammoth ficuses, the heavens were not black. The lights of the sprawling metropolis reflected off the bellies of the eastbound storm clouds, painting the vault of the night with deep and sour yellows that, toward the oceanic west, faded into charcoal gray.

Though familiar to Spencer, the unnatural color of the city sky filled him with a surprising and superstitious dread, for it seemed to be a malevolent firmament under which men were meant to die—and to the sight of which they might wake in Hell. It was a mystery how the yard could remain unlit under that sulfurous glow, yet he could have sworn that it grew blacker the longer he squinted at it.

The stinging in his legs subsided. His hands still ached but not disablingly, and the burning in his face was less intense than it had been.

Inside the dark house, an automatic weapon stuttered briefly, spitting out several rounds. One of the cops must be trigger-happy, shooting at shadows or ghosts. Curious. Hair-trigger nerves were uncommon among special-forces officers.

Spencer scuttled across the sodden grass to the shelter of a nearby triple-trunk ficus. Rising to his feet, with his back against the bark, he surveyed the lawn, the shrubs, and the line of trees along the rear property wall, half convinced he should make a break for it, but also half convinced that he would be spotted and brought down if he stepped into the open.

Flexing his hands to work off the pain, he considered climbing into the web of wood above him and hiding in the higher bowers. Useless, of course. They would find him in the tree, because they would not admit to his escape until they had searched every shadow and cloak of greenery, both high and low.

In the bungalow: voices, a door slamming, not even a pretense of stealth and caution any longer, not after the precipitous gunfire. Still no lights.

Time was running out.

Arrest, revelation, the glare of videocam lights, reporters shouting questions. Intolerable.

He silently cursed himself for being so indecisive.

Rain rattled the leaves above.

Newspaper stories, magazine spreads, the hateful past alive again, the gaping stares of thoughtless strangers to whom he would be the walking, breathing equivalent of a spectacular train wreck.

His booming heart counted cadence for the ever quickening march of his fear.

He could not move. Paralyzed.

Paralysis served him well, however, when a man dressed in black crept past the tree, holding a weapon that resembled an Uzi. Though he was no more than two strides from Spencer, the guy was focused on the house, ready if his quarry crashed through a window into the night, unaware that the very fugitive he sought was within reach. Then the man saw the open window at the bathroom, and he froze.

Spencer was moving before his target began to turn. Anyone with SWAT-team training—whether local cop or federal agent—would not go down easily. The only chance of taking the guy quickly and quietly was to hit him hard while he was in the grip of surprise.

Spencer rammed his right knee into the cop's crotch, putting everything he had behind it, trying to lift the guy off the ground.

Some special-forces officers wore jockstraps with aluminum cups on every enter-and-subdue operation, as surely as they wore bullet-resistant Kevlar body jackets or vests. This one was unprotected. He exhaled explosively, a sound that wouldn't have carried ten feet in the rainy night.

Even as Spencer was driving his knee upward, he seized the automatic weapon with both hands, wrenching it violently clockwise. It twisted out of the other man's grasp before he could convulsively squeeze off a burst of warning fire.

The gunman fell backward on the wet grass. Spencer dropped atop him, carried forward by momentum.

Though the cop tried to cry out, the agony of that intimate blow had robbed him of his voice. He couldn't even inhale.

Spencer could have slammed the weapon—a compact submachine gun, judging by the feel of it—into his adversary's throat, crushing his windpipe, asphyxiating him on his own blood. A blow to the face would have shattered the nose and driven splinters of bone into the brain.

But he didn't want to kill or seriously injure anyone. He just needed time to get the hell out of there. He hammered the gun against the cop's temple, half checking the blow but knocking the poor bastard unconscious.

The guy was wearing night-vision goggles. The SWAT team was conducting a night stalk with full technological assistance, which was why no lights had come on in the house. They had the vision of cats, and Spencer was the mouse.

He rolled onto the grass, rose into a crouch, clutching the submachine gun in both hands. It was an Uzi: He recognized the shape and heft of it. He swept the muzzle left and right, anticipating the charge of another adversary. No one came at him.

Perhaps five seconds had passed since the man in black had crept past the ficus tree.

Spencer sprinted across the lawn, away from the bungalow, into flowers and shrubs. Greenery lashed his legs. Woody azaleas poked his calves, snagged his jeans.

He dropped the Uzi. He wasn't going to shoot at anyone. Even if it meant being taken into custody and exposed to the news media, he would surrender rather than use the gun.

He waded through the shrubs, between two trees, past a eugenia with phosphorescent white blossoms, and reached the property wall.

He was as good as gone. If they spotted him now, they wouldn't shoot him in the back. They'd shout a warning, identify themselves, order him to freeze, and come after him, but they wouldn't shoot.

The stucco-sheathed, concrete-block wall was six feet high, capped with bull-nose bricks that were slippery with rain. He got a grip, pulled himself up, scrabbling at the stucco with the toes of his athletic shoes.

As he slid onto the top of the wall, belly against the cold bricks, and drew up his legs, gunfire erupted behind him. Bullets smacked into the concrete blocks, so close that chips of stucco sprayed his face.

Nobody shouted a goddamned warning.

He rolled off the wall into the neighboring property, and automatic weapons chattered again—a longer burst than before.

Submachine guns in a residential neighborhood. Craziness. What the hell kind of cops were these?

He fell into a tangle of rosebushes. It was winter; the roses had been pruned; even in the colder months, however, the California climate was sufficiently mild to encourage some growth, and thorny trailers snared his clothes, pricked his skin.

Voices, flat and strange, muffled by the static of the rain, came from beyond the wall: "This way, back here, come on!"

Spencer sprang to his feet and flailed through the rose brambles. A spiny trailer scraped the unscarred side of his face and curled around his head as if intent on fitting him with a crown, and he broke free only at the cost of punctured hands.

He was in the backyard of another house. Lights in some of the ground-floor rooms. A face at a rain-jeweled window. A young girl. Spencer had the terrible feeling that he'd be putting her in mortal jeopardy if he didn't get out of there before his pursuers arrived.

∽

After negotiating a maze of yards, block walls, wrought-iron fences, cul-de-sacs, and service alleys, never sure if he had lost his pursuers or if they were, in fact, at his heels, Spencer found the street on which he had parked the Explorer. He ran to it and jerked on the door.

Locked, of course.

He fumbled in his pockets for the keys. Couldn't find them. He hoped to God he hadn't lost them along the way.

Rocky was watching him through the driver's window. Apparently he found Spencer's frantic search amusing. He was grinning.

Spencer glanced back along the rain-swept street. Deserted.

One more pocket. Yes. He pressed the deactivating button on the key chain. The security system issued an electronic bleat, the locks popped open, and he clambered into the truck.

As he tried to start the engine, the keys slipped through his wet fingers and fell to the floor.

"Damn!"

Reacting to his master's fear, no longer amused, Rocky huddled timidly in the corner formed by the passenger seat and the door. He made a thin, interrogatory sound of concern.

Though Spencer's hands tingled from the rubber pellets that had stung them, they were no longer numb. Yet he fumbled after the keys for what seemed an age.

Maybe it was best to lie on the seats, out of sight, and keep Rocky below window level. Wait for the cops to come . . . and go. If they arrived just as he was pulling away from the curb, they would suspect he was the one who had been in Valerie's house, and they would stop him one way or another.

On the other hand, he had stumbled into a major operation with a lot of manpower. They weren't going to give up easily. While he was hiding in the truck, they might cordon off the area and initiate a house-to-house search. They would also inspect parked cars as best they could, peering in windows; he would be pinned by a flashlight beam, trapped in his own vehicle.

The engine started with a roar.

He popped the hand brake, shifted gears, and pulled away from the curb, switching on windshield wipers and headlights as he went. He had parked near the corner, so he hung a U-turn.

He glanced at the rearview mirror, the side mirror. No armed men in black uniforms.

A couple of cars sped through the intersection, heading south on the other avenue. Plumes of spray fanned behind them.

Without even pausing at the stop sign, Spencer turned right and entered the southbound flow of traffic, away from Valerie's neighborhood. He resisted the urge to tramp the accelerator into the floorboards. He couldn't risk being stopped for speeding.

"What the hell?" he asked shakily.

The dog replied with a soft whine.

"What's she done, why're they after her?"

Water trickled down his brow into his eyes. He was soaked. He shook his head, and a spray of cold water flew from his hair, spattering the dashboard, the upholstery, and the dog.

Rocky flinched.

Spencer turned up the heater.

He drove five blocks and made two changes of direction before he began to feel safe.

"Who is she? What the *hell* has she done?"

Rocky had adopted his master's change of mood. He no longer huddled in the corner. Having resumed his vigilant posture in the center of his seat, he was wary but not fearful. He divided his attention between the storm-drenched city ahead and Spencer, favoring the former with guarded anticipation and the latter with a cocked-head expression of puzzlement.

"Jesus, what was I doing there anyway?" Spencer wondered aloud.

Though bathed in hot air from the dashboard vents, he continued to shiver. Part of his chill had nothing to do with being rain-soaked, and no quantity of heat could dispel it.

"Didn't belong there, shouldn't have gone. Do *you* have a clue what I was doing in that place, pal? Hmmmm? Because I sure as hell don't. That was *stupid*."

He reduced speed to negotiate a flooded intersection, where an armada of trash was adrift on the dirty water.

His face felt hot. He glanced at Rocky.

He had just lied to the dog.

Long ago he had sworn never to lie to himself. He kept that oath only somewhat more faithfully than the average drunkard kept his New Year's Eve resolution never to allow demon rum to touch his lips again. In fact, he probably indulged in less self-delusion and self-deception than most people did, but he could not claim, with a straight face, that he invariably told himself the truth. Or even that he invariably wanted to hear it. What it came down to was that he *tried* always to be truthful with himself, but he often accepted a half-truth and a wink instead of the real thing—and he could live comfortably with whatever omission the wink implied.

But he never lied to the dog.

Never.

Theirs was the only entirely honest relationship that Spencer had ever known; therefore, it was special to him. No. More than merely special. Sacred.

Rocky, with his hugely expressive eyes and guileless heart, with his body language and his soul-revealing tail, was incapable of deceit. If he'd been able to talk, he would have been perfectly ingenuous because he was a perfect innocent. Lying to the dog was worse than lying to a small child. Hell, he wouldn't have felt as bad if he had lied to God, because God unquestionably expected less of him than did poor Rocky.

Never lie to the dog.

"Okay," he said, braking for a red traffic light, "so I know why I went to her house. I know what I was looking for."

Rocky regarded him with interest.

"You want me to say it, huh?"

The dog waited.

"That's important to you, is it—for me to say it?"

The dog chuffed, licked his chops, cocked his head.

"All right. I went to her house because—"

The dog stared.

"—because she's a very nice looking woman."

The rain drummed. The windshield wipers thumped.

"Okay, she's pretty but she's not gorgeous. It isn't her looks. There's just . . . something about her. She's special."

The idling engine rumbled.

Spencer sighed and said, "Okay, I'll be straight this time. Right to the heart of it, huh? No more dancing around the edges. I went to her house because—"

Rocky stared.

"—because I wanted to find a life."

The dog looked away from him, toward the street ahead, evidently satisfied with that final explanation.

Spencer thought about what he had revealed to himself by being honest with Rocky. *I wanted to find a life.*

He didn't know whether to laugh at himself or weep. In the end, he did neither. He just moved on, which was what he'd been doing for at least the past sixteen years.

The traffic light turned green.

With Rocky looking ahead, only ahead, Spencer drove home through the streaming night, through the loneliness of the vast city, under a strangely mottled sky that was as yellow as a rancid egg yolk, as gray as crematorium ashes, and fearfully black along one far horizon.

2

AT NINE O'CLOCK, after the fiasco in Santa Monica, eastbound on the freeway, returning to his hotel in Westwood, Roy Miro noticed a Cadillac stopped on the shoulder of the highway. Serpents of red light from its emergency flashers wriggled across his rain-streaked windshield. The rear tire on the driver's side was flat.

A woman sat behind the steering wheel, evidently waiting for help. She appeared to be the only person in the car.

The thought of a woman alone in such circumstances, in *any* part of greater Los Angeles, worried Roy. These days, the City of Angels wasn't the easygoing place it had once been—and the hope of actually finding anyone living even an approximation of an angelic existence was slim indeed. Devils, yes: Those were relatively easy to locate.

He stopped on the shoulder ahead of the Cadillac.

The downpour was heavier than it had been earlier. A wind had sailed in from the ocean. Silvery sheets of rain, billowing like the transparent canvases of a ghost ship, flapped through the darkness.

He plucked his floppy-brimmed vinyl hat off the passenger seat and squashed it down on his head. As always in bad weather, he was wearing a raincoat and galoshes. In spite of his precautionary dress, he was going to get soaked, but he couldn't in good conscience drive on as if he'd never seen the stranded motorist.

As Roy walked back to the Cadillac, the passing traffic cast an all but continuous spray of filthy water across his legs, pasting his pants to his skin. Well, the suit needed to be dry-cleaned anyway.

When he reached the car, the woman did not put down her window. Staring warily at him through the glass, she reflexively checked the door locks to be sure they were engaged.

He wasn't offended by her suspicion. She was merely wise to the ways of the city and understandably skeptical of his intentions.

He raised his voice to be heard through the closed window: "You need some help?"

She held up a cellular phone. "Called a service station. They said they'll send somebody."

Roy glanced toward the oncoming traffic in the eastbound lanes. "How long have they kept you waiting?"

After a hesitation, she said exasperatedly, "Forever."

"I'll change the tire. You don't have to get out or give me your keys. This car—I've driven one like it. There's a trunk-release knob. Just pop it, so I can get the jack and the spare."

"You could get hurt," she said.

The narrow shoulder offered little safety margin, and the fast-moving traffic *was* unnervingly close. "I've got flares," he said.

Turning away before she could object, Roy hurried to his own car and retrieved all six flares from the roadside-emergency kit in the trunk. He strung them out along the freeway for fifty yards behind the Cadillac, closing off most of the nearest traffic lane.

If a drunk driver barreled out of the night, of course, no precautions would be sufficient. And these days it seemed that sober motorists were outnumbered by those who were high on booze or drugs.

It was an age plagued by social irresponsibility—which was why Roy tried to be a good Samaritan whenever an opportunity arose. If everyone lit just one little candle, what a bright world it would be: He really believed in that.

The woman had released the trunk lock. The lid was ajar.

Roy Miro was happier than he had been all day. Battered by wind and rain, splashed by the passing traffic, he labored with a smile. The more hardship involved, the more rewarding the good deed. As he struggled with a tight lug nut, the wrench slipped and he skinned one knuckle; instead of cursing, he began to whistle while he worked.

When the job was done, the woman lowered the window two inches, so he didn't have to shout. "You're all set," he said.

Sheepishly, she began to apologize for having been so wary of him, but he interrupted to assure her that he understood.

She reminded Roy of his mother, which made him feel even better about helping her. She was attractive, in her early fifties, perhaps twenty years older than Roy, with auburn hair and blue eyes. His mother had been a brunette with hazel eyes, but this woman and his mother had in common an aura of gentleness and refinement.

"This is my husband's business card," she said, passing it through the gap in the window. "He's an accountant. If you need any advice along those lines, no charge."

"I haven't done all that much," Roy said, accepting the card.

"These days, running into someone like you, it's a miracle. I'd have called Sam instead of that damn service station, but he's working late at a client's. Seems we work around the clock these days."

"This recession," Roy sympathized.

"Isn't it ever going to end?" she wondered, rummaging in her purse for something more.

He cupped the business card in his hand to protect it from the rain, turning it so the red glow of the nearest flare illuminated the print. The husband had an office in Century City, where rents were high; no wonder the poor guy was working late to remain afloat.

"And here's my card," the woman said, extracting it from her purse and passing it to him.

Penelope Bettonfield. Interior Designer. 213-555-6868.

She said, "I work out of my home. Used to have an office, but this dreadful recession . . ." She sighed and smiled up at him through the partly open window. "Anyway, if I can ever be of help . . ."

He fished one of his own cards from his wallet and passed it in to her. She thanked him again, closed her window, and drove away.

Roy walked back along the highway, clearing the flares off the pavement so they would not continue to obstruct traffic.

In his car once more, heading for his hotel in Westwood, he was exhilarated to have lit his one little candle for the day. Sometimes he wondered if there was any hope for modern society, if it was going to spiral down into a hell of hatred and crime and greed—but then he encountered someone like Penelope Bettonfield, with her sweet smile and her aura of gentleness and refinement, and he found it possible to be hopeful again. She was a caring person who would repay his kindness to her by being kind to someone else.

In spite of Mrs. Bettonfield, Roy's fine mood didn't last. By the time he left the freeway for Wilshire Boulevard and drove into Westwood, a sadness had crept over him.

He saw signs of social devolution everywhere. Spray-painted graffiti defaced the retaining walls of the freeway exit ramp and obscured the directions on a couple of traffic signs, in an area of the city previously spared such dreary vandalism. A homeless man, pushing a shopping cart full of pathetic possessions, trudged through the rain, his face expressionless, as if he were a zombie shuffling along the aisles of a Kmart in Hell.

At a stoplight, in the lane beside Roy, a car full of fierce-looking young men—skinheads, each with one glittering earring—glared at him malevolently, perhaps trying to decide if he looked like a Jew. They mouthed obscenities with care, to be sure he could read their lips.

He passed a movie theater where the films were all swill of one kind or another. Extravaganzas of violence. Seamy tales of raw sex. Films from big studios, with famous stars, but swill nonetheless.

Gradually, his impression of his encounter with Mrs. Bettonfield changed. He remembered what she'd said about the recession, about the long hours that she and her husband were working, about the poor economy that had forced her to close her design office and run her faltering business from her home. She was such a nice lady. He was saddened to think that she had financial worries. Like all of them, she was a victim of the system, trapped in a society that was awash in drugs and guns but that was bereft of compassion and commitment to high ideals. She deserved better.

By the time he reached his hotel, the Westwood Marquis, Roy was in no mood to go to his room, order a late dinner from room service, and turn in for the night—which was what he'd been planning to do. He drove past the place, kept going to Sunset Boulevard, turned left, and just cruised in circles for a while.

Eventually he parked at the curb two blocks from UCLA, but he didn't switch off the engine. He clambered across the gearshift into the passenger seat, where the steering wheel would not interfere with his work.

His cellular phone was fully charged. He unplugged it from the cigarette lighter.

From the backseat, he retrieved an attaché case. He opened it on his lap, revealing a compact computer with a built-in modem. He plugged it into the cigarette lighter and switched it on. The display screen lit. The basic menu appeared, from which he made a selection.

He married the cellular phone to the modem, and then called the direct-access number that would link his terminal with the dual Cray supercomputers in the home office. In seconds, the connection was made, and the familiar security litany began with three words that appeared on his screen: WHO GOES THERE?

He typed his name: ROY MIRO.

YOUR IDENTIFICATION NUMBER?

Roy provided it.

YOUR PERSONAL CODE PHRASE?

POOH, he typed, which he had chosen as his code because it was the name of his favorite fictional character of all time, the honey-seeking and unfailingly good-natured bear.

RIGHT THUMBPRINT PLEASE.

A two-inch-square white box appeared in the upper-right quadrant of the blue screen. He pressed his thumb in the indicated space and waited while sensors in the monitor modeled the whorls in his skin by directing microbursts of intense light at them and then contrasting the comparative shadowiness of the troughs to the marginally more reflective ridges. After a minute, a soft beep indicated that the scanning was completed. When he lifted his thumb, a detailed black-line image of his print filled the center of the white box. After an additional thirty seconds, the print vanished from the screen; it had been digitized, transmitted by phone to the home-office computer, electronically compared to his print on file, and approved.

Roy had access to considerably more sophisticated technology than the average hacker with a few thousand dollars and the address of the nearest Computer City store. Neither the electronics in his attaché case nor the software that had been installed in the machine could be purchased by the general public.

A message appeared on the display: ACCESS TO MAMA IS GRANTED.

Mama was the name of the home-office computer. Three thousand miles away on the East Coast, all her programs were now available for Roy's use, through his cellular phone. A long menu appeared on the screen before him. He scrolled through, found a program titled LOCATE, and selected it.

He typed in a telephone number and requested the street address at which it was located.

While he waited for Mama to access phone company records and trace the listing, Roy studied the storm-lashed street. At that moment, no pedestrians or moving cars were in sight. Some houses were dark, and the lights of the others were dimmed by the seemingly eternal torrents of rain. He could almost believe that a strange, silent apocalypse had transpired, eliminating all human life on earth while leaving the works of civilization untouched.

A real apocalypse *was* coming, he supposed. Sooner than later, a great war: nation against nation or race against race, religions clashing violently or ideology battling ideology. Humanity was drawn to turmoil and self-destruction as inevitably as the earth was drawn to complete its annual revolution of the sun.

His sadness deepened.

Under the telephone number on the video display, the correct name appeared. The address, however, was listed as unpublished by request of the customer.

Roy instructed the home-office computer to access and search the phone company's electronically stored installation and billing records to find the address. Such an invasion of private-sector data was illegal, of course, without a court order, but Mama was exceedingly discreet. Because all the computer systems in the national telephone network were already in Mama's directory of previously violated entities, she was able to enter any of them virtually instantaneously, explore at will, retrieve whatever was requested, and disengage without leaving the slightest trace that she had been there; Mama was a ghost in their machines.

In seconds, a Beverly Hills address appeared on the screen.

He cleared the screen and then asked Mama for a street map of Beverly Hills. She supplied it after a brief hesitation. Seen in its entirety, it was too compressed to be read.

Roy typed in the address that he'd been given. The computer filled the screen with the quadrant that was of interest to him, and then with a quarter of that quadrant. The house was only a couple of blocks south of Wilshire Boulevard, in the less prestigious "flats" of Beverly Hills, and easy to find.

He typed POOH OUT, which disengaged his portable terminal from Mama in her cool, dry bunker in Virginia.

∽

The large brick house—which was painted white, with hunter-green shutters—stood behind a white picket fence. The front lawn featured two enormous bare-limbed sycamores.

Lights were on inside, but only at the back of the house and only on the first floor.

Standing at the front door, sheltered from the rain by a deep portico supported on tall white columns, Roy could hear music inside: a Beatles number, "When I'm Sixty-four." He was thirty-three; the Beatles were before his time, but he liked their music because much of it embodied an endearing compassion.

Softly humming along with the lads from Liverpool, Roy slipped a credit card between the door and the jamb. He worked it upward until it forced open the first—and least formidable—of the two locks. He wedged the card in place to hold the simple spring latch out of the niche in the striker plate.

To open the heavy-duty deadbolt, he needed a more sophisticated tool than a credit card: a Lockaid lock-release gun, sold only to law-enforcement agencies. He slipped the thin pick of the gun into the key channel, under the pin tumblers, and pulled the trigger. The flat steel spring in the Lockaid caused the pick to jump upward and to lodge some of the pins at the shear line. He had to pull the trigger half a dozen times to fully disengage the lock.

The snapping of hammer against spring and the clicking of pick against pin tumblers were not thunderous sounds, by any measure, but he was grateful for the cover provided by the music. "When I'm Sixty-four" ended as he opened the door. Before his credit card could fall, he caught it, froze, and waited for the next song. To the opening bars of "Lovely Rita," he stepped across the threshold.

He put the lock-release gun on the floor, to the right of the entrance. Quietly, he closed the door behind him.

The foyer welcomed him with gloom. He stood with his back against the door, letting his eyes adjust to the shadows.

When he was confident that he would not blindly knock over any furniture, he proceeded from room to room, toward the light at the back of the house.

He regretted that his clothes were so saturated and his galoshes so dirty. He was probably making a mess of the carpet.

She was in the kitchen, at the sink, washing a head of lettuce, her back to the swinging door through which he entered. Judging by the vegetables on the cutting board, she was preparing a salad.

Easing the door shut behind him, hoping to avoid startling her, he debated whether or not to announce himself. He wanted her to know that it was a concerned friend who had come to comfort her, not a stranger with sick motives.

She turned off the running water and placed the lettuce in a plastic colander to drain. Wiping her hands on a dish towel, turning away from the sink, she finally discovered him as "Lovely Rita" drew to an end.

Mrs. Bettonfield looked surprised but not, in the first instant, afraid—which was, he knew, a tribute to his appealing, soft-featured face. He was slightly pudgy, with dimples, and had skin so beardless that it was almost as smooth as a boy's. With his twinkling blue eyes and warm smile, he would make a convincing Santa Claus in another thirty years. He believed that his kindheartedness and his genuine love of people were also apparent, because strangers usually warmed to him more quickly than a merry face alone could explain.

While Roy still was able to believe that her wide-eyed surprise would fade into a smile of welcome rather than a grimace of fear, he raised the Beretta 93-R and shot her twice in the chest. A silencer was screwed to the barrel; both rounds made only soft popping sounds.

Penelope Bettonfield dropped to the floor and lay motionless on her side, with her hands still entangled in the dish towel. Her eyes were open, staring across the floor at his wet, dirty galoshes.

The Beatles began "Good Morning, Good Morning." It must be the *Sgt. Pepper* album.

He crossed the kitchen, put the pistol on the counter, and crouched beside Mrs. Bettonfield. He pulled off one of his supple leather gloves and placed his fingertips to her throat, searching for a pulse in her carotid artery. She was dead.

One of the two rounds was so perfectly placed that it must have pierced her heart. Consequently, with circulation halted in an instant, she had not bled much.

Her death had been a graceful escape: quick and clean, painless and without fear.

He pulled on his right glove again, then rubbed gently at her neck where he had touched it. Gloved, he had no concern that his fingerprints might be lifted off the body by laser technology.

Precautions must be taken. Not every judge and juror would be able to grasp the purity of his motives.

He closed the lid over her left eye and held it in place for a minute or so, to be sure that it would stay shut.

"Sleep, dear lady," he said with a mixture of affection and regret, as he also closed the lid over her right eye. "No more worrying about finances, no more working late, no more stress and strife. You were too good for this world."

It was both a sad and a joyous moment. Sad, because her beauty and elegance no longer brightened the world; nevermore would her smile lift anyone's spirits; her courtesy and consideration would no longer counter the tides of barbarity washing over this troubled society. Joyous, because she would never again be afraid, spill tears, know grief, feel pain.

"Good Morning, Good Morning" gave way to the marvelously bouncy, syncopated reprise of "Sgt. Pepper's Lonely Hearts Club Band," which was better than the first rendition of the song at the start of the album and which seemed a suitably upbeat celebration of Mrs. Bettonfield's passage to a better world.

Roy pulled out one of the chairs from the kitchen table, sat, and removed his galoshes. He rolled up the damp and muddy legs of his trousers as well, determined to cause no more mess.

The reprise of the album theme song was short, and by the time he got to his feet again, "A Day in the Life" had begun. That was a singularly melancholy piece, too somber to be in sync with the moment. He had to shut it off before it depressed him. He was a sensitive man, more vulnerable than most to the emotional effects of music, poetry, fine paintings, fiction, and the other arts.

He found the central music system in a long wall of beautifully crafted mahogany cabinets in the study. He stopped the music and searched two drawers that were filled with compact discs. Still in the mood for the Beatles, he selected *A Hard Day's Night* because none of the songs on that album was downbeat.

Singing along to the title track, Roy returned to the kitchen, where he lifted Mrs. Bettonfield off the floor. She was more petite than she had seemed when he'd been talking with her through the car window. She weighed no more than a hundred and five pounds, with slender wrists, a swan neck, and delicate features. Roy was deeply touched by the woman's fragility, and he bore her in his arms with more than mere care and respect, almost with reverence.

Nudging light switches with his shoulder, he carried Penelope Bettonfield to the front of the house, upstairs, along the hallway, checking door by door until he found the master bedroom. There, he placed her gently on a chaise lounge.

He folded back the quilted bedspread and then the bedclothes, revealing the bottom sheet. He plumped the pillows, which were in Egyptian-cotton shams trimmed with cut-work lace as lovely as any he had ever seen.

He took off Mrs. Bettonfield's shoes and put them in her closet. Her feet were as small as those of a girl.

Leaving her fully dressed, he carried Penelope to the bed and put her down on her back, with her head elevated on two pillows. He left the spread folded at the bottom of the bed, but he drew the blanket cover, blanket, and top sheet over her breasts. Her arms remained free.

With a brush that he found in the master bathroom, he smoothed her hair. The Beatles were singing "If I Fell" when he began to groom her, but they were well into "I'm Happy Just to Dance with You" by the time her lustrous auburn locks were perfectly arranged around her lovely face.

After switching on the bronze floor lamp that stood beside the chaise lounge, he turned off the harsher ceiling light. Soft shadows fell across the recumbent woman, like the enfolding wings of angels who had come to carry her away from this vale of tears and into a higher land of eternal peace.

He went to the Louis XVI vanity, removed its matching chair, and put it beside the bed. He sat next to Mrs. Bettonfield, stripped off his gloves, and took one of her hands in both of his. Her flesh was cooling but still somewhat warm.

He couldn't linger for long. There was much yet to do and not a lot of time in which to do it. Nevertheless, he wanted to spend a few minutes of quality time with Mrs. Bettonfield.

While the Beatles sang "And I Love Her" and "Tell Me Why," Roy Miro tenderly held his late friend's hand and took a moment to appreciate the exquisite furniture, the paintings, the art objects, the warm color scheme, and the array of fabrics in different but wonderfully complementary patterns and textures.

"It's so very unfair that you had to close your shop," he told Penelope. "You were a fine interior designer. You really were, dear lady. You really were."

The Beatles sang.

Rain beat upon the windows.

Roy's heart swelled with emotion.

3

Rocky recognized the route home. Periodically, as they passed one landmark or another, he chuffed softly with pleasure.

Spencer lived in a part of Malibu that was without glamour but that had its own wild beauty.

All the forty-room Mediterranean and French mansions, the ultramodern cliff-side dwellings of tinted glass and redwood and steel, the Cape Cod cottages as large as ocean liners, the twenty-thousand-square-foot Southwest adobes with authentic lodgepole ceilings and authentic twenty-seat personal screening rooms with THX sound, were on the beaches, on the bluffs above the beaches—and inland of the Pacific Coast Highway, on hills with a view of the sea.

Spencer's place was east of any home that *Architectural Digest* would choose to photograph, halfway up an unfashionable and sparsely populated canyon. The two-lane blacktop was textured by patches atop patches and by numerous cracks courtesy of the earthquakes that regularly quivered through the entire coast. A pipe-and-chain-link gate, between a pair of mammoth eucalyptuses, marked the entrance to his two-hundred-yard-long gravel driveway.

Wired to the gate was a rusted sign with fading red letters: DANGER / ATTACK DOG. He had fixed it there when he first purchased the place, long before Rocky had come to live with him. There had been no dog then, let alone one trained to kill. The sign was an empty threat, but effective. No one ever bothered him in his retreat.

The gate was not electrically operated. He had to get out in the rain to unlock it and to relock it after he'd driven through.

With only one bedroom, a living room, and a large kitchen, the structure at the end of the driveway was not a house, really, but a cabin. The cedar-clad exterior, perched on a stone foundation to foil termites, weathered to a lustrous silver gray, might have appeared shabby to an unappreciative eye; to Spencer it was beautiful and full of character in the wash of the Explorer's headlights.

The cabin was sheltered—surrounded, shrouded, *encased*—by a eucalyptus grove. The trees were red gums, safe from the Australian beetles that had been devouring California blue gums for more than a decade. They had not been topped since Spencer had bought the place.

Beyond the grove, brush and scrub oak covered the canyon floor and the steep slopes to the ridges. Summer through autumn, leeched of moisture by dry Santa Ana winds, the hills and the ravines became tinder. Twice in eight years, firefighters had ordered Spencer to evacuate, when blazes in neighboring canyons might have swept down on him as mercilessly as judgment day. Wind-driven flames could move at express-train speeds. One night they might overwhelm him in his sleep. But the beauty and privacy of the canyon justified the risk.

At various times in his life, he had fought hard to stay alive, but he was not afraid to die. Sometimes he even embraced the thought of going to sleep and never waking. When fears of fire troubled him, he worried not about himself but about Rocky.

That Wednesday night in February, the burning season was months away. Every tree and bush and blade of wild grass dripped rain and seemed as if it would be forever impervious to fire.

The house was cold. It could be heated by a big river-rock fireplace in the living room, but each room also had its own in-wall electric heater. Spencer preferred the dancing light, the crackle, and the smell of a log fire, but he switched on the heaters because he was in a hurry.

After changing from his damp clothes into a comfortable gray jogging suit and athletic socks, he brewed a pot of coffee. For Rocky, he set out a bowl of orange juice.

The mutt had many peculiarities besides a taste for orange juice. For one thing, though he enjoyed going for walks during the day, he had none of a dog's usual frisky interest in the nocturnal world, preferring to keep at least a window between himself and the night; if he *had* to go outside after sunset, he stayed close to Spencer and regarded the darkness with suspicion. Then there was Paul Simon. Rocky was indifferent to most music, but Simon's voice enchanted him; if Spencer put on a Simon album, especially *Graceland*, Rocky would sit in front of the speakers, staring intently, or pace the floor in lazy, looping patterns—off the beat, lost in reverie—to "Diamonds on the Soles of Her Shoes" or "You Can Call Me Al." Not a doggy thing to do. Less doggy still was his bashfulness about bodily functions, for he wouldn't make his toilet if watched; Spencer had to turn his back before Rocky would get down to business.

Sometimes Spencer thought that the dog, having suffered a hard life until two years ago and having had little reason to find joy in a canine's place in the world, wanted to be a human being.

That was a big mistake. People were more likely to live a dog's life, in the negative sense of the phrase, than were most dogs.

"Greater self-awareness," he'd told Rocky on a night when sleep wouldn't come, "doesn't make a species any happier, pal. If it did, we'd have fewer psychiatrists and barrooms than you dogs have—and it's not that way, is it?"

Now, as Rocky lapped at the juice in the bowl on the kitchen floor, Spencer carried a mug of coffee to the expansive L-shaped desk in one corner of the living room. Two computers with large hard-disk capacities, a full-color laser printer, and other pieces of equipment were arrayed from one end of the work surface to the other.

That corner of the living room was his office, though he had not held a real job in ten months. Since leaving the Los Angeles Police Department—where, during his last two years, he'd been on assignment to the California Multi-Agency Task Force on Computer Crime—he had spent several hours a day on-line with his own computers.

Sometimes he researched subjects of interest to him, through Prodigy and Genie. More often, however, he explored ways to gain unapproved access to private and government computers that were protected by sophisticated security programs.

Once entry was achieved, he was engaged in illegal activity. He never destroyed any company's or agency's files, never inserted false data. Still, he was guilty of trespassing in private domains.

He could live with that.

He was not seeking material rewards. His compensation was knowledge—and the occasional satisfaction of righting a wrong.

Like the Beckwatt case.

The previous December, when a serial child molester—Henry Beckwatt—was to be released from prison after serving less than five years, the California State Parole Board had refused, in the interest of prisoners' rights, to divulge the name of the community in which he would be residing during the term of his parole. Because Beckwatt had beaten some of his victims and expressed no remorse, his pending release raised anxiety levels in parents statewide.

Taking great pains to cover his tracks, Spencer had first gained entry to the Los Angeles Police Department's computers, stepped from there to the state attorney general's system in Sacramento, and from there into the parole board's computer, where he finessed the address to which Beckwatt would be paroled. Anonymous tips to a few reporters forced the parole board to delay action until a secret new placement could be worked out. During the following five weeks, Spencer exposed three more addresses for Beckwatt, shortly after each was arranged.

Although officials had been in a frenzy to uncover an imagined snitch within the parole system, no one had wondered, at least not publicly, if the leak had been from their electronic-data files, sprung by a clever hacker. Finally admitting defeat, they paroled Beckwatt to an empty care-taker's house on the grounds of San Quentin.

In a couple of years, when his period of post-prison supervision ended, Beckwatt would be free to prowl again, and he would surely destroy more children psychologically if not physically. For the time being, however, he was unable to settle into a lair in the middle of a neighborhood of unsus-pecting innocents.

If Spencer could have discovered a way to access God's computer, he would have tampered with Henry Beckwatt's destiny by giving him an immediate and mortal stroke or by walking him into the path of a run-away truck. He wouldn't have hesitated to ensure the justice that modern society, in its Freudian confusion and moral paralysis, found difficult to impose.

He was not a hero, not a scarred and computer-wielding cousin of Bat-man, not out to save the world. Mostly, he sailed cyberspace—that eerie dimension of energy and information within computers and computer networks—simply because it fascinated him as much as Tahiti and far Tor-tuga fascinated some people, enticed him in the way that the moon and Mars enticed the men and women who became astronauts.

Perhaps the most appealing aspect of that other dimension was the po-tential for exploration and discovery that it offered—*without direct human interaction.* When Spencer avoided computer billboards and other user-to-user conversations, cyberspace was an uninhabited universe, created by human beings yet strangely devoid of them. He wandered through vast structures of data, which were infinitely more grand than the pyramids of Egypt, the ruins of ancient Rome, or the rococo hives of the world's great cities—yet saw no human face, heard no human voice. He was Columbus without shipmates, Magellan walking alone across electronic highways and through metropolises of data as unpopulated as ghost towns in the Nevada wastelands.

Now, he sat before one of his computers, switched it on, and sipped coffee while it went through its start-up procedures. These included the Norton AntiVirus program, to be sure that none of his files had been con-taminated by a destructive bug during his previous venture into the na-tional data webs. The machine was uninfected.

The first telephone number that he entered was for a service offering twenty-four-hour-a-day stock market quotations. In seconds, the con-nection was made, and a greeting appeared on his computer screen: WELCOME TO WORLDWIDE STOCK MARKET INFORMATION, INC.

Using his subscriber ID, Spencer requested information about Japa-nese stocks. Simultaneously he activated a parallel program that he had designed himself and that searched the open phone line for the subtle electronic signature of a listening device. Worldwide Stock Market Information was a legitimate data service, and no police agency had reason to eavesdrop on its lines; therefore, evidence of a tap would indicate that his own telephone was being monitored.

Rocky padded in from the kitchen and rubbed his head against Spencer's leg. The mutt couldn't have finished his orange juice so quickly. He was evidently more lonely than thirsty.

Keeping his attention on the video display, waiting for an alarm or an all-clear, Spencer reached down with one hand and gently scratched behind the dog's ears.

Nothing he had done as a hacker could have drawn the attention of the authorities, but caution was advisable. In recent years, the National Security Agency, the Federal Bureau of Investigation, and other organizations had established computer-crime divisions, all of which zealously prosecuted offenders.

Sometimes they were almost criminally zealous. Like every overstaffed government agency, each computer-crime project was eager to justify its ever increasing budget. Every year a greater number of arrests and convictions was required to support the contention that electronic theft and vandalism were escalating at a frightening rate. Consequently, from time to time, hackers who had stolen nothing and who had wrought no destruction were brought to trial on flimsy charges. They weren't prosecuted with any intention that, by their example, they would deter crime; their convictions were sought merely to create the statistics that ensured higher funding for the project.

Some of them were sent to prison.

Sacrifices on the altars of bureaucracy.

Martyrs to the cyberspace underground.

Spencer was determined never to become one of them.

As the rain rattled against the cabin roof and the wind stirred a whispery chorus of lamenting ghosts from the eucalyptus grove, he waited, with his gaze fixed on the upper-right corner of the video screen. In red letters, a single word appeared: CLEAR.

No taps were in operation.

After logging off Worldwide Stock Market, he dialed the main computer of the California Multi-Agency Task Force on Computer Crime. He entered that system by a deeply concealed back door that he had inserted prior to resigning as second in command of the unit.

Because he was accepted at the system-manager level (the highest security clearance), all functions were available to him. He could use the task force's computer as long as he wanted, for whatever purpose he wished, and his presence wouldn't be observed or recorded.

He had no interest in their files. He used their computer only as a jumping-off point into the Los Angeles Police Department system, to which they had direct access. The irony of employing a computer-crime unit's hardware and software to commit even a minor computer crime was appealing.

It was also dangerous.

Nearly everything that was fun, of course, was also a little dangerous: riding roller coasters, skydiving, gambling, sex.

From the LAPD system, he entered the California Department of Motor Vehicles computer in Sacramento. He got such a kick from making those leaps that he felt almost as though he had traveled physically, teleporting from his canyon in Malibu to Los Angeles to Sacramento, in the manner of a character in a science fiction novel.

Rocky jumped onto his hind legs, planted his forepaws on the edge of the desk, and peered at the computer screen.

"You wouldn't enjoy this," Spencer said.

Rocky looked at him and issued a short, soft whine.

"I'm sure you'd get a lot more pleasure from chewing on that new rawhide bone I got you."

Peering at the screen again, Rocky inquisitively cocked his furry head.

"Or I could put on some Paul Simon for you."

Another whine. Longer and louder than before.

Sighing, Spencer pulled another chair next to his own. "All right. When a fella has a bad case of the lonelies, I guess chewing on a rawhide bone just isn't as good as having a little company. Never works for me, anyway."

Rocky hopped into the chair, panting and grinning.

Together, they went voyaging in cyberspace, plunging illegally into the galaxy of DMV records, searching for Valerie Keene.

They found her in seconds. Spencer had hoped for an address different from the one he already knew, but he was disappointed. She was listed at the bungalow in Santa Monica, where he had discovered unfurnished rooms and the photo of a cockroach nailed to one wall.

According to the data that scrolled up the screen, she had a Class C license, without restrictions. It would expire in a little less than four years. She had applied for the license and taken a written test in early December, two months ago.

Her middle name was Ann.

She was twenty-nine. Spencer had guessed twenty-five.

Her driving record was free of violations.

In the event that she was gravely injured and her own life could not be saved, she had authorized the donation of her vital organs.

Otherwise, the DMV offered little information about her:

SEX:	F	HAIR:	BRN	EYES:	BRN
HT:	5-4	WT:	115		

That bureaucratic thumbnail description wouldn't be of much help when Spencer needed to describe her to someone. It was insufficient to conjure an image that included the things that truly distinguished her: the direct and clear-eyed stare, the slightly lopsided smile, the dimple in her right cheek, the delicate line of her jaw.

Since last year, with federal funding from the National Crime and Terrorism Prevention Act, the California DMV had been digitizing and electronically storing photographs and thumbprints of new and renewing drivers. Eventually, there would be mug shots and prints on file for every resident with a driver's license, though the vast majority had never been accused of a crime, let alone convicted.

Spencer considered this the first step toward a national ID card, an internal passport of the type that had been required in the communist states before they had collapsed, and he was opposed to it on principle. In this instance, however, his principles didn't prevent him from calling up the photo from Valerie's license.

The screen flickered, and she appeared. Smiling.

The banshee eucalyptuses whisper-wailed complaints of eternity's indifference, and the rain drummed, drummed.

Spencer realized that he was holding his breath. He exhaled.

Peripherally, he was aware of Rocky staring at him curiously, then at the screen, then at him again.

He picked up the mug and sipped some black coffee. His hand was shaking.

Valerie had known that authorities of one kind or another were hunting her, and she had known that they were getting close—because she had vacated her bungalow only hours before they'd come for her. If she was innocent, why would she settle for the unstable and fear-filled life of a fugitive?

Putting the mug aside and his fingers to the keyboard, he asked for a hard copy of the photo on the screen.

The laser printer hummed. A single sheet of white paper slid out of the machine.

Valerie. Smiling.

In Santa Monica, no one had called for surrender before the assault on the bungalow had begun. When the attackers burst inside, there had been no warning shouts of *Police!* Yet Spencer was certain that those men had been officers of one law-enforcement agency or another because of their uniformlike dress, night-vision goggles, weaponry, and military methodology.

Valerie. Smiling.

That soft-voiced woman with whom Spencer had talked last night at The Red Door had seemed gentle and honest, less capable of deceit than were most people. First thing, she had looked boldly at his scar and had asked about it, not with pity welling in her eyes, not with an edge of morbid curiosity in her voice, but in the same way that she might have asked where he'd bought the shirt he'd been wearing. Most people studied the scar surreptitiously and managed to speak of it, if at all, only when they realized that he was aware of their intense curiosity. Valerie's frankness had been refreshing. When he'd told her only that he'd been in an accident when he was a child, Valerie had sensed that he either didn't want or wasn't able to talk about it, and she had dropped the subject as if it mattered no more than his hairstyle. Thereafter, he never caught her gaze straying to the pallid brand on his face; more important, he never had the feeling that she was struggling *not* to look. She found other things about him more interesting than that pale welt from ear to chin.

Valerie. In black and white.

He could not believe that this woman was capable of committing a major crime, and certainly not one so heinous that a SWAT team would come after her in utmost silence, with submachine guns and every high-tech advantage.

She might be traveling with someone dangerous.

Spencer doubted that. He reviewed the few clues: one set of dinnerware, one drinking glass, one set of stainless steel flatware, an air mattress adequate for one but too small for two.

Yet the possibility remained: She might not be alone, and the person with her might rate the extreme caution of the SWAT team.

The photo, printed from the computer screen, was too dark to do her justice. Spencer directed the laser printer to produce another, just a shade lighter than the first.

That printout was better, and he asked for five more copies.

Until he held her likeness in his hands, Spencer had not been consciously aware that he was going to follow Valerie Keene wherever she had gone, find her, and help her. Regardless of what she might have done, even if she was guilty of a crime, regardless of the cost to himself, whether or not she could ever care for him, Spencer was going to stand with this woman against whatever darkness she faced.

As he realized the deeper implications of the commitment that he was making, a chill of wonder shivered him, for until that moment he had thought of himself as a thoroughly modern man who believed in no one and nothing, neither in God Almighty nor in himself.

Softly, touched by awe and unable fully to understand his own motivations, he said, "I'll be damned."

The dog sneezed.

4

B Y THE TIME the Beatles were singing "I'll Cry Instead," Roy Miro detected a cooling in the dead woman's hand that began to seep into his own flesh.

He let go of her and put on his gloves. He wiped her hands with one corner of the top sheet to smear any oils from his own skin that might have left the patterns of his fingertips.

Filled with conflicting emotions—grief at the death of a good woman, joy at her release from a world of pain and disappointment—he went downstairs to the kitchen. He wanted to be in a position to hear the automatic garage door when Penelope's husband came home.

A few spots of blood had congealed on the tile floor. Roy used paper towels and a spray bottle of Fantastik, which he found in the cabinet under the kitchen sink, to clean away the mess.

After he wiped up the dirty prints of his galoshes as well, he noticed that the stainless steel sink wasn't as well kept as it could have been, and he scrubbed until it was spotless.

The window in the microwave was smeared. It sparkled when he was done with it.

By the time the Beatles were halfway through "I'll Be Back" and Roy had wiped down the front of the Sub-Zero refrigerator, the garage door rumbled upward. He threw the used paper towels into the trash compactor, put away the Fantastik, and retrieved the Beretta that he had left on the counter after delivering Penelope from her suffering.

The kitchen and garage were separated only by a small laundry room. He turned to that closed door.

The rumble of the car engine echoed off the garage walls as Sam Bettonfield drove inside. The engine cut off. The big door clattered and creaked as it rolled down behind the car.

Home from the accountant wars at last. Weary of working late, crunching numbers. Weary of paying high office rents in Century City, trying to stay afloat in a system that valued money more than people.

In the garage, a car door slammed.

Burned out from the stress of life in a city that was riddled with injustice and at war with itself, Sam would be looking forward to a drink, a kiss from Penelope, a late dinner, perhaps an hour of television. Those simple pleasures and eight hours of restful sleep constituted the poor man's only respite from his greedy and demanding clients—and his sleep was likely to be tormented by bad dreams.

Roy had something better to offer. Blessed escape.

The sound of a key in the lock between the garage and the house, the *clack* of the deadbolt, a door opening: Sam entered the laundry.

Roy raised the Beretta as the inner door opened.

Wearing a raincoat, carrying a briefcase, Sam stepped into the kitchen. He was a balding man with quick dark eyes. He looked startled but sounded at ease. "You must have the wrong house."

Eyes misting with tears, Roy said, "I know what you're going through," and he squeezed off three quick shots.

Sam was not a large man, perhaps fifty pounds heavier than his wife. Nevertheless, getting him upstairs to the bedroom, wrestling him out of his raincoat, pulling off his shoes, and hoisting him into bed was not easy. When the task had been accomplished, Roy felt good about himself because he knew that he had done the right thing by placing Sam and Penelope together and in dignified circumstances.

He pulled the bedclothes over Sam's chest. The top sheet was trimmed with cut-work lace to match the pillow shams, so the dead couple appeared to be dressed in fancy surplices of the sort that angels might wear.

The Beatles had stopped singing a while ago. Outside, the soft and somber sound of the rain was as cold as the city that received it—as relentless as the passage of time and the fading of all light.

Though he had done a caring thing, and though there was joy in the end of these people's suffering, Roy was sad. It was a strangely sweet sadness, and the tears that it wrung from him were cleansing.

Eventually he went downstairs to clean up the few drops of Sam's blood that spotted the kitchen floor. He found the vacuum cleaner in the big closet under the stairs, and he swept away the dirt that he had tracked on the carpet when he'd first come into the house.

In Penelope's purse, he searched for the business card that he had given her. The name on it was phony, but he retrieved it anyway.

Finally, using the telephone in the study, he dialed 911.

When a policewoman answered, Roy said, "It's very sad here. It's very sad. Someone should come right away."

He did not return the handset to the cradle, but put it down on the desk, leaving the line open. The Bettonfields' address should have appeared on a computer screen in front of the policewoman who had answered the call, but Roy didn't want to take a chance that Sam and Penelope might be there for hours or even days before they were found. They were good people and did not deserve the indignity of being discovered stiff, gray, and reeking of decomposition.

He carried his galoshes and shoes to the front door, where he quickly put them on again. He remembered to pick up the lock-release gun from the foyer floor.

He walked through the rain to his car and drove away from there.

According to his watch, the time was twenty minutes past ten. Although it was three hours later on the East Coast, Roy was sure that his contact in Virginia would be waiting.

At the first red traffic light, he popped open the attaché case on the passenger seat. He plugged in the computer, which was still married to the cellular phone; he didn't separate the devices because he needed both. With a few quick keystrokes, he set up the cellular unit to respond to preprogrammed vocal instructions and to function as a speakerphone, which freed both his hands for driving.

As the traffic light turned green, he crossed the intersection and made the long-distance call by saying, "Please connect," and then reciting the number in Virginia.

After the second ring, the familiar voice of Thomas Summerton came down the line, recognizable by a single word, as smooth and as southern as pecan butter. "Hello?"

Roy said, "May I speak to Jerry, please?"

"Sorry, wrong number." Summerton hung up.

Roy terminated the resultant dial tone by saying: "Please disconnect now."

In ten minutes, Summerton would call back from a secure phone, and they could speak freely without fear of being recorded.

Roy drove past the glitzy shops on Rodeo Drive to Santa Monica Boulevard, and then west into residential streets. Large, expensive houses stood among huge trees, palaces of privilege that he found offensive.

When the phone rang, he didn't reach for the keypad but said, "Please accept call."

The connection was made with an audible click.

"Please scramble now," Roy said.

The computer beeped to indicate that everything he said would be rendered unintelligible to anyone between him and Summerton. As it was transmitted, their speech would be broken into small pieces of sound and rearranged by a randomlike control factor. Both phones were synchronized with the *same* control factor, so the meaningless streams of transmitted sound would be reassembled into intelligible speech when received.

"I've seen the early report on Santa Monica," Summerton said.

"According to neighbors, she was there this morning. But she must've skipped by the time we set up surveillance this afternoon."

"What tipped her off?"

"I swear she has a sixth sense about us." Roy turned west on Sunset Boulevard, joining the heavy flow of traffic that gilded the wet pavement with headlight beams. "You heard about the man who showed up?"

"And got away."

"We weren't sloppy."

"So he was just lucky?"

"No. Worse than that. He knew what he was doing."

"You saying he's somebody with a history?"

"Yeah."

"Local, state, or federal history?"

"He took out a team member, neat as you please."

"So he's had a few lessons beyond the local level."

Roy turned right off Sunset Boulevard onto a less traveled street, where mansions were hidden behind walls, high hedges, and wind-tossed trees. "If we're able to chase him down, what's our priority with him?"

Summerton considered for a moment before he spoke. "Find out who he is, who he's working for."

"Then detain him?"

"No. Too much is at stake. Make him disappear."

The serpentine streets wound through the wooded hills, among secluded estates, overhung by dripping branches, through blind turn after blind turn.

Roy said, "Does this change our priority with the woman?"

"No. Whack her on sight. Anything else happening at your end?"

Roy thought of Mr. and Mrs. Bettonfield, but he didn't mention them. The extreme kindness he had extended to them had nothing to do with his job, and Summerton would not understand.

Instead, Roy said, "She left something for us."

Summerton said nothing, perhaps because he intuited what the woman had left.

Roy said, "A photo of a cockroach, nailed to the wall."

"Whack her hard," Summerton said, and he hung up.

As Roy followed a long curve under drooping magnolia boughs, past a wrought-iron fence beyond which a replica of Tara stood spotlighted in the rain-swept darkness, he said, "Cease scrambling."

The computer beeped to indicate compliance.

"Please connect," he said, and recited the telephone number that would bring him into Mama's arms.

The video display flickered. When Roy glanced at the screen, he saw the opening question: WHO GOES THERE?

Though the phone would react to vocal commands, Mama would not; therefore, Roy pulled off the narrow road and stopped in a driveway, before a pair of nine-foot-high wrought-iron gates, to type in his responses to the security interrogation. After the transmission of his thumbprint, he was granted access to Mama in Virginia.

From her basic menu, he chose FIELD OFFICES. From that submenu, he chose LOS ANGELES, and he was thereby connected to the largest of Mama's babies on the West Coast.

He went through a few menus in the Los Angeles computer until he arrived at the files of the photo-analysis department. The file that interested him was currently in play, as he knew it would be, and he tapped in to observe.

The screen of his portable computer went to black and white, and then it filled with a photograph of a man's head from the neck up. His face was half turned away from the camera, dappled with shadows, blurred by a curtain of rain.

Roy was disappointed. He had hoped for a clearer picture.

This was dismayingly like an impressionist painting: in general, recognizable; in specific, mysterious.

Earlier in the evening, in Santa Monica, the surveillance team had taken photographs of the stranger who had gone into the bungalow minutes prior to the SWAT team assault. The night, the heavy rain, and the overgrown trees that prevented the streetlamps from casting much light on the sidewalk—all conspired to make it difficult to get a clear look at the man. Furthermore, they had not been expecting him, had thought that he was only an ordinary pedestrian who would pass by, and had been unpleasantly surprised when he'd turned in at the woman's house. Consequently, they had gotten precious few shots, none of quality, and none that revealed the full face of the mystery man, though the camera had been equipped with a telephoto lens.

The best of the photographs already had been scanned into the local-office computer, where it was being processed by an enhancement program. The computer would attempt to identify rain distortion and eliminate it. Then it would gradually lighten all areas of the shot uniformly, until it was able to identify biological structures in the deepest shadows that fell across the face; employing its extensive knowledge of human skull formation—with an enormous catalogue of the variations that occurred between the sexes, among the races, and among age groups—the computer would interpret the structures it glimpsed and develop them on a best-guess basis.

The process was laborious even at the lightning speed with which the program operated. Any photograph could ultimately be broken down into tiny dots of light and shadow called pixels: puzzle pieces that were identically shaped but varied subtly in texture and shading. Every one of the hundreds of thousands of pixels in this photograph had to be analyzed, to decipher not merely what it represented but what its undistorted relationship was to each of the many pixels surrounding it, which meant that the computer had to make hundreds of millions of comparisons and decisions in order to clarify the image.

Even then, there was no guarantee that the face finally rising from the murk would be an entirely accurate depiction of the man who had been photographed. Any analysis of this kind was as much an art—or guess-work—as it was a reliable technological process. Roy had seen instances in which a computer-enhanced portrait was as off the mark as any amateur artist's paint-by-the-numbers canvas of the Arc de Triomphe or of Manhattan at twilight. However, the face that they eventually got from the computer most likely would be so close to the man's true appearance as to be an exact likeness.

Now, as the computer made decisions and adjusted thousands of pixels, the image on the video display rippled from left to right. Still disappointing. Although changes had occurred, their effect was imperceptible. Roy was unable to see how the man's face was any different from what it had been before the adjustment.

For the next several hours, the image on the screen would ripple every six to ten seconds. The cumulative effect could be appreciated only by checking it at widely spaced intervals.

Roy backed out of the driveway, leaving the computer plugged in and the VDT angled toward him.

For a while he chased his headlights up and down hills, around blind turns, searching for a way out of the folded darkness, where the tree-filtered lights of cloistered mansions hinted at mysterious lives of wealth and power beyond his understanding.

From time to time, he glanced at the computer screen. The rippling face. Half averted. Shadowy and strange.

When at last he found Sunset Boulevard again and then the lower streets of Westwood, not far from his hotel, he was relieved to be back among people who were more like himself than those who lived in the monied hills. In the lower lands, the citizens knew suffering and uncertainty; they were people whose lives he could affect for the better, people to whom he could bring a measure of justice and mercy—one way or another.

The face on the computer screen was still that of a phantom, amorphous and possibly malignant. The face of chaos.

The stranger was a man who, like the fugitive woman, stood in the way of order, stability, and justice. He might be evil or merely troubled and confused. In the end, it didn't matter which.

"I'll give you peace," Roy Miro promised, glancing at the slowly mutating face on the video display terminal. "I'll find you and give you peace."

5

WHILE HOOVES OF RAIN beat across the roof, while the troll-deep voice of the wind grumbled at the windows, and while the dog lay curled and dozing on the adjacent chair, Spencer used his computer expertise to try to build a file on Valerie Keene.

According to the records of the Department of Motor Vehicles, the driver's license for which she'd applied had been her first, not a renewal, and to get it, she had supplied a Social Security card as proof of identity. The DMV had verified that her name and number were indeed paired in the Social Security Administration's files.

That gave Spencer four indices with which to locate her in other data-bases where she was likely to appear: name, date of birth, driver's license number, and Social Security number. Learning more about her should be a snap.

Last year, with much patience and cunning, he'd made a game of get-ting into all the major nationwide credit-reporting agencies—like TRW—which were among the most secure of all systems. Now, he wormed into the largest of those apples again, seeking Valerie Ann Keene.

Their files included forty-two women by that name, fifty-nine when the surname was spelled either "Keene" or "Keane," and sixty-four when a third spelling—"Keen"—was added. Spencer entered her Social Secu-rity number, expecting to winnow away sixty-three of the sixty-four, but *none* had the same number as that in the DMV records.

Frowning at the screen, he entered Valerie's birthday and asked the system to locate her with that. One of the sixty-four Valeries was born on the same day of the same month as the woman whom he was hunting—but twenty years earlier.

With the dog snoring beside him, he entered the driver's license num-ber and waited while the system cross-checked the Valeries. Of those who were licensed drivers, five were in California, but none had a number that matched hers. Another dead end.

Convinced that mistakes must have been made in the data entries, Spencer examined the file for each of the five California Valeries, looking for a driver's license or date of birth that was one number different from the information he had gotten out of the DMV. He was sure he would discover that a data-entry clerk had typed a six when a nine was required or had transposed two numbers.

Nothing. No mistakes. And judging by the information in each file, none of those women could possibly be the right Valerie.

Incredibly, the Valerie Ann Keene who had recently worked at The Red Door was absent from credit-agency files, utterly without a credit history. That was possible only if she had never purchased anything on time payments, had never possessed a credit card of any kind, had never opened a checking or savings account, and had never been the subject of a background check by an employer or landlord.

To be twenty-nine years old without acquiring a credit history in modern America, she would have to have been a Gypsy or a jobless vagrant most of her life, at least since she'd been a teenager. Manifestly she had not been any such thing.

Okay. Think. The raid on her bungalow meant one kind of police agency or another was after her. So she must be a wanted felon with a criminal record.

Spencer returned along electronic freeways to the Los Angeles Police Department computer, through which he searched city, county, and state court records to see if anyone by the name of Valerie Ann Keene had ever been convicted of a crime or had an outstanding arrest warrant in those jurisdictions.

The city system flashed NEGATIVE on the video screen.

NO FILE, reported the county.

NOT FOUND, said the state.

Nothing, nada, zero, zip.

Using the LAPD's electronic information-sharing arrangement with the FBI, he accessed the Washington-based Justice Department files of people convicted of federal offenses. She wasn't included in those, either.

In addition to its famous ten-most-wanted list, the FBI was, at any given time, seeking hundreds of other people related to criminal investigations—either suspects or potential witnesses. Spencer inquired if her name appeared on any of those lists, but it did not.

She was a woman without a past.

Yet something that she'd done had made her a wanted woman. Desperately wanted.

∽

Spencer did not get to bed until ten minutes past one o'clock in the morning.

Although he was exhausted, and although the rhythm of the rain should have served as a sedative, he couldn't sleep. He lay on his back, staring alternately at the shadowy ceiling and at the thrashing foliage of the trees beyond the window, listening to the meaningless monologue of the blustery wind.

At first he could think of nothing but the woman. The look of her. Those eyes. That voice. That smile. The mystery.

In time, however, his thoughts drifted to the past, as they did too often, too easily. For him, reminiscence was a highway with one destination: that certain summer night when he was fourteen, when a dark world became darker, when everything he knew was proved false, when hope died and a dread of destiny became his constant companion, when he awakened to the cry of a persistent owl whose single inquiry thereafter became the central question of his own life.

Rocky, who was usually so well attuned to his master's moods, was still restlessly pacing; he seemed to be unaware that Spencer was sinking into the quiet anguish of stubborn memory and that he needed company. The dog didn't respond to his name when called.

In the gloom, Rocky padded restlessly back and forth between the open bedroom door (where he stood on the threshold and listened to the storm that huffed in the fireplace chimney) and the bedroom window (where he put his forepaws upon the sill and stared out at the rampage of the wind through the eucalyptus grove). Although he neither whined nor grumbled, he had about him an air of anxiety, as if the bad weather had blown an unwanted memory out of his own past, leaving him bedeviled and unable to regain the peace he had known while dozing on the chair in the living room.

"Here, boy," Spencer said softly. "Come here."

Unheeding, the dog padded to the door, a shadow among shadows.

Tuesday evening, Spencer had gone to The Red Door to talk about a night in July, sixteen years past. Instead, he met Valerie Keene and, to his surprise, talked of other things. That distant July, however, still haunted him.

"Rocky, come here." Spencer patted the mattress.

A minute or so of further encouragement finally brought the dog onto the bed. Rocky lay with his head on Spencer's chest, shivering at first but quickly soothed by his master's hand. One ear up, one ear down, he was attentive to the story that he'd heard on countless nights like this, when he was the entire audience, and on nights when he accompanied Spencer into barrooms, where drinks were bought for strangers who would listen in an alcoholic haze.

"I was fourteen," Spencer began. "It was the middle of July, and the night was warm, humid. I was asleep under just one sheet, with my bedroom window open so the air could circulate. I remember . . . I was

Suddenly the night is profoundly quiet, uncannily still, as if the distant bleat of fear was, in fact, the sound of creation's engines grinding to a halt. The stars are hard points of light that have stopped twinkling, and the moon might well be painted on canvas. The landscape—trees, shrubs, summer flowers, fields, hills, and far mountains—appears to be nothing but crystalized shadows in various dark hues, as brittle as ice. The air must still be warm, but I am nonetheless frigid.

I quietly close the window, turn away from it, and move toward the bed again. I feel heavy-eyed, wearier than I've ever been.

But then I realize that I'm in a strange state of denial, that my weariness is less physical than psychological, that I desire sleep more than I really need it. Sleep is an escape. From fear. I'm shaking but not because I'm cold. The air is as warm as it was earlier. I'm shaking with fear.

Fear of what? I can't quite identify the source of my anxiety.

I know that the thing I heard was no ordinary wild cry. It reverberates in my mind, an icy sound that recalls something I've heard once before, although I can't remember what, when, where. The longer the forlorn wail echoes in my memory, the faster my heart beats.

I desperately want to lie down, forget the cry, the night, the owl and his question, but I know I can't sleep.

I'm wearing only briefs, so I quickly pull on a pair of jeans. Now that I'm committed to act, denial and sleep have no attraction for me. In fact, I'm in the grip of an urgency at least as strange as the previous denial. Bare-chested and barefoot, I'm drawn out of my bedroom by intense curiosity, by the sense of post-midnight adventure that all boys share—and by a terrible truth, which I don't yet know that I know.

Beyond my door, the house is cool, because my room is the only one not air-conditioned. For several summers, I've closed the vents against that chill flow because I prefer the benefits of fresh air even on a humid July night . . . and because, for some years, I've been unable to sleep with the hiss and hum that the icy air makes as it rushes through the ductwork and seethes through the vanes in the vent grille. I've long been afraid that this incessant if subtle noise will mask some other sound in the night that I must hear in order to survive. I have no idea what that other sound would be. It's a groundless and childish fear, and I'm embarrassed by it. Yet it dictates my sleeping habits.

The upstairs hallway is silvered with moonlight, which streams through a pair of skylights. Here and there along both walls, the polished-pine floor glimmers softly. Down the middle of the hall is an intricately patterned Persian runner, in which the curved and curled and undulant shapes absorb the radiance of the full moon and glow dimly with it: Hundreds of pale, luminous coelenterate forms seem to be not immediately under my feet but well below me, as if I am not on a carpet but am walking Christlike on the surface of a tidepool while gazing down at the mysterious denizens at the bottom.

dreaming about my mother, who'd been dead more than six years by then, but I can't remember anything that happened in the dream, only the warmth of it, the contentment, the comfort of being with her . . . and maybe the music of her laughter. She had a wonderful laugh. But it was another sound that woke me, not because it was loud but because it was recurring—so hollow and strange. I sat up in bed, confused, half drugged with sleep, but not frightened at all. I heard someone asking 'Who?' again and again. There would be a pause, silence, but then it would repeat as before: 'Who, who, who?' Of course, as I came all the way awake, I realized it was an owl perched on the roof, just above my open window . . ."

Spencer was again drawn to that distant July night, like an asteroid captured by the greater gravity of the earth and doomed to a declining orbit that would end in impact.

. . . it's an owl perched on the roof, just above my open window, calling out in the night for whatever reason owls call out.

In the humid dark, I get up from my bed and go to the bathroom, expecting the hooting to stop when the hungry owl takes wing and goes hunting for mice again. But even after I return to bed, he seems to be content on the roof and pleased by his one-word, one-note song.

Finally, I go to the open window and quietly slide up the double-hung screen, trying not to startle him into flight. But when I lean outside, turning my head to look up, half expecting to see his talons hooked over the shingles and curled in toward the eaves, another and far different cry arises before I can say "Shoo" or the owl can ask "Who." This new sound is thin and bleak, a fragile wail of terror from a far place in the summer night. I look out toward the barn, which stands two hundred yards behind the house, toward the moonlit fields beyond the barn, toward the wooded hills beyond the fields. The cry comes again, shorter this time, but even more pathetic and therefore more piercing.

Having lived in the country since the day I was born, I know that nature is one great killing ground, governed by the cruelest of all laws—the law of natural selection—and ruled by the ruthless. Many nights, I've heard the eerie, quavery yawling of coyote packs chasing prey and celebrating slaughter. The triumphant shriek of a mountain lion after it has torn the life out of a rabbit sometimes echoes out of the highlands, a sound which makes it easy to believe that Hell is real and that the damned have flung open the gates.

This cry that catches my attention as I lean out the window—and that silences the owl on the roof—comes not from a predator but from prey. It's the voice of something weak, vulnerable. The forests and fields are filled with timid and meek creatures, which live only to perish violently, which do so every hour of every day without surcease, whose terror may actually be noticed by a god who knows of every sparrow's fall but seems unmoved.

I pass my father's room. The door is closed.
I reach the head of the stairs, where I hesitate.
The house is silent.
I descend the stairs, quaking, rubbing my bare arms with my hands, wondering at my inexplicable fear. Perhaps even at that moment, I dimly realize that I am going down to a place from which I'll never again quite be able to ascend. . . .

With the dog as his confessor, Spencer spun his story all the way through that long-ago night, to the hidden door, to the secret place, to the beating heart of the nightmare. As he recounted the experience, step by barefoot step, his voice faded to a whisper.

When he finished, he was in a temporary state of grace that would burn away with the coming of the dawn, but it was even sweeter for being so tenuous and brief. Purged, he was at last able to close his eyes and know that dreamless sleep would come to him.

In the morning he would begin to search for the woman.

He had the uneasy feeling that he was walking into a living hell to rival the one that he had so often described to the patient dog. He could do nothing else. Only one acceptable road lay ahead of him, and he was compelled to follow it.

Now sleep.

Rain washed the world, and its susurration was the sound of absolution—though some stains could never be permanently removed.

6

I N THE MORNING, Spencer had a few tiny bruises and red marks on
his face and hands, from the sting-grenade pellets. Compared with
his scar, they would draw no comments.

For breakfast, he had English muffins and coffee at his desk in the living room while he hacked into the county tax collector's computer. He discovered that the bungalow in Santa Monica, where Valerie had been living until the previous day, was owned by the Louis and Mae Lee Family Trust. Property tax bills were mailed in care of something called China Dream, in West Hollywood.

Out of curiosity, he requested a list of other properties—if any—owned by that trust. There were fourteen: five more homes in Santa Monica; a pair of eight-unit apartment buildings in Westwood; three single-family homes in Bel Air; and four adjacent commercial buildings in West Hollywood, including the address for China Dream.

Louis and Mae Lee had done all right for themselves.

After switching off the computer, Spencer stared at the blank screen and finished his coffee. It was bitter. He drank it anyway.

By ten o'clock, he and Rocky were heading south on the Pacific Coast Highway. Traffic passed him at every opportunity, because he obeyed the speed limit.

The storm had moved east during the night, taking every cloud with it. The morning sun was white, and in its hard light, the westward-tilting shadows had edges as sharp as steel blades. The Pacific was bottle green and slate gray.

Spencer tuned the radio to an all-news station. He hoped to hear a story about the SWAT-team raid the night before and to learn who had been in charge of it and why Valerie was wanted.

The news reader informed him that taxes were going up again. The economy was slipping deeper into recession. The government was further restricting gun ownership and television violence. Robbery, rape, and homicide rates were at all-time highs. The Chinese were accusing us of possessing "orbiting laser death rays," and we were accusing them of the same. Some people believed that the world would end in fire; others said ice; both were testifying before Congress on behalf of competing legislative agendas designed to save the world.

When he found himself listening to a story about a dog show that was being picketed by protesters who were demanding an end to selective breeding and to the "exploitation of animal beauty in an exhibitionistic performance no less repugnant than the degrading of young women in topless bars," Spencer knew that there would be no report of the incident at the bungalow in Santa Monica. Surely a SWAT-team operation would rate higher on any reporter's agenda than unseemly displays of canine comeliness.

Either the media had found nothing newsworthy in an assault on a private home by cops with machine guns—or the agency conducting the operation had done a first-rate job of misdirecting the press. They had turned what should have been a public spectacle into what amounted to a covert action.

He switched off the radio and entered the Santa Monica Freeway. East by northeast, in the lower hills, the China Dream awaited them.

To Rocky, he said, "What's your opinion of this dog-show thing?"

Rocky looked at him curiously.

"You're a dog, after all. You must have an opinion. These are your people being exploited."

Either he was a dog of extreme circumspection when it came to discussing current affairs or he was just a carefree, culturally disengaged mutt with no positions on the weightiest social issues of his time and species.

"I would hate to think," Spencer said, "that you are a dropout, resigned to the status of a lumpen mammal, unconcerned about being exploited, all fur and no fury."

Rocky peered forward at the highway again.

"Aren't you outraged that purebred females are forbidden to have sex with mongrels like you, forced to submit only to purebred males? Just to make puppies destined for the degradation of showrings?"

The mutt's tail thumped against the passenger door.

"Good dog." Spencer held the steering wheel with his left hand and petted Rocky with his right. The dog submitted with pleasure. Thump-thump went the tail. "A good, accepting dog. You don't even think it's strange that your master talks to himself."

They exited the freeway at Robertson Boulevard and drove toward the fabled hills.

After the night of rain and wind, the sprawling metropolis was as free of smog as the seacoast from which they had traveled. The palms, ficuses, magnolias, and early-blooming bottlebrush trees with red flowers were so green and gleaming that they appeared to have been hand-polished, leaf by leaf, frond by frond. The streets were washed clean, the glass walls of the tall buildings sparkled in the sunshine, birds wheeled across the piercingly blue sky, and it was easy to be deceived into believing that all was right with the world.

⌒

Thursday morning, while other agents used the assets of several law-enforcement organizations to search for the nine-year-old Pontiac that was registered to Valerie Keene, Roy Miro personally took charge of the effort to identify the man who had nearly been captured in the previous night's operation. From his Westwood hotel, he drove into the heart of Los Angeles, to the agency's California headquarters.

Downtown, the volume of office space occupied by city, county, state, and federal governments was rivaled only by the space occupied by banks. At lunchtime the conversation in the restaurants was more often than not about money—massive, raw slabs of money—whether the diners were from the political or the financial community.

In this opulent wallow, the agency owned a handsome ten-story building on a desirable street near city hall. Bankers, politicians, bureaucrats, and wine-swilling derelicts shared the sidewalks with mutual respect—except for those regrettable occasions when one of them suddenly snapped, screamed incoherent deprecations, and savagely stabbed one of his fellow Angelenos. The wielder of the knife (or gun or blunt instrument) frequently suffered delusions of persecution by extraterrestrials or the CIA and was more likely to be a derelict than a banker, or a politician, or a bureaucrat.

Just six months ago, however, a middle-aged banker had gone on a killing spree with two 9mm pistols. The incident had traumatized the entire society of downtown vagrants and had made them more wary of the unpredictable "suits" who shared the streets with them.

The agency's building—clad in limestone, with acres of bronze windows as dark as any movie star's sunglasses—did not bear the agency's name. The people with whom Roy worked weren't glory seekers; they preferred to function in obscurity. Besides, the agency that employed them did not officially exist, was funded by the clandestine redirection of money from other bureaus that were under the control of the Justice Department, and actually had no name itself.

Over the main entrance, the street address gleamed in polished copper numbers. Under the numbers were four names and one ampersand, also in copper: CARVER, GUNMANN, GARROTE & HEMLOCK.

A passerby, if he wondered about the building's occupant, might think it was a partnership of attorneys or accountants. If he made inquiries of the uniformed guard in the lobby, he would be told that the firm was an "international property-management company."

Roy drove down a ramp to the underground parking facility. At the bottom of the ramp, the way was barred by a sturdy steel gate.

He gained admittance neither by plucking a time-stamped ticket from an automatic dispenser nor by identifying himself to a guard in a booth. Instead, he stared directly into the lens of a high-definition video camera that was mounted on a post two feet from the side window of his car and waited to be recognized.

The image of his face was transmitted to a windowless room in the basement. There, Roy knew, a guard at a display terminal watched as the computer dropped everything out of the image except the eyes, enlarged them without compromising the high resolution, scanned the striation and vessel patterns of the retinas, compared them with on-file retinal patterns, and acknowledged Roy as one of the select.

The guard then pushed a button to raise the gate.

The entire procedure could have been accomplished without the guard—if not for one contingency against which precautions had to be taken. An operative bent on penetrating the agency might have killed Roy, cut out his eyes, and held them up to the camera to be scanned. While the computer conceivably could have been deceived, a guard surely would have noticed this messy ruse.

It was unlikely that anyone would go to such extremes to breach the agency's security. But not impossible. These days, sociopaths of singular viciousness were loose in the land.

Roy drove into the subterranean garage. By the time he parked and got out of the car, the steel gate had clattered shut again. The dangers of Los Angeles, of democracy run amok, were locked out.

His footsteps echoed off the concrete walls and the low ceiling, and he knew that the guard in the basement room could hear them too. The garage was under audio as well as video surveillance.

Access to the high-security elevator was achieved by pressing his right thumb to the glass face of a print scanner. A camera above the lift doors gazed down at him, so the distant guard could prevent anyone from entering merely by placing a severed thumb to the glass.

No matter how smart machines eventually became, human beings would always be needed. Sometimes that thought encouraged Roy. Sometimes it depressed him, though he wasn't sure why.

He rode the elevator to the fourth floor, which was shared by Document Analysis, Substance Analysis, and Photo Analysis.

In the Photo Analysis computer lab, two young men and a middle-aged woman were working at arcane tasks. They all smiled and said good morning, because Roy had one of those faces that encouraged smiles and familiarity.

Melissa Wicklun, their chief photo analyst in Los Angeles, was sitting at the desk in her office, which was in a corner of the lab. The office had no windows to the outside but featured two glass walls through which she could watch her subordinates in the larger room.

When Roy knocked on the glass door, she looked up from a file that she was reading. "Come in."

Melissa, a blonde in her early thirties, was at the same time an elf and a succubus. Her green eyes were large and guileless—yet simultaneously smoky, mysterious. Her nose was pert—but her mouth was sensuous, the essence of all erotic orifices. She had large breasts, a slim waist, and long legs—but she chose to conceal those attributes in loose white blouses, white lab coats, and baggy chinos. In her scuffed Nikes, her feet were no doubt so feminine and delicate that Roy would have been delighted to spend hours kissing them.

He had never made a pass at her, because she was reserved and businesslike—and because he suspected that she was a lesbian. He had nothing against lesbians. Live and let live. At the same time, however, he was loath to reveal his interest only to be rejected.

Melissa said crisply, "Good morning, Roy."

"How have you been? Good heavens, you know that I haven't been in L.A., haven't seen you since—"

"I was just examining the file." Straight to business. She was never interested in small talk. "We have a finished enhancement."

When Melissa was talking, Roy was never able to decide whether to look at her eyes or her mouth. Her gaze was direct, with a challenge that he found appealing. But her lips were so deliciously ripe.

She pushed a photograph across the desk.

Roy looked away from her lips.

The picture was a drastically improved, full-color version of the shot that he had seen on his attaché case computer terminal the night before: a man's head from the neck up, in profile. Shadows still dappled the face, but they were lighter and less obscuring than they had been. The blurring screen of rain had been removed entirely.

"It's a fine piece of work," Roy said. "But it still doesn't give us a good enough look at him to make an identification."

"On the contrary, it tells us a lot about him," Melissa said. "He's between twenty-eight and thirty-two."

"How do you figure?"

"Computer projection based on an analysis of lines radiating from the corner of his eye, percentage of gray in his hair, and the apparent degree of firmness of facial muscles and throat skin."

"That's projecting quite a lot from such few—"

"Not at all," she interrupted. "The system makes analytic projections operating from a ten-megabyte database of biological information, and I'd pretty much bet the house on what it says."

He was thrilled by the way her supple lips formed the words "ten-megabyte database of biological information." Her mouth was better than her eyes. Perfect. He cleared his throat. "Well—"

"Brown hair, brown eyes."

Roy frowned. "The hair, okay. But you can't see his eyes here."

Rising from her chair, Melissa took the photograph out of his hand and put it on the desk. With a pencil, she pointed to the beginning curve of the man's eyeball as viewed from the side. "He's not looking at the camera, so if you or I examined the photo under a microscope, we still wouldn't be able to see enough of the iris to determine color. But even from an oblique perspective like this, the computer can detect a few pixels of color."

"So he has brown eyes."

"Dark brown." She put down the pencil and stood with her left hand fisted on her hip, as delicate as a flower and as resolute as an army general. "Absolutely dark brown."

Roy liked her unshakable self-confidence, the brisk certitude with which she spoke. And that *mouth*.

"Based on the computer's analysis of his physical relationship to measurable objects in the photograph, he's five feet eleven inches tall." She clipped her words, so the facts came out of her with the staccato energy of bullets from a submachine gun. "He weighs one hundred and sixty-five, give or take five pounds. He's Caucasian, clean-shaven, in good physical shape, recently had a haircut."

"Anything else?"

From the file folder, Melissa removed another photograph. "This is him. From the front, straight on. His full face."

Roy looked up from the new photo, surprised. "I didn't know we got a shot like this."

"We didn't," she said, studying the portrait with evident pride. "This isn't an actual photograph. It's a projection of what the guy ought to look like, based on what the computer can determine of his bone structure and fat-deposit patterns from the partial profile."

"It can do that?"

"It's a recent innovation in the program."

"Reliable?"

"Considering the view the computer had to work with in this case," she assured Roy, "there's a ninety-four-percent probability that this face will precisely match the real face in any ninety of one hundred reference details."

"I guess that's better than a police artist's sketch," he said.

"Much better." After a beat, she said, "Is something wrong?"

Roy realized that she had shifted her gaze from the computer portrait to him—and that he was staring at her mouth.

"Uh," he said, looking down at the full portrait of the mystery man, "I was wondering . . . what's this line across his right cheek?"

"A scar."

"Really? You're sure? From the ear to the point of the chin?"

"A major scar," she said, opening a desk drawer. "Cicatricial welt—mostly smooth tissue, crimped here and there along the edges."

Roy referred to the original profile shot and saw that a portion of the scar was there, although he had not correctly identified it. "I thought it was just a line of light between shadows, light from the streetlamp, falling across his cheek."

"No."

"It couldn't be that?"

"No. A scar," Melissa said firmly, and she took a Kleenex from a box in the open drawer.

"This is great. Makes for an easier ID. This guy seems to've had special-forces training, either military or paramilitary, and with a scar like this—it's a good bet he was wounded while on duty. Badly wounded. Maybe badly enough that he was discharged or retired on psychological if not physical disability."

"Police and military organizations keep records forever."

"Exactly. We'll have him in seventy-two hours. Hell, forty-eight." Roy looked up from the portrait. "Thanks, Melissa."

She was wiping her mouth with the Kleenex. She didn't have to be concerned about smearing her lipstick, because she wasn't wearing any. She didn't need lipstick. It couldn't improve her.

Roy was fascinated by the way in which her full and pliant lips compressed so tenderly under the soft Kleenex.

He realized that he was staring and that again she was aware of it. His gaze drifted up to her eyes.

Melissa blushed faintly, looked away from him, and threw the crumpled Kleenex in the waste can.

"May I keep this copy?" he asked, indicating the full-face computer-generated portrait.

Withdrawing a manila envelope from beneath the file folder on the desk, handing it to him, she said, "I've put five prints in here, plus two diskettes that contain the portrait."

"Thanks, Melissa."

"Sure."

The warm pink blush was still on her cheeks.

Roy felt that he had penetrated her cool, businesslike veneer for the first time since he'd known her, and that he was in touch, however tenuously, with the inner Melissa, with the exquisitely sensuous self that she usually strove to conceal. He wondered if he should ask her for a date.

Turning his head, he looked through the glass walls at the workers in the computer lab, certain that they must be aware of the erotic tension in their boss's office. All three seemed to be absorbed in their work.

When Roy turned to Melissa Wicklun again, prepared to ask her to dinner, she was surreptitiously wiping at one corner of her mouth with a fingertip. She tried to cover by spreading her hand across her mouth and faking a cough.

With dismay, Roy realized that the woman had misinterpreted his salacious stare. Apparently she thought that his attention had been drawn to her mouth by a smear or crumb of food left over, perhaps, from a midmorning doughnut.

She had been oblivious of his lust. If she *was* a lesbian, she must have assumed that Roy knew as much and would have no interest in her. If she wasn't a lesbian, perhaps she simply couldn't imagine being attracted—or being an object of desire—to a man with round cheeks, a soft chin, and ten extra pounds on his waist. He had met with that prejudice before: looksism. Many women, brainwashed by a consumer culture that sold the wrong values, were interested only in men like those who appeared in advertisements for Marlboro or Calvin Klein. They could not understand that a man with the merry face of a favorite uncle might be kinder, wiser, more compassionate, and a better lover than a hunk who spent too much time at the gym. How sad to think that Melissa might be that shallow. How very sad.

"Can I help you with anything else?" she asked.

"No, this is fine. This is a lot. We'll nail him with this."

She nodded.

"I have to get down to the print lab, see if they got anything off that flashlight or bathroom window."

"Yes, of course," she said awkwardly.

He indulged in one last look at her *perfect* mouth, sighed, and said, "See you later."

After he had stepped out of her office, closed the door behind him, and crossed two-thirds of the long computer lab, he looked back, half hoping that she would be staring wistfully after him. Instead, she was sitting at her desk again, holding a compact in one hand, examining her mouth in that small mirror.

℘

China Dream was a West Hollywood restaurant in a quaint three-story brick building, in an area of trendy shops. Spencer parked a block away, left Rocky in the truck again, and walked back.

The air was pleasantly warm. The breeze was refreshing. It was one of those days when the struggles of life seemed worth waging.

The restaurant was not yet open for lunch. Nevertheless, the door was unlocked, and he went inside.

The China Dream indulged in none of the decor common to many Chinese restaurants: no dragons or foo dogs, no brass ideograms on the walls. It was starkly modern, pearl gray and black, with white linen on the thirty to forty tables. The only Chinese art object was a life-size, carved-wood statue of a gentle-faced, robed woman holding what appeared to be an inverted bottle or a gourd; it was standing just inside the door.

Two Asian men in their twenties were arranging flatware and wineglasses. A third man, Asian but a decade older than his coworkers, was rapidly folding white cloth napkins into fanciful, peaked shapes. His hands were as dexterous as those of a magician. All three men wore black shoes, black slacks, white shirts, and black ties.

Smiling, the oldest approached Spencer. "Sorry, sir. We don't open for lunch until eleven-thirty."

He had a mellow voice and only a faint accent.

"I'm here to see Louis Lee, if I may," Spencer said.

"Do you have an appointment, sir?"

"No, I'm afraid not."

"Can you please tell me what you wish to discuss with him?"

"A tenant who lives in one of his rental properties."

The man nodded. "May I assume this would be Ms. Valerie Keene?"

The soft voice, smile, and unfailing politeness combined to project an image of humility, which was like a veil that made it more difficult to see, until now, that the napkin folder was also quite intelligent and observant.

"Yes," Spencer said. "My name's Spencer Grant. I'm a . . . I'm a friend of Valerie's. I'm worried about her."

From a pocket of his trousers, the man withdrew an object about the size—but less than the thickness—of a deck of cards. It was hinged at one end; unfolded, it proved to be the smallest cellular telephone that Spencer had ever seen.

Aware of Spencer's interest, the man said, "Made in Korea."

"Very James Bond."

"Mr. Lee has just begun to import them."

"I thought he was a restaurateur."

"Yes, sir. But he is many things." The napkin folder pushed a single button, waited while the seven-digit programmed number was transmitted, and then surprised Spencer again by speaking in neither English nor Chinese, but in French, to the person on the other end.

Collapsing the phone and tucking it into his pocket, the napkin folder said, "Mr. Lee will see you, sir. This way, please."

Spencer followed him among the tables, to the right rear corner of the front room, through a swinging door with a round window in the center, into clouds of appetizing aromas: garlic, onions, ginger, hot peanut oil, mushroom soup, roasting duck, almond essence.

The immense and spotlessly clean kitchen was filled with ovens, cook-tops, griddles, huge woks, deep fryers, warming tables, sinks, chopping blocks. Sparkling white ceramic tile and stainless steel dominated. At least a dozen chefs and cooks and assistants, dressed in white from head to foot, were busy at a variety of culinary tasks.

The operation was as organized and precise as the mechanism in an elaborate Swiss clock with twirling ballerina dolls, marching toy soldiers, prancing wooden horses. Reliably tick-tick-ticking along.

Spencer trailed his escort through another swinging door, into a corridor, past storage rooms and staff rest rooms, to an elevator. He expected to go up. In silence, they went down one floor. When the doors opened, the escort motioned for Spencer to exit first.

The basement was not dank and dreary. They were in a mahogany-paneled lounge with handsome teak chairs upholstered in teal fabric.

The receptionist at the teak and polished-steel desk was a man: Asian, totally bald, six feet tall, with broad shoulders and a thick neck. He was typing furiously at a computer keyboard. When he turned from the keyboard and smiled, his gray suit jacket stretched tautly across a concealed handgun in a shoulder holster.

He said, "Good morning," and Spencer replied in kind.

"Can we go in?" asked the napkin folder.

The bald man nodded. "Everything's fine."

As the escort led Spencer to an inner door, an electrically operated deadbolt clacked open, triggered by the receptionist.

Behind them, the bald man began to type again. His fingers raced across the keys. If he could use a gun as well as he could type, he would be a deadly adversary.

Beyond the lounge, they followed a white corridor with a gray vinyl-tile floor. It served windowless offices on both sides. Most of the doors were open, and Spencer saw men and women—many but not all of them Asian—working at desks, filing cabinets, and computers just like office workers in the real world.

The door at the end of the hall led into Louis Lee's office, which was another surprise. Travertine floor. A beautiful Persian carpet: mostly grays, lavender, and greens. Tapestry-covered walls. Early-nineteenth-century French furniture, with elaborate marquetry and ormolu. Leather-bound books in cases with glass doors. The large room was warmly but not brightly lighted by Tiffany floor and table lamps, some with stained-glass and some with blown-glass shades, and Spencer was sure that none was a reproduction.

"Mr. Lee, this is Mr. Grant," said the escort.

The man who came out from behind the ornate desk was five feet seven, slender, in his fifties. His thick jet-black hair had begun to turn gray at the temples. He wore black wingtips, dark blue trousers with suspenders, a white shirt, a bow tie with small red polka dots against a blue background, and horn-rimmed glasses.

"Welcome, Mr. Grant." He had a musical accent as European as it was Chinese. His hand was small, but his grip was firm.

"Thank you for seeing me," Spencer said, feeling as disoriented as he might have felt if he had followed Alice's white rabbit into this window-less, Tiffany-illumined hole.

Lee's eyes were anthracite black. They fixed Spencer with a stare that penetrated him almost as effectively as a scalpel.

The escort and erstwhile napkin folder stood to one side of the door, his hands clasped behind him. He had not grown, but he now seemed as much of a bodyguard as the huge, bald receptionist.

Louis Lee invited Spencer to one of a pair of armchairs that faced each other across a low table. A nearby Tiffany floor lamp cast blue, green, and scarlet light.

Lee took the chair opposite Spencer and sat very erect. With his spectacles, bow tie, and suspenders, and with the backdrop of books, he might have been a professor of literature in the study of his home, near the campus of Yale or another Ivy League university.

His manner was reserved but friendly. "So you are a friend of Ms. Keene's? Perhaps you went to high school together? College?"

"No, sir. I haven't known her that long. I met her where she works. I'm a recent . . . friend. But I do care about her and . . . well, I'm concerned that something's happened to her."

"What do you think might have happened to her?"

"I don't know. But I'm sure you're aware of the SWAT-team raid on your house last night, the bungalow she was renting from you."

Lee was silent for a moment. Then: "Yes, the authorities came to my own home last evening, after the raid, to ask about her."

"Mr. Lee, these authorities . . . who were they?"

"Three men. They claimed to be with the FBI."

"Claimed?"

"They showed me credentials, but they were lying."

Frowning, Spencer said, "How can you be sure of that?"

"In my life, I've had considerable experience of deceit and treachery," Lee said. He didn't seem either angry or bitter. "I've developed a good nose for it."

Spencer wondered if that was as much a warning as it was an explanation. Whichever the case, he knew that he was not in the presence of an ordinary businessman. "If they weren't actually government agents—"

"Oh, I'm sure they were government agents. However, I believe the FBI credentials were simply a convenience."

"Yes, but if they were with another bureau, why not flash their real ID?"

Lee shrugged. "Rogue agents, operating without the authority of their bureau, hoping to confiscate a cache of drug profits for their own benefit, would have reason to mislead with false ID."

Spencer knew that such things had happened. "But I don't . . . I *can't* believe that Valerie is involved with drug peddling."

"I'm sure she isn't. If I'd thought so, I wouldn't have rented to her. Those people are scum—corrupting children, ruining lives. Besides, although Ms. Keene paid her rent in cash, she wasn't rolling in money. And she worked at a full-time job."

"So if these weren't, let's say, rogue Drug Enforcement Administration operatives looking to line their own pockets with cocaine profits, and if they weren't actually with the FBI—who were they?"

Louis Lee shifted slightly in his chair, still sitting erect but tilting his head in such a way that reflections of the stained-glass Tiffany lamp painted both lenses of his spectacles and obscured his eyes. "Sometimes a government—or a bureau within a government—becomes frustrated when it has to play by the rules. With oceans of tax money washing around, with bookkeeping systems that would be laughable in any private enterprise, it's easy for some government officials to fund covert organizations to achieve results that can't be achieved through legal means."

"Mr. Lee, do you read a lot of espionage novels?"

Louis Lee smiled thinly. "They're not of interest to me."

"Excuse me, sir, but this sounds a little paranoid."

"It's only experience speaking."

"Then your life's been even more interesting than I'd guess from appearances."

"Yes," Lee said, but didn't elaborate. After a pause, with his eyes still hidden by the patterns of reflected color that glimmered in his eyeglasses, he continued: "The larger a government, the more likely it is to be riddled with such covert organizations—some small but some not. We have a very big government, Mr. Grant."

"Yes, but—"

"Direct and indirect taxes require the average citizen to work from January until the middle of July to pay for that government. *Then* working men and women begin to labor for themselves."

"I've heard that figure too."

"When government grows so large, it also grows arrogant."

Louis Lee did not seem to be a fanatic. No anger or bitterness strained his voice. In fact, although he chose to surround himself with highly ornamented French furniture, he had a calm air of Zen simplicity and a distinctly Asian resignation to the ways of the world. He seemed more of a pragmatist than a crusader.

"Ms. Keene's enemies, Mr. Grant, are my enemies too."

"And mine."

"However, I don't intend to make a target of myself—as you are doing. Last night, I didn't express my doubt about their credentials when they presented themselves as FBI agents. That would not have been prudent. I was unhelpful, yes, but *cooperatively* unhelpful—if you know what I mean."

Spencer sighed and slumped in his chair.

Leaning forward with his hands on his knees, his intense black eyes becoming visible again as the reflections of the lamp moved off his glasses, Lee said, "You were the man in her house last night."

Spencer was surprised again. "How do you know anyone was there?"

"They were asking about a man she might have been living with. Your height, weight. What were you doing there, if I may ask?"

"She was late for work. I was worried about her. I went to her place to see if anything was wrong."

"You work at The Red Door too?"

"No. I was waiting there for her." That was all he chose to say. The rest was too complicated—and embarrassing. "What can you tell me about Valerie that might help me locate her?"

"Nothing, really."

"I only want to help her, Mr. Lee."

"I believe you."

"Well, sir, then why not cooperate with me? What was on her renter's application? Previous residence, previous jobs, credit references—anything like that would be helpful."

The businessman leaned back, moving his small hands from his knees to the arms of his chair. "There was no renter's application."

"With as many properties as you have, sir, I'm sure whoever manages them must use applications."

Louis Lee raised his eyebrows, which was a theatrical expression for such a placid man. "You've done some research on me. Very good. Well, in Ms. Keene's case, there was no application, because she was recommended by someone at The Red Door who's also a tenant of mine."

Spencer thought of the beautiful waitress who appeared to be half Vietnamese and half black. "Would that be Rosie?"

"It would."

"She was friends with Valerie?"

"She is. I met Ms. Keene and approved of her. She impressed me as a reliable person. That's all I needed to know about her."

Spencer said, "I've got to speak to Rosie."

"No doubt she'll be working again this evening."

"I need to talk to her before this evening. Partly because of this conversation with you, Mr. Lee, I have the distinct feeling that I'm being hunted and that time may be running out."

"I think that's an accurate assessment."

"Then I'll need her last name, sir, and her address."

Louis Lee was silent for so long that Spencer grew nervous. Finally: "Mr. Grant, I was born in China. When I was a child, we fled the Communists and emigrated to Hanoi, Vietnam, which was then controlled by the French. We lost everything—but that was better than being among the tens of millions liquidated by Chairman Mao."

Although Spencer was unsure what the businessman's personal history might have to do with his own problems, he knew there would be a connection and that it would soon become apparent. Louis Lee was Chinese but not inscrutable. Indeed, he was as direct, in his way, as was any rural New Englander.

"Chinese in Vietnam were oppressed. Life was hard. But the French promised to protect us from the Communists. They failed. When Vietnam was partitioned in nineteen fifty-four, I was still a young boy. Again we fled, to South Vietnam—and lost everything."

"I see."

"No. You begin to perceive. But you don't yet see. Within a year, civil war began. In nineteen fifty-nine, my younger sister was killed in the street by sniper fire. Three years later, one week after John Kennedy promised that the United States would ensure our freedom, my father was killed by a terrorist bomb on a Saigon bus."

Lee closed his eyes and folded his hands in his lap. He almost seemed to be meditating rather than remembering.

Spencer waited.

"By late April, nineteen seventy-five, when Saigon fell, I was thirty, with four children, my wife Mae. My mother was still alive, and one of my three brothers, two of his children. Ten of us. After six months of terror, my mother, brother, one of my nieces, and one of my sons were dead. I failed to save them. The remaining six of us . . . we joined thirty-two others in an attempt to escape by sea."

"Boat people," Spencer said respectfully, for in his own way he knew what it meant to be cut off from one's past, adrift and afraid, struggling daily to survive.

Eyes still closed, speaking as serenely as if recounting the details of a walk in the country, Lee said: "In bad weather, pirates tried to board our vessel. Vietcong gunboat. Same as pirates. They would have killed the men, raped and killed the women, stolen our meager possessions. Eighteen of our thirty-eight perished attempting to repel them. One was my son. Ten years old. Shot. I could do nothing. The rest of us were saved because the weather grew so bad, so quickly—the gunboat withdrew to save itself. The storm separated us from the pirates. Two people were washed overboard in high waves. Leaving eighteen. When good weather returned, our boat was damaged, no engine or sails, no radio, far out on the South China Sea."

Spencer could no longer bear to look at the placid man. But he was incapable of looking away.

"We were adrift six days in fierce heat. No fresh water. Little food. One woman and four children died before we crossed a sea-lane and were rescued by a U.S. Navy ship. One of the children who died of thirst was my daughter. I couldn't save her. I wasn't able to save anyone. Of the ten in my family who survived the fall of Saigon, four remained to be pulled from that boat. My wife, my remaining daughter—who was then my only child—one of my nieces. And me."

"I'm sorry," Spencer said, and those words were so inadequate that he wished he hadn't spoken them.

Louis Lee opened his eyes. "Nine other people were rescued from that disintegrating boat, more than twenty years ago. As I did, they took American first names, and today all nine are partners with me in the restaurant, other businesses. I consider them my family also. We're a nation unto ourselves, Mr. Grant. I am an American because I believe in America's ideals. I love this country, its people. I do not love its government. I can't love what I can't trust, and I will never trust a government again, anywhere. That disturbs you?"

"Yes. It's understandable. But depressing."

"As individuals, as families, as neighbors, as members of one community," Lee said, "people of all races and political views are usually decent, kind, compassionate. But in large corporations or governments, when great power accumulates in their hands, some become monsters even with good intentions. I can't be loyal to monsters. But I will be loyal to my family, my neighbors, my community."

"Fair enough, I guess."

"Rosie, the waitress at The Red Door, was not one of the people on that boat with us. Her mother was Vietnamese, however, and her father was an American who died over there, so she is a member of my community."

Spencer had been so mesmerized by Louis Lee's story that he had forgotten the request that had triggered those grisly recollections. He wanted to talk to Rosie as soon as possible. He needed her last name and address.

"Rosie must not be any more involved in this than she is now," Lee said. "She's told these phony FBI men that she knows little about Ms. Keene, and I don't want you to drag her deeper into this."

"I only want to ask her a few questions."

"If the wrong people saw you with her and identified you as the man at the house last night, they'd think Rosie was more than just a friend at work to Ms. Keene—though that is, in fact, all she was."

"I'll be discreet, Mr. Lee."

"Yes. That is the only choice I'm giving you."

A door opened softly, and Spencer turned in his armchair to see the napkin folder, his polite escort from the front door of the restaurant, returning to the room. He hadn't heard the man leave.

"She remembers him. It's arranged," the escort told Louis Lee, as he approached Spencer and handed him a piece of notepaper.

"At one o'clock," Louis Lee said, "Rosie will meet you at that address. It's not her apartment—in case her place is being watched."

The swiftness with which a meeting had been arranged, without a word between Lee and the other man, seemed magical to Spencer.

"She will not be followed," Lee said, getting up from his chair. "Make sure that you are not followed, either."

Also rising, Spencer said, "Mr. Lee, you and your family . . ."

"Yes?"

"Impressive."

Louis Lee bowed slightly from the waist. Then, turning away and walking to his desk, he said, "One more thing, Mr. Grant."

When Lee opened a desk drawer, Spencer had the crazy feeling that this soft-spoken, mild-looking, professorial gentleman was going to withdraw a silencer-equipped gun and shoot him dead. Paranoia was like an injection of amphetamines administered directly to his heart.

Lee came up with what appeared to be a jade medallion on a gold chain. "I sometimes give one of these to people who seem to need it."

Half afraid that the two men would hear his heart thundering, Spencer joined Lee at the desk and accepted the gift.

It was two inches in diameter. Carved on one side was the head of a dragon. On the other side was an equally stylized pheasant.

"This looks too expensive to—"

"It's only soapstone. Pheasants and dragons, Mr. Grant. You need their power. Pheasants and dragons. Prosperity and long life."

Dangling the medallion from its chain, Spencer said, "A charm?"

"Effective," Lee said. "Did you see the Quan Yin when you came in the restaurant?"

"Excuse me?"

"The wooden statue, by the front door?"

"Yes, I did. The woman with the gentle face."

"A spirit resides in her and prevents enemies from crossing my threshold." Lee was as solemn as when he'd recounted his escape from Vietnam. "She is especially good at barring envious people, and envy is second only to self-pity as the most dangerous of all emotions."

"After a life like yours, you can believe in this?"

"We must believe in something, Mr. Grant."

They shook hands.

Carrying the notepaper and the medallion, Spencer followed the escort out of the room.

In the elevator, recalling the brief exchange between the escort and the bald man when they had first entered the reception lounge, Spencer said, "I was scanned for weapons on the way down, wasn't I?"

The escort seemed amused by the question but didn't answer.

A minute later, at the front door, Spencer paused to study the Quan Yin. "He really thinks she works, keeps out his enemies?"

"If he thinks so, then she must," said the escort. "Mr. Lee is a great man."

Spencer looked at him. "You were in the boat?"

"I was only eight. My mother was the woman who died of thirst the day before we were rescued."

"He says he saved no one."

"He saved us all," the escort said, and he opened the door.

On the sidewalk in front of the restaurant, half blinded by the harsh sunlight, jarred by the noise of the passing traffic and a jet overhead, Spencer felt as if he had awakened suddenly from a dream. Or had just plunged into one.

During the entire time he'd been in the restaurant and the rooms beneath it, no one had looked at his scar.

He turned and gazed through the glass door of the restaurant.

The man whose mother had died of thirst on the South China Sea now stood among the tables again, folding white cloth napkins into fanciful, peaked shapes.

∽

The print lab, where David Davis and a young male assistant were waiting for Roy Miro, was one of four rooms occupied by Fingerprint Analysis. Image-processing computers, high-definition monitors, and more exotic pieces of equipment were provided in generous quantity.

Davis was preparing to develop latent fingerprints on the bathroom window that had been carefully removed from the Santa Monica bungalow. It lay on the marble top of a lab bench—the entire frame, with the glass intact and the corroded brass piano hinge attached.

"This one's important," Roy warned as he approached them.

"Of course, yes, every case is important," Davis said.

"This one's *more* important. And urgent."

Roy disliked Davis, not merely because the man had an annoying name, but because he was exhaustingly enthusiastic. Tall, thin, storklike, with wiry blond hair, David Davis never merely walked anywhere but bustled, scurried, sprinted. Instead of just turning, he always seemed to *spin*. He never pointed at anything but *thrust* a finger at it. To Roy Miro, who avoided extremes of appearance and of public behavior, Davis was embarrassingly theatrical.

The assistant—known to Roy only as Wertz—was a pale creature who wore his lab coat as if it were the cassock of a humble novice in a seminary. When he wasn't rushing off to fetch something for Davis, he orbited his boss with fidgety reverence. He made Roy sick.

"The flashlight gave us nothing," David Davis said, flamboyantly whirling one hand to indicate a big zero. "Zero! Not even a partial. Crap. A piece of *crap*—that flashlight! No smooth surface on it. Brushed steel, ribbed steel, checked steel, but no *smooth* steel."

"Too bad," Roy said.

"Too bad?" Davis said, eyes widening as if Roy had responded to news of the Pope's assassination with a shrug and a chuckle. "It's as if the damned thing was *designed* for burglars and thugs—the official Mafia flashlight, for God's sake."

Wertz mumbled an affirmative, "For God's sake."

"So let's do the window," Roy said impatiently.

"Yes, we have big hopes for the window," Davis said, his head bobbing up and down like that of a parrot listening to reggae music. "Lacquer. Painted with multiple coats of mustard-yellow lacquer to resist the steam from the shower, you see. Smooth." Davis beamed at the small window that lay on the marble lab bench. "If there's anything on it, we'll fume it up."

"The quicker the better," Roy stressed.

In one corner of the room, under a ventilation hood, stood an empty ten-gallon fish tank. Wearing surgical gloves, handling the window by the edges, Wertz conveyed it to the tank. A smaller object would have been suspended on wires, with spring-loaded clips. The window was too heavy and cumbersome for that, so Wertz stood it in the tank, at an angle, against one of the glass walls. It just fit.

Davis put three cotton balls in a petri dish and placed the dish in the bottom of the tank. He used a pipette to transfer a few drops of liquid cyanoacrylate methyl ester to the cotton. With a second pipette, he applied a similar quantity of sodium hydroxide solution.

Immediately, a cloud of cyanoacrylate fumes billowed through the fish tank, up toward the ventilation hood.

Latent prints, left by small amounts of skin oils and sweat and dirt, were generally invisible to the naked eye until developed with one of several substances: powders, iodine, silver nitrate solution, ninhydrin solution—or cyanoacrylate fumes, which often achieved the best results on nonporous materials like glass, metal, plastic, and hard lacquers. The fumes readily condensed into resin on any surface but more heavily on the oils of which latent prints were formed.

The process could take as little as thirty minutes. If they left the window in the tank more than sixty minutes, so much resin might be deposited that print details would be lost. Davis settled on forty minutes and left Wertz to watch over the fuming.

Those were forty cruel minutes for Roy, because David Davis, a techno geek without equal, insisted on demonstrating some new, state-of-the-art lab equipment. With much gesticulating and exclaiming, his eyes as beady and bright as those of a bird, the technician dwelt on every mechanical detail at excruciating length.

By the time Wertz announced that the window was out of the fish tank, Roy was exhausted from being attentive to Davis. Wistfully, he recalled the Bettonfields' bedroom the night before: holding lovely Penelope's hand, listening to the Beatles. He'd been so relaxed.

The dead were often better company than the living.

Wertz led them to the photography table, on which lay the bathroom window. A Polaroid CU-5 was fixed to a rack over the table, lens downward, to take closeups of any prints that might be found.

The side of the window that was facing up had been on the inside of the bungalow, and the mystery man must have touched it when he escaped. The outside, of course, had been washed with rain.

Although a black background would have been ideal, the mustard-yellow lacquer should have been sufficiently dark to contrast with a friction-ridge pattern of white cyanoacrylate deposits. A close examination revealed nothing on either the frame or the glass itself.

Wertz switched off the overhead fluorescent panels, leaving the lab dark except for what little daylight leaked around the closed Levolor blinds. His pale face seemed vaguely phosphorescent in the murk, like the flesh of a creature that lived in a deep-sea trench.

"A little oblique light will make something pop up," Davis said.

A halogen lamp, with a cone-shaped shade and a flexible metal cable for a neck, hung on a wall bracket nearby. Davis unhooked it, switched it on, and slowly moved it around the bathroom window, aiming the focused light at severe angles across the frame.

"Nothing," Roy said impatiently.

"Let's try the glass," Davis said, angling light from first one direction then another, studying the pane as he'd studied the frame.

Nothing.

"Magnetic powder," Davis said. "That's the ticket."

Wertz flicked on the fluorescent lights. He went to a supply cabinet and returned with a jar of magnetic powder and a magnetic applicator called a Magna-Brush, which Roy had seen used before.

Streamers of black powder flowed in rays from the applicator and stuck where there were traces of grease or oil, but loose grains were drawn back by the magnetized brush. The advantage of the magnetized over other fingerprint powders was that it did not leave the suspect surface coated with excess material.

Wertz covered every inch of the frame and pane. No prints.

"Okay, all right, fine, so be it!" Davis exclaimed, rubbing his long-fingered hands together, bobbing his head, happily rising to the challenge. "Shoot, we're not stumped yet. Damned if we are! This is what makes the job fun."

"If it's easy, it's for assholes," Wertz said with a grin, obviously repeating one of their favorite aphorisms.

"Exactly!" Davis said. "Right you are, young master Wertz. And we are not just *any* assholes."

The challenge seemed to have made them dangerously giddy.

Roy looked pointedly at his wristwatch.

While Wertz put away the Magna-Brush and jar of powder, David Davis pulled on a pair of latex gloves and carefully transferred the window to an adjoining room that was smaller than the main lab. He stood it in a metal sink and snatched one of two plastic laboratory wash bottles that stood on the counter, with which he washed down the lacquered frame and glass. "Methanol solution of rhodamine 6G," Davis explained, as though Roy would know what that was or as if he might even keep it in his refrigerator at home.

Wertz came in just then and said, "I used to know a Rhodamine, lived in apartment 6G, just across the hall."

"This smell like her?" Davis asked.

"She was more pungent," Wertz said, and he laughed with Davis.

Nerd humor. Roy found it tedious, not funny. He supposed he should be relieved about that.

Trading the first wash bottle for the second, David Davis said, "Straight methanol. Washes away excess rhodamine."

"Rhodamine always went to excess, and you couldn't wash her away for weeks," said Wertz, and they laughed again.

Sometimes Roy hated his job.

Wertz powered up a water-cooled argon ion laser generator that stood along one wall. He fiddled with the controls.

Davis carried the window to the laser-examination table.

Satisfied that the machine was ready, Wertz distributed laser goggles. Davis switched off the fluorescents. The only light was the pale wedge that came through the door from the adjoining lab.

Putting on his goggles, Roy crowded close to the table with the two technicians.

Davis switched on the laser. As the eerie beam of light played across the bottom of the window frame, a print appeared almost at once, limed in rhodamine: strange, luminescent whorls.

"There's the sonofabitch!" Davis said.

"Could be anybody's print," Roy said. "We'll see."

Wertz said, "That one looks like a thumb."

The light moved on. More prints magically glowed around the handle and the latch hasp in the center of the bottom member of the frame. A cluster: some partial, some smeared, some whole and clear.

"If I was a betting man," Davis said, "I'd wager a bundle that the window had been cleaned recently, wiped with a cloth, which gives us a pristine field. I'd bet all these prints belong to the same person, were laid down at the same time, by your man last night. They were harder to detect than usual because there wasn't much oil on his fingertips."

"Yeah, that's right, he'd just been walking in the rain," Wertz said excitedly.

Davis said, "And maybe he dried his hands on something when he entered the house."

"There aren't any oil glands in the underside of the hand," Wertz felt obliged to tell Roy. "Fingertips get oily from touching the face, the hair, other parts of the body. Human beings seem to be incessantly touching themselves."

"Hey, now," Davis said in a mock-stern voice, "none of that *here*, young master Wertz."

They both laughed.

The goggles pinched the bridge of Roy's nose. They were giving him a headache.

Under the lambent light of the laser, another print appeared.

Even Mother Teresa on powerful methamphetamines would have been stricken by depression in the company of David Davis and the Wertz thing. Nevertheless, Roy felt his spirits rise with the appearance of each new luminous print.

The mystery man would not be a mystery much longer.

7

T HE DAY WAS MILD, though not warm enough for sunbathing. At
Venice Beach, however, Spencer saw six well-tanned young
women in bikinis and two guys in flowered Hawaiian swim trunks,
all lying on big towels and soaking up the rays, goose-pimpled but game.

Two muscular, barefoot men in shorts had set up a volleyball net in
the sand. They were playing an energetic game, with much leaping,
whooping, and grunting. On the paved promenade, a few people glided
along on roller skates and Rollerblades, some in swimwear and some not.
A bearded man, wearing jeans and a black T-shirt, was flying a red kite
with a long tail of red ribbons.

Everyone was too old for high school, old enough so they should have
been at work on a Thursday afternoon. Spencer wondered how many
were victims of the latest recession and how many were just perpetual ado-
lescents who scammed a living from parents or society. California had
long been home to a sizable community of the latter and, with its economic policies, had recently created the former in hordes to rival the af-
fluent legions that it had spawned in previous decades.

On a grassy area adjacent to the sand, Rosie was sitting on a concrete-
and-redwood bench, with her back to the matching picnic table. The
feathery shadows of an enormous palm tree caressed her.

In white sandals, white slacks, and a purple blouse, she was even more
exotic and strikingly beautiful than she had been in the moody Deco lighting at The Red Door. The blood of her Vietnamese mother and that of
her African-American father were both visible in her features, yet she
didn't call to mind either of the ethnic heritages that she embodied. Instead, she seemed to be the exquisite Eve of a new race: a perfect, innocent woman made for a new Eden.

The peace of the innocent didn't fill her, however. She looked tense
and hostile as she stared out to sea, no less so when she turned and saw
Spencer approaching. But then she smiled broadly when she saw Rocky.
"What a cutie!" She leaned forward on the bench and made come-to-me
motions with her hands. "Here, baby. Here, cutie."

Rocky had been happily padding along, tail wagging, taking in the beach scene—but he froze when confronted by the reaching, cooing beauty on the bench. His tail slipped between his legs, fell still. He tensed and prepared to spring away if she moved toward him.

"What's his name?" Rosie asked.

"Rocky. He's shy." Spencer sat on the other end of the bench.

"Come here, Rocky," she coaxed. "Come here, you sweet thing."

Rocky cocked his head and studied her warily.

"What's wrong, cutie? Don't you want to be cuddled and petted?"

Rocky whined. He dropped low on his front paws and wiggled his rear end, though he couldn't bring himself to wag his tail. Indeed, he wanted to be cuddled. He just didn't quite trust her.

"The more you come on to him," Spencer advised, "the more he'll withdraw. Ignore him, and there's a chance he'll decide you're okay."

When Rosie stopped coaxing and sat up straight again, Rocky was frightened by the sudden movement. He scrambled backward a few feet and studied her more warily than before.

"Has he always been this shy?" Rosie asked.

"Since I've known him. He's four or five years old, but I've only had him for two. Saw one of those little spots the newspaper runs every Friday for the animal shelter. Nobody would adopt him, so they were going to have to put him to sleep."

"He's so cute. Anyone would adopt him."

"He was a lot worse then."

"You can't mean he'd bite anyone. Not this sweetie."

"No. Never tried to bite. He was too beaten down for that. He whined and trembled anytime you tried to approach him. When you touched him, he just sort of curled into a ball, closed his eyes, and whimpered, shivering like crazy, as if it hurt to be touched."

"Abused?" she said grimly.

"Yeah. Normally, the people at the pound wouldn't have featured him in the paper. He wasn't a good prospect for adoption. They told me— when a dog's as emotionally crippled as he was, it's usually best not even to try to place him, just put him to sleep."

Still watching the dog as he watched her, Rosie asked, "What happened to him?"

"I didn't ask. Didn't want to know. There are too many things in life I wish I'd never learned . . . 'cause now I can't forget."

The woman looked away from the dog and met Spencer's eyes.

He said, "Ignorance isn't bliss, but sometimes . . ."

". . . ignorance makes it possible for us to sleep at night," she finished.

She was in her late twenties, perhaps thirty. She had been well out of infancy when bombs and gunfire shattered the Asian days, when Saigon fell, when conquering soldiers seized the spoils of war in drunken celebration, when the reeducation camps opened. Maybe as old as eight or nine. Pretty even then: silky black hair, enormous eyes. And far too old for the memories of those terrors ever to fade, as did the forgotten pain of birth and the night fears of the crib.

Last evening at The Red Door, when Rosie had said that Valerie Keene's past was full of suffering, she hadn't merely been guessing or expressing an intuition. She had meant that she'd seen a torment in Valerie that was akin to her own pain.

Spencer looked away from her and stared at the combers that broke gently on the shore. They cast an ever changing lacework of foam across the sand.

"Anyway," he said, "if you ignore Rocky, he might come around. Probably not. But he might."

He shifted his gaze to the red kite. It bobbed and darted on rising thermals, high in the blue sky.

"Why do you want to help Val?" she asked finally.

"Because she's in trouble. And like you said yourself last night, she's special."

"You like her."

"Yes. No. Well, not in the way you mean."

"In what way, then?" Rosie asked.

Spencer couldn't explain what he couldn't understand.

He looked down from the red kite but not at the woman. Rocky was creeping past the far end of the bench, watching Rosie intently as she studiously ignored him. The dog was keeping well out of her reach in case she suddenly turned and snatched at him.

"Why do you want to help her?" Rosie pressed.

The dog was close enough to hear him.

Never lie to the dog.

As he had admitted in the truck last night, Spencer said, "Because I want to find a life."

"And you think you can find it by helping her?"

"Yes."

"How?"

"I don't know."

The dog crept out of sight, circling the bench behind them.

Rosie said, "You think she's part of this life you're looking for. But what if she isn't?"

He stared at the roller skaters on the promenade. They were gliding away from him, as if they were gossamer people blown by the wind, gliding, gliding away.

At last he said, "Then I'll be no worse off than I am now."

"And her?"

"I don't want anything from her that she doesn't want to give."

After a silence, she said, "You're a strange one, Spencer."

"I know."

"Very strange. Are you also special?"

"Me? No."

"Special like Valerie?"

"No."

"She deserves special."

"I'm not."

He heard stealthy sounds behind them, and he knew the dog was squirming on its belly, under the bench on the other side of the picnic table, under the table itself, trying to get closer to the woman, the better to detect and ponder her scent.

"She *did* talk to you quite a while Tuesday night," Rosie said.

He said nothing, letting her make up her mind about him.

"And I saw . . . a couple of times . . . you made her laugh."

He waited.

"Okay," Rosie said, "since Mr. Lee called, I've been trying to remember anything Val said that might help you find her. But there's not much. We liked each other right off, we got close pretty quickly. But mostly we just talked about work, about movies and books, about stuff in the news and things *now*, not about things in the past."

"Where'd she live before she moved to Santa Monica?"

"She never said."

"You didn't ask? You think it might've been somewhere around Los Angeles?"

"No. She wasn't familiar with the city."

"She ever mention where she was born, where she grew up?"

"I don't know why, but I think it was back east somewhere."

"She ever tell you anything about her mom and dad, about having any brothers or sisters?"

"No. But when anyone was talking about family, she'd get this sadness in her eyes. I think maybe . . . her folks are all dead."

He looked at Rosie. "You didn't ask her about them?"

"No. It's just a feeling."

"Was she ever married?"

"Maybe. I didn't ask."

"For a friend, there's a lot you didn't ask."

Rosie nodded. "Because I knew she couldn't tell me the truth. I don't have that many close friends, Mr. Grant, so I didn't want to spoil our relationship by putting her in a position where she'd have to lie to me."

Spencer put his right hand to his face. In the warm air, the scar felt icy under his fingertips.

The bearded man slowly reeled in the kite. That big red diamond blazed against the sky. Its tail of ribbons fluttered like flames.

"So," Spencer said, "you sensed she was running from something?"

"I figured it might be a bad husband, you know, who beat her."

"Do wives regularly run away, start their lives over from scratch, because of a bad husband, instead of just divorcing him?"

"They do in the movies," she said. "If he's violent enough."

Rocky had slipped out from under the table. He appeared at Spencer's side, having fully circled them. His tail was no longer between his legs, but he wasn't wagging it, either. He watched Rosie intently as he continued to slink around to the front of the table.

Pretending to be unaware of the dog, Rosie said, "I don't know if it helps . . . but from little things she said, I think she knows Las Vegas. She's been there more than once, maybe a lot of times."

"Could she have lived there?"

Rosie shrugged. "She liked games. She's good at games. Scrabble, checkers, Monopoly . . . And sometimes we played cards—five-hundred rummy or two-hand pinochle. You should see her shuffle and deal out cards. She can really make them fly through her hands."

"You think she picked that up in Vegas?"

She shrugged again.

Rocky sat on the grass in front of Rosie and stared at her with obvious yearning, but he remained ten feet away, safely out of reach.

"He's decided he can't trust me," she said.

"Nothing personal," Spencer assured her, getting to his feet.

"Maybe he knows."

"Knows what?"

"Animals know things," she said solemnly. "They can see into a person. They see the stains."

"All Rocky sees is a beautiful lady who wants to cuddle him, and he's going crazy because there's nothing to fear but fear itself."

As if he understood his master, Rocky whined pathetically.

"He sees the stains," she said softly. "He knows."

"All I see," Spencer said, "is a lovely woman on a sunny day."

"A person does terrible things to survive."

"That's true of everyone," he said, though he sensed that she was talking to herself more than to him. "Old stains, long faded."

"Never entirely." She seemed no longer to be staring at the dog but at something on the far side of an invisible bridge of time.

Though he was reluctant to leave her in that suddenly strange mood, Spencer could think of nothing more to say.

Where the white sand met the grass, the bearded man cranked the reel in his hands and appeared to be fishing the heavens. The blood-red kite gradually descended, its tail snapping like a whip of fire.

Finally Spencer thanked Rosie for talking with him. She wished him luck, and he walked away with Rocky.

The dog repeatedly stopped to glance back at the woman on the bench, then scurried to catch up with Spencer. When they had covered fifty yards and were halfway to the parking lot, Rocky issued a short yelp of decision and bolted back to the picnic table.

Spencer turned to watch.

In the last few feet, the mutt lost courage. He skidded nearly to a halt and approached her with his head lowered timidly, with much shivering and tail wagging.

Rosie slipped off the bench onto the grass, and pulled Rocky into her arms. Her sweet, clean laughter trilled across the park.

"Good dog," Spencer said quietly.

The muscular volleyball players took a break from their game to get a couple of cans of Pepsi out of a Styrofoam cooler.

Having reeled his kite all the way to the earth, the bearded man headed for the parking lot by a route that brought him past Spencer. He looked like a mad prophet: untrimmed; unwashed; with deeply set, wild blue eyes; a beaky nose; pale lips; broken, yellow teeth. On his black T-shirt, in red letters, were five words: ANOTHER BEAUTIFUL DAY IN HELL. He cast a fierce glance at Spencer, clutched his kite as if he thought every blackguard in creation wanted nothing more than to steal it, and stalked out of the park.

Spencer realized he had put a hand over his scar when the man had glanced at him. He lowered it.

Rosie was standing a few steps in front of the picnic table now, shooing Rocky away, apparently admonishing him not to keep his master waiting. She was beyond the reach of the palm shadows, in sunlight.

As the dog reluctantly left his new friend and trotted toward his master, Spencer was once again aware of the woman's exceptional beauty, which was far greater than Valerie's. And if it was the role of savior and healer that he yearned to fill, this woman most likely needed him more than the one he sought. Yet he was drawn to Valerie, not to Rosie, for reasons he could not explain—except to accuse himself of obsession, of being swept away by the fathomless currents of his subconscious, regardless of where they might take him.

The dog reached him, panting and grinning.

Rosie raised one hand over her head and waved good-bye.

Spencer waved too.

Maybe his search for Valerie Keene wasn't merely an obsession. He had the uncanny feeling that he was the kite and that she was the reel. Some strange power—call it destiny—turned the crank, wound the line around the spool, drawing him inexorably toward her, and he had no choice in the matter whatsoever.

While the sea rolled in from faraway China and lapped at the beach, while the sunshine traveled ninety-three million miles through airless space to caress the golden bodies of the young women in their bikinis, Spencer and Rocky walked back to the truck.

∽

With Roy Miro trailing after him at a more sedate pace, David Davis rushed into the main data processing room with the photographs of the two best prints on the bathroom window. He took them to Nella Shire, at one of the workstations. "One is clearly a thumb, clearly, no question," Davis told her. "The other might be an index finger."

Shire was about forty-five, with a face as sharp as that of a fox, frizzy orange hair, and green fingernail polish. Her half-walled cubicle was decorated with three photographs clipped from bodybuilding magazines: hugely pumped-up men in bikini briefs.

Noticing the musclemen, Davis frowned and said, "Ms. Shire, I've told you this is unacceptable. You must remove these pinups."

"The human body is art."

Davis was red-faced. "You *know* this can be construed as sexual harassment in the workplace."

"Yeah?" She took the fingerprint photos from him. "By who?"

"By any male worker in this room, that's by *whom*."

"None of the men working here looks like these hunks. Until one of them does, nobody has anything to worry about from me."

Davis tore one of the clippings from the cubicle wall, then another. "The last thing I need is a notation on my management record, saying I allowed harassment in my division."

Although Roy believed in the law of which Nella Shire was in violation, he was aware of the irony of Davis worrying about his management record being soiled by a tolerance-of-harassment entry. After all, the nameless agency for which they worked was an illegal organization, answering to no elected official; therefore, every act of Davis's working day was in violation of one law or another.

Of course, like nearly all of the agency's personnel, Davis didn't know that he was an instrument of a conspiracy. He received his paycheck from the Department of Justice and thought he was on their records as an employee. He had signed a secrecy oath, but he believed that he was part of a legal—if potentially controversial—offensive against organized crime and international terrorism.

As Davis tore the third pinup off the cubicle walls and wadded it in his fist, Nella Shire said, "Maybe you hate those pictures so much because they turn *you* on, which is something you can't accept about yourself. Did you ever think of that?" She glanced at the fingerprint photos. "So what do you want me to do with these?"

Roy saw that David Davis had to struggle not to answer with the first thing that came to his mind.

Instead, Davis said, "We need to know whose prints these are. Go through Mama, get on-line with the FBI's Automated Identification Division. Start with the Latent Descriptor Index."

The Federal Bureau of Investigation had one hundred ninety million fingerprints on file. Though its newest computer could make thousands of comparisons a minute, a lot of time could be expended if it had to shuffle through its entire vast storehouse of prints.

With the help of clever software called the Latent Descriptor Index, the field of search could be drastically reduced and results achieved quickly. If they had been seeking suspects in a series of killings, they would have listed the prime characteristics of the crimes—the sex and age of each victim, the methods of murder, any similarities in the conditions of the corpses, the locations at which the bodies had been found—and the index would have compared those facts to the modus operandi of known offenders, eventually producing a list of suspects and their fingerprints. Then a few hundred—or even just a few—comparisons might be necessary instead of millions.

Nella Shire turned to her computer and said, "So give me the telltales, and I'll create a three-oh-two."

"We aren't seeking a known criminal," Davis said.

Roy said, "We think our man was in special forces, or maybe he had special-weapons-and-tactics training."

"Those guys are all hardbodies, for sure," Shire said, eliciting a scowl from David Davis. "Army, navy, marines, or air force?"

"We don't know," Roy said. "Maybe he was never in the service. Could have been with a state or local police department. Could have been a Bureau agent, as far as we know, or DEA or ATF."

"The way this works," Shire said impatiently, "is, I need to put in telltales that limit the field."

A hundred million of the prints in the Bureau's system were in criminal-history files, which left ninety million that covered federal employees, military personnel, intelligence services, state and local law-enforcement officers, and registered aliens. If they knew that their mystery man was, say, an ex-marine, they wouldn't have to search most of those ninety million files.

Roy opened the envelope that Melissa Wicklun had given him a short while ago, in Photo Analysis. He took out one of the computer-projected portraits of the man they were hunting. On the back of it was the data that the photo-analysis software had deduced from the rain-veiled profile of the man at the bungalow the previous night.

"Male, Caucasian, twenty-eight to thirty-two," Roy said.

Nella Shire typed swiftly. A list appeared on the screen.

"Five feet eleven inches tall," Roy continued. "One hundred and sixty-five pounds, give or take five. Brown hair, brown eyes."

He turned the photo over to stare at the full-face portrait, and David Davis bent down to look as well. "Severe facial scarring," Roy said. "Right side. Beginning at the ear, terminating near the chin."

"Was that sustained on duty?" Davis wondered.

"Probably. So a conditional telltale might be an honorable early discharge or even a service disability."

"Whether he was discharged or disabled," Davis said excitedly, "you can bet he was required to undergo psychological counseling. A scar like this—it's a terrible blow to self-esteem. Terrible."

Nella Shire swiveled in her chair, snatched the portrait out of Roy's hand, and looked at it. "I don't know . . . I think it makes him look sexy. Dangerous and sexy."

Ignoring her, Davis said, "The government's very concerned about self-esteem these days. A lack of self-esteem is the root of crime and social unrest. You can't hold up a bank or mug an old lady unless you first think you're nothing but a lowlife thief."

"Yeah?" Nella Shire said, returning the portrait to Roy. "Well, I've known a thousand jerks who thought they were God's best work."

Davis said firmly, "Make psychological counseling a telltale."

She added that item to her list. "Anything else?"

"That's all," Roy said. "How long is this going to take?"

Shire read through the list on the screen. "Hard to say. No more than eight or ten hours. Maybe less. Maybe a lot less. Could be, in an hour or two, I'll have his name, address, phone number, and be able to tell you which side of his pants he hangs on."

David Davis, still clutching a fistful of crumpled musclemen and worried about his management record, appeared offended by her remark.

Roy was merely intrigued. "Really? Maybe only an hour or two?"

"Why would I be jerking your chain?" she asked impatiently.

"Then I'll hang around. We need this guy real bad."

"He's almost yours," Nella Shire promised as she set to work.

At three o'clock they had a late lunch on the back porch while the long shadows of eucalyptuses crept up the canyon in the yellowing light of the westering sun. Sitting in a rocking chair, Spencer ate a ham-and-cheese sandwich and drank a bottle of beer. After polishing off a bowl of Purina, Rocky used his grin, his best sad-eyed look, his most pathetic whine, his wagging tail, and a master thespian's store of tricks to cadge bits of the sandwich.

"Laurence Olivier had nothing on you," Spencer told him.

When the sandwich was gone, Rocky padded down the porch steps and started across the backyard toward the nearest cluster of wild brush, characteristically seeking privacy for his toilet.

"Wait, wait, wait," Spencer said, and the dog stopped to look at him. "You'll come back with your coat full of burrs, and it'll take me an hour to comb them all out. I don't have time for that."

He got up from the rocking chair, turned his back to the dog, and stared at the cabin wall while he finished the last of the beer.

When Rocky returned, they went inside, leaving the tree shadows to grow unwatched.

While the dog napped on the sofa, Spencer sat at the computer and began his search for Valerie Keene. From that bungalow in Santa Monica, she could have gone anywhere in the world, and he would have been as well advised to start looking in far Borneo as in nearby Ventura. Therefore, he could only go backward, into the past.

He had a single clue: Vegas. *Cards. She can really make them fly through her hands.*

Her familiarity with Vegas and her facility with cards might mean that she had lived there and earned her living as a dealer.

By his usual route, Spencer hacked into the main LAPD computer. From there he springboarded into an interstate police data-sharing network, which he had often used before, and bounced across borders into the computer of the Clark County Sheriff's Department in Nevada, which had jurisdiction over the city of Las Vegas.

On the sofa, the snoring dog pumped his legs, chasing rabbits in his sleep. In Rocky's case, the rabbits were probably chasing him.

After exploring the sheriff's computer for a while and finding his way into—among other things—the department's personnel records, Spencer finally discovered a file labeled NEV CODES. He was pretty sure he knew what it was, and he wanted in.

NEV CODES was specially protected. To use it, he required an access number. Incredibly, in many police agencies, that would be either an officer's badge number or, in the case of office workers, an employee ID number—all obtainable from personnel records, which were not well guarded. He had already collected a few badge numbers in case he needed them. Now he used one, and NEV CODES opened to him.

It was a list of numerical codes with which he could access the computer-stored data of any government agency in the state of Nevada. In a wink he followed the cyberspace highway from Las Vegas to the Nevada Gaming Commission in Carson City, the capital.

The commission licensed all casinos in the state and enforced the laws and regulations that governed them. Anyone who wished to invest—or serve as an executive—in the gaming industry was required to submit to a background investigation and to be proved free of ties to known criminals. In the 1970s, a strengthened commission squeezed out most of the mobsters and Mafia front men who had founded Nevada's biggest industry, in favor of companies like Metro-Goldwyn-Mayer and Hilton Hotels.

It was logical to suppose that other casino employees below management level—from pit bosses to cocktail waitresses—underwent similar although less exhaustive background checks and were issued ID cards. Spencer explored menus and directories, and in another twenty minutes, he found the records that he needed.

The data related to casino-employee work permits was divided into three primary files: Expired, Current, Pending. Because Valerie had been working at The Red Door in Santa Monica for two months, Spencer accessed the Expired list first.

In his rambles through cyberspace, he had seen few files so extensively cross-referenced as this one—and those others had been related to grave national defense matters. The system allowed him to search for a subject in the Expired category by means of twenty-two indices ranging from eye color to most recent place of employment.

He typed VALERIE ANN KEENE.

In a few seconds the system replied: UNKNOWN.

He shifted to the file labeled Current and typed in her name.

UNKNOWN.

Spencer tried the Pending file with the same result. Valerie Ann Keene was unknown to the Nevada gaming authorities.

For a moment he stared at the screen, despondent because his only clue had proved to be a dead end. Then he realized that a woman on the run was unlikely to use the same name everywhere she went and thereby make herself easy to track. If Valerie had lived and worked in Vegas, her name almost surely had been different then.

To find her in the file, Spencer would have to be clever.

§

While waiting for Nella Shire to find the scarred man, Roy Miro was in terrible danger of being dragooned into hours of sociable conversation with David Davis. He would almost rather have eaten a cyanide-laced muffin and washed it down with a big, frosty beaker of carbolic acid than spend any more time with the fingerprint maven.

Claiming not to have slept the night before, when in fact he had slept the innocent sleep of a saint after the priceless gift he had given to Penelope Bettonfield and her husband, Roy charmed Davis into offering the use of his office. "I insist, I really do, I will listen to no argument, none!" Davis said with considerable gesturing and bobbing of his head. "I've got a couch in there. You can stretch out on it, you won't be inconveniencing me. I've got plenty of lab work to do. I don't need to be at my desk today."

Roy didn't expect to sleep. In the cool dimness of the office, with the California sun banished by the tightly closed Levolors, he thought he would lie on his back, stare at the ceiling, visualize the nexus of his spiritual being—where his soul connected with the mysterious power that ruled the cosmos—and meditate on the meaning of existence. He pursued deeper self-awareness every day. He was a seeker, and the search for enlightenment was endlessly exciting to him. Strangely, however, he fell asleep.

He dreamed of a perfect world. There was no greed or envy or despair, because everyone was identical to everyone else. There was a single sex, and human beings reproduced by discreet parthenogenesis in the privacy of their bathrooms—though not often. The only skin color was a pale and slightly radiant blue. Everyone was beautiful in an androgynous way. No one was dumb, but no one was too smart, either. Everyone wore the same clothes and lived in houses that all looked alike. Every Friday evening, there was a planetwide bingo game, which everyone won, and on Saturdays—

Wertz woke him, and Roy was paralyzed by terror because he confused the dream and reality. Gazing up into the slug-pale, moon-round face of Davis's assistant, which was revealed by a desk lamp, Roy thought that he himself, along with everyone else in the world, looked exactly like Wertz. He tried to scream but couldn't find his voice.

Then Wertz spoke, bringing Roy fully awake: "Mrs. Shire's found him. The scarred man. She's found him."

Alternately yawning and grimacing at the sour taste in his mouth, Roy followed Wertz to the data processing room. David Davis and Nella Shire were standing at her workstation, each with a sheaf of papers. In the fluorescent glare, Roy squinted with discomfort, then with interest, as Davis passed to him, page by page, computer printouts on which both he and Nella Shire commented excitedly.

"His name's Spencer Grant," Davis said. "No middle name. At eighteen, out of high school, he joined the army."

"High IQ, equally high motivation," Mrs. Shire said. "He applied for special-forces training. Army Rangers."

"He left the army after six years," Davis said, passing another printout to Roy, "used his service benefits to go to UCLA."

Scanning the latest page, Roy said, "Majored in criminology."

"Minored in criminal psychology," said Davis. "Went to school year-round, kept a heavy class load, got a degree in three years."

"Young man in a hurry," Wertz said, apparently so they would remember that he was part of the team and would not, accidentally, step on him and crush him like a bug.

As Davis handed Roy another page, Nella Shire said, "Then he applied to the L.A. Police Academy. Graduated at the top of his class."

"One day, after less than a year on the street," Davis said, "he walked into the middle of a carjacking in progress. Two armed men. They saw him coming, tried to take the woman motorist hostage."

"He killed them both," Shire said. "The woman wasn't scratched."

"Grant get crucified?"

"No. Everyone felt these were righteous shootings."

Glancing at another page that Davis handed to him, Roy said, "According to this, he was transferred off the street."

"Grant has computer skills and high aptitude," Davis said, "so they put him on a computer-crime task force. Strictly desk work."

Roy frowned. "Why? Was he traumatized by the shootings?"

"Some of them can't handle it," Wertz said knowingly. "They don't have the right stuff, don't have the stomach for it, they just come apart."

"According to the records from his mandatory therapy sessions," Nella Shire said, "he wasn't traumatized. He handled it well. He asked for the transfer, but not because he was traumatized."

"Probably in denial," Wertz said, "being macho, too ashamed of his weakness to admit to it."

"Whatever the reason," Davis said, "he asked for the transfer. Then, ten months ago, after putting in twenty-one months with the task force, he just up and resigned from the LAPD altogether."

"Where's he working now?" Roy asked.

"We don't know that, but we *do* know where he lives," David Davis said, producing another printout with a dramatic flourish.

Staring at the address, Roy said, "You're sure this is our man?"

Shire shuffled her own sheaf of papers. She produced a high-resolution printout of a Los Angeles Police Department personnel fingerprint ID sheet while Davis provided the photos of the prints they had lifted from the frame of the bathroom window.

Davis said, "If you know how to make comparisons, you'll see the computer's right when it says they're a perfect match. Perfect. This is our guy. No doubt about it, none."

Handing another printout to Roy, Nella Shire said, "This is his most recent photo ID from the police records."

Full face and in profile, Grant bore an uncanny resemblance to the computer-projected portrait that had been given to Roy by Melissa Wicklun in Photo Analysis.

"Is this a recent photo?" Roy asked.

"The most recent the LAPD has on file," Shire said.

"Taken a long time after the carjacking incident?"

"That would have been two and a half years ago. Yeah, I'm sure this picture is a lot more recent than that. Why?"

"The scar looks fully healed," Roy noted.

"Oh," Davis said, "he didn't get the scar in that shootout, no, not then. He's had it a long time, a very long time, had it when he entered the army. It's from a childhood injury."

Roy looked up from the picture. "What injury?"

Davis shrugged his angular shoulders, and his long arms flapped against his white lab coat. "We don't know. None of the records tell us about it.

They just list it as his most prominent identifying feature. 'Cicatricial scar from right ear to point of chin, result of childhood injury.' That's all."

"He looks like Igor," Wertz said with a snicker.

"I think he's sexy," Nella Shire disagreed.

"Igor," Wertz insisted.

Roy turned to him. "Igor who?"

"Igor. You remember—from those old Frankenstein movies, Dr. Frankenstein's sidekick. Igor. The grisly old hunchback with the twisted neck."

"I don't care for that kind of entertainment," Roy said. "It glorifies violence and deformity. It's sick." Studying the photo, Roy wondered how young Spencer Grant had been when he'd suffered such a grievous wound. Just a boy, apparently. "The poor kid," he said. "The poor, poor kid. What quality of life could he have had with a face as damaged as that? What psychological burdens does he carry?"

Frowning, Wertz said, "I thought this was a bad guy, mixed up in terrorism somehow?"

"Even bad guys," Roy said patiently, "deserve compassion. This man has suffered. You can see that. I need to get my hands on him, yes, and be sure that society's safe from him—but he still deserves to be treated with compassion, with as much mercy as possible."

Davis and Wertz stared uncomprehendingly.

But Nella Shire said, "You're a nice man, Roy."

Roy shrugged.

"No," she said, "you really are. It makes me feel good to know there are men like you in law enforcement."

The heat of a blush rose in Roy's face. "Well, thank you, that's very kind, but there's nothing special about me."

Because Nella was clearly not a lesbian, even though she was as much as fifteen years older than he, Roy wished that at least one feature about her was as attractive as Melissa Wicklun's exquisite mouth. But her hair was too frizzy and too orange. Her eyes were too cold a blue, her nose and chin too pointed, her lips too severe. Her body was reasonably well proportioned but not exceptional in any regard.

"Well," Roy said with a sigh, "I'd better pay a visit to this Mr. Grant, ask him what he was doing in Santa Monica last night."

∽

Sitting at the computer in his Malibu cabin but prowling deep into the Nevada Gaming Commission in Carson City, Spencer searched the file of current casino-worker permits by asking to be given the names of all card dealers who were female, between the ages of twenty-eight and thirty, five feet four inches tall, one hundred ten to one hundred twenty pounds, with brown hair and brown eyes. Those were sufficient parameters to result in a comparatively small number of candidates—just fourteen. He directed the computer to print the list of names in alphabetical order.

He started at the top of the printout and summoned the file on Janet Francine Arbonhall. The first page of the electronic dossier that appeared on the screen featured her basic physical description, the date on which her work permit had been approved, and a full-face photograph. She looked nothing like Valerie, so Spencer exited her file without reading it.

He called up another file: Theresa Elisabeth Dunbury. Not her.

Bianca Marie Haguerro. Not her, either.

Corrine Serise Huddleston. No.

Laura Linsey Langston. No.

Rachael Sarah Marks. Nothing like Valerie.

Jacqueline Ethel Mung. Seven down and seven to go.

Hannah May Rainey.

On the screen, Valerie Ann Keene appeared, her hair different from the way she had worn it at The Red Door, lovely but unsmiling.

Spencer ordered a complete printout of Hannah May Rainey's file, which was only three pages long. He read it end to end while the woman continued to stare at him from the computer.

Under the Rainey name, she had worked for over four months of the previous year as a blackjack dealer in the casino of the Mirage Hotel in Las Vegas. Her last day on the job had been November 26, not quite two and a half months ago, and according to the casino manager's report to the commission, she had quit without notice.

They—whoever "they" might be—must have tracked her down on the twenty-sixth of November, and she must have eluded them as they were reaching out for her, just as she eluded them in Santa Monica.

In a corner of the parking garage beneath the agency's building in downtown Los Angeles, Roy Miro had a final word with the three agents who would accompany him to Spencer Grant's house and take the man into custody. Because their agency did not officially exist, the word "custody" was being stretched beyond its usual definition; "kidnapping" was a more accurate description of their intentions.

Roy had no problem with either term. Morality was relative, and nothing done in the service of correct ideals could be a crime.

They were all carrying Drug Enforcement Administration credentials, so Grant would believe that he was being taken to a federal facility to be questioned—and that upon arrival there, he would be permitted to call an attorney. Actually, he was more likely to see the Lord God Almighty on a golden airborne throne than anyone with a law degree.

Using whatever methods might be necessary to obtain truthful answers, they would question him about his relationship with the woman and her current whereabouts. When they had what they needed—or were convinced that they had squeezed out of him all that he knew—they would dispose of him.

Roy would conduct the disposal himself, releasing the poor scarred devil from the misery of this troubled world.

The first of the other three agents, Cal Dormon, wore white slacks and a white shirt with the logo of a pizza parlor stitched on the breast. He would be driving a small white van with a matching logo, which was one of many magnetic-mat signs that could be attached to the vehicle to change its character, depending on what was needed for any particular operation.

Alfonse Johnson was dressed in work shoes, khaki slacks, and a denim jacket. Mike Vecchio wore sweats and a pair of Nikes.

Roy was the only one of them in a suit. Because he had napped fully clothed on Davis's couch, however, he didn't fit the stereotype of a neat and well-pressed federal agent.

"All right, this isn't like last night," Roy said. They had all been part of the SWAT team in Santa Monica. "We need to *talk* to this guy."

The previous night, if any of them had seen the woman, he would have cut her down instantly. For the benefit of any local police who might have shown up, a weapon would have been planted in her hand: a Desert Eagle .50 Magnum, such a powerful handgun that a shot from it would leave an exit wound as large as a man's fist, a piece obviously meant solely for killing people. The story would have been that the agent had gunned her down in self-defense.

"But we can't let him slip away," Roy continued. "And he's a boy with schooling, as well trained as any of you, so he might not just hold out his hands for the bracelets. If you can't make him behave and he looks to be gone, then shoot his legs out from under him. Chop him up good if you have to. He isn't going to need to walk again anyway. Just don't get carried away—okay? Remember, we absolutely *must* talk to him."

∽

Spencer had obtained all the information of interest to him that was contained in the files of the Nevada Gaming Commission. He retreated along the cyberspace highways as far as the Los Angeles Police Department computer.

From there he linked with the Santa Monica Police Department and examined its file of cases initiated within the past twenty-four hours. No case could be referenced either by the name Valerie Ann Keene or by the street address of the bungalow that she had been renting.

He exited the case files and checked call reports for Wednesday night, because it was possible that SMPD officers had answered a call related to the fracas at the bungalow but had not given the incident a case number. This time, he found the address.

The last of the officer's notations indicated why no case number had been assigned: ATF OP IN PROG. FED ASSERTED. Which meant: Bureau of Alcohol, Tobacco and Firearms operation in progress; federal jurisdiction asserted.

The local cops had been frozen out.

On the nearby couch, Rocky exploded from sleep with a shrill yelp, fell to the floor, scrambled to his feet, started to chase his tail, then whipped his head left and right in confusion, searching for whatever threat had pursued him out of his dream.

"Just a nightmare," Spencer assured the dog.

Rocky looked at him doubtfully and whined.

"What was it this time—a giant prehistoric cat?"

The mutt padded quickly across the room and jumped up to plant his forepaws on a windowsill. He stared out at the driveway and the surrounding woods.

The short February day was drawing toward a colorful twilight. The undersides of the eucalyptuses' oval leaves, which were usually silver, now reflected the golden light that poured through gaps in the foliage; they glimmered in a faint breeze, so it appeared as if the trees had been hung with ornaments for the Christmas season that was now more than a month past.

Rocky whined worriedly again.

"A pterodactyl cat?" Spencer suggested. "Huge wings and giant fangs and a purr loud enough to crack stone?"

Not amused, the dog dropped from the window and hurried into the kitchen. He was always like this when he woke abruptly from a bad dream.

He would circle the house, from window to window, convinced that the enemy in the land of dreams was every bit as dangerous to him in the real world.

Spencer looked at the computer screen again.

ATF OP IN PROG. FED ASSERTED.

Something was wrong.

If the SWAT team that hit the bungalow the previous night had been composed of agents of the Bureau of Alcohol, Tobacco and Firearms, why had the men who showed up at Louis Lee's home in Bel Air been carrying FBI credentials? The former bureau was under the control of the United States Secretary of the Treasury, while the latter was ultimately answerable to the Attorney General—though changes in that structure were being contemplated. The different organizations sometimes cooperated in operations of mutual interest; however, considering the usual intensity of interagency rivalry and suspicion, *both* would have had representatives present at the questioning of Louis Lee or of anyone else from whom a lead might have been developed.

Grumbling to himself as if he were the White Rabbit running late for tea with the Mad Hatter, Rocky scampered out of the kitchen and hurried through the open door to the bedroom.

ATF OP IN PROG.

Something wrong . . .

The FBI was by far the more powerful of the two bureaus, and if it was interested enough to be on the scene, it would never agree to surrender all jurisdiction entirely to the ATF. In fact, there was legislation being written in Congress, at the request of the White House, to fold the ATF into the FBI. The cop's note in the SMPD call report should have read: FBI/ATF OP IN PROG.

Brooding about all that, Spencer retreated from Santa Monica to the LAPD, floated there a moment as he tried to decide if he was finished, then backed into the task-force computer, closing doors as he went, neatly cleaning up any traces of his invasion.

Rocky bolted out of the bedroom, past Spencer, to the living room window once more.

Home again, Spencer shut down his computer. He got up from the desk and went to the window to stand beside Rocky.

The tip of the dog's black nose was against the glass. One ear up, one down.

"What do you dream about?" Spencer wondered.

Rocky whimpered softly, his attention fixed on the deep purple shadows and the golden glimmerings of the twilit eucalyptus grove.

"Fanciful monsters, things that could never be?" Spencer asked. "Or just . . . the past?"

The dog was shivering.

Spencer put one hand on the nape of Rocky's neck and stroked him gently.

The dog glanced up, then immediately returned his attention to the eucalyptuses, perhaps because a great darkness was descending slowly over the shrinking twilight. Rocky had always been afraid of the night.

8

THE FADING LIGHT congealed into a luminous red scum across the western sky. The crimson sun was reflected by every microscopic particle of pollution and water vapor in the air, so it seemed as though the city lay under a thin mist of blood.

Cal Dormon retrieved a large pizza box from the back of the white van and walked toward the house.

Roy Miro was on the other side of the street from the van, having entered the block from the opposite direction. He got out of his car and quietly closed the door.

By now, Johnson and Vecchio would have made their way to the back of the house by neighboring properties.

Roy started across the street.

Dormon was halfway along the front walk. He didn't have a pizza in the box, but a Desert Eagle .44 Magnum pistol equipped with a heavy-duty sound suppressor. The uniform and the prop were solely to allay suspicion if Spencer Grant happened to glance out a window just as Dormon was approaching the house.

Roy reached the back of the white van.

Dormon was at the front stoop.

Putting one hand across his mouth as if to muffle a cough, Roy spoke into the transmitter microphone that was clipped to his shirt cuff. "Count five and go," he whispered to the men at the back of the house.

At the front door, Cal Dormon didn't bother to ring the bell or knock. He tried the knob. The lock must have been engaged, because he opened the pizza box, let it fall to the ground, and brought up the powerful Israeli pistol.

Roy picked up his pace, no longer casual.

In spite of its high-quality silencer, the .44 emitted a hard thud each time it was fired. The sound wasn't like gunfire, but it was loud enough to draw the attention of passersby if there had been any. The gun was, after all, a door-buster: Three quick rounds tore the hell out of the jamb and striker plate. Even if the deadbolt remained intact, the notch in which it had been seated was not a notch any more; it was just a bristle of splinters.

Dormon went inside, with Roy behind him, and a guy in stocking feet was coming up from a blue vinyl Barcalounger, a can of beer in one hand, wearing faded jeans and a T-shirt, saying "Jesus Christ," looking terrified and bewildered because the last bits of wood and brass from the door had just hit the living room carpet around him. Dormon drove him backward into the chair again, hard enough to knock the breath out of him, and the can of beer tumbled to the floor, rolled across the carpet, spewing gouts of foam.

The guy wasn't Spencer Grant.

Holding his silencer-fitted Beretta in both hands, Roy quickly crossed the living room, went through an archway into a dining room, and then through an open door into a kitchen.

A blonde of about thirty was facedown on the kitchen floor, her head turned toward Roy, her left arm extended as she tried to recover a butcher knife that had been knocked out of her hand and that was an inch or two beyond her reach. She couldn't move toward it, because Vecchio had a knee in the small of her back and the muzzle of his pistol against her neck, just behind her left ear.

"You bastard, you bastard, you *bastard*," the woman squealed. Her shrill words were neither loud nor clear, because her face was jammed against the linoleum. And she couldn't draw much breath with Vecchio's knee in her back.

"Easy, lady, easy," Vecchio said. "Be still, damn it!"

Alfonse Johnson was one step inside the back door, which must have been unlocked because they hadn't needed to break it down. Johnson was covering the only other person in the room: a little girl, perhaps five, who stood with her back pressed into a corner, wide-eyed and pale, too frightened yet to cry.

The air smelled of hot tomato sauce and onions. On the cutting board were sliced green peppers. The woman had been making dinner.

"Come on," Roy said to Johnson.

Together, they searched the rest of the house, moving fast. The element of surprise was gone, but momentum was still on their side. Hall closet. Bathroom. Girl's bedroom: teddy bears and dolls, the closet door standing open, nobody there. Another small room: a sewing machine, a half-finished green dress on a dressmaker's dummy, closet packed full, no place for anyone to hide. Then the master bedroom, closet, closet, bathroom: nobody.

Johnson said, "Unless that's him in a blond wig on the kitchen floor . . ."

Roy returned to the living room, where the guy in the lounge chair was tilted as far back as he could go, staring into the bore of the .44 while Cal Dormon screamed in his face, spraying him with spittle: "One more time. You hear me, asshole? I'm asking just one more time—where is he?"

"I told you," the guy said, "Jesus, nobody's here but us."

"Where's Grant?" Dormon insisted.

The man was shaking as if the Barcalounger was equipped with a vibrating massage unit. "I don't know him, I swear, never heard of him. So will you just, will you just please, will you point that cannon somewhere else?"

Roy was saddened that it was so often necessary to deny people their dignity in order to get them to cooperate. He left Johnson in the living room with Dormon and returned to the kitchen.

The woman was still flat on the floor, with Vecchio's knee in her back, but she was no longer trying to reach the butcher knife. She wasn't calling him a bastard any more, either. Fury having given way to fear, she was begging him not to hurt her little girl.

The child was in the corner, sucking on her thumb. Tears tracked down her cheeks, but she made no sound.

Roy picked up the butcher knife and put it on the counter, out of the woman's reach.

She rolled one eye to look up at him. "Don't hurt my baby."

"We aren't going to hurt anyone," Roy said.

He went to the little girl, crouched beside her, and said in his softest voice, "Are you scared, honey?"

She turned her eyes from her mother to Roy.

"Of course, you're scared, aren't you?" he said.

With her thumb stuck in her mouth, sucking fiercely, she nodded.

"Well, there's no reason to be scared of me. I'd never hurt a fly. Not even if it buzzed and buzzed around my face and danced in my ears and went skiing down my nose."

The child stared solemnly at him through tears.

Roy said, "When a mosquito lands on me and tries to take a bite, do I swat him? Noooooo. I lay out a tiny napkin for him, a teeny tiny little knife and fork, and I say, 'No one in this world should go hungry. Dinner's on me, Mr. Mosquito.' "

The tears seemed to be clearing from her eyes.

"I remember one time," Roy told her, "when this elephant was on his way to a supermarket to buy peanuts. He was in ever so great a hurry, and he just ran my car off the road. Most people, they would have followed that elephant to the market and punched him right on the tender tip of his trunk. But did I do that? Noooooo. 'When an elephant is out of peanuts,' I told myself, 'he just can't be held responsible for his actions.' However, I must admit I drove to that market after him and let the air out of the tires on his bicycle, but that was not done in anger. I only wanted to keep him off the road until he'd had time to eat some peanuts and calm down."

She was an adorable child. He wished he could see her smile.

"Now," he said, "do you really think I'd hurt anyone?"

The girl shook her head: no.

"Then give me your hand, honey," Roy said.

She let him take her left hand, the one without a wet thumb, and he led her across the kitchen.

Vecchio released the mother. The woman scrambled to her knees and, weeping, embraced the child.

Letting go of the girl's hand and crouching again, touched by the mother's tears, Roy said, "I'm sorry. I abhor violence, I really do. But we thought a dangerous man was here, and we couldn't very well just knock and ask him to come out and play. You understand?"

The woman's lower lip quivered. "I . . . I don't know. Who are you, what do you want?"

"What's your name?"

"Mary. Mary Z-Zelinsky."

"Your husband's name?"

"Peter."

Mary Zelinsky had a lovely nose. The bridge was a perfect wedge, all the lines straight and true. Such delicate nostrils. A septum that seemed crafted of finest porcelain. He didn't think he had ever seen a nose quite as wonderful before.

Smiling, he said, "Well, Mary, we need to know where he is."

"Who?" the woman asked.

"I'm sure you know who. Spencer Grant, of course."

"I don't know him."

Just as she answered him, he looked up from her nose into her eyes, and he saw no deception there.

"I've never heard of him," she said.

To Vecchio, Roy said, "Turn the gas off under that tomato sauce. I'm afraid it's going to burn."

"I swear I've never heard of him," the woman insisted.

Roy was inclined to believe her. Helen of Troy could not have had a nose any finer than Mary Zelinsky's. Of course, indirectly, Helen of Troy had been responsible for the deaths of thousands, and many others had suffered because of her, so beauty was no guarantee of innocence. And in the tens of centuries since the time of Helen, human beings had become masters at the concealment of evil, so even the most guileless-looking creatures sometimes proved to be depraved.

Roy had to be sure, so he said, "If I feel you're lying to me—"

"I'm not lying," Mary said tremulously.

He held up one hand to silence her, and he continued where he had been interrupted:

"—I might take this precious girl to her room, undress her—"

The woman closed her eyes tightly, in horror, as if she could block out the scene that he was so delicately describing for her.

"—and there, among the teddy bears and dolls, I could teach her some grown-up games."

The woman's nostrils flared with terror. Hers really was an exquisite nose.

"Now, Mary, look me in the eyes," he said, "and tell me again if you know a man named Spencer Grant."

She opened her eyes and met his gaze.

They were face-to-face.

He put one hand on the child's head, stroked her hair, smiled.

Mary Zelinsky clutched her daughter with pitiful desperation. "I swear to God I never heard of him. I don't know him. I don't understand what's happening here."

"I believe you," he said. "Rest easy, Mary. I believe you, dear lady. I'm sorry it was necessary to resort to such crudity."

Though the tone of his voice was tender and apologetic, a tide of rage washed through Roy. His fury was directed at Grant, who had somehow hoodwinked them, not at this woman or her daughter or her hapless husband in the Barcalounger.

Although Roy strove to repress his anger, the woman must have glimpsed it in his eyes, which were ordinarily of such a kindly aspect, for she flinched from him.

At the stove, where he had turned off the gas under the sauce and under a pot of boiling water as well, Vecchio said, "He doesn't live here any more."

"I don't think he ever did," Roy said tightly.

∽

Spencer took two suitcases from the closet, considered them, put the smaller of the two aside, and opened the larger bag on his bed. He selected enough clothes for a week. He didn't own a suit, a white shirt, or even one necktie. In his closet hung half a dozen pairs of blue jeans, half a dozen pairs of tan chinos, khaki shirts, and denim shirts. In the top drawer of the highboy, he kept four warm sweaters—two blue, two green—and he packed one of each.

While Spencer filled the suitcase, Rocky paced from room to room, standing worried sentry duty at every window he could reach. The poor mutt was having a hard time shaking off the nightmare.

§

Leaving his men to watch over the Zelinsky family, Roy stepped out of the house and crossed the street toward his car.

The twilight had darkened from red to deep purple. The streetlamps had come on. The air was still, and for a moment the silence was almost as deep as if he had been in a country field.

They were lucky that the Zelinskys' neighbors had not heard anything to arouse suspicion.

On the other hand, no lights showed in the houses flanking the Zelinsky place. Many families in that pleasant middle-class neighborhood were probably able to maintain their standard of living only if both husband and wife held full-time jobs. In fact, in this precarious economy, with take-home pay declining, many were holding on by their fingernails even with two breadwinners. Now, at the height of the rush hour, two-thirds of the homes on both sides of the street were dark, untenanted; their owners were battling freeway traffic, picking up their kids at sitters and day schools that they could not easily afford, and struggling to get home to enjoy a few hours of peace before climbing back on the treadmill in the morning.

Sometimes Roy was so sensitive to the plight of the average person that he was brought to tears.

Right now, however, he could not allow himself to surrender to the empathy that came so easily to him. He had to find Spencer Grant.

In the car, after starting the engine and slipping into the passenger seat, he plugged in the attaché case computer. He married the cellular telephone to it.

He called Mama and asked her to find a phone number for Spencer Grant, in the greater L.A. area, and from the center of her web in Virginia, she began the search. He hoped to get an address for Grant from the phone company, as he had gotten one for the Bettonfields.

David Davis and Nella Shire would have left the downtown office for the day, so he couldn't call there to rail at them. In any case, the problem wasn't their fault, though he would have liked to place the blame on Davis—and on Wertz, whose first name was probably Igor.

In a few minutes, Mama reported that no one named Spencer Grant possessed a telephone, listed or unlisted, in the Los Angeles area.

Roy didn't believe it. He fully trusted Mama. The problem wasn't with her. She was as faultless as his own dear, departed mother had been. But Grant was clever. Too damned clever.

Roy asked Mama to search telephone-company *billing* records for the same name. Grant might have been listed under a pseudonym, but before providing service, the phone company had surely required the signature of a real person with a good credit history.

As Mama worked, Roy watched a car cruise past and pull into a driveway a few houses farther along the street.

Night ruled the city. To the far edge of the western horizon, twilight had abdicated; no trace of its royal-purple light remained.

The display screen flashed dimly, and Roy looked down at the computer on his lap. According to Mama, Spencer Grant's name did not appear in telephone billing records, either.

First, the guy had gone back into his employment files in the LAPD computer and inserted the Zelinsky address, evidently chosen at random, in place of his own. And now, although he still lived in the L.A. area and almost certainly had a telephone, he had expunged his name from the records of whichever company—Pacific Bell or GTE—provided his local service.

Grant seemed to be trying to make himself invisible.

"Who the hell is this guy?" Roy wondered aloud.

Because of what Nella Shire had found, Roy had been convinced that he knew the man he was seeking. Now he suddenly felt that he didn't know Spencer Grant at all, not in any fundamental sense. He knew only generalities, superficialities—but it was in the details where his damnation might lie.

What had Grant been doing at the bungalow in Santa Monica? How was he involved with the woman? What did he know?

Getting answers to those questions was of increasing urgency.

Two more cars disappeared into garages at different houses.

Roy sensed that his chances of finding Grant were diminishing with the passage of time.

Feverishly, he considered his options, and then went through Mama to penetrate the computer at the California Department of Motor Vehicles in Sacramento. In moments, a picture of Grant was on his display screen, one taken by the DMV specifically for a new driver's license. All vital statistics were provided. And a street address.

"All right," Roy said softly, as if to speak loudly would be to undo this bit of good luck.

He ordered and received three printouts of the data on the screen, exited the DMV, said good-bye to Mama, switched off the computer, and went back across the street to the Zelinsky house.

Mary, Peter, and the daughter sat on the living room sofa. They were pale, silent, holding hands. They looked like three ghosts in a celestial waiting room, anticipating the imminent arrival of their judgment documents, more than half expecting to be served with one-way tickets to Hell.

Dormon, Johnson, and Vecchio stood guard, heavily armed and expressionless. Without comment, Roy gave them printouts of the new address for Grant that he had gotten from the DMV.

With a few questions, he established that both Mary and Peter Zelinsky were out of work and on unemployment compensation. That was why they were at home, about to have dinner, when most neighbors were still in schools of steel fish on the concrete seas of the freeway system. They had been searching the want ads in the Los Angeles *Times* every day, applying for new jobs at numerous companies, and worrying so unrelentingly about the future that the explosive arrival of Dormon, Johnson, Vecchio, and Roy had seemed, on some level, not surprising but a natural progression of their ongoing catastrophe.

Roy was prepared to flash his Drug Enforcement Administration ID and to use every technique of intimidation in his repertoire to reduce the Zelinsky family to total submission and to ensure that they never filed a complaint, either with the local police or with the federal government. However, they were obviously already so cowed by the economic turmoil that had taken their jobs—and by city life in general—that Roy did not need to provide even phony identification.

They would be grateful to escape from this encounter with their lives. They would meekly repair their front door, clean up the mess, and probably conclude that they had been terrorized by drug dealers who had burst into the wrong house in search of a hated competitor.

No one filed complaints against drug dealers. Drug dealers in modern America were akin to a force of nature. It made as much sense—and was far safer—to file an angry complaint about a hurricane, a tornado, a lightning storm.

Adopting the imperious manner of a cocaine king, Roy warned them: "Unless you want to see what it's like having your brains blown out, better sit still for ten minutes after we leave. Zelinsky, you have a watch. You think you can count off ten minutes?"

"Yes, sir," Peter Zelinsky said.

Mary would not look at Roy. She kept her head down. He could not see much of her splendid nose.

"You know I'm serious?" Roy asked the husband, and was answered with a nod. "Are you going to be a good boy?"

"We don't want any trouble."

"I'm glad to hear that."

The reflexive meekness of these people was a sorry comment on the brutalization of American society. It depressed Roy.

On the other hand, their pliability made his job a hell of a lot easier than it otherwise might have been.

He followed Dormon, Johnson, and Vecchio outside, and he was the last to drive away. He glanced repeatedly at the house, but no faces appeared at the door or at any of the windows.

A disaster had been narrowly averted.

Roy, who prided himself on his generally even temper, could not remember being as angry with anyone in a long time as he was with Spencer Grant. He couldn't wait to get his hands on the guy.

∽

Spencer packed a canvas satchel with several cans of dog food, a box of biscuit treats, a new rawhide bone, Rocky's water and food bowls, and a rubber toy that looked convincingly like a cheeseburger in a sesame-seed bun. He stood the satchel beside his own suitcase, near the front door.

The dog was still checking the windows from time to time, but not as obsessively as before. For the most part, he had overcome the nameless terror that propelled him out of his dream. Now his fear was of a more mundane and quieter variety: the anxiety that always possessed him when he sensed that they were about to do something out of their daily routine, a wariness of change. He padded after Spencer to see if any alarming actions were being taken, returned repeatedly to the suitcase to sniff it, and visited his favorite corners of the house to sigh over them as though he suspected that he might never have the chance to enjoy their comforts again.

Spencer removed a laptop computer from a storage shelf above his desk and put it beside the satchel and suitcase. He'd purchased it in September, so he could develop his own programs while sitting on the porch, enjoying the fresh air and the soothing susurration of autumn breezes stirring the eucalyptus grove. Now it would keep him wired into the great American info network during his travels.

He returned to his desk and switched on the larger computer. He made floppy-disk copies of some of the programs he had designed, including the one that could detect the faint electronic signature of an eavesdropper on a phone line being used for a computer-to-computer dialogue. Another would warn him if, while he was hacking, someone began hunting him down with sophisticated trace-back technology.

Rocky was at a window again, alternately grumbling and whining softly at the night.

§

At the west end of the San Fernando Valley, Roy drove into hills and across canyons. He was not yet beyond the web of interlocking cities, but there were pockets of primordial blackness between the clustered lights of the suburban blaze.

This time, he would proceed with more caution than he had shown previously. If the address from the DMV proved to be the home of another family who, like the Zelinskys, had never heard of Spencer Grant, Roy preferred to find that out *before* he smashed down their door, terrorized them with guns, ruined the spaghetti sauce that was on the stove, and risked being shot by an irate homeowner who perhaps also happened to be a heavily armed fanatic of one kind or another.

In this age of impending social chaos, breaking into a private home—whether behind the authority of a genuine badge or not—was a riskier business than it had once been. The residents might be anything from child-molesting worshipers of Satan to cohabiting serial killers with cannibalistic tendencies, refrigerators full of body parts, and eating utensils prettily hand-carved out of human bones. On the cusp of the millennium, some damned strange people were loose out there in fun-house America.

Following a two-lane road into a dark hollow that was threaded with gossamer fog, Roy began to suspect he wouldn't be confronted with an ordinary suburban house or with the simple question of whether or not it was occupied by Spencer Grant. Something else awaited him.

The blacktop became one lane of loose gravel, flanked by sickly palms that had not been trimmed in years and that sported long ruffs of dead fronds. At last it came to a gate in a chain-link fence.

The phony pizza-shop truck was already there; its red taillights were refracted by the thin mist. Roy checked his rearview mirror and saw headlights a hundred yards behind him: Johnson and Vecchio.

He walked to the gate. Cal Dormon was waiting for him.

Beyond the chain-link, in the headlight-silvered fog, strange machines moved rhythmically, in counterpoint to one another, like giant prehistoric birds bobbing for worms in the soil. Wellhead pumps. It was a producing oil field, of which many were scattered throughout southern California.

Johnson and Vecchio joined Roy and Dormon at the gate.

"Oil wells," Vecchio said.

"Goddamned oil wells," Johnson said.

"Just a bunch of goddamned oil wells," Vecchio said.

At Roy's direction, Dormon went to the van to get flashlights and a bolt cutter. It was not just a fake pizza-delivery truck, but a well-equipped support unit with all the tools and electronic gear that might be needed in a field operation.

"We going in there?" Vecchio asked. "Why?"

"There might be a caretaker's cottage," Roy said. "Grant might be an on-site caretaker, living here."

Roy sensed that they were as anxious as he to avoid being made fools of twice in one evening. Nevertheless, they knew, as he did, that Grant had likely inserted a phony address in his DMV records and that the chance of finding him in the oil field was between slim and nil.

After Dormon snapped the gate chain, they followed the gravel lane, using their flashlights to probe between the seesawing pumps. In places, the previous night's torrential rain had washed away the gravel, leaving mud. By the time they looped through the creaking-squeaking-clicking machinery and returned to the gate, without finding a caretaker, Roy had ruined his new shoes.

In silence, they cleaned off their shoes as best they could by shuffling their feet in the wild grass beside the lane.

While the others waited to be told what to do next, Roy returned to his car. He intended to link with Mama and find another address for Spencer snake-humping-crap-eating-piece-of-human-garbage Grant.

He was angry, which wasn't good. Anger inhibited clear thinking. No problem had ever been solved in a rage.

He breathed deeply, inhaling both air and tranquility. With each exhalation, he expelled his tension. He visualized tranquility as a pale-peach vapor; he saw tension, however, as a bile-green mist that seethed from his nostrils in twin plumes.

From a book of Tibetan wisdom, he had learned this meditative technique of managing his emotions. Maybe it was a Chinese book. Or Indian. He wasn't sure. He had explored many Eastern philosophies in his endless search for deeper self-awareness and transcendence.

When he got in the car, his pager was beeping. He unclipped it from the sun visor. In the message window he saw the name Kleck and a telephone number in the 714 area code.

John Kleck was leading the search for the nine-year-old Pontiac registered to "Valerie Keene." If she'd followed her usual pattern, the car had been abandoned in a parking lot or along a city street.

When Roy called the number on the pager, the answering voice was unmistakably Kleck's. He was in his twenties, thin and gangly, with a huge Adam's apple and a face resembling that of a trout, but his voice was deep, mellifluous, and impressive.

"It's me," Roy said. "Where are you?"

The words rolled off Kleck's tongue with sonorous splendor: "John Wayne Airport, down in Orange County." The search had begun in L.A. but had been widening all day. "The Pontiac's here, in one of the long-term parking garages. We're collecting the names of the airline ticket agents working yesterday afternoon and evening. We've got photographs of her. Someone may remember selling her a ticket."

"Follow through, but it's a dead end. She's too smart to dump the car where she made her next connection. It's misdirection. She knows we can't be sure, so we'll have to waste time checking it out."

"We're also trying to talk to all the cabdrivers who worked the airport during that time. Maybe she didn't fly out but took a taxi."

"Better carry it one step further. She might have walked from the airport to one of the hotels around there. See if any doormen, parking valets, or bellmen remember her asking for a cab."

"Will do," Kleck said. "She's not going to get far this time, Roy. We're going to stay right on her ass."

Roy might have been reassured by Kleck's confidence and by the rich timbre of his voice—if he hadn't known that Kleck looked like a fish trying to swallow a cantaloupe. "Later." He hung up.

He married the phone to the attaché case computer, started the car, and linked with Mama in Virginia. He gave her a daunting task, even considering her considerable talents and connections: Search for Spencer Grant in the computerized records of water and power companies, gas companies, tax collectors' offices; in fact, search the electronic files of every state, county, regional, and city agency, as well as those of any company regulated by any public agency in Ventura, Kern, Los Angeles, Orange, San Diego, Riverside, and San Bernardino Counties; furthermore, access customer records of every banking institution in California—their checking, savings, loan, and credit-card accounts; on a national level, search Social Security Administration and Internal Revenue Agency files beginning with California and working eastward state by state.

Finally, after indicating that he would call in the morning for the results of Mama's investigation, he closed the electronic door in Virginia. He switched off his computer.

The fog was growing thicker and the air chillier by the minute. The three men were still waiting for him by the gate, shivering.

"We might as well wrap it up for tonight," Roy told them. "Get a fresh start in the morning."

They looked relieved. Who knew where Grant might send them next?

Roy slapped their backs and gave them cheerful encouragement as they returned to their vehicles. He wanted them to feel good about themselves. Everyone had a right to feel good about himself.

In his car, reversing along the gravel to the two-lane blacktop, Roy breathed deeply, slowly. In with the pale-peach vapor of blessed tranquility. Out with the bile-green mist of anger, tension, stress. Peach in. Green out. Peach in.

He was still furious.

○

Because they had eaten a late lunch, Spencer drove across a long stretch of barren Mojave, all the way to Barstow, before pulling off Interstate 15 and stopping for dinner. At the drive-through window of a McDonald's, he ordered a Big Mac, fries, and a small vanilla milkshake for himself. Rather than fuss with the cans of dog food in the canvas satchel, he also ordered two hamburgers and a large water for Rocky—then relented and ordered a second vanilla shake.

He parked at the rear of the well-lighted restaurant lot, left the engine running to keep the Explorer warm, and sat in the cargo area to eat, with his back against the front seat and legs stretched out in front of him. Rocky licked his chops in anticipation as the paper bags were opened and the truck filled with wonderful aromas. Spencer had folded down the rear seats before leaving Malibu, so even with the suitcase and other gear, he and the dog had plenty of room.

He opened Rocky's burgers and put them on their wrappers. By the time Spencer had extracted his own Big Mac from its container and had taken a single bite, Rocky had wolfed down the meat patties that he'd been given and most of one bun, which was all the bread he wanted. He gazed yearningly at Spencer's sandwich, and he whined.

"Mine," Spencer said.

Rocky whined again. Not a frightened whine. Not a whine of pain. It was a whine that said oh-look-at-poor-cute-me-and-realize-how-much-I'd-like-that-hamburger-and-cheese-and-special-sauce-and-maybe-even-the-pickles.

"Do you understand the meaning of *mine?*"

Rocky looked at the bag of french fries in Spencer's lap.

"Mine."

The dog looked dubious.

"Yours," Spencer said, pointing to the uneaten hamburger bun.

Rocky sorrowfully regarded the dry bun—then the juicy Big Mac.

After taking another bite and washing it down with some vanilla milk-shake, Spencer checked his watch. "We'll gas up and be back on the interstate by nine o'clock. It's about a hundred and sixty miles to Las Vegas. Even without pushing hard, we can make it by midnight."

Rocky was fixated on the french fries again.

Spencer relented and dropped four of them onto one of the burger wrappers. "You ever been to Vegas?" he asked.

The four fries had vanished. Rocky stared longingly at the others that bristled from the bag in his master's lap.

"It's a tough town. And I've got a bad feeling that things are going to get nasty for us real fast once we get there."

Spencer finished his sandwich, fries, and milkshake, sharing no more of anything in spite of the mutt's reproachful expression. He gathered up the paper debris and put it in one of the bags.

"I want to make this clear to you, pal. Whoever's after her—they're damned powerful. Dangerous. Trigger-happy, on edge—the way they shot at shadows last night. Must be a lot at stake for them."

Spencer took the lid off the second vanilla milkshake, and the dog cocked his head with interest.

"See what I saved for you? Now, aren't you ashamed for thinking bad thoughts about me when I wouldn't give you more fries?"

Spencer held the container so Rocky wouldn't tip it over.

The dog attacked the milkshake with the fastest tongue west of Kansas City, consuming it in a frenzy of lapping, and in seconds his snout went deep into the cup in quest of the swiftly vanishing treat.

"If they had that house under observation last night, maybe they have a photograph of me."

Withdrawing from the cup, Rocky stared curiously at Spencer. The mutt's snout was smeared with milkshake.

"You have disgusting table manners."

Rocky stuck his snout back in the cup, and the Explorer was filled with the slurping noises of canine gluttony.

"If they have a photo, they'll find me eventually. And trying to get a lead on Valerie by going back into her past, I'm liable to blunder across a tripwire and call attention to myself."

The cup was empty, and Rocky was no longer interested in it. With an amazing extended rotation of his tongue, he licked most of the mess off his snout.

"Whoever she's up against, I'm the world's biggest fool to think I can handle them. I know that. I'm *acutely* aware of that. But here I am, on my way to Vegas, just the same."

Rocky hacked. Milkshake residue was cloying in his throat.

Spencer opened the cup of water and held it while the dog drank.

"What I'm doing, getting involved like this . . . it's not really fair to you. I'm aware of that too."

Rocky wanted no more water. His entire muzzle was dripping.

After capping the cup again, Spencer put it in the bag of trash. He picked up a handful of paper napkins and took Rocky by the collar.

"Come here, slob."

Rocky patiently allowed his snout and chin to be blotted dry.

Eye-to-eye with the dog, Spencer said, "You're the best friend I have. Do you know that? Of course, you know. I'm the best friend you have too. And if I get myself killed—who'll take care of you?"

The dog solemnly met Spencer's gaze, as if aware that the issue at hand was important.

"Don't tell me you can take care of yourself. You're better than when I took you in—but you're not self-sufficient yet. You probably never will be."

The dog chuffed as if to disagree, but they both knew the truth.

"If anything happens to me, I think you'll come apart. Revert. Be like you were in the pound. And who else will ever give you the time and attention you'll need to come back again? Hmmm? Nobody."

He let go of the collar.

"So I want you to know I'm not as good a friend to you as I ought to be. I want to have a chance with this woman. I want to find out if she's special enough to care about . . . about someone like me. I'm willing to risk my life to find that out . . . but I shouldn't be willing to risk yours too."

Never lie to the dog.

"I don't have it in me to be as faithful a friend as you can be. I'm just a human being, after all. Look deep enough inside any of us, you'll find a selfish bastard."

Rocky wagged his tail.

"Stop that. Are you trying to make me feel even worse?"

With his tail swishing furiously back and forth, Rocky clambered into Spencer's lap to be petted.

Spencer sighed. "Well, I'll just have to avoid getting killed."

Never lie to the dog.

"Though I think the odds are against me," he added.

§

In the suburban maze of the valley once more, Roy Miro cruised through a series of commercial districts, unsure where one community ended and the next began. He was still angry but also on the edge of a depression. With increasing desperation, he sought a convenience store, where he could expect to find a full array of newspaper-vending machines. He needed a *special* newspaper.

Interestingly, in two widely separated neighborhoods, he passed what he was certain were two sophisticated surveillance operations.

The first was being conducted out of a tricked-up van with an extended wheelbase and chrome-plated wire wheels. The side of the vehicle had been decorated with an airbrush mural of palm trees, waves breaking on a beach, and a red sunset. Two surfboards were strapped to the luggage rack on the roof. To the uninitiated, it might appear to belong to a surf Gypsy who'd won the lottery.

The clues to the van's real purpose were apparent to Roy. All glass on the vehicle, including the windshield, was heavily tinted, but two large windows on the side, around which the mural wrapped, were so black that they had to be two-way mirrors disguised with a layer of tinted film on the exterior, making it impossible to see inside, but providing agents in the van—and their video cameras—a clear view of the world beyond. Four spotlights were side by side on the roof, above the windshield; none was lit, but each bulb was seated in a cone-shaped fixture, like a small megaphone, which might have been a reflector that focused the beam forward—although, in fact, it was no such thing. One cone would be the antenna for a microwave transceiver linked to computers inside the van, allowing high volumes of encoded data to be received and sent from—or to—more than one communicant at a time. The remaining three cones were collection dishes for directional microphones.

One unlit spotlight was turned not toward the front of the van, as it should have been and as the other three were, but toward a busy sandwich shop—Submarine Dive—across the street. The agents were recording the jumble of conversations among the eight or ten people socializing on the sidewalk in front of the place. Later, a computer would analyze the host of voices: It would isolate each speaker, identify him with a number, associate one number to another based on word flow and inflection, delete most background noise such as traffic and wind, and record each conversation as a separate track.

The second surveillance operation was a mile from the first, on a cross street. It was being run out of a van disguised as a commercial vehicle that supposedly belonged to a glass-and-mirror company called Jerry's Glass Magic. Two-way mirrors were featured boldly on the side, incorporated into the fictitious company's logo.

Roy was always gladdened to see surveillance teams, especially super-high-tech units, because they were likely to be federal rather than local. Their discreet presence indicated that *somebody* cared about social stability and peace in the streets.

When he saw them, he usually felt safer—and less alone.

Tonight, however, his spirits were not lifted. Tonight, he was caught in a whirlpool of negative emotions. Tonight, he could not find solace in the surveillance teams, in the good work he was doing for Thomas Summerton, or in anything else that this world had to offer.

He needed to locate his center, open the door in his soul, and stand face-to-face with the cosmic.

Before he spotted a 7-Eleven or any other convenience store, Roy saw a post office, which had what he needed. In front of it were ten or twelve battered newspaper-vending machines.

He parked at a red curb, left the car, and checked the machines. He wasn't interested in the *Times* or the *Daily News*. What he required could be found only in the alternative press. Most such publications sold sex: focusing on swinging singles, mate-swapping couples, gays—or on adult entertainment and services. He ignored the salacious tabloids. Sex would never suffice when the soul sought transcendence.

Many large cities supported a weekly New Age newspaper that reported on natural foods, holistic healing, and spiritual matters ranging from reincarnation therapy to spirit channeling.

Los Angeles had three.

Roy bought them all and returned to the car.

By the dim glow of the ceiling light, he flipped through each publication, scanning only the space ads and classifieds. Gurus, swamis, psychics, Tarot-card readers, acupuncturists, herbalists to movie stars, channelers, aura interpreters, palm readers, chaos-theory dice counselors, past-life guides, high-colonic therapists, and other specialists offered their services in heartening numbers.

Roy lived in Washington, D.C., but his work took him all over the country. He had visited all the sacred places where the land, like a giant battery, accumulated vast stores of spiritual energy: Santa Fe, Taos, Woodstock, Key West, Spirit Lake, Meteor Crater, and others. He'd had moving experiences in those hallowed confluences of cosmic energy—yet he had long suspected that Los Angeles was an undiscovered nexus as powerful as any. Now, the sheer plenitude of consciousness-raising guides in the ads strengthened his suspicion.

From the myriad choices, Roy selected The Place Of The Way in Burbank. He was intrigued that they had capitalized every word in the name of their establishment, instead of using lowercase for the preposition and second article. They offered numerous methods for "seeking the self and finding the eye of the universal storm," not from a shabby storefront but "from the peaceful sphere of our home." He also liked the proprietors' names—and that they were thoughtful enough to identify themselves in their ad: Guinevere and Chester.

He checked his watch. Past nine o'clock.

Still parked illegally in front of the post office, he called the number in the ad. A man answered: "This is Chester at The Place Of The Way. How may I assist you?"

Roy apologized for calling at that hour, since The Place Of The Way was located in their home, but he explained that he was slipping into a spiritual void and needed to find firm ground as quickly as possible. He was grateful to be assured that Chester and Guinevere fulfilled their mission at all hours. After he received directions, he estimated that he could be at their door by ten o'clock.

He arrived at nine-fifty.

The attractive two-story Spanish house had a tile roof and deep-set leaded windows. In the artful landscape lighting, lush palms and Australian tree ferns threw mysterious shadows against pale-yellow stucco walls.

When Roy rang the bell, he noticed an alarm-company sticker on the window next to the door. A moment later, Chester spoke to him from an intercom box. "Who's there, please?"

Roy was only mildly surprised that an enlightened couple like this, in touch with their psychic talents, found it necessary to take security precautions. Such was the sorry state of the world in which they lived. Even mystics were marked for mayhem.

Smiling and friendly, Chester welcomed Roy into The Place Of The Way. He was potbellied, about fifty, mostly bald but with a Friar Tuck fringe of hair, deeply tanned in midwinter, bearish and strong looking in spite of his gut. He wore Rocksports, khaki slacks, and a khaki shirt with the sleeves rolled to expose thick, hairy forearms.

Chester led Roy through rooms with yellow pine floors buffed to a high polish, Navajo rugs, and rough-hewn furniture that looked more suitable to a lodge in the Sangre de Cristo Mountains than to a home in

Burbank. Beyond the family room, which boasted a giant-screen TV, they entered a vestibule and then a round room that was about twelve feet in diameter, with white walls and no windows other than the round skylight in the domed ceiling.

A round pine table stood in the center of the round room. Chester indicated a chair at the table. Roy sat. Chester offered a beverage—"anything from diet Coke to herbal tea"—but Roy declined because his only thirst was of the soul.

In the center of the table was a basket of plaited palm leaves, which Chester indicated. "I'm only an assistant in these matters. Guinevere is the spiritual adept. Her hands must never touch money. Though she's transcended earthly concerns, she must eat, of course."

"Of course," Roy said.

From his wallet, Roy extracted three hundred dollars and put the cash in the basket. Chester seemed to be pleasantly surprised by the offering, but Roy had always believed that a person could expect only the quality of enlightenment for which he was willing to pay.

Chester left the room with the basket.

From the ceiling, pin spots had washed the walls with arcs of white light. Now they dimmed until the chamber filled with shadows and a moody amber radiance that approximated candlelight.

"Hi, I'm Guinevere! No, please, don't get up."

Breezing into the room with girlish insouciance, head held high, shoulders back, she went around the table to a chair opposite the one in which Roy sat.

Guinevere, about forty, was exceedingly beautiful, in spite of wearing her long blond hair in medusan cascades of cornrows, which Roy disliked. Her jade-green eyes flared with inner light, and every angle of her face was reminiscent of every mythological goddess Roy had seen portrayed in classical art. In tight blue jeans and a snug white T-shirt, her lean and supple body moved with fluid grace, and her large breasts swayed alluringly. He could see the points of her nipples straining against her cotton shirt.

"How ya doin'?" she asked perkily.

"Not so good."

"We'll fix that. What's your name?"

"Roy."

"What are you seeking, Roy?"

"I want a world with justice and peace, a world that's perfect in every way. But people are flawed. There's so little perfection anywhere. Yet I want it so badly. Sometimes I get depressed."

"You need to understand the meaning of the world's imperfection and your own obsession with it. What road of enlightenment do you prefer to take?"

"Any road, all roads."

"Excellent!" said the beautiful Nordic Rastafarian, with such enthusiasm that her cornrows bounced and swayed, and the clusters of red beads dangling from the ends clicked together. "Maybe we'll start with crystals."

Chester returned, pushing a large wheeled box around the table to Guinevere's right side.

Roy saw that it was a gray-and-black metal tool cabinet: four feet high, three feet wide, two feet deep, with doors on the bottom third and drawers of various widths and depths above the doors. The Sears Craftsman logo gleamed dully in the amber light.

While Chester sat in the third and last chair, which was two feet to the left and a foot behind the woman, Guinevere opened one of the drawers in the cabinet and removed a crystal sphere slightly larger than a billiard ball. Cupping it in both hands, she held it out to Roy, and he accepted it.

"Your aura's dark, disturbed. Let's clean that up first. Hold this crystal in both hands, close your eyes, seek a meditative calm. Think about only one thing, only this clean image: hills covered with snow. Gently rolling hills with fresh snow, whiter than sugar, softer than flour. Gentle hills to all horizons, hills upon hills, mantled with new snow, white on white, under a white sky, snowflakes drifting down, whiteness through whiteness over whiteness on whiteness . . ."

Guinevere went on like that for a while, but Roy couldn't see the snow-mantled hills or the falling snow regardless of how hard he tried. Instead, in his mind's eye, he could see only one thing: her hands. Her lovely hands. Her incredible *hands*.

She was altogether so spectacular looking that he hadn't noticed her hands until she was passing the crystal ball to him. He had never seen hands like hers. Exceptional hands. His mouth went dry at the mere thought of kissing her palms, and his heart pounded fiercely at the memory of her slender fingers. They had seemed *perfect*.

"Okay, that's better," Guinevere said cheerily, after a time. "Your aura's much lighter. You can open your eyes now."

He was afraid that he had imagined the perfection of her hands and that when he saw them again he would discover that they were no different from the hands of other women—not the hands of an angel after all. Oh, but they *were*. Delicate, graceful, ethereal. They took the crystal ball from him, returned it to the open drawer of the tool cabinet, and then gestured—like the spreading wings of doves—to seven new crystals that she had placed on a square of black velvet in the center of the table while his eyes had been closed.

"Arrange these in any pattern that seems appropriate to you," she said, "and then I'll read them."

The objects appeared to be half-inch-thick crystal snowflakes that had been sold as Christmas ornaments. None was like another.

As Roy tried to focus on the task before him, his gaze kept sliding surreptitiously to Guinevere's hands. Each time he glimpsed them, his breath caught in his throat. His own hands were trembling, and he wondered if she noticed.

Guinevere progressed from crystals to the reading of his aura through prismatic lenses, to Tarot cards, to rune stones, and her fabulous hands became ever more beautiful. Somehow he answered her questions, followed instructions, and appeared to be listening to the wisdom that she imparted. She must have thought him dim-witted or drunk, because his speech was thick and his eyelids drooped as he became increasingly intoxicated by the sight of her hands.

Roy glanced guiltily at Chester, suddenly certain that the man—perhaps Guinevere's husband—was angrily aware of the lascivious desire that her hands engendered. But Chester wasn't paying attention to either of them. His bald head was bowed, and he was cleaning the fingernails of his left hand with the fingernails of his right.

Roy was convinced that the Mother of God could not have had hands more gentle than Guinevere's, nor could the greatest succubus in Hell have had hands more erotic. Guinevere's hands were, to her, what Melissa Wicklun's sensuous lips were to *her*, oh, but a thousand times more so, *ten thousand* times more so. Perfect, perfect, perfect.

She shook the bag of runes and cast them again.

Roy wondered if he dared ask for a palm reading. She would have to hold his hands in hers.

He shivered at that delicious thought, and a spiral of dizziness spun through him. He could not walk out of that room and leave her to touch other men with those exquisite, unearthly hands.

He reached under his suit jacket, drew the Beretta from his shoulder holster, and said, "Chester."

The bald man looked up, and Roy shot him in the face. Chester tipped backward in his chair, out of sight, and thudded to the floor.

The silencer needed to be replaced soon. The baffles were worn from use. The muffled shot had been loud enough to carry out of the room, though fortunately not beyond the walls of the house.

Guinevere was gazing at the rune stones on the table when Roy shot Chester. She must have been deeply immersed in her reading, for she seemed confused when she looked up and saw the gun.

Before she could raise her hands in defense and force Roy to damage them, which was unthinkable, he shot her in the forehead. She crashed backward in her chair, joining Chester on the floor.

Roy put the gun away, got up, went around the table. Chester and Guinevere stared, unblinking, at the skylight and the infinite night beyond. They had died instantly, so the scene was almost bloodless. Their deaths had been quick and painless.

The moment, as always, was sad and joyous. Sad, because the world had lost two enlightened people who were kind of heart and deep-seeing. Joyous, because Guinevere and Chester no longer had to live in a society of the unenlightened and uncaring.

Roy envied them.

He withdrew his gloves from an inside coat pocket and dressed his hands for the tender ceremony ahead.

He tipped Guinevere's chair back onto its feet. Holding her in it, he pushed the chair to the table, wedging the dead woman in a seated position. Her head flopped forward, chin on her breast, and her cornrows rattled softly, falling like a beaded curtain to conceal her face. He lifted her right arm, which hung at her side, and put it on the table, then her left.

Her hands. For a while he stared at her hands, which were as appealing in death as in life. Graceful. Elegant. Radiant.

They gave him hope. If perfection could exist anywhere, in any form, no matter how small, even in a pair of hands, then his dream of an *entirely* perfect world might one day be realized.

He put his own hands atop hers. Even through his gloves, the contact was electrifying. He shuddered with pleasure.

Dealing with Chester was more difficult because of his greater weight. Nevertheless, Roy managed to move him around the table until he was opposite Guinevere, but slumped in his own chair rather than in the one Roy had been using.

In the kitchen, Roy explored the cabinets and pantry, collecting what he needed to finish the ceremony. He looked in the garage as well, for the final implement he required. Then he carried those items to the round room and placed them atop the wheeled chest in which Guinevere stored her divining aids.

He used a dish towel to wipe off the chair in which he had been sitting, for at the time he had not been wearing gloves and might have left fingerprints. He also buffed that side of the table, the crystal ball, and the snowflake crystals that he had arranged earlier for the psychic reading. He had touched nothing else in the room.

For a few minutes he pulled open drawers and doors in the tool chest, examining the magical contents, until he found an item that seemed appropriate to the circumstances. It was a pentalpha, also called a pentagram, in green on a field of black felt, used in more serious matters—such as attempted communication with the spirits of the dead—than the mere reading of runes, crystals, and Tarot cards.

Unfolded, it was an eighteen-inch square. He placed it in the center of the table, as a symbol of the life beyond this one.

He plugged in the small electric reciprocating saw that he had found among the tools in the garage, and he relieved Guinevere of her right hand. Gently, he placed the hand in a rectangular Tupperware container on another soft dish towel that he had arranged as a bed for it. He snapped the lid on the container.

Although he wanted to take her left hand, too, he felt that it would be selfish to insist on possessing both. The right thing was to leave one with the body, so the police and coroner and mortician and everyone else who dealt with Guinevere's remains would know that she'd possessed the most beautiful hands in the world.

He lifted Chester's arms onto the table. He placed the dead man's right hand over Guinevere's left, on top of the pentalpha, to express his conviction that they were together in the next world.

Roy wished he had the psychic power or purity or whatever was required to be able to channel the spirits of the dead. He would have channeled Guinevere there and then, to ask if she would really mind if he acquired her left hand as well.

He sighed, picked up the Tupperware container, and reluctantly left the round room. In the kitchen, he phoned 911 and spoke to the police operator: "The Place Of The Way is just a place now. It's very sad. Please come."

Leaving the telephone off the hook, he snatched another dish towel from a drawer and hurried to the front door. As far as he could recall, when he had first entered the house and followed Chester to the round room, he had touched nothing. Now, he needed only to wipe the doorbell-push and drop the dish towel on the way to his car.

He drove out of Burbank, over the hills, into the Los Angeles basin, through a seedy section of Hollywood. The bright splashes of graffiti on walls and highway structures, the cars full of young thugs cruising in search of trouble, the pornographic bookstores and movie theaters, the empty shops and the littered gutters and the other evidence of economic and moral collapse, the hatred and envy and greed and lust that thickened the air more effectively than the smog—none of that dismayed him for the time being, because he carried with him an object of such perfect beauty that it proved there was a powerful and wise creative force at work in the universe. He had evidence of God's existence secured in a Tupperware container.

∽

Out on the vast Mojave, where the night ruled, where the works of humankind were limited to the dark highway and the vehicles upon it, where the radio reception of distant stations was poor, Spencer found his thoughts drawn, against his will, to the deeper darkness and even stranger silence of that night sixteen years in the past. Once captured in that loop of memory, he could not escape until he had purged himself by talking about what he had seen and endured.

The barren plains and hills provided no convenient taverns to serve as confessionals. The only sympathetic ears were those of the dog.

. . . bare-chested and barefoot, I descend the stairs, shivering, rubbing my arms, wondering why I'm so afraid. Perhaps even at that moment, I dimly realize that I'm going down to a place from which I'll never be able to ascend.

I'm drawn forward by the cry that I heard while leaning out the window to find the owl. Although it was brief and came just twice, and then only faintly, it was so piercing and pathetic that the memory of it bewitches me, the way a fourteen-year-old boy can sometimes be seduced as easily by the prospect of strangeness and terror as by the mysteries of sex.

Off the stairs. Through rooms where the moonlit windows glow softly, like video screens, and where the museum-quality Stickley furniture is visible only as angular black shadows within the blue-black gloom. Past artworks by Edward Hopper and Thomas Hart Benton and Steven Ackblom, from the latter of which peer vaguely luminous faces with eerie expressions as inscrutable as the ideograms of an alien language evolved on a world millions of light-years from earth.

In the kitchen, the honed-limestone floor is cold beneath my feet. During the long day and all night it has absorbed the chill from the Freon-cooled air, and now it steals the heat from my soles.

Beside the back door, a small red light burns on the security-system keypad. In the readout window are three words in radiant green letters: ARMED AND SECURE. *I key in the code to disarm the system. The red light turns green. The words change:* READY TO ARM.

This is no ordinary farmhouse. It isn't the home of folks who earn their living from the bounty of the land and who have simple tastes. There are treasures within—fine furnishings and art—and even in rural Colorado, precautions must be taken.

I disengage both deadbolts, open the door, and step onto the back porch, out of the frigid house, into the sultry July night. I walk barefoot across the boards to the steps, down to the flagstone patio that surrounds the swimming pool, past the darkly glimmering water in the pool, into the yard, almost like a boy sleepwalking while in a dream, drawn through the silence by the remembered cry.

The ghostly silver face of the full moon behind me casts its reflection on every blade of grass, so the lawn appears to be filmed by a frost far out of season. Strangely, I am suddenly afraid not merely for myself but for my mother, although she has been dead for more than six years and is far beyond the reach of any danger. My fear becomes so intense that I am halted by it. Halfway across the backyard, I stand alert and still in the uncertain silence. My moonshadow is a blot on the faux frost before me.

Ahead of me looms the barn, where no animals or hay or tractors have been kept for at least fifteen years, since before I was born. To anyone driving past on the county road, the property looks like a farm, but it isn't what it appears to be. Nothing is what it appears to be.

The night is hot, and sweat beads on my face and bare chest. Nevertheless, the stubborn chill is beneath my skin and in my blood and in the deepest hollows of my boyish bones, and the July heat can't dispel it.

It occurs to me that I'm chilled because, for some reason, I'm remembering too clearly the late-winter coldness of the bleak day in March, six years ago, when they found my mother after she had been missing for three days. Rather, they had found her brutalized body, crumpled in a ditch along a back road, eighty miles from home, where she had been dumped by the sonofabitch who kidnapped and killed her. Only eight years old, I'd been too young to understand the full meaning of death. And no one dared tell me, that day, how savagely she'd been treated, how terribly she had suffered; those were horrors still to be revealed to me by a few of my schoolmates—who had the capacity for cruelty that is possessed only by certain children and by those adults who, on some primitive level, have never matured. Yet, even in my youth and innocence, I had understood enough of death to realize at once that I would never see my mother again, and the chill of that March day had been the most penetrating cold that I'd ever known.

Now I stand on the moonlit lawn, wondering why my thoughts leap repeatedly to my lost mother, why the eerie cry that I heard when I leaned out my bedroom window strikes me as both infinitely strange and familiar, why I fear for my mother even though she's dead, and why I fear so intensely for my own life when the summer night holds no immediate threat that I can see.

I begin to move again, toward the barn, which has become the focus of my attention, though initially I had thought that the cry had come from some animal out in the fields or in the lower hills. My shadow floats ahead of me, so that no step I take is on the carpet of moonlight but, instead, into a darkness of my own making.

Instead of going directly to the huge main doors in the south wall of the barn, in which a smaller, man-size door is inset, I obey instinct and head toward the southeast corner, crossing the macadam driveway that leads past the house and garage. In grass again, I round the corner of the barn and follow the east wall, stealthy in my bare feet, treading on the cushion of my moonshadow all the way to the northeast corner.

There I halt, because a vehicle I've never seen before is parked behind the barn: a customized Chevy van that no doubt isn't charcoal, as it appears to be, for the moonlight alchemizes every color into silver or gray. Painted on the side is a rainbow, which also seems to be in shades of gray. The rear door stands open. The silence is deep.

No one is in sight.

Even at the impressionable age of fourteen, with a childhood of Halloweens and nightmares behind me, I've never known strangeness and terror to be more seductive, and I can't resist their perverse allure. I take one step toward the van, and—

—something slices the air close overhead with a whoosh and a flutter, startling me. I stumble, fall, roll, and look up in time to see enormous white wings spread above me. A shadow sweeps over the moonlit grass, and I have the crazy notion that my mother, in some angelic form, has swooped down from Heaven to warn me away from the van. Then the celestial presence arcs higher into the darkness, and I see that it's only a great white owl, with a wingspan of five feet, sailing the summer night in search of field mice or other prey.

The owl vanishes.

The night remains.

I rise to my feet.

I creep toward the van, powerfully drawn by the mystery of it, by the promise of adventure. And by a terrible truth, which I don't yet know that I know.

The sound of the owl's wings, though so recent and frightening, doesn't remain with me. But that pitiful cry, heard at the open window, echoes unrelentingly in my memory. Perhaps I'm beginning to acknowledge that it wasn't the plaint of any wild animal meeting its end in the fields and forests, but the wretched and desperate plea of a human being in the grip of extreme terror. . . .

In the Explorer, speeding across the moonlit Mojave, wingless but now as wise as any owl, Spencer followed insistent memory all the way into the heart of darkness, to the flash of steel from out of shadows, to the sudden pain and the scent of hot blood, to the wound that would become his scar, forcing himself toward the ultimate revelation that always eluded him.

It eluded him again.

He could recall nothing of what happened in the final moments of that hellish, long-ago encounter, after he pulled the trigger of the revolver and returned to the slaughterhouse. The police had told him how it must have ended. He had read accounts of what he'd done, by writers who based their articles and books upon the evidence. But none of them had been there. They couldn't know the truth beyond a doubt. Only he had been there. Up to a point, his memories were so vivid as to be profoundly tormenting, but memory ended at a black hole of amnesia; after sixteen years, he'd still not been able to focus even one beam of light into that darkness.

If he ever recalled the rest, he might earn lasting peace. Or remembrance might destroy him. In that black tunnel of amnesia, he might find a shame with which he could not live, and the memory might be less desirable than a self-administered bullet to the brain.

Nevertheless, by periodically unburdening himself of everything that he *did* remember, he always found temporary relief from anguish. He found it again in the Mojave Desert, at fifty-five miles an hour.

When Spencer glanced at Rocky, he saw that the dog was curled on the other seat, dozing. The mutt's position seemed awkward, if not precarious, with his tail dangling down into the leg space under the dashboard, but he was evidently comfortable.

Spencer supposed that the rhythms of his speech and the tone of his voice, after countless repetitions of his story over the years, had become soporific whenever he turned to that subject. The poor dog couldn't have stayed awake even if they'd been in a thunderstorm.

Or perhaps, for some time, he had not actually been talking aloud. Perhaps his soliloquy had early faded to a whisper and then into silence while he continued to speak only with an inner voice. The identity of his confessor didn't matter—a dog was as acceptable as a stranger in a barroom—so it followed that it was not important to him if his confessor listened. Having a willing listener was merely an excuse to talk *himself* through it once more, in search of temporary absolution or—if he could shine a light into that final darkness—a permanent peace of one kind or another.

He was fifty miles from Vegas.

Windblown tumbleweeds as big as wheelbarrows rolled across the highway, through his headlight beams, from nowhere to nowhere.

The clear, dry desert air did little to inhibit his view of the universe. Millions of stars blazed from horizon to horizon, beautiful but cold, alluring but unreachable, shedding surprisingly little light on the alkaline plains that flanked the highway—and, for all their grandeur, revealing nothing.

∽

When Roy Miro woke in his Westwood hotel room, the digital clock on the nightstand read 4:19. He had slept less than five hours, but he felt rested, so he switched on the lamp.

He threw back the covers, sat on the edge of the bed in his pajamas, squinted as his eyes adjusted to the brightness—then smiled at the Tupperware container that stood beside the clock. The plastic was translucent, so he could see only a vague shape within.

He put the container on his lap and removed the lid. Guinevere's hand. He felt blessed to possess an object of such great beauty.

How sad, however, that its ravishing splendor wouldn't last much longer. In twenty-four hours, if not sooner, the hand would have deteriorated visibly. Its comeliness would be but a memory.

Already it had undergone a color change. Fortunately, a certain chalkiness only emphasized the exquisite bone structure in the long, elegantly tapered fingers.

Reluctantly, Roy replaced the lid, made sure the seal was tight, and put the container aside.

He went into the living room of the two-room suite. His attaché case computer and cellular phone were already connected, plugged in, and arranged on a luncheon table by a large window.

Soon he was in touch with Mama. He requested the results of the investigation that he'd asked her to undertake the previous evening, when he and his men had discovered that the DMV address for Spencer Grant was an uninhabited oil field.

He had been so furious then.

He was calm now. Cool. In control.

Reading Mama's report from the screen, tapping the PAGE DOWN key each time he wanted to continue, Roy quickly saw that the search for Spencer Grant's true address hadn't been easy.

During Grant's months with the California Multi-Agency Task Force on Computer Crime, he'd learned a lot about the nationwide Infonet and the vulnerabilities of the thousands of computer systems it comprised. Evidently, he had acquired codes-and-procedures books and master programming atlases for the computer systems of various telephone companies, credit agencies, and government offices. Then he must have managed to carry or electronically transmit them from the task-force offices to his own computer.

After quitting his job, he had erased every reference to his whereabouts from public and private records. His name appeared only in his military,

DMV, Social Security, and police department files, and in every case the given address was one of the two that had already proved to be false. The national file of the Internal Revenue Service contained other men with his name; however, none was his age, had his Social Security number, lived in California, or had paid withholding taxes as an employee of the LAPD. Grant was missing, as well, from the records of the State of California tax authorities.

If nothing else, he was apparently a tax evader. Roy hated tax evaders. They were the epitome of social irresponsibility.

According to Mama, no utility company currently billed Spencer Grant—yet no matter where he lived, he needed electricity, water, telephone, garbage pickup, and probably natural gas. Even if he had erased his name from billing lists to avoid paying for utilities, he couldn't exit their *service* records without triggering disconnection of essential services. Yet he could not be found.

Mama assumed two possibilities. First: Grant was honest enough to pay for utilities; however, he altered the companies' billing and service records to transfer his accounts to a false name that he had created for himself. The sole purpose of those actions would be to further his apparent goal of disappearing from public record, making himself hard to find if any police agency or governmental body wanted to talk to him. Like now. Or, second: He was dishonest, eliminating himself from billing records, paying for nothing—while maintaining service under a false name. In either case, he and his address were *somewhere* in those companies' files, under the name that was his secret identity; he could be located if his alias could be uncovered.

Roy froze Mama's report and returned to the bedroom to get the envelope that contained the computer-projected portrait of Spencer Grant. This man was an unusually crafty adversary. Roy wanted to have the clever bastard's face for reference while reading about him.

At the computer again, he paged forward in the report.

Mama had been unable to find an account for Spencer Grant at any bank or savings and loan association. Either he paid for everything with cash, or he maintained accounts under an alias. Probably the former. There was unmistakable paranoia in this man's actions, so he wouldn't trust his funds in a bank under any circumstances.

Roy glanced at the portrait beside the computer. Grant's eyes *did* look strange. Feverish. No doubt about it. A trace of madness in his eyes. Maybe even more than a trace.

Because Grant might have formed an S-chapter corporation through which he did his banking and bill paying, Mama had searched the files of the California Secretary of the Treasury and various regulatory bodies, seeking his name as a registered corporate officer. Nothing.

Every bank account had to be tied to a Social Security number, so Mama looked for a savings or checking account with Grant's number, regardless of the name under which the money was deposited. Nothing.

He might own the home in which he lived, so Mama had checked property tax records in the counties that Roy targeted. Nothing. If he *did* own a home, he held title under a false name.

Another hope: If Grant had ever taken a university class or been a hospital patient, he might not have remembered that he'd supplied his home address on applications and admissions forms, and he might not have deleted them. Most educational and medical institutions were regulated by federal laws; therefore, their records were accessible to numerous government agencies. Considering the number of such institutions even in a limited geographical area, Mama needed the patience of a saint or a machine, the latter of which she possessed. And for all her efforts, she found nothing.

Roy glanced at the portrait of Spencer Grant. He was beginning to think that this man was not merely mentally disturbed, but something far darker than that. An actively *evil* person. Anyone this obsessed with his privacy was surely an enemy of the people.

Chilled, Roy returned his attention to the computer.

When Mama undertook a search as extensive as the one that Roy had requested of her and when that search was fruitless, she didn't give up. She was programmed to apply her spare logic circuits—during periods of lighter work and between assignments—to riffle through a large store of mailing lists that the agency had accumulated, looking for the name that couldn't be found elsewhere. Name soup. That was what the lists were called. They were lifted from book and record clubs, national magazines, Publishers Clearing House, major political parties, catalogue-sales companies peddling everything from sexy lingerie to electronic gadgetry to meat by mail, interest groups like antique-car enthusiasts and stamp collectors, as well as from numerous other sources.

In the name soup, Mama had found a Spencer Grant different from the others in the Internal Revenue Service records.

Intrigued, Roy sat up straighter in his chair.

Almost two years ago, *this* Spencer Grant had ordered a dog toy from a mail-order catalogue aimed at pet owners: a hard-rubber, musical bone. The address on that list was in California. Malibu.

Mama had returned to the utility companies' files, to see whether services were maintained at that address. They were.

The electrical connection was in the name of Stewart Peck.

The water service and trash collection account was in the name of Mr. Henry Holden.

Natural gas was billed to James Gable.

The telephone company provided service to one John Humphrey. They also billed a cellular phone to William Clark at that address.

AT&T provided long-distance service for Wayne Gregory.

Property tax records listed the owner as Robert Tracy.

Mama had found the scarred man.

In spite of his efforts to vanish behind an elaborate screen of multifarious identities, though he had diligently attempted to erase his past and to make his current existence as difficult to prove as that of the Loch Ness monster, and though he had nearly succeeded in being as elusive as a ghost, he had been tripped up by a musical rubber bone. A dog toy. Grant had seemed inhumanly clever, but the simple human desire to please a beloved pet had brought him down.

9

Roy Miro watched from the blue shadows of the eucalyptus grove, enjoying the medicinal but pleasant odor of the oil-rich leaves.

The rapidly assembled SWAT team hit the cabin an hour after dawn, when the canyon was quiet except for the faintest rustle of the trees in an offshore breeze. The stillness was broken by shattering glass, the *whomp* of stun grenades, and the crash of the front and back doors going down simultaneously.

The place was small, and the initial search required little more than a minute. Toting a Micro Uzi, wearing a Kevlar jacket so heavy that it appeared to be capable of stopping even Teflon-coated slugs, Alfonse Johnson stepped out onto the back porch to signal that the cabin was deserted.

Dismayed, Roy came out of the grove and followed Johnson through the rear entrance into the kitchen, where shards of glass crunched under his shoes.

"He's taken a trip somewhere," Johnson said.

"How do you figure?"

"In here."

Roy followed Johnson into the only bedroom. It was almost as sparsely furnished as a monk's cell. No art brightened the roughly plastered walls. Instead of drapes or curtains, white vinyl blinds hung at the windows.

A suitcase stood near the bed, in front of the only nightstand.

"Must have decided he didn't need that one," said Johnson.

The simple cotton bedspread was slightly mussed—as if Grant had put another suitcase there to pack for his trip.

The closet door stood open. A few shirts, jeans, and chinos hung from the wooden rod, but half the hangers were empty.

One by one, Roy pulled out the drawers on a highboy. They contained a few items of clothing—mostly socks and underwear. A belt. One green sweater, one blue.

Even the contents of a large suitcase, if returned to the drawers, would not have filled them. Therefore, Grant had either packed two or more suitcases—or his clothing and home-decorating budgets were equally frugal.

"Any signs of a dog?" Roy asked.

Johnson shook his head. "Not that I noticed."

"Look around, inside and out," Roy ordered, leaving the bedroom.

Three members of the SWAT team, men with whom Roy had not worked before, were standing in the living room. They were tall, beefy guys. In that confined space, their protective gear, combat boots, and bristling weapons made them appear to be even larger than they were. With no one to shoot or subdue, they were as awkward and uncertain as professional wrestlers invited to tea with the octogenarian members of a ladies' knitting club.

Roy was about to send them outside when he saw that the screen was lit on one of the computers in the array of electronic equipment that covered the surface of an L-shaped corner desk. White letters glowed on a blue background.

"Who turned that on?" he asked the three men.

They gazed at the computer, baffled.

"Must've been on when we came in," one of them said.

"Wouldn't you have noticed?"

"Maybe not."

"Grant must've left in a hurry," said another.

Alfonse Johnson, just entering the room, disagreed: "It wasn't on when I came through the front door. I'd bet anything."

Roy went to the desk. On the computer screen was the same number repeated three times down the center:

31

31

31

Suddenly the numbers changed, beginning at the top, continuing slowly down the column, until all were the same:

32

32

32

Simultaneously with the appearance of the third thirty-two, a soft *whirrrrr* arose from one of the electronic devices on the large desk. It lasted only a couple of seconds, and Roy couldn't identify the unit in which it originated.

The numbers changed from top to bottom, as before: 33, 33, 33. Again: that whispery two-second *whirrrr*.

Although Roy was far better acquainted with the capabilities and operation of sophisticated computers than was the average citizen, he had never seen most of the gadgetry on the desk. Some items appeared to be homemade. Small red and green bulbs shone on several peculiar devices, indicating that they were powered up. Tangles of cables, in various diameters, linked much of the familiar equipment with the units that were mysterious to him.

34

34

34

Whirrrr.

Something important was happening. Intuition told Roy that much. But *what?* He couldn't understand, and with growing urgency he studied the equipment.

On the screen, the numbers advanced, from top to bottom, until all of them were thirty-five. *Whirrrr.*

If the numbers had been descending, Roy might have thought that he was watching a countdown toward a detonation. A bomb. Of course, no cosmic law required that a time bomb had to be triggered at the end of a count*down*. Why not a count*up?* Start at zero, detonate at one hundred. Or at fifty. Or forty.

36

36

36

Whirrrr.

No, not a bomb. That didn't make sense. Why would Grant want to blow up his own home?

Easy question. Because he was crazy. Paranoid. Remember the eyes in the computer-generated portrait: feverish, touched with madness.

Thirty-seven, top to bottom. *Whirrrr.*

Roy started exploring the tangle of cables, hoping to learn something from the way in which the devices were linked.

A fly crept along his left temple. He brushed impatiently at it. Not a fly. A bead of sweat.

"What's wrong?" Alfonse Johnson asked. He loomed at Roy's side—abnormally tall, armored, and armed, as if he were a basketball player from some future society in which the game had evolved into a form of mortal combat.

On the screen, the count had reached forty. Roy paused with his hands full of cables, listened to the *whirrrrr*, and was relieved when the cabin didn't blow up.

If it wasn't a bomb, what was it?

To grasp what was happening, he needed to think like Grant. Try to imagine how a paranoid sociopath might view the world. Look out through the eyes of madness. Not easy.

Well, all right, even if Grant was psychotic, he was also cunning, so after nearly being apprehended in the assault on the bungalow Wednesday night in Santa Monica, he had figured that a surveillance unit had photographed him and that he had become the subject of an intense search. He was an ex-cop, after all. He knew the routine. Although he'd spent the past year performing a gradual disappearing act from every public record, he hadn't yet taken the final step into invisibility, and he'd been acutely aware that they would find his cabin sooner or later.

"What's wrong?" Johnson repeated.

Grant would have expected them to break into his home in the same manner as they had broken into the bungalow. An entire SWAT team. Searching the place. Milling around.

Roy's mouth was dry. His heart was racing. "Check the door frame. We must've set off an alarm."

"Alarm? In this old shack?" Johnson said doubtfully.

"Do it," Roy ordered.

Johnson hurried away.

Roy frantically sorted through the loops and knots of cables. The computer in action was the one with the most powerful logic unit among Grant's collection. It was connected to a lot of things, including an unmarked green box that was, in turn, linked to a modem that was itself linked to a six-line telephone.

For the first time he realized that one of the red power-on lights gleaming in the equipment was actually the in-use indicator on line one of the telephone. An outgoing call was in progress.

He picked up the handset and listened. Data transmission was under way in the form of a cascade of electronic tones, a high-speed language of weird music without melody or rhythm.

"Magnetic contact here on the doorsill!" Johnson called from the front entrance.

"Visible wires?" Roy asked, dropping the telephone handset into the cradle.

"Yeah. And this was just hooked up. Bright, new copper at the contact point."

"Follow the wires," Roy said.

He glanced at the computer again.

On the screen, the count was up to forty-five.

Roy returned to the green box that linked computer and modem, and he grabbed another gray cable that led from it to something that he had not yet found. He traced it across the desk, through snarled cords, behind equipment, to the edge of the desk, and then to the floor.

On the other side of the room, Johnson was ripping up the alarm wire from the baseboard to which it was stapled, and winding it around one gloved fist. The other three men were watching him and edging backward, out of the way.

Roy followed the gray cable along the floor. It disappeared behind a tall bookcase.

Following the alarm wire, Johnson reached the other side of the same bookcase.

Roy jerked on the gray cable, and Johnson jerked on the alarm wire. Books wobbled noisily on the next to the highest shelf.

Roy looked up from the cable on which his attention had been fixed. Almost directly in front of him, slightly higher than eye level, a one-inch lens peered darkly at him from between the spines of thick volumes of history. He pulled books off the shelf, revealing a compact videocamera.

"What the hell's this?" Johnson asked.

On the display screen, the count had just reached forty-eight at the top of the column.

"When you broke the magnetic contact at the door, you started the videocamera," Roy explained.

He dropped the cable and snatched another book from the shelf.

Johnson said, "So we just destroy the videotape, and no one knows we were here."

Opening the book and tearing off one corner of a page, Roy said, "It's not so easy as that. When you turned on the camera, you also activated the computer, the whole system, and it placed an outgoing phone call."

"What system?"

"The videocamera feeds to that oblong green box on the desk."

"Yeah? What's it do?"

After working up a thick gob of saliva, Roy spat on the page fragment that he had torn from the book, and he pasted the paper to the lens. "I'm not sure exactly what it does, but somehow the box processes the video image, translates it from visuals to another form of information, and feeds it to the computer."

He stepped to the display screen. He was less tense than he had been before finding the camera, for now he knew what was happening. He wasn't happy about it—but at least he understood.

51
50
50

The second number changed to fifty-one. Then the third.
Whirrrrr.
"Every four or five seconds, the computer freezes a frame's worth of data from the videotape and sends it back to the green box. That's when the first number changes."

They waited. Not long.

52
51
51

"The green box," Roy continued, "passes that frame of data to the modem, and that's when the second number changes."

52
52
51

"The modem translates the data into tonal code, sends it to the telephone, then the third number changes and—"

52
52
52

"—at the far end of the phone line, the process is reversed, translating the encoded data back into a picture again."

"Picture?" Johnson said. "Pictures of us?"

"He's just received his fifty-second picture since you entered the cabin."

"Damn."

"Fifty of them were nice and clear—before I blocked the camera lens."

"Where? Where's he receiving them?"

"We'll have to trace the phone call the computer made when you broke down the door," Roy said, pointing to the red indicator light on line one of the six-line phone. "Grant didn't want to meet us face-to-face, but he wanted to know what we look like."

"So he's looking at printouts of us right now?"

"Probably not. The other end could be just as automated as this. But he'll stop by there eventually to see if anything's been transmitted. By then, with a little luck, we'll find the phone to which the call was placed, and we'll be waiting there for him."

The three other men had backed farther away from the computers. They regarded the equipment with superstition.

One of them said, "Who *is* this guy?"

Roy said, "He's nothing special. Just a sick and hateful man."

"Why didn't you pull the plug the minute you realized he was filming us?" Johnson demanded.

"He already had us by then, so it didn't matter. And maybe he set up the system so the hard disk will erase if the plug is pulled. Then we wouldn't know what programs and information had been in the machine. As long as the system's intact, we might get a pretty good idea of what this guy's been up to here. Maybe we can reconstruct his activities for the past few days, weeks, even months. We should be able to turn up a few clues about where he's gone—and maybe even find the woman through him."

55
55
55

Whirrrrr.

The screen flashed, and Roy flinched. The column of numbers was replaced by three words: THE MAGIC NUMBER.

The phone disconnected. The red indicator light on line one blinked off.

"That's all right," Roy said. "We can still trace it through the phone company's automated records."

The display screen went blank again.

"What's happening?" Johnson asked.

Two new words appeared: BRAIN DEAD.

Roy said, "You sonofabitch, bastard, scar-faced geek!"

Alfonse Johnson backed off a step, obviously surprised by such fury in a man who had always been good-natured and even-tempered.

Roy pulled the chair out from the desk and sat down. As he put his hands to the keyboard, BRAIN DEAD blinked off the screen.

A field of soft blue confronted him.

Cursing, Roy tried to call up a basic menu.

Blue. Serene blue.

His fingers flew over the keys.

Serene. Unchanging. Blue.

The hard disk was blank. Even the operating system, which was surely still intact, was frozen and dysfunctional.

Grant had cleaned up after himself, and then he had mocked them with the BRAIN DEAD announcement.

Breathe deeply. Slowly and deeply. Inhale the pale-peach vapor of tranquility. Exhale the bile-green mist of anger and tension. In with the good, out with the bad.

§

When Spencer and Rocky had arrived in Vegas near midnight, the towering ramparts of blinking-rippling-swirling-pulsing neon along the famous Strip had made the night nearly as bright as a sunny day. Even at that hour, traffic clogged Las Vegas Boulevard South. Swarms of people had filled the sidewalks, their faces strange and sometimes demonic in the reflected phantasmagoria of neon; they churned from casino to casino and then back again, like insects seeking something that only insects could want or understand.

The frenetic energy of the scene had disturbed Rocky. Even viewing it from the safety of the Explorer, with the windows tightly closed, the dog had begun to shiver before they had gone far. Then he'd whimpered and turned his head anxiously left and right, as if certain that a vicious attack was imminent, but unable to discern from which direction to expect danger. Perhaps, with a sixth sense, the mutt had perceived the fevered need of the most compulsive gamblers, the predatory greed of con men and prostitutes, and the desperation of the big losers in the crowd.

They had driven out of the turmoil and had stayed overnight in a motel on Maryland Parkway, two long blocks from the Strip. Without a casino or cocktail lounge, the place was quiet.

Exhausted, Spencer had found that sleep came easily even on the too-soft bed. He dreamed of a red door, which he opened repeatedly, ten times, twenty, a hundred. Sometimes he found only darkness on the other side, a blackness that smelled of blood and that wrenched a sudden thunder from his heart. Sometimes Valerie Keene was there, but when he reached for her, she receded, and the door slammed shut.

Friday morning, after shaving and showering, Spencer filled one bowl with dog food, another with water, put them on the floor by the bed, and went to the door. "They have a coffee shop. I'll have breakfast, and we'll check out when I get back."

The dog didn't want to be left alone. He whined pleadingly.

"You're safe here," Spencer said.

Guardedly, he opened the door, expecting Rocky to rush outside.

Instead of making a break for freedom, the dog sat on his butt, huddled pathetically, and hung his head.

Spencer stepped outside onto the covered promenade. He looked back into the room.

Rocky hadn't moved. His head hung low. He was shivering.

Sighing, Spencer reentered the room and closed the door. "Okay, have your breakfast, then come with me while I have mine."

Rocky rolled his eyes to watch from under his furry brows as his master settled in the armchair. He went to his food bowl, glanced at Spencer, then looked back uneasily at the door.

"I'm not going anywhere," Spencer assured him.

Instead of wolfing down his food as usual, Rocky ate with a delicacy and at a pace not characteristically canine. As if he believed that this would be his last meal, he savored it.

When the mutt was finally finished, Spencer rinsed the bowls, dried them, and loaded all the luggage into the Explorer.

In February, Vegas could be as warm as a late-spring day, but the high desert was also subject to an inconstant winter that had sharp teeth when it chose to bite. That Friday morning, the sky was gray, and the temperature was in the low forties. From the western mountains came a wind as cold as a pit boss's heart.

After the luggage was loaded, they visited a suitably private corner of a brushy vacant lot behind the motel. Spencer stood guard, with his back turned and his shoulders hunched and his hands jammed in his jeans pockets, while Rocky attended to the call of nature.

With that moment successfully negotiated, they returned to the Explorer, and Spencer drove from the south wing of the motel to the north wing, where the coffee shop was located. He parked at the curb, facing the big plate-glass windows.

Inside the restaurant, he selected a booth by the windows, in a direct line with the Explorer, which was less than twenty feet away. Rocky sat as tall as he could in the passenger seat of the truck, watching his master through the windshield.

Spencer ordered eggs, home fries, toast, coffee. While he ate, he glanced frequently at the Explorer, and Rocky was always watching.

A few times, Spencer waved.

The dog liked that. He wagged his tail every time that Spencer acknowledged him. Once, he put his paws on the dashboard and pressed his nose to the windshield, grinning.

"What did they do to you, pal? What did they do to make you like this?" Spencer wondered aloud, over his coffee, as he watched the adoring dog.

∽

Roy Miro left Alfonse Johnson and the other men to search every inch of the cabin in Malibu while he returned to Los Angeles. With luck, they would find something in Grant's belongings that would shed light upon his psychology, reveal an unknown aspect of his past, or give them a lead on his whereabouts.

Agents in the downtown office were already penetrating the phone company system to trace the call placed earlier by Grant's computer. Grant had probably covered his trail. They would be lucky if they discovered, even by this time tomorrow, at what number and location he had received those fifty images from the videocamera.

Driving south on the Coast Highway, toward L.A., Roy put his cellular unit on speakerphone mode and called Kleck in Orange County.

Although he sounded weary, John Kleck was in fine, deep voice. "I'm getting to hate this tricky bitch," he said, referring to the woman who had been Valerie Keene until she abandoned her car at John Wayne Airport on Wednesday and became, yet again, someone new.

As he listened, Roy had difficulty picturing the thin, gangly young agent with the startled-trout face. Because of the reverberant bass voice, it was easier to believe that Kleck was a tall, broad-chested, black rock singer from the doo-wop era.

Every report that Kleck delivered sounded vitally important—even when he had nothing to report. Like now. Kleck and his team still had no idea where the woman had gone.

"We're widening the search to rental-car agencies countywide," Kleck intoned. "Also checking stolen-car reports. Any set of wheels heisted anytime Wednesday—we're putting it on our must-find sheet."

"She never stole a car before," Roy noted.

"Which is why she might this time—to keep us off balance. I'm just worried she hitchhiked. Can't track her on the thumb express."

"If she hitchhiked, with all the crazies out there these days," Roy said, "then we don't have to worry about her any more. She's already been raped, murdered, beheaded, gutted, and dismembered."

"That's all right with me," Kleck said. "Just so I can get a piece of the body for a positive ID."

After talking to Kleck, though the morning was still fresh, Roy was convinced that the day would feature nothing but bad news.

Negative thinking usually wasn't his style. He loathed negative thinkers. If too many of them radiated pessimism at the same time, they could distort the fabric of reality, resulting in earthquakes, tornadoes, train wrecks, plane crashes, acid rain, cancer clusters, disruptions in microwave communications, and a dangerous surliness in the general population. Yet he couldn't shake his bad mood.

Seeking to lift his spirits, he drove with only his left hand until he'd gently extracted Guinevere's treasure from the Tupperware container and put it on the seat beside him.

Five exquisite digits. Perfect, natural, unpainted fingernails, each with its precisely symmetrical, crescent-shaped lunula. And the fourteen finest phalanges that he'd ever seen: None was a millimeter more or less than ideal length. Across the gracefully arched back of the hand, pulling the skin taut: the five most flawlessly formed metacarpals he ever hoped to see. The skin was pale but unblemished, as smooth as melted wax from the candles on God's own high table.

Driving east, heading downtown, Roy let his gaze drift now and then to Guinevere's treasure, and with each stolen glimpse, his mood improved. By the time he was near Parker Center, the administrative headquarters of the Los Angeles Police Department, he was buoyant.

Reluctantly, while stopped at a traffic light, he returned the hand to the container. He put that reliquary and its precious contents under the driver's seat.

At Parker Center, after leaving his car in a visitor's stall, he took an elevator from the garage and, using his FBI credentials, went up to the fifth floor. The appointment was with Captain Harris Descoteaux, who was in his office and waiting.

Roy had spoken briefly to Descoteaux from Malibu, so it was no surprise that the captain was black. He had that almost glossy, midnight-dark, beautiful skin sometimes enjoyed by those of Caribbean extraction, and although he evidently had been an Angeleno for years, a faint island lilt still lent a musical quality to his speech.

In navy-blue slacks, striped suspenders, white shirt, and blue tie with diagonal red stripes, Descoteaux had the poise, dignity, and gravitas of a Supreme Court justice, even though his sleeves were rolled up and his jacket was hanging on the back of his chair.

After shaking Roy's hand, Harris Descoteaux indicated the only visitor's chair and said, "Please sit down."

The small office was not equal to the man who occupied it. Poorly ventilated. Poorly lighted. Shabbily furnished.

Roy felt sorry for Descoteaux. No government employee at the executive level, whether in a law-enforcement organization or not, should have to work in such a cramped office. Public service was a noble calling, and Roy was of the opinion that those who were willing to serve should be treated with respect, gratitude, and generosity.

Settling into the chair behind the desk, Descoteaux said, "The Bureau verifies your ID, but they won't say what case you're on."

"National security matter," Roy assured him.

Any query about Roy that was placed with the FBI would have been routed to Cassandra Solinko, a valued administrative assistant to the director. She would support the lie (though not in writing) that Roy was a Bureau agent; however, she could not discuss the nature of his investigation, because she didn't know what the hell he was doing.

Descoteaux frowned. "Security matter—that's pretty vague."

If Roy got into deep trouble—the kind to inspire congressional investigations and newspaper headlines—Cassandra Solinko would deny that she'd ever verified his claim to be with the FBI. If she was disbelieved and subpoenaed to testify about what little she knew of Roy and his nameless agency, there was a stunningly high statistical probability that she would suffer a deadly cerebral embolism, or a massive cardiac infarction, or a high-speed, head-on collision with a bridge abutment. She was aware of the consequences of cooperation.

"Sorry, Captain Descoteaux, but I can't be more specific."

Roy would experience consequences similar to Ms. Solinko's if he himself screwed up. Public service could sometimes be a brutally stressful career—which was one reason why comfortable offices, a generous package of fringe benefits, and virtually unlimited perks were, in Roy's estimation, entirely justified.

Descoteaux didn't like being frozen out. Trading his frown for a smile, speaking with soft island ease, he said, "It's difficult to lend assistance without knowing the whole picture."

It would be easy to succumb to Descoteaux's charm, to mistake his deliberate yet fluid movements for the sloth of a tropical soul, and

to be deceived by his musical voice into believing that he was a frivolous man.

Roy saw the truth, however, in the captain's eyes, which were huge, as
black and liquid as ink, as direct and penetrating as those in a Rembrandt
portrait. His eyes revealed an intelligence, patience, and relentless curiosity that defined the kind of man who posed the greatest threat to
someone in Roy's line of work.

Returning Descoteaux's smile with an even sweeter smile of his own,
convinced that his younger-slimmer-Santa-Claus look was a match for
Caribbean charm, Roy said, "Actually, I don't need help, not in the sense
of services and support. Just a little information."

"Be pleased to provide it, if I can," said the captain.

The wattage of their two smiles had temporarily rectified the problem
of inadequate lighting in the small office.

"Before you were promoted to central administration," Roy said, "I
believe you were a division captain."

"Yes. I commanded the West Los Angeles Division."

"Do you remember a young officer who served under you for a little
more than a year—Spencer Grant?"

Descoteaux's eyes widened slightly. "Yes, of course, I remember
Spence. I remember him well."

"Was he a good cop?"

"The best," Descoteaux said without hesitation. "Police academy,
criminology degree, army special services—he had *substance.*"

"A very competent man, then?"

" 'Competence' is hardly an adequate word in Spence's case."

"And intelligent?"

"Extremely so."

"The two carjackers he killed—was that a righteous shooting?"

"Hell, yes, as righteous as they get. One perp was wanted for murder,
and there were three felony warrants out on the second loser. Both were
carrying, shot at him. Spence had no choice. The review board cleared
him as quick as God let Saint Peter into Heaven."

Roy said, "Yet he didn't go back out on the street."

"He didn't want to carry a gun any more."

"He'd been a U.S. Army Ranger."

Descoteaux nodded. "He was in action a few times—in Central
America and the Middle East. He'd had to kill before, and finally
he was forced to admit to himself he couldn't make a career of the
service."

"Because of how killing made him feel."

"No. More because . . . I think because he wasn't always convinced that the killing was justified, no matter what the politicians said. But I'm guessing. I don't know for sure what his thinking was."

"A man has trouble using a gun against another human being—that's understandable," Roy said. "But the same man trading the army for the police department—that baffles me."

"As a cop, he thought he'd have more control over when to use deadly force. Anyway, it was his dream. Dreams die hard."

"Being a cop was his dream?"

"Not necessarily a cop. Just being the good guy in a uniform, risking his life to help people, saving lives, upholding the law."

"Altruistic young man," Roy said with an edge of sarcasm.

"We get some. Fact is, a lot are like that—in the beginning, at least." He stared at his coal-black hands, which were folded on the green blotter on his desk. "In Spence's case, high ideals led him to the army, then the force . . . but there was something more than that. Somehow . . . by helping people in all the ways a cop can help, Spence was trying to understand himself, come to terms with himself."

Roy said, "So he's psychologically troubled?"

"Not in any way that would prevent him from being a good cop."

"Oh? Then what is it he's trying to understand about himself?"

"I don't know. It goes back, I think."

"Back?"

"The past. He carries it like a ton of stone on his shoulders."

"Something to do with the scar?" Roy asked.

"Everything to do with it, I suspect."

Descoteaux looked up from his hands. His huge, dark eyes were full of compassion. They were exceptional, expressive eyes. Roy might have wanted to possess them if they had belonged to a woman.

"How was he scarred, how did it happen?" Roy asked.

"All he ever said was he'd been in an accident when he was a boy. A car accident, I guess. He didn't really want to talk about it."

"He have any close friends on the force?"

"Not close, no. He was a likable guy. But self-contained."

"A loner," Roy said, nodding with understanding.

"No. Not the way you mean it. He'll never wind up in a tower with a rifle, shooting everyone in sight. People liked him, and he liked people. He just had this . . . reserve."

"After the shooting, he wanted a desk job. Specifically, he applied for a transfer to the Task Force on Computer Crime."

"No, *they* came to *him*. Most people would be surprised—but I'm sure you're aware—we have officers with degrees in law, psychology, and criminology like Spence. Many get the education not because they want to change careers or move up to administration. They want to stay on the street. They love their work, and they think a little advanced education will help them do a better job. They're committed, dedicated. They only want to be *cops*, and they—"

"Admirable, I'm sure. Though some might see them as hard-core reactionaries, unable to give up the *power* of being a cop."

Descoteaux blinked. "Well, anyway, if one of them wants off the street, he doesn't wind up processing paperwork. The department uses his knowledge. The Administrative Office, Internal Affairs, Organized Crime Intelligence Division, most divisions of the Detective Services Group—they all wanted Spence. He chose the task force."

"He didn't perhaps *solicit* the interest of the task force?"

"He didn't need to solicit. Like I said, they came to him."

"Before he went to the task force, had he been a computer nut?"

"Nut?" Descoteaux was no longer able to repress his impatience. "He knew how to use computers on the job, but he wasn't obsessed with them. Spence wasn't a nut about anything. He's a very solid man, dependable, together."

"Except that—and these are your words—he's still trying to understand himself, come to terms with himself."

"Aren't we all?" the captain said crisply. He rose and turned from Roy to the small window beside his desk. The angled slats of the blind were dusty. He stared between them at the smog-cloaked city.

Roy waited. It was best to let Descoteaux have his tantrum. The poor man had earned it. His office was dreadfully small. He didn't even have a private bathroom with it.

Turning to face Roy again, the captain said, "I don't know what you think Spence has done. And there's no point in my asking—"

"National security," Roy confirmed smugly.

"—but you're wrong about him. He's not a man who's ever going to turn bad."

Roy raised his eyebrows. "What makes you so sure of that?"

"Because he agonizes."

"Does he? About what?"

"About what's right, what's wrong. About what he does, the decisions he makes. Quietly, privately—but he agonizes."

"Don't we all?" Roy said, getting to his feet.

"No," Descoteaux said. "Not these days. Most people believe everything's relative, including morality."

Roy didn't think Descoteaux was in a hand-shaking mood, so he just said, "Well, thank you for your time, Captain."

"Whatever the crime, Mr. Miro, the kind of man you want to be looking for is one who's absolutely certain of his righteousness."

"I'll keep that in mind."

"No one's more dangerous than a man who's convinced of his own moral superiority," Descoteaux said pointedly.

"How true," Roy replied, opening the door.

"Someone like Spence—he's not the enemy. In fact, people like that are the only reason the whole damn civilization hasn't fallen down around our ears already."

Stepping into the hall, Roy said, "Have a nice day."

"Whatever side Spence settles on," said Descoteaux with quiet but unmistakable belligerence, "I'd bet my ass it's the right side."

Roy closed the office door behind him. By the time he reached the elevators, he'd decided to have Harris Descoteaux killed. Maybe he would do it himself, as soon as he had dealt with Spencer Grant.

On the way to his car, he cooled down. On the street once more, with Guinevere's treasure on the car seat beside him exerting its calming influence, Roy was sufficiently in control again to realize that summary execution wasn't an appropriate response to Descoteaux's insulting insinuations. Greater punishments than death were within his power to bestow.

∽

The three wings of the two-story apartment complex embraced a modest swimming pool. Cold wind chopped the water into wavelets that slapped at the blue tile under the coping, and Spencer detected the scent of chlorine as he crossed the courtyard.

The burned-out sky was lower than it had been before breakfast, as if it were a pall of gray ashes settling toward the earth. The lush fronds of the wind-tossed palm trees rustled and clicked and clattered with what might have been a storm warning.

Padding along at Spencer's side, Rocky sneezed a couple of times at the chlorine smell, but he was unfazed by the thrashing palms. He had never met a tree that scared him. Which was not to say that such a devil tree didn't exist. When he was in one of his stranger moods, when he had the heebie-jeebies and sensed evil mojo at work in every shadow, when the circumstances were *just right*, he probably could be terrorized by a wilted sapling in a five-inch pot.

According to the information that Valerie—then calling herself Hannah May Rainey—had supplied to obtain a work card for a job as a dealer in a casino, she'd lived at this apartment complex. Unit 2-D.

The apartments on the second floor opened onto a roofed balcony that overlooked the courtyard and that sheltered the walkway in front of the ground-floor units. As Spencer and Rocky climbed concrete stairs, wind rattled a loose picket in the rust-spotted iron railing.

He'd brought Rocky because a cute dog was a great icebreaker. People tended to trust a man who was trusted by a dog, and they were more likely to open up and talk to a stranger who had an appealing mutt at his side—even if that stranger had a dark intensity about him and a scar from ear to chin. Such was the power of canine charm.

Hannah-Valerie's former apartment was in the center wing of the U-shaped structure, at the rear of the courtyard. A large window to the right of the door was covered by draperies. To the left, a small window revealed a kitchen. The name above the doorbell was Traven.

Spencer rang the bell and waited.

His highest hope was that Valerie had shared the apartment and that the other tenant remained in residence. She had lived there at least four months, the duration of her employment at the Mirage. In that much time, though Valerie would have been living as much of a lie as in California, her roommate might have made an observation that would enable Spencer to track her backward from Nevada, the same way that Rosie had pointed him from Santa Monica to Vegas.

He rang the bell again.

Odd as it was to try to find her by seeking to learn where she'd come from instead of where she'd gone, Spencer had no better choice. He didn't have the resources to track her forward from Santa Monica. Besides, by going backward, he was less likely to collide with the federal agents—or whatever they were—following her.

He had heard the doorbell ringing inside. Nevertheless, he tried knocking.

The knock was answered—though not by anyone in Valerie's former apartment. Farther to the right along the balcony, the door to 2-E opened, and a gray-haired woman in her seventies leaned her head out to peek at him. "Can I help you?"

"I'm looking for Miss Traven."

"Oh, she works the early shift at Caesars Palace. Won't be home for hours yet."

She moved into the doorway: a short, plump, sweet-faced woman in clunky orthopedic shoes, support stockings as thick as dinosaur hide, a yellow-and-gray housedress, and a forest-green cardigan.

Spencer said, "Well, who I'm really looking for is—"

Rocky, hiding behind Spencer, risked poking his head around his master's legs to get a look at the grandmotherly soul from 2-E, and the old woman squealed with delight when she spotted him. Although she toddled more than walked, she launched herself off the threshold with the exuberance of a child who didn't know the meaning of the word "arthritis." Burbling baby talk, she approached at a velocity that startled Spencer and alarmed the hell out of Rocky. The dog yelped, the woman bore down on them with exclamations of adoration, the dog tried to climb Spencer's right leg as if to hide under his jacket, the woman said "Sweetums, sweetums, sweetums," and Rocky dropped to the balcony floor in a swoon of terror and curled into a ball and crossed his forepaws over his eyes and prepared himself for the inevitability of violent death.

∽

Bosley Donner's left leg slipped off the foot brace on his electric wheelchair and scraped along the walkway. Laughing, letting his chair coast to a halt, Donner lifted his unfeeling leg with both hands and slammed it back where it belonged.

Equipped with a high-capacity battery and a golf-cart propulsion system, Donner's transportation was capable of considerably greater speeds than any ordinary electric wheelchair. Roy Miro caught up with him, breathing heavily.

"I told you this baby can *move*," Donner said.

"Yes. I see. Impressive," Roy puffed.

They were in the backyard of Donner's four-acre estate in Bel Air, where a wide ribbon of brick-colored concrete had been installed to allow the disabled owner to access every corner of his elaborately landscaped property. The walkway rose and fell repeatedly, passed through a tunnel under one end of the pool patio, and serpentined among phoenix palms, queen palms, king palms, huge Indian laurels, and melaleucas in their jackets of shaggy bark. Evidently, Donner had designed the walkway to serve as his private roller coaster.

"It's illegal, you know," Donner said.

"Illegal?"

"It's against the law to modify a wheelchair the way I've done."

"Well, yes, I can see why it would be."

"You can?" Donner was amazed. "I can't. It's *my* chair."

"Whipping around this track the way you do, you could wind up not just a paraplegic but a quadriplegic."

Donner grinned and shrugged. "Then I'd computerize the chair so I could operate it with vocal commands."

At thirty-two, Bosley Donner had been without the use of his legs for eight years, after taking a chunk of shrapnel in the spine during a Middle East police action that had involved the unit of U.S. Army Rangers in which he had served. He was stocky, deeply tanned, with brush-cut blond hair and blue-gray eyes that were even merrier than Roy's. If he'd ever been depressed about his disability, he had gotten over it long ago—or maybe he'd learned to hide it well.

Roy disliked the man because of his extravagant lifestyle, his annoyingly high spirits, his unspeakably garish Hawaiian shirt—and for other reasons not quite definable. "But is this recklessness socially responsible?"

Donner frowned with confusion, but then his face brightened. "Oh, you mean I might be a burden to society. Hell, I'd never use government health care anyway. They'd triage me into the grave in six seconds flat. Look around, Mr. Miro. I can pay what's necessary. Come on, I want to show you the temple. It's really something."

Rapidly gaining speed, Donner streaked away from Roy, downhill through feathery palm shadows and spangles of red-gold sunshine.

Straining to repress his annoyance, Roy followed.

After being discharged from the army, Donner had fallen back on a lifelong talent for drawing inventive cartoon characters. His portfolio had won him a job with a greeting card company. In his spare time, he developed a comic strip and was offered a contract by the first newspaper syndicate to see it. Within two years, he was the hottest cartoonist in the country. Now, through those widely loved cartoon characters—which Roy found idiotic—Bosley Donner was an industry: best-selling books, TV shows, toys, T-shirts, his own line of greeting cards, product endorsements, records, and much more.

At the bottom of a long slope, the walkway led to a balustraded garden temple in the classical style. Five columns stood on a limestone floor, supporting a heavy cornice and a dome with a ball finial. The structure was surrounded by English primrose laden with blossoms in intense shades of yellow, red, pink, and purple.

Donner sat in his chair, in the center of the open-air temple, swathed in shadows, waiting for Roy. In that setting, he should have been a mysterious figure; however, his stockiness and broad face and brush-cut hair and loud Hawaiian shirt all combined to make him seem like one of his own cartoon characters.

Stepping into the temple, Roy said, "You were telling me about Spencer Grant."

"Was I?" Donner said with a note of irony.

In fact, for the past twenty minutes, while leading Roy on a chase around the estate, Donner had said quite a lot about Grant—with whom he had served in the Army Rangers—and yet had said nothing that revealed either the inner man or any important details of his life prior to joining the army.

"I liked Hollywood," Donner said. "He was the quietest man I've ever known, one of the most polite, one of the smartest—and sure as hell the most self-effacing. Last guy in the world to brag. And he could be a lot of fun when he was in the right mood. But he was very self-contained. No one ever really got to know him."

"Hollywood?" Roy asked.

"That's just a name we had for him, when we wanted to kid him. He loved old movies. I mean, he was almost obsessed with them."

"Any particular kind of movies?"

"Suspense flicks and dramas with old-fashioned heroes. These days, he said, movies have forgotten what heroes are all about."

"How so?"

"He said heroes used to have a better sense of right and wrong than they do now. He loved *North by Northwest, Notorious, To Kill a Mockingbird*, because the heroes had strong principles, morals. They used their wits more than guns."

"Now," Roy said, "you have movies where a couple of buddy cops smash and shoot up half a city to get one bad guy—"

"—use four-letter words, all kinds of trash talk—"

"—jump into bed with women they met only two hours ago—"

"—and strut around with half their clothes off to show their muscles, totally *full* of themselves."

Roy nodded. "He had a point."

"Hollywood's favorite old movie stars were Cary Grant and Spencer Tracy, so of course he took a lot of ribbing about that."

Roy was surprised that his and the scarred man's opinions of current movies were in harmony. He was disturbed to find himself in agreement on *any* issue with a dangerous sociopath like Grant.

Thus preoccupied, he'd only half heard what Donner had told him. "I'm sorry—took a lot of ribbing about what?"

"Well, it wasn't particularly funny that Spencer Tracy and Cary Grant must've been his mom's favorite stars too, or that she named him after them. But a guy like Hollywood, as modest and quiet as he was, shy around girls, a guy who didn't hardly seem to *have* an ego—well, it just struck us funny that he identified so strongly with a couple of movie stars, the heroes they played. He was still nineteen when he went into Ranger training, but in most ways he seemed twenty years older than the rest of us. You could see the kid in him only when he was talking about old movies or watching them."

Roy sensed that what he had just learned was of great importance—but he didn't understand why. He stood on the brink of a revelation yet could not quite see the shape of it.

He held his breath, afraid that even exhaling would blow him away from the understanding that seemed within reach.

A warm breeze soughed through the temple.

On the limestone floor near Roy's left foot, a slow black beetle crawled laboriously toward its own strange destiny.

Then, almost eerily, Roy heard himself asking a question that he had not first consciously considered. "You're sure his mother named him after Spencer Tracy and Cary Grant?"

"Isn't it obvious?" Donner replied.

"Is it?"

"It is to me."

"He actually told you that's why she named him what she did?"

"I guess so. I don't remember. But he must have."

The soft breeze soughed, the beetle crawled, and a chill of enlightenment shivered through Roy.

Bosley Donner said, "You haven't seen the waterfall yet. It's terrific. It's really, really neat. Come on, you've got to see it."

The wheelchair purred out of the temple.

Roy turned to watch between the limestone columns as Donner sped recklessly along another down-sloping pathway into the cool shadows of a green glen. His brightly patterned Hawaiian shirt seemed to flare with fire when he flashed through shafts of red-gold sunshine, and then he vanished past a stand of Australian tree ferns.

By now Roy understood the primary thing about Bosley Donner that so annoyed him: The cartoonist was just too damned self-confident and independent. Even disabled, he was utterly self-possessed and self-sufficient.

Such people were a grave danger to the system. Civil order was not sustainable in a society populated by rugged individualists. The dependency of the people was the source of the state's power, and if the state didn't have enormous power, progress could not be achieved or peace sustained in the streets.

He might have followed Donner and terminated him in the name of social stability, lest others be inspired by the cartoonist's example, but the risk of being observed by witnesses was too great. A couple of gardeners were at work on the grounds, and Mrs. Donner or a member of the household staff might be looking out a window at the most inconvenient of all moments.

Besides, chilled and excited by what he believed he'd discovered about Spencer Grant, Roy was eager to confirm his suspicion.

He left the temple, being careful not to crush the slow black beetle, and turned in the opposite direction from that in which Donner had vanished. He swiftly ascended to higher levels of the backyard, hurried past the side of the enormous house, and got in his car, which was parked in the circular driveway.

From the manila envelope that Melissa Wicklun had given him, he withdrew one of the pictures of Grant and put it on the seat. But for the terrible scar, that face initially had seemed quite ordinary. Now he knew that it was the face of a monster.

From the same envelope, he took a printout of the report that he'd requested from Mama the previous night and that he'd read off the computer screen in his hotel a few hours ago. He paged to the false names under which Grant had acquired and paid for utilities.

Stewart Peck
Henry Holden
James Gable
John Humphrey
William Clark
Wayne Gregory
Robert Tracy

Roy withdrew a pen from his inside jacket pocket and rearranged first and last names into a new list of his own:

Gregory Peck
William Holden
Clark Gable
James Stewart
John Wayne

That left Roy with four names from the original list: Henry, Humphrey, Robert, and Tracy.

Tracy, of course, matched the bastard's first name—Spencer. And for a purpose that neither Mama nor Roy had yet discovered, the tricky, scar-faced son of a bitch was probably using another false identity that incorporated the name Cary, which was missing from the first list but was the logical match for his last name—Grant.

That left Henry, Humphrey, and Robert.

Henry. No doubt Grant sometimes operated under the name Fonda, perhaps with a first name lifted from Burt Lancaster or Gary Cooper.

Humphrey. In some circle, somewhere, Grant was known as Mr. Bogart—first name courtesy of yet another movie star of yesteryear.

Robert. Eventually they were certain to find that Grant also employed the surname Mitchum or Montgomery.

As casually as other men changed shirts, Spencer Grant changed identities.

They were searching for a phantom.

Although he couldn't yet prove it, Roy was now convinced that the name Spencer Grant was as phony as all the others. Grant was not the surname that this man had inherited from his father, nor was Spencer the Christian name that his mother had given him. He had named himself after favorite actors who had played old-fashioned heroes.

His real name was cipher. His real name was mystery, shadow, ghost, smoke.

Roy picked up the computer-enhanced portrait and studied the scarred face.

This dark-eyed cipher had joined the army under the name Spencer Grant, when he was just eighteen. What teenager knew how to establish a false identity, with convincing credentials, and get away with it? What had this enigmatic man been running from at even that young age?

How in the *hell* was he involved with the woman?

∾

On the sofa, Rocky lay on his back, all four legs in the air, paws limp, his head in Theda Davidowitz's ample lap, gazing up in rapture at the plump, gray-haired woman. Theda stroked his tummy, scratched under his chin, and called him "sweetums" and "cutie" and "pretty eyes" and "snookums." She told him that he was God's own little furry angel, the handsomest canine in all creation, wonderful, marvelous, cuddly, adorable, perfect. She fed him thin little slices of ham, and he took each morsel from her fingertips with a delicacy more characteristic of a duchess than of a dog.

Ensconced in an overstuffed armchair with antimacassars on the back and arms, Spencer sipped from a cup of rich coffee that Theda had improved with a pinch of cinnamon. On the table beside his chair, a china pot held additional coffee. A plate was heaped with homemade chocolate-chip cookies. He had politely declined imported English tea biscuits, Italian anisette biscotti, a slice of lemon-coconut cake, a blueberry muffin, gingersnaps, shortbread, and a raisin scone; exhausted by Theda's hospitable perseverance, he had at last agreed to a cookie, only to be presented with twelve of them, each the size of a saucer.

Between cooing at the dog and urging Spencer to eat another cookie, Theda revealed that she was seventy-six and that her husband—Bernie—had died eleven years ago. She and Bernie had brought two children into the world: Rachel and Robert. Robert—the finest boy who ever lived, thoughtful and kind—served in Vietnam, was a *hero*, won more medals than you would believe . . . and died there. Rachel—oh, you should have seen her, so beautiful, her picture was there on the mantel, but it didn't do her justice, no photo could do her justice—had been killed in a traffic accident fourteen years ago. It was a terrible thing to outlive your children; it made you wonder if God was paying attention. Theda and Bernie had lived most of their married life in California, where Bernie had been an accountant and she'd been a third-grade teacher. On retirement, they sold their home, reaped a big capital gain, and moved to Vegas not because they were gamblers—well, twenty dollars, wasted on slot machines, once a month—but because real estate was cheap compared with California. Retirees had moved there by the thousands for that very reason. She and Bernie bought a small house for cash and were still able to bank sixty percent of what they'd gotten from the sale of their home in California. Bernie died three years later. He was the sweetest man, gentle and considerate, the greatest good fortune in her life had been to marry him—and after his death, the house was too large for a widow, so Theda sold it and moved to the apartment. For ten years, she'd had a dog—his name was Sparkle and it suited him, he was an adorable cocker spaniel—but, two months ago, Sparkle had gone the way of all things. God, how she'd cried, a foolish old woman, cried rivers, but she'd loved him. Since then she'd occupied herself with cleaning, baking, watching TV, and playing cards with friends twice a week. She hadn't considered getting another dog after Sparkle, because she wouldn't outlive another pet, and she didn't want to die and leave a sad little dog to fend for itself. Then she saw Rocky, and her heart melted, and now she knew she would have to get another dog. If she got one from the pound, a cute pooch destined to be put to sleep anyway, then every good day she could give him was more than he would have had without her. And who knew? Maybe she *would* outlive another pet and make a home for him until *his* time came, because two of her friends were in their mid-eighties and still going strong.

To please her, Spencer had a third cup of coffee and a second of the immense chocolate-chip cookies.

Rocky was gracious enough to accept more paper-thin slices of ham and submit to more belly stroking and chin scratching. From time to time he rolled his eyes toward Spencer, as if to say, *Why didn't you tell me about this lady a long time ago?*

Spencer had never seen the dog so completely, quickly charmed as he'd been by Theda. When his tail periodically swished back and forth, the motion was so vigorous that the upholstery was in danger of being worn to tatters.

"What I wanted to ask you," Spencer said when Theda paused for breath, "is if you knew a young woman who lived in the next apartment until late last November. Her name was Hannah Rainey and she—"

At the mention of Hannah—whom Spencer knew as Valerie—Theda launched into an enthusiastic monologue seasoned with superlatives. This girl, this special girl, oh, she'd been the best neighbor, so considerate, such a good heart in that dear girl. Hannah worked at the Mirage, a blackjack dealer on the graveyard shift, and she slept mornings through early afternoons. More often than not, Hannah and Theda had eaten dinner together, sometimes in Theda's apartment, sometimes in Hannah's. Last October Theda had been desperately ill with the flu and Hannah had looked after her, nursed her, been like a *daughter* to her. No, Hannah never talked about her past, never said where she was from, never talked about family, because she was trying to put something terrible behind her—that much was obvious—and she was looking only to the future, always forward, never back. For a while Theda had figured maybe it was an abusive husband, still out there somewhere, stalking her, and she'd had to leave her old life to avoid being killed. These days, you heard so much about such things, the world was a mess, everything turned upside down, getting worse all the time. Then the Drug Enforcement Administration had raided Hannah's apartment last November, at eleven in the morning, when she should have been sound asleep, but the girl was gone, packed up and moved overnight, without a word to her friend Theda, as if she'd known that she was about to be found. The federal agents were furious, and they questioned Theda at length, as if she might be a criminal mastermind herself, for God's sake. They said Hannah Rainey was a fugitive from justice, a partner in one of the most successful cocaine-importing rings in the country, and that she had shot and killed two undercover police officers in a sting operation that had gone sour.

"So she's wanted for murder?" Spencer asked.

Making a fist of one liver-spotted hand, stamping one foot so hard that her orthopedic shoe hammered the floor with a resounding *thud* in spite of the carpet, Theda Davidowitz said, "Bullshit!"

 ∾

Eve Marie Jammer worked in a windowless chamber at the bottom of an office tower, four stories below downtown Las Vegas. Sometimes she thought of herself as being like the hunchback of Notre Dame in his bell tower, or like the phantom in his lonely realm beneath the Paris Opera House, or like Dracula in the solitude of his crypt: a figure of mystery, in possession of terrible secrets. One day, she hoped to be feared more intensely, by more people, than all those who had feared the hunchback, the phantom, and the count combined.

Unlike the monsters in movies, Eve Jammer was not physically disfigured. She was thirty-three, an ex-showgirl, blond, green-eyed, breathtaking. Her face caused men to turn their heads and walk into lampposts. Her perfectly proportioned body existed nowhere else but in the moist, erotic dreams of pubescent boys.

She was aware of her exceptional beauty. She reveled in it, for it was a source of power, and Eve loved nothing as much as power.

In her deep domain, the walls and the concrete floor were gray, and the banks of fluorescent bulbs shed a cold, unflattering light in which she was nonetheless gorgeous. Though the space was heated, and though she occasionally turned the thermostat to ninety degrees, the concrete vault resisted every effort to warm it, and Eve often wore a sweater to ward off the chill. As the sole worker in her office, she shared the room only with a few varieties of spiders, all unwelcome, which no quantity of insecticide could eradicate entirely.

That Friday morning in February, Eve was diligently tending the banks of recording machines on the metal shelves that nearly covered one wall. One hundred twenty-eight private telephone lines served her bunker, and all but two were connected to recorders, although not all the recorders were on active status. Currently, the agency had eighty taps operating in Las Vegas.

The sophisticated recording devices employed laser discs rather than tape, and all the phone taps were voice activated, so the discs would not become filled with long stretches of silence. Because of the enormous capacity for data storage allowed by the laser format, the discs seldom had to be replaced.

Nevertheless, Eve checked the digital readout on each machine, which indicated available recording capacity. And although an alarm would draw attention to any malfunctioning recorder, she tested each unit to be certain that it was working. If even one disc or machine failed, the agency might lose information of incalculable value: Las Vegas was the heart of the country's underground economy, which meant that it was a nexus of criminal activity and political conspiracy.

Casino gambling was primarily a cash business, and Las Vegas was like a huge, brightly lighted pleasure ship afloat on a sea of coins and paper currency. Even the casinos that were owned by respectable conglomerates were believed to be skimming fifteen to thirty percent of receipts, which never appeared on their books or tax returns. A portion of that secret treasure circulated through the local economy.

Then there were tips. Tens of millions in gratuities were given by winning gamblers to card dealers and roulette croupiers and craps-table crews, and most of that vanished into the deep pockets of the city. To obtain a three- or five-year contract as the maître d' at main showrooms in most major hotels, a winning applicant had to pay a quarter million in cash—or more—as "key money" to those who were in a position to grant the job; tips reaped from tourists seeking good seats for the shows quickly made the investment pay off.

The most beautiful call girls, referred by casino management to high rollers, could make half a million a year—tax free.

Houses frequently were bought with hundred-dollar bills packed in grocery bags or Styrofoam coolers. Each such sale was by private contract, with no escrow company involved and no official recording of a new deed, which prevented any taxing authority from discovering either that a seller had made a capital gain or that a buyer had made the purchase with undeclared income. Some of the finest mansions in the city had changed hands three or four times over two decades, but the name on the deed of record remained that of the original owner, to whom all official notices were mailed even after his death.

The IRS and numerous other federal agencies maintained large offices in Vegas. Nothing interested the government more than money—especially money from which it had never taken its bite.

The high rise above Eve's windowless realm was occupied by an agency that maintained as formidable a presence in Las Vegas as any arm of government. She was supposed to believe that she worked for a secret though legitimate operation of the National Security Agency, but she knew that was not the truth. This was a nameless outfit, engaged in wide-ranging and mysterious tasks, intricately structured, operating outside the law, manipulating legislative and judicial branches of government (perhaps the executive branch as well), acting as judge and jury and executioner when it wished—a discreet gestapo.

They had put her in one of the most sensitive positions in the Vegas office partly because of her father's influence. However, they also trusted her in that subterranean recording studio because they thought that she was too dumb to realize the personal advantage to be made of the information therein. Her face was the purest distillation of male sex fantasies, and her legs were the most lithe and erotic ever to grace a Vegas stage, and her breasts were enormous, defiantly upswept—so they assumed that she was barely bright enough to change the laser discs from time to time and, when necessary, to call an in-house technician to repair malfunctioning machines.

Although Eve had developed a convincing dumb-blonde act, she was smarter than any of the Machiavellian crowd in the offices above her. During two years with the agency, she had secretly listened to the wiretaps on the most important of the casino owners, Mafia bosses, businessmen, and politicians being monitored.

She had profited by obtaining the details of secret corporate-stock manipulations, which allowed her to buy and sell for her own portfolio without risk. She was well informed about the guaranteed point spreads on national sporting events on those occasions when they were rigged to ensure gigantic profits for certain casino sports books. Usually, when a boxer had been paid to take a dive, Eve had placed a wager on his opponent—through a sports book in Reno, where her amazing luck was less likely to be noticed by anyone she knew.

Most of the people under agency surveillance were sufficiently experienced—and larcenous—to know the danger of conducting illegal activities over the phone, so they monitored their own lines twenty-four hours a day for evidence of electronic eavesdropping. Some of them also used scrambling devices. They were, therefore, arrogantly convinced that their communications couldn't be intercepted.

However, the agency employed technology available nowhere else outside the inner sanctums of the Pentagon. No detection equipment in existence could sniff out the electronic spoor of their devices. To Eve's certain knowledge, they operated an undiscovered tap on the "secure" phone of the special agent in charge of the Las Vegas office of the FBI; she wouldn't have been surprised to learn that the agency enjoyed equal coverage of the director of the Bureau in Washington.

In two years, making a long series of small profits that no one noticed, she had amassed more than five million dollars. Her only large score had been a million in cash, which had been intended as a payoff from the Chicago mob to a United States Senator on a fact-finding junket to Vegas. After covering her tracks by destroying the laser disc on which a conversation about the bribe had been recorded, Eve intercepted the two couriers in a hotel elevator on their way from a penthouse suite to the lobby. They were carrying the money in a canvas book bag that was decorated with the face of Mickey Mouse. Big guys. Hard faces. Cold eyes. Brightly patterned Italian silk shirts under black linen sport coats. Eve was rummaging in her big straw purse even as she entered the elevator, but the two thugs could see only her boobs stretching the low neckline of her sweater. Because they might have been quicker than they looked, she didn't risk taking the Korth .38 out of the handbag, just shot them through the straw, two rounds each. They hit the floor so hard that the elevator shook, and then the money was hers.

The only thing she regretted about the operation was the third man. He was a little guy with thinning hair and bags under his eyes, squeezing into the corner of the cab as if trying to make himself too small to be noticed. According to the tag pinned to his shirt, he was with a convention of dentists and his name was Thurmon Stookey. The poor bastard was a witness. After stopping the elevator between the twelfth and eleventh floors, Eve shot him in the head, but she didn't like doing it.

After she reloaded the Korth and stuffed the ruined straw purse into the canvas book bag with the money, she descended to the ninth floor. She was prepared to kill anyone who might be waiting in the elevator alcove—but, thank God, no one was there. Minutes later she was out of the hotel, heading home, with one million bucks and a handy Mickey Mouse tote bag.

She felt terrible about Thurmon Stookey. He shouldn't have been in that elevator. The wrong place, the wrong time. Blind fate. Life sure was full of surprises. In her entire thirty-three years, Eve Jammer had killed only five people, and Thurmon Stookey had been the sole innocent bystander among them. Nevertheless, for a while, she kept seeing the little guy's face in her mind's eye, as he had looked before she'd wasted him, and it had taken her the better part of a day to stop feeling bad about what had happened to him.

Within a year, she would not need to kill anyone again. She would be able to order people to carry out executions for her.

Soon, though unknown to the general populace, Eve Jammer would be the most feared person in the country, and safely beyond the reach of all enemies. The money she socked away was growing geometrically, but it was not money that would make her untouchable. Her *real* power would come from the trove of incriminating evidence on politicians, businessmen, and celebrities that she had transmitted at high speed, in the form of supercompressed digitized data, from the discs in her bunker to an automated recording device of her own, on a dedicated telephone line, in a bungalow in Boulder City that she had leased through an elaborate series of corporate blinds and false identities.

This was, after all, the Information Age, which had followed the Service Age, which itself had replaced the Industrial Age. She'd read all about it in *Fortune* and *Forbes* and *Business Week*. The future was now, and information was wealth.

Information was power.

Eve had finished examining the eighty active recorders and had begun to select new material for transmission to Boulder City when an electronic tone alerted her to a significant development on one of the taps.

If she had been out of the office, at home or elsewhere, the computer would have alerted her by beeper, whereupon she would have returned to the office immediately. She didn't mind being on call twenty-four hours a day. That was preferable to having assistants manning the room on two other shifts, because she simply didn't *trust* anyone else with the sensitive information on the discs.

A blinking red light drew her to the correct machine. She pushed a button to turn off the alarm.

On the front of the recorder, a label provided information about the wiretap. The first line was a case-file number. The next two lines were the address at which the tap was located. On the fourth line was the name of the subject being monitored: THEDA DAVIDOWITZ.

The surveillance of Mrs. Davidowitz was not the standard fishing expedition in which every word of every conversation was preserved on disc. After all, she was only an elderly widow, an ordinary prole whose general activities were no threat to the system—and therefore were of no interest to the agency. By merest chance, Davidowitz had established a short-lived friendship with the woman who was, at the moment, the most urgently sought fugitive in the nation, and the agency was interested in the widow only in the unlikely event that she received a telephone call or was paid a visit by her special friend. Monitoring the old woman's dreary chats with other friends and neighbors would have been a waste of time.

Instead, the bunker's autonomous computer, which controlled all the recording machines, was programmed to monitor the Davidowitz wiretap continuously and to activate the laser disc only upon the recognition of a key word that was related to the fugitive. That recognition had occurred moments ago. Now the key word appeared on a small display screen on the recorder: HANNAH.

Eve pressed a button marked MONITOR and heard Theda Davidowitz talking to someone in her living room on the other side of the city.

In the handset of each telephone in the widow's apartment, the standard microphone had been replaced with one that could pick up not only what was said in a phone conversation but what was said in any of her rooms, even when none of the phones was in use, and pass it down the line to a monitoring station on a continuous basis. This was a variation on a device known in the intelligence trade as an infinity transmitter.

The agency used infinity transmitters that were considerably improved over the models available on the open market. This one could operate twenty-four hours a day without compromising the function of the telephone in which it was concealed; therefore, Mrs. Davidowitz always heard a dial tone when she picked up a receiver, and callers trying to reach her were never frustrated by a busy signal related to the infinity transmitter's operation.

Eve Jammer listened patiently as the old woman rambled on about Hannah Rainey. Davidowitz was obviously talking *about* rather than *to* her friend the fugitive.

When the widow paused, a young-sounding man in the room with her asked a question about Hannah. Before Davidowitz answered, she called her visitor "my pretty-eyed snookie-wookums" and asked him to "give me a kissie, come on, give me a little lick, show Theda you love her, you little sweetums, sweet little sweetums, yeah, that's right, shake that tail and give Theda a little lick, a little kissie."

"Good God," Eve said, grimacing with disgust. Davidowitz was going on eighty. From the sound of him, the man with her was forty or fifty years her junior. Sick. Sick and perverted. What was the world coming to?

⌇

"A cockroach," Theda said as she gently rubbed Rocky's tummy. "Big. About four or five feet long, not counting the antennae."

After the Drug Enforcement Administration raided Hannah Rainey's place with a force of eight agents and discovered that she'd already fled, they grilled Theda and other neighbors for hours, asking the dumbest questions, all those grown men insisting Hannah was a dangerous criminal, when anyone who had ever met the precious girl for five minutes knew she was *incapable* of dealing drugs and murdering police officers. What absolute, total, stupid, silly nonsense. Then, unable to learn anything from neighbors, the agents had spent still more hours in Hannah's apartment, searching for God-knew-what.

Later that same evening, long after the Keystone Kops had departed—such a loud, rude group of nitwits—Theda went to 2-D with the spare key that Hannah had given her. Instead of breaking down the door to get into the apartment, the DEA had smashed the big window in the dining area that overlooked the balcony and courtyard. The landlord already had boarded over the window with sheets of plywood, until the glazier could fix it. But the front door was intact, and the lock hadn't been changed, so Theda let herself in. The apartment—unlike Theda's own—was rented furnished. Hannah had always kept it spotless, treated the furniture as though it were her own, a fastidious and *thoughtful* girl, so Theda wanted to see what damage the nitwits had done and be sure that the landlord didn't try to blame it on Hannah. In case Hannah turned up, Theda would testify about her immaculate housekeeping and her respect for the landlord's property. By God, she wouldn't let them make the dear girl pay for the damage *plus* stand trial for murdering police officers whom she obviously never murdered. And, of course, the apartment was a mess, the agents were pigs: They had ground out cigarettes on the kitchen floor, spilled cups of take-out coffee from the diner down the block, and even left the toilet unflushed, if you could believe such a thing, since they were grown men and must have had mothers who taught them *something*. But the strangest thing was the cockroach, which they'd drawn on a bedroom wall, with one of those wide-point felt-tip markers.

"Not well drawn, you understand, more or less just the outline of a cockroach, but you could see what it was meant to be," Theda said. "Just a sort of line drawing but ugly all the same. What on earth were those nitwits trying to prove, scrawling on the walls?"

Spencer was pretty sure that Hannah-Valerie herself had drawn the cockroach—just as she had nailed the textbook photograph of a roach to the wall of the bungalow in Santa Monica. He sensed it was meant to taunt and aggravate the men who had come looking for her, though he had no idea what it signified or why she knew that it would anger her pursuers.

∽

Sitting at her desk in her windowless jurisdiction, Eve Jammer telephoned the operations office, upstairs, on the ground floor of the Las Vegas quarters of Carver, Gunmann, Garrote & Hemlock. The morning duty officer was John Cottcole, and Eve alerted him to the situation at Theda Davidowitz's apartment.

Cottcole was electrified by the news and unable to conceal his excitement. He was shouting orders to people in his office even while he was still on the line with Eve.

"Ms. Jammer," Cottcole said, "I'll want a copy of that disc, every word on that disc, you understand?"

"Sure," she said, but he hung up even as she was replying.

They thought that Eve didn't know who Hannah Rainey had been before becoming Hannah Rainey, but she knew the whole story. She also knew that there was an enormous opportunity for her in that case, a chance to hasten the growth of her fortune and power, but she hadn't quite yet decided how to exploit it.

A fat spider scurried across her desk.

She slammed one hand down, crushing the bug against her palm.

⌒

Driving back to Spencer Grant's cabin in Malibu, Roy Miro opened the Tupperware container. He needed the mood boost that the sight of Guinevere's treasure was sure to give him.

He was shocked and dismayed to see a bluish-greenish-brownish spot of discoloration spreading from the web between the first and second fingers. He hadn't expected anything like that for *hours* yet. He was irrationally upset with the dead woman for being so fragile.

Although he told himself that the spot of corruption was small, that the rest of the hand was still exquisite, that he should focus more on the unchanged and perfect form of it than on the coloration, Roy could not rekindle his previous passion for Guinevere's treasure. In fact, though it didn't yet emit a foul odor, it wasn't a treasure any longer: It was just garbage.

Deeply saddened, he put the lid on the plastic box.

He drove another couple of miles before pulling off Pacific Coast Highway and parking in the lot at the foot of a public pier. But for his sedan, the lot was empty.

Taking the Tupperware container with him, he got out of the car, climbed the steps to the pier, and walked toward the end.

His footsteps echoed hollowly off the boardwalk. Under those tightly set beams, breakers rolled between the pilings, rumbling and sloshing.

The pier was deserted. No fishermen. No young lovers leaning against the railing. No tourists. Roy was alone with his corrupted treasure and with his thoughts.

At the end of the pier he stood for a moment, gazing at the vast expanse of glimmering water and at the azure heavens that curved down to meet it at the far horizon. The sky would be there tomorrow and a thousand years from tomorrow, and the sea would roll eternally, but all else passed away.

He strove to avoid negative thoughts. It wasn't easy.

He opened the Tupperware container and threw the five-fingered garbage into the Pacific. It disappeared into the golden spangles of sunlight that gilded the backs of the low waves.

He wasn't concerned that his fingerprints might be lifted by laser from the pallid skin of the severed hand. If the fish didn't eat that last bit of Guinevere, the salt water would scrub away evidence of his touch.

He tossed the Tupperware container and its lid into the sea as well, although he was stricken with a pang of guilt even as the two objects arced toward the waves. He was usually sensitive to the environment, and he never littered.

He was not concerned about the hand, because it was organic. It would become a part of the ocean, and the ocean would not be changed.

Plastic, however, would take more than three hundred years to completely disintegrate. And throughout that period, toxic chemicals would leech from it into the suffering sea.

He should have dumped the Tupperware in one of the trash cans that stood at intervals along the pier railing.

Well. Too late. He was human. That was always the problem.

For a while Roy leaned against the railing. He stared into an infinity of sky and water, brooding about the human condition.

As far as Roy was concerned, the saddest thing in the world was that human beings, for all their ardent striving and desire, could never achieve physical, emotional, or intellectual perfection. The species was doomed to imperfection; it thrashed forever in despair or denial of that fact.

Though she had been undeniably attractive, Guinevere had been perfect in only one regard. Her hands.

Now those were gone too.

Even so, she had been one of the fortunate, because the vast majority of people were imperfect in *every* detail. They would never know the singular confidence and pleasure that must surely arise from the possession of even one flawless feature.

Roy was blessed with a repetitive dream, which came to him two or three nights every month, and from which he always woke in a state of rapture. In the dream, he searched the world over for women like Guinevere, and from each he harvested her perfect feature: from this one, a pair of ears so beautiful that they made his foolish heart pound almost painfully; from that one, the most exquisite ankles that it was within the mind of man to contemplate; from yet another, the snow-white, sculptured teeth of a goddess. He kept these treasures in magic jars, where they did not in the least deteriorate, and when he had collected all the parts of an ideal woman, he assembled them into the lover for whom he had always longed. She was so radiant in her unearthly perfection that he was half blinded when he looked upon her, and her slightest touch was purest ecstasy.

Unfortunately, he always woke from the paradise of her arms.

In life he would never know such beauty. Dreams were the only refuge for a man who would settle for nothing less than perfection.

Gazing into the sea and sky. A solitary man at the end of a deserted pier. Imperfect in every aspect of his own face and form. Aching for the unattainable.

He knew that he was both a romantic and a tragic figure. There were those who would even call him a fool. But at least he dared to dream and to dream big.

Sighing, he turned away from the uncaring sea and walked back to his car in the parking lot.

Behind the steering wheel, after he switched on the engine but before he put the car in gear, Roy allowed himself to withdraw the color snapshot from his wallet. He had carried it with him for more than a year, and he had studied it often. Indeed, it had such power to mesmerize him that he could have spent half the day staring at it in dreamy contemplation.

The photo was of the woman who had most recently called herself Valerie Ann Keene. She was attractive by anyone's standards, perhaps even as attractive as Guinevere.

What made her special, however, what filled Roy with reverence for the divine power that had created humankind, was her perfect eyes. They were more arresting and compelling than even the eyes of Captain Harris Descoteaux of the Los Angeles Police Department.

Dark yet limpid, enormous yet perfectly proportioned to her face, direct yet enigmatic, they were eyes that had seen what lay at the heart of all meaningful mysteries. They were the eyes of a sinless soul yet somehow also the eyes of a shameless voluptuary, simultaneously coy and direct, eyes to which every deceit was as transparent as glass, filled with spirituality and sexuality and a complete understanding of destiny.

He was confident that in reality her eyes would be more, not less, powerful than they were in the snapshot. He had seen other photographs of her, as well as numerous videotapes, and each image had battered his heart more punishingly than the one before it.

When he found her, he would kill her for the agency and for Thomas Summerton and for all those well-meaning others who labored to make this a better country and a better world. She had earned no mercy. Except for her single perfect feature, she was an evil woman.

But after Roy had fulfilled his duty, he would take her eyes. He deserved them. For too brief a time, those enchanting eyes would bring him desperately needed solace in a world that was sometimes too cruel and cold to bear, even for someone with an attitude as positive as that which he cultivated.

∽

By the time Spencer was able to make it to the front door of the apartment with Rocky in his arms (the dog might not have left under his own power), Theda filled a plastic bag with the remaining ten chocolate-chip cookies from the plate beside the armchair, and she insisted that he take them. She also toddled into the kitchen and returned with a homemade blueberry muffin in a small brown paper bag—and then made another trip to bring him two slices of lemon-coconut cake in a Tupperware container.

Spencer protested only the cake, because he wouldn't be able to return the container to her.

"Nonsense," she said. "You don't need to return it. I've got enough Tupperware to last two lifetimes. For years I collected and collected it, because you can keep just anything in Tupperware, it has so many uses, but enough is enough, and I have more than enough, so just enjoy the cake and throw the container away. Enjoy!"

In addition to all the edible treats, Spencer had acquired two pieces of information about Hannah-Valerie. The first was Theda's story about the portrait of the cockroach on the wall of Hannah's bedroom, but he still didn't know what to make of that. The second concerned something that Theda remembered Hannah saying during idle dinner conversation one evening shortly before packing up her things and dusting Vegas off her heels. They had been discussing places in which they had always dreamed of living, and although Theda couldn't make up her mind between Hawaii and England, Hannah had been adamant that only the small coastal town of Carmel, California, had all the peace and beauty that anyone could ever desire.

Spencer supposed that Carmel was a long shot, but at the moment it was the best lead he had. On one hand, she hadn't gone straight there from Las Vegas; she had stopped in the Los Angeles metropolitan area and tried to make a life as Valerie Keene. On the other hand, perhaps now, after her mysterious enemies had found her twice in large cities, she would decide to see if they could locate her as easily in a far smaller community.

Theda had not informed the band of loud, rude, window-shattering nitwits about Hannah's mention of Carmel. Maybe that gave Spencer an advantage.

He was loath to leave her alone with the memories of her beloved husband, long-mourned children, and vanished friend. Nevertheless, thanking her effusively, he stepped across the threshold onto the balcony and walked to the stairs that led down into the courtyard.

The mottled gray-black sky and the blustery wind surprised him, for when he had been in Thedaworld, he had all but forgotten that anything else existed beyond its walls. The crowns of the palms still thrashed, and the air was chiller than before.

Carrying a seventy-pound dog, a plastic bag full of cookies, a blueberry muffin in a paper sack, and a Tupperware container heavy with cake, he found the stairs precarious. He lugged Rocky all the way to the bottom, however, because he was certain that the dog would race straight back to Thedaworld if put down on the balcony.

When Spencer finally released the mutt, Rocky turned and gazed longingly up the stairs toward that little piece of canine heaven.

"Time to plunge back into reality," Spencer said.

The dog whined.

Spencer walked toward the front of the complex, under the wind-whipped trees. Halfway past the swimming pool he looked back.

Rocky was still at the stairs.

"Hey, pal."

Rocky looked at him.

"Whose hound are you anyway?"

An expression of doggy guilt overcame the mutt, and at last he padded toward Spencer.

"Lassie would never leave Timmy, even for God's *own* grandmother."

Rocky sneezed, sneezed, and sneezed again at the pungent scent of chlorine.

"What if," Spencer said as the dog caught up to him, "I'd been trapped here, under an overturned tractor, unable to save myself, or maybe cornered by an angry bear?"

Rocky whined as if in apology.

"Accepted," Spencer said.

On the street, in the Explorer again, Spencer said, "Actually, I'm proud of you, pal."

Rocky cocked his head.

Starting the engine, Spencer said, "You're getting more sociable every day. If I didn't know better, I'd think you've been raiding my cash supply to pay for some high-priced Beverly Hills therapist."

Half a block ahead, a mold-green Chevy rounded the corner in a high-speed slide, tires screaming and smoking, and almost rolled like a stock car in a demolition derby. Somehow it stayed on two wheels, accelerated toward them, and shrieked to a stop at the curb on the other side of the street.

Spencer assumed the car was driven by a drunk or by a kid hopped up on something stronger than Pepsi—until the doors flew open and four men, of a type he recognized too well, exploded out of it. They hurried toward the entrance to the apartment-house courtyard.

Spencer popped the hand brake and shifted into drive.

One of the running men spotted him, pointed, shouted. All four of them turned toward the Explorer.

"Better hold tight, pal."

Spencer tramped on the accelerator, and the Explorer shot into the street, away from the men, toward the corner.

He heard gunfire.

10

A BULLET SMACKED INTO the tailgate of the Explorer. Another ricocheted off metal with a piercing whine. The fuel tank didn't explode. No glass shattered. No tires blew out. Spencer hung a hard right turn past the coffee shop on the corner, felt the truck lifting, trying to tip over, so he pushed it into a slide instead. Rubber barked against blacktop as the rear tires stuttered sideways across the pavement. Then they were into the side street, out of sight of the gunmen, and Spencer accelerated.

Rocky, who was afraid of darkness and wind and lightning and cats and being seen at his toilet, among a dauntingly long list of other things, was not in the least frightened by the gunfire or by Spencer's stunt driving. He sat up straight, his claws sunk into the upholstery, swaying with the movement of the truck, panting and grinning.

Glancing at the speedometer, Spencer saw that they were doing sixty-five in a thirty-mile-per-hour zone. He accelerated.

In the passenger seat, Rocky did something that he had never done before: He began to bob his head up and down, as if encouraging Spencer to greater speed, *yesyesyesyes.*

"This is serious stuff," Spencer reminded him.

Rocky chuffed, as though scoffing at the danger.

"They must have been running audio surveillance on Theda's apartment."

Yesyesyesyesyes.

"Wasting precious resources monitoring *Theda*—and ever since last November? What the *hell* do they want with Valerie, what's so damned important that it's worth all this?"

Spencer looked at the rearview mirror. One and a half blocks behind them, the Chevy rounded the corner at the coffee shop.

He had wanted to get two blocks away before swinging left, out of sight, hoping that the trigger-happy torpedoes in the mold-green sedan would be deceived into thinking that he had turned at the first cross street rather than the second. Now they were on to him again. The Chevy was closing the distance between them, and it was a hell of a lot faster than it looked, a souped-up street rod disguised as one of the stripped-down wheezemobiles that the government assigned to Agriculture Department inspectors and agents of the Bureau of Dental Floss Management.

Though in their sights, Spencer hung a left at the end of the second block, as planned. This time he entered the new street in a wide turn to avoid another time-wasting, tire-stressing slide.

Nevertheless, he was going so fast that he spooked the driver of an approaching Honda. The guy wheeled hard right, bounced up onto the sidewalk, grazed a fire hydrant, and rammed a sagging chain-link fence that surrounded an abandoned service station.

From the corner of his eye, Spencer saw Rocky leaning against the passenger door, pushed there by centrifugal force, yet bobbing his head enthusiastically: *Yesyesyesyesyes.*

Pillowy hammers of cold wind buffeted the Explorer. From out of several empty acres on the right, dense clouds of sand churned into the street.

Vegas had grown haphazardly across the floor of a vast desert valley, and even most of the developed sectors of the city embraced big expanses of barren land. At a glance they seemed to be only enormous vacant lots— but, in fact, they were manifestations of the brooding desert, which was just biding its time. When the wind blew hard enough, the encircled desert angrily flung off its thin disguise, storming into the surrounding neighborhoods.

Half blinded by the seething tempest of sand, with shatters of dust hissing across the windshield, Spencer prayed for more: more wind, more clouds of grit. He wanted to vanish like a ghost ship disappearing into a fog.

He glanced at the rearview mirror. Behind him, visibility was limited to ten or fifteen feet.

He started to accelerate but reconsidered. Already he was plunging into the dry blizzard at suicidal speed. The street was no more visible ahead than it was behind. If he encountered a stopped or slow-moving vehicle, or if he suddenly crossed an intersection against the flow of traffic, the least of his worries would be the four homicidal men in the supercharged fedwagon.

One day, when the axis of the earth shifted just the tiniest fraction of a degree or when the jet streams of the upper troposphere suddenly deepened and accelerated for reasons mysterious, the wind and desert would no doubt conspire to tumble Vegas into ruin and bury the remains beneath billions of cubic yards of dry, white, triumphant sand. Maybe that moment had arrived.

Something thumped into the back end of the Explorer, jolting Spencer. The rearview mirror. The Chevy. On his ass. The fedwagon receded a few feet into the swirling sand, then leaped forward again, tapping the truck, maybe trying to make him spin out, maybe just letting him know they were there.

He was aware of Rocky looking at him, so he looked at Rocky.

The dog seemed to be saying, *Okay, now what?*

They passed the last of the undeveloped land and exploded into a silent clarity of sandless air. In the cold steely light of the pending storm, they had to abandon all hope of slipping away like Lawrence of Arabia into the swirling silicate cloaks of the desert.

An intersection lay half a block ahead. The signal light was red. The flow of traffic was against him.

He kept his foot on the accelerator, praying for a gap in the passing traffic, but at the last moment he rammed the brake pedal to the floor, to avoid colliding with a bus. The Explorer seemed to lift onto its front wheels, then rocked to a halt in a shallow drainage swale that marked the brink of the intersection.

Rocky yelped, lost his grip on the upholstery, and slid into the leg space in front of his seat, under the dashboard.

Belching pale-blue fumes, the bus trundled past in the nearest of the four traffic lanes.

Rocky eeled around in the cramped leg space and grinned up at Spencer. "Stay there, pal. It's safer."

Ignoring the advice, the dog scrambled onto the seat again as Spencer accelerated into traffic in the reeking wake of the bus.

As Spencer turned right and swung around the bus, the rearview mirror captured the mold-green sedan bouncing across the same shallow swale in the pavement and arcing right into the street, as smoothly as if it were airborne.

"That sonofabitch knows how to drive."

Behind him, the Chevy appeared around the side of the city bus. It was coming fast.

Spencer was less concerned about losing them than about being shot at again before he could get away.

They would have to be crazy to open fire from a moving car, in traffic, where stray bullets could kill uninvolved motorists or pedestrians. This wasn't Chicago in the Roaring Twenties, wasn't Beirut or Belfast, wasn't even Los Angeles, for God's sake.

On the other hand, they hadn't hesitated to blast away at him on the street in front of Theda Davidowitz's apartment building. *Shot* at him. No questions first. No polite reading of his constitutional rights. Hell, they hadn't even made a serious effort to confirm that he was, in fact, the person they believed him to be. They wanted him badly enough to risk killing the wrong man.

They seemed convinced that he'd learned something of staggering importance about Valerie and that he must be terminated. In truth, he knew less about the woman's past than he knew about Rocky's.

If they ran him down in traffic and shot him, they would flash real or fake ID from one federal agency or another, and no one would hold them responsible for murder. They would claim that Spencer had been a fugitive, armed and dangerous, a cop killer. No doubt they'd be able to produce a warrant for his arrest, issued after the fact and postdated, and they would clamp his dead hand around a drop gun that could be linked to a series of unsolved homicides.

He accelerated through a yellow traffic light as it turned red. The Chevy stayed close behind him.

If they didn't kill him on the spot, but wounded him and took him alive, they would probably haul him away to a soundproofed room and use creative methods of interrogation. His protestations of ignorance would not be believed, and they would kill him slowly, by degrees, in a vain attempt to extract secrets that he didn't possess.

He had no gun of his own. He had only his hands. His training. And a dog. "We're in big trouble," he told Rocky.

～

In the cozy kitchen of the cabin in the Malibu canyon, Roy Miro sat alone at the dining table, sorting through forty photographs. His men had found them in a shoe box on the top shelf in the bedroom closet. Thirty-nine of the pictures were loose, and the fortieth was in an envelope.

Six of the loose snapshots were of a dog—mixed breed, tan and black, with one floppy ear. It was most likely the pet for which Grant had bought the musical rubber bone from the mail-order firm that still kept his name and address on file two years later.

Thirty-three of the remaining photographs were of the same woman. In some she appeared to be as young as twenty, in others as old as her early thirties. Here: wearing blue jeans and a reindeer sweater, decorating a Christmas tree. And here: in a simple summer dress and white shoes, holding a white purse, smiling at the camera, dappled in sun and shadow, standing by a tree that was dripping clusters of white flowers. In more than a few, she was grooming horses, riding horses, or feeding apples to them.

Something about her haunted Roy, but he couldn't understand why she so affected him.

She was an undeniably attractive woman, but she was far from drop-dead gorgeous. Though shapely, blond, blue-eyed, she nonetheless lacked any single transcendent feature that would have put her in the pantheon of true beauty.

Her smile was the only truly striking thing about her. It was the most consistent element of her appearance from one snapshot to the next: warm, open, easy, a charming smile that never seemed to be false, that revealed a gentle heart.

A smile, however, was not a *feature*. That was especially true in this woman's case, for her lips weren't particularly luscious, as were Melissa Wicklun's lips. Nothing about the set or width of her mouth, the contours of her philtrum, or the shape of her teeth was even intriguing, let alone electrifying. Her smile was greater than the sum of its parts, like the dazzling reflection of sunlight on the otherwise unremarkable surface of a pond.

He could find nothing about her that he yearned to possess.

Yet she haunted him. Though he doubted that he had ever met her, he felt that he ought to know who she was. Somewhere, he had seen her before.

Staring at her face, at her radiant smile, he sensed a terrible presence hovering over her, just beyond the frame of the photograph. A cold darkness was descending, of which she was unaware.

The newest of the photographs were at least twenty years old, and many were surely three decades out of the darkroom tray. The colors of even the more recent shots were faded. The older ones held only the faintest suggestions of color, were mostly gray and white, and were slightly yellowed in places.

Roy turned each photo over, hoping to find a few identifying words on the reverse, but the backs were all blank. Not even a single name or date.

Two of the pictures showed her with a young boy. Roy was so mystified by his strong response to the woman's face and so fixated on figuring out why she seemed familiar that he did not at first realize that the boy was Spencer Grant. When he made the connection, he put the two snapshots side by side on the table.

It was Grant in the days before he had sustained his scar.

In his case, more than with most people, the face of the man reflected the child he had been.

He was about six or seven years old in the first photo, a skinny kid in swimming trunks, dripping wet, standing by the edge of a pool. The woman was in a one-piece bathing suit beside him, playing a silly practical joke for the camera: one hand behind Grant's head, two of her fingers secretly raised and spread to make it appear as though he had a small pair of horns or antennae.

In the second photograph, the woman and the boy were sitting at a picnic table. The kid was a year or two older than in the first picture, wearing jeans, a T-shirt, and a baseball cap. She had one arm around him, pulling him against her side, knocking his cap askew.

In both snapshots, the woman's smile was as radiant as in all those without the boy, but her face was also brightened by affection and love. Roy felt confident that he'd found Spencer Grant's mother.

He remained baffled, however, as to why the woman was familiar to him. Eerily familiar. The longer he stared at the pictures of her, with or without the boy at her side, the more certain he became that he knew her—and that the context in which he had previously seen her was deeply disturbing, dark, and strange.

He turned his attention again to the snapshot in which mother and son stood beside the swimming pool. In the background, at some distance, was a large barn; even in the faded photograph, traces of red paint were visible on its high, blank walls.

The woman, the boy, the barn.

On a deep subconscious level, a memory must have stirred, for suddenly the skin prickled across Roy's scalp.

The woman. The boy. The barn.

A chill quivered through him.

He looked up from the photographs on the kitchen table, at the window above the sink, at the crowded grove of trees beyond the window, at the meager coins of noontime sunlight tumbling through the wealth of shadows, and he willed memory to glimmer forth, as well, from the eucalyptic dark.

The woman. The boy. The barn.

For all his straining, enlightenment eluded him, although another chill walked through his bones.

The barn.

∾

Through residential streets of stucco homes, where cacti and yucca plants and hardy olive trees were featured in low-maintenance desert landscaping, through a shopping center parking lot, through an industrial area, through the maze of a self-storage yard filled with corrugated-steel sheds, off the pavement and through a sprawling park, where the fronds of the palms tossed and lashed in a frenzied welcome to the on-coming storm, Spencer sought without success to shake off the pursuing Chevrolet.

Sooner or later, they were going to cross the path of a police patrol. As soon as one unit of local cops became involved, Spencer would find it even more difficult to get away.

Disoriented by the twisting route taken to elude his pursuers, Spencer was surprised to be flashing past one of the newest resort hotels, on the right. Las Vegas Boulevard South was only a few hundred yards ahead. The traffic light was red, but he decided to bet everything that it would change by the time he got there.

The Chevy remained close behind him. If he stopped, the bastards would be out of their car and all over the Explorer, bristling with more guns than a porcupine had quills.

Three hundred yards to the intersection. Two hundred fifty.

The signal was still red. Cross traffic wasn't as heavy as it could get farther north along the Strip, but it was not light, either.

Running out of time, Spencer slowed slightly, enough to allow him-self more maneuverability at the moment of decision but not enough to encourage the driver of the Chevy to try to pull alongside him.

A hundred yards. Seventy-five. Fifty.

Lady Luck wasn't with him. He was still playing the green, but the red kept turning up.

A gasoline tanker truck was approaching the intersection from the left, taking advantage of the rare chance to make a little speed on the Strip, going faster than the legal limit.

Rocky began bobbing his head up and down again.

Finally the driver of the tanker saw the Explorer coming and tried to brake quickly without jackknifing.

"All right, okay, okay, gonna make it," Spencer heard himself saying, almost chanting, as if he were crazily determined to shape reality with positive thought.

Never lie to the dog.

"We're in deep shit, pal," he amended as he curved into the intersec-tion in a wide arc, around the front of the oncoming truck.

As panic shifted his perceptions into slo-mo, Spencer saw the tanker sweep toward them, the giant tires rolling and bouncing and rolling and bouncing while the terrified driver adroitly pumped the brakes as much as he dared. And now it was not merely approaching but looming over them, huge, an inexorable and inescapable behemoth, far bigger than it had seemed only a split second ago, and now bigger still, towering, immense. Good God, it seemed bigger than a jumbo jet, and he was nothing but a bug on the runway. The Explorer began to cant to starboard, as if it would tip over, and Spencer corrected with a slight pull to the right and a tap of the brakes. The energy of the aborted rollover was channeled into a slide, however, and the back end traveled sideways with a shriek of tormented tires. The steering wheel spun back and forth through his sweat-dampened hands. The Explorer was out of control, and the gasoline tanker was on top of them, as large as God, but at least they were sliding in the right direction, away from the big rig, although probably not fast enough to escape it. Then the sixteen-wheel monster shrieked by with only inches to spare, a curved wall of polished steel passing in a mirrored blur, in a gale of wind that Spencer was certain he could feel even through the tightly closed windows.

The Explorer spun three hundred sixty degrees, then kept going for another ninety. It shuddered to a halt, facing the opposite direction—and on the far side of the divided boulevard—from the gasoline tanker, even as that behemoth was still passing it.

The southbound traffic, into the lanes of which Spencer had careened, stopped before running him down, although not without a chorus of screaming brakes and blaring horns.

Rocky was on the floor again.

Spencer didn't know if the dog had been thrown off the seat again or, in a sudden attack of prudence, had scrambled down there.

He said, "Stay!" even as Rocky clambered up onto the seat.

The roar of an engine. From the left. Coming across the broad intersection. The Chevy. Hurtling past the back of the halted tanker, toward the side of the Explorer.

He jammed his foot down hard on the accelerator. The tires spun, then rubber got a bite of pavement. The Explorer bulleted south on the boulevard—just as the Chevy shot past the rear bumper. With a cold squeal, metal kissed metal.

Gunshots erupted. Three or four rounds. None seemed to strike the Explorer.

Rocky remained on the seat, panting, claws dug in, determined to hold fast this time.

Spencer was headed out of Vegas, which was both good and bad. It was good because as he proceeded farther south, toward the open desert and the last entrance to Interstate 15, the risk of being brought to a stop by a traffic jam would quickly diminish. It was bad, however, because beyond the forest of hotels, the barren land would provide few easy routes of escape and even fewer places to hide. Out on the vast panoramas of the Mojave, the thugs in the Chevy could slip a mile or two behind and still keep a watch on him.

Nevertheless, leaving town was the only sane choice. The turmoil at the intersection behind him was sure to bring the cops.

As he was speeding past the newest hotel-casino in town—which included a two-hundred-acre amusement park, Spaceport Vegas—his only sane choice became no real choice at all. From across the boulevard, a hundred yards ahead, a northbound car swung out of the oncoming traffic, jumped the far side of the low median strip, smashed through a row of shrubs, and bounced into the southbound lanes. It slid to a stop at an angle, blocking the way, ready to ram Spencer if he tried to squeeze around either end of it.

He stopped thirty yards from the blockade.

The new car was a Chrysler but, otherwise, so like the Chevy that the two might have been born of the same factory.

The driver stayed behind the wheel of the Chrysler, but the other doors opened. Big, troublesome-looking men got out.

The rearview mirror revealed what he'd expected: The Chevy also had halted at an angle across the boulevard, fifteen yards behind him. Men were getting out of that vehicle too—and they had guns.

In front of him, the men at the Chrysler had guns too. Somehow that didn't come as a surprise.

✿

The final picture had been kept in a white envelope, which had been fastened shut with a length of Scotch tape.

Because of the shape and thinness of the object, Roy knew that it was another photograph before he opened the envelope, though it was larger than a snapshot. As he peeled off the tape, he expected to find a five-by-seven studio portrait of the mother, a memento of special importance to Grant.

It was a black-and-white studio photograph, sure enough, but it was of a man in his middle thirties.

For a strange moment, for Roy, there was neither a eucalyptus grove beyond the windows nor a window through which to see it. The kitchen itself faded from his awareness, until nothing existed except him and that single picture, to which he related even more powerfully than to the photos of the woman.

He could breathe but shallowly.

If anyone had entered the room to ask a question, he could not have spoken.

He felt detached from reality, as if in a fever, but he was not feverish. Indeed, he was cold, though not uncomfortably so: It was the cold of a watchful chameleon, pretending to be stone on a stone, on an autumn morning; it was a cold that invigorated, that focused his entire consciousness, that contracted the gears of his mind and allowed his thoughts to spin without friction. His heart didn't race, as it would have in a fever. Indeed, his pulse rate declined, until it was as ponderously slow as that of a sleeper, and throughout his body, each beat reverberated like a recording of a cathedral bell played at quarter speed: protracted, solemn, heavy tolling.

Obviously, the shot had been taken by a talented professional, under studio conditions, with much attention to the lighting and to the selection of the ideal lens. The subject, wearing a white shirt open at the throat and a leather jacket, was presented from the waist up, posed against a white wall, arms folded across his chest. He was strikingly handsome, with thick dark hair combed straight back from his forehead. The publicity photograph, of a type usually associated with young actors, was a blatant glamour shot but a good one, because the subject possessed natural glamour, an aura of mystery and drama that the photographer didn't have to create with bravura technique.

The portrait was a study in light and shadow, with more of the latter than the former. Peculiar shadows, cast by objects beyond the frame, appeared to swarm across the wall, drawn to the man as night itself was drawn across the evening sky by the terrible weight of the sinking sun.

His direct and piercing stare, the firm set of his mouth, his aristocratic features, and even his deceptively casual posture seemed to reveal a man who had never known self-doubt, depression, or fear. He was more than merely confident and self-possessed. In the photo, he projected a subtle but unmistakable arrogance. His expression seemed to say that, without exception, he regarded all other members of the human race with amusement and contempt.

Yet he remained enormously appealing, as though his intelligence and experience had earned him the right to feel superior. Studying the photograph, Roy sensed that here was a man who would make an interesting, unpredictable, entertaining friend. Peering out from his shadows, this singular individual had an animal magnetism that made his expression of contempt seem inoffensive. Indeed, an air of arrogance seemed *right* for him—just as any lion must walk with feline arrogance if it was to seem at all like a lion.

Gradually, the spell cast by the photograph diminished in power but didn't altogether fade. The kitchen reestablished itself from the mists of Roy's fixation, as did the window and the eucalyptuses.

He knew this man. He had seen him before.

A long time ago . . .

Familiarity was part of the reason that the picture affected him so strongly. As with the woman, however, Roy was unable to put a name to the face or to recall the circumstances under which he had seen this person previously.

He wished the photographer had allowed more light to reach his subject's face. But the shadows seemed to love the dark-eyed man.

Roy placed that photo on the kitchen table, beside the snapshot of the mother and her son at poolside.

The woman. The boy. The barn in the background. The man in the shadows.

☙

At a full stop on Las Vegas Boulevard South, confronted by armed men in front of and behind him, Spencer pounded the horn, pulled the wheel hard to the right, and tramped on the accelerator. The Explorer rocketed toward the amusement park, Spaceport Vegas, pressing him and Rocky against their seats as if they were astronauts moonward bound.

The cocksure boldness of the gunmen proved that they *were* feds of some kind, even if they used fake credentials to conceal their true identity. They would never ambush him on a major street, before witnesses, unless they were confident of pulling rank on local cops.

On the sidewalk in front of Spaceport Vegas, on their way from casino to casino, pedestrians scattered, and the Explorer shot into a driveway posted for buses only, though no buses were in sight.

Perhaps because of the February cold snap and the pending storm, or maybe because it was only noon, Spaceport Vegas wasn't open. The ticket booths were shuttered, and the thrill rides that were high enough to be seen behind the park walls were in suspended animation.

Nevertheless, neon and futuristic applications of fiber optics throbbed and flashed along the perimeter wall, which was nine feet high and painted like the armored hull of a starfighter. A photosensitive cell must have switched on the lights, mistaking the midday gloom of the advancing storm for the onset of evening.

Spencer drove between two rocket-shaped ticket booths, toward a twelve-foot-diameter tunnel of polished steel that penetrated the park walls. In blue neon, the words TIME TUNNEL TO SPACEPORT VEGAS promised more escape than he needed.

He flew up the gentle ramp, never tapping the brakes, and raced unheeding through time.

The massive pipe was two hundred feet long. Tubes of brilliant blue neon curved up the walls, across the ceiling. They blinked in rapid sequence from the entrance to the exit, creating an illusion of a funnel of lightning.

Under ordinary circumstances, patrons were conveyed into the park on lumbering trams, but the half-blinding surges of light were more effective at greater speed. Spencer's eyes throbbed, and he could almost believe that he *had* been catapulted into a distant era.

Rocky was doing the head-bobbing bit again.

"Never knew I had a dog," Spencer said, "with a need for speed."

He fled into the far reaches of the park, where the lights had not been activated like those on the wall and in the tunnel. The deserted and seemingly endless midway rose and fell, narrowed and widened and narrowed again, and repeatedly looped back on itself.

Spaceport Vegas featured corkscrew roller coasters, dive-bombers, scramblers, whips, and the other usual gut churners, all tricked up with lavish science fiction facades, gimmicks, and names. Lightsled to Ganymede. Hyperspace Hammer. Solar Radiation Hell. Asteroid Collision. Devolution Drop. The park also offered elaborate flight-simulator adventures and virtual-reality experiences in buildings of futuristic or bizarrely alien architecture: Planet of the Snakemen, Blood Moon, Vortex Blaster, Deathworld. At Robot Wars, homicidal machines with red eyes guarded the entrance, and the portal to Star Monster looked like a glistening orifice at one end or the other of an extraterrestrial leviathan's digestive tract.

Under the bleak sky, swept by cold wind, with the gray prestorm light sucking the color out of everything, the future as imagined by the creators of Spaceport Vegas was unremittingly hostile.

Curiously, that made it appear more realistic to Spencer, more like a true vision and less like an amusement park than its designers ever intended. Alien, machine, and human predators were everywhere on the prowl. Cosmic disasters loomed at every turn: The Exploding Sun, Comet Strike, Time Snap, The Big Bang, Wasteland. The End of Time was on the same avenue of the midway that offered an adventure called Extinction. It was possible to look at the ominous attractions and believe that this grim future—in its mood if not its specifics—was sufficiently terrifying to be one that contemporary society might make for itself.

In search of a service exit, Spencer drove recklessly along the winding promenades, weaving among the attractions. He repeatedly glimpsed the

Chevy and the Chrysler between the rides and the exotic structures, though never dangerously close. They were like sharks cruising in the distance. Each time he spotted them, he whipped out of sight into another branch of the midway maze.

Around the corner from the Galactic Prison, past the Palace of the Parasites, beyond a screen of ficus trees and a red-flowering oleander hedge that were surely drab compared with the shrubs that grew on the planets of the Crab Nebula, he found a two-lane service road that marked the back of the park. He followed it.

To his left were the trees, aligned twenty feet on center, with the six-foot-high hedge between the trunks. On his right, instead of the neon-lit wall that was featured in the public portions of the perimeter, a chain-link fence rose ten feet high, topped with coils of barbed wire, and beyond it lay a sward of desert scrub.

He rounded a corner, and a hundred yards ahead was a pipe-and-chain-link gate, on wheels, controlled by overhead hydraulic arms. It would roll out of the way at the touch of the right remote-control device—which Spencer didn't possess.

He increased speed. He'd have to ram the gate.

Reverting to his customary prudence, the dog scrambled off the passenger seat and curled in the leg space before he could be thrown there by the upcoming impact.

"Neurotic but not stupid," Spencer said approvingly.

He was more than halfway to the gate when he caught a flicker of motion out of the corner of his left eye. The Chrysler erupted from between two ficus trees, tearing the hell out of the oleander hedge, and crashed into the service way in showers of green leaves and red flowers. It crossed Spencer's wake and rammed the fence so hard that the chain-link billowed, as if made of cloth, to the end of the lane.

The Explorer trailed that billow by a split second and hit the gate with enough force to crumple the hood without popping it open, to make Spencer's restraining harness tighten painfully across his chest, to knock the breath out of him, to clack his teeth together, to make his luggage rattle under the restraining net in the cargo area—but not hard enough to take out the gate. That barrier was torqued, sagging, half collapsed, trailing tangles of barbed wire like dreadlocks—but still intact.

He shifted gears and shot backward as if he were a cannonball returning to the barrel in a counterclockwise world.

The hitmen in the Chrysler were opening the doors, getting out, drawing their guns—until they saw the truck reversing toward them. They reversed too, scrambling inside the car, pulling the doors shut.

He rammed backward into the sedan, and the collision was loud enough to convince him that he'd overdone it, disabled the Explorer.

When he shifted into drive, however, the truck sprang forward. No tires were flat or obstructed by crumpled fenders. No windows had shattered. No smell of gasoline, so the tank wasn't ruptured. The battered Explorer rattled, clinked, ticked, and creaked—but it *moved*, with power and grace.

The second impact took down the gate. The truck clambered over the fallen chain-link, away from Spaceport Vegas, into an enormous plot of desert scrub on which no one had yet built a theme park, a hotel, a casino, or a parking lot.

Engaging the four-wheel drive, Spencer angled west, away from the Strip, toward Interstate 15.

He remembered Rocky and glanced down at the leg space in front of the passenger seat. The dog was curled up, with his eyes squeezed shut, as if anticipating another collision.

"It's okay, pal."

Rocky continued to grimace in anticipation of disaster.

"Trust me."

Rocky opened his eyes and returned to his seat, where the vinyl upholstery had been well scratched and punctured by his claws.

They rocked and rolled across the eroded and barren land, to the base of the superhighway.

A steep slope of gravel and shale rose thirty or forty feet to the east–west lanes. Even if he could find a break in the guardrail above him, no escape could be found—and certainly no salvation—on that highway. The people who were seeking him would establish checkpoints in both directions.

After a brief hesitation, he turned south, following the base of the elevated interstate.

From the east, across the white sand and the pink-gray slate, came the mold-green Chevrolet. It was like a heat mirage, although the day was cool. The low dunes and shallow washes would defeat it. The Explorer was made for overland travel; the Chevrolet was not.

Spencer came to a waterless riverbed, which the interstate crossed on a low concrete bridge. He drove into that declivity, onto a soft bed of silt, where driftwood slept and where dead tumbleweeds moved as ceaselessly as strange shadows in a bad dream.

He followed the dry wash under the interstate, west into the inhospitable Mojave.

The forbidding sky, as hard and dark as sarcophagus granite, hung within inches of the iron mountains. Desolate plains rose gradually toward those more sterile elevations, with a steadily decreasing burden of withered mesquite, dry bunchgrass, and cactus.

He drove out of the arroyo but continued to follow it upslope, toward distant peaks as bare as ancient bones.

The Chevrolet was no longer in sight.

Finally, when he was sure that he was far beyond the casual notice of any surveillance teams posted to watch the traffic on the interstate, he turned south and paralleled that highway. Without it as a reference, he would be lost. Whirling dust devils spun across the desert, masking the telltale plumes cast up behind the Explorer.

Although no rain yet fell, lightning scored the sky. The shadows of low stone formations leaped, fell back, and leaped again across the alabaster land.

Rocky's cloaks of courage had been cast off as the Explorer's speed had fallen. He was huddled once more in folds of cold timidity. He whined periodically and looked at his master for reassurance.

The sky cracked with fissures of fire.

∽

Roy Miro pushed the troubling photographs aside and set up his attaché case computer on the kitchen table in the Malibu cabin. He plugged it into a wall outlet and connected with Mama in Virginia.

When Spencer Grant had joined the United States Army, as a boy of eighteen, more than twelve years ago, he must have completed the standard enlistment forms. Among other things, he'd been required to provide information about his schooling, his place of birth, his father's name, his mother's maiden name, and his next of kin.

The recruiting officer through whom he had enlisted would have verified that basic information. It would have been verified again, at a higher level, prior to Grant's induction into the service.

If "Spencer Grant" was a phony identity, the boy would have had considerable difficulty getting into the army with it. Nevertheless, Roy remained convinced that it was not the name on Grant's original birth certificate, and he was determined to discover what that birth name had been.

At Roy's request, Mama accessed the Department of Defense dead files on former army personnel. She brought Spencer Grant's basic information sheet onto the display screen.

According to the data on the VDT, Grant's mother's name, which he had given to the army, was Jennifer Corrine Porth.

The young recruit had listed her as "deceased."

The father was said to be "unknown."

Roy blinked in surprise at the screen. UNKNOWN.

That was extraordinary. Grant had not simply claimed to be a bastard child, but had implied that his mother's promiscuity had made it impossible to pinpoint the man who fathered him. Anyone else might have cited a false name, a convenient fictional father, to spare himself and his late mother some embarrassment.

Logically, if the father was genuinely unknown, Spencer's last name should have been Porth. Therefore, either his mother borrowed the "Grant" from a favorite movie star, as Bosley Donner believed she'd done, or she named her son after one of the men in her life even without being certain that he had fathered the boy.

Or the "unknown" was a lie, and the name "Spencer Grant" was just another false identity, perhaps the first of many, that this phantom had manufactured for himself.

At the time of Grant's enlistment, with his mother already dead and his father unknown, he had given his next of kin as "Ethel Marie and George Daniel Porth, grandparents." They had to be his mother's parents, since Porth was also her maiden name.

Roy noticed that the address for Ethel and George Porth—in San Francisco—had been the same as Grant's current address at the time that he'd enlisted. Apparently the grandparents had taken him in, subsequent to the death of his mother, whenever that had been.

If anyone knew the true story of Grant's provenance and the source of his scar, it would be Ethel and George Porth. Assuming that they actually existed and were not just names on a form that a recruitment officer had failed to verify twelve years ago.

Roy asked for a printout of the pertinent portion of Grant's service file. Even with what seemed to be a good lead in the Porths, Roy wasn't confident of learning anything in San Francisco that would give more substance to this elusive phantom whom he'd first glimpsed less than forty-eight hours ago in the rainy night in Santa Monica.

Having erased himself entirely from all utility-company records, from property tax rolls, and even from the Internal Revenue Service files—why had Grant allowed his name to remain in the DMV, Social Security Administration, LAPD, and military files? He had tampered with those records to the extent of replacing his true address with a series of phony addresses, but he could have entirely eliminated them. He had the knowledge and the skill to do so. Therefore, he must have maintained a presence in some data banks for a purpose.

Roy felt that somehow he was playing into Grant's hands even by try-ing to track him down.

Frustrated, he turned his attention once more to the two most affect-ing of the forty photographs. The woman, the boy, and the barn in the background. The man in the shadows.

∽

On all sides of the Explorer lay sand as white as powdered bones, ash-gray volcanic rock, and slopes of shale shattered by millions of years of heat, cold, and quaking earth. The few plants were crisp and bristly. Except for the dust and vegetation stirred by the wind, the only movement was the creeping and slithering of scorpions, spiders, scarabs, poisonous snakes, and the other cold-blooded or bloodless creatures that thrived in that arid wasteland.

Silvery quills and nibs of lightning flashed continually, and fast-moving thunderheads as black as ink wrote a promise of rain across the sky. The bellies of the clouds hung heavy. With great crashes of thunder, the storm struggled to create itself.

Captured between the dead earth and tumultuous heavens, Spencer paralleled the distant interstate highway as much as possible. He detoured only when the contours of the land required compromise.

Rocky sat with head bowed, gazing at his paws rather than at the stormy day. His flanks quivered as currents of fear flowed through him like electricity through a closed circuit.

On another day, in a different place and in a different storm, Spencer would have kept up a steady line of patter to soothe the dog. Now, how-ever, he was in a mood that darkened with the sky, and he was able to focus only on his own turmoil.

For the woman, he had walked away from his life, such as it was. He had left behind the quiet comfort of the cabin, the beauty of the eucalyp-tus grove, the peace of the canyon—and most likely he would never be able to return to that. He had made a target of himself and had put his precious anonymity in jeopardy.

He regretted none of that—because he still had the hope of gaining a real life with some kind of meaning and purpose. Although he had wanted to help the woman, he had also wanted to help himself.

But the stakes suddenly had been raised. Death and disclosure were not the only risks he was going to have to take if he continued to involve himself in Valerie Keene's problems. Sooner or later, he was going to have to kill someone. They would give him no choice.

After escaping the assault on the bungalow in Santa Monica on Wednesday night, he had avoided thinking about the most disturbing implications of the SWAT team's extreme violence. Now he recalled the gunfire directed at imagined targets inside the dark house and the rounds fired at him as he had scaled the property wall.

That was not merely the response of a few edgy law-enforcement officers intimidated by their quarry. It was a criminally excessive use of force, evidence of an agency out of control and arrogantly confident that it wasn't accountable for any atrocities it committed.

A short while ago, he had encountered equivalent arrogance in the reckless behavior of the men who harried him out of Las Vegas.

He thought about Louis Lee in that elegant office under China Dream. The restaurateur had said that governments, when big enough, often ceased to play by the codes of justice under which they were established.

All governments, even democracies, maintained control by the threat of violence and imprisonment. When that threat was divorced from the rule of law, however, even if with the best of intentions, there was a fearfully thin line between a federal agent and a thug.

If Spencer located Valerie and learned why she was on the run, helping her would not be simply a matter of dipping into his cash reserves and finding the best attorney to represent her. Naively, that had been his nebulous plan, on those few occasions when he had bothered to think about what he might do if he tracked her down.

But the ruthlessness of these enemies ruled out a solution in any court of law.

Faced with the choice of violence or flight, he would always choose to flee and risk a bullet in the back—at least when no life but his own was at stake. When he eventually took responsibility for this woman's life, however, he could not expect her to turn her own back on a gun; sooner or later he would have to meet the violence of those men with violence of his own.

Brooding about that, Spencer drove south between the too-solid desert and the amorphous sky. The distant highway was only barely visible to the east, and no clear path lay before him.

Out of the west came rain in blinding cataracts of rare ferocity for the Mojave, a towering gray tide behind which the desert began to disappear.

Spencer could smell the rain even though it hadn't reached them yet. It was a cold, wet, ozone-tainted scent, refreshing at first but then strange and profoundly chilling.

"It's not that I'm worried about being able to kill someone if it comes to that," he told the huddled dog.

The gray wall rushed toward them, faster by the second, and it seemed to be more than mere rain that loomed. It was the future too, and it was all that he feared knowing about the past.

"I've done it before. I can do it again if I have to."

Over the rumble of the Explorer's engine, he could hear the rain now, like a million pounding hearts.

"And if some sonofabitch deserves killing, I can do him and feel no guilt, no remorse. Sometimes it's right. It's justice. I don't have a problem with that."

The rain swept over them, billowing like a magician's scarves, bringing sorcerous change. The pale land darkened dramatically with the first splash. In the peculiar storm light, the desiccated vegetation, more brown than green, suddenly became glossy, verdant; in seconds, withered leaves and grass appeared to swell into plump tropical forms, though it was all illusion.

Switching on the windshield wipers, shifting the Explorer into four-wheel drive, Spencer said, "What worries me . . . what scares me is . . . maybe I waste some sonofabitch who deserves it . . . some piece of walking garbage . . . and *this* time I like it."

The downpour could have been no less cataclysmic than that which had launched Noah upon the Flood, and the fierce drumming of rain on the truck was deafening. The storm-cowed dog probably could not hear his master above the roar, yet Spencer used Rocky's presence as an excuse to acknowledge a truth that he preferred not to hear, speaking aloud because he might lie if he spoke only to himself.

"I never liked it before. Never felt like a hero for doing it. But it didn't sicken me, either. I didn't puke or lose any sleep over it. So . . . what if the next time . . . or the time after that . . . ?"

Beneath the glowering thunderheads, in the velvet-heavy shrouds of rain, the early afternoon had grown as dark as twilight. Driving out of murk into mystery, he switched on the headlights, surprised to find that both had survived the impact with the amusement-park gate.

Rain fell straight to the earth in such tremendous tonnage that it dissolved and washed away the wind that had previously stirred the desert into sand spouts.

They came to a ten-foot-deep wash with gently sloping walls. In the headlight beams, a stream of silvery water, a foot wide and a few inches deep, glimmered along the center of that depression. Spencer crossed the twenty-foot-wide arroyo to higher ground on the far side.

As the Explorer crested the second bank, a series of massive lightning bolts blazed across the desert, accompanied by crashes of thunder that vibrated through the truck. The rain came down even harder than before, harder than he had ever seen it fall.

Driving with one hand, Spencer stroked Rocky's head. The dog was too frightened to look up or to lean into the consoling hand.

They went no more than fifty yards from the first arroyo when Spencer saw the earth moving ahead of them. It rolled sinuously, as though swarms of giant serpents were traveling just below the surface of the desert. By the time he braked to a full stop, the headlights revealed a less fanciful but no less frightening explanation: The earth wasn't moving, but a swift muddy river was churning from west to east along the gently sloping plain, blocking travel to the south.

The depths of this new arroyo were mostly hidden. The racing water was already within a few inches of its banks.

Such torrents couldn't have risen just since the storm had swept across the plains minutes ago. The runoff was from the mountains, where rain had been falling for a while and where the stony, treeless slopes absorbed little of it. The desert seldom received downpours of that magnitude; but on rare occasions, with breathtaking suddenness, flash floods could inundate even portions of the elevated interstate highway or pour into low-lying areas of the now distant Las Vegas Strip and sweep cars out of casino parking lots.

Spencer couldn't judge the depth of the water. It might have been two feet or twenty.

Even if only two feet deep, the water was moving so fast, with such power, that he didn't dare attempt to ford it. The second wash was wider than the first, forty feet across. Before he'd traveled half that distance, the truck would be lifted and carried downriver, rolling and bobbing, as if it were driftwood.

He backed the Explorer away from the churning flow, turned, and retraced his route, arriving at the first arroyo, to the south, more quickly than he expected. In the brief time since he had crossed it, the silvery freshet had become a turbulent river that nearly filled the wash.

Bracketed by impassable cataracts, Spencer was no longer able to parallel the distant north–south interstate.

He considered parking right there, to wait for the storm to pass. When the rain ended, the arroyos would empty as swiftly as they had filled. But he sensed that the situation was more dangerous than it appeared.

He opened the door, stepped into the downpour, and was soaked by the time he walked to the front of the Explorer. The pummeling rain hammered a chill deep into his flesh.

The cold and the wet contributed to his misery less than did the incredible *noise*. The oppressive roar of the storm blocked all other sounds.

The rattle of the rain against the desert, the swash and rumble of the river, and the booming thunder combined to make the vast Mojave as confining and claustrophobia-inducing as the interior of a stuntman's barrel on the brink of Niagara.

He wanted a better view of the surging flux than he'd gotten from inside the truck, but a closer look alarmed him. Moment by moment, water lapped higher on the banks of the wash; soon it would flood across the plain. Sections of the soft arroyo walls collapsed, dissolved into the muddy currents, and were carried away. Even as the violent gush eroded a wider channel, it swelled tremendously in volume, simultaneously rising and growing broader. Spencer turned from the first arroyo and hurried toward the second, to the south of the truck. He reached that other impromptu river sooner than he expected. It was brimming and widening like the first channel. Fifty yards had separated the two arroyos when he'd first driven between them, but that gap had shrunk to thirty.

Thirty yards was still a considerable distance. He found it difficult to believe that those two spates were powerful enough to eat through so much remaining land and ultimately converge.

Then, immediately in front of his shoes, a crack opened in the ground. A long, jagged leer. The earth grinned, and a six-foot-wide slab of riverbank collapsed into the onrushing water.

Spencer stumbled backward, out of immediate danger. The sodden land around him was turning mushy underfoot.

The unthinkable suddenly seemed inevitable. Large portions of the desert were all shale and volcanic rock and quartzite, but he had the misfortune to be caught in a cloudburst while traveling over a fathomless sea of sand. Unless a hidden spine of rock was buried between the two arroyos, the intervening land might indeed be washed away and the entire plain recontoured, depending on how long the storm raged at its current intensity.

The impossibly heavy downfall abruptly grew heavier still.

He sprinted for the Explorer, clambered inside, and pulled his door shut. Shivering, streaming water, he backed the truck farther from the northern arroyo, afraid that the wheels would be undermined.

With head still downcast, from under his lowered brow, Rocky looked up worriedly at his master.

"Have to drive between arroyos, east or west," Spencer thought aloud, "while there's still something to drive on."

The windshield wipers weren't coping well with the cascades that poured across the glass, and the rain-blurred landscape settled into deeper degrees of false twilight. He tried turning the wiper control to a higher setting. It was already as high as it would go.

"Shouldn't head toward lower land. Water's gaining velocity as it goes. More likely to wash out down there."

He switched the headlamps to high beams. The extra light didn't clarify anything: It bounced off the skeins of rain, so the way ahead seemed to be obscured by curtain after curtain of mirrored beads. He selected the low beams again.

"Safer ground uphill. Ought to be more rock."

The dog only trembled.

"The space between arroyos will probably widen out."

Spencer shifted gears again. The plain sloped gradually up to the west, into obscure terrain.

As giant needles of lightning stitched the heavens to the earth, he drove into the resultant narrow pocket of gloom.

∽

At Roy Miro's direction, agents in San Francisco were seeking Ethel and George Porth, the maternal grandparents who had raised Spencer Grant following the death of his mother. Meanwhile, Roy drove to the offices of Dr. Nero Mondello in Beverly Hills.

Mondello was the most prominent plastic surgeon in a community where God's work was revised more frequently than anywhere except Palm Springs and Palm Beach. On a misshapen nose, he could perform miracles equivalent to those that Michelangelo had performed on giant cubes of Carrara marble—though Mondello's fees were substantially higher than those of the Italian master.

He had agreed to make changes in a busy schedule to meet with Roy, because he believed that he was assisting the FBI in a desperate search for a particularly savage serial killer.

They met in the doctor's spacious inner office: white marble floor, white walls and ceiling, white shell sconces. Two abstract paintings hung in white frames: The only color was white, and the artist achieved his effects solely with the textures of the heavily layered pigment. Two whitewashed lacewood chairs with white leather cushions flanked a glass-and-steel table and stood before a whitewashed burled-wood desk, against a backdrop of white silk draperies.

Roy sat in one of the lacewood chairs, like a blot of soil in all that whiteness, and wondered what view would be revealed if the draperies were opened. He had the crazy notion that beyond the window, in downtown Beverly Hills, lay a landscape swaddled in snow.

Other than the photographs of Spencer Grant that Roy had brought with him, the only object on the polished surface of the desk was a single blood-red rose in a Waterford cut-crystal vase. The flower was a testament to the possibility of perfection—and drew the visitor's attention to the man who sat beyond it, behind the desk.

Tall, slender, handsome, fortyish, Dr. Nero Mondello was the focal point of his bleached domain. With his thick jet-black hair combed back from his forehead, warm-toned olive complexion, and eyes the precise purple-black of ripe plums, the surgeon had an impact almost as powerful as that of a spirit manifestation. He wore a white lab coat over a white shirt and red silk necktie. Around the face of his gold Rolex, matched diamonds sparkled as though charged with supernatural energy.

The room and the man were no less impressive for being blatantly theatrical. Mondello was in the business of replacing nature's truth with convincing illusions, and all good magicians were theatrical.

Studying the DMV photograph of Grant and the computer-generated portrait, Mondello said, "Yes, this would have been a dreadful wound, quite terrible."

"What might've caused it?" Roy asked.

Mondello opened a desk drawer and removed a magnifying glass with a silver handle. He studied the photographs more closely.

At last he said, "It was more a cut than a tear, so it must have been a relatively sharp instrument."

"A knife?"

"Or glass. But it wasn't an entirely even cutting edge. Very sharp but slightly irregular like glass—or a serrated blade. An even blade would produce a cleaner wound and a narrower scar."

Watching Mondello pore over the photographs, Roy realized that the surgeon's facial features were so refined and so uncannily well proportioned that a talented colleague had been at work on them.

"It's a cicatricial scar."

"Excuse me?" Roy said.

"Connective tissue that's contracted—pinched or wrinkled," Mondello said, without looking up from the photographs. "Though this one is relatively smooth, considering its width." He returned the magnifying glass to the drawer. "I can't tell you much more—except that it's not a recent scar."

"Could surgery eliminate it, skin grafts?"

"Not entirely, but it could be made far less visible, just a thin line, a thread of discoloration."

"Painful?" Roy asked.

"Yes, but this"—he tapped the photo—"wouldn't require a long series of surgeries over a number of years, as burns might."

Mondello's face was exceptional because the proportions were so studied, as though the guiding aesthetic behind his surgery had been not merely the intuition of an artist but the logical rigor of a mathematician. The doctor had remade himself with the same iron control that great politicians applied to society to transform its imperfect citizens into better people. Roy had long understood that human beings were so deeply flawed that no society could have perfect justice without imposing mathematically rigorous planning and stern guidance from the top. Yet he'd never perceived, until now, that his passion for ideal beauty and his desire for justice were both aspects of the same longing for Utopia.

Sometimes Roy was amazed by his intellectual complexity.

"Why," he asked Mondello, "would a man live with that scar if it could be made all but invisible? Aside, that is, from being unable to pay for the surgery."

"Oh, cost wouldn't be a deterrent. If the patient had no money and the government wouldn't pay, he'd still receive treatment. Most surgeons have always dedicated a portion of their professional time to charity work like this."

"Then why?"

Mondello shrugged and pushed the photographs across the desk. "Perhaps he's afraid of pain."

"I don't think so. Not this man."

"Or afraid of doctors, hospitals, sharp instruments, anesthesia. There are countless phobias that prevent people from having surgery."

"This man's not a phobic personality," Roy said, returning the photos to the manila envelope.

"Could be guilt. If he lived through an accident in which others were killed, he could have survivor's guilt. Especially if loved ones died. He feels he's no better than they were, and he wonders why he was spared when they were taken. He feels guilty just for living. Suffering with the scar is a way of atoning."

Frowning, Roy got to his feet. "Maybe."

"I've had patients with that problem. They didn't want surgery because survivor's guilt led them to feel they deserved their scars."

"That doesn't sound right, either. Not for this guy."

"If he's not either phobic or suffering from survivor's guilt," said Mondello, coming around the desk and walking Roy to the door, "then you can bet it's guilt over *something*. He's punishing himself with the scar. Reminding himself of something he would like to forget but feels obligated to remember. I've seen that before as well."

As the surgeon talked, Roy studied his face, fascinated by the finely honed bone structure. He wondered how much of the effect had been achieved with real bone and how much with plastic implants, but he knew that it would be gauche to ask.

At the door, he said, "Doctor, do you believe in perfection?"

Pausing with his hand on the doorknob, Mondello appeared mildly puzzled. "Perfection?"

"Personal and societal perfection. A better world."

"Well . . . I believe in always striving for it."

"Good." Roy smiled. "I knew you did."

"But I don't believe it can be achieved."

Roy's smile froze. "Oh, but I've seen perfection now and then. Not perfection in the whole of anything, perhaps, but in part."

Mondello smiled indulgently and shook his head. "One man's idea of perfect order is another man's chaos. One man's vision of perfect beauty is another man's notion of deformity."

Roy did not appreciate such talk. The implication was that any Utopia was also Hell. Eager to convince Mondello of an alternate view, he said, "Perfect beauty exists in nature."

"There's always a flaw. Nature abhors symmetry, smoothness, straight lines, order—all the things we associate with beauty."

"I recently saw a woman with perfect hands. Flawless hands, without a blemish, exquisitely shaped."

"A cosmetic surgeon looks at the human form with a more critical eye than other people do. I'd have seen a lot of flaws, I'm sure."

The doctor's smugness irritated Roy, and he said, "I wish I'd brought those hands to you—the one, anyway. If I'd brought it, if you'd seen it, you would have agreed."

Suddenly Roy realized that he had come close to revealing things that would have necessitated the surgeon's immediate execution.

Concerned that his agitated state of mind would lead him to make another and more egregious error, Roy dawdled no longer. He thanked Mondello for his cooperation, and he got out of the white room.

In the medical building parking lot, the February sunshine was more white than golden, with a harsh edge, and a border of palm trees cast eastward-leaning shadows. The afternoon was turning cool.

As he twisted the key in the ignition and started the car, his pager beeped. He checked the small display window, saw a number with the prefix of the regional offices in downtown Los Angeles, and made the call on his cellular phone.

They had big news for him. Spencer Grant had almost been chased down in Las Vegas; he was now on the run, overland, across the Mojave Desert. A Learjet was standing by at LAX to take Roy to Nevada.

Driving up the barely perceptible slope between two rushing rivers, on a steadily narrowing peninsula of sodden sand, searching for an intruding formation of rock on which to batten down and wait out the storm, Spencer was hampered by decreasing visibility. The clouds were so thick, so black, that daylight on the desert was as murky as that a few fathoms under any sea. Rain fell in Biblical quantities, overwhelming the wind-shield wipers, and although the headlights were on, clear glimpses of the ground ahead were brief.

Great fiery lashes tortured the sky. The blinding pyrotechnics esca-lated into nearly continuous chain lightning, and brilliant links rattled down the heavens as though an evil angel, imprisoned in the storm, were angrily testing his bonds. Even then, the inconstant light illuminated nothing while swarms of stroboscopic shadows flickered across the land-scape, adding to the gloom and confusion.

Suddenly, ahead and a quarter mile to the west, at ground level, a blue light appeared as if from out of another dimension. At once, it moved off to the south at high speed.

Spencer squinted through rain and shadow, trying to discern the na-ture and size of the light source. The details remained obscure.

The blue traveler turned east, proceeded a few hundred yards, then swung north toward the Explorer. Spherical. Incandescent.

"What the hell?" Spencer slowed the Explorer to a crawl to watch the eerie luminosity.

When it was still a hundred yards from him, the thing swerved west, toward the place where it had first appeared, then dwindled past that point, rose, flared, and vanished.

Even before the first light winked out, Spencer saw a second from the corner of his eye. He stopped and looked west-northwest.

The new object—blue, throbbing—moved incredibly fast, on an er-ratic serpentine course that brought it closer before it angled east. Abruptly it spun like pinwheel fireworks and disappeared.

Both objects had been silent, gliding like apparitions across the storm-washed desert.

The skin prickled on his arms and along the nape of his neck.

For the past few days, although he was usually skeptical of all things mystical, he had felt that he was venturing into the unknown, the uncanny. In his country, in his time, real life had become a dark fantasy, as full of sorcery as any novel about lands where wizards ruled, dragons roamed, and trolls ate children. Wednesday night, he had stepped through an invisible doorway that separated his lifelong reality from another place. In this new reality, Valerie was his destiny. Once found, she would be a magic lens that would forever alter his vision. All that was mysterious would become clear, but things long known and understood would become mysterious once more.

He felt all that in his bones, as an arthritic man might feel the approach of a storm before the first cloud crossed the horizon. He felt more than understood it, and the visitations of the two blue spheres seemed to confirm that he was on the right trail to find Valerie, traveling to a strange place that would transform him.

He glanced at his four-legged companion, hoping that Rocky was staring toward where the second light had vanished. He needed confirmation that he had not imagined the thing, even if his only reassurance came from a dog. But Rocky was huddled and shivering in terror. His head remained bowed, and his eyes were downcast.

To the right of the Explorer, lightning was reflected in raging water. The river was much closer than he expected. The right-hand arroyo had widened dramatically in the past minute.

Hunched over the wheel, he angled to the new midpoint of the ever narrower strip of high ground and drove forward, seeking stable rock, wondering if the mysterious Mojave had more surprises for him.

The third blue enigma plunged out of the sky, as fast and plumb as an express elevator, two hundred yards ahead and to the left. It halted smoothly and hovered just above the ground, revolving rapidly.

Spencer's heart thudded painfully against his ribs. He eased off the accelerator. He was balanced between wonder and dread.

The glowing object shot straight at him: as large as the truck, still without detail, silent, otherworldly, on a collision course. He tramped the accelerator. The light swerved to counter his move, swelled brighter, filled the Explorer with blue-blue light. To make a smaller target of himself, he turned right, braked hard, putting the back end of the truck to the oncoming object. It struck without force but with sprays of sapphire sparks, and scores of electrical arcs blazed from one prominent point of the truck to another.

Spencer was encapsulated in a dazzling blue sphere of hissing, crackling light. And knew what it was. One of the rarest of all weather phenomena. Ball lightning. It wasn't a conscious entity, not the extraterrestrial force he had half imagined, neither stalking nor seducing him. It was simply one more element of the storm, as impersonal as ordinary lightning, thunder, rain.

Perched on four tires, the Explorer was safe. As soon as the ball burst upon them, its energy began to dissipate. Sizzling and snapping, it swiftly faded to a fainter blue: dimmer, dimmer.

His heart had been pounding with a strange jubilation, as though he desperately wanted to encounter something paranormal, even if it proved hostile, rather than return to a life without wonder. Though rare, ball lightning was too mundane to satisfy his expectations, and disappointment brought his heart rate almost back to normal.

With a jolt, the front of the truck dropped precipitously, and the cab tipped forward. As a final arc of electricity crackled from the left headlight rim to the top right corner of the windshield frame, dirty water sloshed over the hood.

In his panic, as he had tried to avoid the blue light, Spencer had swung too far to the right, braking at the brink of the arroyo. The soft wall of sand was eroding beneath him.

His heart raced again, his disappointment forgotten.

He shifted into reverse and *eased* down on the accelerator. The truck moved backward, up the disintegrating slope.

Another slab of the bank gave way. The Explorer tipped farther forward. Water surged across the hood, almost to the windshield.

Spencer abandoned caution, accelerated hard. The truck *jumped* backward. Out of the water. Tires eating through the soft, wet ground. Tipping back, back, almost horizontal again.

The arroyo wall was too unstable to endure. The churning wheels destabilized the gelatinous ground. Engine shrieking, tires spinning in the treacherous muck, the Explorer slid into the flood, protesting as noisily as a mastodon being sucked into a tar pit.

"Sonofabitch." Spencer inhaled deeply and held his breath as though he were a schoolboy leaping into a pond.

The truck splashed beneath the surface, fully submerged.

Unnerved by the calamitous sound and motion, Rocky wailed in misery, as though responding not only to current events but to the cumulative terrors of his entire troubled life.

The Explorer broke the surface, wallowing like a boat in rough seas. The windows were closed, preventing an inrush of cold water, but the engine had gone dead.

The truck was swept downstream, pitching and yawing, riding higher in the flood than Spencer had expected. The choppy surface lapped four to six inches below the sill of his side window.

He was assaulted by liquid noises, a symphonic Chinese water torture: the hollow paradiddle of rain on the roof, the whoosh and swish and plash and gurgle of the churning flow against the Explorer.

Above all the competing sounds, a drizzling noise drew Spencer's attention, because it was intimate, not muffled by sheet metal or glass. The maracas of a rattlesnake wouldn't have been more alarming. Somewhere, water was getting into the truck.

The breach wasn't catastrophic—a drizzle, not a gush. With every pound of water taken aboard, however, the truck would ride lower, until it sank. Then it would tumble along the river bottom, pushed rather than buoyed, body crumpling, windows shattering.

Both front doors were secure. No leaks.

As the truck heaved and plunged downstream, Spencer turned in his seat, snared by his safety harness, and examined the cargo hold. All windows were intact. The tailgate wasn't leaking. The backseat was folded down, so he couldn't see the floor concealed under it, but he doubted that the river was getting through the rear doors, either.

When he faced front again, his feet sloshed in an inch of water.

Rocky whined, and Spencer said, "It's okay."

Don't alarm the dog. Don't lie, but don't alarm.

Heater. The engine was dead, but the heater still functioned. The river was invading through the lower vents. Spencer switched off the system, closed the air intakes. The drizzle was silenced.

As the truck pitched, the headlights slashed the bruised sky and glistered in the mortal torrents of rain. Then the truck yawed, and the beams cut wildly left and right, seeming to carve the arroyo walls; slabs of earth crashed into the dirty tide, spewing gouts of pearlescent foam. He killed the lights, and the resultant gray-on-gray world was less chaotic.

The windshield wipers were running on battery power. He didn't switch them off. He needed to see what was coming, as best he could.

He would be less stressed—and no worse off—if he lowered his head and closed his eyes, like Rocky, and waited for fate to deal with him as it wished. A week ago, he might have done that. Now he peered forward anxiously, hands locked to the useless steering wheel.

He was surprised by the fierceness of his desire to survive. Until he had walked into The Red Door, he had expected nothing from life: only to keep a degree of dignity and to die without shame.

Blackened tumbleweed, thorny limbs of uprooted cacti, masses of desert bunchgrass that might have been the blond hair of drowned women, and pale driftwood rode the rolling river with the Explorer, scraping and thumping against it. In emotional turmoil equal to the tumult of the natural world, Spencer knew that he had been traveling the years as if he himself were driftwood, but at last he was *alive*.

The watercourse abruptly dropped ten or twelve feet, and the truck sailed over a roaring cataract, airborne, tipping forward. It dove into the rampaging water, into a diluvial darkness. Spencer was first jerked forward in his harness, then slammed backward. His head bounced off the headrest. The Explorer failed to hit bottom, exploded through the surface, and rollicked on downriver.

Rocky was still on the passenger seat, huddled and miserable, claws hooked in the upholstery.

Spencer gently stroked and squeezed the back of the mutt's neck.

Rocky didn't raise his bowed head but turned toward his master and rolled his eyes to look up from under his brow.

Interstate 15 was a quarter mile ahead. Spencer was stunned that the truck had been carried so far in so little time. The currents were even faster than they seemed.

The highway spanned the arroyo—usually a dry wash—on massive concrete columns. Through the smeary windshield and heavy rain, the bridge supports appeared to be absurdly numerous, as if government engineers had designed the structure primarily to funnel millions of dollars ·to a senator's nephew in the concrete business.

The central passage between the bridge supports was broad enough to let five trucks pass abreast. But half the flood churned through the narrower races between the closely ranked columns on each side of the main channel. Impact with the bridge supports would be deadly.

Swooping, plunging, they rode a series of rapids. Water splashed against the windows. The river picked up speed. A lot of speed.

Rocky was shaking more violently than ever and panting raggedly.

"Easy, pal, easy. You better not pee on the seat. You hear?"

On I–15, the headlights of big rigs and cars moved through the storm-darkened day. Emergency flashers threw red light into the rain where motorists had stopped on the shoulder to wait out the downpour.

The bridge loomed. Exploding ceaselessly against the concrete columns, the river threw sheets of spray into the rain-choked air.

The truck had attained a fearful velocity, *shooting* downstream. It rolled violently, and waves of nausea swelled through Spencer.

"Better not pee on the seat," he repeated, no longer speaking only to the dog.

He reached under his fleece-lined denim jacket, under his soaked shirt, and withdrew the jade-green soapstone medallion that hung on a gold chain around his neck. On one side was the carved head of a dragon. On the other side was an equally stylized pheasant.

Spencer vividly recalled the elegant, windowless office beneath China Dream. Louis Lee's smile. The bow tie, suspenders. The gentle voice: *I sometimes give one of these to people who seem to need it.*

Without slipping the chain over his head, he held the medallion in one hand. He felt childish, but he held it tightly nonetheless.

The bridge was fifty yards ahead. The Explorer was going to pass dangerously close to the forest of columns on the right.

Pheasants and dragons. Prosperity and long life.

He remembered the statue of Quan Yin by the front door of the restaurant. Serene but vigilant. Guarding against envious people.

After a life like yours, you can believe in this?

We must believe in something, Mr. Grant.

Ten yards from the bridge, ferocious currents caught the truck, lifted it, dropped it, tipped it half onto its right side, rolled it back to the left, and slapped loudly against the doors.

Sailing out of the storm into the eclipsing shadow of the highway above, they passed the first of the bridge columns in the row immediately to the right. Passed the second. At horrendous speed. The river was so high that the solid underside of the bridge was only a foot above the truck. They surged nearer to the columns, bulleting past the third, the fourth, nearer still.

Pheasants and dragons. Pheasants and dragons.

The currents pulled the truck away from the concrete supports and dropped it into a sudden swale in the turbulent surface, where it wallowed with filthy water to its windowsills. The river teased Spencer with the possibility of safe passage in that trough, pushing them along as if they were on a bobsled in a luge chute—but then it mocked his brief flicker of hope by lifting the truck again and tossing it passenger-side-first into the next column. The crash was as loud as a bomb blast, metal shrieked, and Rocky howled.

The impact pitched Spencer to his left, a move that the safety harness couldn't check. The side of his head slammed into the window. In spite of all the other clamor, he heard the tempered glass webbing with a million hairline cracks, a sound like a crisp slice of toast being crushed with a sudden clench of a fist.

Cursing, he put his left hand to the side of his head. No blood. Only a rapid throbbing that was in time with his heartbeat.

The window was a mosaic of thousands of tiny chips of glass, held together by the gummy film in the center of the sandwiched pane.

Miraculously, the windows on Rocky's side were undamaged. But the front door bulged inward. Water dribbled around the frame.

Rocky lifted his head, suddenly afraid *not* to look. He whimpered as he peered at the wild river, at the low concrete ceiling, and at the rectangle of cheerless gray storm light beyond the bridge.

"Hell," Spencer said, "pee on the seat if you want to."

The truck sank into another swale.

They were two-thirds of the way through the tunnel.

A hissing, needle-thin stream of water *squirted* through a tiny breach in the twisted door frame. Rocky yelped as it spattered him.

When the truck soared out of the trough, it wasn't thrown into the columns after all. Worse, the river heaved as if passing over an enormous obstruction on the floor of the wash, and it slammed the Explorer straight up into the low concrete underside of the bridge.

Braced with both hands on the steering wheel, determined not to be thrown into the side window, Spencer was unprepared for the upward rush. He dropped in his seat as the roof crumpled inward, but he was not quick enough. The ceiling cracked against the top of his skull.

Bright bolts of pain flashed behind his eyes, along his spine. Blood streamed down his face. Scalding tears. His vision blurred.

The river carried the truck down from the underside of the bridge, and Spencer tried to push up in his seat. The effort made him dizzy, so he slumped again, breathing hard.

His tears swiftly darkened, as if polluted. His blurred vision faded. Soon the tears were as black as ink, and he was blind.

The prospect of blindness panicked him, and panic opened a door to understanding: He wasn't blind, thank God, but he *was* passing out.

He held desperately to consciousness. If he fainted, he might never wake. He balanced on the edge of a swoon. Then hundreds of gray dots appeared in the blackness, expanded into elaborate matrices of light and shadow, until he could see the interior of the truck.

Pulling himself up in the seat as far as the crumpled roof would allow, he again almost passed out. Gingerly, he touched his bleeding scalp. The wound seeped rather than gushed, not a mortal laceration.

They were in the open once more. Rain hammered on the truck.

The battery wasn't dead yet. Wipers still swept the windshield.

The Explorer gamely wallowed down the center of the river, which was broader than ever. Perhaps a hundred twenty feet wide. Brimming against its banks, within inches of spilling over. God knew how deep it might be. The water was calmer than it had been but moving fast.

Gazing worriedly at the liquid road ahead, Rocky made pitiful sounds of distress. He wasn't bobbing his head, wasn't delighted by their speed, as on the streets of Vegas. He didn't seem to trust nature as much as he had trusted his master.

"Good old Mr. Rocky Dog," Spencer said affectionately, and was unnerved to hear that his speech was slurred.

In spite of Rocky's concern, Spencer couldn't see any unusual dangers immediately ahead, nothing like the bridge. For a couple of miles the flow appeared to proceed unimpeded, until it vanished into rain, mist, and the iron-colored light of thunderhead-filtered sun.

Desert plains lay on both sides, bleak but not entirely barren. Mesquite bristled. Clumps of wiry grass. Outcroppings of gnarled rock also grew out of the plains. They were natural formations but achieved the strange geometry of ancient Druid structures.

A new pain blossomed in Spencer's skull. Irresistible darkness flowered behind his eyes. He might have been out for a minute or an hour. He didn't dream. He just went away into a timeless dark.

When he revived, cool air fluttered feebly across his brow, and cold rain spattered his face. The many liquid voices of the river grumbled, hissed, and chuckled louder than before.

He sat for a while, wondering why the sound was so much louder. His thoughts were muddled. Eventually, he realized that the side window had collapsed while he'd been unconscious. Gummy laces of highly fragmented tempered glass lay in his lap.

Water was ankle-deep on the floor. His feet were half numb with cold. He propped them on the brake pedal and flexed his toes in his saturated shoes. The Explorer was riding lower than when last he'd noticed. The water was only an inch below the bottom of the window. Though moving fast, the river was less turbulent, perhaps because it had broadened. If the arroyo narrowed or the terrain changed, the flow might become tempestuous again, lap inside, and sink them.

Spencer was barely clearheaded enough to know that he should be alarmed. Nevertheless, he could muster only a mild concern.

He should find a way to seal the dangerous gap where the window had been. But the problem seemed insurmountable. For one thing, he would have to move to accomplish it, and he didn't want to move.

All he wanted to do was sleep. He was so tired. Exhausted.

His head lolled to the right against the headrest, and he saw the dog sitting on the passenger seat. "How you doin', fur butt?" he asked thickly, as if he had been pouring down beer after beer.

Rocky glanced at him, then looked again at the river ahead.

"Don't be afraid, pal. He wins if you're afraid. Don't let the bastard win. Can't let him win. Got to find Valerie. Before he does. He's out there. He's forever . . . on the prowl. . . ."

With the woman on his mind and a deep uneasiness in his heart, Spencer Grant rode through the glistening day, muttering feverishly, searching for something unknown, unknowable. The vigilant dog sat silently beside him. Rain ticked on the crumpled roof of the truck.

Maybe he passed out again, maybe he only closed his eyes, but when his feet slipped off the brake pedal and splashed into water that was now halfway up his calves, Spencer lifted his throbbing head and saw that the windshield wipers had stopped. Dead battery.

The river was as fast as an express train. Some turbulence had returned. Muddy water licked at the sill of the broken window.

Inches beyond that gap, a dead rat floated on the surface of the flow, pacing the truck. Long and sleek. One unblinking, glassy eye fixed on Spencer. Lips skinned back from sharp teeth. The long, disgusting tail was as stiff as wire, strangely curled and kinked.

The sight of the rat alarmed Spencer as he had not been alarmed by the flood lapping at the windowsill. With the breathless, heart-pounding fear familiar from nightmares, he knew he would die if the rat washed into the truck, because it was not merely a rat. It was Death. It was a cry in the night and the hoot of an owl, a flashing blade and the smell of hot blood, it was the catacombs, it was the smell of lime and worse, it was the door out of boyhood innocence, the passageway to Hell, the room at the end of nowhere: It was all that in the cold flesh of one dead rodent. If it touched him, he'd scream until his lungs burst, and his last breath would be darkness.

If only he could find an object with which to reach through the window and shove the thing away without having to touch it directly. But he was too weak to search for anything that could serve as a prod. His hands lay in his lap, palms up, and even contracting his fingers into fists required more strength than he possessed.

Maybe more damage had been done than he had first realized, when the top of his head had hit the ceiling. He wondered if paralysis had begun to creep through him. If so, he wondered if it mattered.

Lightning scarred the sky. A bright reflection transformed the rat's tenebrous eye into a flaring white orb that seemed to swivel in the socket to glare even more directly at Spencer.

He sensed that his fixation on the rat would draw it toward him, that his horrified gaze was a magnet to its iron-black eye. He looked away from it. Ahead. At the river.

Though he was sweating profusely, he was colder than ever. Even his scar was cold, not ablaze any longer. The coldest part of him. His skin was ice, but his scar was frozen steel.

Blinking away the rain as it slanted through the window, Spencer watched the river gain speed, racing toward the only interesting feature in an otherwise tedious landscape of gently declining plains.

North to south across the Mojave, vanishing in mist, a spine of rock jutted as high as twenty or thirty feet in some places, as low as three feet in others. Though it was a natural geological feature, the formation was

weathered curiously, with wind-carved windows, and appeared to be the ruined ramparts of an immense fortification erected and destroyed in a war-
ring age a thousand years prior to recorded history. Along some of the
highest portions of the expanse were suggestions of crumbling and unevenly
crenelated parapets. In places the wall was breached from top to bottom, as
though an enemy army had battered into the fortress at those points.

Spencer concentrated on the fantasy of the ancient castle, superim-
posing it upon the escarpment of stone, to distract himself from the dead
rat floating just beyond the broken window at his side.

In his mental confusion, he was not initially concerned that the river
was carrying him toward those battlements. Gradually, however, he realized that the approaching encounter might be as devastating to the truck
as had been the brutal game of pinball with the bridge. If the currents
conveyed the Explorer through one of the sluiceways and along the river,
the queer rock formations would be just interesting scenery. But if the
truck clipped one of those natural gateposts . . .

The spine of rock traversed the arroyo but was breached in three
places by the flow. The widest gap was fifty feet across and lay to the right,
framed by the south shore and by a six-foot-wide, twenty-foot-high tower
of dark stone that rose from the water. The narrowest passage, not even
eight feet wide, lay in the center, between that first tower and another pile
of rocks ten feet wide and twelve high. Between *that* pile and the left-hand
shore, where the battlements soared again and ran uninterrupted far to
the north, lay the third passage, which must have been twenty to thirty
feet across.

"Gonna make it." He tried to reach out to the dog. Couldn't.

With a hundred yards to go, the Explorer seemed to be drifting swiftly
toward the southernmost and widest gateway.

Spencer wasn't able to stop himself from glancing to the left. Through
the missing window. At the rat. Floating. Closer than before. The stiff tail
was mottled pink and black.

A memory scuttled through his mind: *rats in a cramped place, hateful red
eyes in the shadows, rats in the catacombs, down in the catacombs, and ahead lies
the room at the end of nowhere.*

With a quiver of revulsion, he looked forward. The windshield was
blurred by rain. Nevertheless, he could see too much. Having closed
within fifty yards of the point at which the river divided, the truck no
longer sailed toward the widest passage. It angled left, toward the center
gate, the most dangerous of the three.

The channel narrowed. The water accelerated.

"Hold on, pal. Hold on."

Spencer hoped to be carried sharply to the left, past the center gate, into the north passage. Twenty yards from the sluiceways, the lateral drift of the truck slowed. It would never reach the north gate. It was going to race through the center.

Fifteen yards. Ten.

Even to transit the center passage, they would need some luck. At the moment, they were rocketing toward the twenty-foot-high gatepost of solid rock on the right of that opening.

Maybe they would just graze the pillar or even slide by with a finger's width to spare.

They were so close that Spencer could no longer see the base of the stone tower past the front of the Explorer. "Please, God."

The bumper rammed the rock as though to cleave it. The impact was so great that Rocky slid onto the floor again. The right front fender tore loose, flew away. The hood buckled as if made of tinfoil. The windshield imploded, but instead of spraying Spencer, tempered glass cascaded over the dashboard in glutinous, prickly wads.

For an instant after the collision, the Explorer was at a dead stop in the water and at an angle to the direction of the flow. Then the raging current caught the side of the truck and began to push the back end around to the left.

Spencer opened his eyes and watched in disbelief as the Explorer turned crosswise to the flow. It could never pass sideways between the two masses of rock and through the center sluiceway. The gap was too narrow; the truck would wedge tight. Then the rampaging river would hammer the passenger side until it flooded the interior or maybe hurled a driftwood log through the open window at his head.

Shuddering, grinding, the front of the Explorer worked along the rock, deeper into the passage, and the back end continued to arc to the left. The river pushed hard on the passenger side, surging halfway up the windows. In turn, as the driver's side of the truck was shoved fully around toward the narrow sluiceway, it created a small swell that rose over the windowsill. The back end slammed into the second gatepost, and water poured inside, onto Spencer, carrying the dead rodent, which had remained in the orbit of the truck.

The rat slipped greasily through his upturned palms and onto the seat between his legs. Its stiff tail trailed across his right hand.

The catacombs. The fiery eyes watching from the shadows. The room, the room, the room at the end of nowhere.

He tried to scream, but what he heard was a choked and broken sobbing, like that of a child terrified beyond endurance.

Possibly half paralyzed from the blow to his head, without a doubt paralyzed by fear, he still managed a spasmodic twitch of both hands, casting the rat off the seat. It splashed into a calf-deep pool of muddy water on the floor. Now it was out of sight. But not gone. Down there. Floating between his legs.

Don't think about that.

He was as dizzy as if he had spent hours on a carousel, and a fun-house darkness was bleeding in at the edges of his vision.

He wasn't sobbing any more. He repeated the same two words, in a hoarse, agonized voice: "I'm sorry, I'm sorry, I'm sorry. . . ."

In his deepening delirium, he knew that he was not apologizing to the dog or to Valerie Keene, whom he would now never save, but to his mother for not having saved her, either. She had been dead for more than twenty-two years. He had been only eight years old when she'd died, too small to have saved her, too small then to feel such enormous guilt now, yet "I'm sorry" spilled from his lips.

The river industriously shoved the Explorer deeper into the sluiceway, although the truck was now entirely crosswise to the flow. Both front and rear bumpers scraped and rattled along the rock walls. The tortured Ford squealed, groaned, creaked: It was at most one inch shorter from back to front than the width of the water-smoothed gap through which it was struggling to be borne. The river wiggled it, wrenched it, alternately jammed and finessed it, crumpled it at each end to force it forward a foot, an inch, grudgingly forward.

Simultaneously, gradually, the tremendous power of the thwarted currents actually lifted the truck a foot. The dark water surged against the passenger side, no longer halfway up the windows on that flank but swirling at the base of them.

Rocky remained down in the half-flooded leg space, enduring.

When Spencer had quelled his dizziness with sheer willpower, he saw that the spine of rock bisecting the arroyo was not as thick as he had thought. From the entrance to the exit of the sluiceway, that corridor of stone would measure no more than twelve feet.

The jackhammering river pushed the Explorer nine feet into the passage, and then with a *skreek* of tearing metal and an ugly binding sound, the truck wedged tight. If it had made only three more feet, the Explorer would have flowed with the river once more, clear and free. So close.

Now that the truck was held fast, no longer protesting the grip of the rock, the rain was again the loudest sound in the day. It was more thunderous than before, although falling no harder. Maybe it only *seemed* louder because he was sick to death of it.

Rocky had scrambled onto the seat again, out of the water on the floor, dripping and miserable.

"I'm so sorry," Spencer said.

Fending off despair and the insistent darkness that constricted his vision, incapable of meeting the dog's trusting eyes, Spencer turned to the side window, to the river, which so recently he had feared and hated but which he now longed to embrace.

The river wasn't there.

He thought he was hallucinating.

Far away, veiled by furies of rain, a range of desert mountains defined the horizon, and the highest elevations were lost in clouds. No river dwindled from him toward those distant peaks. In fact, nothing whatsoever seemed to lie between the truck and the mountains. The vista was like a painting in which the artist had left the foreground of the canvas entirely blank.

Then, almost dreamily, Spencer realized that he had not seen what was there to see. His perception had been hampered as much by his expectations as by his befuddled senses. The canvas wasn't blank after all. Spencer needed only to alter his point of view, lower his gaze from his own plane, to see the thousand-foot chasm into which the river plunged.

The miles-long spine of weathered rock that he had thought marched across otherwise flat desert terrain was actually the irregular parapet of a perilous cliff. On his side, the sandy plain had eroded, over eons, to a somewhat lower level than the rock. On the other side was not another plain but a sheer face of stone, down which the river fell with a cataclysmic roar.

He had also wrongly assumed that the increased rumble of rain was imaginary. In fact, the greater roar was a trio of waterfalls, altogether more than one hundred feet across, crashing a hundred stories to the valley floor below.

Spencer couldn't see the foaming cataracts, because the Explorer was suspended directly over them. He lacked the strength to pull himself against the door and lean out the window to look. With the flood pushing hard against the passenger side, as well as slipping under it and away, the truck actually hung half *in* the narrowest of the three falls, prevented from being carried over the brink only by the jaws of the rock vise.

He wondered how in God's name he was going to get out of the truck and out of the river alive. Then he rejected all consideration of the challenge. The fearfulness of it sapped what meager energy he still had. He must rest first, think later.

From where Spencer slumped in the driver's seat, though he had no view of the river gone vertical, he could see the broad valley beneath him and the serpentine course of the water as it flowed horizontally again across the lower land. That long drop and the tilted panorama at the bottom caused a new attack of vertigo, and he turned away to avoid passing out.

Too late. The motion of a phantom carousel afflicted him, and the spinning view of rock and rain became a tight spiral of darkness into which he tumbled, around and around and down and away.

. . . and there in the night behind the barn, I'm still spooked by the swooping angel that was only an owl. Inexplicably, when the vision of my mother in celestial robes and wings proves to be a fantasy, I am overcome by another image of her: bloody, crumpled, naked, dead in a ditch, eighty miles from home, as she had been found six years before. I never actually saw her that way, not even in a newspaper photograph, only heard the scene described by a few kids in school, vicious little bastards. Yet, after the owl has vanished into the moonlight, I can't retain the vision of an angel, though I try, and I can't shed the gruesome mental picture of the battered corpse, although both images are products of my imagination and should be subject to my control.

Bare-chested and barefoot, I move farther behind the barn, which hasn't been a real working barn for more than fifteen years. It's a well-known place to me, part of my life since I can remember—yet tonight it seems different from the barn I've always known, changed in some way that I can't define but that makes me uneasy.

It's a strange night, stranger than I yet realize. And I'm a strange boy, full of questions I've never dared to ask myself, seeking answers in that July darkness when the answers are within me, if I would only look for them there. I am a strange boy who feels the warp in the wood of a life gone wrong, but who convinces himself that the warped line is really true and straight. I am a strange boy who keeps secrets from himself—and keeps them as well as the world keeps the secret of its meaning.

In the eerily quiet night, behind the barn, I creep cautiously toward the Chevy van, which I've never seen before. No one is behind the wheel or in the other front seat. When I place my hand on the hood, it's warm with engine heat. The metal is still cooling with faint ticks and pings. I slip past the rainbow mural on the side of the van to the open rear door.

Although the interior of the cargo section is dark, enough pale moonlight filters back from the windshield to reveal that no one is in there, either. I'm also able to see this is only a two-seater, with no apparent amenities, though the customized exterior led me to expect a plush recreational vehicle.

I still sense there's something ominous about the van—other than the simple fact that it doesn't belong here. Seeking a reason for that ominousness, leaning through the open door, squinting, wishing I'd brought a flashlight, I'm hit by the stink of urine. Someone has pissed in the back of the van. Weird. Jesus. Of course, maybe it's only a dog that made the mess, which isn't so weird after all, but it's still disgusting.

Holding my breath, wrinkling my nose, I step back from the door and hunker down to get a closer look at the license plate. It's from Colorado, not out of state.

I stand.

I listen. Silence.

The barn waits.

Like many barns built in snow country, it had been essentially windowless when constructed. Even after the radical conversion of the interior, the only windows are two on the first floor, the south side, and four second-floor panes in this face. Those four above me are tall and wide to capture the north light from dawn to dusk.

The windows are dark. The barn is silent.

The north wall features a single entrance. One man-size door.

After moving around to the far side of the van, finding no one there, either, I'm indecisive for precious seconds.

From a distance of twenty feet, under a moon that seems to conceal as much with its shadows as it reveals with its milky light, I nevertheless can see that the north door is ajar.

On some deep level, perhaps I know what I should do, what I must do. But the part of me that keeps secrets so well is insistent that I return to my bed, forget the cry that woke me from a dream of my mother, and sleep the last of the night away. In the morning, of course, I'll have to continue living in the dream that I've made for myself, a prisoner of this life of self-deception, with truth and reality tucked into a forgotten pocket at the back of my mind. Maybe the burden of that pocket has become too heavy for the fabric to contain it, and maybe the threads of the seams have begun to break. On some deep level, maybe I have decided to end my waking dream.

Or maybe the choice I make is preordained, having less to do with either my subconscious agonies or my conscience than with the track of destiny on which I've traveled since the day I was born. Maybe choice is an illusion, and maybe the only routes we can take in life are those marked on a map at the moment of our conception. I pray to God that destiny isn't a thing of iron, that it can be flexed and reshaped, that it bends to the power of mercy, honesty, kindness, and virtue—because otherwise, I can't tolerate the person I will become, the things I will do, or the end that will be mine.

That hot July night, beaded with sweat but chilled, fourteen in moonlight, I am thinking about none of that: no brooding about hidden secrets or destiny. That night, I'm driven by emotion rather than intellect, by sheer intuition rather than reason, by need rather than curiosity. I'm only fourteen years old, after all. Only fourteen.

The barn waits.

I go to the door, which is ajar.

I listen at the gap between the door and the jamb.

Silence within.

I push the door inward. The hinges are well oiled, my feet are bare, and I enter with a silence as perfect as that of the darkness that welcomes me. . . .

Spencer opened his eyes from the dark interior of the barn in the dream to the dark interior of the rock-pinned Explorer, and he realized that night had come to the desert. He had been unconscious for at least five or six hours.

His head was tipped forward, his chin on his chest. He gazed down into his own upturned palms, chalk white and supplicant.

The rat was on the floor. Couldn't see it. But it was there. In the darkness. Floating.

Don't think about that.

The rain had stopped. No drumming on the roof.

He was thirsty. Parched. Raspy tongue. Chapped lips.

The truck rocked slightly. The river was trying to push it over the cliff. The tireless damned river.

No. That couldn't be the explanation. The roar of the waterfall was gone. The night was silent. No thunder. No lightning. No water sounds out there any more.

He ached all over. His head and neck were the worst.

He could barely find the strength to look up from his hands.

Rocky was gone.

The passenger door hung open.

The truck rocked again. Rattled and creaked.

The woman appeared at the bottom of the open door. First her head, then her shoulders, as if she were levitating up out of the flood. Except, judging by the comparative quiet, the flood was gone.

Because his eyes were adapted to darkness and cool moonlight shone between ragged clouds, Spencer was able to recognize her.

In a voice as dry as cinders, but without a slur, he said, "Hi."

"Hi, yourself," she said.

"Come in."

"Thank you, I think I will."

"This is nice," he said.

"You like it here?"

"Better than the other dream."

She levered herself into the truck, and it wobbled more than before, grinding against rock at both ends.

The motion disturbed him—not because he was concerned that the truck would shift and break loose and fall, but because it stirred up his vertigo again. He was afraid of spiraling out of this dream, back into the nightmare of July and Colorado.

Sitting where Rocky had once sat, she remained still for a moment, waiting for the truck to stop moving. "This is one tricky damned situation you've gotten into."

"Ball lightning," he said.

"Excuse me?"

"Ball lightning."

"Of course."

"Knocked the truck into the arroyo."

"Why not," she said.

It was so hard to think, to express himself clearly. Thinking hurt. Thinking made him dizzy.

"Thought it was aliens," he explained.

"Aliens?"

"Little guys. Big eyes. Spielberg."

"Why would you think it was aliens?"

"Because you're wonderful," he said, though the words didn't convey what he meant. In spite of the poor light, he could see that the look she gave him was peculiar. Straining to find better words, made dizzier by the effort, he said, "Wonderful things must happen around you . . . happen around you all the time."

"Oh, yeah, I'm the center of a regular *festival*."

"You must know some wonderful thing. That's why they're after you. Because you know some wonderful thing."

"You been taking drugs?"

"I could use a couple aspirin. Anyway . . . they're not after you because you're a bad person."

"Aren't they?"

"No. Because you're not. A bad person, I mean."

She leaned toward him and put a hand against his forehead. Even her light touch made him wince with pain.

"How do you know I'm not a bad person?" she asked.

"You were nice to me."

"Maybe it was an act."

She produced a penlight from her jacket, peeled back his left eyelid, directed the beam at his eye. The light hurt. Everything hurt. The cool air hurt his face. Pain accelerated his vertigo.

"You were nice to Theda."

"Maybe that was an act too," she said, now examining his right eye with the penlight.

"Can't fool Theda."

"Why not?"

"She's wise."

"Well, that's true."

"And she makes *huge* cookies."

Finished examining his eyes, she tipped his head forward to have a look at the gash in the top of his skull. "Nasty. Coagulated now, but it needs cleaned and stitched."

"Ouch!"

"How long were you bleeding?"

"Dreams don't hurt."

"Do you think you lost a lot of blood?"

"This hurts."

"'Cause you're not dreaming."

He licked his chapped lips. His tongue was dry. "Thirsty."

"I'll get you a drink in just a minute," she said, putting two fingers under his chin and tipping his head up again.

All this head tipping was making him dangerously dizzy, but he managed to say, "Not dreaming? You're sure?"

"Positive." She touched his upturned right palm. "Can you squeeze my hand?"

"Yes."

"Go ahead."

"All right."

"I mean now."

"Oh." He closed his hand around hers.

"That's not bad," she said.

"It's nice."

"A good grip. Probably no spinal damage. I expected the worst."

She had a warm, strong hand. He said, "Nice."

He closed his eyes. An inner darkness leaped at him. He opened his eyes at once, before he could fall back into the dream.

"You can let go of my hand now," she said.

"Not a dream, huh?"

"No dream."

She clicked on the penlight again and directed it down between his seat and the center console.

"This is really strange," he said.

She was peering along the narrow shaft of light.

"Not dreaming," he said, "must be hallucinating."

She popped the release button that disengaged the buckle on his safety harness from the latch between his seat and the console.

"It's okay," he said.

"What's okay?" she asked, switching off the light and returning it to her jacket pocket.

"That you peed on the seat."

She laughed.

"I like to hear you laugh."

She was still laughing as she carefully extricated him from the harness.

"You've never laughed before," he said.

"Well," she said, "not much recently."

"Not ever before. You've never barked either."

She laughed again.

"I'm going to get you a new rawhide bone."

"You're very kind."

He said, "This is damned interesting."

"That's for sure."

"It's so real."

"Seems *un*real to me."

Even though Spencer remained mostly passive through the process, getting out of the harness left him so dizzy that he saw three of the woman and three of every shadow in the car, like superimposed images on a photograph.

Afraid that he would pass out before he had a chance to express himself, he spoke in a raspy rush of words: "You're a real friend, pal, you really are, you're a perfect friend."

"We'll see if that's how it turns out."

"You're the only friend I have."

"Okay, my friend, now we've come to the hard part. How the hell am I going to get you out of this junker when you can't help yourself at all?"

"I can help myself."

"You think you can?"

"I was an Army Ranger once. And a cop."

"Yes, I know."

"I've been trained in tae kwon do."

"That would really be handy if we were under assault by a bunch of ninja assassins. But can you help me get you out of here?"

"A little."

"I guess we've got to give it a try."

"Okay."

"Can you lift your legs out of there, swing them to me?"

"Don't want to disturb the rat."

"There's a rat?"

"He's dead already but . . . you know."

"Of course."

"I'm very dizzy."

"Then let's wait a minute, rest a minute."

"Very, very dizzy."

"Just take it easy."

"Good-bye," he said, and surrendered to a black vortex that spun him around and away. For some reason, as he went, he thought of Dorothy and Toto and Oz.

The back door of the barn opens into a short hallway. I step inside. No lights. No windows. The green glow from the security-system readout—NOT READY TO ARM—in the right-hand wall provides just enough light for me to see that I am alone in the corridor. I don't ease the door all the way shut behind me but leave it ajar, as I found it.

The floor appears to be black beneath me, but I'm on polished pine. To the left are a bathroom and a room where art supplies are stored. Those doorways are barely discernible in the faint green wash, which is like the unearthly illumination in a dream, less like real light than like a lingering memory of neon. To the right is a file room. Ahead, at the end of the hallway, is the door to the large first-floor gallery, where a switchback staircase leads to my father's studio. That upper chamber occupies the entire second floor and features the big north-facing windows under which the van is parked outside.

I listen to the hallway darkness.

It doesn't speak or breathe.

The light switch is to the right, but I leave it untouched.

In the green-black gloom, I ease the bathroom door all the way open. Step inside. Wait for a sound, a sense of movement, a blow. Nothing.

The supply room is also deserted.

I move to the right side of the hall and quietly open the door to the file room. I step across the threshold.

The overhead fluorescent tubes are dark, but there is other light where no light should be. Yellow and sour. Dim and strange. From a mysterious source at the far end of the room.

A long worktable occupies the center of that rectangular space. Two chairs. File cabinets stand against one of the long walls.

My heart is knocking so hard it shakes my arms. I make fists of my hands and hold them at my sides, struggling to control myself.

I decide to return to the house, to bed, to sleep.

Then I'm at the far end of the file room, though I don't recall having taken a single step in that direction. I seem to have walked those twenty feet in a sudden spell of sleep. Called forward by something, someone. As if responding to a powerful hypnotic command. To a wordless, silent summons.

I am standing in front of a knotty-pine cabinet that extends from floor to ceiling and from corner to corner of the thirteen-foot-wide room. The cabinet features three pairs of tall, narrow doors.

The center pair stand open.

Behind those doors, there should be nothing but shelves. On the shelves should be boxes of old tax records, correspondence, and dead files no longer kept in the metal cabinets along the other wall.

This night, the shelves and their contents, along with the back wall of the pine cabinet, have been pushed backward four or five feet into a secret space behind the file room, into a hidden chamber I've never seen before. The sour yellow light comes from a place beyond the closet.

Before me is the essence of all boyish fantasies: the secret passage to a world of danger and adventure, to far stars, to stars farther still, to the very center of the earth, to lands of trolls or pirates or intelligent apes or robots, to the distant future or to the age of dinosaurs. Here is a stairway to mystery, a tunnel through which I might set out upon heroic quests, or a way station on a strange highway to dimensions unknown.

Briefly, I thrill to the thought of what exotic travels and magical discoveries might lay ahead. But instinct quickly tells me that on the far side of this secret passage, there is something stranger and deadlier than an alien world or a Morlock dungeon. I want to return to the house, to my bedroom, to the protection of my sheets, immediately, as fast as I can run. The perverse allure of terror and the unknown deserts me, and I'm suddenly eager to leave this waking dream for the less threatening lands to be found on the dark side of sleep.

Although I can't recall crossing the threshold, I find myself inside the tall cabinet instead of hurrying to the house, through the night, the moonlight, and the owl shadows. I blink, and then I find that I've gone farther still, not back one step but forward into the secret space beyond.

It's a vestibule of sorts, six feet by six feet. Concrete floor. Concrete-block walls. Bare yellow bulb in a ceiling socket.

A cursory investigation reveals that the back wall of the pine cabinet, complete with the attached and laden shelves, is fitted with small concealed wheels. It's been shoved inward on a pair of sliding-door tracks.

To the right is a door out of the vestibule. An ordinary door in many ways. Heavy, judging by the look of it. Solid wood. Brass hardware. It's painted white, and in places the paint is yellowed with age. However, though it's more white and grimy yellow than it is anything else, tonight this is neither a white nor a yellow door. A series of bloody handprints arcs from the area around the brass knob across the upper portion of the door, and their bright patterns render the color of the background unimportant. Eight, ten, twelve, or more impressions of a woman's hands. Palms and spread fingers. Each hand partially overlapping the one before it. Some smeared, some as clear as police-file prints. All glistening, wet. All fresh. Those scarlet images bring to mind the spread wings of a bird leaping into flight, fleeing to the sky, in a flutter of fear. Staring at them, I am mesmerized, unable to get my breath, my heart storming, because the handprints convey an unbearable sense of the woman's terror, desperation, and frantic resistance to the prospect of being forced beyond the gray concrete vestibule of this secret world.

I can't go forward. Can't. Won't. I'm just a boy, barefoot, unarmed, afraid, not ready for the truth.

I don't remember moving my right hand, but now it's on the brass knob. I open the red door.

PART TWO

TO THE SOURCE OF THE FLOW

On the road that I have taken,
one day, walking, I awaken,
amazed to see where I have come,
where I'm going, where I'm from.

This is not the path I thought.
This is not the place I sought.
This is not the dream I bought,
just a fever of fate I've caught.

I'll change highways in a while,
at the crossroads, one more mile.
My path is lit by my own fire.
I'm going only where I desire.

On the road that I have taken,
one day, walking, I awaken.
One day, walking, I awaken,
on the road that I have taken.

—*The Book of Counted Sorrows*

11

FRIDAY AFTERNOON, after discussing Spencer Grant's scar with Dr. Mondello, Roy Miro left Los Angeles International aboard an agency Learjet, with a glass of properly chilled Robert Mondavi chardonnay in one hand and a bowl of shelled pistachios in his lap. He was the only passenger, and he expected to be in Las Vegas in an hour.

A few minutes short of his destination, his flight was diverted to Flagstaff, Arizona. Flash floods, spawned by the worst storm to batter Nevada in a decade, had inundated lower areas of Las Vegas. Also, lightning had damaged vital electronic systems at the airport, McCarran International, forcing a suspension of service.

By the time the jet was on the ground in Flagstaff, the official word was that McCarran would resume operations in two hours or less. Roy remained aboard, so he would not waste precious minutes returning from the terminal when the pilot learned that McCarran was up and running again.

He passed the time, at first, by linking to Mama in Virginia and using her extensive data-bank connections to teach a lesson to Captain Harris Descoteaux, the Los Angeles police officer who had irritated him earlier in the day. Descoteaux had too little respect for higher authority. Soon, however, in addition to a Caribbean lilt, his voice would have a new note of humility.

Later, Roy watched a PBS documentary on one of three television sets that served the passenger compartment of the Lear. The program was about Dr. Jack Kevorkian—dubbed Dr. Death by the media—who had made it his mission in life to assist the terminally ill when they expressed a desire to commit suicide, though he was persecuted by the law for doing so.

Roy was enthralled by the documentary. More than once, he was moved to tears. By the middle of the program, he was compelled to lean forward from his chair and place one hand flat on the screen each time Jack Kevorkian appeared in closeup. With his palm against the blessed image of the doctor's face, Roy could *feel* the purity of the man, a saintly aura, a thrill of spiritual power.

In a fair world, in a society based on true justice, Kevorkian would have been left to do his work in peace. Roy was depressed to hear about the man's suffering at the hands of regressive forces.

He took solace, however, from the knowledge that the day was swiftly approaching when a man like Kevorkian would never again be treated as a pariah. He would be embraced by a grateful nation and provided with an office, facilities, and salary commensurate with his contribution to a better world.

The world was so full of suffering and injustice that *anyone* who wanted to be assisted in suicide, terminally ill or not, should have that assistance. Roy passionately believed that even those who were chronically but not terminally ill, including many of the elderly, should be granted eternal rest if they wished to have it.

Those who didn't see the wisdom of self-elimination should not be abandoned, either. They should be given free counseling, until they could perceive the immeasurable beauty of the gift that they were being offered.

Hand on the screen. Kevorkian in closeup. *Feel* the power.

The day would come when the disabled would suffer no more pain or indignities. No more wheelchairs or leg braces. No more Seeing Eye dogs. No more hearing aids, prosthetic limbs, no more grueling sessions with speech therapists. Only the peace of endless sleep.

Dr. Jack Kevorkian's face filled the screen. Smiling. Oh, that smile.

Roy put *both* hands to the warm glass. He opened his heart and permitted that fabulous smile to flow into him. He unchained his soul and allowed Kevorkian's spiritual power to lift him up.

Eventually the science of genetic engineering would ensure that none but healthy children were born, and eventually they would all be beautiful, as well as strong and sound. They would be *perfect*. Until that day came, however, Roy saw a need for an assisted-suicide program for infants born with less than the full use of their five senses and all four limbs. He was even ahead of Kevorkian on this.

In fact, when his hard work with the agency was done, when the country had the compassionate government that it deserved and was on the threshold of Utopia, he would like to spend the rest of his life serving in a suicide-assistance program for infants. He could not imagine anything more rewarding than holding a defective baby in his arms while a lethal injection was administered, comforting the child as it passed from imperfect flesh to a transcendent spiritual plane.

His heart swelled with love for those less fortunate than he. The halt and blind. The maimed and the ill and the elderly and the depressed and the learning impaired.

After two hours on the ground in Flagstaff, by the time McCarran re-opened and the Learjet departed for a second try at Las Vegas, the documentary had ended. Kevorkian's smile was no longer to be seen. Nevertheless, Roy remained in a state of rapture that he was sure would last for at least several days.

The power was now in him. He would experience no more failure, no more setbacks.

In flight, he received a telephone call from the agent seeking Ethel and George Porth, the grandparents who had raised Spencer Grant after the death of his mother. According to county property records, the Porths had once owned the house at the San Francisco address in Grant's military records, but they had sold it ten years ago. The buyers had resold it seven years thereafter, and the new owners, in residence just three years, had never heard of the Porths and had no clue as to their whereabouts. The agent was continuing the search.

Roy had every confidence that they would find the Porths. The tide had turned in their favor. *Feel* the power.

By the time the Learjet landed in Las Vegas, night had fallen. Although the sky was overcast, the rain had stopped.

Roy was met at the debarkation gate by a driver who looked like a Spam loaf in a suit. He said only that his name was Prock and that the car was in front of the terminal. Glowering, he stalked away, expecting to be followed, clearly uninterested in small talk, as rude as the most arrogant maître d' in New York City.

Roy decided to be amused rather than insulted.

The nondescript Chevrolet was parked illegally in the loading zone. Although Prock seemed bigger than the car that he was driving, somehow he fit inside.

The air was chilly, but Roy found it invigorating.

Because Prock kept the heater turned up high, the interior of the Chevy was stuffy, but Roy chose to think of it as cozy.

He was in a brilliant mood.

They went downtown with illegal haste.

Though Prock stayed on secondary streets and kept away from the busy hotels and casinos, the glare of those neon-lined avenues was reflected on the bellies of the low clouds. The red-orange-green-yellow sky might have seemed like a vision of Hell to a gambler who had just lost next week's grocery money, but Roy found it festive.

After delivering Roy to the agency's downtown headquarters, Prock drove off to deliver his baggage to the hotel for him.

On the fifth floor of the high rise, Bobby Dubois was waiting. Dubois, the evening duty officer, was a tall, lanky Texan with mud-brown eyes and hair the color of range dust, on whom clothes hung like thrift-shop castaways on a stick-and-straw scarecrow. Although big-boned, rough-hewn, with a mottled complexion, with jug-handle ears, with teeth as crooked as the tombstones in a cow-town cemetery, with not a single feature that even the kindest critic could deem perfect, Dubois had a good-old-boy charm and an easy manner that distracted attention from the fact he was a biological tragedy.

Sometimes Roy was surprised that he could be around Dubois for long periods, yet resist the urge to commit a mercy killing.

"That boy, he's some cute sonofabitch, the way he drove out of that roadblock and into the amusement park," Dubois said as he led Roy down the hall from his office to the satellite-surveillance room. "And that dog of his, just bobbin' its head up and down, up and down, like one of them spring-necked novelties that people put on the rear-window shelves in their cars. That dog, he got palsy or what?"

"I don't know," Roy said.

"My granpap, he once had a dog with palsy. Name was Scooter, but we called him Boomer 'cause he could cut the godawfulest loud farts. I'm talkin' about the dog, you understand, not my granpap."

"Of course," Roy said as they reached the door at the end of the hall.

"Boomer got palsied his last year," Dubois said, hesitating with his hand on the doorknob. "'Course he was older than dirt by then, so it wasn't any surprise. You should've seen that poor hound shake. Palsied up somethin' fierce. Let me tell you, Roy, when old Boomer lifted a hind leg and let go with his stream, all palsied like he was—you dived for cover or wished you was in another county."

"Sounds like someone should have put him to sleep," Roy said as Dubois opened the door.

The Texan followed Roy into the satellite-surveillance center. "Nah, Boomer was a good old dog. If the tables had been turned, that old hound wouldn't never have taken a gun and put granpap to sleep."

Roy really *was* in a good mood. He could have listened to Bobby Dubois for hours.

The satellite-surveillance center was forty feet by sixty feet. Only two of the twelve computer workstations in the middle of the room were manned, both by women wearing headsets and murmuring into mouthpieces as they studied the data streaming across their VDTs. A third technician was working at a light table, examining several large photographic negatives through a magnifying glass.

One of the two longer walls was largely occupied by an immense screen on which was projected a map of the world. Cloud formations were superimposed on it, along with green lettering that indicated weather conditions planetwide.

Red, blue, white, yellow, and green lights blinked steadily, revealing the current positions of scores of satellites. Many were electronic-communications packages handling microwave relays of telephone, television, and radio signals. Others were engaged in topographical mapping, oil exploration, meteorology, astronomy, international espionage, and domestic surveillance, among numerous other tasks.

The owners of those satellites ranged from public corporations to government agencies and military services. Some were the property of nations other than the United States or of businesses based beyond U.S. shores. Regardless of the ownership or origin, however, every satellite on that wall display could be accessed and used by the agency, and the legitimate operators usually remained unaware that their systems had been invaded.

At a U-shaped control console in front of the huge screen, Bobby Dubois said, "The sonofabitch rode straight out of Spaceport Vegas off into the desert, and our boys weren't equipped to chase around playin' Lawrence of Arabia."

"Did you put up a chopper to track him?"

"Weather turned bad too fast. A real toad-drowner, rain comin' down like every angel in Heaven was takin' a leak at the same time."

Dubois pushed a button on the console, and the map of the world faded from the wall. An actual satellite view of Oregon, Idaho, California, and Nevada appeared in its place. Seen from orbit, the boundaries of those four states would have been difficult to define, so borders were overlaid in orange lines.

Western and southern Oregon, southern Idaho, northern through central California, and all of Nevada were concealed below a dense layer of clouds.

"This here's a direct satellite feed. There's just a three-minute delay for transmission and then conversion of the digital code back into images again," said Dubois.

Along eastern Nevada and eastern Idaho, soft pulses of light rippled through the clouds. Roy knew that he was seeing lightning from above the storm. It was strangely beautiful.

"Right now, the only storm activity is out on the eastern edge of the front. 'Cept for an isolated patch of spit-thin rain here and there, things are pretty quiet all the way back to the ass-end of Oregon. But we can't just do a look-down for the sonofabitch, not even with infrared. It'd be like trying to see the bottom of a soup bowl through clam chowder."

"How long until clear skies?" Roy asked.

"There's a kick-ass wind at higher altitudes, pushing the front east–southeast, so we should have a clear look at the whole Mojave and surrounding territory before dawn."

A surveillance subject, sitting in bright sunshine and reading a newspaper, could be filmed from a satellite with sufficiently high resolution that the headlines on his paper would be legible. However, in clear weather, in an unpopulated wasteland that boasted no animals as large as a man, locating and identifying a moving object as large as a Ford Explorer would not be easy, because the territory to be examined was so vast. Nevertheless, it could be done.

Roy said, "He could leave the desert for one highway or another, put the pedal to the metal, and be long gone by morning."

"Damn few paved roads in this part of the state. We got lookout teams in every direction, on every serious highway and sorry strip of blacktop. Interstate Fifteen, Federal Highway Ninety-five, Federal Highway Ninety-three. Plus State Routes One-forty-six, One-fifty-six, One-fifty-eight, One-sixty, One-sixty-eight, and One-sixty-nine. Lookin' for a green Ford Explorer with some body damage fore and aft. Lookin' for a man with a dog in *any* vehicle. Lookin' for a man with a big facial scar. Hell, we got this whole part of the state locked down tighter than a mosquito's butt."

"Unless he already got off the desert and back onto a highway before you put your men in place."

"We moved quick. Anyway, in a storm as bad as that one, goin' overland, he made piss-poor time. Fact is, he's damn lucky if he didn't bog down somewhere, four-wheel drive or no four-wheel drive. We'll nail the sonofabitch tomorrow."

"I hope you're right," Roy said.

"I'd bet my pecker on it."

"And they say Las Vegas locals aren't big gamblers."

"How's he tied up with the woman anyway?"

"I wish I knew," Roy said, watching as lightning flowered softly under the clouds on the leading edge of the storm front. "What about this tape of the conversation between Grant and the old woman?"

"You want to hear that?"

"Yes."

"It starts from when he first says the name Hannah Rainey."

"Let's give it a listen," Roy said, turning away from the wall display.

All the way down the hall, into the elevator, and down to the deepest subterranean level of the building, Dubois talked about the best places to get good chili in Vegas, as though he had reason to believe that Roy cared. "There's this joint on Paradise Road, the chili's so hot some folks been known to spontaneously combust from eatin' it, *whoosh*, they just go up like torches."

The elevator reached the subbasement.

"We're talkin' chili that makes you sweat from your fingernails, makes your belly button pop out like a meat thermometer."

The doors slid open.

Roy stepped into a windowless concrete room.

Along the far wall were scores of recording machines.

In the middle of the room, rising from a computer workstation, was the most stunningly gorgeous woman Roy had ever seen, blond and green-eyed, so beautiful that she took his breath away, so beautiful that she set his heart to racing and sent his blood pressure soaring high into the stroke-risk zone, so achingly beautiful that no words could adequately describe her—nor could any music ever written be sweet enough to celebrate her—so beautiful and so incomparable that he couldn't breathe or speak, so radiant that she blinded him to the dreariness of that bunker and left him surrounded by her magnificent light.

ᔓ

The flood had disappeared over the cliff like bathwater down a tub drain. The arroyo was now merely an enormous ditch.

To a considerable depth, the soil was mostly sand, extremely porous, so the rain had not puddled on it. The downpour had filtered quickly into a deep aquifer. The surface had dried out and firmed up almost as rapidly as the empty channel had previously turned into a racing, spumous river.

Nevertheless, before she had risked taking the Range Rover into the channel, although the machine was as surefooted as a tank, she had walked the route from the eroded arroyo wall to the Explorer and checked the condition of the ground. Satisfied that the bed of the ghost river wasn't muddy or soft and that it would provide sufficient traction, she had driven the Rover into that declivity and had backed between the two columns of rock to the suspended Explorer.

Even now, after rescuing the dog and putting him in the back of the Rover, and after disentangling Grant from his safety harness, she was amazed by the precarious position in which the Explorer had come to rest. She was tempted to lean past the unconscious man and look through the gaping hole where the side window had been, but even if she could have seen much in the darkness, she knew that she wouldn't enjoy the view.

The flood tide had lifted the truck more than ten feet above the floor of the arroyo before wedging it in that pincer of stone, on the brink of the cliff. Now that the river had vanished beneath it, the Explorer hung up there, its four wheels in midair, as though gripped in a pair of tweezers that belonged to a giant.

When she'd first seen it, she'd stood in childlike wonder, mouth open and eyes wide. She was no less astonished than she would have been if she'd seen a flying saucer and its unearthly crew.

She'd been certain that Grant had been swept out of the truck and carried to his death. Or that he was dead inside.

To get up to his truck, she'd had to back her Rover under it, putting the rear wheels uncomfortably close to the edge of the cliff. Then she had stood on the roof, which brought her head just to the bottom of the Explorer's front passenger door. She had reached up to the handle and, in spite of the awkward angle, had managed to open the door.

Water poured out, but the dog was what startled her. Whimpering and miserable, huddled on the passenger seat, he had peered down at her with a mixture of alarm and yearning.

She didn't want him jumping onto the Rover. He might slip on that smooth surface and fracture a leg, or tumble and break his neck.

Although the pooch hadn't looked as if he would perform any canine stunts, she had warned him to stay where he was. She climbed down from the Rover, drove it forward five yards, turned it around to direct the headlights on the ground under the Explorer, got out again, and coaxed the dog to jump to the sandy riverbed.

He needed a *lot* of coaxing. Poised on the edge of the seat, he repeatedly built up the courage to jump. But each time, he turned his head away at the last moment and shrank back, as if he were facing a chasm instead of a ten- or twelve-foot drop.

Finally, she remembered how Theda Davidowitz had often talked to Sparkle, and she tried the same approach with this dog: "Come on, sweetums, come to mama, come on. Little sweetums, little pretty-eyed snookie-wookums."

In the truck above, the pooch pricked one ear and regarded her with acute interest.

"Come here, come on, snookums, little sweetums."

He began to quiver with excitement.

"Come to mama. Come on, little pretty eyes."

The dog crouched on the seat, muscles tensed, poised to leap.

"Come give mama a kissie, little cutie, little cutie baby."

She felt idiotic, but the dog jumped. He sprang out of the open door of the Explorer, sailed in a long graceful arc through the night air, and landed on all fours.

He was so startled by his own agility and bravery that he turned to look up at the truck and then sat down as if in shock. He flopped onto his side, breathing hard.

She had to carry him to the Rover and lay him in the cargo area directly behind the front seat. He repeatedly rolled his eyes at her, and he licked her hand once.

"You're a strange one," she said, and the dog sighed.

Then she had turned the Rover around again, backed it under the suspended Explorer, and climbed up to find Spencer Grant slumped behind the steering wheel, woozily conscious.

Now he was out cold again. He was murmuring to someone in a dream, and she wondered how she would get him out of the Explorer if he didn't revive soon.

She tried talking to him and shaking him gently, but she wasn't able to get a response from him. He was already damp and shivering, so there was no point in scooping a handful of water off the floor and splashing his face.

His injuries needed to be treated as soon as possible, but that was not the primary reason that she was anxious to get him into the Rover and away from there. Dangerous people were searching for him. With their resources, even hampered by weather and terrain, they would find him if she didn't quickly move him to a secure place.

Grant solved her dilemma not merely by regaining consciousness but by virtually *exploding* out of his unnatural sleep. With a gasp and a wordless cry, he bolted upright in his seat, bathed in a sudden sweat yet shuddering so furiously that his teeth chattered.

He was face-to-face with her, inches away, and even in the poor light, she saw the horror in his eyes. Worse, there was a bleakness that transmitted his chill deep into her own heart.

He spoke urgently, though exhaustion and thirst had reduced his voice to a coarse whisper: "*Nobody knows.*"

"It's all right," she said.

"*Nobody. Nobody knows.*"

"Easy. You'll be okay."

"*Nobody knows,*" he insisted, and he seemed to be caught between fear and grief, between terror and tears.

A terrible hopelessness informed his tortured voice and every aspect of his face to such an extent that she was struck speechless. It seemed foolish to continue to repeat meaningless reassurances to a man who appeared to have been granted a vision of the cankerous souls in Hades.

Though he looked into her eyes, Spencer seemed to be gazing at someone or something far away, and he was speaking in a rush of words, more to himself than to her: "*It's a chain, iron chain, it runs through me, through my brain, my heart, through my guts, a chain, no way to get loose, no escape.*"

He was scaring her. She hadn't thought that she could be scared any more, at least not easily, certainly not with mere words. But he was scaring her witless.

"Come on, Spencer," she said. "Let's go. Okay? Help me get you out of here."

∽

When the slightly chubby, twinkly-eyed man stepped out of the elevator with Bobby Dubois into the windowless subbasement, he halted in his tracks and gazed at Eve as a starving man might have stared at a bowl of peaches and cream.

Eve Jammer was accustomed to having a powerful effect on men. When she had been a topless showgirl on the Las Vegas stage, she had been one beauty among many—yet the eyes of all the men had followed her nearly to the exclusion of the other women, as though something about her face and body was not just more appealing to the eye but so harmonious that it was like a secret siren's song. She drew men's eyes to herself as inevitably as a skillful hypnotist could capture a subject's mind by swinging a gold medallion on a chain or simply with the sinuous movements of his hands.

Even poor little Thurmon Stookey—the dentist who'd had the bad luck to be in the same hotel elevator with the two gorillas from whom Eve had taken the million in cash—had been vulnerable to her charms at a time when he should have been too terrified to entertain the slightest thought of sex. With the two goons dead on the elevator floor and the Korth .38 pointed at his face, Stookey had let his eyes drift from the bore of the revolver to the lush cleavage revealed by Eve's low-cut sweater. Judging by the glimmer that had come into his myopic eyes just as she'd squeezed the trigger, Eve figured that the dentist's final thought had not been *God help me* but *What a set.*

No man had ever affected Eve to even a small fraction of the extent to which she affected most men. Indeed, she could take or leave most men.

Her interest was drawn only to those from whom she might extract money or from whom she might learn the tricks of obtaining and holding on to power. Her ultimate goal was to be extremely rich and feared, not loved. Being an object of fear, totally in control, having the power of life and death over others: *That* was infinitely more erotic than *any* man's body or lovemaking skills could ever be.

Still, when she was introduced to Roy Miro, she felt something unusual. A flutter of the heart. A mild disorientation that was not in the least unpleasant.

What she was feeling couldn't have been called desire. Eve's desires were all exhaustively mapped and labeled, and the periodic satisfaction of each was achieved with mathematical calculation, to a schedule as precise as that kept by a fascist train conductor. She had no time or patience for spontaneity in either business or personal affairs; the intrusion of unplanned passion would have been as repulsive to her as being forced to eat worms.

Undeniably, however, she felt *something* from the first moment she saw Roy Miro. And minute by minute, as they discussed the Grant-Davidowitz tape and then listened to it, her peculiar interest in him increased. An unfamiliar thrill of anticipation coursed through her as she wondered where events were leading.

For the life of her, she couldn't figure out what qualities of the man inspired her fascination. He was rather pleasant looking, with merry blue eyes, a choirboy face, and a sweet smile—but he was not handsome in the usual sense of the word. He was fifteen pounds overweight, somewhat pale, and he didn't appear to be rich. He dressed with less flair than any Nazarene passing out religious publications door-to-door.

Frequently Miro asked her to replay a passage of the Grant-Davidowitz recording, as though it contained a clue that required pondering, but she knew that he had become preoccupied with her and had missed something.

For both Eve and Miro, Bobby Dubois pretty much ceased to exist. In spite of his height and physical awkwardness, in spite of his colorful and ceaseless chatter, Dubois was of no more interest to either of them than were the bunker's plain concrete walls.

When everything on the recording had been played and replayed, Miro went through some shuffle and jive to the effect that he was unable to do anything about Grant for the time being, except wait: wait for him to surface; wait for the skies to clear so a satellite search could begin; wait for search teams already in the field to turn up something; wait for agents investigating other aspects of the case, in other cities, to get back to him. Then he asked Eve if she was free for dinner.

She accepted the invitation with an uncharacteristic lack of coyness. She had a growing sense that what she responded to in the man was some secret power that he possessed, a strength that was mostly hidden and that could be glimpsed only in the self-confidence of his easy smile and in those blue-blue eyes that never revealed anything but amusement, as if this man expected always to have the last laugh.

Although Miro had been assigned a car from the agency pool while he was in Vegas, he rode in her own Honda to a favorite restaurant of hers on Flamingo Road. Reflections of a sea of neon rolled in tidal patterns across low clouds, and the night seemed filled with magic.

She expected to get to know him better over dinner and a couple of glasses of wine—and to understand, by dessert, why he fascinated her. However, his skills as a conversationalist were equivalent to his looks: pleasant enough, but far from beguiling. Nothing that Miro said, nothing that he did, no gesture, no look brought Eve any closer to understanding the curious attraction that he held for her.

By the time they left the restaurant and crossed the parking lot toward her car, she was frustrated and confused. She didn't know whether she should invite him back to her place or not. She didn't want sex with him. It wasn't that kind of attraction, exactly. Of course, some men revealed their truest selves when they had sex: by what they liked to do, by how they did it, by what they said and how they acted both during and after. But she didn't want to take him home, do it with him, get all sweaty, go the whole disgusting route, and *still* not understand what it was about him that so intrigued her.

She was in a dilemma.

Then, as they drew near to her car, with the cold wind soughing in a nearby row of palm trees and the air scented with the aroma of charcoal-broiled steaks from the restaurant, Roy Miro did the most unexpected and outrageous thing that Eve had ever seen in thirty-three years of outrageous experience.

∽

An immeasurable time after getting down from the Explorer and into the Range Rover—which could have been an hour or two minutes or thirty days and thirty nights, for all he knew—Spencer woke and saw a herd of tumbleweed pacing them. The shadows of mesquite and paddle-leaf cactus leaped through the headlights.

He rolled his head to the left, against the back of the seat, and saw Valerie behind the wheel. "Hi."

"Hi, there."

"How'd you get here?"

"That's too complicated for you right now."

"I'm a complicated guy."

"I don't doubt it."

"Where we going?"

"Away."

"Good."

"How're you feeling?"

"Woozy."

"Don't pee on the seat," she said with obvious amusement.

He said, "I'll try not to."

"Good."

"Where's my dog?"

"Who do you think's licking your ear?"

"Oh."

"He's right there behind you."

"Hi, pal."

"What's his name?" she asked.

"Rocky."

"You've got to be kidding."

"About what?"

"The name. Doesn't fit."

"I named him that so he'd have more confidence."

"Isn't working," she said.

Strange rock formations loomed, like temples to gods forgotten before human beings had been capable of conceiving the idea of time and counting the passage of days. They awed him, and she drove among them with great expertise, whipping left and right, down a long hill, onto a vast, dark flatness.

"Never knew his real name," Spencer said.

"Real name?"

"Puppy name. Before the pound."

"Wasn't Rocky."

"Probably not."

"What was it before Spencer?"

"He was never named Spencer."

"So you're clearheaded enough to be evasive."

"Not really. Just habit. What's your name?"

"Valerie Keene."

"Liar."

He went away for a while. When he came around again, there was still desert: sand and stone, scrub and tumbleweed, darkness pierced by head-lights.

"Valerie," he said.

"Yeah?"

"What's your real name?"

"Bess."

"Bess what?"

"Bess Baer."

"Spell it."

"B-A-E-R."

"Really?"

"Really. For now."

"What's that mean?"

"It means what it means."

"It means that's your name now, after Valerie."

"So?"

"What was your name before Valerie?"

"Hannah Rainey."

"Oh, yeah," he said, realizing that he was firing on only four of six cylinders. "Before that?"

"Gina Delucio."

"Was that real?"

"It felt real."

"Is that the name you were born with?"

"You mean my puppy name?"

"Yeah. That your puppy name?"

"Nobody's called me by my puppy name since before I was in the pound," she said.

"You're very funny."

"You like funny women?"

"I must."

" 'And then the funny woman,' " she said, as if reading from a printed page, " 'and the cowardly dog and the mysterious man rode off into the desert in search of their real names.' "

"In search of a place to puke."

"Oh, no."

"Oh, yes."

She applied the brakes, and he flung open the door.

Later, when he woke, still riding through the dark desert, he said, "I have the most god-awful taste in my mouth."

"I don't doubt it."

"What's your name?"

"Bess."

"Bullshit."

"No, Baer. Bess Baer. What's your name?"

"My faithful Indian sidekick calls me Kemosabe."

"How do you feel?"

"Like shit," he said.

"Well, that's what 'Kemosabe' means."

"Are we ever going to stop?"

"Not while we have cloud cover."

"What've clouds got to do with anything?"

"Satellites," she said.

"You are the strangest woman I've ever known."

"Just wait."

"How the *hell* did you find me?"

"Maybe I'm psychic."

"Are you psychic?"

"No."

He sighed and closed his eyes. He could almost imagine that he was on a merry-go-round. "*I* was supposed to find *you*."

"Surprise."

"I wanted to help you."

"Thanks."

He let go of his grip on the world of the waking. For a while all was silent and serene. Then he walked out of the darkness and opened the red door. There were rats in the catacombs.

∽

Roy did a crazy thing. Even as he was doing it, he was amazed at the risk he was taking.

He decided that he should be himself in front of Eve Jammer. His real self. His deeply committed, compassionate, caring self that was never more than half revealed in the bland, bureaucratic functionary that he appeared to be to most people.

Roy was willing to take risks with this stunning woman, because he sensed that her mind was as marvelous as her ravishing face and body. The woman within, so close to emotional and intellectual perfection, would understand him as no one else ever had.

Over dinner, they had not found the key that would open the doors in their souls and let them merge, which was their destiny. As they were leaving the restaurant, Roy was concerned that their moment of opportunity would pass and that their destiny would be thwarted, so he tapped the power of Dr. Kevorkian, which he'd recently absorbed from the television in the Learjet. He found the courage to reveal his true heart to Eve and force the fulfillment of their destiny.

Behind the restaurant, a blue Dodge van was parked three spaces to the right of Eve's Honda, and a man and woman were getting out of it, on their way to dinner. They were in their forties, and the man was in a wheelchair. He was being lowered from a side door of the van on an electric lift, which he operated without assistance.

Otherwise, the parking lot was deserted.

To Eve, Roy said, "Come with me a minute. Come say hello."

"Huh?"

Roy walked directly to the Dodge. "Good evening," he said as he reached under his coat to his shoulder holster.

The couple looked up at him, and both said, "Good evening," with a thread of puzzlement sewn through their voices, as if trying to recall where they had met him before.

"I feel your pain," Roy said as he drew his pistol.

He shot the man in the head.

His second round hit the woman in the throat, but it didn't finish her. She fell to the ground, twitching grotesquely.

Roy stepped past the dead man in the wheelchair. To the woman on the ground, he said, "Sorry," and then he shot her again.

The new silencer on the Beretta worked well. With the February wind moaning through the palm fronds, none of the three shots would have been audible farther than ten feet away.

Roy turned to Eve Jammer.

She looked thunderstruck.

He wondered if he had been too impulsive for a first date.

"So sad," he said, "the quality of life that some people are forced to endure."

Eve looked up from the bodies and met Roy's eyes. She didn't scream or even speak. Of course, she might have been in shock. But he didn't think that was the case. She seemed to want to understand.

Maybe everything would be all right after all.

"Can't leave them like this." He holstered his gun and pulled on his gloves. "They have a right to be treated with dignity."

The remote-control unit that operated the wheelchair lift was attached to the arm of the chair. Roy pressed a button and sent the dead man back up from the parking lot.

He climbed into the van through the double-wide sliding door, which had been pushed to one side. When the wheelchair completed its ascent, he rolled it inside.

Assuming that the man and woman were husband and wife, Roy planned the tableau accordingly. The situation was so public that he didn't have time to be original. He would have to repeat what he had done with the Bettonfields on Wednesday evening in Beverly Hills.

Tall lampposts were spaced around the parking lot. Just enough bluish light came through the open door to allow him to do his work.

He lifted the dead man out of the chair and placed him faceup on the floor. The van was uncarpeted. Roy was remorseful about that, but he had no padding or blankets with which to make the couple's final rest more comfortable.

He pushed the chair into a corner, out of the way.

Outside again, while Eve watched, Roy lifted the dead woman and put her into the van. He climbed in after her and arranged her beside her husband. He folded her right hand around her husband's left.

Both of the woman's eyes were open, as was one of her husband's, and Roy was about to press them shut with his gloved fingers when a better idea occurred to him. He peeled up the husband's closed eyelid and waited to see if it would remain open. It did. He turned the man's head to the left and the woman's head to the right, so they were gazing into each other's eyes, into the eternity that they now shared in a far better realm than Las Vegas, Nevada, far better than any place in this dismal, imperfect world.

He crouched at the feet of the cadavers for a moment, admiring his work. The tenderness expressed by their positions was enormously pleasing to him. Obviously, they had been in love and were now together forever, as any lovers would wish to be.

Eve Jammer stood at the open door, staring at the dead couple. Even the desert wind seemed to be aware of her exceptional beauty and to treasure it, for her golden hair was shaped into exquisitely tapered streamers. She appeared not windblown but wind*adored*.

"It's so sad," Roy said. "What quality of life could they have had—with him imprisoned in a wheelchair, and with her tied to him by bonds of love? Their lives were so limited by his infirmities, their futures tethered to that damned chair. How much better now."

Without saying a word, Eve turned away and walked to the Honda.

Roy got out of the Dodge van and, after one last look at the loving couple, closed the sliding door.

Eve was waiting behind the wheel of her car, with the engine running. If she had been frightened of him, she would have tried to drive away without him or would have run back to the restaurant.

He got in the Honda and buckled his safety harness.

They sat in silence.

Clearly, she intuited that he was no murderer, that what he had done was a moral act, and that he operated on a higher plane than did the average man. Her silence was only indicative of her struggle to translate her intuition into intellectual concepts and thereby more fully understand him.

She drove out of the parking lot.

Roy took off his leather gloves and returned them to the inside coat pocket from which he had gotten them.

For a while, Eve followed a random route through a series of residential neighborhoods, just driving to drive, going nowhere yet.

To Roy, the lights in all the huddled houses no longer seemed to be either warm or mysterious, as they had seemed on other nights and in other neighborhoods, in other cities, when he had cruised similar streets alone. Now they were merely sad: terribly sad little lights that inadequately illuminated the sad little lives of people who would never enjoy a passionate commitment to an ideal, not of the sort that so enriched Roy's life, sad little people who would never rise above the herd as he had risen, who would never experience a transcendent relationship with anyone as exceptional as Eve Jammer.

When at last the time seemed right, he said, "I yearn for a better world. But more than better, Eve. Oh, much more."

She didn't reply.

"Perfection," he said quietly but with great conviction, "in all things. Perfect laws and perfect justice. Perfect beauty. I dream of a perfect society, where everyone enjoys perfect health, perfect equality, in which the economy hums always like a perfectly tuned machine, where everyone lives in harmony with everyone else and with nature. Where no offense is ever given or taken. Where all dreams are perfectly rational and considerate. Where *all* dreams come true."

He was so moved by his soliloquy that his voice became thick toward the end of it, and he had to blink back tears.

Still she said nothing.

Night streets. Lighted windows. Little houses, little lives. So much confusion, sadness, yearning, and alienation in those houses.

"I do what I can," he said, "to make an ideal world. I scrub away some of its imperfect elements and push it inch by grudging inch toward perfection. Oh, not that I think I can change the world. Not alone, not me, and not even a thousand or a hundred thousand like me. But I light a little candle whenever I can, one little candle after another, pushing back the darkness one small shadow at a time."

They were on the east side of town, almost at the city limits, cruising into higher land and less populated neighborhoods than they had traveled previously. At an intersection, she suddenly made a U-turn and headed back into the sea of lights from which they'd come.

"You may say I'm a dreamer," Roy admitted. "But I'm not the only one. I think you're a dreamer too, Eve, in your own special way. If you can admit being a dreamer . . . maybe if all of us dreamers can admit it and join together, the world could someday live as one."

Her silence was now profound.

He dared to look at her, and she was more devastating than he had remembered. His heart thudded slow and heavy, weighed down by the sweet burden of her beauty.

When at last she spoke, her voice was quavery. "You didn't take anything from them."

It wasn't fear that made her words shimmer as they passed along her elegant throat and across her ripe lips but, rather, a tremendous excitement. And her tremulous voice in turn excited Roy. He said, "No. Nothing."

"Not even the money from her purse or his wallet."

"Of course not. I'm not a taker, Eve. I'm a giver."

"I've never seen . . ." She seemed unable to find the words even to describe what he had done.

"Yes, I know," he said, delighted to see how completely he had swept her away.

". . . never seen such . . ."

"Yes."

". . . never such . . ."

"I know, dear one. I know."

". . . such *power,*" she said.

That was not the word he had thought that she was searching for. But she had pronounced it with such passion, imbued it with so much erotic energy, he could not be disappointed that she had yet to grasp the full meaning of what he had done.

"They're just going out for dinner," she said excitedly. She had begun to drive too fast, recklessly. "Just going out to dinner, an ordinary night, nothing special, and—*wham!*—you whack them! Just like that, Jesus, take them out, and not even to get anything that belongs to them, not even because they crossed you or anything like that. Just for me. Just for me, to show me who you really *are.*"

"Well, yes, for you," he said. "But not only for you, Eve. Don't you see? I removed two imperfect lives from creation, inching the world closer to perfection. And at the same time, I relieved those two sad people of the burden of this cruel life, this imperfect world, where nothing could ever be as they hoped. I gave to the world, and I gave to those poor people, and there were no losers."

"You're like the wind," she said breathlessly, "like a fantastic storm wind, hurricane, tornado, except there's no weatherman to warn anyone you're coming. You've got the power of the storm, you're a force of nature—sweeping out of nowhere, for no reason. *Wham!*"

Worried that she was missing the point, Roy said, "Wait, wait a minute, Eve, listen to me."

She was so excited that she couldn't drive any more. She angled the Honda to the curb, tramped the brakes so hard that Roy would have been pitched into the windshield if his harness hadn't been buckled.

Slamming the gearshift into park with nearly enough force to snap it off, she turned to him. "You're an earthquake, just like an earthquake. People can be walking along, carefree, sun shining, birds singing—and then the ground opens and just swallows them up."

She laughed with delight. Hers was a girlish, trilling, musical laugh, so infectious that he had difficulty not laughing with her.

He took her hands in his. They were elegant, long-fingered, as exquisitely shaped as the hands of Guinevere, and the touch of them was more than any man deserved.

Unfortunately, the radius and ulna, above the perfectly shaped carpals of her wrist, were not of the supreme caliber of the bones in her hands. He was careful not to look at them. Or touch them.

"Eve, listen. You must understand. It's extremely important that you understand."

She grew solemn at once, realizing that they had reached a most serious point in their relationship. She was even more beautiful when somber than when laughing.

He said, "You're right, this is a great power. The greatest of all powers, and that's why you've got to be clear about it."

Although the only light in the car came from the instrument panel, her green eyes blazed as if with the reflection of summer sun. They were perfect eyes, as flawless and compelling as those of the woman for whom he had been hunting this past year, whose photograph he carried in his wallet.

Eve's left *brow* was perfect too. But a slight irregularity marred her right superciliary arch, above her eye socket: It was regrettably too prominent, only fractionally more so than the left, formed with barely half a gram too much bone, but nevertheless out of balance and shy of the perfection on the left.

That was okay. He could live with that. He would just focus on her angelic eyes below her brow, and on each of her incomparable hands below her knobby radius and ulna. Though flawed, she was the only woman he'd ever seen with more than one perfect feature. Ever, ever, ever. And her treasures weren't limited to her hands and eyes.

"Unlike other power, Eve, this doesn't flow from anger," he explained, wanting this precious woman to understand his mission and his innermost self. "It doesn't come from hatred, either. It's not the power of rage, envy, bitterness, greed. It's not like the power some people find in courage or honor—or that they gain from a belief in God. It transcends those powers, Eve. Do you know what it is?"

She was rapt, unable to speak. She only shook her head: no.

"My power," he said, "is the power of compassion."

"Compassion," she whispered.

"Compassion. If you try to understand other people, to feel their pain, to really *know* the anguish of their lives, to love them in spite of their faults, you're overcome by such pity, such *intense* pity, it's intolerable. It must be relieved. So you tap into the immeasurable, inexhaustible power of compassion. You *act* to relieve suffering, to ease the world a hairsbreadth closer to perfection."

"Compassion," she whispered again, as if she had never heard the word before, or as if he had shown her a definition of it that she had never previously appreciated.

Roy could not look away from her mouth as she repeated the word twice again. Her lips were divine. He couldn't imagine why he had thought that Melissa Wicklun's lips were perfect, for Eve's lips made Melissa's seem less attractive than those of a leprous toad. These were lips beside which the ripest plum would look as withered as a prune, beside which the sweetest strawberry would look sour.

Playing Henry Higgins to her Eliza Doolittle, he continued her first lesson in moral refinement: "When you're motivated solely by compassion, when no personal gain is involved, then *any* act is moral, utterly moral, and you owe no explanations to anyone, ever. Acting from compassion, you're freed forever from doubt, and that is a power like no other."

"Any act," she said, so overcome by the concept that she could barely find enough breath to speak.

"Any," he assured her.

She licked her lips.

Oh, God, her tongue was so delicate, glistened so intriguingly, slipped so sensuously across her lips, was so *perfectly* tapered that a faint sigh of ecstasy escaped him before he was quite aware of it.

Perfect lips. Perfect tongue. If only her chin had not been tragically fleshy. Others might think it was the chin of a goddess, but Roy was cursed with a greater sensitivity to imperfection than were other men. He was acutely aware of the smidgin of excess fat that lent her chin a barely perceptible *puffy* look. He would just have to focus on her lips, on her tongue, and not allow his gaze to drift down from there.

"How many have you done?" she asked.

"Done? Oh. You mean, like back at the restaurant."

"Yes. How many?"

"Well, I don't count them. That would seem . . . I don't know . . . it would seem prideful. I don't want praise. No. My satisfaction is just in doing what I know is right. It's a very private satisfaction."

"How many?" she persisted. "A rough estimate."

"Oh, I don't know. Over the years . . . a couple of hundred, a few hundred, something like that."

She closed her eyes and shivered. "When you do them . . . just before you do them and they look in your eyes, are they afraid?"

"Yes, but I wish they weren't. I wish they could see that I know their anguish, that I'm acting from compassion, that it's going to be quick and painless."

With her own eyes closed, half swooning, she said, "They look into your eyes, and they see the power you have over them, the power of a *storm*, and they're afraid."

He released her right hand and pointed his forefinger at the flat section of bone immediately above the root of her perfect nose. It was a nose that made all the other fine noses seem as unformed as the "nose" on a coconut shell. Slowly, he moved his finger toward her face as he said, "You. Have. The. Most. Exquisite. Glabella. I. Have. Ever. Seen."

With the last word, he touched his finger to her glabella, the flat portion of the front skull bone between her unimpeachable left superciliary arch and her unfortunately bony right superciliary arch, directly above her nose.

Although her eyes were closed, Eve didn't flinch with surprise at his touch. She seemed to have developed such a closeness to him, so quickly, that she was aware of his every intention and slightest movement without the aid of vision—and without relying on any of the other five senses, for that matter.

He took his finger off her glabella. "Do you believe in fate?"

"Yes."

"We *are* fate."

She opened her eyes and said, "Let's go back to my place."

On the trip to her house, she broke traffic laws by the score. Roy didn't approve, but he withheld his criticism.

She lived in a small two-story house in a recently completed tract. It was nearly identical to the other houses on the street.

Roy had expected glamour. Disappointed, he reminded himself that Eve, though stunning, was but another woefully underpaid bureaucrat.

As they waited in the Honda, in the driveway, for the automatic garage door to finish lifting out of the way, he said, "How did a woman like you wind up working in the agency?"

"I wanted the job, and my father had the influence to make it happen," she said, driving into the garage.

"Who's your father?"

"He's a rotten sonofabitch," she said. "I hate him. Let's not go into all that, Roy, please. Don't ruin the mood."

The last thing that he wanted to do was ruin the mood.

Out of the car, at the door between the garage and the house, as Eve fumbled in her purse for keys, she was suddenly nervous and clumsy. She turned to him, leaned close. "Oh, God, I can't stop thinking about it, how you did them, how you just walked up and did them. Such *power* in the way you did it."

She was virtually smouldering with desire. He could feel the heat rolling off her, driving the February chill out of the garage.

"You have so much to teach me," she said.

A turning point in their relationship had arrived. Roy needed to explain one more thing about himself. He'd been delaying bringing it up, for fear she would not understand this one quirk as easily as she had absorbed and accepted what he'd had to say about the power of compassion. But he could delay no longer.

As Eve returned her attention to her purse and at last extracted the ring of keys from it, Roy said, "I want to see you undressed."

"Yes, darling, yes," she said, and the keys clinked noisily as she searched for the right one on the ring.

He said, "I want to see you entirely nude."

"Entirely, yes, all for you."

"I have to know how much of the rest of you is as perfect as the perfect parts that I can already see."

"You're so sweet," she said, hastily inserting the correct key into the dead-bolt lock.

"From the soles of your feet to the curve of your spine, to the backs of your ears, to the pores in the skin of your scalp. I want to see every inch of you, nothing hidden, nothing at all."

Throwing open the unlocked door, rushing inside, switching on a kitchen light, she said, "Oh, you are too much, you are so *strong*. Every crevice, darling, every inch and fold and crevice."

As she dropped her purse and keys on the kitchen table and began to strip out of her coat, he followed her inside and said, "But that doesn't mean *I* want to undress or . . . or anything."

That stopped her. She blinked at him.

He said, "I want to see. And touch you, but not much of that. Just a little touching, when something looks perfect, to feel if the skin is as smooth and silky as it appears, to test the resilience, to feel if the muscle tension is as wonderful as it looks. You don't have to touch me at all." He hurried on, afraid that he was losing her. "I want to make love to you, to the perfect parts of you, make passionate love with my eyes, with a few quick touches, perhaps, but with nothing else. I don't want to spoil it by doing . . . what other people do. Don't want to debase it. Don't need that sort of thing."

She stared at him so long that he almost turned and fled.

Suddenly Eve squealed shrilly, and Roy took a step back, more than half afraid of her. Offended and humiliated, she might fling herself at him and claw his face, tear at his eyes.

Then, to his astonishment, he realized that she was laughing, though not cruelly, not laughing at him. She was laughing with pure joy. She hugged herself and squealed as if she were a schoolgirl, and her sublime green eyes shone with delight.

"My God," she said tremulously, "you're even better than you seemed, even better than I thought, better than I could ever hope. You're perfect, Roy, you're perfect, perfect."

He smiled uncertainly. He was still not entirely free of the fear that she was going to claw him.

Eve grabbed his right hand, pulled him through the kitchen, across a dining room, snapping on lights and talking as she went: "I was willing . . . if you wanted *that*. But that's not what I want, either, all that pawing and squeezing, all that sweating, it *disgusts* me, having another person's sweat all over me, all slick and sticky with another person's sweat, I can't stand that, it *sickens* me."

"Fluids," he said with revulsion, "how can there be anything *sexy* about another person's fluids, exchanging fluids?"

With growing excitement, pulling him into a hallway, Eve said, "Fluids, my God, doesn't it make you want to die, just *die*, with all the fluids that have to be involved, so much that's *wet*. They all want to lick and suck my breasts, all that saliva, it's so hideous, and shoving their tongues in my mouth—"

"*Spittle!*" he said, grimacing. "What's so erotic about swapping spit, for God's sake?"

They had reached the threshold of her bedroom. He stopped her on the brink of the paradise that they were about to create together.

"If I ever kiss you," he promised, "it'll be a dry kiss, as dry as paper, dry as sand."

Eve was shaking with excitement.

"No tongue," he swore. "Even the lips mustn't be moist."

"And never lips to lips—"

"—because then even in a dry kiss—"

"—we'd be swapping—"

"—breath for breath—"

"—and there's moisture in breath—"

"—vapors from the lungs," he said.

With a gladdening of his heart almost too sweet to endure, Roy knew that this splendid woman was, indeed, more like him than he ever could have hoped when he first stepped out of that elevator and saw her. They were two voices in harmony, two hearts beating in unison, two souls soaring to the same song, emphatically simpatico.

"No man has ever been in this bedroom," she said, leading him across the threshold. "Only you. Only you."

The portion of the walls immediately to the left and right of the bed, as well as the area of the ceiling directly above it, was mirrored. Otherwise, the walls and ceiling were upholstered with midnight-blue satin the precise shade of the carpet. A single chair stood in a corner, upholstered in silvery silk. The two windows were covered with polished-nickel blinds. The bed was sleek and modern, with radius footboard, bookcase headboard, tall flanking cabinets, and a light bridge; it was finished with several coats of high-gloss, midnight-blue lacquer in which glimmered silvery speckles like stars. Above the headboard was another mirror. Instead of a bedspread, she had a silver-fox fur throw—"Just fake fur," she assured him when he expressed concern about the rights of helpless animals—which was the most lustrous and luxurious thing he had ever seen.

Here was the glamour for which Roy had yearned.

The computerized lighting was voice-activated. It offered six distinct moods through clever combinations of strategically placed halogen pin spots (with a variety of colored lenses), mirror-framing neon in three colors (that could be displayed singly or two or three at a time), and imaginative applications of fiber optics. Furthermore, each mood could be subtly adjusted by a voice-activated rheostat that responded to the commands "up" and "down."

When Eve touched a button on the headboard, the tambour doors on the tall bed-flanking cabinets hummed up, out of sight. Shelves were revealed, laden with bottles of lotions and scented oils, ten or twelve rubber phalluses in various sizes and colors, and a collection of battery-powered and hand-operated sex toys that were bewildering in their design and complexity.

Eve switched on a CD player with a hundred-disc carousel and set it for random play. "It's loaded with everything from Rod Stewart to Metallica, Elton John, Garth Brooks, the Beatles, the Bee Gees, Bruce Springsteen, Bob Seger, Screamin' Jay Hawkins, James Brown and the Famous Flames, and Bach's *Goldberg Variations*. Somehow it's more exciting when there's so many different kinds of music and when you never know what will be playing next."

After taking off his topcoat but not his suit jacket, Roy Miro moved the upholstered chair out of the corner. He positioned it to one side of the bed, near the footboard, to ensure a glorious view yet to avoid, as much as possible, casting his reflections in the mirrors and spoiling the multitudinous images of *her* perfection.

He sat in the chair and smiled.

She stood beside the bed, fully clothed, while Elton John sang about healing hands. "This is like a dream. To be here, doing exactly what I like to do, but with someone who can appreciate me—"

"I appreciate you, I do."

"—who can adore me—"

"I adore you."

"—who can surrender to me—"

"I'm yours."

"—without soiling the beauty of it."

"No fluids. No pawing."

"Suddenly," she said, "I'm as shy as a virgin."

"I could stare at you for hours, fully clothed."

She tore off her blouse so violently that buttons popped and the fabric ripped. In a minute she was completely nude, and more of what had been hidden proved to be perfect than imperfect.

Reveling in his gasp of pleased disbelief, she said, "You see why I don't like to make love in the usual way? When I have me, what do I need with anyone else?"

Thereafter, she turned from him and proceeded as she would have done if he'd not been there. Clearly, she took intense satisfaction from knowing that she could hold him totally in her power without ever having to touch him.

She stood before the mirror, examining herself from every angle, caressing herself tenderly, wonderingly, and her rapture at what she saw was so exciting to Roy that he could draw only shallow breaths.

When she finally went to the bed, with Bruce Springsteen singing about whiskey and cars, she cast off the silver-fox throw. For just a moment, Roy was disappointed, for he had wanted to see her writhing upon those lustrous pelts, whether faux or real. But she pulled back the top sheet and the lower sheet as well, revealing a black rubber mattress cover that instantly intrigued him.

From a shelf in one of the open cabinets, she removed a bottle of jewel-pure amber oil, unscrewed the cap, and poured a small pool of it in the center of the bed. A subtle and appealing fragrance, as light and fresh as a spring breeze, drifted to Roy: not a floral scent, but spices—cinnamon, ginger, and other, more exotic ingredients.

While James Brown sang about urgent desire, Eve rolled onto the big bed, straddling the puddle of oil. She anointed her hands and began working the amber essence into her flawless skin. For fifteen minutes, her hands moved knowingly over every curve and plane of her body, lingering at each lovely, yielding roundness and at each shadowy, mysterious cleft. More often than not, what Eve touched was perfect. But when she touched a part that was beneath Roy's standards and dismaying to him, he focused on her hands, for they themselves were without flaw—at least below the too-bony radii and ulnae.

The sight of Eve upon the glistening black rubber, her lush body all gold and pink, slick with a fluid that was satisfyingly pure and not of human origin, had elevated Roy Miro to a spiritual plane that he had never before attained, not even by the use of secret Eastern techniques of meditation, not even when a channeler had once brought forth the spirit of his dead mother at a séance in Pacific Heights, not even with peyote or vibrating crystals or high-colonic therapy administered by an innocent-looking twenty-year-old technician dressed accommodatingly as a Girl Scout. And judging by the lazy pace that she had set, Eve expected to spend hours in the exploration of her magnificent self.

Consequently, Roy did something that he had never done before. He took his pager from his pocket, and because there was no way to switch off the beeper on this particular model, he popped open the plastic plate on the back and removed the batteries.

For one night, his country would have to get along without him, and suffering humanity would have to make do without its champion.

✧

Pain brought Spencer out of a black-and-white dream featuring surreal architecture and mutant biology, all the more disturbing for the lack of color. His entire body was a mass of chronic aches, dull and relentlessly throbbing, but a sharp pain in the top of his head was what broke the chains of his unnatural sleep.

It was still night. Or night again. He didn't know which.

He was lying on his back, on an air mattress, under a blanket. His shoulders and head were elevated by a pillow and by something under the pillow.

The soft hissing sound and characteristic eerie glow of a Coleman lantern identified the light source somewhere behind him.

The lambent light revealed weather-smoothed rock formations to the left and right. Directly ahead of him lay a slab of what he supposed was the Mojave with an icing of night, which the beams of the lantern couldn't melt. Overhead, stretched from one thrust of rock to the other, was a cover of desert-camouflage canvas.

Another sharp pain lanced across his scalp.

"Be still," she said.

He realized that his pillow rested on her crossed legs and that his head lay in her lap.

"What're you doing?" He was spooked by the weakness of his own voice.

She said, "Sewing up this laceration."

"You can't do that."

"It keeps breaking open and bleeding."

"I'm not a quilt."

"What's that supposed to mean?"

"You're not a doctor."

"Aren't I?"

"Are you?"

"No. *Be still.*"

"It hurts."

"Of course."

"It'll get infected," he worried.

"I shaved the area first, then sterilized it."

"You shaved my *head?*"

"Just one little spot, around the gash."

"Do you have *any* idea what you're doing?"

"You mean in terms of barbering or doctoring?"

"Either one."

"I've got a little basic knowledge."

"Ouch, damn it!"

"If you're going to be such a baby, I'll use a spritz of local anesthetic."

"You have that? Why didn't you use it?"

"You were already unconscious."

He closed his eyes, walked through a black-and-white place made of bones, under an arch of skulls, and then opened his eyes again and said, "Well, I'm not now."

"You're not what?"

"Unconscious," he said.

"You just were again. A few minutes passed between our last exchange and this one. And while you were out that time, I almost finished. Another stitch and I'm through."

"Why'd we stop?"

"You weren't traveling well."

"Sure, I was."

"You needed some treatment. Now you need rest. Besides, the cloud cover is breaking up fast."

"Got to go. Early bird gets the tomato."

"Tomato? That's interesting."

He frowned. "I say tomato? Why're you trying to confuse me?"

"Because it's so easy. There—the last suture."

Spencer closed his grainy eyes. In the somber black-and-white world, jackals with human faces were prowling the vine-tangled rubble of a once great cathedral. He could hear children crying in rooms hidden beneath the ruins.

When he opened his eyes, he found that he was lying flat. His head was now elevated only a couple of inches on the pillow.

Valerie was sitting on the ground beside him, watching over him. Her dark hair fell softly along one side of her face, and she was pretty in the lamplight.

"You're pretty in the lamplight," he said.

"Next you'll be asking if I'm an Aquarius or a Capricorn."

"Nah, I don't give a shit."

She laughed.

"I like your laugh," he said.

She smiled, turned her head, and ruminated on the dark desert.

He said, "What do you like about me?"

"I like your dog."

"He's a great dog. What else?"

Looking at him again, she said, "You've got nice eyes."

"I do?"

"Honest eyes."

"Are they? Used to have nice hair too. All shaved off now. I was butchered."

"Barbered. Just one small spot."

"Barbered and then butchered. What are you doing out here in the desert?"

She stared at him awhile, then looked away without answering.

He wouldn't let her off that easily. "What are you doing out here? I'll just keep asking until the repetition drives you insane. What are you doing out here?"

"Saving your ass."

"Tricky. I mean, what were you doing here in the first place?"

"Looking for you."

"Why?" he wondered.

"Because you've been looking for me."

"But how'd you find me, for God's sake?"

"Ouija board."

"I don't think I can believe anything you say."

"You're right. It was Tarot cards."

"Who're we running from?"

She shrugged. The desert engaged her attention again. At last she said, "History, I guess."

"There you go, trying to confuse me again."

"Specifically, the cockroach."

"We're running from a cockroach?"

"That's what I call him, 'cause it infuriates him."

His gaze rolled from Valerie to the tarp that hung ten feet above them. "Why the roof?"

"Blends with the terrain. It's a heat-dispersing fabric too, so we won't show up strong on any infrared look-down."

"Look-down?"

"Eyes in the sky."

"God?"

"No, the cockroach."

"The cockroach has eyes in the sky?"

"He and his people, yeah."

Spencer thought about that. Finally he said, "I'm not sure if I'm awake or dreaming."

"Some days," she said, "neither am I."

In the black-and-white world, the sky seethed with eyes, and a great white owl flew overhead, casting a moonshadow in the shape of an angel.

∽

Eve's desire was insatiable, and her energy was inexhaustible, as though each protracted bout of ecstasy electrified rather than enervated her. At the end of an hour, she seemed more vital than ever, more beautiful, aglow.

Before Roy's adoring eyes, her incredible body seemed to be sculpted and pumped up by her ceaseless rhythmic flexing-contracting-flexing, by her writhing-thrashing-thrusting, just as a long session of lifting weights pumped up a bodybuilder. After years of exploring all the ways she could satisfy herself, she enjoyed a flexibility that Roy judged to be somewhere between that of a gold-medal Olympic gymnast and a carnival contortionist, combined with the endurance of an Alaskan dogsled team. There was no doubt whatsoever that a session in bed with herself provided a thorough workout for every muscle from her radiant head to her cute toes.

Regardless of the astounding knots into which she tied herself, regardless of the bizarre intimacies she took with herself, she never looked at all grotesque or absurd, but unfailingly beautiful, from any angle, in even the most unlikely acts. She was always milk and honey on that black rubber, peaches and cream, flowing and smooth, the most desirable creature ever to grace the earth.

Halfway through the second hour, Roy was convinced that sixty percent of this angel's features—body and face overall—were perfect by even the most stringent standards. Another thirty-five percent of her was not perfect but so *close* to perfect as to break his heart, and only five percent was plain.

Nothing about her—no slightest line or concavity or convexity—was ugly.

Roy was certain that Eve must soon stop pleasuring herself or otherwise collapse unconscious. But by the end of the second hour, she seemed to have more appetite and capacity than when she'd begun. The power of her sensuality was so great that every piece of music was changed by her horizontal dance, until it seemed that all of it, even the Bach, had been expressly composed as the score for a pornographic movie. From time to time she called out the number of a new lighting arrangement, said "up" or "down" to the rheostat, and her selection was always the most flattering for the next position into which she folded herself.

She was thrilled by watching herself in the mirrors. And by watching herself watch herself. And by watching herself as she watched herself watching herself. The infinity of images bounced back and forth between the mirrors on opposite walls, until she could believe that she had filled the universe with replications of herself. The mirrors seemed magical, transmitting all the energy of each reflection back into her own dynamic flesh, overloading her with power, until she was a runaway blond engine of eroticism.

Sometime during the third hour, batteries gave out in a few of her favorite toys, gears froze in others, and she surrendered herself once more to the expertise of her own bare hands. For a while, in fact, her hands seemed to be separate entities from her, each alive in its own right. They were in such a frenzy of lust that they couldn't occupy themselves with just one of her many treasures for any length of time; they kept sliding over her ample curves, up-around-down her oiled skin, massaging and tweaking and caressing and stroking one delight after another. They were like a pair of starving diners at a fabulous smorgasbord that had been prepared to celebrate the imminence of Armageddon, allowed only precious seconds to gorge themselves before all was obliterated by a sun gone nova.

But the sun did not go nova, of course, and eventually—if gradually—those matchless hands slowed, slowed, finally stopped, and were sated. As was their mistress.

For a while, after it was over, Roy couldn't get up from his chair. He couldn't even slump back from the edge of it. He was numb, paralyzed, tingling strangely in every extremity.

In time, Eve rose from the bed and stepped into the adjoining bathroom. When she returned, carrying two plush towels—one damp, one dry—she was no longer gleaming with oil. With the damp cloth, she removed the glistening residue from the rubber mattress cover, then carefully wiped it down with the dry towel. She replaced the bottom sheet that she had earlier cast off.

Roy joined her on the bed. Eve lay on her back, her head on a pillow. He stretched out beside her, on his back, his head on another pillow. She was still gloriously nude, and he remained fully clothed—though at some point during the night, he had loosened his necktie by an inch.

Neither of them made the mistake of trying to comment upon what had transpired. Mere words could not have done the experience justice and might have made a nearly religious odyssey seem somehow tawdry. Anyway, Roy already knew that it had been good for Eve; and as for himself, well, he had seen more physical human perfection in those few hours—and in *action*—than in his entire life theretofore.

After a while, gazing at his darling's reflection on the ceiling as she stared at his, Roy began to talk, and the night entered a new phase of communion that was nearly as intimate, intense, and life-changing as the more physical phase that had preceded it. He spoke further about the power of compassion, refining the concept for her. He told her that humankind always hungered for perfection. People would endure unendurable pain, accept awful deprivation, countenance savage brutalities, live in constant and abject terror—if only they were convinced that their sufferings were the tolls that must be paid on the highway to Utopia, to Heaven on earth.

A person motivated by compassion—yet who was also aware of the masses' willingness to suffer—could change the world. Although he, Roy Miro of the merry blue eyes and Santa Claus smile, did not believe that he possessed the charisma to be that leader of leaders who would launch the next crusade for perfection, he hoped to be one who served that special person and served him well.

"I light my little candles," he said. "One at a time."

For hours Roy talked while Eve interjected numerous questions and perceptive comments. He was excited to see how she thrilled to his ideas almost as she had thrilled to her battery-powered toys and to her own practiced hands.

She was especially moved when he explained how an enlightened society ought to expand on the work of Dr. Kevorkian, compassionately assisting in the self-destruction not solely of suicidal people but also of those poor souls who were deeply depressed, offering easy exits not only to the terminally ill but to the chronically ill, the disabled, the maimed, the psychologically impaired.

And when Roy talked about his concept for a suicide-assistance program for infants, to bring a compassionate solution to the problem of babies born with even the slightest defects that might affect their lives, Eve made a few breathless sounds similar to those that had escaped her in the throes of passion. She pressed her hands to her breasts once more, though this time only in an attempt to quiet the fierce pounding of her heart.

As Eve filled her hands with her bosoms, Roy could not take his eyes off the reflection of her that hovered above him. For a moment he thought that he might weep at the sight of her sixty-percent-perfect face and form.

Sometime before dawn, intellectual orgasms sent them spiraling into sleep, as physical orgasms had not the power to do. Roy was so fulfilled that he didn't even dream.

Hours later, Eve woke him. She had already showered and dressed for the day.

"You've never been more radiant," he told her.

"You've changed my life," she said.

"And you mine."

Although she was late for work in her concrete bunker, she drove him to the Strip hotel at which Prock, his taciturn driver from the previous night, had left his luggage. It was Saturday, but Eve worked seven days a week. Roy admired her commitment.

The desert morning was bright. The sky was a cool, serene blue.

At the hotel, under the entrance portico, before Roy got out of the car, he and Eve made plans to see each other soon, to experience again the pleasures of the night just past.

He stood by the front entrance to watch her drive away. When she was gone, he went inside. He passed the front desk, crossed the raucous casino, and took an elevator to the thirty-sixth and highest floor in the main tower.

He didn't recall putting one foot in front of the other since getting out of her car. As far as he knew, he had floated into the elevator.

He had never imagined that his pursuit of the fugitive bitch and the scarred man would lead him to the most perfect woman in existence. Destiny was a funny thing.

When the doors opened at the thirty-sixth floor, Roy stepped into a long corridor with custom-sculpted, tone-on-tone, wall-to-wall Edward Fields carpet. Wide enough to be considered a gallery rather than a hallway, the space was furnished with early-nineteenth-century French antiques and paintings of some quality from the same period.

This was one of three floors originally designed to offer huge luxury suites, free of charge, to high rollers who were willing to wager fortunes at the games downstairs. The thirty-fifth and thirty-fourth floors still served that function. However, since the agency had purchased the resort for its moneymaking and money-laundering potential, the suites on the top floor had been set aside for the convenience of out-of-town operatives of a certain executive level.

The thirty-sixth floor was served by its own concierge, who was established in a cozy office across from the elevator. Roy picked up the key to his suite from the man on duty, Henri, who didn't so much as raise an eyebrow over the rumpled condition of his guest's suit.

Key in hand, on his way to his rooms, whistling softly, Roy looked forward to a hot shower, a shave, and a lavish room-service breakfast. But when he opened the gilded door and went into the suite, he found two local agents waiting for him. They were in a state of acute but respectful consternation, and only when Roy saw them did he remember that his pager was in one of his jacket pockets and the batteries in another.

"We've been looking everywhere for you since four o'clock this morning," said one of his visitors.

"We've located Grant's Explorer," said the second.

"Abandoned," said the first. "There's a ground search under way for him—"

"—though he might be dead—"

"—or rescued—"

"—because it looks like someone got there before us—"

"—anyway, there are other tire tracks—"

"—so we don't have much time, we've got to move."

In his mind's eye, Roy pictured Eve Jammer: golden and pink, oiled and limber, writhing on black rubber, more perfect than not. That would sustain him, no matter how bad the day proved to be.

∽

Spencer woke in the purple shade under the camouflage tarp, but the desert beyond was bathed in harsh white sunshine.

The light stung his eyes, forcing him to squint, although that pain was as nothing compared with the headache that cleaved his brow from temple to temple, on a slight diagonal. Against the backs of his eyeballs, red lights spun with the abrasiveness of razor-blade pinwheels.

He was hot as well. Burning up. Though he suspected that the day was not especially warm.

Thirsty. His tongue felt swollen. It was stuck to the roof of his mouth. His throat was scratchy, raw.

He was still lying on an air mattress, with his head on a meager pillow, under a blanket in spite of the insufferable heat—but he was no longer lying alone. The woman was snuggled against his right side, exerting a sweet pressure against his flank, hip, thigh. Somehow he had gotten his right arm around her without meeting an objection—*Way to go, Spence, my man!*—and now he relished the feel of her under his hand: so warm, so soft, so sleek, so furry.

Uncommonly furry for a woman.

He turned his head and saw Rocky.

"Hi, pal."

Talking was painful. Each word was a spiny burr being torn out of his throat. His own speech echoed piercingly through his skull, as though it had been stepped up by amplifiers inside his sinus cavities.

The dog licked Spencer's right ear.

Whispering to spare his throat, he said, "Yeah, I love you too."

"Am I interrupting anything?" Valerie asked, dropping to her knees at his left side.

"Just a boy and his dog, hangin' out together."

"How're you feeling?"

"Lousy."

"Are you allergic to any drugs?"

"Hate the taste of Pepto-Bismol."

"Are you allergic to any antibiotics?"

"Everything's spinning."

"Are you allergic to any antibiotics?"

"Strawberries give me hives."

"Are you delirious or just difficult?"

"Both."

Maybe he drifted away for a while, because the next thing he knew, she was giving him an injection in his left arm. He smelled the alcohol with which she had swabbed the area over the vein.

"Antibiotic?" he whispered.

"Liquified strawberries."

The dog was no longer lying at Spencer's side. He was sitting next to the woman, watching with interest as she withdrew the needle from his master's arm.

Spencer said, "I have an infection?"

"Maybe secondary. I'm taking no chances."

"You a nurse?"

"Not a doctor, not a nurse."

"How do you know what to do?"

"He tells me," she said, indicating Rocky.

"Always joking. Must be a comedian."

"Yes, but licensed to give injections. Do you think you can hold down some water?"

"How about bacon and eggs?"

"Water seems hard enough. Last time, you spit it up."

"Disgusting."

"You apologized."

"I'm a gentleman."

Even with her assistance, he was tested to his limits merely by the effort required to sit up. He choked on the water a couple of times, but it tasted cool and sweet, and he thought he would be able to keep it in his stomach.

After she eased him flat onto his back again, he said, "Tell me the truth."

"If I know it."

"Am I dying?"

"No."

"We have one rule around here," he said.

"Which is?"

"Never lie to the dog."

She looked at Rocky.

The mutt wagged his tail.

"Lie to yourself. Lie to me. But never lie to the dog."

"As rules go, it seems pretty sensible," she said.

"So am I dying?"

"I don't know."

"That's better," Spencer said, and he passed out.

∽

Roy Miro took fifteen minutes to shave, brush his teeth, and shower. He changed into chinos, a red cotton sweater, and a tan corduroy jacket. He had no time for the breakfast that he so badly wanted. The concierge, Henri, provided him with two chocolate-almond croissants in a white paper bag and two cups of the finest Colombian coffee in a disposable plastic thermos.

In a corner of the hotel parking lot, a Bell JetRanger executive helicopter was waiting for Roy. As on the jet from L.A., he was the only person in the plushly upholstered passenger cabin.

On the flight out to the discovery in the Mojave, Roy ate both croissants and drank the black coffee while using his attaché case computer to connect to Mama. He reviewed the overnight developments in the investigation.

Not much had happened. Back in southern California, John Kleck had not turned up any leads that might tell them where the woman had gone after abandoning her car at the airport in Orange County. Likewise, they had not succeeded in tracing the telephone number to which Grant's cleverly programmed system had faxed photos of Roy and his men from the Malibu cabin.

The biggest news, which wasn't much, came from San Francisco. The agent tracking down George and Ethel Porth—the grandparents who evidently had raised Spencer Grant following his mother's passing—now knew, from public records, that a death certificate had been issued for Ethel ten years ago. Evidently that was why her husband sold the house at that time. George Porth had died, too, just three years ago. Now that the agent couldn't hope to talk with the Porths about their grandson, he was pursuing other avenues of investigation.

Through Mama, Roy routed a message to the agent's E-mail number in San Francisco, suggesting that he check the records of the probate court to determine if the grandson had been an heir to either the estate of Ethel Porth or that of her husband. Maybe the Porths had not known their grandson as "Spencer Grant" and had used his real name in their wills. If for some inexplicable reason they had aided and abetted his use of that false identity for purposes including enlistment in the military, they nevertheless might have cited his real name when disposing of their estates.

It wasn't much of a lead, but it was worth checking out.

As Roy unplugged the computer and closed it, the pilot of the Jet-Ranger alerted him, by way of the public-address system, that they were one minute from their destination. "Coming up on our right."

Roy leaned to the window beside his seat. They were paralleling a wide arroyo, heading almost due east across the desert.

The glare of sun on sand was intense. He took sunglasses from an inner jacket pocket and put them on.

Ahead, three Jeep wagons, all agency hardware, were clustered in the middle of the dry wash. Eight men were waiting around the vehicles, and most of them were watching the approaching helicopter.

The JetRanger swept over the Jeeps and agents, and suddenly the land below dropped a thousand feet as the chopper soared across the brink of a precipice. Roy's stomach dropped, too, because of the abrupt change in perspective and because of something that he had glimpsed but couldn't quite believe that he had really seen.

High over the valley floor, the pilot entered a wide starboard turn and brought Roy around for a better look at the place where the arroyo met the edge of the cliff. In fact, using the two towers of rock in the middle of the dry wash as a visual fulcrum, he flew a full three-hundred-sixty-degree circle. Roy had a chance to see the Explorer from every amazing angle.

He took off his sunglasses. The truck was still there in the full glare of daylight. He put the glasses on as the JetRanger brought him around again and landed in the arroyo, near the Jeeps.

Disembarking from the chopper, Roy was met by Ted Tavelov, the agent in charge at the site. Tavelov was shorter and twenty years older than Roy, lean and sun browned; he had leathery skin and a dry-as-beef-jerky look from having spent too many years outdoors in the desert. He was dressed in cowboy boots, jeans, a blue flannel shirt, and a Stetson. Although the day was cool, Tavelov wore no jacket, as if he had stored up so much Mojave heat in his sun-cured flesh that he would never again be cold.

As they walked toward the Explorer, the chopper engine fell silent behind them. The rotors wheezed more slowly to a halt.

Roy said, "There's no sign of either the man or the dog, so I hear."

"Nothing in there but a dead rat."

"Was the water really *that* high when it jammed the truck between those rocks?"

"Yep. Sometime yesterday afternoon, at the height of the storm."

"Then maybe he was washed out, went over the falls."

"Not if he stayed buckled up."

"Well, farther up the river, maybe he tried to swim for shore."

"Man would have to be a fool to try swimming in a flash flood, the water moving like an express train. This man a fool?"

"No."

"See these tracks here," Tavelov said, pointing to tire marks in the silt of the arroyo bed. "Even what little wind there's been since the storm has worn 'em down some. But you can still see where somebody drove down the south bank, under the Explorer, probably stood on the roof of his vehicle to get up there."

"When would the arroyo have dried up enough for that?"

"Water level drops fast when the rain stops. And this ground, deep sand—it dries out quick. Say . . . seven or eight last night."

Standing deep inside the rock-walled passage, gazing up at the Explorer, Roy said, "Grant could've climbed down and walked away before the other vehicle got here."

"Fact is, you'll see some vague footprints that *don't* belong to the first group of my hopeless asshole assistants who tramped up the scene. And judging by 'em, you might make a case that a woman drove in here and took him away. Him and the dog. And his luggage."

Roy frowned. "A woman?"

"One set of prints is of a size that you know it's got to be a man. Even big women don't often have feet as big as would be in proportion to the rest of 'em. The second set is small prints, which might be those of a boy, say ten to thirteen. But I doubt any boy was drivin' on his own out here. Some small men have feet might step into shoes that size. But not many. So most likely it was a woman."

If a woman had come to Grant's rescue, Roy was obliged to wonder if she was *the* woman, the fugitive. That raised anew the questions that had plagued him since Wednesday night: Who *was* Spencer Grant, what in the hell did the bastard have to do with the woman, what sort of wild card was he, was he likely to screw up their operations, and would he put them all at risk of exposure?

Yesterday, when Roy had stood in Eve's bunker, listening to the laser-disc recording, he'd been more baffled than enlightened by what he'd heard. Judging by the questions and the few comments that Grant managed to insert into Davidowitz's monologue, he knew little about "Hannah Rainey," but for mysterious reasons, he was busily learning everything he could. Until then, Roy had assumed that Grant and the woman already had some kind of close relationship; so the task had been to determine the nature of that relationship and to figure how much sensitive information the woman had shared with Grant. But if the guy didn't already know her, why had he been at her bungalow that rainy night, and why had he made it his personal crusade to find her?

Roy didn't want to believe that the woman had shown up here in the arroyo, because to believe it was to be even more confused. "So you're saying what—that he called someone on his cellular and she came right out to get him?"

Tavelov was not rattled by Roy's sarcasm. "Could've been some desert rat, likes living out where there aren't phones, electricity. There are some. Though none I know about for twenty miles. Or it could've been an off-roader, just having himself some fun."

"In a storm."

"Storm was over. Anyway, the world's full of fools."

"And whoever it is just happens to stumble across the Explorer. In this whole vast desert."

Tavelov shrugged. "We found the truck. It's your job, making sense of it."

Walking back to the entrance of the rock-walled sluiceway, staring at the far riverbank, Roy said, "Whoever she was, she drove into the arroyo from the south, then also drove out to the south. Can we follow those tire tracks?"

"Yep, you can—pretty clear for maybe four hundred yards, then spotty for another two hundred. Then they vanish. The wind wiped 'em out in some places. Other places, ground's too hard to take tracks."

"Well, let's search farther out, see if the tracks reappear."

"Already tried. While we were waiting."

Tavelov gave an edge to the word "waiting."

Roy said, "My damn pager was broken, and I didn't know it."

"By foot and chopper, we pretty much had a good look-around in every direction to the south bank of the wash. Went three miles east, three south, three west."

"Well," Roy said, "extend the search. Go out six miles and see if you can pick up the trail again."

"Just going to be a waste of time."

Roy thought of Eve as she had been last night, and that memory gave him the strength to remain calm, to smile, and to say, with characteristic pleasantness, "Probably is a waste of time, probably is. But I guess we've got to try anyway."

"Wind's picking up."

"Maybe it is."

"Definitely picking up. Going to erase everything."

Perfection on black rubber.

Roy said, "Then let's try to stay ahead of it. Bring in more men, another chopper, push out *ten* miles in each direction."

❦

Spencer was not awake. But he wasn't asleep, either. He was taking a drunkard's walk along the thin line between.

He heard himself mumbling. He couldn't make much sense of what he was saying. Yet he was ever in the grip of a feverish urgency, certain there was something important that he must tell someone—although what that vital information was, and to whom he must impart it, eluded him.

Occasionally he opened his eyes. Blurry vision. He blinked. Squinted. Couldn't see well enough to be sure even if it was daytime or if the light came from the Coleman lantern.

Always, Valerie was there. Close enough for him to know, even with his vision so poor, that it was her. Sometimes she was wiping his face with a damp cloth, sometimes changing a cool compress on his forehead. Sometimes she was just watching, and he sensed that she was worried, though he couldn't clearly see her expression.

Once, when he swam up from his personal darkness and stared out through the distorting pools that shimmered in his eye sockets, Valerie was turned half away from him, busy at a hidden task. Behind him, farther back under the camouflage tarp, the Rover's engine was idling. He heard another familiar sound: the soft but unmistakable *tick-tickety-tick* of well-practiced fingers flying over a computer keyboard. Odd.

From time to time, she talked to him. Those were the moments when he was best able to focus his mind and to mumble something that was halfway comprehensible, though he still faded in and out.

Once he faded in to hear himself asking, ". . . how'd you find me . . . out here . . . way out here . . . between nothing and nowhere?"

"Bug on your Explorer."

"Cockroach?"

"The other kind of bug."

"Spider?"

"Electronic."

"Bug on my truck?"

"That's right. I put it there."

"Like . . . you mean . . . a transmitter thing?" he asked fuzzily.

"Just like a transmitter thing."

"Why?"

"Because you followed me home."

"When?"

"Tuesday night. No point denying it."

"Oh, yeah. Night we met."

"You make it sound almost romantic."

"Was for me."

Valerie was silent. Finally she said, "You're not kidding, are you?"

"Liked you right off."

After another silence, she said, "You come to The Red Door, chat me up, seem like just a nice customer, then you follow me home."

The full meaning of her revelations was sinking in gradually, and a slow-dawning amazement was overtaking him. "You knew?"

"You were good. But if I couldn't spot a tail, I'd have been dead a long time ago."

"The bug. How?"

"How did I plant it? Went out the back door while you were sitting across the street in your truck. Hot-wired somebody's car a block or so away, drove to my street, parked up the block from you, waited till you left, then followed you."

"Followed *me?*"

"What's good for the goose."

"Followed me . . . Malibu?"

"Followed you Malibu."

"And I never saw."

"Well, you weren't expecting to be followed."

"Jesus."

"I climbed your gate, waited till all the lights were out in your cabin."

"Jesus."

"Fixed the transmitter to the undercarriage of your truck, wired it to work off the battery."

"You just happened to have a transmitter."

"You'd be surprised what I just happen to have."

"Maybe not any more."

Although Spencer didn't want to leave her, Valerie grew blurrier and faded into shadows. He drifted into his inner darkness once more.

Later he must have swum up again, because she was shimmering in front of him. He heard himself say, "Bug on my truck," with amazement.

"I had to know who you were, why you were following me. I knew you weren't one of *them*."

He said weakly, "Cockroach's people."

"That's right."

"Coulda been one of them."

"No, because you'd have blown my brains out the first time you were close enough to do it."

"They don't like you, huh?"

"Not much. So I wondered who you were."

"Now you know."

"Not really. You're a mystery, Spencer Grant."

"*Me* a mystery!" He laughed. Pain hammered across his entire head when he laughed, but he laughed anyway. "Least you have a name for me."

"Sure. But no more real than those you have for me."

"It's real."

"Sure."

"Legal name. Spencer Grant. Guaranteed."

"Maybe. But who were you before you were a cop, before you went to UCLA, way back before you were in the army?"

"You know all about me."

"Not all. Just what you've left on the records, just as much as you wanted anybody to find. Following me home, you spooked me, so I started checking you out."

"You moved out of the bungalow because of me."

"Didn't know who the hell you were. But I figured if you could find me, so could they. Again."

"And they did."

"The very next day."

"So when I spooked you . . . I saved you."

"You could look at it that way."

"Without me, you'd have been there."

"Maybe."

"When the SWAT team hit."

"Probably."

"Seems like it's all sort of . . . meant to be."

"But what were *you* doing there," she asked.

"Well . . ."

"In my house."

"You were gone."

"So?"

"Wasn't your place any more."

"Did you know it wasn't my place any more when you went in?"

The full meaning of her revelations kept giving him delayed jolts. He blinked furiously, vainly trying to see her face clearly. "Jesus, if you bugged my truck . . . !"

"What?"

"Then were you following me Wednesday night?"

She said, "Yeah. Seeing what you were all about."

"From Malibu . . . ?"

"To The Red Door."

"Then back to your place in Santa Monica?"

"I wasn't *inside* like you were."

"But you saw it go down, the assault."

"From a distance. Don't change the subject."

"What subject?" he asked, genuinely confused.

"You were going to explain why you broke into my house Wednesday night," she reminded him. She wasn't angry. Her voice wasn't sharp. He would have felt better if she'd been flat-out angry with him.

"You . . . you didn't show up at work."

"So you break into my house?"

"Didn't break in."

"Have I forgotten that I sent you an invitation?"

"Door was unlocked."

"Every unlocked door is an invitation to you?"

"I was . . . worried."

"Yeah, worried. Come on, tell me the truth. What were you looking for in my house that night?"

"I was . . ."

"You were what?"

"I needed . . ."

"What? What did you need in my house?"

Spencer wasn't sure whether he was dying from his injuries or from embarrassment. Whatever the case, he lost consciousness.

∽

The Bell JetRanger transported Roy Miro from the dry wash in the open desert straight to the landing pad on the roof of the agency's high rise in downtown Las Vegas. While a ground and air search was being conducted in the Mojave for the woman and the vehicle that had taken Spencer Grant away from the wreckage of his Explorer, Roy spent Saturday afternoon in the fifth-floor satellite-surveillance center.

While he worked, he ate a substantial lunch that he ordered from the commissary, to compensate for missing the lavish breakfast about which he'd fantasized. Besides, later he would need all the energy that he was able to muster, when he went home with Eve Jammer again.

The previous evening, when Bobby Dubois had brought Roy to that same room, it had been quiet, operating with a minimal staff. Now every computer and other piece of equipment was manned, and murmured conversations were being conducted throughout the large chamber.

Most likely, the vehicle they were seeking had traveled a considerable distance during the night, in spite of the inhospitable terrain. Grant and the woman might even have gotten far enough to pick up a highway beyond the surveillance posts that the agency had established on every route out of the southern half of the state, in which case they had slipped through the net again.

On the other hand, perhaps they hadn't gotten far at all. They might have bogged down. They might have had mechanical failure.

Perhaps Grant had been injured in the Explorer. According to Ted Tavelov, bloodstains discolored the driver's seat, and it didn't appear as if the blood had come from the dead rat. If Grant was in bad shape, maybe he'd been *unable* to travel far.

Roy was determined to think positively. The world was what you made it—or tried to make it. His entire life was committed to that philosophy.

Of the available satellites in geosynchronous orbits that kept them positioned over the western and southwestern United States at all times, three were capable of the intense degree of surveillance that Roy Miro wished to conduct of the state of Nevada and of all neighboring states. One of those three space-based observation posts was under the control of the Drug Enforcement Administration. One was owned by the Environmental Protection Agency. The third was a military venture officially shared by the army, navy, air force, marines, and coast guard—but it was, in fact, under the iron-fisted political control of the office of the Chairman of the Joint Chiefs of Staff.

No contest. The Environmental Protection Agency.

The Drug Enforcement Administration, in spite of the dedication of its agents and largely because of meddling politicians, had pretty much failed in its assigned mission. And the military services, at least in these years following the end of the Cold War, were confused as to their purpose, underfunded, and moribund.

By contrast, the Environmental Protection Agency was fulfilling its mission to an unprecedented degree for a government agency, in part because there was no well-organized criminal element or interest group opposed to it, and because many of its workers were motivated by a fierce desire to save the natural world. The EPA cooperated so successfully with the Department of Justice that a citizen who even inadvertently contaminated protected wetlands was at risk of spending more time in prison than would a doped-up gangsta dude who killed a 7-Eleven clerk, a pregnant mother, two nuns, and a kitten while he was stealing forty dollars and a Mars bar.

Consequently, because shining success bred increased budgets and the greatest access to additional off-budget funding, the EPA owned the finest of hardware, from office equipment to orbital surveillance satellites. If any federal bureaucracy were to obtain independent control of nuclear weapons, it would be the EPA, although it was the least likely to use them—except, perhaps, in a turf dispute with the Department of the Interior.

To find Spencer Grant and the woman, therefore, the agency was using the EPA surveillance satellite—Earthguard 3—which was in a geosynchronous orbit over the western United States. To seize complete and uncontested use of that asset, Mama infiltrated EPA computers and fed them false data to the effect that Earthguard 3 had experienced sudden, total systems failure. Scientists at EPA satellite-tracking facilities had immediately mounted a campaign to diagnose the ills of Earthguard 3 by long-distance telemechanical testing. However, Mama had secretly intercepted all commands sent to that eighty-million-dollar package of sophisticated electronics—and she would continue to do so until the agency no longer needed Earthguard 3, at which time she would allow it to go on-line again for the EPA.

From space, the agency could now conduct a supramagnified visual inspection of a multistate area. It could focus all the way down to a square-meter-by-square-meter search pattern if the need arose to get in that tight on a suspect vehicle or person.

Earthguard 3 also provided two methods of highly advanced night surveillance. Using profile-guided infrared, it could differentiate between a vehicle and stationary sources of radiant heat by the very fact of the target's mobility and by its distinct thermal signature. The system also could employ a variation on Star Tron night-vision technology to magnify ambient light by a factor of eighteen thousand, making a night scene appear nearly as bright as an overcast day—although with a monochromatic, eerie green cast.

All images were automatically processed through an enhancement program aboard the satellite prior to encoding and transmission. And upon receipt in the Vegas control center, an equally automated but more sophisticated enhancement program, run on the latest-generation Cray supercomputer, further clarified the high-definition video image before projecting it on the wall display. If additional clarification was desired, stills taken from the tape could be subjected to more enhancement procedures under the supervision of talented technicians.

The effectiveness of satellite surveillance—whether infrared, night-vision, or ordinary telescopic photography—varied according to the territory under scrutiny. Generally, the more populated an area, the less successful a space-based search for anything as small as a single individual or vehicle, because there were far too many objects in motion and too many heat sources to be sorted through and analyzed either accurately or on a timely basis. Towns were easier to observe than cities, rural areas easier than towns, and open highways could be monitored better than metropolitan streets.

If Spencer Grant and the woman had been delayed in their flight, as Roy hoped, they were still in ideal territory to be located and tracked by Earthguard 3. Barren, unpopulated desert.

Saturday afternoon through evening, as suspect vehicles were spotted, they were either studied and eliminated or maintained on an under-observation list until a determination could be made that their occupants didn't fit the fugitive-party profile: woman, man, and dog.

After watching the big wall display for hours, Roy was impressed by how *perfect* their part of the world appeared to be from orbit. All colors were soft and subdued, and all shapes appeared harmonious.

The illusion of perfection was more convincing when Earthguard was surveying larger rather than smaller areas and was, therefore, using the lowest magnification. It was *most* convincing when the image was in infrared. The less he was able to detect obvious signs of human civilization, the closer to perfection the planet appeared.

Perhaps those extremists who insisted that the population of the earth be expediently reduced by ninety percent, by any means, to save the ecology were onto something. What quality of life could anyone have in a world that civilization had utterly despoiled?

If such a program of population reduction was ever instituted, he would take deep personal satisfaction in helping to administer it, although the work would be exhausting and often thankless.

The day waned without either the ground or air search turning up a trace of the fugitives. At nightfall the hunt was called off until dawn. And Earthguard 3, with all its eyes and all its ways of seeing, was no more successful than the men on foot and the helicopter crews, though at least it could continue searching throughout the night.

Roy remained in the satellite-surveillance center until almost eight o'clock, when he left with Eve Jammer for dinner at an Armenian restaurant. Over a tasty fattoush salad and then superb rack of lamb, they discussed the concept of massive and rapid population reduction. They imagined ways in which it might be achieved without undesirable side effects, such as nuclear radiation and uncontrollable riots in the streets. And they conceived *several* fair methods of determining which ten percent of the population would survive to carry on a less chaotic and drastically perfected version of the human saga. They sketched possible symbols for the population-reduction movement, composed inspiring slogans, and debated what the uniforms ought to look like. They were in a state of high excitement by the time they left the restaurant to go to Eve's place. They might have killed any cop who had been foolish enough to stop them for doing seventy miles an hour through hospital and residential zones.

✌

The stained and shadowed walls had faces. Strange, embedded faces. Half-seen, tortured expressions. Mouths open in cries for mercy that were never answered. Hands. Reaching hands. Silently beseeching. Ghostly white tableaux, streaked gray and rust-red in some places, mottled brown and yellow in others. Face by face and body beside body, some limbs overlapping, but always the posture of the supplicant, always the expressions of despairing beggars: pleading, imploring, praying.

"*Nobody knows . . . nobody knows . . .*"

"Spencer? Can you hear me, Spencer?"

Valerie's voice echoed down a long tunnel to him as he walked in a place between wakefulness and true sleep, between denial and acceptance, between one hell and another.

"Easy now, easy, don't be afraid, it's okay, you're dreaming."

"No. See? See? Here in the catacombs, here, the catacombs."

"Only a dream."

"Like in school, in the book, pictures, like in Rome, martyrs, down in the catacombs, but worse, worse, worse . . ."

"You can walk away from there. It's only a dream."

He heard his own voice diminishing from a shout to a withered, miserable cry: "Oh God, oh my God, *oh my God!*"

"Here, take my hand. Spencer, can you hear me? Hold my hand. I'm here. I'm with you."

"They were so afraid, afraid, all alone and afraid. See how afraid they are? Alone, no one to hear, no one, nobody ever knew, so afraid. Oh, Jesus, Jesus, help me, Jesus."

"Come on, hold my hand, that's it, that's good, hold tight. I'm right here with you. You aren't alone any more, Spencer."

He held on to her warm hand, and somehow she led him away from the blind white faces, the silent cries.

By the power of her hand, Spencer drifted, lighter than air, up from the deep place, through darkness, through a red door. Not the door with wet handprints on the aged-white background. This door was entirely red, dry, with a film of dust. It opened into sapphire-blue light, black booths and chairs, polished-steel trim, mirrored walls. Deserted bandstand. A handful of people drinking quietly at tables. In jeans and a suede jacket instead of slit skirt and black sweater, she sat on a barstool beside him, because business was slow. He was lying on an air mattress, sweating yet chilled, and she was perched on a stool, yet they were at the same level, holding hands, talking easily, as though they were old friends, with the hiss of the Coleman lantern in the background.

He knew he was delirious. He didn't care. She was so pretty.

"Why did you go into my house Wednesday night?"

"Already told you?"

"No. You keep avoiding an answer."

"Needed to know about you."

"Why?"

"You hate me?"

"Of course not. I just want to understand."

"Went to your place, sting grenades coming through the windows."

"You could've walked away when you realized what trouble I was."

"No, can't let you end up in a ditch, eighty miles from home."

"What?"

"Or in catacombs."

"After you knew I was trouble, why'd you wade in deeper?"

"Told you. I liked you first time we met."

"That was just Tuesday night! I'm a stranger to you."

"I want . . ."

"What?"

"I want . . . a life."

"You don't have a life?"

"A life . . . with hope."

The cocktail lounge dissolved, and the blue light changed to sour yellow. The stained and shadowed walls had faces. White faces, death masks, mouths open in voiceless terror, silently beseeching.

A spider followed the electrical cord that hung in loops from the ceiling, and its exaggerated shadow scurried across the stained white faces of the innocent.

Later, in the cocktail lounge again, he said to her, "You're a good person."

"You can't know that."

"Theda."

"Theda thinks everyone's a good person."

"She was so sick. You took care of her."

"Only for a couple of weeks."

"Day and night."

"Wasn't that big a deal."

"Now me."

"I haven't pulled you through yet."

"More I learn about you, the better you are."

She said, "Hell, maybe I *am* a saint."

"No. Just a good person. Too sarcastic to be a saint."

She laughed. "I can't help liking you, Spencer Grant."

"This is nice. Getting to know each other."

"Is that what we're doing?"

Impulsively, he said, "I love you."

Valerie was silent for so long that Spencer thought he'd lost consciousness again.

At last she said, "You're delirious."

"Not about this."

"I'll change the compress on your forehead."

"I love you."

"You better be quiet, try to get some rest."

"I'll always love you."

"Be quiet, you strange man," she said with what he believed and hoped was affection. "Just be quiet and rest."

"Always," he repeated.

Having confessed that the hope he sought was her, Spencer was so greatly relieved that he sank into a darkness without catacombs.

A long time later, not certain if he was awake or asleep, in a half-light that might have been dawn, dusk, lamp glow, or the cold and sourceless luminosity of a dream, Spencer was surprised to hear himself say, "Michael."

"Ah, you're back," she said.

"Michael."

"No one here's named Michael."

"You need to know about him," Spencer warned.

"Okay. Tell me."

He wished he could see her. There was only light and shadow, not even a blurred shape any more.

He said, "You need to know if . . . if you're going to be with me."

"Tell me," she encouraged.

"Don't hate me when you know."

"I'm not an easy hater. Trust me, Spencer. Trust me and talk to me. Who is Michael?"

His voice was fragile. "Died when he was fourteen."

"Michael was a friend?"

"He was me. Died fourteen . . . wasn't buried till he was sixteen."

"Michael was you?"

"Walking around dead two years, then I was Spencer."

"What was your . . . what was Michael's last name?"

He knew then that he must be awake, not dreaming, because he had never felt as bad in a dream as he felt at that moment. The need to reveal could no longer be repressed, yet revelation was agony. His heart beat hard and fast, though it was pierced by secrets as painful as needles. "His last name . . . was the devil's name."

"What was the devil's name?"

Spencer was silent, trying to speak but unable.

"What was the devil's name?" she asked again.

"Ackblom," he said, spitting out the hated syllables.

"Ackblom? Why do you say that's the name of the devil?"

"Don't you remember? Didn't you ever hear?"

"I guess you'll have to tell me."

"Before Michael was Spencer," said Spencer, "he had a dad. Like other boys . . . had a dad . . . but not like other dads. His f-father's name was . . . was . . . his name was Steven. Steven Ackblom. The artist."

"Oh, my God."

"Don't be afraid of me," he pleaded, his voice breaking apart, word by desperate word.

"You're the boy?"

"Don't hate me."

"You're that boy."

"Don't hate me."

"Why would I hate you?"

"Because . . . I'm the boy."

"The boy who was a hero," she said.

"No."

"Yes, you were."

"I couldn't save them."

"But you saved all those who might've come after them."

The sound of his own voice chilled him deeper than cold rain had chilled him earlier. "Couldn't save them."

"It's all right."

"Couldn't save them." He felt a hand upon his face. Upon his scar. Tracing the hot line of his cicatricial brand.

She said, "You poor bastard. You poor, sweet bastard."

∽

Saturday night, perched on the edge of a chair in Eve Jammer's bedroom, Roy Miro saw examples of perfection that even the best-equipped surveillance satellite could not have shown him.

This time, Eve didn't pull the satin sheets back to reveal black rubber and didn't use scented oils. She had a new—and stranger—set of toys. And although Roy was surprised to discover that it was possible, Eve achieved greater heights of self-gratification and had a greater erotic impact on him than she had managed the night before.

After a night of cataloguing Eve's perfections, Roy required the greatest patience for the imperfect day that followed.

Through Sunday morning and afternoon, satellite surveillance, helicopters, and on-foot search teams had no more success locating the fugitives than they'd had on Saturday.

Operatives in Carmel, California—sent there following Theda Davidowitz's revelation to Grant that "Hannah Rainey" had thought it was the ideal place to live—were enjoying the natural beauty and the refreshing winter fog. Of the woman, however, they had seen no sign.

From Orange County, John Kleck issued another important-sounding report to the effect that he had come up with no leads whatsoever.

In San Francisco, the agent who had tracked down the Porths, only to discover that they had died years ago, had gained access to probate records. He'd learned that Ethel Porth's estate had passed entirely to George; George's estate had passed to their grandson—Spencer Grant of Malibu, California, sole issue of the Porths' only child, Jennifer. Nothing had been found to indicate that Grant had ever gone by another name or that his father's identity was known.

From a corner of the satellite-surveillance control center, Roy spoke by telephone with Thomas Summerton. Although it was Sunday, Summerton was in his office in Washington rather than at his estate in Virginia. As security conscious as ever, he treated Roy's call as a wrong number, then phoned back on a deep-cover line a while later, using a scrambling device matched to Roy's.

"Hell of a mess in Arizona," Summerton said. He was furious.

Roy didn't know what his boss was talking about.

Summerton said, "Rich asshole activist out there, thinks he can save the world. You see the news?"

"Too busy," Roy said.

"This asshole—he's gotten some evidence that would embarrass me on the Texas situation last year. He's been feeling out some people about how best to break the story. So we were going to hit him quick, make sure there was evidence of drug dealing on his property."

"The asset-forfeiture provision?"

"Yeah. Seize everything. When his family has nothing to live on and he doesn't have the assets to pay for a serious defense, he'll come around. They usually do. But then the operation went wrong."

They usually do, Roy thought wearily. But he didn't speak his mind. He knew Summerton wouldn't appreciate candor. Besides, that thought had been a prime example of shamefully negative thinking.

"Now," Summerton said dourly, "an FBI agent's dead, out there in Arizona."

"A real one or a floater like me?"

"A real one. The asshole activist's wife and boy are dead in the front yard too, and he's sniping from the house, so we can't hide the bodies from the TV cameras down the block. And anyway, a neighbor has it all on videotape!"

"Did the guy kill his own wife and kid?"

"I wish. But maybe it can still look that way."

"Even with videotape?"

"You've been around long enough to know photographic evidence rarely clinches anything. Look at the Rodney King video. Hell, look at the Zapruder film of the Kennedy hit." Summerton sighed. "So I hope you've got good news for me, Roy, something to cheer me up."

Being Summerton's right-hand man was getting to be dreary work. Roy wished that he could report *some* progress on his current case.

"Well," Summerton said, just before hanging up, "right now no news seems like good news to me."

Later, prior to leaving the Vegas offices on Sunday evening, Roy decided to ask Mama to use Nexis and other data-search services to scan for "Jennifer Corrine Porth" in all media data banks that were offered on various information networks—and to report by morning. The past fifteen to twenty years' issues of many major newspapers and magazines, including the *New York Times*, were electronically stored and available for on-line research. In a previous perusal of those resources, Mama had turned up the name "Spencer Grant" only related to the killing of the two carjackers in Los Angeles a few years ago. But she might have more luck with the mother's name.

If Jennifer Corrine Porth had died in a colorful fashion—or if she'd had even a middle-level reputation in business, government, or the arts—

her death would have made a few major newspapers. And if Mama located any stories about her or any long obituaries, a valuable reference to Jennifer's only surviving child might be buried in them.

Roy stubbornly clung to positive thinking. He was confident that Mama would find a reference to Jennifer and break the case wide open.

The woman. The boy. The barn in the background. The man in the shadows.

He didn't have to take the photographs out of the envelope in which he was keeping them to recall those images with total clarity. The pictures teased his memory, for he knew that he'd seen the people in them before. A long time ago. In some compelling context.

Sunday night, Eve helped to keep Roy's spirits high and his thoughts on a positive track. Aware that she was adored and that Roy's adoration gave her total power over him, she worked herself into a frenzy that exceeded anything he had seen before.

For part of their unforgettable third encounter, he sat on the closed lid of the toilet, watching, while she proved that a shower stall could be as conducive to erotic games as any fur-draped, satin-sheeted, or rubber-covered bed.

He was astounded that anyone would have thought to invent and manufacture many of the water toys in her collection. Those devices were cleverly designed, intriguingly flexible, glistening with such lifelike need, convincingly *biological* in their battery- or hand-powered throbbing, mysterious and thrilling in their serpentine-knobby-dimpled-rubbery complexity. Roy was able to identify with them as if they were extensions of the body—part human, part machine—that he sometimes inhabited in dreams. When Eve handled those toys, Roy felt as though her perfect hands were fondling portions of his own anatomy by remote control.

In the blurring steam, the hot water, and the lather of scented soap, Eve seemed to be ninety percent perfect rather than just sixty percent. She was as unreal as an idealized woman in a painting.

Nothing this side of death could have been more fulfilling for Roy than watching Eve methodically stimulate one exquisite anatomical feature at a time, in each case with a device that seemed to be the amputated but functioning organ of a superlover from the future. Roy was able to focus his observations so tightly that Eve herself ceased to exist for him, and each sensuous encounter in the large shower stall—with bench and grab bars—was between one perfect body part and its fleshless analogue: erotic geometry, prurient physics, a study in the fluid dynamics of insatiable lust. The experience was untainted by personality or by any other human trait or association. Roy was transported into extreme realms of voyeuristic pleasure so intense that he almost screamed with the pain of his joy.

∽

Spencer woke when the sun was above the eastern mountains. The light was coppery, and long morning shadows spilled westward across the badlands from every thrust of rock and impertinence of gnarled vegetation.

His vision wasn't blurred. The sun no longer stung his eyes.

Out at the edge of the shade that was provided by the tarp, Valerie sat on the ground, her back to him. She was bent to a task that he couldn't see.

Rocky was sitting at Valerie's side, his back also to Spencer.

An engine was idling. Spencer had the strength to lift his head and turn toward the sound. The Range Rover. Behind him, deeper in the tarp-covered niche. An orange utility cord led from the open driver's door of the Rover to Valerie.

Spencer felt dreadful, but he was grateful for the improvement in his condition since his most recent bout of consciousness. His skull no longer seemed about to explode; his headache was down to a dull thump over his right eye. Dry mouth. Chapped lips. But his throat wasn't hot and achy any more.

The morning was genuinely warm. The heat wasn't from a fever, because his forehead felt cool. He threw back the blanket.

He yawned, stretched—and groaned. His muscles ached, but after the battering he had taken, that was to be expected.

Alerted by Spencer's groan, Rocky hurried to him. The mutt was grinning, trembling, whipping his tail from side to side, in a frenzy of delight to see his master awake.

Spencer endured an enthusiastic face licking before he managed to get a grip on the dog's collar and hold him at tongue's length.

Looking over her shoulder, Valerie said, "Good morning."

She was as lovely in the early sun as she had been in lamplight.

He almost repeated that sentiment aloud but was disconcerted by a dim memory of having said too much already, when he had been out of his head. He suspected himself not merely of having revealed secrets that he would rather have kept but of having been artlessly candid about his feelings for her, as ingenuous as an infatuated puppy.

As he sat up, denying the dog another lick at his face, Spencer said, "No offense, pal, but you stink something fierce."

He got to his knees, rose to his feet, and swayed for a moment.

"Dizzy?" Valerie asked.

"No. That's gone."

"Good. I think you had a bad concussion. I'm no doctor—as you made clear. But I've got some reference books with me."

"Just a little weak now. Hungry. Starving, in fact."

"That's a good sign, I think."

Now that Rocky was no longer in his face, Spencer realized that the dog didn't stink. He himself was the offending party: the wet-mud fragrance of the river, the sourness of several fever sweats.

Valerie returned to her work.

Being careful to stay upwind of her, and trying not to let the playful mutt trip him, Spencer shuffled to the edge of the shaded enclosure to see what the woman was doing.

A computer sat on a black plastic mat on the ground. It wasn't a laptop but a full PC with a MasterPiece surge protector between the logic unit and the color monitor. The keyboard was on her lap.

It was remarkable to see such an elaborate high-tech workstation plunked down in the middle of a primitive landscape that had remained largely unchanged for hundreds of thousands if not millions of years.

"How many megabytes?" he asked.

"Not mega. Giga. Ten gigabytes."

"You need all that?"

"Some of the programs I use are pretty damn complex. They fill up a lot of hard disk."

The orange electrical cord from the Rover was plugged into the logic unit. Another orange cord led from the back of the logic unit to a peculiar device sitting in the sunlight ten feet beyond the shade line of their tarp-covered hideaway: It looked like an inverted Frisbee with a flared rather than inward-curling rim; underneath, at its center, it was fixed to a ball joint, which was in turn fixed to a four-inch flexible black metal arm, which disappeared into a gray box approximately a foot square and four inches deep.

Busy at the keyboard, Valerie answered his question before he could ask it. "Satellite up-link."

"You talking to aliens?" he asked, only half joking.

"Right now, to the dee-oh-dee computer," she said, pausing to study the data that scrolled up the screen.

"Dee-oh-dee?" he wondered.

"Department of Defense."

DOD.

He squatted on his haunches. "Are you a government agent?"

"I didn't say I was talking to the DOD computer with the DOD's permission. Or knowledge, for that matter. I up-linked to a phone-company satellite, accessed one of their lines reserved for systems testing, called in to the DOD deep computer in Arlington, Virginia."

"Deep," he mused.

"Heavily secured."

"I bet that's not a number you got from directory assistance."

"Phone number's not the hardest part. It's more difficult to get the operating codes that let you use their system once you're into it. Without them, being able to make the connection wouldn't matter."

"And you have those codes?"

"I've had full access to DOD for fourteen months." Her fingers flew over the keyboard again. "Hardest to get is the access code to the program with which they periodically change all the *other* access codes. But if you don't have *that* sucker, you can't stay current unless they send you a new invitation every once in a while."

"So fourteen months ago, you just happened to find all these numbers and whatnot scrawled on a rest room wall?"

"Three people I loved gave their lives for those codes."

That response, though delivered in no graver a tone of voice than anything else Valerie had said, carried an emotional weight that left Spencer silent and pondering for a while.

A foot-long lizard—mostly brown, flecked with black and gold—slithered from under a nearby rock into the sunshine and scampered across the warm sand. When it saw Valerie, it froze and watched her. Its silver-and-green eyes were protuberant, with pebbly lids.

Rocky saw the lizard too. He retreated behind his master.

Spencer found himself smiling at the reptile, although he was not sure why he should be so pleased by its sudden appearance. Then he realized that he was unconsciously fingering the carved soapstone medallion that hung against his chest, and he understood. Louis Lee. Pheasants and dragons. Prosperity and long life.

Three people I loved gave their lives for those codes.

Spencer's smile faded. To Valerie, he said, "What are you?"

Without looking up from the display screen, she said, "You mean, am I an international terrorist or a good patriotic American?"

"Well, I wouldn't put it like that."

Instead of answering him, she said, "Over the past five days, I tried to learn what I could about you. Not very damn much. You've just about erased yourself from official existence. So I think I've got a right to ask the same question: What are *you?*"

He shrugged. "Just someone who values his privacy."

"Sure. And what I am is a concerned and interested citizen—not a whole lot different from you."

"Except I don't know how to get into DOD."

"You fiddled with your military records."

"That's an easy-access database compared with the big muddy you're wading in right now. What the hell are you looking for?"

"The DOD tracks every satellite in orbit: civilian, government, military—both domestic and foreign. I'm one-stop shopping for all the satellites with the surveillance capabilities to look down into this little corner of the world and find us if we go out and about."

"I thought that was part of a dream," he said uneasily, "that talk about eyes in the sky."

"You'd be surprised what's up there. 'Surprised' is one word. As for surveillance, there are probably two to six satellites with that capability in orbit over the western and southwestern states."

Rattled, he said, "What happens when you identify them?"

"The DOD will have their access codes. I'll use those to up-link to each satellite, poke around in its current programs, and see if it's looking for us."

"This awesome lady here pokes around in satellites," he said to Rocky, but the dog seemed less impressed than his master was, as if canines had been up to similar shenanigans for ages. To Valerie, Spencer said, "I don't think the word 'hacker' is adequate for you."

"So . . . what did they call people like me when you were on that computer-crime task force?"

"I don't think we even conceived there *were* people like you."

"Well, we're here."

"They'd really hunt us with satellites?" he asked doubtfully. "I mean, we're not that important—are we?"

"They think I am. And you've got them totally confused. They can't figure out how the hell you fit in. Until they get an idea what you're all about, they'll figure you're as dangerous to them as I am—maybe more so. The unknown—that's you, from their viewpoint—is always more frightening than the known."

He mulled that over. "Who're these people you're talking about?"

"Maybe you're safer if you don't know."

Spencer opened his mouth to respond, then held his silence. He didn't want to argue. Not yet, anyway. First, he needed to clean up and get something to eat.

Without pausing in her work, Valerie explained that plastic jugs of bottled water, a basin, liquid soap, sponges, and a clean towel were just inside the Rover's tailgate. "Don't use a lot of water. It's our drinking supply if we have to be out here a few more days."

Rocky followed his master to the truck, glancing back nervously at the lizard in the sun.

Spencer discovered that Valerie had salvaged his belongings from the Explorer. He was able to shave and change into clean clothes, in addition to taking a sponge bath. He felt refreshed, and he could no longer smell his own body odor. He couldn't get his hair quite as clean as he would have liked, however, because his scalp was tender, not just around the sutured laceration but across the entire crown of his head.

The Rover was a truck-style station wagon, like the Explorer, and it was packed solid with gear and supplies from the tailgate to within two feet of the front seats. The food was just where a well-organized person would stow it: in boxes and coolers immediately behind the two-foot clear space, easily accessible from either the driver's or passenger's seat.

Most of the provisions were canned and bottled, except for boxes of crackers. Because Spencer was too hungry to take the time to cook, he selected two small tins of Vienna sausages, two snack-size packets of cheese crackers, and a single-serving lunch-box can of pears.

In one of the Styrofoam coolers, also within easy reach of the front seats, he found weapons. A SIG 9mm pistol. A Micro Uzi that appeared to have been illegally converted for full automatic fire. There were spare magazines of ammunition for both.

Spencer stared at the weapons, then turned to look through the windshield at the woman sitting with her computer, twenty feet away.

That Valerie was skilled at many things, Spencer had no doubt. She seemed so well prepared for every contingency that she could serve as the paradigm not only for all Girl Scouts but for doomsday survivalists. She was clever, intelligent, funny, daring, courageous, and easy to look at in lamplight, in sunlight, in any light at all. Undoubtedly she was also practiced in the use of both the pistol and the submachine gun, because otherwise she was too practical to be in possession of them: She simply wouldn't waste space on tools that she couldn't use, and she wouldn't risk the penalties for possession of a fully automatic Uzi unless she was able—and willing—to fire it.

Spencer wondered if she had ever been forced to shoot at another human being. He hoped not. And he hoped that she would never be driven to such an extreme. Sadly, however, life seemed to be handing her nothing but extremes.

He opened a tin of sausages with the ring tab on top. Resisting an urge to wolf down the contents in a single great mouthful, he ate one of the miniature frankfurters, then another. Nothing had ever tasted half as good. He popped the third in his mouth as he returned to Valerie.

Rocky danced and whimpered at his side, begging for his share.

"Mine," Spencer said.

Though he hunkered down beside Valerie, he didn't speak to her. She seemed especially focused on the cryptic data that filled the display screen.

The lizard was in the sun, alert and poised to flee, at the same spot where it had been almost half an hour earlier. Tiny dinosaur.

Spencer opened a second can of sausages, shared two with the dog, and was just finishing the last of the rest when Valerie jerked in surprise.

She gasped. *"Oh, shit!"*

The lizard vanished under the rock from which it had appeared.

Spencer glimpsed a word flashing on the display screen: LOCKON.

Valerie hit the power switch on the logic unit.

Just before the screen went dead, Spencer saw two more words flash under the first: TRACE BACK.

Valerie exploded to her feet, yanked both utility-cord plugs from the computer, and sprinted into the sun, to the microwave dish. "Load everything into the Rover!"

Getting to his feet, Spencer said, "What's happening?"

"They're using an EPA satellite." She had already retrieved the microwave dish and had turned toward him. "And they're running some sort of weird damned security program. Locks onto any invasive signal and traces back." Hurrying past him, she said, "Help me pack. Move, damn it, *move!*"

He balanced the keyboard on top of the monitor and picked up the entire workstation, including the rubber mat beneath it. Following Valerie to the Rover, his bruised muscles protesting at the demand for haste, he said, "They found us?"

"Bastards!" she fumed.

"Maybe you switched off in time."

"No."

"How can they be sure it's us?"

"They'll know."

"It was just a microwave signal, no fingerprints on it."

"They're coming," she insisted.

∽

Sunday night, their third night together, Eve Jammer and Roy Miro had begun their passionate but contact-free lovemaking earlier in the evening than they had done previously. Therefore, although that session was the longest and most ardent to date, they concluded before midnight. Thereafter, they lay chastely side by side on her bed, in the soft blue glow of indirect neon, each of them guarded by the loving eyes of the other's reflection in the ceiling mirror. Eve was as naked as the day that she'd slipped into the world, and Roy was fully clothed. In time they enjoyed a deep and restful sleep.

Because he had brought an overnight bag, Roy was able to get ready for work in the morning without returning to his hotel suite on the Strip. He showered in the guest bath, rather than in Eve's, for he had no desire to undress and reveal his many imperfections, from his stubby toes to his knobby knees, to his paunch, to the spray of freckles and the two moles on his chest. Besides, neither of them wanted to follow the other's session in any shower stall. If he were to stand on tiles wet with her bathwater or vice versa . . . well, in a subtle but disturbing way, that act would violate the satisfyingly dry relationship, free of fluid exchanges, which they had established and on which they thrived.

He supposed some people would think them mad. But anyone who was truly in love would understand.

With no need to go to the hotel, Roy arrived at the satellite-communications room early Monday. When he walked through the door, he knew that something exciting had transpired only moments before. Several people were gathered down front, gazing up at the wall display, and the buzz of conversation had a positive sound.

Ken Hyckman, the morning duty officer, was smiling broadly. Clearly eager to be the first to impart the good news, he waved at Roy to come down to the U-shaped control console.

Hyckman was a tall, blandly handsome, blown-dry type. He looked as if he had joined the agency following an attempt at a career as a TV news anchorman.

According to Eve, Hyckman had made several passes at her, but she had put a chill on him each time. If Roy had thought that Ken Hyckman was in any way a threat to Eve, he would have blown the bastard's head off right there, and to hell with the consequences. He found considerable peace of mind, however, in the knowledge that he had fallen in love with a woman who could pretty much take care of herself.

"We found them!" Hyckman announced as Roy approached him at the control console. "She up-linked to Earthguard to see if we were using it for satellite surveillance."

"How do you know it's her?"

"It's her *style.*"

"Admittedly, she's a bold one," Roy said. "But I hope you've got more to go on than sheer instinct."

"Well, hell, the up-link was from the middle of nowhere. Who else would it be?" Hyckman asked, pointing at the wall.

The orbital view currently on display was a simple, enhanced, tele-scopic look-down that included the southern halves of Nevada and Utah, plus the northern third of Arizona. Las Vegas was in the lower left corner. The three red and two white rings of a small, flashing bul-l's-eye marked the remote position from which the up-link had been initiated.

Hyckman said, "One hundred and fifteen miles north-northeast of Vegas, in desert flats northeast of Pahroc Summit and northwest of Oak Springs Summit. Middle of nowhere, like I told you."

"It's an EPA satellite we're using," Roy reminded him. "Could have been an EPA employee trying to up-link to get an aerial view of his work site beamed down to a computer there. Or a spectrographic analysis of the terrain. Or a hundred other things."

"EPA employee? But it's the middle of nowhere," Hyckman said. He seemed stuck on that phrase, as though repeating the haunting lyrics of an old song. "Middle of nowhere."

"Curiously enough," Roy said with a warm smile that took the sting out of his sarcasm, "a lot of environmental research is done in the field, right out there in the *environment,* and you'd be amazed if you knew how much of the planet is in the middle of nowhere."

"Yeah, maybe so. But if it was somebody legitimate, a scientist or something, why terminate contact so fast, before doing anything?"

"Now *that* is the first shred of meat you've provided," Roy said. "But it's not enough to nourish a certainty."

Hyckman looked bewildered. "What?"

Instead of explaining, Roy said, "What's with the bull's-eye? Targets are always marked with a white cross."

Grinning, pleased with himself, Hyckman said, "I thought this was more interesting, adds a little fun."

"Looks like a video game," Roy said.

"Thanks," Hyckman said, interpreting the slight as a compliment.

"Factoring in magnification," Roy said, "what altitude does this view represent?"

"Twenty thousand feet."

"Much too high. Bring us down to five thousand."

"We're in the process right now," Hyckman said, indicating some of the people working at the computers in the center of the room.

A cool, soft, female voice came from the control-center address sys-tem: *"Higher-magnification view coming up."*

～

The terrain was rugged, if not forbidding, but Valerie drove as she might have driven on a smooth ribbon of freeway blacktop. The tortured Rover leaped and plunged, rocked and swayed, bounced and shuddered across that inhospitable land, rattling and creaking as if at any moment it would explode like the overstressed springs and gearwheels of a clockwork toy.

Spencer occupied the passenger seat, with the SIG 9mm pistol in his right hand. The Micro Uzi was on the floor between his feet.

Rocky sat behind them, in the narrow clear space between the back of the front seat and the mass of gear that filled the rest of the cargo area all the way to the tailgate. The dog's good ear was pricked, because he was interested in their lurching progress, and his other ear flapped like a rag.

"Can't we slow down a little?" Spencer asked. He had to raise his voice to be heard above the tumult: the roaring engine, the tires stuttering across a washboard gully.

Valerie leaned over the steering wheel, looked up at the sky, craned her head left and right. "Wide and blue. No clouds anywhere, damn it. I was hoping we wouldn't have to make a run for it until we had clouds again."

"Does it matter? What about the infrared surveillance you were talking about, the way they can see through clouds?"

Looking ahead again as the Range Rover chewed its way up the gully wall, she said, "That's a threat when we're sitting still, in the middle of nowhere, the only unnatural heat source for miles. But it's not much good to them when we're on the move. Especially not if we were on a highway, with other cars, where they can't analyze the Rover's heat signature and distinguish it in traffic."

The top of the gully wall proved to be a low ridge, over which they shot with sufficient speed to be airborne for a second or two. They slammed front-tires-first onto a long, gradual slope of gray-black-pink shale.

Slivers of shale, spun up by the tires, showered against the undercarriage, and Valerie shouted to be heard above a hard clatter as loud as a hailstorm: "With a sky that blue, we have more to worry about than infrared. They have a clear, bare-eyed look-down at us."

"You think they've already seen us?"

"You can bet your ass they're already *looking* for us," she said, barely audible because of the machine-gun shatters of shale that volleyed beneath them.

"Eyes in the sky," he said, more to himself than to her.

The world seemed upside down: Blue heavens had become the place where demons lived.

Valerie shouted: "Yeah, they're looking. And for sure, it won't be much longer till we're spotted, considering we're the only moving thing, other than snakes and jackrabbits, for at least five miles in any direction."

The Rover roared off the shale onto softer soil, and the sudden diminution of noise was such a relief that the usual tumult, which had earlier been so annoying, now seemed by comparison like the music of a string quartet.

Valerie said, "Damn! I only up-linked to confirm that it was clear. I didn't really think they'd still be there, still tying up a satellite for a third day. And I sure as hell didn't think they'd be locking on incoming signals."

"Three days?"

"Yeah, they probably started surveillance before dawn Saturday, as soon as the storm passed and the sky cleared. Oh, man, they must want us even worse than I thought."

"What day is this?" he asked uneasily.

"Monday."

"I was sure this was Sunday."

"You were dead to the world a lot longer than you think. Since sometime Friday afternoon."

Even if unconsciousness had healed into ordinary sleep sometime during the previous night, he had been pretty much out of his head for forty-eight to sixty hours. Because he valued self-control so highly, the contemplation of such a lengthy delirium made him queasy.

He remembered some of what he'd said when he'd been out of his head. He wondered what else he had told her that he couldn't recall.

Looking at the sky again, Valerie said, "I *hate* these bastards!"

"Who are they?" he asked, not for the first time.

"You don't want to know," she said, as before. "As soon as you know, you're a dead man."

"Looks like there's a good chance I'm already a dead man. And I sure wouldn't want them to whack me and never know who they were."

She mulled that over as she accelerated up another hill, a long one this time. "Okay. You've got a point. But later. Right now, I've got to concentrate on getting us out of this mess."

"There's a way out?"

"Between slim and none—but a way."

"I thought, with that satellite, they were going to spot us any second now."

"They will. But the nearest place the bastards have any men is probably back in Vegas, a hundred and ten miles from here, maybe even a hundred twenty. That's how far I got Friday night, before I decided that staying on the move was making you worse. By the time they get a hit squad together and fly in here after us, we've got two hours minimum, two and a half max."

"To do what?"

"To lose them again," she said somewhat impatiently.

"How do we lose them if they're watching us from outer space, for God's sake?" he demanded.

"Boy, does *that* sound paranoid," she said.

"It's not paranoid, it's what they're *doing*."

"I know, I know. But it sure sounds crazy, doesn't it?" She adopted a voice not dissimilar from that of Goofy, the Disney cartoon character. "Watching us from outer space, funny little men in pointy hats, with ray guns, gonna steal our women, destroy the world."

Behind them, Rocky woofed softly, intrigued by the Goofy voice.

She dropped the funny voice. "Are we living in screwed-up times or what? God in Heaven, are we ever."

As they crested the top of the long hill, giving the springs another hard workout, Spencer said, "One minute I think I know you, and the next minute I don't know you at all."

"Good. Keeps you alert. We need to be alert."

"You suddenly seem to think this is funny."

"Oh, sometimes I can't *feel* the humor any more than you're able to right now. But we live in God's amusement park. Take it too seriously, you'll go nuts. On some level, everything's funny, even the blood and the dying. Don't you think so?"

"No. No, I don't."

"Then how do you ever get along?" she asked, but not in the least flippantly, with total seriousness now.

"It hasn't been easy."

The broad, flat top of the hill featured more brush than they had yet encountered. Valerie didn't let up on the accelerator, and the Rover smashed through everything in its way.

Spencer persisted: "How will we lose them if they're watching us from outer space?"

"Trick 'em."

"How?"

"With some clever moves."

"Such as?"

"I don't know yet."

He wouldn't relent: "When will you know?"

"I sure hope before our two hours are up." She frowned at the odometer. "Seems like we ought to've gone six miles."

"Seems like a hundred. Much more of this damn bouncing, and my headache's going to come back hard."

The broad top of the hill didn't drop off abruptly but melted into a long, descending slope that was covered with tall grass as dry, pale, and translucent as insect wings. At the bottom were two lanes of blacktop that led east and west.

"What's that?" he wondered.

"Old Federal Highway Ninety-three," she said.

"You knew it was there? How?"

"Either I studied a map while you were out of your head—or I'm just dead-on psychic."

"Probably both," he said, for again she had surprised him.

○

Because the view from five thousand feet didn't provide adequate resolution of car-size objects at ground level, Roy requested that the system focus down to one thousand feet.

For clarity, that extreme degree of magnification required more than the usual amount of image enhancement. The additional processing of the incoming Earthguard transmission required so much computer capacity that other agency work was halted to free the Cray for this urgent task. Otherwise, more minutes of delay would have occurred between receipt of an image and its projection in the control center.

Less than a minute passed before the cool, almost whispery, female voice again spoke softly from the public-address system: *"Suspect vehicle acquired."*

Ken Hyckman dashed away from the control console into the two rows of computers, all of which were manned. He returned within another minute, boyish and buoyant. "We've got her."

"We can't know yet," Roy cautioned.

"Oh, we've got her, all right," Hyckman said excitedly, turning to beam at the wall display. "What other vehicle would be out there, on the move, in the same area where somebody tried to up-link?"

"Could still be some EPA scientist."

"Suddenly on the run?"

"Maybe just moving around."

"Moving *real* fast for the terrain."

"Well, there aren't any speed limits out there."

"Too coincidental," said Hyckman. "It's her."

"We'll see."

With a ripple, beginning at the left and moving to the right across the wall display, the image changed. The new view shifted, blurred, shifted, cleared, shifted, blurred, cleared again—and they were looking down from one thousand feet onto rough terrain.

A vehicle of unidentifiable type and make, obviously with off-road capability, raced across a table of brush-covered land. It was still a woefully tiny object seen from that altitude.

"Focus down to five hundred feet," Roy ordered.

"Higher-magnification view coming up."

After a brief delay, the display rippled left to right again. The image blurred, shifted, blurred, cleared.

Earthguard 3 was not directly over the moving target but in a geo-synchronous orbit to the east and north. Therefore, the target was observed at an angle, which required additional automated processing of the image to eliminate distortions caused by the perspective. The result, however, was a picture that included not only the rectangular forms of the roof and hood but a severe angular view of one flank of the vehicle.

Although Roy knew that an element of distortion still remained, he was half convinced that he could see a couple of brighter spots glimmering in that fleet shadow, which might have been driver's-side windows reflecting the morning sun.

As the suspect vehicle reached the brink of the hill and began to descend a long slope, Roy peered at the foremost of those possible windows and wondered if, indeed, the woman waited to be discovered on the other side of a pane of sun-bronzed glass. Had they found her at last?

The target was approaching a highway.

"What road is that?" Roy demanded. "Give us some overlays, let's identify this. Quickly."

Hyckman pressed a console key and spoke into the microphone.

On the wall, by the time the suspect turned east onto the two-lane highway, a multicolored overlay identified a few topographical features— as well as Federal Highway 93.

ဢ

When Valerie didn't hesitate before turning east on the highway, Spencer said, "Why not west?"

"Because there's nothing in that direction but Nevada badlands. First town is over two hundred miles. Warm Springs, they call it, but it's so small it might as well be Warm *Spit*. We'd never get that far. Lonely, empty land. There's a thousand places they could hit us between here and there, and no one would ever see what happened. We'd just disappear off the face of the earth."

"So where are we headed?"

"It's several miles to Caliente, then ten more to Panaca—"

"They don't sound like metropolises, either."

"Then we cross the border into Utah. Modena, Newcastle—they aren't exactly cities that never sleep. But after Newcastle, there's Cedar City."

"Big time."

"Fourteen thousand people or thereabouts," she said. "Which is maybe all the bigger we need to give us a chance to slip surveillance long enough to get out of the Rover and into something else."

The two-lane blacktop featured frequent subsidence swales, lumpy patches, and unrepaired potholes. Along both shoulders, the pavement was deteriorating. As an obstacle course, it provided no challenge to the Rover—though after the jolting overland journey, Spencer wished the truck had cushier springs and shock absorbers.

Regardless of the road condition, Valerie kept the pedal down, maintaining a speed that was punishing if not reckless.

"I hope this pavement gets better soon," he said.

"Judging by the map, it probably gets worse after Panaca. From there on, all the way into Cedar City, it's just state routes."

"And how far to Cedar City?"

"About a hundred and twenty miles," she said, as though that was not bad news.

He gaped at her in disbelief. "You've got to be kidding. Even with luck, on roads like this—roads worse than this!—we'll need two hours to get there."

"We're doing seventy now."

"And it feels like a hundred and seventy!" His voice quavered as the tires jittered over a section of pavement that was as runneled as corduroy.

Her voice vibrating too, she said, "Boy, I hope you don't have hemorrhoids."

"You won't be able to keep up this speed all the way. We'll be getting into Cedar City with that hit squad right on our ass."

She shrugged. "Well, I'll bet people around there could use some excitement. Been a long time since last summer's Shakespeare Festival."

∽

At Roy's request, the magnification had been increased again to provide a view equivalent to the one that they would have had if they really had been two hundred feet above the target. Image enhancement became more difficult with each incremental increase in magnification—but fortunately there was enough additional logic-unit capacity to avoid a further processing delay.

The scale of the wall display was so much larger than before that the target rapidly progressed across the width, vanishing off the right-hand edge. But it reappeared from the left as Earthguard projected a new segment of territory that lay immediately east of the one out of which the target had driven.

The truck was rushing east, instead of south as before, so the angle now revealed some of the windshield, across which played reflections of sunlight and shadow.

"Target profile identified as that of a late-model Range Rover."

Roy Miro stared at the wall display, trying to make up his mind whether to bet the bank that the suspect vehicle contained at least the woman, if not also the scarred man.

Occasionally he glimpsed dark figures within the Rover, but he couldn't identify them. He couldn't even see well enough to be sure how many people were in the damn thing or what sex they were.

Further magnification would require long, tedious enhancement sessions. By the time they were able to obtain a more detailed look inside that vehicle, the driver would have been able to reach—and get lost in— any of half a dozen major cities.

If he committed men and equipment to stopping the Range Rover, and if the occupants proved to be innocent people, he would forfeit any chance of nailing the woman. She might break cover while he was distracted, might slip down into Arizona or back into California.

"Target's speed is seventy-two miles per hour."

To justify going after the Rover, a lot of assumptions had to be made, with little or no supporting evidence. That Spencer Grant had survived when his Explorer had been swept away in a flash flood. That somehow he had been able to alert the woman to his whereabouts. That she had rendezvoused with him in the desert, and that they had driven away together in her vehicle. That the woman, realizing the agency might resort to orbital-surveillance resources to locate her, had gone to ground early Saturday, before the cloud cover dissipated. That this morning she had broken cover, had started up-linking with available surveillance satellites to determine if anyone was still looking specifically for her, had been surprised by the trace-back program, and had just minutes ago begun to run for her life.

That was a series of assumptions long enough to make Roy uneasy.

"Target's speed is seventy-four miles per hour."

"Too damn fast for the roads in that area," Ken Hyckman said. "It's her, and she's scared."

Saturday and Sunday, Earthguard had discovered two hundred sixteen suspect vehicles in the designated search zone, most of which had been engaged in off-road recreation of one kind or another. The drivers and passengers eventually had gotten out of their vehicles, been observed either by satellite or chopper overflight, and proved not to be Grant or the woman. This might be number two hundred seventeen on that list of false alarms.

"Target's speed is seventy-six miles per hour."

On the other hand, this was the best suspect they'd had in more than two days of searching.

And ever since Friday afternoon in Flagstaff, Arizona, the power of Kevorkian had been with him. It had brought him to Eve and had changed his life. He should trust in it to guide his decisions.

He closed his eyes, took several deep breaths, and said, "Let's put a team together and go after them."

"Yes!" Ken Hyckman said, punching one fist into the air in an annoying, adolescent expression of enthusiasm.

"Twelve men, full assault gear," Roy said, "leaving in fifteen minutes or less. Arrange transport from the roof here, so we don't waste time. Two large executive choppers."

"You got it," Hyckman promised.

"Make sure they understand to terminate the woman on sight."

"Of course."

"With extreme prejudice."

Hyckman nodded.

"Give her no chance—*no chance*—to slip loose again. But we have to take Grant alive, interrogate him, find out how he fits into all this, who the sonofabitch is working for."

"To give you the quality of satellite look-down you'll need in the field," Hyckman said, "we'll have to remote-program Earthguard to alter its orbit temporarily, nail it specifically to that Rover."

"Do it," Roy said.

12

B<small>Y THAT</small> M<small>ONDAY MORNING</small> in February, Captain Harris Descoteaux, of the Los Angeles Police Department, would not have been surprised to discover that he had died the previous Friday and had been in Hell ever since. The outrages perpetrated upon him would have occupied the time and energies of numerous clever, malicious, industrious demons.

At eleven-thirty Friday night, as Harris was making love to his wife, Jessica, and as their daughters—Willa and Ondine—were asleep or watching television in other bedrooms, an FBI special-weapons-and-tactics team, in a joint operation between the FBI and the Drug Enforcement Administration, raided the Descoteaux house on a quiet street in Burbank. The assault was executed with the stalwart commitment and merciless force exhibited by any platoon of United States Marines in any battle in any war in the country's history.

On all sides of the house, with a synchronization that would have been envied by the most demanding symphony-orchestra conductor, stun grenades were launched through windows. The blasts of sound instantly disoriented Harris, Jessica, and their daughters, and also temporarily impaired their motor-nerve functions.

Even as porcelain figurines toppled and paintings clattered against walls in response to those shock waves, the front and back doors were battered down. Heavily armed men in black helmets and bullet-resistant vests swarmed into the Descoteaux residence and dispersed like a doomsday tide through its rooms.

One moment, in romantically soft amber lamplight, Harris was in the arms of his wife, gliding back and forth on the sweet dissolving edge of bliss. The next moment, passion having turned to terror, he was staggering around in the infuriatingly *dim* lamplight, naked and confused. His limbs twitched, his knees repeatedly buckled, and the room seemed to tumble like a giant barrel in a carnival fun house.

Though his ears were ringing, he heard men shouting elsewhere in the house: "FBI! FBI! FBI!" The booming voices weren't reassuring. Addled by a stun grenade, he couldn't think what those letters meant.

He remembered the nightstand. His revolver. Loaded.

He couldn't recall how to open a drawer. Suddenly it seemed to require superhuman intelligence, the dexterity of a torch juggler.

Then the bedroom was crowded with men as big as professional football players, all shouting at once. They forced Harris to lie facedown on the floor, with his hands behind his head.

His mind cleared. He remembered the meaning of FBI. Terror and confusion didn't evaporate, but diminished to fear and bafflement.

A helicopter roared into position above the house. Searchlights swept the yard. Over the furious pounding of the rotors, Harris heard a sound so cold that he felt as if ice had formed in his blood: his daughters, screaming as the doors to their rooms crashed open.

Being required to lie naked on the floor while Jessica was rousted from bed, equally naked, was deeply humiliating. They made her stand in a corner, with only her hands to cover herself, while they searched the bed for weapons. After an eternity, they tossed a blanket to her, and she wrapped herself in it.

Harris was eventually permitted to sit on the edge of the bed, still naked, burning with humiliation. They presented the search warrant, and he was surprised to find his name and address. He had assumed that they had invaded the wrong house. He explained that he was an LAPD captain, but they already knew and were unmoved.

At last Harris was permitted to dress in gray exercise sweats. He and Jessica were taken into the living room.

Ondine and Willa were huddled on the sofa, hugging each other for emotional support. The girls tried to rush to their parents but were restrained by officers who ordered them to remain seated.

Ondine was thirteen, and Willa was fourteen. Both girls had their mother's beauty. Ondine was dressed for bed in panties and a T-shirt that featured the face of a rap singer. Willa was wearing a cut-off T-shirt, cut-off pajama bottoms, and yellow knee socks.

Some officers were looking at the girls in a way they had no right to look. Harris asked that his daughters be allowed to put on robes, but he was ignored. While Jessica was taken to an armchair, Harris was flanked by two men who tried to lead him out of the room.

When he again requested that the girls be given robes and was ignored, he pulled away from his escorts, indignant. His indignation was interpreted as resistance. He was hit in the stomach with the butt of an assault rifle, driven to his knees, and handcuffed.

In the garage, a man who identified himself as "Agent Gurland" was at the workbench, examining a hundred plastic-wrapped kilos of cocaine, worth millions. Harris stared in disbelief, with a growing chill, as he was told that the coke had been found in his garage.

"I'm innocent. I'm a cop. I've been set up. This is nuts!"

Gurland perfunctorily recited a list of constitutional rights.

Harris was infuriated by their indifference to everything he said. His anger and frustration earned him more rough handling as he was escorted out of the house to a car at the curb. Along the street, neighbors had come onto their lawns and porches to watch.

He was taken to a federal detention facility. There he was permitted to call his attorney—who was his brother, Darius.

By virtue of being a policeman, and therefore endangered if confined with cop-hating felons, he expected to be segregated in the lockup. Instead, he was put into a holding cell with six men waiting to be charged on offenses ranging from interstate transportation of illegal drugs to the hatchet murder of a federal marshal.

All claimed that they were being railroaded. Although a few were *obviously* bad pieces of work, the captain found himself more than half believing their protestations of innocence.

At two-thirty Saturday morning, sitting across from Harris at a scarred Formica-topped table in a lawyer-client conference room, Darius said, "This is total bullshit, total, it stinks, it really *reeks*. You're the most honest man I've ever known, a straight arrow since you were a kid. You made it *hell* for a brother to measure up. You're an annoying goddamned *saint*, is what you are! Anyone who says you're a cocaine dealer is a moron or a liar. Listen, don't worry about this, don't worry for a minute, a second, a nanosecond. You have an exemplary past, not a stain, the record of an annoying goddamned saint. We'll get low bail, and eventually we'll convince them it's a mistake or a conspiracy. Listen, I swear to you, it's never going to go to trial, on our mother's grave, I swear to you."

Darius was five years younger than Harris but resembled him to such an extent that they seemed to be twins. He was also as brilliant as he was hyperkinetic, a fine criminal trial attorney. If Darius said there was no reason to worry, Harris would try not to worry.

"Listen, if it's a conspiracy," Darius said, "who's behind it? What walking slime would do this? Why? What enemies have you made?"

"I can't think of any. Not any who're capable of this."

"It's total bullshit. We'll have them crawling on their bellies to apologize, the bastards, the morons, the ignorant geeks. This *burns* me. Even saints make enemies, Harris."

"I can't point a finger," Harris insisted.

"Maybe saints *especially* make enemies."

Less than eight hours later, shortly after ten o'clock Saturday morning, with his brother at his side, Harris was brought before a judge. He was ordered held for trial. The federal prosecutor wanted a ten-million-dollar bail, but Darius argued for Harris's release on his own recognizance. Bail was set at five hundred thousand, which Darius considered acceptable because Harris would be free upon posting ten percent to a bondsman's ninety.

Harris and Jessica had seventy-three thousand in stocks and savings accounts. Since Harris didn't intend to flee prosecution, they would get their money back when he went to court.

The situation wasn't ideal. But before they could proceed to structure a legal counteroffensive and get the charges dismissed, Harris had to regain his freedom and escape the extraordinary danger faced by a police officer in jail. At least events were finally moving in the right direction.

Seven hours later, at five o'clock Saturday afternoon, Harris was taken from the holding cell to the lawyer-client conference room, where Darius was waiting for him again—with bad news. The FBI had persuaded a judge that probable cause existed to conclude that the Descoteaux house had been used for illegal purposes, thus permitting immediate application of federal property-forfeiture statutes. The FBI and DEA then acquired liens against the house and its contents.

To protect the government's interests, federal marshals had evicted Jessica, Willa, and Ondine, permitting them to pack only a few articles of clothing. The locks had been changed. At least for the time being, guards were posted at the property.

Darius said, "This is crap. Okay, maybe it doesn't technically violate the recent Supreme Court decision on forfeiture, but it sure as hell violates the *spirit*. For one thing, the court said they now have to give the property owner a notice of intent to seize."

"Intent to seize?" Harris said, bewildered.

"Of course, they'll say they served that notice at the same time as the eviction order, which they did. But the court clearly meant there should be a decent interval between notice and eviction."

Harris didn't understand. "Evicted Jessica and the girls?"

"Don't worry about them," Darius said. "They're staying with Bonnie and me. They're all right."

"How can they evict them?"

"Until the Supreme Court rules on other aspects of forfeiture laws, if it ever does, eviction can still take place prior to the hearing, which is unfair. Unfair? Jesus, it's worse than unfair, it's totalitarian. At least these days you get a hearing, which wasn't required till recently. You'll go before a judge in ten days, and he'll listen to your argument against forfeiture."

"It's my house."

"That's no argument. We'll do better than that."

"But it's my house."

"I have to tell you, the hearing doesn't mean much. The feds will pull every trick in the book to be sure it's assigned to a judge with a strong history of endorsing the forfeiture laws. I'll try to prevent that, try to get you a judge who still remembers this is supposed to be a democracy. But the reality is, ninety-nine percent of the time, the feds get the judge they want. We'll have a hearing, but the ruling is almost certain to be against us and in favor of forfeiture."

Harris was having difficulty absorbing the horror of what his brother had told him. Shaking his head, he said, "They can't put my family out of the house. I haven't been convicted of anything."

"You're a cop. You must know how the forfeiture laws work. They've been on the books ten years, growing broader every year."

"I'm a cop, yes, not a prosecutor. I get the bad guys, and the district attorney's office decides under what laws to prosecute."

"Then this will be an unpleasant lesson. See . . . to lose your property under forfeiture statutes, you don't have to be convicted."

"They can take my property even if I'm found innocent?" Harris said, and he was sure that he was having a nightmare based on some Kafka short story he'd read in college.

"Harris, listen very closely here. Forget about conviction or acquittal. *They can take your property and not even charge you with a crime.* Without taking you to court. Of course, you *have* been charged, which gives them an even stronger hand."

"Wait, wait. How did this happen?"

"If there's evidence of any nature that the property was used for an illegal purpose, *even one of which you have no knowledge*, that's sufficient probable cause for forfeiture. Isn't that a cute touch? You don't even have to know about it, to lose your property."

"No, I mean, *how did this happen in America?*"

"The war against drugs. That's what the forfeiture laws were written for. To come down hard on drug dealers, break them."

Darius was more subdued than on his previous visit that morning. His hyperkinetic nature was expressed not primarily in his usual, voluble flow of words as much as in his ceaseless fidgeting.

Harris was as alarmed by the change in his brother as by what he was learning. "This evidence, the cocaine, was *planted*."

"You know that, I know that. But the court has to see you prove it before it'll reverse a forfeiture."

"You mean, I'm guilty till proven innocent."

"That's the way the forfeiture laws work. But at least you've been charged with a crime. You'll have your day in court. By proving you're innocent in a criminal trial, you'll indirectly have a chance to prove forfeiture was unjustified. Now, I hope to God they don't drop the charges."

Harris blinked in surprise. "You hope they *don't* drop them?"

"If they drop the charges, no criminal trial. Then the best chance you'll ever have to get your house back is at the upcoming hearing I mentioned."

"My *best* chance? At this rigged hearing?"

"Not rigged exactly. Just in front of *their* judge."

"What's the difference?"

Darius nodded wearily. "Not much. And once forfeiture is approved in that hearing, if you didn't have a criminal trial in which to state your case, you'd have to initiate legal action, sue the FBI and the DEA, to get the forfeiture overturned. That would be an uphill battle. Government attorneys would repeatedly attempt to have your suit dismissed—until they found a sympathetic court. Even if you got a jury or panel of judges to overturn the forfeiture, the government would appeal and appeal, trying to exhaust you."

"But if they dropped the charges against me, how could they still keep my house?" He understood what his brother had told him. He just didn't understand the logic or the justice of it.

"Like I explained," Darius said patiently, "all they have to show is evidence the *property* was used for illegal purposes. Not that you or any member of your family was involved in that activity."

"But then who would they claim was stashing cocaine there?"

Darius sighed. "They don't have to name anyone."

Astonished, reluctantly accepting the full monstrousness of it at last, Harris said, "They can seize my house by claiming someone was dealing drugs out of it—but not have to name a suspect?"

"As long as they have evidence, yes."

"The evidence was planted!"

"Like I explained already, you'd have to prove that to a court."

"But if they don't charge me with a crime, I might never get *into* a court with a suit of my own."

"Right." Darius smiled humorlessly. "Now you see why I hope to God they don't drop the charges. Now you understand the rules."

"Rules?" Harris said. "These aren't rules. This is *madness.*"

He needed to pace, work off a sudden dark energy that filled him. His anger and outrage were so great that his knees were weak when he tried to stand. Halfway to his feet, he was forced to sit again, as if suffering the effects of another stun grenade.

"You okay?" Darius worried.

"But these laws were only supposed to target major drug dealers, racketeers, Mafia."

"Sure. People who might liquidate property, flee the country before they went to trial. That was the original intent when the laws were passed. But now there are two hundred federal offenses, not just drug offenses, that allow property forfeiture without trial, and they were used fifty thousand times last year."

"Fifty thousand!"

"It's becoming a major source of funding for law enforcement. Once liquidated, eighty percent of seized assets goes to the police agencies in the case, twenty percent to the prosecutor."

They sat in silence. The old-fashioned wall clock ticked softly. The sound brought to mind the image of a time bomb, and Harris felt as though he were, in fact, sitting on just such an explosive device.

No less angry than he had been but more in control of his anger, he said at last, "They're going to sell my house, aren't they?"

"Well, at least this is a federal seizure. If it was under the California forfeiture law, it'd be gone ten days after the hearing. Feds give us more time."

"They'll sell it."

"Listen, we'll do everything we can to overturn before then. . . ." Darius's voiced trailed away. He was no longer able to look his brother in the eyes. Finally he said, "And even after assets are liquidated, if you can overturn, then you can get compensation—though not for any costs you incurred related to the forfeiture."

"But I can kiss my house good-bye. I might get money back but not my house. And I can't get back all the *time* this will take."

"There's legislation in Congress to reform these laws."

"Reform? Not toss them out completely?"

"No. The government likes the laws too much. Even the proposed reforms don't go far enough and don't have wide support yet."

"Evicted my family," Harris said, still gripped by disbelief.

"Harris, I feel rotten. I'll do everything I can, I'll be a tiger on their ass, I swear, but I ought to be able to do *more*."

Harris's hands were fisted again on the table. "None of this is your fault, little brother. You didn't write the laws. We'll . . . just cope. Somehow, we'll cope. The important thing now is to post bail, so I can get out of here."

Darius put the heels of his coal-black hands to his eyes and pressed gently, as if trying to banish his weariness. Like Harris, he hadn't slept the previous night. "That's going to take until Monday. I'll go to my bank first thing Monday morning—"

"No, no. You don't have to put up your money for bail. We've got it. Didn't Jessica tell you? And our bank's open Saturdays."

"She told me. But—"

"Not open now, but it was earlier. God, I wanted out today."

Lowering his hands from his face, Darius met his brother's eyes with reluctance. "Harris, they've impounded your bank accounts too."

"They can't do that," he said angrily, but no longer with any conviction. "Can they?"

"Savings, checking, all of it, whether it was a joint account with Jessie, in your name, or just in her name. They're calling it all illegal drug profits, even the Christmas-club account."

Harris felt as if he'd been hit in the face. A strange numbness began to spread through him. "Darius, I can't . . . I can't let you put up all the bail. Not fifty thousand. We have some stocks—"

"Your brokerage account's impounded too, pending forfeiture."

Harris stared at the clock. The second hand twitched around the face. The time-bomb sound seemed louder, louder.

Reaching across the conference-room table, putting his hands over Harris's fists, Darius said, "Big brother, I swear, we'll get through this together."

"With everything impounded . . . we have nothing but the cash in my wallet and Jessica's purse. Jesus. Maybe just her purse. My wallet is in the nightstand drawer at home, if she didn't think to bring it when . . . when they made her and the girls leave."

"So Bonnie and I are putting up bail, and we don't want any argument about it," Darius said.

Tick . . . tick . . . tick . . .

Harris's entire face was numb. The back of his neck was numb, pebbled with gooseflesh. Numb and cold.

Darius squeezed his brother's hands reassuringly once more, and then finally let go.

Harris said, "How are Jessica and I going to rent a place if we can't put together first month, last month, and security deposit?"

"You'll move in with Bonnie and me for the duration. That's already been settled."

"Your house isn't that big. You don't have room for four more."

"Jessie and the girls are already with us. You're just one more. Sure, it'll be tight, but we'll be fine. Nobody'll mind if it's a bit of a squeeze. We're family. We're in this together."

"But this might take months to get resolved. My God, it could take *years*, couldn't it?"

Tick . . . tick . . . tick . . .

Later, as Darius was about to leave, he said, "I want you to think hard about enemies, Harris. This isn't all just a big mistake. This took planning, cunning, and contacts. Somewhere, you've got a smart and powerful enemy, whether you realize it or not. Think about it. If you come up with any names, that might help me."

Saturday night, Harris shared a windowless four-bed cell with two alleged murderers and with a rapist who bragged about assaulting women in ten states. He slept only fitfully.

Sunday night, he slept much better, only because he was by then utterly exhausted. Dreams tormented him. All were nightmares, and in each, sooner or later, there was a clock ticking, ticking.

Monday, he was up at dawn, eager to be free. He was loath to let Darius and Bonnie tie up so much money to make his bail. Of course, he had no intention of fleeing jurisdiction, so they wouldn't lose their funds. And he had developed a prison claustrophobia that, if it continued to worsen, would soon be intolerable.

Though his situation was dreadful, unthinkable, he nevertheless took some solace from the certainty that the worst was behind him. Everything had been taken away—or soon would be taken. He was at the bottom, and in spite of the long fight ahead, he had nowhere to go but up.

That was Monday morning. Early.

ॐ

At Caliente, Nevada, the federal highway angled north, but at Panaca they left it for a state route that turned east toward the Utah border. The rural highway carried them into higher land that had a stark, cauldron-of-creation quality, almost pre-Mesozoic, even though it was forested with pine and spruce.

As crazy as it sounded, Spencer was nevertheless completely convinced by Valerie's fear of satellite surveillance. All was blue above, with no monstrous mechanical presences hovering like something out of *Star Wars*, but he was uncomfortably aware of being watched, mile by lonely mile.

Regardless of the eye in the sky and the professional killers who might be en route to Utah to intercept them, Spencer was ravenous. Two small cans of Vienna sausages had not satisfied his hunger. He ate cheese crackers and washed them down with a Coke.

Behind the front seats, sitting erect in his narrow quarters, Rocky was so enthusiastic about Valerie's way with a Rover that he expressed no interest in the cheese crackers. He grinned broadly. His head bobbed up and down, up and down.

"What's with the dog?" she asked.

"He likes the way you drive. He has a need for speed."

"Really? He's such a frightened little guy most of the time."

"I just found out about this speed thing myself," Spencer said.

"Why's he so afraid of everything?"

"He was abused before he wound up in the pound, before I brought him home. I don't know what's in his past."

"Well, it's nice to see him enjoying himself so much."

Rocky's head bobbed enthusiastically.

As tree shadows flickered across the roadway, Spencer said, "I don't know what's in your past, either." Instead of responding, she eased down on the accelerator, but Spencer persisted: "Who are you running from? Now they're my enemies too. I have a right to know."

She stared intently at the road. "They don't have a name."

"What—a secret society of fanatical assassins, like in an old Fu Manchu novel?"

"More or less." She was serious. "It's a nameless government agency, financed by misdirected appropriations intended for lots of other programs. Also by hundreds of millions of dollars a year from cases involving the asset-forfeiture laws. Originally it was intended to be used to conceal the illegal actions and botched operations of government bureaus and agencies ranging from the post office to the FBI. A political pressure-release valve."

"An independent cover-up squad."

"Then if a reporter or anybody discovered evidence of a cover-up in a case that, say, the FBI had investigated, that cover-up couldn't be traced to anyone in the FBI itself. This independent group covers the Bureau's ass, so the Bureau never has to destroy evidence, bribe judges, intimidate witnesses, all that nasty stuff. The perpetrators are mysterious, nameless. No proof they're government employees."

The sky was still blue and cloudless, but the day seemed darker than it had been before.

Spencer said, "There's enough paranoia in this concept for half a dozen Oliver Stone movies."

"Stone sees the shadow of the oppressor but doesn't understand who casts it," she said. "Hell, even the average FBI or ATF agent is unaware this agency exists. It operates at a very high level."

"How high?" he wondered.

"Its top officers answer to Thomas Summerton."

Spencer frowned. "Is that name supposed to mean something?"

"He's independently wealthy, a major political fund-raiser and wheeler-dealer. And currently the first deputy attorney general."

"Of what?"

"Of the Kingdom of Oz—what do you think?" she said impatiently. "First Deputy Attorney General of the United States!"

"You've got to be putting me on."

"Look it up in an almanac, read a newspaper."

"I don't mean you're kidding about him being the first deputy. I mean, about him being involved in a conspiracy like this."

"I know it for a fact. I know *him*. Personally."

"But in that position, he's the second most powerful person in the Department of Justice. The next link up the chain from him . . ."

"Curdles your blood, doesn't it?"

"Are you saying the attorney general knows about this?"

She shook her head. "I don't know. I hope not. I've never seen any evidence. But I don't rule out anything any more."

Ahead, in the westbound lane, a gray Chevrolet van topped a hill and came toward them. Spencer didn't like the looks of it. According to Valerie's schedule, they weren't likely to be in immediate danger for the better part of two hours yet. But she might be wrong. Maybe the agency didn't have to fly in thugs from Vegas. Maybe it already had operatives in the area.

He wanted to tell her to turn off the road at once. They had to put trees between themselves and any fusillade of machine-gun fire directed at them. But there was nowhere to go: no connecting road in sight and a six-foot drop beyond the narrow shoulder.

He put his hand on the SIG 9mm pistol that lay in his lap.

As the oncoming Chevy passed the Rover, the driver gave them a look of astonished recognition. He was big. About forty. A broad, hard face. His eyes widened, and his mouth opened as he spoke to another man in the van with him, and then he was gone.

Spencer turned in his seat to look after the Chevy, but because of Rocky and half a ton of gear, he wasn't able to see through the tailgate window. He peered in his side mirror and watched the van as it dwindled westward behind them. No brake lights. It wasn't turning to follow the Rover.

Belatedly, he realized that the driver's look of astonishment had nothing to do with recognition. The man simply had been amazed by how fast they were going. According to the speedometer, Valerie was pressing eighty-five miles per hour, thirty over the legal speed limit and fifteen or twenty too fast for the condition of the road.

Spencer's heart was thudding. Not because of her driving.

Valerie met his eyes again. She was clearly aware of the fear that had gripped him. "I warned you that you didn't really want to know who they are." She turned her attention to the highway. "Kind of gives you the heebie-jeebies, doesn't it?"

"Heebie-jeebies doesn't quite describe it. I feel as if . . ."

"You've been given an ice-water enema?" she suggested.

"You find even *this* funny?"

"On one level."

"Not me. Jesus. If the attorney general knows," he said, "then the *next* link up the chain—"

"The President of the United States."

"I don't know what's worse: that maybe the president and the attorney general sanction an agency like you described . . . or that it operates at such a high level *without* their knowledge. Because if they don't know, and they stumble across its existence—"

"They're dead meat."

"And if they don't know, then the people who're running this country aren't the people we elected."

"I can't say it goes as high as the attorney general. And I don't have a clue about Oval Office involvement. I hope not. But—"

"But you don't rule out anything any more," he finished for her.

"Not after what I've been through. These days, I don't really trust anyone but God and myself. Lately I'm not so sure about God."

⟋

Down in the concrete aural cavity, where the agency listened to Las Vegas with a multitude of secret ears, Roy Miro said good-bye to Eve Jammer.

There were no tears, no qualms at being separated and possibly never seeing each other again. They were confident of being together soon. Roy was still energized by the spiritual power of Kevorkian, felt all but immortal. For her part, Eve seemed never to have realized that she *could* die or that anything she truly wanted—such as Roy—could be denied her.

They stood close. He put down his attaché case to be able to hold her flawless hands, and he said, "I'll try to be back here this evening, but there's no guarantee."

"I'll miss you," she said huskily. "But if you can't make it, I'll do something to remember you by, something that will remind me how exciting you are and make me even more eager to have you back."

"What? Tell me what you're going to do, so I can carry the image in my mind, an image of you to make the time away pass faster."

He was surprised at how good he was at this love talk. He had always known that he was a shameless romantic, but he had never been sure that he would know how to act when and if he ever found a woman who measured up to his standards.

"I don't want to tell you now," she said playfully. "I want you to dream, wonder, imagine. Because when you get back and I tell you—*then* we'll have the most thrilling night we've had yet."

The heat pouring off Eve was incredible. Roy wanted nothing more than to close his eyes and melt in her radiance.

He kissed her on the cheek. His lips were chapped from the desert air, and her skin was hot. It was a deliciously dry kiss.

Turning away from her was agony. At the elevator, as the doors slid open, he looked back.

She was poised on one foot, the other raised. On the concrete floor was a black spider.

"Darling, no!" he said.

She looked up at him, baffled.

"A spider is a *perfect* little creation, Mother Nature at her best. A spinner of beautiful webs. A perfectly engineered killing machine. Its kind have been here since before the first man ever walked the earth. It deserves to live in peace."

"I don't like them much," she said with the cutest little pout that Roy had ever seen.

"When I get back, we'll examine one together, under a magnifying glass," he promised. "You'll see how perfect it is, how compact and efficient and functional. Once I show you how perfect arachnids are, they'll never seem the same to you again. You'll cherish them."

"Well," she said reluctantly, "all right," and she carefully stepped over the spider instead of tramping on it.

Full of love, Roy rode the elevator to the top floor of the high rise. He climbed a service staircase to the roof.

Eight of the twelve men in the strike force had already boarded the first of the two customized executive helicopters. With a hard clatter of rotors, the craft lifted into the sky, up and away.

The second—and identical—chopper was hovering at the north side of the building. When the landing pad was clear, the helicopter descended to pick up the four other men, all of whom were in civilian clothes but were carrying duffel bags full of weapons and gear.

Roy boarded last and sat at the back of the cabin. The seat across the aisle and the two in the forward row were empty.

As the craft took off, he opened his attaché case and plugged the computer power and transmission cables into outlets in the back wall of the cabin. He divorced the cellular telephone from the workstation and put it on the seat across the aisle. He no longer needed it. Instead, he was using the chopper's communications system. A phone keypad appeared right on the display screen. After putting a call through to Mama in Virginia, he identified himself as "Pooh," provided a thumbprint, and accessed the satellite-surveillance center in the Las Vegas branch of the agency.

A miniature version of the scene on the surveillance-center wall screen appeared on Roy's VDT. The Range Rover was moving at reckless speeds, which strongly indicated that the woman was behind the wheel. It was past Panaca, Nevada, bulleting toward the Utah border.

⌢

"Something like this agency was bound to come along sooner or later," she said as they approached the Utah border. "By insisting on a perfect world, we've opened the door to fascism."

"I'm not sure I follow that." He wasn't certain that he wanted to follow it, either. She spoke with unsettling conviction.

"There've been so many laws written by so many idealists with competing visions of Utopia that nobody can get through a single day without inadvertently and unknowingly breaking a score of them."

"Cops are asked to enforce tens of thousands of laws," Spencer agreed, "more than they can keep track of."

"So they tend to lose a true sense of their mission. They lose focus. You saw it happening when you were a cop, didn't you?"

"Sure. There's been some controversy, several times, about LAPD intelligence operations that targeted legitimate citizens' groups."

"Because those particular groups at that particular time were on the 'wrong' side of sensitive issues. Government has politicized every aspect of life, including law-enforcement agencies, and all of us are going to suffer for it, regardless of our political views."

"Most cops are good guys."

"I know that. But tell me something: These days, the cops who rise to the top in the system . . . are they usually the best, or are they more often the ones who're politically astute, the great schmoozers. Are they ass kissers who know how to handle a senator, a congressman, a mayor, a city councilman, and political activists of all stripes?"

"Maybe it's always been that way."

"No. We'll probably never again see men like Elliot Ness in charge of anything—but there used to be a lot like him. Cops used to respect the brass they served. Is it always that way now?"

Spencer didn't even have to answer that one.

Valerie said, "Now it's the politicized cops who set agendas, allocate resources. It's worst at the federal level. Fortunes are spent chasing violators of vaguely written laws against hate crimes, pornography, pollution, product mislabeling, sexual harassment. Don't get me wrong. I'd love to see the world rid of every bigot, pornographer, polluter, snake-oil peddler, every jerk who harasses a woman. But at the same time, we're living with the highest rates of murder, rape, and robbery of any society in history."

The more passionately Valerie spoke, the faster she drove.

Spencer winced every time he looked away from her face to the road over which they hurtled. If she lost control, if they spun out and flew off the blacktop into those towering spruces, they wouldn't have to worry about hit squads coming in from Las Vegas.

Behind them, however, Rocky was exuberant.

She said, "The streets aren't safe. Some places, people aren't even safe in their own homes. Federal law-enforcement agencies have lost focus. When they lose focus, they make mistakes and need to be bailed out of scandals to save politicians' hides—cop politicians, as well as the appointed and elected kind."

"Which is where this agency without a name comes in."

"To sweep up the dirt, hide it under the rug—so no politicians have to put their fingerprints on the broom," she said bitterly.

They crossed into Utah.

～

They were still over the outskirts of North Las Vegas, only a few minutes into the flight, when the copilot came to the rear of the passenger compartment. He was carrying a security phone with a built-in scrambler, which he plugged in and handed to Roy.

The phone had a headset, leaving Roy's hands free. The cabin was heavily insulated, and the saucer-size earphones were of such high quality that he could hear no engine or rotor noise, although he could feel the separate vibrations of both through his seat.

Gary Duvall—the agent in northern California who had been assigned to look into the matter of Ethel and George Porth—was calling. But not from California. He was now in Denver, Colorado.

The assumption had been made that the Porths had already been living in San Francisco when their daughter had died and when their grandson had first come to live with them. That assumption had turned out to be false.

Duvall had finally located one of the Porths' former neighbors in San Francisco, who had remembered that Ethel and George had moved there from Denver. By then their daughter had been dead a long time, and their grandson, Spencer, was sixteen.

"A long time?" Roy said doubtfully. "But I thought the boy lost his mother when he was fourteen, in the same car accident where he got his scar. That's just two years earlier."

"No. Not just two years. Not a car accident."

Duvall had unearthed a secret, and he was clearly one of those people who relished being in possession of secrets. The childish I-know-something-that-you-don't-know tone of his voice indicated that he would parcel out his treasured information in order to savor each little revelation.

Sighing, Roy leaned back in his seat. "Tell me."

"I flew to Denver," Duvall said, "to see if maybe the Porths had sold a house here the same year they bought one in San Francisco. They had. So I tried to find some Denver neighbors who remembered them. No problem. I found several. People don't move as often here as in California. And they recalled the Porths and the boy because it was such sensational stuff, what happened to them."

Sighing again, Roy opened the manila envelope in which he was still carrying some of the photographs that he had found in the shoe box in Spencer Grant's Malibu cabin.

"The mother, Jennifer, she died when the boy was eight," Duvall said. "And it wasn't in any accident."

Roy slid the four photos out of the envelope. The topmost was the snapshot taken when the woman was perhaps twenty. She was wearing a simple summer dress, dappled in sun and shadow, standing by a tree that was dripping clusters of white flowers.

"Jenny was a horsewoman," Duvall said, and Roy remembered the other pictures with horses. "Rode them, bred them. The night she died, she went to a meeting of the county breeder's association."

"This was in Denver, somewhere around Denver?"

"No, that's where her parents lived. Jenny's home was in Vail, on a small ranch just outside Vail, Colorado. She showed up at that meeting of the breeder's association, but she never came home again."

The second photograph was of Jennifer and her son at the picnic table. She was hugging the boy. His baseball cap was askew.

Duvall said, "Her car was found abandoned. There was a manhunt for her. But she wasn't anywhere near home. A week later, someone finally discovered her body in a ditch, eighty miles from Vail."

As when he'd sat at the kitchen table in the Malibu cabin on Friday morning and had sorted through the photographs for the first time, Roy was overcome by a haunting sense that the woman's face was familiar. Every word that Duvall spoke brought Roy closer to the enlightenment that had eluded him three mornings ago.

Duvall's voice now came through the headphones with a strange, seductive softness: "She was found naked. Tortured, molested. Back then, it was the most savage murder anyone had ever seen. Even these days, when we've seen it all, the details would give you nightmares."

The third snapshot showed Jennifer and the boy at poolside. She held one hand behind her son's head, making horns with two fingers. The barn loomed in the background.

"Every indication was . . . she'd fallen victim to some transient," said Duvall, pouring out the details in ever smaller drops as his flask of secrets slowly emptied. "A sociopath. Some guy with a car but no permanent address, roaming the interstate highways. It was a relatively new syndrome then, twenty-two years ago, but police had started to see it often enough to recognize it: the footloose serial killer, no ties to family or community, a shark out of his school."

The woman. The boy. The barn in the background.

"The crime wasn't solved for a while. For six years, in fact."

The vibrations from the helicopter engine and rotors traveled through the frame of the craft, up Roy's seat, into his bones, and carried with them a chill. A not unpleasant chill.

"The boy and his father continued to live on the ranch," Duvall said. "There *was* a father."

The woman. The boy. The barn in the background.

Roy turned up the fourth and final photograph.

The man in the shadows. That piercing stare.

"The boy's name wasn't Spencer. Michael," Gary Duvall revealed.

The black-and-white studio photograph of the man in his middle thirties was moody: a fine study in contrasts, sunlight and darkness. Peculiar shadows, cast by unidentifiable objects beyond the frame, appeared to swarm across the wall, drawn by the subject, as if this were a man who commanded the night and all its powers.

"The boy's name was Michael—"

"Ackblom." Roy was at last able to recognize the subject in spite of the shadows that hid at least half the face. "Michael Ackblom. His father was Steven Ackblom, the painter. The murderer."

"That's right," Duvall said, sounding disappointed that he had not been able to hold off that secret for another second or two.

"Refresh my memory. How many bodies did they eventually find?"

"Forty-one," Duvall said. "And they've always thought there were more somewhere else."

" 'They were all so beautiful in their pain, and all like angels when they died,' " Roy quoted.

"You remember that?" Duvall said in surprise.

"It's the only thing Ackblom said in court."

"It's just about the only thing he said to the cops or his lawyer or anyone. He didn't feel that he'd done anything so wrong, but he acknowledged as how he understood why society thought he had. So he pleaded guilty, confessed, and accepted sentencing."

" 'They were all so beautiful in their pain, and all like angels when they died,' " Roy whispered.

※

As the Rover raced through the Utah morning, sunshine angled among the needled branches of the evergreens, flaring and flickering across the windshield. To Spencer, the swift play of bright light and shadow was as frenetic and disorienting as the pulsing of a stroboscopic lamp in a dark nightclub.

Even as he closed his eyes against that assault, he realized that he was bothered more by the association that each white flare triggered in his memory than he was by the sunshine itself. To his mind's eye, every lambent glint and glimmer was the flash of hard, cold steel out of catacomb gloom.

He never ceased to be amazed and distressed by how completely the past remained alive in the present and by how the struggle to forget was an inducement to memory.

Tracing his scar with the fingertips of his right hand, he said, "Give me an example. Tell me about one of the scandals this nameless agency smoothed over."

She hesitated. "David Koresh. The Branch Davidian compound. Waco, Texas."

Her words startled him into opening his eyes even in the bright steel blades of sunshine and the dark-blood shadows. He stared at her in disbelief. "Koresh was a maniac!"

"No argument from me. He was four different kinds of maniac, as far as I know, and I sure wouldn't disagree that the world is better off with him out of it."

"Me neither."

"But if the Bureau of Alcohol, Tobacco and Firearms wanted him on weapons charges, they could've collared him at a bar in Waco, where he often went to hear a band he liked—and *then* they could've entered the compound, with him out of the way. Instead of storming his place with a SWAT team. There were children in there, for God's sake."

"Endangered children," he reminded her.

"They sure were. They were burned to death."

"Low blow," he said accusingly, playing devil's advocate.

"The government never produced any illegal weapons. At the trial they claimed to've found guns converted to full automatic fire, but there are lots of discrepancies. The Texas Rangers recovered only two guns for each sect member—all legal. Texas is a big gun state. Seventeen million people, over sixty million guns—four per resident. People in the sect had half the guns in the *average* Texas household."

"Okay, this was in the newspapers. And the child-abuse stories turned out to have no apparent substance. That's been reported—even if not widely. It's a tragedy, for those dead kids *and* for the ATF. But what exactly did this nameless agency cover up? It was an ugly, very public mess for the government. Seems like they did a bad job making the ATF look good in this."

"Oh, but they were brilliant at concealing the most explosive aspect of the case. An element in ATF loyal to Tom Summerton instead of to the current director intended to use Koresh as a test case for applying asset-forfeiture laws to religious organizations."

As Utah rolled under their wheels and they drew nearer to Modena, Spencer continued to finger his scar while he thought about what she had revealed.

The trees had thinned out. The pines and spruces were too far from the highway to cast shadows across the pavement, and the sword dance of sunlight had ended. Yet Spencer noted that Valerie squinted at the road ahead and flinched slightly from time to time, as though she was threatened by her own blades of memory.

Behind them, Rocky seemed oblivious of the sobering weight of their conversation. Whatever its drawbacks, there were also many advantages to the canine condition.

At last Spencer said, "Targeting religious groups for asset seizure, even fringe figures like Koresh—that's a major bombshell if it's true. It shows utter contempt for the Constitution."

"There are lots of cults and splinter sects these days, with millions in assets. That Korean minister—Reverend Moon? I'll bet his church has hundreds of millions on U.S. soil. If any religious organization is involved in criminal activity, its tax-free status is revoked. Then if the ATF or FBI has a lien for asset forfeiture, it'll be first in line, even ahead of the IRS, to grab everything."

"A steady cash flow to buy more toys and better office furniture for the bureaus involved," he said ruminatively. "And help to keep this nameless agency afloat. Even make it grow. While lots of local police forces—the guys who have to deal with real hard-core crime, street gangs, murder, rape—they're all so starved for funds they can't have pay raises or buy new equipment."

As Modena passed by in four blinks of an eye, Valerie said, "And the accountability provisions of federal and state forfeiture laws are dismal. Seized assets are inadequately tracked—so a percentage just vanishes into the pockets of some of the officials involved."

"Legalized theft."

"No one's ever caught, so it might as well be legal. Anyway, Summerton's element in ATF planned to plant drugs, phony records of major drug sales, and lots of illegal weapons in the Mount Carmel Center—Koresh's compound—after the success of the initial assault."

"But the initial assault failed."

"Koresh was more unstable than they realized. So innocent ATF agents were killed. And innocent children. It became a media circus. With everyone watching, Summerton's goons couldn't plant the drugs and guns. The operation was abandoned. But by then there was a paper trail inside ATF: secret memos, reports, files. All that had to be eliminated quickly. A couple of *people* were also eliminated, people who knew too much and might squeal."

"And you're saying this nameless agency cleaned up that mess."

"I'm not *saying* they did. They really *did.*"

"How do you fit into all this? How do you know Summerton?"

She chewed on her lower lip and seemed to be thinking hard about how much she should reveal.

He said, "Who *are* you, Valerie Keene? Who are you, Hannah Rainey? Who are you, Bess Baer?"

"Who are *you*, Spencer Grant?" she asked angrily, but her anger was false.

"Unless I'm mistaken, I told you a name, a real and true name, when I was out of my head, last night or the night before."

She hesitated, nodded, but kept her eyes on the road.

He found his voice diminishing to a softness barely louder than a murmur, and though he was unable to force himself to speak louder, he knew that she heard every word he said. "Michael Ackblom. It's a name I've hated for more than half my life. It hasn't even been my legal name for fourteen years, not since my grandparents helped me apply to a court to have it changed. And since the day the judge granted that change, it's a name I've never spoken, not once in all that time. Until I told you."

He fell into a silence.

She didn't speak, as though in spite of the silence, she knew that he wasn't finished.

The things that Spencer needed to say to her were more easily said in a liberating delirium like the one in which he'd made his previous revelations. Now he was inhibited by a reserve that resulted less from shyness than from an acute awareness that he was a damaged man and that she deserved someone finer than he could ever be.

"And even if I hadn't been delirious," he continued, "I would've told you anyway, sooner or later. Because I don't want to keep any secrets from you."

How difficult it sometimes could be to say the things that most deeply and urgently needed to be said. If given a choice, he wouldn't have selected either that time or that place to say any of it: on a lonely Utah highway, watched and pursued, hurtling toward likely death or toward an unexpected gift of freedom—and in either case toward the unknown. Life chose its consequential moments, however, without the consultation of those who lived them. And the pain of speaking from the heart was always, in the end, more endurable than the suffering that was the price of silence.

He took a deep breath. "What I'm trying to say to you . . . it's so presumptuous. Worse than that. Foolish, ridiculous. For God's sake, I can't even describe what I feel for you because I don't have the words. There might not even be words for it. All I know is that what I feel is wonderful, strange, different from anything I ever expected to feel, different from anything people are *supposed* to feel."

She kept her attention on the highway, which allowed Spencer to look at her as he spoke. The sheen of her dark hair, the delicacy of her profile, and the strength of her beautiful sun-browned hands on the steering wheel encouraged him to continue. If she had met his eyes at that moment, however, he might have been too intimidated to express the rest of what he longed to say.

"Crazier still, I can't tell you *why* I feel this way about you. It's just there. Inside me. It's a feeling that just sprang up. Not there one moment . . . but there the next, as if it had always been there. As if *you'd* always been there, or as if I'd spent my life waiting for you to be there."

The more words that tumbled from him and the faster they came, the more he feared that he would never be able to find the *right* words. At least she seemed to know that she should not respond or, worse, encourage him. He was balanced so precariously on the high wire of revelation that the slightest blow, although unintended, would knock him off.

"I don't know. I'm so awkward at this. The problem is I'm just fourteen years old when it comes to this, when it comes to emotion, frozen back there in adolescence, as inarticulate as a boy about this sort of thing. And if I can't explain what I feel or why I feel it—then how can I expect you ever to feel anything in return? Jesus. I was right: 'Presumptuous' is the wrong word. 'Foolish' is better."

He retreated to the safety of silence again. But he didn't dare linger in silence, because he would soon lose the will to break it.

"Foolish or not, I've got hope now, and I'm going to hold onto it until you tell me to let go. I'll tell you all about Michael Ackblom, the boy who used to be. I'll tell you everything you want to know, everything you can bear to hear. But I want the same thing from you. I want to know all there is to know. No secrets. This is an end to secrets. Here, now, from this moment on, no secrets. Whatever we can have together—if we can have anything at all—has to be honest, true, clean, shining, like nothing I've known before."

The speed of the Rover had fallen while he talked.

His latest silence was not just another pause between painful attempts to express himself, and she seemed to be aware of its new quality. She looked at him. Her lovely, dark eyes shone with the warmth and kindness to which he had responded in The Red Door less than a week ago, when he'd first met her.

When the warmth threatened to well into tears, she turned her attention to the road once more.

Since encountering her again in the arroyo on Friday night, he had not until now seen quite that same exceptionally kind and open spirit; of necessity, it had been masked by doubt, by caution. She hadn't trusted him any more, after he'd followed her home from work. Her life had taught her to be cynical and suspicious of others, as surely as his life had taught him to be afraid of what he might one day find crouched and waiting within himself.

She became aware that she'd let their speed fall. She tramped on the accelerator, and the Rover surged forward.

Spencer waited.

Trees crowded close to the highway again. Filleting blades of light flashed across the glass, spattering quick sprays of shadows behind them.

"My name," she said, "is Eleanor. People used to call me Ellie. Ellie Summerton."

"Not . . . his daughter?"

"No. Thank God, no. His daughter-in-law. My maiden name was Golding. Eleanor Golding. I was married to Tom's son, only child. Danny Summerton. Danny's dead now. Been dead for fourteen months." Her voice was pulled between anger and sadness, and often the balance in the contest shifted in the middle of a word, stretching it and distorting it. "Some days it seems he's only been gone a week or so, and some days it feels like he's been gone forever. Danny knew too much. And he was going to talk. He was killed to shut him up."

"Summerton . . . killed his own son?"

Her voice became so cold that anger seemed to have won forever against the insistent pull of sadness. "He's even worse than that. He ordered someone else to do it. My mom and dad were killed too . . . just because they happened to be in the way when the agency men came for Danny."

Her voice was colder than ever, and she was whiter than pale. During his days as a policeman, Spencer had seen a few faces as white as Ellie's was at that moment—but they had all been faces in one morgue or another.

"I was there. I escaped," she said. "I was lucky. That's what I've been telling myself ever since. Lucky."

⌀

". . . but Michael had no peace, even once he'd gone to Denver to live with his grandparents, the Porths," Gary Duvall said. "Every kid in school knew the name Ackblom. An unusual name. And the father was a famous artist even before he became a famous murderer, killed his wife and forty-one others. Besides, the kid's picture had been in all the papers. Boy hero. He was an object of unending curiosity. Everyone stared. And every time it seemed the media would leave him alone, there would be another flare-up of interest, and they'd be hounding him again, even though he was just a kid, for God's sake."

"Journalists," Roy said scornfully. "You know what they're like. Cold bastards. Only the story matters. They have no compassion."

"The kid had been through a similar hell, unwanted notoriety, when he'd been eight years old, after his mother's body was found in that ditch. This time it was tearing him apart. The grandparents were retired, could live anywhere, so after almost two years they decided to get Michael out of Colorado altogether. A new city, new state, new start. That's what they told neighbors—but they wouldn't tell anyone where they were going. They uprooted themselves and left their friends for the sake of the boy. They must've figured that was the only way he'd have a chance to make a normal life for himself."

"New city, new state, new start—and even a new name," Roy said. "They legally changed it, didn't they?"

"Right here in Denver, before they moved away. Given the circumstances, the court record of the change is sealed, of course."

"Of course."

"But I've reviewed it. Michael Steven Ackblom became Spencer Grant, no middle name or even initial. An odd choice. It seems to have been a name the boy came up with himself, but I don't know where he got it."

"From old movies he liked."

"Huh?"

"Good work. Thanks, Gary."

Roy disconnected with the touch of a button, but he didn't take off the telephone headset.

He stared at the photograph of Steven Ackblom. The man in the shadows.

Engines, rotors, powerful desires, and sympathy for the devil vibrated in Roy's bones. He shivered with a not unpleasant chill.

They were all so beautiful in their pain, and all like angels when they died.

※

Here and there in the gloom beneath the trees, where shadows held back the sun through most or all of the day, patches of white snow shone like bone in the carcass of the earth.

The true desert was behind them. Winter had come to this area, had been driven back by an early thaw, and would no doubt come again before true spring. But now the sky was blue, on a day when Spencer would have welcomed bitterly cold wind and dense swirls of snow to blind all eyes above.

"Danny was a brilliant software designer," Ellie said. "He'd been a computer nerd since junior high. Me too. Since the eighth grade, I've lived and breathed computers. We met in college. My being a hacker, deep into that world, which is mostly guys—that's what drew Danny to me."

Spencer remembered how Ellie had looked as she'd sat on desert sand; at the edge of the morning sun, bent over a computer, up-linking to satellites, dazzling in her expertise, her limpid eyes alight with the pleasure that she got from being so skillful at the task, with a curve of hair like a raven's wing against her cheek.

Whatever she might believe, her status as a hacker had not been the only thing that had drawn Danny to her. She was compelling for many reasons, but most of all because she seemed, at all times, more *alive* than most other people.

Her attention was on the highway, but she was clearly having difficulty treating the past with detachment and was struggling not to become lost in it. "After graduate school, Danny had job offers, but his father was relentless about him coming to work at the Bureau of Alcohol, Tobacco and Firearms. Back then, years before he went to the Department of Justice, Tom Summerton was Director of the ATF."

"But that was in a different administration."

"Oh, in Tom's case, it doesn't matter much who's in power in Washington, either party, left or right. He's always appointed to an important position in what they laughingly call 'public service.' Twenty years ago, he inherited over one billion dollars, which is now probably two, and he gives huge amounts to both parties. He's clever enough to position himself as nonpartisan, a statesman rather than a politician, a man who knows how to get things done, no ideological axe to grind, only wants to make a better world."

"That's a hard act to pull off," Spencer said.

"Easy for him. Because he believes in nothing. Except himself. And power. Power is his food, drink, love, sex. *Using* power is the thrill, not forwarding the ideals it serves. In Washington, a lust for power keeps the devil busy buying souls, but Tom is so ambitious he must have collected a record price for his."

Responding to the simmering fury in the undertone of her voice, Spencer said, "Did you always hate him?"

"Yes," Ellie said forthrightly. "Quietly despised the stinking sonofabitch. I didn't want Danny to work at ATF, because he was too innocent, naive, too easily taken in by his old man."

"What did he do there?"

"Developed Mama. The computer system, the software to run it—which they later called Mama. It was supposed to be the biggest, baddest anticrime data resource in the world, a system that could process billions of bytes at record speeds, link together federal and state and local law enforcement with ease, eliminate duplication of effort, and finally give the good guys an edge."

"Very stirring."

"Isn't it? And Mama turned out awesome. But Tom never intended her to serve any legit branch of government. He used ATF resources to develop her, yeah, but his intention all along was to make Mama the core of this nameless agency."

"So Danny realized it had gone sour?"

"Maybe he knew but didn't want to admit. He stayed with it."

"How long?"

"Too long," she said sadly. "Until his dad had left the ATF and moved to the Department of Justice, a full year after Mama and the agency were in place. But eventually he accepted that Mama's entire purpose was to make it possible for the government to *commit* crimes and not be caught. He was eaten alive with anger, self-disgust."

"And when he wanted out, they wouldn't let him go."

"We didn't realize there was no leaving. I mean, Tom is a piece of walking shit, but he was still Danny's *father.* And Danny was his only child. Danny's mother died when he was young. Cancer. So it seemed like Danny was all Tom had."

Following the violent death of his own mother, Spencer and his father also were drawn closer in the aftermath. Or so it had seemed. Until a certain night in July.

Ellie said, "Then it became obvious—this work with the agency was mandatory lifetime employment."

"Like being the personal attorney to a Mafia don."

"The only way out was to go public, blow the whole dirty business wide open. Secretly Danny prepared his own file of Mama's software and a history of the cover-ups the agency was involved with."

"You realized the danger?"

"On one level. But deep down inside, I think both of us, to different degrees, had trouble believing Tom would have Danny killed. We were twenty-eight, for God's sake. Death was an abstract concept to us. At twenty-eight, who really believes he's ever going to die?"

"And then the hit men showed up."

"No SWAT team. More subtle. Three men on Thanksgiving evening. The year before last. My folks' place in Connecticut. My dad is . . . was a doctor. A doctor's life, especially in a small town, isn't his own. Even on Thanksgiving. So . . . near the end of dinner, I was in the kitchen . . . getting the pumpkin pie . . . when the doorbell rang. . . ."

For once, Spencer didn't want to look at her lovely face. He closed his eyes.

Ellie took a deep breath and went on: "The kitchen was at the end of the hall from the foyer. I pushed the swinging door aside to see who our visitor was, just as my mother opened . . . just as she opened the front door."

Spencer waited for her to tell it at her own pace. If he had made the correct assumptions about the sequence of events since that door had been opened, fourteen months in the past, this was the first time that she had described those murders to anyone. Between then and now, she had been on the run, unable to fully trust another human being and unwilling to risk the lives of innocent people by involving them in her personal tragedy.

"Two men at the front door. Nothing special about them. Could have been Dad's patients, for all I knew. First one was wearing a red-plaid hunting jacket. He said something to Mom, then came inside, pushing her back, a gun in his hand. Never heard a shot. Silencer. But I saw . . . a spray of blood . . . the back of her head blowing out."

With his eyes closed against the sight of Ellie's face, Spencer could clearly visualize that Connecticut foyer and the horror that she described.

"Dad and Danny were in the dining room. I screamed, 'Run, get away.' I knew it was the agency. I didn't go out the rear door. Instinct, maybe. I'd have been killed on the back porch. Ran into the laundry room off the kitchen, then into the garage and out the side garage door. The house is on two acres, lots of lawn, but I got to the fence between our place and the Doyle house. I was going over it, almost over it, when a bullet ricocheted off the wrought iron. Somebody shooting from behind our house. Another silencer. No sound but the slug smacking iron. I was frantic, ran across the Doyles' yard. Nobody home, away at their kids' place for the holiday, windows dark. I ran through a gate, into St. George's Wood. Presbyterian church sits on six or eight acres, surrounded by woods—mostly pines, sycamores. Ran a ways. Stopped in the trees. Looked back. Thought one of them would be after me. But I was alone. I guess I'd been too fast or maybe they didn't want to chase me in public, waving guns. And just then snow started falling, just *then*, big fat flakes. . . ."

Behind his closed eyes, Spencer could see her on that distant night, in that faraway place: alone in darkness, without a coat, shivering, breathless, terrified. Abruptly, torrents of white flakes spiraled through the bare limbs of the sycamores, and the timing made the snow seem more than merely a sudden change of weather, gave it the significance of an omen.

"There was something uncanny about it . . . sort of eerie . . . ," Ellie said, confirming what Spencer sensed that she had felt and what he himself might have felt under those circumstances. "I don't know . . . can't explain it . . . the snow was like a curtain coming down, a stage curtain, the end of an act, end of *something*. I knew then they were all dead. Not just my mother. Dad and Danny too."

Her voice trembled with grief. Talking for the first time about those killings, she had reopened the scabs that had formed over her raw pain, as he had known she would.

Reluctantly he opened his eyes and looked at her.

She was beyond pale now. Ashen. Tears shimmered in her eyes, but her cheeks were still dry.

"Want me to drive?" he asked.

"No. Better if I do. Keeps me focused here and now . . . instead of too much back then."

A roadside sign indicated that they were eight miles from the town of Newcastle.

Spencer stared out the side window at a landscape that seemed barren in spite of the many trees and murky in spite of the sunshine.

Ellie said, "Then in the street, beyond the trees, a car roared by, really moving. It went under a streetlamp, and I was close enough to see the man in the front passenger seat. Red hunting jacket. The driver, one more in the backseat—three altogether. After they went past, I ran through the trees, toward the street, going to shout for help, for the police, but I stopped before I got there. I knew who'd done it . . . the agency, Tom. But no proof."

"What about Danny's files?"

"Back in Washington. A set of diskettes hidden in our apartment, another set in a bank safe-deposit box. And I knew Tom must already have both sets, or he wouldn't have been so . . . bold. If I went to the cops, if I surfaced anywhere, Tom would get me. Sooner or later. It would look like an accident or suicide. So I went back to the house. Back through St. George's Wood, the gate at the Doyle house, over the iron fence. At our house, I almost couldn't force myself through the kitchen . . . the hall . . . to Mom in the foyer. Even after all this time, when I try to picture my mother's face, I can't see it without the wound, the blood, the bone structure distorted by the bullets. Those bastards haven't even left me with a clean memory of my mother's face . . . just that awful, bloody *thing*."

For a while she couldn't go on.

Aware of Ellie's anguish, Rocky mewled softly. He was no longer bobbing and grinning. He huddled in his narrow space, head down, both ears limp. His love of speed was outweighed by his sensitivity to the woman's pain.

Two miles from Newcastle, Ellie at last continued: "And in the dining room, Danny and Dad were dead, shot repeatedly in the head, not to be sure they were dead . . . just for the sheer savagery. I had to . . . to touch the bodies, take the money out of their wallets. I was going to need every dollar I could get. Raided Mom's purse, jewelry box. Opened the safe in Dad's den, took his coin collection. Jesus, I felt like a thief, worse than a thief . . . a grave robber. I didn't pack my suitcase, just left with what I was wearing, partly because I started to get spooked that the killers would come back. But also because . . . it was so silent in that house, just me and the bodies and the snow falling past the windows, so *quiet,* as if not only Mom and Dad and Danny were dead, but as if the whole world had died, the end of everything, and I was the last one left, alone."

Newcastle was a repeat of Modena. Small. Isolated. It offered no place to hide from people who could look down on the whole world as if they were gods.

Ellie said, "I left the house in our Honda, Danny's and mine, but I knew I had to get rid of it in a few hours. When Tom realized I hadn't gone to the cops, the whole agency would be looking for me, and they'd have a description of the car, the plate number."

He looked at her again. Her eyes were no longer watery. She had repressed her grief with a fierce weight of anger.

He said, "What do the police think happened in that house, to Danny and your folks? Where do they think you are? Not Summerton's people. I mean the *real* police."

"I suspect Tom intended to make it look as if a well-organized group of terrorists wasted us as a way of punishing him. Oh, he could've milked that for sympathy! And used the sympathy to weasel more power for himself inside the Department of Justice."

"But with you gone, they couldn't plant their phony evidence, because you might show up to refute it."

"Yeah. Later, the media decided that Danny and my folks . . . well, you know, it was one of those deplorable acts of senseless violence we see so often, blah-blah-blah. Terrible, sick, blah-blah-blah, but only a three-day story. As for me . . . obviously I'd been taken away, raped and murdered, my body left where it might never be found."

"That was fourteen months ago?" he asked. "And the agency's still this hot to get you?"

"I have some significant codes they don't know I have, things Danny and I memorized . . . a lot of knowledge. I don't have hard proof against them. But I *know* everything about them, which makes me dangerous enough. Tom will never stop looking, as long as he lives."

∽

Like a great black wasp, the helicopter droned across the Nevada badlands.

Roy was still wearing the telephone headset with the saucer-size earphones, blocking out the engine and rotor noise to concentrate on the photograph of Steven Ackblom. The loudest sound in his private realm was the slow, heavy thudding of his heart.

When Ackblom's secret work had been exposed, Roy had been only sixteen years old and still confused about the meaning of life and about his own place in the world. He was drawn to beautiful things: the paintings of Childe Hassam and so many others, classical music, antique French furniture, Chinese porcelain, lyrical poetry. He was always a happy boy when alone in his room, with Beethoven or Bach on the stereo, gazing at the color photographs in a book about Fabergé eggs, Paul Storr silver, or Sung Dynasty porcelains. Likewise, he was happy when he was wandering alone through an art museum. He was seldom happy around people, however, although he wanted desperately to have friends and to be liked. In his expansive but guarded heart, young Roy was convinced that he had been born to make an important contribution to the world, and he knew that when he discovered what his contribution would be, he then would become widely admired and loved. Nevertheless, at sixteen and bedeviled by the impatience of youth, he was enormously frustrated by the need to wait for his purpose and his destiny to be revealed to him.

He had been fascinated by the newspaper accounts of the Ackblom tragedy, because in the mystery of the artist's double life, he had sensed a resolution to his own deep confusion. He acquired two books with color plates of Ackblom's art—and responded powerfully to the work. Though Ackblom's pictures were beautiful, even ennobling, Roy's enthusiasm wasn't aroused only by the paintings themselves. He was also affected by the artist's inner struggle, which he inferred from the paintings and which he believed to be similar to his own.

Basically, Steven Ackblom was preoccupied with two subjects and produced two types of paintings.

Although only in his mid-thirties, he had been obsessed enough to produce an enormous body of work, consisting half of exceptionally beautiful still lifes. Fruit, vegetables, stones, flowers, pebbles, the contents of a sewing box, buttons, tools, plates, a collection of old bottles, bottle caps—humble and exalted objects alike were rendered in remarkable detail, so realistic that they seemed three-dimensional. In fact, each item attained a hyperreality, appeared to be more real than the object that had served as the model for it, and possessed an eerie beauty. Ackblom never resorted to the forced beauty of sentimentality or unrestrained romanticism; his vision was always convincing, moving, and sometimes breathtaking.

The subjects of the remainder of the paintings were people: portraits of individuals and of groups containing three to seven subjects. More frequently, they were faces rather than full figures, but when they were figures, they were invariably nudes. Sometimes Ackblom's men, women, and children were ethereally beautiful on the surface, though their comeliness was always tainted by a subtle but terrible pressure within them, as if some monstrous possessing spirit might explode from their fragile flesh at any moment. This pressure distorted a feature here and there, not dramatically but just enough to rob them of perfect beauty. And sometimes the artist portrayed ugly—even grotesque—individuals, within whom there was also fearful pressure, though its effect was to force a feature here and there to conform to an ideal of beauty. Their malformed countenances were all the more chilling for being, in some aspects, lightly touched by grace. As a consequence of the conflict between inner and outer realities, the people in both types of portraits were enormously expressive, although their expressions were more mysterious and haunting than any that enlivened the faces of real human beings.

Seizing on those portraits, the news media had been quick to make the most obvious interpretation. They claimed that the artist—himself a handsome man—had been painting his own demon within, crying out for help or issuing a warning regarding his true nature.

Although he was only sixteen, Roy Miro understood that Ackblom's paintings were not about the artist himself, but about the world as he perceived it. Ackblom had no need to cry out for help or to warn anyone, for he didn't see himself as demonic. Taken as a whole, what his art said was that no human being could ever achieve the perfect beauty of even the humblest object in the inanimate world.

Ackblom's great paintings helped young Roy to understand why he was delighted to be alone with the artistic works of human beings, yet was often unhappy in the company of human beings themselves. No work of art could be flawless, because an imperfect human being had created it. Yet art was the distillation of the best in humanity. Therefore, works of art were closer to perfection than those who created them.

Favoring the inanimate over the animate was all right. It was acceptable to value art above people.

That was the first lesson he learned from Steven Ackblom.

Wanting to know more about the man, Roy had discovered that the artist was, not surprisingly, extremely private and seldom spoke to anyone for publication. Roy managed to find two interviews. In one, Ackblom held forth with great feeling and compassion about the misery of the human condition. One quotation seemed to leap from the text: "Love is the most human of all emotions because love is messy. And of all the things we can feel with our minds and bodies, severe pain is the purest, for it drives everything else from our awareness and focuses us as perfectly as we can ever be focused."

Ackblom had pleaded guilty to the murders of his wife and forty-one others, rather than face a lengthy trial that he couldn't win. In the courtroom, entering his plea, the painter had disgusted and angered the judge by saying, of his forty-two victims: "They were all so beautiful in their pain, and all like angels when they died."

Roy began to understand what Ackblom had been doing in those rooms under the barn. In subjecting his victims to torture, the artist was trying to focus them toward a moment of perfection, when they would briefly shine—even though still alive—with a beauty equal to that of inanimate objects.

Purity and beauty were the same thing. Pure lines, pure forms, pure light, pure color, pure sound, pure emotion, pure thought, pure faith, pure ideals. However, human beings were capable of achieving purity, in any thought or endeavor, only rarely and only in extreme circumstances— which made the human condition pitiable.

That was the second lesson he learned from Steven Ackblom.

For a few years, Roy's heartfelt pity for humanity intensified and matured. One day shortly after his twentieth birthday, as a bud suddenly blossoms into a full-blown rose, his pity became compassion. He considered the latter to be a purer emotion than the former. Pity often entailed a subtle element of disgust for the object of pity or a sense of superiority on the part of the person who felt pity for another. But compassion was an unpolluted, crystalline, piercing empathy for other people, a perfect understanding of their suffering.

Guided by compassion, acting on frequent opportunities to make the world a better place, confident of the purity of his motivation, Roy had then become a more enlightened man than Steven Ackblom. He had found his destiny.

Now, thirteen years later, sitting in the back of the executive helicopter as it carried him toward Utah, Roy smiled at the photograph of the artist in swarming shadows.

Funny how everything in life seemed connected to everything else. A forgotten moment or half-remembered face from the past could suddenly become important again.

The artist had never been so central a figure in Roy's life that he could have been called a mentor or even an inspiration. Roy had never believed that Ackblom was a madman—as the media had portrayed him—but saw him as merely misguided. The best answer to the hopelessness of the human condition was not to grant one moment of pure beauty to each imperfect soul by the elevating effect of severe pain. That was a pathetically transient triumph. The better answer was to identify those most in need of release—then, with dignity and compassion and merciful speed, set them free of their imperfect human condition.

Nevertheless, at a crucial time, the artist had unknowingly taught a few vital truths to a confused boy. Though Steven Ackblom was a misguided and tragic figure, Roy owed him a debt.

It was ironic—and an intriguing example of cosmic justice—that Roy should be the one to rid the world of the troubled and thankless son who had betrayed Ackblom. The artist's quest for human perfection had been misguided but, in Roy's view, well meaning. Their sorry world would inch closer to an ideal state with Michael (now Spencer) removed from it. And pure justice seemed to require that Spencer be removed only subsequent to being subjected to prolonged and severe pain, in a manner that would adequately honor his visionary father.

As Roy took off the telephone headset, he heard the pilot making an announcement on the public-address system. ". . . according to Vegas control, allowing for the target's current speed, we're approximately sixteen minutes from rendezvous. Sixteen minutes to the target."

∽

A sky like blue glass.

Seventeen miles to Cedar City.

They began to encounter more traffic on the two-lane highway. Ellie used the horn to encourage slow vehicles to get out of her way. When the drivers were stubborn, she took nail-biting risks to get around them in no-passing zones or even passed them to the right when the shoulder of the highway was wide enough.

Their speed dropped because of the interference that the traffic posed, but the need for increased recklessness made it seem as though they were actually going faster than ever. Spencer held on to one edge of his seat. In the back, Rocky was bobbing his head again.

"Even without proof," Spencer suggested, "you could go to the press. You could point them in the right direction, put Summerton on the defensive—"

"Tried that twice. First a *New York Times* reporter. Contacted her on her office computer, had an on-line dialogue and set up a meeting at an Indian restaurant. Made it clear if she told anyone, anyone at all, my life *and* hers wouldn't be worth spit. I got there four hours early, watched the place with binoculars from the roof of a building across the street, to be sure she came alone and there wasn't any obvious stakeout. I figured I'd make her wait, go in half an hour late, take the extra time to watch the street. But fifteen minutes after she arrived . . . the restaurant blew up. Gas explosion, so the police said."

"The reporter?"

"Dead. Along with fourteen other people in there."

"Dear God."

"Then, a week later, a guy from the *Washington Post* was supposed to meet me in a public park. I actually set it up with a cellular phone from another rooftop overlooking that site, but not obvious enough to be seen. Made it for six hours later. About an hour and a half go by, and then a water department truck pulls up near the park. The work crew opens a manhole, sets out some safety cones and sawhorses with flashers on them."

"But they weren't really city workers."

"I had a battery-powered multiband scanner with me on that roof. Picked up the frequency they were using to coordinate the phony work crew with a phony lunch wagon on the other side of the park."

"You are something else," he said admiringly.

"Three agents in the park, too, one pretending he's a panhandler, two pretending to be park-service employees doing maintenance. Then the time comes and the reporter shows up, walks to the monument where I told him we'd meet—and the sonofabitch is wired too! I hear him muttering to them that he doesn't see me anywhere, what should he do. And they're calming him, telling him it's cool, he should just wait. The little weasel must've been in Tom Summerton's pocket, called him up right after talking to me."

Ten miles west of Cedar City, they pulled behind a Dodge pickup that was doing ten miles per hour under the legal limit. At the rear window of the cab, two rifles hung in a rack.

The pickup driver let Ellie pound on the horn for a while, mule-stubborn about pulling over to let her by.

"What's wrong with this jerk?" she fumed. She gave him more horn, but he played deaf. "As far as he knows, we have someone dying in here, needs a doctor fast."

"Hell, these days, we could be a couple of lunatic dopers just spoiling for a shootout."

The man in the pickup was moved by neither compassion nor fear. Finally he responded to the horn by putting his arm out the window and flipping Ellie the finger.

Passing to the left was impossible at the moment. Visibility was limited, and what highway they *could* see was occupied by a steady stream of oncoming traffic.

Spencer looked at his watch. They had only fifteen minutes left from the two-hour safety margin that Ellie had estimated.

The man in the pickup, however, seemed to have all the time in the world.

"Jackass," she said, and whipped the Rover to the right, trying to get around the slow vehicle by using the shoulder of the highway.

When she pulled even with the Dodge, it accelerated to match her speed. Twice Ellie pumped more juice to the Rover, twice it leaped forward, and twice the pickup matched her new pace.

The other driver repeatedly glanced away from the road to glare at them. He was in his forties. Under a baseball cap, his face revealed all the intelligence of a shovel.

Clearly, he intended to pace Ellie until the shoulder narrowed and she was forced to fall in behind him again.

Shovelface didn't know what kind of woman he was dealing with, of course, but Ellie promptly showed him. She pulled the Rover to the left, bashing the pickup hard enough to startle the driver into shifting his foot off the accelerator. The pickup lost speed. The Rover shot ahead. Shovelface jammed the pedal again, but he was too late: Ellie swung the Rover onto the pavement, in front of the Dodge.

As the Rover lurched left then right, Rocky yelped with surprise and fell onto his side. He scrambled into a sitting position again and snorted in what might have been either embarrassment or delight.

Spencer looked at his watch. "You think they'll hook up with local cops before they come after us?"

"No. They'll try to keep locals out of it."

"Then what should we be looking for?"

"If they fly in from Vegas—or anywhere else—I think they'll be in a chopper. More maneuverability, flexibility. With satellite tracking, they can pinpoint the Rover, come right in over us, and blow us off the highway, if they get a chance."

Leaning forward, Spencer peered through the windshield at the threatening blue sky.

A horn blared behind them.

"Damn," Ellie said, glancing at her side mirror.

Checking the mirror on his side, Spencer saw that the Dodge had caught up with them. The angry driver was pounding his horn as Ellie had pounded hers earlier.

"We don't need this right now," she worried.

"Okay," Spencer said, "so let's see if he'll take a rain check on a shootout. If we survive the agency, then we'll come back and give him a fair whack at us."

"Think he'd go for that?"

"Seems like a reasonable man."

Pressing the Rover as hard as ever, Ellie managed to glance at Spencer and smile. "You're getting the attitude."

"It's contagious."

Here and there, scattered along both sides of the highway, were businesses, houses. This wasn't quite yet Cedar City, but they were definitely back in civilization.

The slug in the Dodge pickup pounded on the horn with such enthusiasm that every blast must have been sending a thrill through his groin.

✍

On the display screen in the open attaché case, relayed from Las Vegas, was the view from Earthguard, enormously magnified and enhanced, looking down on the state highway just west of Cedar City.

The Range Rover was pulling one reckless stunt after another. Sitting in the back of the chopper, with the open case on his lap, Roy was riveted by the performance, which was like something out of an action movie, though seen from one monotonous angle.

No one drove that fast, weaving lane to lane, sometimes facing down oncoming traffic, unless he was drunk or being pursued. This driver wasn't drunk. There was nothing sloppy about the way the Rover was being handled. It was rash, daredevil driving, but it was also skillful. And from all appearances, the Rover was not being chased.

Roy was finally convinced that the woman was behind the wheel of that vehicle. After being alarmed by the satellite trace-back to her computer, she would never take comfort from the fact that no pursuit car was racing up her tailpipe. She knew that they either would be waiting ahead for her at a roadblock or would take her out from the air. Before either of those things happened, she was trying to get into a town, where she could blend into a busy flow of traffic and use whatever architecture of the urban landscape might help her to escape their eyes.

Cedar City wasn't nearly large enough, of course, to provide her with the opportunities she needed. Evidently she underestimated the power and clarity of surveillance from orbit.

At the front of the chopper's passenger compartment, the four strike force officers were checking their weapons. They distributed spare magazines of ammunition in their pockets.

Civilian clothing was the uniform for this mission. They wanted to get in, nail the woman, capture Grant, and get out before Cedar City law enforcement showed up. If they became involved with the locals, they would only have to deceive them, and deception involved the risk of making mistakes and being unmasked—especially when they had no idea how much Grant knew and what he might say if the cops insisted on talking to him. Besides, dealing with locals also took too much damn time. Both choppers were marked with phony registration numbers to mislead observers. As long as the men wore no identifying clothing or gear, witnesses would have little or nothing useful to tell the police later.

Every member of the strike force, including Roy, was protected by a bullet-resistant body vest under his clothes and was carrying Drug Enforcement Administration ID that could be produced quickly to placate the local authorities if necessary. If they were lucky, however, they would be back in the air three minutes after touching down, with Spencer Grant in custody, with the woman's body, but with no wounded of their own.

The woman was finished. She was still breathing, still had a heartbeat, but in fact she was already stone dead.

On the computer in Roy's lap, Earthguard 3 showed the target drastically slowing. Then the Rover passed another vehicle, perhaps a pickup, on the shoulder of the highway. The pickup increased its speed, too, and suddenly a drag race seemed to be under way.

Frowning, Roy squinted at the display screen.

The pilot announced that they were five minutes from the target.

∽

Cedar City.

There was too much traffic to facilitate their escape, and too little to allow them to blend in and confuse Earthguard. She was also hindered by being on streets with gutters instead of on open highways with wide shoulders. And traffic lights. And that stupid pickup jockey insistently pounding, pounding, pounding his horn.

Ellie turned right at an intersection, frantically surveying both sides of the street. Fast-food restaurants. Service stations. Convenience stores. She had no idea exactly what she was looking for. She only knew that she would recognize it when she saw it: a place or situation that they could turn to their advantage.

She had hoped for time to scout the territory and find a way to get the Rover under cover: a grove of evergreens with a dense canopy of branches, a large parking garage, any place in which they might evade the eyes in the sky and leave the Rover without being spotted. Then they could either buy or heist new wheels, and from orbit they would again be indistinguishable from other vehicles on the highway.

She supposed she would earn a bed of nails in Hades for sure if she killed the creep in the Dodge pickup—but the satisfaction might be worth the price. He hammered on the horn as if he were a confused and angry ape determined to beat the damned thing until it stopped bleating at him.

He also tried to get around them during every break in oncoming traffic, but Ellie swerved to block him. The passenger side of the pickup was badly scraped and crumpled from when she had bashed into it with the Rover, so the guy probably figured that he had nothing to lose by pulling alongside and forcing her to the curb.

She couldn't let him do that. They were quickly running out of time. Having to deal with the ape would consume precious minutes.

"Tell me it's not," Spencer shouted above the blaring horn.

"Not what?"

Then she realized that he was pointing through the windshield. Something in the sky. To the southwest. Two large executive-style helicopters. One behind and to the left of the other. Both black. The polished hulls and windows glistened as if sheathed with ice, and the morning sun shimmered off the whirling rotors. The two craft were like huge insects out of an apocalyptic 1950s science fiction movie about the dangers of nuclear radiation. Less than two miles away.

She saw a U-shaped strip shopping center ahead on the left. Skating on the fragile ice of instinct, she accelerated, hung a hard left through a gap in traffic, and drove into a short access road that served the big parking lot.

Near her right ear, the dog was panting with excitement, and it sounded uncannily like soft laughter: *Heh-heh-heh-heh-heh-heh!*

Spencer still had to shout, because the horn-blower remained close behind them: "What're we doing?"

"Got to get new wheels."

"Out in the open?"

"Only choice."

"They'll see us make the switch."

"Create a diversion."

"How?"

"I'm thinking," she said.

"I was afraid of that."

With only the lightest application of the brakes, she turned right and then sped southward across the blacktop lot, instead of approaching the stores to the east.

The pickup stayed close behind them.

In the southwest sky, the two helicopters were no more than one mile away. They had altered course to follow the Range Rover. They were descending as they approached.

The anchor store in the U-shaped complex was a supermarket in the center of the middle wing. Beyond the glass front and glass doors, the cavernous interior was filled with hard fluorescent light. Flanking that store were smaller businesses, selling clothing and books and records and health foods. Other small stores filled the two end wings.

The hour was still so early that most of the shops had just opened. Only the supermarket had been doing business for any length of time, and there were few parked cars other than the twenty or thirty clustered in front of that central enterprise.

"Gimme the pistol," she said urgently. "Put it on my lap."

Spencer gave the SIG to her, and then he picked up the Micro Uzi from the floor between his feet.

No obvious opportunity for creating a diversion awaited her toward the south. She did a hard, fishtailing U-turn and headed back north toward the center of the parking lot.

That maneuver so surprised the ape that he put his pickup into a slide and almost rolled it in his eagerness to stay behind her. While regaining control, at least, he stopped blowing his horn.

The dog was still panting: *Heh-heh-heh-heh-heh!*

She continued to parallel the street on which they had been traveling when she had spotted the shopping center, staying away from the stores.

She said, "Anything you want to take with you?"

"Just my suitcase."

"You don't need it. I already took the money out."

"You what?"

"The fifty thousand in the false bottom," she said.

"You found my money?" He seemed astonished.

"I found it."

"You took it out of the case?"

"It's right there in the canvas bag behind my seat. With my laptop and some other stuff."

"You found my money?" he repeated disbelievingly.

"We'll talk about it later."

"Bet on it."

The ape in the Dodge was on her case again, blowing his horn, but he was not as close as he had been.

To the southwest, the choppers were less than half a mile away and only about a hundred feet off the ground, angling down.

She said, "You see the bag I mean?"

He looked behind her seat. "Yeah. There past Rocky."

After clashing with the Dodge, she wasn't sure if her door would open easily. She didn't want to have to wrestle with the bag and the door at the same time. "Take it with you when we come to a stop."

"Are we coming to a stop?" he asked.

"Oh, yeah."

A final turn. Hard right. She swung into one of the center aisles in the parking lot. It led directly east, to the front of the supermarket. As she approached the building, she put her hand on the horn and held it there, making even more noise than the ape was making behind her.

"Oh, no," Spencer said, with dawning awareness.

"Diversion!" Ellie shouted.

"This is nuts!"

"No choice!"

"It's still nuts!"

Across the face of the market, sales banners were taped to the big sections of plate glass, advertising Coke and potatoes and toilet tissue and rock salt for home water softeners. Most were along the top half of those tall panes; through the glass, below and between the signs, Ellie could see the checkout stations. In the fluorescent light, a few clerks and customers were looking out, alerted by the strident horns. As she shot toward them, the small ovals of their faces were as luminously white as the painted masks of harlequins. One woman ran, which startled the others into scattering for safety.

She hoped to God they would all manage to get out of the way in time. She didn't want to hurt any innocent bystanders. But she didn't want to be gunned down by the men who would pour out of those helicopters, either.

Do or die.

The Rover was moving fast but not flat-out. The trick was to have enough speed to jump the curb onto the wide promenade in front of the market and get through the glass wall and all the merchandise that was stacked waist-high beyond it. But at too high a speed, she would crash into the checkout stations with deadly impact.

"Gonna make it!" Then she remembered never to lie to the dog. "Probably!"

Over the horns and the sound of the engines, she suddenly heard the *chuda-chuda-chuda* of the choppers. Or maybe she felt more than heard the pressure waves cast off by their rotors. They must be directly over the parking lot.

The front tires rammed the curb, the Range Rover leaped, Rocky yelped, and Ellie simultaneously released the horn and took her foot off the accelerator. She tramped on the brakes as the tires slammed into the concrete. The promenade didn't seem so wide when the Rover was skidding across it at thirty or forty miles an hour, with the scared-pig squeal of hot rubber on pavement, not so very wide at all, hell, not nearly wide *enough*. Her sudden awareness of the Rover's oncoming reflection was followed instantly by cascades of glass, ringing down like shattered icicles. They plowed through big wooden pallets, on which were stacked fifty-pound bags of potatoes or some damn thing, and finally took a header into the end of a checkout station. Panels of fiberboard popped apart, the stainless steel grocery chute buckled like gift-wrapping foil, the rubber conveyor belt snapped in two and spun off its rollers and rippled into the air as if it were a giant black flatworm, and the cash register almost toppled to the floor. The impact wasn't as hard as Ellie had feared, and as if to celebrate their safe landing, gay foulards of translucent plastic bags blossomed briefly, with a flourish, in midair, from the pockets of an invisible magician.

"Okay?" she asked, releasing the buckle on her safety harness.

He said, "Next time, I drive."

She tried her door. It protested, screeching and grinding, but neither the brush with the Dodge nor the explosive entry into the market had jammed the latch. Grabbing the SIG 9mm that was trapped between her thighs, she clambered out of the Range Rover.

Spencer had already gotten out of the other side.

The morning was filled with the clatter of helicopters.

∽

The two choppers appeared on the computer screen because they had entered the boundaries of Earthguard's two-hundred-foot look-down. Roy sat in the second of the craft, studying the top of that very machine as it was photographed from orbit, marveling at the strange possibilities of the modern world.

Because the pilot was making a straight-on approach to the target, neither the porthole on the left nor the one on the right gave Roy any view. He stayed with the computer to watch the Range Rover as it strove to elude the pickup truck by weaving back and forth across the shopping-center parking lot. As the pickup tried to get back up to speed after making a bad U-turn, the Rover swung toward the central building in the complex—which was, judging by its size, a supermarket or a discount store like Wal-Mart or Target.

Only at the last moment did Roy realize that the Rover was going to ram the place. When it hit, he expected to see it rebound in a mass of flattened and tangled metal. But it disappeared, merged with the building. With horror, he realized that it had driven through an entrance or a glass wall and that the occupants had survived.

He lifted the open attaché case off his lap, put it on the cabin deck, in the aisle beside his seat, and bolted to his feet in alarm. He did not pause to go through the back-out security procedures with Mama, didn't disconnect, didn't unplug, but stepped over the computer and hurried toward the pilot's cabin.

From what he'd seen on the display, he knew that both choppers had crossed over the power lines at the street. They were above the parking lot, easing toward touchdown, making a forward speed of only two or three miles an hour, all but hovering. They were so *close* to the damn woman, but now she was out of sight.

Once out of sight, she might quickly be out of reach as well. Gone again. No. Intolerable.

Armed and ready for action, the four strike force agents had gotten to their feet and were blocking the aisle near the exit.

"Clear the way, clear the way!"

Roy struggled through the assembled hulks to the head of the aisle, jerked open a door, and leaned into the cramped cockpit.

The pilot's attention was focused on avoiding the parking lot lampposts and the parked cars as he gentled the JetRanger toward the blacktop. But the second man, who was both copilot and navigator, turned in his seat to look at Roy as the door opened.

"She drove into the damned building," Roy said, looking out through the windshield at the shattered glass along the front of the supermarket.

"Wild, huh?" the copilot agreed, grinning.

Too many cars were spread out across the blacktop to allow either chopper to put down directly in front of the market. They were angling toward opposite ends of the building, one to the north and the other to the south.

Pointing at the first craft, with its full complement of eight strike force agents, Roy said, "No, no. Tell him I want him over the building, in back, not here, in back, all eight of his men deployed in back, stopping everyone on foot."

Their pilot was already in radio contact with the pilot of the other craft. While he hovered twenty feet over the parking lot, he repeated Roy's orders into the mouthpiece of his headset.

"They'll try to go through the market and out the back," Roy said, striving to rein in his anger and remain calm. Deep breaths. In with the pale-peach vapor of blessed tranquility. Out with the bile-green mist of anger, tension, stress.

Their chopper was hovering too low for Roy to be able to see over the roof of the market. From the Earthguard look-down on his computer, however, he remembered what lay behind the shopping center: a wide service alley, a concrete-block wall, and then a housing development with numerous trees. Houses and trees. Too many places to hide, too many vehicles to steal.

North of them, just as the first JetRanger was about to touch down on the parking lot and disgorge its men, the pilot got Roy's message. Rotor speed picked up, and the craft began to lift into the air again.

Peach in. Green out.

§

A carpet of brown nuggets had spilled from some of the torn fifty-pound bags, and they crunched under Spencer's shoes as he got out of the Rover and ran between two checkout stations. He carried the canvas bag by its straps. In the other hand, he clutched the Uzi.

He glanced to his left. Ellie was paralleling him in the next checkout lane. The shopping aisles were long and ran front to back of the store. He met Ellie at the head of the nearest aisle.

"Out the back." She hurried toward the rear of the supermarket.

Starting after her, he remembered Rocky. The mutt had gotten out of the Rover behind him. Where was Mr. Rocky Dog?

He stopped, spun around, ran back two steps, and saw the hapless canine in the checkout lane that he himself had used. Rocky was eating some of the brown nuggets that hadn't been crushed under his master's shoes. Dry dog food. Fifty pounds or more of it.

"Rocky!"

The mutt looked up and wagged his tail.

"Come on!"

Rocky didn't even consider the command. He snatched up a few more nuggets, crunching them with delight.

"Rocky!"

The dog regarded him again, one ear up and one down, bushy tail banging against the side of the cashier's counter.

In his sternest voice, Spencer said, "*Mine!*"

Regretful but obedient, a little ashamed, Rocky trotted away from the food. When he saw Ellie, who had stopped halfway down the long aisle to wait for them, he broke into a sprint. Ellie resumed her flight, and Rocky dashed exuberantly past her, unaware that they were running for their lives.

At the end of the aisle, three men rushed into sight from the left and halted when they saw Ellie, Spencer, the dog, the guns. Two were in white uniforms: names stitched on their shirt pockets, employees of the market. The third—in street clothes, with a loaf of French bread in one hand—must have been a customer.

With an alacrity and sinuosity more like that of a cat, Rocky transformed his headlong plunge into an immediate retreat. Eeling around on himself, tail between his legs, almost on his belly, he waddled back toward his master for protection.

The men were startled, not aggressive. But they froze, blocking the way. "*Back off!*" Spencer shouted.

Aiming at the ceiling, he punctuated his demand with a short burst from the Uzi, blowing out a fluorescent strip and precipitating a shower of lightbulb glass and chopped-up acoustic tiles.

Terrified, the three men scattered.

A pair of swinging doors at the back of the market was recessed between dairy cases to the left and lunch-meat-and-cheese coolers to the right. Ellie slammed through the doors. Spencer followed with Rocky. They were in a short hallway, with rooms to both sides.

The sound of the helicopters was muffled there.

At the end of the hallway, they burst into a cavernous room that extended the width of the building: bare concrete walls, fluorescent lights, open rafters instead of a suspended ceiling. An area in the center of the chamber was open, but merchandise in shipping cartons was stacked sixteen feet high in aisles on both sides—additional stock of products from shampoo to fresh produce.

Spencer spotted a few stockroom employees watching warily from between the storage aisles.

Directly ahead, beyond the open work area, was an enormous metal roll-up door through which big trucks could be backed inside and unloaded. To the right of the shipping entrance was a man-size door. They ran to it, opened it, and went outside into the fifty-foot-wide service alley.

No one in sight.

A twenty-foot-deep overhang sprouted from the wall above the roll-up. It extended the length of the market, jutting nearly halfway across the alley, to allow additional trucks to pull under it and unload while protected from the elements. It was also protection from eyes in the sky.

The morning was surprisingly chilly. Though the market and stockroom had been cool, Spencer wasn't prepared for the briskness of the outside air. The temperature must have been in the mid-forties. In more than two hours of breakneck travel, they had come from the edge of a desert into higher altitudes and a different climate.

He saw no point in following the service alley left or right. Both ways, they would only be going around the U-shaped structure to the parking lot out front.

On three sides of the shopping center, a nine-foot-high privacy wall separated it from its neighbors: concrete blocks, painted white, capped with bricks. If it had been six feet, they might have scaled it fast enough to escape. Nine feet, no way in hell. They could throw the canvas bag across, easy enough, but they couldn't simply heave a seventy-pound dog to the other side and hope he landed well.

Out at the front of the supermarket, the pitch of engines from at least one of the helicopters changed. The clatter of its props grew louder. It was coming to the rear of the building.

Ellie dashed to the right, along the shaded back of the market. Spencer knew what she intended. They had one hope. He followed her.

She stopped at the limit of the overhang, which marked the end of the supermarket. Beyond was that portion of the back wall of the shopping center belonging to neighboring businesses.

Ellie glowered at Rocky. "Stay close the building, tight against it," she told him, as if he could understand.

Maybe he could. Ellie hurried out into the sunshine, heeding her own advice, and Rocky trotted between her and Spencer, staying close to the back wall of the shopping center.

Spencer didn't know if satellite surveillance was acute enough to differentiate between them and the structure. He didn't know if the two-foot overhang on the main roof, high above, provided cover. But even if Ellie's strategy was smart, Spencer still *felt* watched.

The stuttering thunder of the chopper grew louder. Judging by the sound, it was up and out of the front parking lot, starting across the roof.

South of the supermarket, the first business was a dry cleaner. A small sign bearing the name of the shop was posted on the employee entrance. Locked.

The sky was full of apocalyptic sound.

Beyond the dry cleaner was a Hallmark card shop. The service door was unlocked. Ellie yanked it open.

∽

Roy Miro leaned through the cockpit door to watch as the other chopper rose higher than the building, hovered for a moment, then angled across the roof toward the back of the supermarket.

Pointing to a clear area of blacktop just south of the market, for the benefit of his own pilot, Roy said, "There, smack in front of Hallmark, put us down right there."

As the pilot took them down the last twenty feet and maneuvered to the desired landing point, Roy joined the four agents at the door in the passenger cabin. Breathing deeply. Peach in. Green out.

He pulled the Beretta from his shoulder holster. The silencer was still fitted to the weapon. He removed it and dropped it in an inside jacket pocket. This wasn't a clandestine operation that required silencers, not with all the attention they were attracting. And the pistol would allow more accuracy without the trajectory distortion caused by a silencer.

They touched down.

One of the strike team agents slid the door out of the way, and they exited rapidly, one after the other, into the battering downdraft from the rotor blades.

∽

As Spencer followed Ellie and Rocky through the door into the back room of the card shop, he glanced up into cannonades of sound. Silhouetted against the icy-blue sky, straight overhead, the outer edges of the rotors appeared first, chopping through the dry Utah air. Then the glide-slope antenna on the nose of the craft eased into view. As the leading edge of the downdraft hit him, he stepped inside and pulled the door shut, barely in time to avoid being seen.

The deadbolt had a brass thumb turn on the inside of the door. Although the hit squad would focus first on the back of the market, Spencer engaged the lock.

They were in a narrow, windowless storeroom that smelled of rose-scented air freshener. Ellie opened the next door before Spencer had closed the first. Beyond the storeroom was a small office with overhead fluorescents. Two desks. A computer. Files.

Two more doors led out of there. One stood half open to a tiny bathroom: toilet and sink. The other connected the office to the shop itself.

The long, narrow store was crowded with pyramidal island displays of cards, carousels of more cards, giftwrap, puzzles, stuffed toys, decorative candles, and novelties. The current promotion was for Valentine's Day, and there was an abundance of overhead banners and decorative wall hangings, all hearts and flowers.

The festiveness of the place was an unsettling reminder that regardless of what happened to him and Ellie and Rocky in the next few minutes, the world would spin on, unheeding. If they were shot dead in Hallmark, their bodies would be hauled away, the blood would be expunged from the carpet, a rose-scented air freshener would be employed in generous sprays, a few more potpourri might be set out for sale, and the stream of lovers coming in to buy cards would continue all but unabated.

Two women, evidently employees, were at the glass storefront, backs turned. They stared out at the activity in the parking lot.

Ellie started toward them.

Following her, Spencer suddenly wondered if she intended to take hostages. He didn't like that idea. Not at all. Jesus, no. These agency people, as she had described them and as he had seen them in action, wouldn't hesitate to blow away a hostage, even a woman or a child, to get at their target—especially not early in an operation, when witnesses were the most confused and no reporters were yet on the scene with cameras.

He didn't want innocent blood on his hands.

Of course, they couldn't merely wait in Hallmark until the agency went away. When they weren't found in the supermarket, the search would surely spread to adjacent stores.

Their best chance to escape was to slip out the front door of the card shop while the hit team's attention remained focused on the supermarket, try to get to a parked car, and hot-wire it. Not much of a chance. As thin as paper, as thin as hope itself. But it was all they had, better than hostages, so he clung to it.

With the chopper landing virtually at the back door, the card shop was so hammered by the screaming of engines and the pounding of rotor blades that it couldn't have been noisier if it had been under an amusement-park roller coaster. The Valentine banners trembled overhead. Hundreds of novelty key rings jangled from the hooks of a display stand. A collection of small ornate picture frames rattled against the glass shelf on which they stood. Even the walls of the store seemed to thrum like drumheads.

The racket was so ungodly that he wondered about the shopping center. It must be cheapjack construction, the worst crap, if one chopper could set up such reverberations in its walls.

They were almost to the front of the store, fifteen feet from the women at the window, when the reason for the fearful tumult became obvious: The second helicopter settled down in front of the shop, beyond the covered promenade, in the parking lot. The store was bracketed by the machines, shaken by cross-vibrations.

Ellie halted at the sight of the chopper.

Rocky seemed less worried by the cacophony than by an unfurled poster of Beethoven—the movie-star Saint Bernard, not the composer of symphonies—and he shied from it, taking refuge behind Ellie's legs.

The two women at the window were still unaware that they had company. They were side by side, chattering excitedly, and though their voices were raised above the clamor of the machines, their words were unintelligible to Spencer.

As he stepped to Ellie's side, gazing at the chopper with dread, he saw a door slide open on the fuselage. Armed men jumped to the blacktop, one after the other. The first was carrying a submachine gun larger than Spencer's Micro Uzi. The second had an automatic rifle. The third toted a pair of grenade-launching rifles, no doubt equipped with stun, sting, or gas payloads. The fourth man was armed with a submachine gun, and the fifth had only a pistol.

The fifth man was the last, and he was different from the four hulks who preceded him. Shorter, somewhat pudgy. He held his pistol to one side, aimed at the ground, and ran with less athletic grace than his companions.

None of the five approached the card shop. They raced toward the front of the supermarket, moving quickly out of view.

The chopper's engine was idling. The blades were still turning, though at a slower speed. The hit team hoped to be in and out fast.

"Ladies," Ellie said.

The women didn't hear her over the still considerable noise of the helicopters and of their own excited conversation.

Ellie raised her voice: "*Ladies, damn it!*"

Startled, exclaiming, wide-eyed, they turned.

Ellie didn't point the SIG 9mm at them, but she made sure they got a good look at it. "Get away from those windows, come here."

They hesitated, glanced at each other, at the pistol.

"I don't want to hurt you." Ellie was unmistakably sincere. "But I'll do what I have to do if you don't *come here right now!*"

The women stepped away from the storefront windows, one of them moving slower than the other. The slowpoke cast a furtive glance at the nearby entrance door.

"Don't even think about it," Ellie told her. "I'll shoot you in the back, so help me God, and if you aren't killed, you'll be in a wheelchair forever. Okay, yeah, that's better, come here."

Spencer stepped aside—and Rocky hid behind him—as Ellie guided the frightened women along the aisle. Halfway through the store, she made them lie facedown, one behind the other, with their heads toward the back wall.

"If either of you looks up anytime in the next fifteen minutes, I'll kill you both," Ellie told them.

Spencer didn't know if she was as sincere this time as when she had told them that she didn't *want* to hurt them, but she sounded as though she were. If he had been one of the women, he wouldn't have raised his head to look around until at least Easter.

Returning to him, Ellie said, "Pilot's still in the chopper."

He moved a few steps closer to the front of the store. Through the side window of the cockpit, one of the crew was visible, probably the copilot. "Two of them, I'm sure."

"They don't take part in the assault?" Ellie asked.

"No, of course not, they're flyers, not gunmen."

She went to the door and looked north toward the front of the supermarket. "Have to do it. No time to think about it. We just have to do it."

Spencer didn't even need to ask her what she was talking about. She was an instinctive survivor with fourteen hard months of combat experience under her belt, and *he* remembered most of what the United States Army Rangers had taught him about strategy and about thinking on his feet. They couldn't go back the way they'd come. Couldn't stay in the card shop, either. Eventually it would be searched. They could no longer hope to reach a car in the parking lot and hot-wire it, behind the backs of the gunmen, because all the cars were parked to the front of the chopper, requiring them to pass in full view of its crew. They were left with one option. One terrible, desperate option. It required boldness, courage—and either a dash of fatalism or an enormous measure of brainless self-confidence. They were both ready to do it.

"Take this," he said, handing her the canvas bag, "this too," and then gave her the Uzi.

As he took the SIG from her and tucked it under the waistband of his jeans, against his belly, she said, "I guess you have to."

"It's a three-second dash, at most, even less for him, but we can't risk him freezing up."

Spencer squatted, scooped up Rocky, and stood with the dog cradled like a child in his arms.

Rocky didn't know whether to wag his tail or be afraid, whether they were having fun or were in big trouble. He was clearly on the brink of sensory overload. In that condition he customarily either went all limp and quivery—or flew into a frenzy of terror.

Ellie eased open the door to check the front of the supermarket.

Glancing at the two women on the floor, Spencer saw that they were obeying the instructions they'd been given.

"Now," Ellie said, stepping outside, holding the door for him.

He went through sideways, so as not to bash Rocky's head into the door frame. Stepping onto the covered shopping promenade, he glanced toward the market. All but one of the gunmen had gone inside. A thug with submachine guns remained outside, facing away from them.

In the chopper, the copilot was looking down at something on his lap, not out the side window of the cockpit.

Half convinced that Rocky weighed seven hundred rather than seventy pounds, Spencer sprinted to the open door in the helicopter fuselage. It was only a thirty-foot dash, even counting the ten-foot width of the promenade, but those were the longest thirty feet in the universe, a quirk of physics, an eerie scientific anomaly, a bizarre distortion in the fabric of creation, stretching ever longer in front of him as he ran—and then he was there, pushing the dog inside, scrambling up and into the craft himself.

Ellie was so close behind him that she might as well have been his backpack. She dropped the canvas bag the moment she was up and across the threshold, but she held on to the Uzi.

Unless someone was crouched behind one of the ten seats, the passenger compartment was deserted. Just to be safe, Ellie moved back down the aisle, checking left and right.

Spencer stepped to the nearby cockpit door, opened it. He was just in time to jam the muzzle of the pistol in the face of the copilot, who was starting to get up from his seat.

"Take us up," Spencer told the pilot.

The two men appeared even more surprised than the women in the card shop.

"Take us up now—*now!*—or I'll blow this asshole's brains out through that window, then *yours!*" Spencer shouted so forcefully that he sprayed the crewmen with spittle and felt the veins in his temples popping up like those in a weight lifter's biceps.

He thought he sounded every bit as frightening as Ellie.

♒

Just inside the shattered glass wall of the supermarket, beside the wrecked Range Rover, in a drift of dog food, Roy and three agents stood with their weapons aimed at a tall man with a flat face, yellow teeth, and coal-black eyes as cold as a viper's. The guy clutched a semiautomatic rifle in both hands, and although he wasn't aiming it at anyone, he looked mean enough and angry enough to use it on the baby Jesus Himself.

He was the driver of the pickup. His Dodge stood abandoned in the parking lot, one door hanging wide open. He had come inside either to seek vengeance for whatever had happened on the highway or to play the hero.

"Drop the gun!" Roy repeated for the third time.

"Says who?"

"Says who?"

"That's right."

"Are you a moron? Am I talking to a blithering *idiot* here? You see four guys holding heavy weapons on you, and you don't understand the logic of dropping that rifle?"

"You cops or what?" asked the viper-eyed man.

Roy wanted to kill him. No more formalities. The guy was too damn stupid to live. He'd be better off dead. A sad case. Society would be better off without him too. Cut him down, right there, right now, and then find the woman and Grant.

The only problem was that Roy's dream of a three-minute mission, in and out and away before the nosy locals showed up, was no longer achievable. The operation had gone sour when the hateful woman had driven into the market, and it was getting more sour by the moment. Hell, it was past sour into bitter. They were going to have to deal with Cedar City cops, and that was going to be more difficult if one of the residents they were sworn to protect was lying dead on a mound of Purina Dog Chow.

If they were going to have to work with locals, he might as well show a badge to this fool. From an inner jacket pocket, he withdrew an ID wallet, flipped it open, and flashed his phony credentials. "Drug Enforcement Administration."

"Well, sure," the man said. "Now, that's all right."

He lowered the gun to the floor, let go of it. Then he actually put one hand to the bill of his baseball cap and tipped it at Roy with what seemed to be sincere respect.

Roy said, "You go sit in the back of your truck. Not inside. In the open, behind the cab. You wait there. You try to leave, that guy outside with a machine gun will cut your legs off at the knees."

"Yes, sir." With convincing solemnity, he tipped his cap again, and then he walked out through the damaged front wall of the store.

Roy almost turned and shot him in the back.

Peach in. Green out.

"Spread out across the front of the store," he told his men, "and wait, keep alert."

The team coming in from the back would search the supermarket exhaustively, flushing out Grant and the woman if they tried to hide anywhere inside. The fugitives would be driven forward and forced either to surrender or to die in a barrage of gunfire.

The woman, of course, would be shot to death whether she tried to surrender or not. They were taking no more chances with her.

"There'll be employees and customers coming through," he called out to his three men as they deployed across the store to both sides of him. "Don't let *anybody* leave. Herd them over near the manager's office. Even if you think they have *no* resemblance to the pair we're looking for, hold them. Even if it's the Pope, you *hold* him."

Outside, the helicopter engine went from a low idle to a loud roar. The pilot revved it. Revved it again.

What the hell?

Frowning, Roy clambered through the debris and went outside to see what was happening.

The agent posted in front of the market was looking toward the Hallmark shop, where the chopper was lifting off.

"What's he doing?" Roy asked.

"Taking off."

"Why?"

"Must be going somewhere."

Another moron. Stay calm. Peach in. Green out.

"Who told him to leave his position, who told him to take off?" Roy demanded.

As soon as the question was put, he knew the answer. He didn't know *how* it was possible, but he knew why the chopper was taking off and who was in it.

He jammed the Beretta into his shoulder holster, wrenched the submachine gun out of the surprised agent's hands, and charged toward the ascending aircraft. He intended to rupture its fuel tanks and bring it to the ground.

Raising the weapon, finger on the trigger, Roy realized there was no way he was ever going to be able to explain his actions to the satisfaction of a straight-arrow Utah cop with no appreciation for the moral ambiguity of federal law enforcement. Shooting at his own helicopter. Jeopardizing his pilot and copilot. Destroying a hugely expensive piece of government machinery. Perhaps causing it to crash into occupied stores. Great, fiery gouts of aviation fuel splashing everything and anyone in their path. Respected Cedar City merchants transformed into human torches, running in circles through the February morning, blazing and shrieking. It would all be colorful and exciting, and nailing the woman would be worth the lives of any number of bystanders, but explaining the catastrophe would be as hopeless as trying to explain the fine points of nuclear physics to the idiot sitting in the back of the Dodge pickup.

And there was at least a fifty-fifty chance that the chief of police would be a clean-cut Mormon who had never tasted an alcoholic drink in his life, who had never smoked, and who would not be tuned in properly to the concepts of untaxable hush money and police-agency collusion. Bet on it. A Mormon.

Reluctantly, Roy lowered the submachine gun.

The chopper rose swiftly.

"Why Utah?" he shouted furiously at the fugitives that he could not see but that he *knew* were frustratingly close.

Peach in. Green out.

He had to calm down. Think cosmically.

The situation would be resolved in his favor. He still had the second chopper to use as a pursuit vehicle. And Earthguard 3 would find it easier to track the JetRanger than the Rover, because the chopper was larger than the truck and because it traveled above all sheltering vegetation and above the distracting movement of ground-level traffic.

Overhead, the hijacked aircraft swung east, across the roof of the card store.

∽

In the passenger cabin, Ellie crouched beside the opening in the fuselage, leaned against the door frame, and looked down at the shopping center roof that passed under her. God, her heart was booming as loud as the rotor blades. She was terrified that the chopper would tip or lurch and that she would fall out.

During the past fourteen months, she had learned more about herself than in the entire previous twenty-eight years. For one thing, her love of life, her sheer joy in *being* alive, was greater than she had ever realized until the three people she had loved most had been taken from her in one brutal, bloody night. In the face of so much death, with her own existence in constant jeopardy, she now savored both the warmth of every sun-filled day and the chill wind of every raging storm, weeds as much as flowers, the bitter and the sweet. She had never been a fraction as aware of her love of freedom—her *need* for freedom—as when she had been forced to fight to keep it. And in those fourteen months, she had been amazed to learn that she had the guts to walk precipices, leap chasms, and grin in the devil's face; amazed to discover that she was not capable of losing hope; amazed to find that she was but one of many fugitives from an imploding world, all of them perpetually on the rim of a black hole and resisting its God-crushing gravity; amazed by how much fear she could tolerate and still thrive.

One day, of course, she would amaze herself straight into a sudden death. Maybe today. Leaning against the frame of the open door in the fuselage. Finished by a bullet or by a long, hard fall.

They traversed the building and moved over the fifty-foot-wide service alley. The other helicopter was down there, parked behind Hallmark. No gunmen were in the immediate vicinity of the craft. Evidently, they had already bailed out and had moved in on the back of the supermarket, under the twenty-foot overhang.

With Spencer giving orders to their own pilot, they hovered in position long enough for Ellie to use the Micro Uzi on the tail assembly of the craft on the ground. The weapon had two magazines, welded at right angles to each other, with a capacity of forty rounds—minus the few that Spencer had fired into the supermarket ceiling. She emptied both magazines, slapped in spares, emptied those too. The bullets destroyed the horizontal stabilizer, damaged the tail rotor, and punched holes in the tail pylon, disabling the aircraft.

If her assault was answered by any return fire, she was unaware of it. The gunmen who had moved off to cover the back of the market were probably too surprised and confused to be sure what to do.

Besides, the entire attack on the grounded chopper had taken only twenty seconds. Then she put the Uzi on the cabin deck and slid the door shut. The pilot, at Spencer's direction, immediately took them due north at high speed.

Rocky was crouched between two of the passenger seats, watching her intently. He was not as exuberant as he had been since they'd fled their camp in Nevada shortly after dawn. He had slipped into his more familiar suit of fretfulness and timidity.

"It's okay, pooch."

His disbelief was unconcealed.

"Well, it sure could be worse," she said.

He whimpered.

"Poor baby."

With both ears drooping, racked by shivers, Rocky was the essence of misery.

"How can I say anything that'll make you feel better," she asked the dog, "if I'm not allowed to lie to you."

From the nearby cockpit door, Spencer said, "That's a pretty grim assessment of our situation, considering we just slipped loose of a damned tight knot."

"We're not out of this mess yet."

"Well, there's something I tell Mr. Rocky Dog now and then, when he's down in the dumps. It's something that helps me a little, though I can't say whether it works for him."

"What?" Ellie asked.

"You've got to remember, whatever happens—it's only life, we all get through it."

13

MONDAY MORNING, after his bail had been posted, crossing the parking lot to his brother's BMW, Harris Descoteaux stopped twice to turn his face to the sun. He basked in its warmth. He had once read that black people, even those as midnight-dark as he was, could get skin cancer from too much sun. Being black was no absolute guarantee against melanoma. Being black, of course, was no guarantee against any misfortune, quite the opposite, so melanoma would have to wait in line with all the other horrors that might befall him. After spending fifty-eight hours in jail, where direct sunlight was more difficult to get than a hit of heroin, he felt as if he wanted to stand in the sun until his skin blistered, until his bones melted, until he became one giant pulsing melanoma. *Anything* was better than being locked away in a sunless prison. He inhaled deeply, too, because the smog-tainted air of Los Angeles smelled so sweet. Like the juice of an exotic fruit. The scent of freedom. He wanted to stretch, run, leap, twirl, whoop, and holler—but there were some things that a man of forty-four simply did not do, regardless of how giddy with freedom he might be.

In the car, as Darius started the engine, Harris put a hand on his arm, staying him for a moment. "Darius, I'll never forget this—what you've done for me, what you're still doing."

"Hey, it's nothing."

"The hell it isn't."

"Well, you'd have done the same for me."

"I think I would've. I hope I would've."

"There you go again, working on sainthood, putting on those robes of modesty. Man, whatever I know about doing the right thing, I learned from you. So what I did here, it's what you would do."

Harris grinned and lightly punched Darius on the shoulder. "I love you, little brother."

"Love you, big brother."

Darius lived in Westwood, and from downtown, the drive could take as little as thirty minutes on a Monday morning, after the rush hour, or more than twice that long. It was always a crapshoot. They had a choice between using Wilshire Boulevard, all the way across the city, or the Santa Monica Freeway. Darius chose Wilshire, because some days the rush hour never ended and the freeway became Hell with talk radio.

For a while, Harris was all right, enjoying his freedom if not the thought of the legal nightmare that lay ahead; however, as they were approaching Fairfax Boulevard, he began to feel ill. The first symptom was a mild but disturbing dizziness, a strange conviction that the city was ever so slowly revolving around them even as they drove through it. The sensation came and went, but each time that it gripped him, he suffered a spell of tachycardia more frantic than the one before it. When his heart fluttered through more beats in a half-minute seizure than the heart of a frightened hummingbird, he was overcome by the peculiar worry that he wasn't getting enough oxygen. When he tried to breathe deeply, he found he could barely breathe at all.

At first he thought that the air in the car was stale. Stuffy, too warm. He didn't want to reveal his distress to his brother—who was on the car phone, taking care of business—so he casually fiddled with the vent controls, until he got a draft of cool air directed at his face. Ventilation didn't help. The air wasn't stuffy but *thick*, like the heavy vapors of something odorless but toxic.

He endured the city revolving around the BMW, his heart bursting into fits of tachycardia, the air so syrup-thick that he could inhale only an inadequate drizzle, the oppressive intensity of light that forced him to squint against the sunshine that he had so recently enjoyed, the feeling that a crushing weight was hovering over him—but then he was enveloped by nausea so intense that he cried out for his brother to pull to the curb. They were crossing Robertson Boulevard. Darius engaged the emergency flashers, swung out of traffic just past the intersection, and stopped in a no-parking zone.

Harris flung open his door, leaned out, regurgitated violently. He had eaten none of the jailhouse breakfast that he'd been offered, so he was racked only by the dry heaves, although they were no less distressing or less exhausting because of that.

The siege passed. He slumped back in his seat, pulled the door shut, and closed his eyes. Shaking.

"Are you all right?" Darius asked worriedly. "Harris? Harris, what's wrong?"

With the spell past, Harris knew he'd been stricken by nothing more— and nothing less—than an attack of prison claustrophobia. It had been infinitely worse, however, than any panic attacks that had plagued him when he had actually been behind bars.

"Harris? Talk to me."

"I'm in prison, little brother."

"We're standing together on this, remember. Together, we're stronger than anybody, always were and always will be."

"I'm in prison," Harris repeated.

"Listen, these charges are bullshit. You were set up. None of this will stick. You're a Teflon defendant. You're not going to spend another day in jail."

Harris opened his eyes. The sunshine was no longer painfully bright. In fact, the February day seemed to have darkened with his mood.

He said, "Never stole a dime in my life. Never cheated on my taxes. Never cheated on my wife. Paid back every loan I ever took. Worked overtime most weeks since I've been a cop. Walked the straight and narrow—and let me tell you, little brother, it hasn't always been easy. Sometimes I get tired, fed up, tempted to take an easier way. I've had bribe money in my hand, and it felt good, but I just couldn't make my hand put it into my pocket. Close. Oh, yes, a lot closer than you ever want to know. And there've been some women . . . they would've been there for me, and I could've put Jessica way back in my mind while I was with them, and maybe I would've cheated on her if the opportunities had been just the littlest bit easier. I know it's in me to do it—"

"Harris—"

"I'm telling you, I've got evil in me as much as anyone, some desires that scare me. Even if I don't give in to them, just *having* them scares the living bejesus out of me sometimes. I'm no saint, the way you kid about. But I've always walked the line, walked that goddamned line. It's a mean mother of a line, straight and narrow, sharp as a razor, cuts right into you when you walk it long enough. You're always bleeding on that line, and sometimes you wonder why you don't just step off and walk in the cool grass. But I've always wanted to be a man our mother could be proud of. I wanted to shine in your eyes too, little brother, in the eyes of my wife and kids. I love you all so damned much, I never wanted any of you to know about any of the ugliness in me."

"The same ugliness that's in all of us, Harris. All of us. So why are you going on like this, doing this to yourself?"

"If I've walked that line, hard as it is, and something like this can happen to *me*, then it can happen to anyone."

Darius regarded him with stubborn perplexity. He was obviously struggling to understand Harris's anguish but was only halfway there.

"Little brother, I'm sure you'll clear me of the charges. No more nights in jail. But you explained the asset-forfeiture laws, and you did a damned good job, made it *too* clear. They have to *prove* I'm a drug dealer to put me back in jail, and they'll never be able to do that because it's all trumped up. But they don't have to prove a damn thing to keep my house, my bank accounts. They only have to show 'reasonable cause' that maybe the house was the site of illegal activity, and they'll say the planted drugs are reasonable cause even if the drugs don't *prove* anything."

"There's that reform law in Congress—"

"Moving slowly."

"Well, you never know. If some sort of reform passes, maybe it'll even tie forfeiture to conviction."

"Can you guarantee I'll get my house back?"

"With your clean record, your years of service—"

Harris gently interrupted: "Darius, under the current law, can you *guarantee* I'll get my house back?"

Darius stared at him in silence. A shimmer of tears blurred his eyes, and he looked away. He was an attorney, and it was his job to obtain justice for his big brother, and he was overwhelmed by the truth that he was all but powerless to assure even minimal fairness.

"If it can happen to me, it can happen to anyone," Harris said. "It could happen to you next. It could happen to my kids someday. Darius . . . maybe I get *something* back from the bastards, say as much as eighty cents on the dollar once all my costs are deducted. And maybe I get my life on track, start to rebuild. But how do I know it won't happen to me again, somewhere down the road?"

Having held back the tears, Darius looked at him again, shocked. "No, that's not possible. This is outrageous, unusual—"

"Why can't it happen again?" Harris persisted. "If it happened once, why not twice?"

Darius had no answer.

"If my house isn't really *my* house, if my bank accounts aren't really mine, if they can take what they want without proving a thing, what's to keep them from coming back? Do you see? I'm in prison, little brother. Maybe I'll never be behind bars again, but I'm in another kind of prison and never going to get free. The prison of expectations. The prison of fear. The prison of doubt, distrust."

Darius put one hand to his forehead, pressed and pulled at his brow, as if he would like to extract from his mind the awareness that Harris had forced upon him.

The car's emergency-flasher indicator blinked rhythmically, in time with a soft but penetrating sound, as if warning of the crisis in Harris Descoteaux's life.

"When the realization began to hit me," Harris said, "back there a few blocks ago, when I began to see what a box I'm in, what a box anyone could be in under these rules, I just was . . . overwhelmed . . . felt so claustrophobic that it made me sick to my stomach."

Darius lowered the hand from his brow. He looked lost. "I don't know what to say."

"I don't think there's anything anyone can say."

For a while they just sat there, with Wilshire Boulevard traffic whizzing by them, with the city so bright and busy all around, with the true darkness of modern life not to be glimpsed in mere palm shadows and awning-shaded shop entrances.

"Let's go home," Harris said.

They drove the rest of the way to Westwood in silence.

Darius's house was a handsome brick-and-clapboard Colonial with a columned portico. The spacious lot featured huge old ficus trees. The limbs were massive yet gracious in their all-encompassing spread, and the roots went back to the Los Angeles of Jean Harlow and Mae West and W. C. Fields, if not further.

It was a major achievement for Darius and Bonnie to have earned such a place in the world, considering how far down the ladder they had started their climb. Of the two Descoteaux brothers, Darius had enjoyed the greater financial success.

As the BMW pulled into the brick driveway, Harris was overcome by regret that his own troubles would inevitably taint the pride and well-earned pleasure that Darius took from that Westwood house and from everything else that he and Bonnie had acquired or achieved. What pride in their struggles and what pleasure in their attainments could survive, undiminished, after the realization that their position was maintained only at the sufferance of mad kings who might confiscate all for a royal purpose or dispatch a deputation of blackguards, under the protective heraldry of the monarch, to lay waste and burn? This beautiful house was only ashes waiting for the fire, and when Darius and Bonnie regarded their handsome residence henceforth, they would be troubled by the faintest scent of smoke, the bitter taste of burnt dreams.

Jessica met them at the door, hugged Harris fiercely, and wept against his shoulder. To have held her any tighter, he would have had to hurt her. She, the girls, his brother, and his sister-in-law were all that he had now. He was not merely without possessions but without his once strong belief in the system of law and justice that had inspired and sustained him during his entire adult life. From that moment on, he would trust in nothing except himself and the few people who were closest to him. Security, if it existed at all, could not be bought, but was a gift to be given only by family and friends.

Bonnie had taken Ondine and Willa to the mall to buy some new clothes for them.

"I should've gone along, but I just couldn't," Jessica said, wiping at the tears in the corners of her eyes. She seemed fragile in a way she had never been before. "I'm still . . . I'm shaking from all this. Harris, when they came on Saturday with . . . with the seizure notice, when they made us move out, we were only allowed to take one suitcase each, clothes and personal stuff, no jewelry, no . . . no anything."

"It's an outrageous abuse of legal process," Darius said angrily and with palpable frustration.

"And they stood over us, watching what we packed," Jessica told Harris. "Those men . . . just standing there, while the girls opened dresser drawers to get their underwear, bras . . ." That memory brought a snarl of outrage to her voice and, for the time being, chased off the emotional fragility that dismayed Harris and that was so unlike her. "It was *disgusting!* They were so arrogant, such bastards about it. I was just waiting for one of the sonsofbitches to touch me, to try to hurry me along with a little hand on the arm, anything like that, because I'd have kicked him in the balls so hard he'd have been wearing dresses and high heels the rest of his life."

He was surprised to hear himself laugh.

Darius laughed too.

Jessica said, "Well, I would have."

"I know," Harris said. "I know you would."

"I don't see what's so funny."

"I don't either, honey, but it is."

"Maybe you've got to have balls to see the humor," Darius said.

That made Harris laugh again.

Shaking her head in amazement at the inexplicable behavior of men in general and these two in particular, Jessica went to the kitchen, where she was preparing the ingredients for a pair of her justly renowned walnut-apple pies. They followed her.

Harris watched her peel an apple. Her hands were trembling.

He said, "Shouldn't the girls be in school? They can wait till the weekend to buy clothes."

Jessica and Darius exchanged a look, and Darius said, "We all felt it was better they stay out of school for a week. Until the press coverage isn't so . . . fresh."

That was something Harris hadn't really thought about: his name and photograph in the newspapers, headlines about a drug-dealing cop, the television anchorpersons conducting their happy talk around lurid accounts of his alleged secret life of crime. Ondine and Willa would have to endure heavy humiliation whenever they returned to school, whether it was tomorrow or next week or a month from now. *Hey, can your dad sell me an ounce of pure white? How much does your old man charge to fix a speeding ticket? Does your daddy just deal in drugs, or can he get a hooker for me?* Dear God. This wound was separate from all others.

Whoever his mysterious enemies were, whoever had done this to him, they must have been aware that they were destroying not only him but his family as well. Though Harris knew nothing else about them, he knew they were utterly without pity and as merciless as snakes.

From the wall phone in the kitchen, he made a call that he had been dreading—to Carl Falkenberg, his boss at Parker Center. He was prepared to use accumulated personal days and vacation, in order not to return to work for three weeks, in the hope that the conspiracy against him would miraculously collapse during that time. But, as he had feared, they were suspending him from duty indefinitely, although with pay. Carl was supportive but uncharacteristically reserved, as if he were responding to every question by reading from a carefully worded selection of answers. Even if the charges against Harris were eventually dropped or if a trial resulted in a verdict of innocence, there would be a parallel investigation by the LAPD Internal Affairs Division, and if its findings discredited him, he would be discharged from duty regardless of the outcome in federal court. Consequently, Carl was keeping a safe professional distance.

Harris hung up, sat at the kitchen table, and quietly conveyed the essence of the conversation to Jessica and Darius. He was aware of an unnerving hollowness in his voice, but he couldn't get rid of it.

"At least it's suspension with pay," Jessica said.

"They have to keep paying me or get in trouble with the union," Harris explained. "It's no gift."

Darius brewed a pot of coffee, and while Jessica continued with her pie-making, he and Harris remained in the kitchen, so the three of them could discuss legal options and strategies. Although the situation was grim, it felt good to be talking about taking action, striking back.

But the hits just kept on coming.

Not even half an hour passed before Carl Falkenberg called to inform Harris that the Internal Revenue Service had served the LAPD with a legal order to garnishee his wages against "possible unpaid taxes from trafficking in illegal drugs." Although his suspension was with pay, his weekly salary would have to be held in trust until the issue of his guilt or innocence was determined in court.

Walking back to the table and sitting opposite his brother again, Harris told them the latest. His voice was now as flat and emotionless as that of a talking machine.

Darius exploded off his chair, furious. "Damn it, this is not right, this does not wash, no way, I'll be damned if it does! Nobody has proved *any-thing*. We'll get this garnishment withdrawn. We'll start on it right now. It might take a few days, but we'll make them eat that piece of paper, Harris, I swear to you that we'll make the bastards eat it." He hurried out of the kitchen, evidently to his study and the telephone there.

For a long spiral of seconds, Harris and Jessica stared at each other. Neither of them spoke. They had been married so long that sometimes they didn't have to speak to know what they would have said to each other.

She returned her attention to the dough in the pie pan, which she had been crimping along the edge with her thumb and forefinger. Ever since Harris had come home, Jessica's hands had been trembling noticeably. Now the tremors were gone. Her hands were steady. He had the terrible feeling that her steadiness was the result of a bleak resignation to the un-beatable superiority of the unknown forces arrayed against them.

He looked out the window beside the table. Sunshine streamed through ficus branches. The flowers in the beds of English primrose were almost Day-Glo bright. The backyard was expansive, well and lushly landscaped, with a swimming pool in the center of a used-brick patio. To every dreamer living in deprivation, that backyard was a perfect symbol of success. A highly motivating image. But Harris Descoteaux knew what it really was. Just another room in the prison.

∽

While the JetRanger flew due north, Ellie sat in one of the two seats in the last row of the passenger cabin. She held the open attaché case on her lap and worked with the computer that was built into it.

She was still marveling over her good fortune. When she had first boarded the chopper and had searched the cabin to be sure no agency men were hiding there, before they had even taken off, she had discovered the computer on the deck at the end of the aisle. She recognized it immediately as hardware developed for the agency, because she'd actually looked over Danny's shoulder when he had been designing some of the critical software for it. She realized that it was plugged in and on-line, but she was too busy to check it out closely until after they got off the ground and disabled the second JetRanger. Safely in the air, northbound toward Salt Lake City, she returned to the computer and was astonished when she realized that the image on the display screen was the satellite look-down of the very shopping center from which they had just escaped. If the agency had temporarily hijacked Earthguard 3 from the EPA to search for her and Spencer, they could only have done so through their omnipotent home-office computer system in Virginia. Mama. Only Mama had such power. The workstation that had been abandoned in the chopper was on-line with Mama, the megabitch herself.

If she had found the computer unplugged, she wouldn't have been able to get into Mama. A thumbprint was required to get on-line. Danny hadn't designed the software, but he had seen a demonstration of it and had told her about it, as excited as a child who had been shown one of the best toys ever. Because her thumbprint was not one of the approved, the hardware would have been useless to her.

Spencer came back down the aisle, with Rocky padding along behind him, and Ellie glanced up from the VDT in surprise. "Shouldn't you be keeping a gun on the crew?"

"I took their headsets away from them, so they can't use the radio. They don't have any weapons up there, and even if they had an arsenal, they might not use it. They're flyboys, not murderous thugs. But they think we *are* murderous thugs, *insane* murderous thugs, and they're nicely respectful."

"Yeah, well, they also know we need them to fly this crate."

As Ellie returned to her work on the computer, Spencer picked up the cellular phone that someone had abandoned on the last seat in the port-side row. He sat across the aisle from her.

"Well, see," he said, "they think I can fly this eggbeater if anything happens to them."

"Can you?" she asked, without shifting her attention from the video display, keeping her fingers busy on the keys.

"No. But when I was a Ranger, I learned a lot about choppers—mostly related to how you sabotage them, boobytrap them, and blow them up. I recognize all the flight instruments, know the names of them. I was real convincing. Fact is, they probably think the only reason I haven't already killed them is because I don't want to have to haul their bodies out of the cockpit and sit in their blood."

"What if they lock the cockpit door?"

"I broke the lock. And they don't have anything in there to wedge the door shut with."

She said, "You're pretty good at this."

"Aw, shucks, not really. What've you got there?"

While Ellie worked, she told him about their good fortune.

"Everything's coming up roses," he said with only a half-note of sarcasm. "What're you doing?"

"Through Mama, I've up-linked to Earthguard, the EPA satellite they've been using to track us. I've gotten into the core of its operating program. All the way to the program-management level."

He whistled in appreciation. "Look, even Mr. Rocky Dog is impressed."

She glanced up and saw that Rocky was grinning. His tail swished back and forth on the deck, thumping into the seats on both sides of the aisle.

"You're going to screw up a hundred-million-dollar satellite, turn it into space junk?" Spencer asked.

"Only for a while. Freeze it up for six hours. By then they won't have a clue where to look for us."

"Ah, go ahead, have fun, screw it up permanently."

"When the agency isn't using it for crap like this, it might actually do some beneficial work."

"So you're a civic-minded individual after all."

"Well, I was a Girl Scout once. It gets in your blood, like a disease."

"Then you probably wouldn't want to go out with me tonight, spray-paint some graffiti on highway overpasses."

"There!" she said, and tapped the ENTER key. She studied the data that came up on the screen and smiled. "Earthguard just shut down for a six-hour nap. They've lost us—except for radar tracking. Are you sure we're keeping due north and high enough for radar to pick us up, like I asked?"

"The boys up front promised me."

"Perfect."

"What did you do before all this?" he asked.

"Freelance software designer, specializing in video games."

"You created video games?"

"Yeah."

"Well, of course, you did."

"I'm serious. I did."

"No, you missed my inflection," he said. "I meant, *of course* you did. It's obvious. And now you're in a real-life video game."

"The way the world's going, everyone'll be living in one big video game eventually, and it's sure as hell not going to be a nice one, not 'Super Mario Brothers' or anything that gentle. More like 'Mortal Kombat.' "

"Now that you've disabled a hundred-million-dollar satellite, what next?"

As they had talked, Ellie had been focused on the VDT. She had retreated from Earthguard, back into Mama. She was calling up menus, one after the other, speed-reading them. "I'm looking around, seeing what's the best damage I can do."

"Mind doing something for me first?"

"Tell me what, while I nose around here."

He told her about the trap that he had set for anyone who might break into his cabin while he was gone.

It was her turn to whistle appreciatively. "God, I'd like to've seen their faces when they figured out what was going down. And what happened to the digitized photographs when they left Malibu?"

"They were transmitted to the Pacific Bell central computer, preceded by a code that activated a program I'd previously designed and secretly buried there. That program allowed them to be received and then re-transmitted to the Illinois Bell central computer, where I buried another little hidden program that came to life in response to the special access code, and it received them from Pacific Bell."

"You think the agency didn't track them that far?"

"Well, to Pacific Bell, sure. But after my little program sent them to Chicago, it erased all record of that call. Then it self-destructed."

"Sometimes a self-destruct can be rebuilt and examined. Then they'd see the instructions about erasing the call to Illinois Bell."

"Not in this case. This was a beautiful little self-destructed program that stayed beautifully self-destructed, I guarantee you. When it dismantled it-self, it also took out a reasonably large block of the Pacific Bell system."

Ellie interrupted her urgent search of Mama's programs to look at him. "How large is reasonably large?"

"About thirty thousand people must've been without telephone ser-vice for two to three hours before they got backup systems on-line."

"You were never a Girl Scout," she said.

"Well, I was never given a chance."

"You learned a lot in that computer-crime task force."

"I was a diligent employee," he admitted.

"More than you learned about helicopters, for sure. So you think those photos are still waiting in the Chicago Bell computer?"

"I'll walk you through the routine, and we'll find out. Might be useful to get a good look at the faces of some of these thugs—for future refer-ence. Don't you think?"

"I think. Tell me what to do."

Three minutes later, the first of the photographs appeared on the video display of the computer in her lap. Spencer leaned across the nar-row aisle from his seat, and she angled the attaché case so they both could see the screen.

"That's my living room," he said.

"You're not deeply interested in decor, are you?"

"My favorite period style is Early Neat."

"More like Late Monastery."

Two men in riot gear were moving through the room quickly enough to be blurred in the still shot.

"Hit the space bar," Spencer said.

She hit the bar, and the next photograph appeared on the screen. They went through the first ten shots in less than a minute. A few provided a clear image of a face or two. But it was difficult to get a sense of what a man looked like when he was wearing a riot helmet with a chin strap.

"Just shuffle through them until we see something new," he said.

Ellie rapidly, repeatedly tapped the space bar, flipping through the photos, until they came to shot number thirty-one. A new man appeared, and he was not in riot gear.

"Sonofabitch," Spencer said.

"I think so," she agreed.

"Let's see thirty-two."

She tapped the space bar.

"Well."

"Yeah."

"Thirty-three."

Tap.

"No doubt about it," she said.

Tap. Thirty-four.

Tap. Thirty-five.

Tap. Thirty-six.

The same man was in shot after shot, moving around the living room of the cabin in Malibu. And he was the last of the five men they had seen getting out of this very helicopter in front of the Hallmark card store a short while ago.

"Weirdest thing of all," Ellie said, "I'll bet we're looking at his picture on *his* computer."

"You're probably sitting in his seat."

"In his helicopter."

Spencer said, "My God, he must be pissed."

Quickly they went through the rest of the photographs. That pudgy-faced, rather jolly-looking fellow was in every shot until he apparently spit on a piece of paper and pasted it to the camera lens.

"I won't forget what he looks like," Spencer said, "but I wish we had a printer, could get a copy of that."

"There's a printer built in," she said, indicating a slot on the side of the attaché case. "I think there's a supply of maybe fifty sheets of eight-and-a-half-by-eleven bond paper. I sort of remember that's what Danny told me about it."

"All I need is one."

"Two. Once for me."

They picked the clearest shot of their benign-looking enemy, and Ellie printed out twice.

"You've never seen him before, huh?" Spencer asked.

"Never."

"Well, I suspect we'll be seeing him again."

Ellie closed out Illinois Bell and returned to Mama's seemingly endless series of menus. The depth and breadth of the megabitch's abilities really did make her seem omnipotent and omniscient.

Settling back into his seat, Spencer said, "Think you can give Mama a terminal stroke?"

She shook her head. "No. Too many redundancies built into her for that."

"A bloody nose, then?"

"At least that much."

She was aware of him staring at her for the better part of a minute, while she worked.

Finally he said, "Have you broken many?"

"Noses? Me?"

"Hearts."

She was amazed to feel a blush rising in her cheeks. "Not me."

"You could. Easy."

She said nothing.

"The dog's listening," he said.

"What?"

"I can only speak the truth."

"I'm no cover girl."

"I love the way you look."

"I'd like a better nose."

"I'll buy you a different one if you want."

"I'll think about it."

"But it's only going to be different. Not any better."

"You're a strange man."

"Besides, I wasn't talking about looks."

She didn't respond, just kept poring through Mama.

He said, "If I was blind, if I'd never seen your face, I already know you well enough that you could still break my heart."

When she was finally able to take a breath, she said, "As soon as they give up on Earthguard, they'll try to get control of another satellite and find us again. So it's time to drop below radar and change course. Better tell the flyboys."

After a hesitation, which might have indicated disappointment in her failure to respond in any expected fashion to the way he had bared his feelings, he said, "Where are we going?"

"As near the Colorado border as this bucket will take us."

"I'll find out how much fuel we have. But why Colorado?"

"Because Denver is the nearest really major city. And if we can get to a major city, I can make contact with people who can help us."

"Do we need help?"

"Haven't you been paying attention?"

"I've got a history with Colorado," he said, and an uneasiness marked his voice.

"I'm aware of that."

"Quite a history."

"Does it matter?"

"Maybe," he said, and he was no longer romancing her. "I guess it shouldn't. It's just a place. . . ."

She met his eyes. "The heat's on us too high right now. We need to get to some people who can hide us out, let things cool off."

"You know people like that?"

"Not until recently. I've always been on my own before. But lately . . . things have changed."

"Who are they?"

"Good people. That's all you need to know for now."

"Then I guess we're going to Denver," he said.

∾

Mormons, Mormons were everywhere, a plague of Mormons, Mormons in neatly pressed uniforms, clean-shaven, clear-eyed, too soft-spoken for cops, so excessively polite that Roy Miro wondered if it was all an act, Mormons to the left of him, Mormons to the right of him, both local and county authorities, and all of them too efficient and by-the-book either to flub their investigation or to let this whole mess be covered over with a wink and a slap on the back. What bothered Roy the most about these particular Mormons was that they robbed him of his usual advantage, because in their company, his affable manner was nothing unusual. His politeness paled in comparison to theirs. His quick and easy smile was only one in a blizzard of smiles full of teeth remarkably whiter than his own. They swarmed through the shopping center and the supermarket, these Mormons, asking their oh-so-polite questions, armed with their small notebooks and Bic pens and direct Mormon stares, and Roy could never be sure that they were buying any part of his cover story or that they were convinced by his impeccable phony credentials.

Hard as he tried, he couldn't figure out how to schmooze with Mormon cops. He wondered if they would respond well and open up to him if he told them how very much he liked their tabernacle choir. He didn't actually like or dislike their choir, however, and he had a feeling that they would know he was lying just to warm them up. The same was true of the Osmonds, the premier Mormon show-business family. He neither liked nor disliked their singing and dancing; they were undeniably talented, but they just weren't to his taste. Marie Osmond had *perfect* legs, legs that he could have spent hours kissing and stroking, legs against which he wished that he could crush handsful of soft red roses—but he was pretty sure that these Mormons were not the type of cops who would enthusiastically join in on a conversation about that sort of thing.

He was certain that not all of the cops were Mormons. The equal-opportunity laws ensured a diverse police force. If he could find those who weren't Mormons, he might be able to establish the degree of rapport necessary to grease the wheels of their investigation, one way or another, and get the hell out of there. But the non-Mormons were indistinguishable from the Mormons because they'd adopted Mormon ways, manners, and mannerisms. The non-Mormons—whoever the cunning bastards might be—were all polite, pressed, well groomed, sober, with infuriatingly well-scrubbed teeth that were free of all telltale nicotine stains. One of the officers was a black man named Hargrave, and Roy was positive that he'd found at least one cop to whom the teachings of Brigham Young were no more important than those of Kali, the malevolent form of the Hindu Mother Goddess, but Hargrave turned out to be perhaps the most Mormon of all Mormons who had ever walked the Mormon Way. Hargrave had a walletful of pictures of his wife and nine children, including two sons who were currently on religious missions in squalid corners of Brazil and Tonga.

Eventually the situation spooked Roy as much as it frustrated him. He felt as if he were in *The Invasion of the Body Snatchers.*

Before the city and county patrol cars had begun to arrive—all well polished and in excellent repair—Roy had used the secure phone in the disabled helicopter to order two more customized JetRangers out of Las Vegas, but the agency had only one more at that office to send him.

"Jesus," Ken Hyckman had said, "you're going through choppers like they're Kleenex." Roy would be continuing the pursuit of the woman and Grant with only nine of his twelve men, which was the maximum number that could be packed into the one new craft.

Although the disabled JetRanger wouldn't be repaired and able to take off from behind the Hallmark store for at least thirty-six hours, the new chopper was already out of Vegas and on its way to Cedar City. Earthguard was being retargeted to track the stolen aircraft. They had suffered a setback, no argument about that, but the situation was by no means an unmitigated disaster. One battle lost—even one *more* battle lost—didn't mean they would lose the war.

He wasn't calmed by inhaling the pale-peach vapor of tranquility and exhaling the bile-green vapor of rage and frustration. He found no comfort in any of the other meditative techniques that for years had worked so reliably. Only one thing kept his counterproductive anger in check: thinking about Eve Jammer in all her glorious sixty-percent perfection. Nude. Oiled. Writhing. Blond splendor on black rubber.

The new helicopter wouldn't reach Cedar City until past noon, but Roy was confident of being able to tough out the Mormons until then. Under their watchful eyes, he wandered among them, answered their questions again and again, examined the contents of the Rover, tagged everything in the vehicle for impoundment, and all the while his head was filled with images of Eve pleasuring herself with her perfect hands and with a variety of devices that had been designed by sexually obsessed inventors whose creative genius exceeded that of Thomas Edison and Albert Einstein combined.

As he was standing at a supermarket checkout counter, examining the computer and the file box of twenty software diskettes that had been removed from the back of the Range Rover, Roy remembered Mama. For one frantic moment of denial, he tried to delude himself into remembering that he had switched off or unplugged the attaché case computer before he had departed the chopper. No good. He could see the video display as it had been when he'd put the workstation on the deck beside his seat before he had hurried to the cockpit: the satellite look-down on the shopping center.

"Holy *shit!*" he exclaimed, and every Mormon cop within hearing twitched as one.

Roy raced to the back of the supermarket, through the stockroom, out the rear door, through the milling strike force agents and cops, to the damaged helicopter, where he could use the secure phone with its scrambling device.

He called Las Vegas and reached Ken Hyckman in the satellite-surveillance center. "We've got trouble—"

Even as Roy started to explain, Hyckman talked over him with pompous ex-anchorman solemnity: "We have trouble here. Earthguard's onboard computer crashed. It inexplicably went off the air. We're working on it, but we—"

Roy interrupted, because he knew the woman must have used his VDT to take out Earthguard. "Ken, listen, my field computer was in that stolen chopper, and it was on-line with Mama."

"Holy shit!" Ken Hyckman said, but in the satellite-surveillance center, there were no Mormon cops to twitch.

"Get on with Mama, have her cut off my unit and block it from ever reaccessing her. *Ever.*"

∽

The JetRanger chattered eastward across Utah, flying as low as one hundred feet above ground level where possible, to avoid radar detection.

Rocky remained with Ellie after Spencer went forward to oversee the crew again. She was too intensely focused on learning as much as she could about Mama's capabilities to be able to pet the pooch or even talk at him a little. His unrewarded company seemed to be a touching and welcome indication that he had come to trust and approve of her.

She might as well have smashed the VDT and spent the time giving the dog a good scratch behind the ears, because before she was able to accomplish anything, the data on the video display vanished and was replaced by a blue field. A question flashed at her in red letters against the blue: WHO GOES THERE?

This development was no surprise. She had expected to be cut off long before she could do any damage to Mama. The system was designed with elaborate redundancies, protections against hacker penetrations, and virus vaccines. Finding a route into Mama's deep program-management level, where major destruction could be wrought, would require not merely hours of diligent probing but days. Ellie had been fortunate to have the time necessary to take out Earthguard, for she could never have achieved such total control of the satellite without Mama's assistance. To attempt not merely to use Mama but to bloody her nose had been overreaching. Nevertheless, doomed as the effort was, Ellie had been obliged to try.

When she had no answer for the red-letter question, the screen went blank and changed from blue to gray. It looked dead. She knew there was no point in trying to reacquire Mama.

She unplugged the computer, put it in the aisle beside her seat, and reached for the dog. He wiggled to her, lashing his tail. As she bent forward to pet him, she noticed a manila envelope on the deck, half under her seat.

After petting and scratching the pooch for a minute or two, Ellie retrieved the envelope from under the seat. It contained four photographs.

She recognized Spencer in spite of how very young he was in the snapshots. Although the man was visible in the boy, he had lost more than youth since the days when those pictures had been taken. More than innocence. More than the effervescent spirit that seemed evident in the smile and body language of the child. Life also had stolen an ineffable quality from him, and the loss was no less apparent for being inexpressible.

Ellie studied the woman's face in the two pictures that showed her with Spencer, and was convinced that they were mother and son. If appearances didn't deceive—and in this instance she sensed that they did not—Spencer's mother had been gentle, kind, soft-spoken, with a girlish sense of fun.

In a third photo, the mother was younger than in the two with Spencer, perhaps twenty, standing alone in front of a tree laden with white flowers. She appeared to be radiantly innocent, not naive but unspoiled and without cynicism. Maybe Ellie was reading too much into a photo, but she perceived in Spencer's mother a vulnerability so poignant that suddenly tears welled in her eyes.

Squinting, biting her lower lip, determined not to weep, she was at last forced to wipe her eyes with the heel of her hand. She wasn't moved solely by Spencer's loss. Staring at the woman in the summer dress, she thought of her own mother, taken from her so brutally.

Ellie stood on the shore of a warm sea of memories, but she couldn't bathe in the comfort of them. Every wave of recollection, regardless of how innocent it seemed, broke on the same dark beach. Her mother's face, in every recaptured moment of the past, was as it had been in death: bloodied, bullet-shattered, with a fixed gaze so full of horror that it seemed as if, at the penultimate moment, the dear woman had glimpsed what lay beyond this world and had seen only a cold, vast emptiness.

Shivering, Ellie turned her eyes away from the snapshot to the starboard porthole beside her seat. The blue sky was as forbidding as an icy sea, and close beneath the low-flying craft passed a meaningless blur of rock, vegetation, and human endeavor.

When she was certain that she was in control of her emotions, Ellie looked again at the woman in the summer dress—and then at the final of the four photographs. She had noted aspects of the mother in the son, but she saw a much greater resemblance between Spencer and the shadow-shrouded man in the fourth picture. She knew this had to be his father, even though she didn't recognize the infamous artist.

The resemblance, however, was limited to the dark hair, darker eyes, the shape of the chin, and a few other features. In Spencer's face, there was none of the arrogance and potential for cruelty that made his father appear to be so cold and forbidding.

Or perhaps she saw those things in Steven Ackblom only because she knew that she was gazing at a monster. If she had come upon the photo without reason to suspect who the man was—or if she had met him in life, at a party or on the street—she might have seen nothing about him that made him more ominous than Spencer or other men.

Ellie was immediately sorry that such a thought had occurred to her, for it encouraged her to wonder if the kind, good man she saw in Spencer was an illusion or, at best, only part of the truth. She realized, somewhat to her surprise, that she did not want to doubt Spencer Grant. Instead, she was eager to believe in him, as she had not believed in anything or anyone for a long time.

If I was blind, if I'd never seen your face, I already know you well enough that you could still break my heart.

Those words had been so sincere, such an uncalculated revelation of his feelings and his vulnerability, that she had been left briefly speechless. Yet she hadn't possessed the courage to give him any reason to believe that she might be capable of reciprocating his feelings for her.

Danny had been dead only fourteen months, and that was, by her standards, far too short a time to grieve. To touch another man this soon, to care, to love—that seemed to be a betrayal of the man whom she had *first* loved and whom she would still love, to the exclusion of all others, were he alive.

On the other hand, fourteen months of loneliness was, by any measure, an eternity.

To be honest with herself, she had to admit that her reticence sprang from more than a concern about the propriety or impropriety of a fourteen-month period of mourning. As fine and loving as Danny had been, he never would have found it possible to bare his heart as directly or as completely as Spencer had done repeatedly since she'd driven him out of that dry wash in the desert. Danny had not been unromantic, but he had expressed his feelings less directly, with thoughtful gifts and kindnesses, rather than with words, as if to say "I love you" would have been to cast a curse upon their relationship. She was unaccustomed to the rough poetry of a man like Spencer, when he spoke from his heart, and she was not sure what she thought of it.

That was a lie. She liked it. More than liked it. In her hardened heart, she was surprised to find a tender place that wasn't merely responsive to Spencer's forthright expressions of love but that longed for more. That longing was like the profound thirst of a desert traveler, and she now realized it was a thirst that had been in need of slaking all her life.

She was reluctant to respond to Spencer not primarily because she might have grieved too short a time for Danny but because she sensed that the first love of her life might eventually prove not to be the greatest. Finding the capacity to love again seemed like a betrayal of Danny. But it was far worse—cruel rejection—to love another *more* than she had loved her murdered husband.

Perhaps that would never happen. If she opened herself to this still mysterious man, perhaps she would ultimately discover that the room he occupied in her heart would never be as large or warm as the one in which Danny had lived and would always live.

In carrying her loyalty to Danny's memory so far, she supposed that she was allowing honest sentiment to degenerate into a sugary pudding of sentimentality. Surely no one was born to love but once and never again, even if fate carried that first love to an early grave. If creation operated on rules that stern, God had built a cold, bleak universe. Surely love—and all emotions—were in one regard like muscles: growing stronger with exercise, withering when not used. Loving Danny might have given her the emotional strength, in the wake of his passing, to love Spencer more.

And to be fair to Danny, he had been raised by a soulless father—and a brittle, socialite mother—in whose icy embrace he'd learned to be self-contained and guarded. He had given her all that he could give, and she had been fortunate and happy in his arms. So happy, in fact, that suddenly she could no longer imagine going through the rest of her life without seeking, from someone else, the gift that Danny had been the first to give her.

How many women had ever affected a man so strongly that he had, after one evening of conversation, given up a comfortable existence and put his life in extreme jeopardy to be with her? She was more than merely mystified and flattered by Spencer's commitment. She felt special, foolish, girlish, reckless. She was reluctantly enchanted.

Frowning, she studied Steven Ackblom's photograph again.

She knew that Spencer's commitment to her—and all that he had done to find her—might be seen as less the result of love than of obsession. In the son of a savage serial killer, any sign of obsession might reasonably be viewed as a cause for alarm, as a reflection of the father's madness.

Ellie returned all four photographs to the envelope. She closed it with its small metal clasp.

She believed Spencer was, in all ways that mattered, *not* his father's son. He was no more dangerous to her than was Mr. Rocky Dog. For three nights in the desert, as she had listened to him murmuring in delirium, between his periodic ascensions to a shaky state of consciousness, she had heard nothing to make her suspect that he was the bad seed of a bad seed.

In reality, even if Spencer was a danger to her, he was no match for the agency when it came to being a threat. The agency was still out there, hunting for them.

What Ellie really needed to worry about was whether she could avoid the agency's goons long enough to discover and enjoy whatever emotional connections might evolve between her and this complex and enigmatic man. By Spencer's own admission, he had secrets that were still unrevealed. More for his sake than hers, those secrets would have to be aired before any future they might have together could be discussed or even discerned; because until he settled his debts with the past, he would never know the peace of mind or the self-respect needed for love to flourish.

She looked out at the sky again.

They flew across Utah in their sleek black machine, strangers in their own land, putting the sun behind them, heading eastward toward the horizon from which, several hours hence, the night would come.

§

Harris Descoteaux showered in the gray and maroon guest bathroom of his brother's Westwood home, but the scent of the jailhouse, which he believed he could detect on himself, was ineradicable. Jessica had packed three changes of clothes for him on Saturday, prior to being evicted from their house in Burbank. From that meager wardrobe, he selected Nikes, gray cords, and a long-sleeve, dark-green knit shirt.

When he told his wife that he was going for a walk, she wanted him to wait until the pies could be taken from the oven, so she could go with him. Darius, busy on the telephone in his study, suggested that he delay leaving for half an hour, so they could walk together. Harris sensed that they were concerned about his despondency. They felt he should not be alone.

He reassured them that he had no intention of throwing himself in front of a truck, that he needed to exercise after a weekend in a cell, and that he wanted to be alone to think. He borrowed one of Darius's leather jackets from the foyer closet and went into the cool February morning.

The residential streets of Westwood were hilly. Within a few blocks, he realized that a weekend spent sitting in a cell actually *had* left his muscles cramped and in need of stretching.

He hadn't been telling the truth when he had said that he wanted to be alone to think. Actually, he wanted to *stop* thinking. Ever since the assault on his house on Friday night, his mind had been spinning ceaselessly. And thinking had gotten him nowhere but into bleaker places within himself.

Even what little sleep he had gotten had been no surcease from worry, for he had dreamed about faceless men in black uniforms and shiny black jackboots. In the nightmares, they buckled Ondine, Willa, and Jessica into collars and leashes, as if dealing with dogs instead of with people, and led them away, leaving Harris alone.

As there was no escape from worry in his sleep, there was none in the company of Jessica or Darius. His brother was ceaselessly working on the case or brooding aloud about offensive and defensive legal strategies. And Jessica was—as Ondine and Willa would be, when they returned from the mall—a constant reminder that he had failed his family. None of them would say anything of that kind, of course, and he knew that the thought would never actually cross their minds. He had done nothing to earn the catastrophe that had befallen them. Yet, though he was blameless, he blamed himself. Somewhere, sometime, someplace, he'd made an enemy whose retribution was psychotically in excess of whatever offense Harris unwittingly had committed. If only he had done one thing differently, avoided one offending statement or act, perhaps none of this would have happened. Every time he thought of Jessica or his daughters, his inadvertent and unavoidable culpability seemed to be a greater sin.

The men in jackboots, though only creatures from his dream, had in a very real sense begun to deny him the comfort of his family without the need to buckle them in leashes and lead them away. His anger and frustration at his powerlessness and his self-inflicted guilt, as surely as bricks and mortar, had become the components of a wall between him and those he loved; and this barrier was likely to become wider and higher with time.

Alone, therefore, he walked the winding streets and the hills of Westwood. Many palms, ficuses, and pines kept the neighborhood California-green in February, but there were also numerous sycamores and maples and birches that were bare-limbed in winter. Harris focused largely on the interesting patterns of sunlight and tree shadows that alternately swagged and filigreed the sidewalk ahead. He tried to use them to induce a state of self-imposed hypnosis, in which all thought was banished except for an awareness of the need to keep putting one foot in front of the other.

He had some success at that game. In a half trance, he was only peripherally aware of the sapphire-blue Toyota that passed him and, abruptly chugging and stalling out, pulled to the curb and stopped nearly a block ahead. A man got out of the car and opened the hood, but Harris remained focused on the tapestry of sun and shade on which he trod.

As Harris passed the front of the Toyota, the stranger turned from his examination of the engine and said, "Sir, may I give you something to think about?"

Harris continued a couple of steps before he realized that the man was speaking to him. Halting, turning, rising from his self-induced hypnosis, he said, "Excuse me?"

The stranger was a tall black man in his late twenties. He was as skinny as a fourteen-year-old, with the somber and intense manner of an elderly man who had seen too much and carried too great a grief all his life. Dressed in black slacks, a black turtleneck sweater, and a black jacket, he seemed to want to project an ominous image. But if that was his intention, it was defeated by his large, bottle-thick glasses, his thinness, and a voice which, while deep, was as velvety and appealing as that of Mel Torme.

"May I give you something to think about?" he asked again, and then he continued without waiting for a response. "What's happened to you couldn't happen to a United States Representative or Senator."

The street was uncannily quiet for being in such a metropolitan area. The sunlight seemed different from what it had been a moment ago. The glimmer that it laid along the curved surfaces of the blue Toyota struck Harris as unnatural.

"Most people are unaware of it," said the stranger, "but for decades, politicians have exempted current and future members of the U.S. Congress from most of the laws they pass. Asset forfeiture, for one. If cops nail a senator peddling cocaine out of his Cadillac by a schoolyard, his car can't be seized the way your house was."

Harris had the peculiar feeling that he had hypnotized himself so well that this tall man in black was an apparition in a trance-state dream.

"You might be able to prosecute him for drug dealing and get a conviction—unless his fellow politicians just censor him or expel him from Congress and, at the same time, arrange his immunity from prosecution. But you couldn't seize his assets for drug dealing or any of the other two hundred offenses for which they seize yours."

Harris said, "Who are you?"

Ignoring the question, the stranger went on in that soft voice: "Politicians pay no Social Security taxes. They have their own retirement fund. And they don't rob it to finance other programs, the way they drain Social Security. *Their* pensions are safe."

Harris looked anxiously around the street to see who might be watching, what other vehicles and men might have accompanied this man. Although the stranger wasn't threatening, the situation itself suddenly seemed ominous. He felt that he was being set up, as if the point of the encounter was to tease from him some seditious statement for which he could be arrested, prosecuted, and imprisoned.

That was an absurd fear. Free speech was still well guaranteed. No citizens of the world were as openly and heatedly opinionated as his countrymen. Recent events obviously had inspired a paranoia over which he needed to gain control.

Yet he remained afraid to speak.

The stranger said, "They exempt themselves from health-care plans they intend to force on you, so someday you'll have to wait months for things like gallbladder surgery, but they'll get the care they need on demand. Somehow we've allowed ourselves to be ruled by the greediest and most envious among us."

Harris found the nerve to speak again, but only to repeat the question he had already asked and to add another. "Who are you? What do you want?"

"I only want to give you something to think about until the next time," said the stranger. Then he turned and slammed shut the hood of the blue Toyota.

Emboldened when the other's back was to him, Harris stepped off the curb and grabbed the man by the arm. "Look here—"

"I have to go," the stranger said. "As far as I know, we're not being watched. The chances are a thousand to one. But with today's technology, you can't be a hundred percent sure any more. Until now, to anyone observing us, you just seem to've struck up a conversation with a guy who has car trouble, offered some assistance. But if we stand here talking any longer, and if someone *is* watching, they'll come in for a closer look and turn on their directional microphones."

He went to the driver's door of his Toyota.

Bewildered, Harris said, "But what was this all about?"

"Be patient, Mr. Descoteaux. Just go with the flow, just ride the wave, and you'll find out."

"What wave?"

Opening the driver's door, the stranger cracked his first smile since he had spoken. "Well, I guess the microwave, the light wave, the waves of the future."

He got in the car, started the engine, and drove away, leaving Harris more bewildered than ever.

The microwave. The light wave. The waves of the future.

What the *hell* had just happened?

Harris Descoteaux turned in a circle, studying the neighborhood, and for the most part it seemed unremarkable. Sky and earth. Houses and trees. Lawns and sidewalks. Sunlight and shadows. But in the fabric of the day, glimmering darkly in the deep warp and woof, were threads of mystery that had not been there earlier.

He walked on. Periodically, however, as he had not done before, he glanced over his shoulder.

ॐ

Roy Miro in the Empire of the Mormons. After dealing with the Cedar City Police and the county sheriff's deputies for nearly two hours, Roy had experienced enough niceness to last him until at least the first of July. He understood the value of a smile, courtesy, and unfailing friendliness, because he used a disarming approach in his own work. But these Mormon cops carried it to extremes. He began to long for the cool indifference of Los Angeles, the hard selfishness of Las Vegas, even the surliness and insanity of New York.

His mood was not enhanced by the news of Earthguard's shutdown. He had been further rattled by subsequently learning that the stolen helicopter had descended to such a low altitude that two military facilities tracking it (in response to urgent agency requests that they believed had come from the Drug Enforcement Administration) had lost the craft. They hadn't been able to reacquire it. The fugitives were gone, and only God and a couple of kidnapped pilots knew where.

Roy dreaded having to make his report to Tom Summerton.

The replacement JetRanger was due from Las Vegas in less than twenty minutes, but he didn't know what he was going to do with it. Park it in the shopping-center lot and sit in it, waiting for someone to sight the fugitives? He might still be there when the time rolled around to do Christmas shopping again. Besides, these Mormon cops would undoubtedly keep bringing him coffee and doughnuts, and they would hang around to help him pass the time.

He was spared all the horrors of continued niceness when Gary Duvall telephoned again from Colorado and put the investigation back on track. The call came through on the scrambler-equipped security phone in the disabled chopper.

Roy sat in the back of the cabin and put on the headset.

"You're not easy to track down," Duvall told him.

"Complications here," Roy said succinctly. "You're still in Colorado? I thought you'd be on your way back to San Francisco by this time."

"I got interested in this Ackblom angle. Always been fascinated by these serial killers. Dahmer, Bundy, that Ed Gein fellow a lot of years ago. Weird stuff. Got me to wondering what in hell the son of a serial killer is doing mixed up with this woman."

"We're all wondering," Roy assured him.

As before, Duvall was going to pay out whatever he had learned in small installments.

"While I was so close, I decide to hop over from Denver to Vail, have a look at the ranch where it happened. It's a quick flight. Almost took longer to board and disembark than it took to get there."

"You're there now?"

"At the ranch? No. I just got back from there. But I'm still in Vail. And wait'll you hear what I discovered."

"I guess I'll have to."

"Huh?"

"Wait," Roy said.

Either missing the sarcasm or ignoring it, Duvall said, "I've got two tasty enchiladas of information to feed you. Enchilada number one—what do you think happened to the ranch after they took all of the bodies out of there and Ackblom went to prison for life?"

"It became a retreat for Carmelite nuns," Roy said.

"Where'd you hear that?" Duvall asked, unaware that Roy's answer had been intended to be humorous. "Aren't any nuns anywhere around the place. There's this couple lives on the ranch, Paul and Anita Dresmund. Been there for years. Fifteen years. Everyone around Vail thinks they own the place, and they don't let on any different. They're only about fifty-five now, but they have the look and style of people who might've been able to retire at forty—which is what they claimed—or never worked at all, lived on inheritance. They're perfect for the job."

"What job?"

"Caretakers."

"Who does own it?"

"That's the creepy part."

"I'm sure it is."

"Part of the Dresmunds' job is to pretend ownership and not reveal they're paid caretakers. They like to ski, live the easy life, and it doesn't bother them to be living in a place with that reputation, so keeping their mouths shut has been easy."

"But they opened up to you?"

"Well, you know, people take FBI credentials and a few threats of criminal charges a lot more seriously than they should," Duvall said.

"Anyway, until about a year and a half ago, they were paid by an attorney in Denver."

"You've got his name?"

"Bentley Lingerhold. But I don't think we'll need to bother with him. Until a year and a half ago, the Dresmunds' checks were issued from a trust fund, the Vail Memorial Trust, overseen by this attorney. I had my field computer with me, got on-line with Mama, had her track it down. It's a defunct entity, but there's still a record of it. Actually, it was managed by another trust that still exists—the Spencer Grant Living Trust."

"Good God," Roy said.

"Stunning, huh?"

"The son still owns that property?"

"Yeah, through other entities he controls. A year and a half ago, ownership was transferred from the Vail Memorial Trust, which was essentially owned by the son, to an offshore corporation on Grand Cayman Island. That's a tax-shelter haven in the Caribbean that—"

"Yes, I know. Go on."

"Since then, the Dresmunds have been getting their checks from something called Vanishment International. Through Mama, I got into the Grand Cayman bank where the account is located. I wasn't able to learn its value or call up any transaction records, but I *was* able to find out that Vanishment is controlled by a Swiss-based holding company: Amelia Earhart Enterprises."

Roy fidgeted in his seat, wishing that he'd brought a pen and notebook to keep all these details straight.

Duvall said, "The grandparents, George and Ethel Porth, formed the Vail Memorial Trust well over fifteen years ago, about six months after the Ackblom story exploded. They used it to manage the property at a one-step remove, to keep their names disassociated from it."

"Why didn't they sell the place?"

"Haven't a clue. Anyway, a year later they set up the Spencer Grant Living Trust for the boy, here in Denver, through this Bentley Lingerhold, just after the kid had his name legally changed. At the same time they put *that* trust in charge of the Vail Memorial Trust. But Vanishment International came into existence just a year and a half ago, long after both grandparents were dead, so you've got to figure that Grant himself set it up and that he's moved most of his assets out of the United States."

"Starting at about the same time he began to eliminate his name from most public records," Roy mused. "Okay, tell me something . . . when you're talking trusts and offshore corporations, you're talking about big money, aren't you?"

"Big," Duvall confirmed.

"Where'd it come from? I mean, I know the father was famous. . . ."

"After the old man pleaded guilty to all those murders, you know what happened to him?"

"Tell me."

"He accepted a sentence of life imprisonment in an institution for the criminally insane. No possibility of parole. He made no arguments, no appeals. The guy was absolutely serene from the moment he was arrested, all the way through the final proceeding. Not one outburst, no expressions of regret."

"No point. He knew he didn't have any defense. He wasn't crazy."

"He wasn't?" Duvall said, surprised.

"Well, not irrational, not babbling or raving or anything like that. He knew he couldn't get off. He was just being realistic."

"I guess so. Anyway, then the grandparents moved to have the son declared the legal owner of Ackblom's assets. In fact, at the Porths' request, the court ultimately divided the liquidated assets—minus the ranch—between the boy and the immediate families of the victims, in those cases where any spouses or children survived them. Want to guess how much they split?"

"No," Roy said. He glanced out the porthole and saw a pair of local cops walking alongside the aircraft, looking it over.

Duvall didn't even hesitate at Roy's "no," but poured out more details: "Well, the money came from selling paintings from Ackblom's personal collection of other artists' work, but mainly from the sale of some of his own paintings that he'd never been willing to put on the market. It totaled a little more than twenty-nine million dollars."

"*After* taxes?"

"See, the value of his paintings *soared* with the notoriety. Seems funny, doesn't it, that anyone would want to hang his work in their homes, knowing what the artist did. You'd think the value of his stuff would just collapse. But there was a frenzy in the art market. Values went through the roof."

Roy remembered the color plates of Ackblom's work that he had studied as a boy, at the time the story broke, and he couldn't quite understand Duvall's point. Ackblom's art was exquisite. If Roy could have afforded to buy them, he would have decorated his own home with dozens of the artist's canvases.

Duvall said, "Prices have continued to climb all these years, though more slowly than in the first year after. The family would have been better off holding onto some of the art. Anyway, the boy ended up with fourteen and a half million after taxes. Unless he lives high on the hog, that ought to have grown into an even more substantial fortune over all these years."

Roy thought of the cabin in Malibu, the cheap furniture and walls without any artwork. "No high living."

"Really? Well, you know, his old man didn't live nearly as high as he could have, either. He refused to have a bigger house, didn't want any live-in servants. Just a day maid and a property foreman who went home at five o'clock. Ackblom said he needed to keep his life as simple as possible to preserve his creative energy." Gary Duvall laughed. "Of course he really just didn't want anyone around at night to catch him at his games under the barn."

Wandering back along the side of the chopper again, the Mormon cops looked up at Roy, where he was watching them from the porthole.

He waved.

They waved and smiled.

"Still," Duvall said, "it's a wonder the wife didn't tumble to it sooner. He'd been experimenting with his 'performance' art for four years before she got wise."

"She wasn't an artist."

"What?"

"She didn't have the vision to anticipate. Without the vision to anticipate . . . she wouldn't become suspicious without good reason."

"Can't say I follow you. Four years, for heaven's sake."

Then six more until the boy had found out. Ten years, forty-two victims, slightly more than four a year.

The numbers, Roy decided, weren't particularly impressive. The factors that made Steven Ackblom one for the record books were his fame *before* his secret life was discovered, his position of respect in his community, his status as a family man (most classic serial killers were loners), and his desire to apply his exceptional talent to the art of torture in order to help his subjects achieve a moment of perfect beauty.

"But why," Roy wondered again, "would the son want to hold on to that property? With all its associations. He wanted to change his name. Why not rid himself of the ranch too?"

"Strange, huh?"

"And if not the son, why not the grandparents? Why didn't they sell it off when they were his legal guardians, make that decision for him? After their daughter was killed there . . . why would they want to have anything to do with the place?"

"There's something there," Duvall said.

"What do you mean?"

"Some explanation. Some reason. Whatever it is, it's weird."

"This caretaker couple—"

"Paul and Anita Dresmund."

"—did they say whether Grant ever comes around?"

"He doesn't. At least, they've never seen anybody with a scar like he's got."

"So who oversees them?"

"Until a year and a half ago, they only ever saw two people related to the Vail Memorial Trust. This lawyer, Lingerhold, or one of his partners would come by twice a year, just to check that the ranch was being maintained, that the Dresmunds were earning their salary and spending the upkeep fund on genuinely needed maintenance."

"And for the past year and a half?"

"Since Vanishment International has owned the place, nobody's come around at all," Duvall said. "God, I'd love to find out how much he's got stashed away in Amelia Earhart Enterprises, but you know we're never going to pry that out of the Swiss."

In recent years, Switzerland had grown alarmed by the large number of cases in which U.S. authorities had sought to seize the Swiss accounts of American citizens by invoking asset-forfeiture statutes without proof of criminal activity. The Swiss increasingly viewed such laws as blunt tools of political repression. Every month they retreated further from their traditional cooperation in criminal cases.

"What's the other taco?" Roy asked.

"Huh?"

"The second taco. You said you had two tacos to feed me."

"Enchiladas," Duvall said. "Two enchiladas of information."

"Well, I'm hungry," Roy said pleasantly. He was proud of his patience, after all the tests to which the Mormon cops had put it. "So why don't you heat up that second enchilada?"

Gary Duvall served it to him, and it was as tasty as promised.

The moment he hung up on Duvall, Roy called the Vegas office and spoke to Ken Hyckman, who would soon conclude his shift as the morning duty officer. "Ken, where's that JetRanger?"

"Ten minutes from you."

"I'm going to send it back with most of the men here."

"You're giving up?"

"You know we've lost radar contact on them."

"Right."

"They're gone, and we're not going to reconnect with them that way. But I have another lead, a good one, and I'm jumping on it. I need a jet."

"Jesus."

"I didn't say I needed to hear a little profanity."

"Sorry."

"What about the Lear I came in on Friday night?"

"It's still here. Serviced and ready."

"Is there anywhere in my vicinity it can land, any military base where I could meet it?"

"Let me check," Hyckman said, and he put Roy on hold.

While he waited, Roy thought about Eve Jammer. He would not be able to return to Las Vegas that evening. He wondered what his blond sweetness would do to remember him and to keep him in her heart. She had said that it would be something special. He assumed she would practice new positions, if there were any, and try out erotic aids that she had never used before, in order to prepare an experience for him that, a night or two hence, would leave him shuddering and breathless as never before. When he attempted to imagine what those erotic aids might be, his mind spun. And his mouth went as dry as sand—which was perfect.

Ken Hyckman came back on the line. "We can put the Lear down right there in Cedar City."

"This burg can take a Lear?"

"Brian Head is just twenty-nine miles east of there."

"Who?"

"Not who. What. First-rate ski resort, lots of pricey homes up on the mountain. Lots of rich people and corporations own condos in Brian Head, bring their jets in to Cedar City and drive up from there. It doesn't have anything like O'Hare or LAX, no bars and newsstands and baggage carousels, but the airfield can handle long landing requirements."

"Is a crew standing by with the Lear?"

"Absolutely. We can get them out of McCarran and to you by one o'clock."

"Terrific. I'll ask one of the grinning gendarmes to drive me to the airfield."

"Who?"

"One of the courteous constables," Roy said. He was in a fine mood again.

"I'm not sure this scrambler is giving me what you're saying."

"One of the Mormon marshals."

Either getting the point or deciding that he didn't need to understand, Hyckman said, "They'll have to file a flight plan here. Where are you going from Cedar City?"

"Denver," Roy said.

∽

Slumped in the last seat in the starboard aisle, Ellie dozed on and off for a couple of hours. In fourteen months as a fugitive, she had learned to put aside her fears and worries, sleeping whenever she had a chance.

Shortly after she woke, while she was stretching and yawning, Spencer returned from an extended visit with the two-man crew. He sat across from her.

As Rocky curled up in the aisle at his feet, Spencer said, "More good news. According to the boys, this is an extensively customized eggbeater. For one thing, they have jumped-up engines on this baby, so we can carry an extra-heavy load, which allows them to saddle her with big auxiliary fuel tanks. She's got a lot more range than the standard model. They're sure they can get us all the way across the border and past Grand Junction before there's any danger of the tanks running dry, if we want to go that far."

"The farther the better," she said. "But not right in or around Grand Junction. We don't want to be seen by a lot of curious people. Better out somewhere, but not so far out that we can't find wheels nearby."

"We won't make it to the Grand Junction area until half an hour or so before twilight. Right now it's only ten past two o'clock. Well, three o'clock in the Mountain Time Zone. Still plenty of time to look at a map and pick a general area to put down."

She pointed to the canvas duffel bag on the seat in front of hers. "Listen, about your fifty thousand dollars—"

He held up one hand to silence her. "I was just startled that you found it, that's all. You had every right and reason to search my luggage after you located me in the desert. You didn't know why the hell I was trying to track you down. In fact, I wouldn't be surprised if you still weren't entirely clear on that."

"You always carry that kind of pocket change?"

"About a year and a half ago," he said, "I started salting cash and gold coins in safe-deposit boxes in California, Nevada, Arizona. Also opened savings accounts in various cities, under false names and Social Security numbers. Shifted everything else out of the country."

"Why?"

"So I could move fast."

"You expected to be on the run like this?"

"No. I just didn't like what I saw happening on that computer-crime task force. They taught me all about computers, including that access to information is the essence of freedom. And yet what they ultimately wanted to do was restrict that access in as many instances as possible and to the greatest extent possible."

Playing devil's advocate, Ellie said, "I thought the idea was just to prevent criminal hackers from using computers to steal and maybe to stop them from vandalizing data banks."

"And I'm all for that kind of crime control. But they want to keep a thumb on *everybody*. Most authorities these days . . . they violate privacy all the time, fishing both openly and secretly in data banks. Everyone from the IRS to the Immigration and Naturalization Service. Even the Bureau of Land Management, for God's sake. They were all helping to fund this regional task force with grants, and they all gave me the creeps."

"You see a new world coming—"

"—like a runaway freight train—"

"—and you don't like the shape of it—"

"—don't think I want to be a part of it."

"Do you see yourself as a cyberpunk, an on-line outlaw?"

"No. Just a survivor."

"Is that why you've been erasing yourself from public record—a little survival insurance?"

No shadow fell across him, but his features seemed to darken. He had looked haggard to begin with, which was understandable after the ordeal of the past few days. But now he was sunken-eyed, gaunt, and older than his years.

He said, "At first I was just . . . getting ready to go away." He sighed and wiped a hand across his face. "This sounds strange maybe. But changing my name from Michael Ackblom to Spencer Grant wasn't enough. Moving from Colorado, starting a new life . . . none of it was ever enough. I couldn't forget who I was . . . whose son I was. So I decided to wipe myself out of existence, painstakingly, methodically, until there was no record in the world that I existed under *any* name. What I'd been learning about computers gave me that power."

"And then? When you were erased?"

"That's what I could never figure out. And then? What next? Wipe myself out for real? Suicide?"

"That's not you." She found her heart sinking at the thought.

"No, not me," he agreed. "I never brooded about eating a shotgun barrel or anything like that. And I had an obligation to Rocky, to be here for him."

Sprawled on the deck, the dog raised his head at the sound of his name. He swished his tail.

"Then, after a while," he continued, "even though I didn't know what I was going to do, I decided there was still virtue in becoming invisible. Just because, as you say, of this new world coming, this brave new high-tech world with all its blessings—and curses."

"Why did you leave your DMV file and your military records partly intact? You could've wiped them out completely, long ago."

He smiled. "Being too clever, maybe. I thought I'd just change my address on them, a few salient details, so they weren't much use to anyone. But by leaving them in place, I could always go back to look at them and see if somebody was searching for me."

"You booby-trapped them?"

"Sort of, yeah. I buried little programs in those computers, very deep, very subtle. Each time anyone goes into my DMV or military files without using a little code I implanted, the system adds one asterisk to the end of the last sentence in the file. The idea was that I'd check once or twice a week, and if I saw asterisks, saw that someone was investigating me . . . well, then maybe it would be time to walk away from the cabin in Malibu and just move on."

"Move on where?"

"Anywhere. Just move on and keep moving."

"Paranoid," she said.

"Damned paranoid."

She laughed quietly. So did he.

He said, "By the time I left that task force, I knew that the way the world's changing, everybody's going to have somebody looking for him sooner or later. And most people, most of the time, are going to wish they hadn't been findable."

Ellie checked her wristwatch. "Maybe we should take a look at that map now."

"They have a slew of maps up front," he said.

She watched him walk forward to the cockpit door. His shoulders were slumped. He moved with evident weariness, and he still appeared to be somewhat stiff from his days of immobility.

Suddenly Ellie was chilled by a feeling that Spencer Grant was not going to make it through this with her, that he was going to die somewhere in the night ahead. The foreboding was perhaps not strong enough to be called an explicit premonition, but it was more powerful than a mere hunch.

The possibility of losing him left her half sick with dread. She knew then that she cared for him even more than she had been able to admit.

When he returned with the map, he said, "What's wrong?"

"Nothing. Why?"

"You look like you've seen a ghost."

"Just tired," she lied. "And starved."

"I can do something about the starved part." As he sat in the seat across the aisle again, he produced four candy bars from the pockets of his fleece-lined denim jacket.

"Where'd you get these?"

"The boys up front have a snack box. They were happy to share. They're really a couple of swell guys."

"Especially with a gun to their heads."

"Especially then," he agreed.

Rocky sat up and cocked his good ear with keen interest when he smelled the candy bars.

"Ours," Spencer said firmly. "When we're out of the air and on the road again, we'll stop and get some real food for you, something healthier than this."

The dog licked his chops.

"Look, pal," Spencer said, "*I* didn't stop in the supermarket to graze on the wreckage, like you did. I need every bite of these, or I'll collapse on my face. Now you just lie down and forget it. Okay?"

Rocky yawned, looked around with pretended disinterest, and stretched out on the deck again.

"You two have an incredible rapport," she said.

"Yeah, we're Siamese twins, separated at birth. You couldn't know that, of course, because he's had a lot of plastic surgery."

She could not take her eyes off his face. More than weariness was visible in it. She could see the certain shadow of death.

Disconcertingly perceptive and alert to her mood, Spencer said, "What?"

"Thanks for the candy."

"It would've been filet mignon if I could've swung it."

He unfolded the map. They held it between their seats, studying the territory around Grand Junction, Colorado.

Twice she dared to look at him, and each glimpse made her heart race with fear. She could too clearly see the skull beneath the skin, the promise of the grave that was usually so well concealed by the mask of life.

She felt ignorant, silly, superstitious, like a foolish child. There were other explanations besides omens and portents and psychic images of tragedy to come. Perhaps, after the Thanksgiving night when Danny and her parents had been snatched away forever, this fear would plague her every time that she crossed the line between caring for people and loving them.

§

Roy landed at Stapleton International Airport in Denver, aboard the Lear-jet, after twenty-five minutes in a holding pattern. The local office of the agency had assigned two operatives to work with him, as he had requested on the scrambler phone while in flight. Both men—Burt Rink and Oliver Fordyce—were waiting in the parking bay as the Lear taxied into it. They were in their early thirties, tall, clean-shaven. They wore black topcoats, dark-blue suits, dark ties, white shirts, and black Oxfords with rubber rather than leather soles. All that was also as Roy had requested.

Rink and Fordyce had new clothes for Roy that were virtually identical to their own outfits. Having shaved and showered aboard the jet during the trip from Cedar City, Roy needed only to change clothes before they could switch from the plane to the black Chrysler super-stretch limousine that was waiting at the foot of the portable stairs.

The day was bone-freezing. The sky was as clear as an arctic sea and deeper than time. Icicles hung along the eaves of building roofs, and banks of snow marked the far limits of runways.

Stapleton was on the northeastern edge of the city, and their appointment with Dr. Sabrina Palma was beyond the *southwest* suburbs. Roy would have insisted on a police escort, under one pretense or another, except that he didn't want to call any more attention to themselves than absolutely necessary.

"It's a four-thirty appointment," Fordyce said as he and Rink settled into the back of the limousine, facing to the rear, where Roy sat facing forward. "We'll make it with a few minutes to spare."

The driver had been instructed not to dawdle. They accelerated away from the Learjet as if they *did* have a police escort.

Rink passed a nine-by-twelve white envelope to Roy. "These are all the documents you required."

"You have your Secret Service credentials?" Roy asked.

From suit-coat pockets, Rink and Fordyce withdrew their ID wallets and flipped them open to reveal holographic identification cards with their photographs and authentic SS badges. Rink's name for the upcoming meeting was Sidney Eugene Tarkenton. Fordyce was Lawrence Albert Olmeyer.

Roy extracted his own ID wallet from among the documents in the white envelope. He was J. Robert Cotter.

"Let's all remember who we are. Be sure to call one another by these names," Roy said. "I don't expect you'll need to say much—or even anything at all. I'll do the talking. You're there primarily to lend the whole thing an air of realism. You'll enter Dr. Palma's office behind me and post yourselves to the left and the right of the door. Stand with your feet about eighteen inches apart, arms down in front of you, one hand clasped over the other. When I introduce you to her, you'll say 'Doctor' and nod or 'Pleased to meet you' and nod. Stoic at all times. About as expressionless as a Buckingham Palace guard. Eyes straight ahead. No fidgeting. If you're asked to sit down, you'll politely say 'No, thank you, Doctor.' Yes, I know, it's ridiculous, but this is how people are used to seeing Secret Service agents in the movies, so any indication that you're a real human being will ring false to her. Is that understood, Sidney?"

"Yes, sir."

"Is that understood, Lawrence?"

"I prefer Larry," said Oliver Fordyce.

"Is that understood, Larry?"

"Yes, sir."

"Good."

Roy withdrew the other documents from the envelope, examined them, and was satisfied.

He was taking one of the greatest risks of his career, but he was remarkably calm. He was not even assigning agents to seek the fugitives in Salt Lake City or anywhere else directly north of Cedar City, because he was confident that their flight in that direction had been a ruse. They had altered course immediately after dropping under the radar floor. He doubted that they would go west, back into Nevada, because that state's empty fastness provided too little cover. Which left south and east. After the two enchiladas of information from Gary Duvall, Roy had reviewed everything he knew about Spencer Grant and had decided that he could accurately predict in which direction the man—and, with luck, the woman—would proceed. East-northeast. Moreover, he had divined *exactly* where Grant would impact at the end of that east-northeast trajectory, even more confidently than he could have plotted the line of a bullet from the barrel of a rifle. Roy was calm not solely because he trusted in his well-exercised powers of deductive reasoning but also because, in this special instance, destiny walked with him as surely as blood flowed in his veins.

"Can I assume that the team I asked for earlier today is on its way to Vail?" he asked.

"Twelve men," said Fordyce.

Glancing at his watch, Rink said, "They should be meeting Duvall there just about now."

For sixteen years, Michael Ackblom—aka "Spencer Grant"—had been denying the deep desire to return to that place, repressing the need, resisting the powerful magnet of the past. Nevertheless, either consciously or unconsciously, he had always known that he must pay a visit to those old haunts sooner or later. Otherwise, he would have sold the property to be rid of that tangible reminder of a time he wanted to forget, just as he had sloughed off his old name for a new one. He retained ownership for the same reason that he'd never sought surgery to have his facial scar minimized. *He's punishing himself with the scar*, Dr. Nero Mondello had said, in his white-on-white office in Beverly Hills. *Reminding himself of something he would like to forget but feels obligated to remember.* As long as Grant had lived in California and had followed a pressure-free daily routine, perhaps he could have indefinitely resisted the call of that killing ground in Colorado. But now he was running for his life and under tremendous pressure, and he had come near enough to his old home to ensure that the siren song of the past would be irresistible. Roy was betting everything that the son of the serial killer would return to the marrow of the nightmare, from which all the blood had sprung.

Spencer Grant had unfinished business at the ranch outside Vail. And only two people in the world knew what it was.

Beyond the heavily tinted windows of the speeding limousine, in the rapidly dwindling winter afternoon, the modern city of Denver appeared to be smoky and as vaguely defined at the edges as piles of ancient ruins entwined with ivy and shrouded with moss.

⌒

West of Grand Junction, inside the Colorado National Monument, the JetRanger landed in an eroded basin between one parenthesis of red rock formations and another of low hills mantled with junipers and pinyon pines. A skin of dry snow, less than half an inch thick, was flayed into crystalline clouds by the downdraft.

A hundred feet away, a green-black screen of trees served as backdrop to the bright silhouette of a white Ford Bronco. A man in a green ski suit stood at the open tailgate, watching the helicopter.

Spencer stayed with the crew while Ellie went outside to have a word with the man at the truck. With the JetRanger engine off and the rotor blades dead, the rock- and tree-rimmed basin was as silent as a deserted cathedral. She could hear nothing but the squeak and crunch of her own footsteps on the snow-filmed, frozen earth.

As she drew close to the Bronco, she saw a tripod with a camera on it. Related gear was spread across the lowered tailgate.

The photographer, bearded and furious, was spouting steam from his nostrils as if about to explode. "You ruined my shot. That pristine swath of snow curving up to that thrusting, fiery rock. Such contrast, such drama. And now *ruined*."

She glanced back at the rock formations beyond the helicopter. They were still fiery, a luminous stained-glass red in the beams of the westering sun, and they were still thrusting. But he was right about the snow: It wasn't pristine any longer.

"Sorry."

"Sorry doesn't cut it," he said sharply.

She studied the snow in the vicinity of the Bronco. As far as she could tell, his were the only footprints in it. He was alone.

"What the hell are you doing out here anyway?" the photographer demanded. "There are sound restrictions here, nothing as noisy as that allowed. This is a wildlife preserve."

"Then cooperate and preserve your own," she said, drawing the SIG 9mm from under her leather jacket.

In the JetRanger again, while Ellie held the pistol and the Micro Uzi, Spencer cut strips out of the upholstery. He used those lengths of leather to bind the wrists of each of the three men to the arms of the passenger seats in which he'd made them sit.

"I won't gag you," he told them. "Nobody's likely to hear you shouting anyway."

"We'll freeze to death," the pilot fretted.

"You'll work your arms loose in half an hour at most. Another half an hour or forty-five minutes to walk out to the highway we crossed over when we flew in. Not nearly enough time to freeze."

"Just to be safe," Ellie assured them, "as soon as we get to a town, we'll call the police and tell them where you are."

Twilight had arrived. Stars were beginning to appear in the deep purple of the eastern sky as it curved down to the horizon.

While Spencer drove the Bronco, Rocky panted in Ellie's ear from the cargo area behind her seat. They found the way overland toward the highway with no difficulty. The route was clearly marked by the tire tracks in the snow that the truck had made on its trip into the picturesque basin.

"Why'd you tell them we'd call the police?" Spencer wondered.

"You want them to freeze?"

"I don't think there's much chance of that."

"I won't risk it."

"Yeah, but these days, it's possible—maybe not likely, but possible—that any call you make to a police department is going to be received on a caller-ID line, not just if you punch nine-one-one. Fact is, a smaller city like Grand Junction, with not so much street crime or so many demands on resources, is a lot more likely to have money to spend on fancy communications systems with all the bells and whistles. You call them, then they know right away the address you're phoning from. It comes up on the screen in front of the police operator. And then they'll know what direction we went, what road we left Grand Junction on."

"I know. But we're not going to make it that simple for them," she said, and explained what she had in mind.

"I like it," he said.

The Rocky Mountain Prison for the Criminally Insane had been constructed in the Great Depression, under the auspices of the Work Projects Administration, and it looked as solid and formidable as the Rockies themselves. It was a squat, rambling building with small, deep-set, barred windows even in the administration wing. The walls were faced with iron-gray granite. An even darker granite had been used for lintels, window stools, door and window surrounds, coins, and carved cornices. The whole pile slumped under a gabled attic and a black slate roof.

The general effect, Roy Miro felt, was as depressing as it was ominous. Without hyperbole, the structure could be said to brood high upon its hillside, as if it were a living creature. In the late-afternoon shadows of the steep slopes that rose behind the prison, its windows were filled with a sour-yellow light that might have been reflected through connecting corridors from the dungeons of some mountain demon who lived deeper in the Rockies.

Approaching the prison in the limousine, standing before it, and walking its public corridors to Dr. Palma's office, Roy was overcome with compassion for the poor souls locked away in that heap of stone. He grieved as well for the equally suffering warders who, in looking after the deranged, were forced to spend so much of their lives in such circumstances. If it had been within his authority to do so, he would have sealed up every last window and vent, with all the inmates and attendants inside, and put them out of their misery with a gentle-acting but lethal gas.

Dr. Sabrina Palma's reception lounge and office were so warmly and luxuriously furnished that, by contrast with the building that sur-

rounded them, they seemed to belong not only in another and more exalted place—a New York penthouse, a Palm Beach bayside mansion—
but in another age than the 1930s, a time warp in which the rest of
the prison seemed still to exist. Sofas and chairs were recognizably by
J. Robert Scott, upholstered in platinum and gold silks. Tables and mirror frames and side chairs were also by J. Robert Scott, done in a variety of exotic woods with bold grains, all either bleached or whitewashed.
The deeply sculpted, beige-on-beige carpet might have been from Edward Fields. At the center of the inner office was a massive Monteverde
& Young desk, in a crescent-moon shape, that must have cost forty thousand dollars.

Roy had never seen an office of any public official to equal those two
rooms, not even in the highest circles of official Washington. He knew at
once what to make of it, and he knew that he had a sword to hold over
Dr. Palma if she gave him any resistance.

Sabrina Palma was the director of the prison medical staff. By virtue
of its being as much hospital as prison, she was also the equivalent of a
warden in any ordinary correctional facility. And she was as striking as her
office. Raven-black hair. Green eyes. Skin as pale and smooth as pooled
milk. Early forties, tall, svelte but shapely. She wore a black knit suit with
a white silk blouse.

After identifying himself, Roy introduced her to Agent Olmeyer—
"Pleased to meet you, Doctor."
—and Agent Tarkenton.
"Doctor."
She invited them all to sit down.
"No, thank you, Doctor," said Olmeyer, and took up a position to the
right of the door that connected the inner and outer offices.
"No, thank you, Doctor," said Tarkenton, and took up a position to
the left of the same door.
Roy proceeded to one of three exquisite chairs in front of Dr. Palma's
desk as she circled to the plush leather throne behind it. She sat in a cascade
of indirect, amber light that made her pale skin glow as if with inner fire.
"I'm here on a matter of the utmost importance," Roy told her in as
gracious a tone as he could command. "We believe—no, we are certain—
that the son of one of your inmates is currently stalking the President of
the United States and intends to assassinate him."

When she heard the name of the would-be assassin and knew the identity of his father, Sabrina Palma raised her eyebrows. After she examined
the documents that Roy withdrew from the white envelope and after she
learned what he expected of her, she excused herself and went to the outer
office to make several urgent telephone calls.

Roy waited in his chair.

Beyond the three narrow windows, spread out across the night below the prison, the lights of Denver gleamed and glittered.

He looked at his watch. By now, on the far side of the Rockies, Duvall and his twelve men ought to have settled inconspicuously into the creeping night. They wanted to be ready, in case the travelers arrived far earlier than anticipated.

∽

The hood of night had fully covered the face of twilight by the time they reached the outskirts of Grand Junction.

With a population of over thirty-five thousand, the city was big enough to delay them. But Ellie had a penlight and the map that she had taken from the helicopter, and she found the simplest route.

Two-thirds of the way around the city, at a multiplex cinema, they stopped to go shopping for a new vehicle. Apparently, none of the shows was either letting out or about to begin, for no moviegoers were arriving or leaving. The sprawling parking lot was full of cars but devoid of people.

"Get an Explorer or a Jeep if you can," she said as he opened the door of the Bronco, letting in a frigid draft. "Something like that. It's more convenient."

"Thieves can't be choosers," he said.

"They have to be." As he got out, she shifted over behind the steering wheel. "Hey, if you're not choosy, then you're not a thief, you're a trash collector."

While Ellie drifted along one aisle, pacing him, Spencer moved boldly from vehicle to vehicle, trying the doors. Each time that he found one unlocked, he leaned inside long enough to check for keys in the ignition, behind the sun visor, and under the driver's seat.

Watching his master through the side windows of the Bronco, Rocky whined as though with concern.

"Dangerous, yes," Ellie said. "I can't lie to the dog. But not half as dangerous as driving through the front of a supermarket with helicopters full of thugs on your tail. You've just got to keep this in perspective."

The fourteenth set of wheels that Spencer tried was a big black Chevy pickup with an extended cab that provided both front and back seats. He climbed into it, pulled the door shut, started the engine, and reversed out of the parking slot.

Ellie parked the Bronco in the space that the Chevy had vacated. They needed only fifteen seconds to transfer the guns, the duffel bag, and the dog to the pickup. Then they were on their way again.

On the east side of the city, they started looking for any motel that appeared to have been recently constructed. The rooms in most older establishments were not computer friendly.

At a self-described "motor lodge" that looked new enough to have held its ribbon-cutting ceremony just hours ago, Ellie left Spencer and Rocky in the pickup while she went into the front office to ask the desk clerk if their accommodations would allow her to use her modem. "I have a report due at my office in Cleveland by morning." In fact, all rooms were properly wired for her needs. Using her Bess Baer ID for the first time, she took a double with a queen-size bed and paid cash in advance.

"How soon can we be on the road again?" Spencer asked as they parked in front of their unit.

"Forty-five minutes tops, probably half an hour," she promised.

"We're miles from where we took the pickup, but I have a bad feeling about hanging around here too long."

"You aren't the only one."

She couldn't help but notice the decor of the room even as she took Spencer's laptop computer out of the duffel bag, put it on the desk next to an arrangement of accessible plugs and phone jacks, and concentrated on getting it ready for business. Blue-and-black-speckled carpet. Blue-and-yellow-striped draperies. Green-and-blue-checkered bedspread. Blue and gold and silver wallpaper in a pale ameboid pattern. It looked like army camouflage for an alien planet.

"While you're working on that," Spencer said, "I'll take Rocky out to do his business. He must be ready to burst."

"Doesn't seem in distress."

"He'd be too embarrassed to let on." At the door, he turned to her again and said, "I saw fast-food places across the street. I'll walk over there and get us some burgers and stuff too, if that sounds like it would hit the spot."

"Just buy plenty," she said.

While Spencer and the pooch were gone, Ellie accessed the AT&T central computer, which she had penetrated a long time ago and had explored in depth. Through AT&T's nationwide linkages, she had been able, in the past, to finesse her way into the computers of several regional phone companies at all ends of the country, although she'd never before tried to slide into the Colorado system. For a hacker as for a concert pianist or an Olympic gymnast, however, training and practice were the keys to success, and she was extremely well trained and well practiced.

When Spencer and Rocky returned after only twenty-five minutes, Ellie was already deep inside the regional system, scrolling rapidly down a dauntingly long list of pay-phone numbers with corresponding addresses that were arranged county by county. She settled on a phone at a service station in Montrose, Colorado, sixty-six miles south of Grand Junction.

Manipulating the main switching system in the regional phone company, she rang the Grand Junction Police while routing the call from their motel room through the service-station pay phone down in Montrose. She called the emergency number, rather than the main police number, just to be sure that the source address would appear onscreen in front of the operator.

"Grand Junction Police."

Ellie began without any preamble: "We hijacked a Bell JetRanger helicopter in Cedar City, Utah, earlier today—" When the police operator attempted to interrupt with questions that would encourage a standard-format report, Ellie shouted the woman down: "Shut up, shut up! I'm only going to say this once, so you better listen, or people will die!" She grinned at Spencer, who was opening bags of wonderfully fragrant food on the dinette table. "The chopper is now on the ground in the Colorado National Monument, with the crew aboard. They're unhurt but tied up. If they have to spend the night out there, they'll freeze to death. I'll describe the landing site just once, and you better get the details right if you want to save their lives."

She gave succinct directions and disconnected.

Two things had been achieved. The three men in the JetRanger would be found soon. And the Grand Junction Police Department had an address in Montrose, sixty-six miles to the south, from which the emergency call had been made, indicating that Ellie and Spencer were either about to flee east on Federal Highway 50, toward Pueblo, or continue south on Federal Highway 550 toward Durango. Several state routes branched off those main arteries as well, providing enough possibilities to keep agency search teams fully occupied. Meanwhile, she and Spencer and Mr. Rocky Dog would be headed to Denver on Interstate 70.

§

Dr. Sabrina Palma was being difficult, which was no surprise to Roy. Before arriving at the prison, he had expected objections to his plans, based on medical, security, and political grounds. The moment he had seen her office, he had known that vital financial considerations would weigh more heavily against him than all the genuinely ethical arguments that she might have pursued.

"I can't conceive of any circumstances, related to the threat against the President, that would require Steven Ackblom's removal from this facility," she said crisply. Though she had returned to the formidable leather chair, she no longer relaxed in it but sat forward on the edge, arms on her crescent desk. Her manicured hands were alternately fisted on her blotter or busy with various pieces of Lalique crystal—small animals, colorful fishes—that were arranged to one side of her blotter. "He's an extremely dangerous individual, an arrogant and utterly selfish man who would never cooperate with you even if there *was* something he could do to help you find his son—though I can't imagine what that would be."

As pleasant as he ever was, Roy said, "Dr. Palma, with all due respect, it isn't for you to imagine or be told how he could help us or how we expect to win his cooperation. This is an urgent matter of national security. I am not permitted to share any details with you, regardless of how much I might want to."

"This man is evil, Mr. Cotter."

"Yes, I'm aware of his history."

"You aren't understanding me—"

Roy gently interrupted, pointing to one of the documents on her desk. "You have read the judicial order, signed by a justice of the Colorado Supreme Court, conveying Steven Ackblom into my temporary custody."

"Yes, but—"

"I assume that when you left the room to make telephone calls, one of them was to confirm that signature?"

"Yes, and it's legitimate. He was still in his office, and he confirmed it personally."

In fact, it was a real signature. That particular justice lived in the agency's pocket.

Sabrina Palma was not satisfied. "But what does your judge know about evil like this? What experience does he have with this particular man?"

Pointing to another document on the desk, Roy said, "And may I assume that you've confirmed the genuineness of the letter from my boss, the secretary of the Treasury? You called Washington?"

"I didn't speak with him, no, of course not."

"He's a busy man. But there must have been an assistant. . . ."

"Yes," the doctor admitted grudgingly. "I spoke with one of his assistants, who verified the request."

The signature of the secretary of the Treasury had been forged. The assistant, one of a swarm of minions, was an agency sympathizer. He was no doubt still standing by in the secretary's office, after hours, to field another call on the private number that Roy had given to Sabrina Palma, just in case she called again.

Pointing to a third document on her desk, Roy said, "And this request from the first deputy attorney general?"

"Yes, I called him."

"I understand you've actually met Mr. Summerton."

"Yes, at a conference on the insanity plea and its effect on the health of the judicial system. About six months ago."

"I trust Mr. Summerton was persuasive."

"Quite. Look, Mr. Cotter, I have a call in to the governor's office, and if we can just wait until—"

"I'm afraid we've no time to wait. As I've told you, the life of the President of the United States is at stake."

"This is a prisoner of exceptional—"

"Dr. Palma," Roy said. His voice now had a steely edge, though he continued to smile. "You do not have to worry about losing your golden goose. I swear to you that he will be back in your care within twenty-four hours."

Her green eyes fixed him with an angry stare, but she did not respond.

"I hadn't heard that Steven Ackblom has continued to paint since his incarceration," Roy said.

Dr. Palma's gaze flicked to the two men at the door, who were in convincingly rigid Secret Service postures, then returned to Roy. "He produces a little work, yes. Not much. Two or three pieces a year."

"Worth millions at the current rate."

"There is nothing unethical going on here, Mr. Cotter."

"I didn't imagine there was," Roy said innocently.

"Of his own free will, without coercion of any sort, Mr. Ackblom assigns all rights to each of his new paintings to this institution—after he tires of it hanging in his cell. The proceeds from their sale are used entirely to supplement the funds that are budgeted to us by the State of Colorado. And these days, in this economy, the state generally underfunds prison operations of all kinds, as if the institutionalized don't deserve adequate care."

Roy slid one hand lightly, appreciatively, *lovingly* along the glass-smooth, radius edge of the forty-thousand-dollar desk. "Yes, I'm sure that without the lagniappe of Ackblom's art, things here would be grim indeed."

She was silent again.

"Tell me, Doctor, in addition to the two or three major pieces that Ackblom produces each year, as he just sort of dabbles in his art to pass his entombed days, are there perhaps sketches, pencil studies, scraps of scrawlings that aren't worth the bother for him to assign to this institution? You know what I mean: insignificant doodlings, preliminaries, worth hardly ten or twenty thousand each, which one might take home to hang on one's bathroom walls? Or even simply incinerate along with the rest of the garbage?"

Her hatred for him was so intense that he would not have been surprised if the blush that rose in her face had been hot enough to make her cotton-white skin explode into flames, as if it were not skin at all but magicians' flashpaper.

"I adore your watch," he said, indicating the Piaget on her slender wrist. The rim of the face was enhanced by alternating diamonds and emeralds.

The fourth document on the desk was a transferral order that acknowledged Roy's legal authority—by direction of the Colorado Supreme Court—to receive Ackblom into his temporary custody. Roy had already signed it in the limousine. Now Dr. Palma signed it too.

Delighted, Roy said, "Is Ackblom on any medications, any antipsychotics, that we should continue to give him?"

She met his eyes again, and her anger was watered down with concern. "No antipsychotics. He doesn't need them. He isn't psychotic by any current psychological definition of the term. Mr. Cotter, I'm trying my best to make you understand this man exhibits none of the classic signs of psychosis. He is that most imprecisely defined creature—a sociopath, yes. But a sociopath by his actions only, by what we know him to have done, not by anything that he says or can be shown to believe. Administer any psychological test you want, and he comes through with flying colors, a perfectly normal guy, well adjusted, balanced, not even markedly neurotic—"

"I understand he's been a model prisoner these sixteen years."

"That means nothing. That's what I'm trying to tell you. Look, I'm a medical doctor and a psychiatrist. But over the years, from observation and experience, I've lost all faith in psychiatry. Freud and Jung—they were both full of shit." That crude word had shocking power, coming from a woman as elegant as she. "Their theories of how the human mind works are worthless, exercises in self-justification, philosophies devised only to excuse their own desires. No one knows how the mind works. Even when we can administer a drug and correct a mental condition, we only know *that* the drug is effective, not *why*. And in Ackblom's case, his behavior isn't based in a physiological problem any more than it is in a psychological problem."

"You have no compassion for him?"

She leaned across her desk, focusing intently on him. "I tell you, Mr. Cotter, there *is* evil in the world. Evil that exists without cause, without rationalization. Evil that doesn't arise from trauma or abuse or deprivation. Steven Ackblom is, in my judgment, a prime example of evil. He is sane, utterly sane. He clearly knows the difference between right and wrong. He chose to do monstrous things, knowing they were monstrous, and even though he felt no psychological compulsion to do them."

"You have no compassion for your patient?" Roy asked again.

"He isn't my patient, Mr. Cotter. He's my prisoner."

"However you choose to look at him, doesn't he deserve some compassion—a man who's fallen from such heights?"

"He deserves to be shot in the head and buried in an unmarked grave," she said bluntly. She was not attractive any more. She looked like a witch, raven-haired and pale, with eyes as green as those of certain cats. "But because Mr. Ackblom entered a guilty plea, and because it was easiest to commit him to this facility, the state supported the fiction that he was a sick man."

Of all the people Roy had met in his busy life, he had disliked few and had hated fewer still. For nearly everyone that he had ever met, he had found compassion in his heart, regardless of their shortcomings or personalities. But he flatly despised Dr. Sabrina Palma.

When he found time in his busy schedule, he would give her a comeuppance that would make what he'd done to Harris Descoteaux seem merciful.

"Even if you can't find some compassion for the Steven Ackblom who killed those people," Roy said, rising from his chair, "I would think you could find some for the Steven Ackblom who has been so generous to you."

"He is evil." She was unrelenting. "He deserves no compassion. Just use him however you must, then return him."

"Well, maybe you *do* know a thing or two about evil, Doctor."

"The advantage I've taken of the arrangement here," she said coolly, "is a sin, Mr. Cotter. I know that. And one way or another, I'll pay for the sin. But there's a difference between a sinful act, which springs from weakness, and one that's pure evil. I am able to recognize that difference."

"How handy for you," he said, and began to gather up the papers from her desk.

৯

They sat on the motel bed, chowing down on Burger King burgers, french fries, and chocolate-chip cookies. Rocky ate off a torn paper bag on the floor.

That morning in the desert, now hardly twelve hours behind them, seemed to be an eternity in the past. Ellie and Spencer had learned so much about each other that they could eat in silence, enjoying the food, without feeling the least awkward together.

He surprised her, however, when, toward the end of their hurried meal, he expressed the desire to stop at the ranch outside Vail, on their way to Denver. And "surprised" was not the word for it when he told her that he still owned the place.

"Maybe I've always known that I'd have to go back eventually," he said, unable to look at her.

He put the last of his dinner aside, appetite lost. Sitting lotus-fashion on the bed, he folded his hands on his right knee and stared at them as if they were more mysterious than artifacts from lost Atlantis.

"In the beginning," he continued, "my grandparents held on to the place because they didn't want anyone to buy it and maybe make some god-awful tourist attraction out of it. Or let the news media into those underground rooms for more morbid stories. The bodies had been removed, everything cleaned out, but it was still the *place*, could still attract media interest. After I went into therapy, which I stayed with for about a year, the therapist felt we should keep the property until I was ready to go back."

"Why?" Ellie wondered. "Why ever go back?"

He hesitated. Then: "Because part of that night is a blank to me. I've never been able to remember what happened toward the end, after I shot him. . . ."

"What do you mean? You shot him, and you ran for help, and that was the end of it."

"No."

"What?"

He shook his head. Still staring at his hands. Very still hands. Like hands of carved marble, resting on his knee.

Finally he said, "That's what I've got to find out. I've got to go back there, back down there, and find out. Because if I don't, I'm never going to be . . . right with myself . . . or any good for you."

"You can't go back there, not with the agency after you."

"They wouldn't look for us there. They can't have found out who I was. Who I really am. Michael. They can't know that."

"They might," she said.

She went to the duffel bag and got the envelope of photographs that she had found on the deck of the JetRanger, half under her seat. She presented them to him.

"They found these in a shoe box in my cabin," he said. "They probably just took them for reference. You wouldn't recognize . . . my father. No one would. Not from this shot."

"You can't be sure."

"Anyway, I don't own the property under any identity they would associate with me, even if somehow they got into sealed court records and found out I'd changed my name from Ackblom. I hold it through an offshore corporation."

"The agency is damned resourceful, Spencer."

Looking up from his hands, he met her eyes. "All right, I'm willing to believe they're resourceful enough to uncover all of it—given enough time. But surely not this quickly. That just means I've got more reason than ever to go there tonight. When am I going to have a chance again, after we go to Denver and to wherever we'll go after that? By the time I can return to Vail again, maybe they *will* have discovered I still own the ranch. Then I'll never be able to go back and finish this. We pass right by Vail on the way to Denver. It's off Interstate Seventy."

"I know," she said shakily, remembering that moment in the helicopter, somewhere over Utah, when she had sensed that he might not live through the night to share the morning with her.

He said, "If you don't want to go there with me, we can work that out too. But . . . even if I could be sure the agency would never learn about the place, I'd have to go back tonight. Ellie, if I don't go back now, when I have the guts to face it, I might never work up the courage later. It's taken sixteen years this time."

She sat for a while, staring at her own hands. Then she got up and went to the laptop, which was still plugged in and connected to the modem. She switched it on.

He followed her to the desk. "What're you doing?"

"What's the address of the ranch?" she asked.

It was a rural address, rather than a street number. He gave it to her, then again after she asked him to repeat it. "But why? What's this about?"

"What's the name of the offshore company?"

"Vanishment International."

"You're kidding."

"No."

"And that's the name on the deed now—Vanishment International? That's how it would show on the tax records?"

"Yeah." Spencer pulled up another chair beside hers and sat on it as Rocky came sniffing around to see if they had more food. "Ellie, will you open up?"

"I'm going to try to crack into public land records out there," she said. "I need to call up a parcel map if I can get one. I've got to figure out the exact geographic coordinates of the place."

"Is all that supposed to mean something?"

"By God, if we're going in there, if we're taking a risk like that, then we're going to be as heavily armed as possible." She was talking to herself more than to him. "We're going to be ready to defend ourselves against anything."

"What're you talking about?"

"Too complicated. Later. Now I need some silence."

Her quick hands worked magic on the keyboard. Spencer watched the screen as Ellie moved from Grand Junction to the courthouse computer in Vail. Then she peeled the county's data-system onion one layer at a time.

Wearing a slightly large suit of clothes provided by the agency and a top-coat identical to those of his three companions, in shackles and handcuffs, the famous and infamous Steven Ackblom sat beside Roy in the back of the limousine.

The artist was fifty-three but appeared to be only a few years older than when he had been on the front pages of newspapers, where the sensation mongers had variously dubbed him the Vampire of Vail, the Madman of the Mountains, and the Psycho Michelangelo. Although a trace of gray had appeared at his temples, his hair was otherwise black and glossy and not in the least receding. His handsome face was remarkably smooth and youthful, and his brow was unmarked. A soft smile line curved downward from the outer flare of each nostril, and fans of fine crinkles spread at the outer corners of his eyes: None of that aged him whatsoever; in fact, it gave the impression that he suffered few troubles but enjoyed many sources of amusement.

As in the photograph that Roy had found in the Malibu cabin and as in all the pictures that had appeared in newspapers and magazines sixteen years ago, Steven Ackblom's eyes were his most commanding feature. Nevertheless, the arrogance that Roy had perceived even in the shadowy publicity still was not there now, if it ever had been; in its place was a quiet self-confidence. Likewise, the menace that could be read into any photograph, when one knew the accomplishments of the man, was not in the least visible in person. His gaze was direct and clear, but not threatening. Roy had been surprised and not displeased to discover an uncommon gentleness in Ackblom's eyes, and a poignant empathy as well, from which it was easy to infer that he was a person of considerable wisdom, whose understanding of the human condition was deep, complete.

Even in the limousine's odd and inadequate illumination, which came from the recessed lights under the heel-kicks of the car seats and from the low-wattage sconces in the doorposts, Ackblom was a presence to be reckoned with—although in no way that the press, in its sensation seeking, had begun to touch upon. He was quiet, but his taciturnity had no quality of inarticulateness or distraction. Quite the opposite: His silences spoke more than other men's most polished flights of oratory, and he was always and unmistakably observant and alert. He moved little, never fidgeted. Occasionally, when he accompanied a comment with a gesture, the movement of his cuffed hands was so economical that the chain between his wrists clinked softly if at all. His stillness was not rigid but relaxed, not limp but full of quiescent power. It was impossible to sit at his side and be unaware that he possessed tremendous intelligence: He all but hummed with it, as if his mind was a dynamic machine of such omnipotence that it could move worlds and alter the cosmos.

In his entire thirty-three years, Roy Miro had met only two people whose mere physical presence had engendered in him an approximation of love. The first had been Eve Marie Jammer. The second was Steven Ackblom. Both in the same week. In this wondrous February, destiny had become, indeed, his cloak and his companion. He sat at Steven Ackblom's side, discreetly enthralled. He wanted desperately to make the artist aware that he, Roy Miro, was a person of profound insights and exceptional accomplishments.

Rink and Fordyce (Tarkenton and Olmeyer had ceased to exist upon leaving Dr. Palma's office) seemed not to be as charmed by Ackblom as Roy was—or charmed at all. Sitting in the rear-facing seats, they appeared uninterested in what the artist had to say. Fordyce closed his eyes for long periods of time, as though meditating. Rink stared out the window, although he could have seen nothing whatsoever of the night through the darkly tinted glass. On those rare occasions when a gesture of Ackblom's rang a soft clink from his cuffs, and on those even rarer occasions when he shifted his feet enough to rattle the shackles that connected his ankles, Fordyce's eye popped open like the counterbalanced eyes of a doll, and Rink's head snapped from the unseen night to the artist. Otherwise they seemed to pay no attention to him.

Depressingly, Rink and Fordyce clearly had formed their opinions of Ackblom based on what drivel they had gleaned from the media, not from what they could observe for themselves. Their denseness was no surprise, of course. Rink and Fordyce were men not of ideas but of action, not of passion but of crude desire. The agency had need of their type, although they were sadly without vision, pitiable creatures of woeful limitations who would one day inch the world closer to perfection by departing it.

"At the time, I was quite young, only two years older than your son," Roy said, "but I understood what you were trying to achieve."

"And what was that?" Ackblom asked. His voice was in the lower tenor range, mellow, with a timbre that suggested he might have had a career as a singer if he'd wished.

Roy explained his theories about the artist's work: that those eerie and compelling portraits weren't about people's hateful desires building like boiler pressure beneath their beautiful surfaces, but were meant to be viewed *with* the still lifes and, together, were a statement about the human desire—and struggle—for perfection. "And if your work with living subjects resulted in their attainment of a perfect beauty, even for a brief time before they died, then your crimes weren't crimes at all but acts of charity, acts of profound compassion, because too few people in this world will ever know any moment of perfection in their entire lives. Through torture, you gave those forty-one—your wife as well, I assume—a transcendent experience. Had they lived, they might eventually have thanked you."

Roy was speaking sincerely, although previously he had believed that Ackblom had been misguided in the means by which he had pursued the grail of perfection. That was before he had met the man. Now, he felt ashamed of his woeful underestimation of the artist's talent and keen perception.

In the rear-facing seats, neither Rink nor Fordyce evinced any surprise or interest in anything that Roy said. In their service with the agency, they had heard so many outrageous lies, all so well and sincerely delivered, that they undoubtedly believed their boss was only playing with Ackblom, cleverly manipulating a madman into the degree of cooperation required from him to ensure the success of the current operation. Roy was in the singular and thrilling position of being able to express his deepest feelings, with the knowledge that Ackblom would fully comprehend him even while Rink and Fordyce would think he was engaged only in Machiavellian games.

Roy did not go so far as to reveal his personal commitment to compassionate treatment of the sadder cases that he met in his many travels. Stories like those about the Bettonfields in Beverly Hills, Chester and Guinevere in Burbank, and the paraplegic and his wife outside the restaurant in Vegas might strike even Rink and Fordyce as too specific in detail to be impromptu fabrications invented to win the artist's confidence.

"The world would be an infinitely better place," Roy opined, restricting his observations to safely general concepts, "if the breeding stock of humanity was thinned out. Eliminate the most imperfect specimens first. Always working up from the bottom. Until those permitted to survive are the people who most closely meet the standards for the ideal citizens needed to build a gentler and more enlightened society. Don't you agree?"

"The process would certainly be fascinating," Ackblom replied.

Roy took the comment to be approving. "Yes, wouldn't it?"

"Always supposing that one was on the committee of eliminators," the artist said, "and not among those to be judged."

"Well, of course, that's a given."

Ackblom favored him with a smile. "Then what fun."

They were driving over the mountains on Interstate 70, rather than flying to Vail. The trip would require less than two hours by car. Returning across Denver from the prison to Stapleton, waiting for flight clearance, and making the journey by air would actually have taken longer. Besides, the limousine was more intimate and quieter than the jet. Roy was able to spend more quality time with the artist than he would have been able to enjoy in the Lear.

Gradually, mile by mile, Roy Miro came to understand why Steven Ackblom affected him as powerfully as Eve had affected him. Although the artist was a handsome man, nothing about his physical appearance could qualify as a perfect feature. Yet in some way, he *was* perfect. Roy sensed it. A radiance. A subtle harmony. Soothing vibrations. In some aspect of his being, Ackblom was without the slightest flaw. For the time being, the artist's perfect quality or virtue remained tantalizingly mysterious, but Roy was confident of discovering it by the time they arrived at the ranch outside Vail.

The limousine cruised into ever higher mountains, through vast primeval forests encrusted with snow, upward into silvery moonlight—all of which the tinted windows reduced to a smoky blur. The tires hummed.

∽

While Spencer drove the stolen black pickup east on Interstate 70 out of Grand Junction, Ellie slumped in her seat and worked feverishly on the laptop, which she had plugged into the cigarette lighter. The computer was elevated on a pillow that they had filched from the motel. Periodically she consulted a printout of the parcel map and other information that she had obtained about the ranch.

"What're you doing?" he asked again.

"Calculations."

"What calculations?"

"Ssshhhhh. Rocky's sleeping on the backseat."

From her duffel bag, she had produced diskettes of software which she'd installed in the machine. Evidently they were programs of her own design, adapted to his laptop while he had lingered in delirium for more than two days in the Mojave. When he had asked her why she had backed up her own computer—now gone with the Rover—with his quite different system, she had said, "Former Girl Scout. Remember? We always like to be prepared."

He had no idea what her software allowed her to do. Across the screen flickered formulas and graphs. Holographic globes of the earth revolved at her command, and from them she extracted areas for enlargement and closer examination.

Vail was only three hours away. Spencer wished that they could use the time to talk, to discover more about each other. Three hours was such a short time—especially if it proved to be the last three hours they ever had together.

14

WHEN HE RETURNED to his brother's house from his walk through the hilly streets of Westwood, Harris Descoteaux did not mention the encounter with the tall man in the blue Toyota. For one thing, it seemed half like a dream. Improbable. Besides, he hadn't been able to make up his mind whether that stranger had been a friend or an enemy. He didn't want to alarm Darius or Jessica.

Late that afternoon, after Ondine and Willa returned from the mall with their aunt and after Darius and Bonnie's son, Martin, came home from school, Darius decided that they needed to have a little fun. He insisted on packing everyone—the seven of them—into the VW Microbus, which he had so lovingly restored with his own hands, to go to a movie and then to dinner at Hamlet Gardens.

Neither Harris nor Jessica wanted to go to movies and dinners in restaurants when every dollar spent was a dollar that they were mooching. Not even Ondine and Willa, as resilient as any teenagers, had yet bounced back from the trauma of the SWAT attack on Friday or from having been put out of their own home by federal marshals.

Darius was adamant that a movie and dinner at Hamlet Gardens were precisely the right medicines for what ailed them. And his persistence was one of the qualities that made him an exceptional attorney.

That was how, at six-fifteen Monday evening, Harris came to be in a theater with a boisterous crowd, unable to grasp the humor in scenes that everyone else found hilarious, and succumbing to another attack of claustrophobia. The darkness. So many people in one room. The body heat of the crowd. He was afflicted, first, by an inability to draw a deep breath and then by a mild dizziness. He feared that worse would swiftly follow. He whispered to Jessica that he had to use the bathroom. When worry crossed her face, he patted her arm and smiled reassuringly, and then he got the hell out of there.

The men's room was deserted. At one of the four sinks, Harris turned on the cold water. He bent over the bowl and splashed his face repeatedly, trying to cool down from the overheated theater and chase away the dizziness.

The noise of the running water prevented him from hearing the other man enter. When he looked up, he was no longer alone.

About thirty, Asian, wearing loafers and jeans and a dark-blue sweater with prancing red reindeer, the stranger stood two sinks away. He was combing his hair. He met Harris's eyes in the mirror, and he smiled. "Sir, may I give you something to think about?"

Harris recognized the question as the very one with which the tall man in the blue Toyota had initially addressed him. Startled, he backed away from the sink so fast that he crashed against the swinging door at one of the toilet stalls. He tottered, almost fell, but caught the hingeless side of the jamb to keep his balance.

"For a while the Japanese economy was so hot that it gave the world the idea that maybe big government and big business must work hand in glove."

"Who are you?" Harris asked, quicker off the mark with this man than he had been with the first.

Ignoring the question, the smiling stranger said, "So now we hear about national industrial policies. Big business and government strike deals every day. Push my social programs and enhance my power, says the politician, and I'll guarantee your profit."

"What does any of this matter to me?"

"Be patient, Mr. Descoteaux."

"But—"

"Union members get screwed because government conspires with their bosses. Small businessmen get screwed, everyone too little to play in the hundred-billion-dollar league. Now the secretary of defense wants to use the military as an arm of economic policy."

Harris returned to the sink, where he had left the cold water running. He turned it off.

"A business-government alliance, enforced by the military and domestic police—once, this was called fascism. Will we see fascism in our time, Mr. Descoteaux? Or is this something new, not to worry?"

Harris was trembling. He realized that his face and hands were dripping, and he yanked paper towels from the dispenser.

"And if it's something new, Mr. Descoteaux, is it going to be something good? Maybe. Maybe we'll go through a time of adjustment, and thereafter everything will be delightful." He nodded, smiling, as if considering that possibility. "Or maybe this new thing will turn out to be a new kind of hell."

"I don't care about any of this," Harris said angrily. "I'm not political."

"You don't need to be. To protect yourself, you need only to be informed."

"Look, whoever you are, I just want my house back. I want my life like it was. I want to go on just the way everything was."

"That will never transpire, Mr. Descoteaux."

"Why is this happening to me?"

"Have you read the novels of Philip K. Dick, Mr. Descoteaux?"

"Who? No."

Harris felt more than ever as if he had crossed into White Rabbit and Cheshire Cat territory.

The stranger shook his head with dismay. "The futuristic world Mr. Dick wrote about is the world we're sliding into. It's a scary place, this Dicksian world. More than ever, a person needs friends."

"Are you a friend?" Harris demanded. "Who are you people?"

"Be patient and consider what I've said."

The man started for the door.

Harris reached out to stop him but decided against it. A moment later he was alone.

His bowels were suddenly in turmoil. He hadn't lied to Jessica after all: He really did need to use the bathroom.

♒

Approaching Vail, high in the western Rockies, Roy Miro used the phone in the limousine to call the number of the cellular unit that Gary Duvall had given him earlier.

"Clear?" he asked.

"No sign of them yet," Duvall said.

"We're almost there."

"You really think they're going to show?"

The stolen JetRanger and its crew had been found in the Colorado National Monument. A call from the woman to the Grand Junction police had been traced to Montrose, indicating that she and Spencer Grant were fleeing south toward Durango. Roy didn't believe it. He knew that telephone calls could be deceptively routed with the assistance of a computer. He trusted not in a traced call but in the power of the past; where the past and the present met, he would find the fugitives.

"They'll show," Roy said. "Cosmic forces are with us tonight."

"Cosmic forces?" Duvall said, as if playing into a joke, waiting for the punch line.

"They'll show," Roy repeated, and he disconnected.

Beside Roy, Steven Ackblom sat silent and serene.

"We'll be there in just a few minutes," Roy told him.

Ackblom smiled. "There's no place like home."

Spencer had been driving for nearly an hour and a half before Ellie switched off the computer and unplugged it from the cigarette lighter. A dew of perspiration beaded her forehead, although the interior of the truck was not overheated.

"God knows if I'm mounting a good defense or planning a double suicide," she said. "Could go either way. But now it's there for us to use if we have to."

"Use what?"

"I'm not going to tell you," she said bluntly. "It'll take too much time. Besides, you'd try to talk me out of it. Which would be a waste of time. I know the arguments against it, and I've already rejected them."

"And this makes an argument so much easier—when you handle both sides of it."

She remained somber. "If worse comes to worst, I'll have no choice but to use it, no matter how insane that seems."

Rocky had awakened in the backseat a short while ago, and to him, Spencer said, "Pal, you're not confused back there, are you?"

"Ask me anything else but not about *that*," Ellie said. "If I talk about it, if I even think too much about it, then I'll be too damn scared to do it when the time comes, *if* the time comes. I hope to God we don't need it."

Spencer had never heard her babble before. She usually kept tight control of herself. Now she was spooking him.

Panting, Rocky poked his head between the front seats. One ear up, one down: refreshed and interested.

"I didn't think you were confused," Spencer told him. "Me, I'm twice as befuddled as a lightning bug bashing itself to bits to get out of an old mayonnaise jar. But I suppose that higher forms of intelligence, like the canine species, would have no trouble figuring out what she's ranting about."

Ellie stared at the road ahead, rubbing absentmindedly at her chin with the knuckles of her right hand.

She had said that he could ask her about anything except *that*, whatever *that* might be, so he took her up on it. "Where was 'Bess Baer' going to settle down before I mucked things up? Where were you going to take that Rover and make a new life?"

"Wasn't going to settle again," she said, proving that she was listening. "I gave up on that. Sooner or later, they find me if I stay in one place too long. I spent a lot of the money I had . . . and some from friends . . . to buy that Rover and the gear in it. With that, I figured I could keep moving and go just about anywhere."

"I'll pay for the Rover."

"That's not what I was after."

"I know. But what's mine is yours anyway."

"Oh? When did that happen?"

"No strings attached," he said.

"I like to pay my own way."

"No point discussing it."

"What you say is final, huh?"

"No. What the dog says is final."

"This was Rocky's decision?"

"He takes care of all my finances."

Rocky grinned. He liked hearing his name.

"Because it's Rocky's idea," she said, "I'll keep an open mind."

Spencer said, "Why do you call Summerton a cockroach? Why does that annoy him particularly?"

"Tom's got a phobia about insects. All kinds of insects. Even a house-fly can make him squirm. But he's especially uptight about cockroaches. When he sees one—and they used to have an infestation at the ATF when he was there—he goes off the deep end. It's almost comic. Like in a cartoon when an elephant spots a mouse. Anyway, a few weeks after . . . after Danny and my folks were killed, and after I gave up trying to approach reporters with what I knew, I called old Tom at his office in the Department of Justice, just rang him up from a pay phone in midtown Chicago."

"Good grief."

"The most private of his private lines, the one he picks up himself. Surprised him. He tried to play innocent, keep me talking until he could have me whacked right at that pay phone. I told him he shouldn't be so afraid of cockroaches, since he was one himself. Told him that someday I'll stomp him flat, kill him. And I meant what I said. Someday, somehow, I'll send him straight to Hell."

Spencer glanced at her. She was staring at the night ahead, still brooding. Slender, so pleasing to the eye, in some ways as delicate as any flower, she was nevertheless as fierce and tough as any special-forces soldier that Spencer had ever known.

He loved her beyond all reason, without reservation, without qualification, with a passion immeasurable, loved every aspect of her face, loved the sound of her voice, loved her singular vitality, loved the kindness of her heart and the agility of her mind, loved her so purely and intensely that sometimes when he looked at her, a hush seemed to fall across the world. He prayed that she was a favored child of fate, destined to have a long life, because if she died before he did, there would be no hope for him, no hope at all.

He drove east into the night, past Rifle and Silt and New Castle and Glenwood Springs. The interstate highway frequently followed the bottoms of deep, narrow canyons with sheer walls of seamed stone. In daylight, it was some of the most breathtaking scenery on the planet. In February darkness, those soaring ramparts of rock pressed close, black monoliths that denied him the choice of going left or right and that funneled him toward higher places, toward dire confrontations so inevitable that they seemed to have been waiting to unfold since before the universe had exploded into existence. From the floor of that crevasse, only a ribbon of sky was visible, sprinkled with a meagerness of stars, as though Heaven could accommodate no more souls and would soon close its gates forever.

§

Roy touched a button in the armrest. Beside him, the car window purred down. "Is it as you remember?" he asked the artist.

As they turned off the two-lane country road, Ackblom leaned past Roy to look outside.

Toward the front of the property, untrammeled snow mantled the paddocks that surrounded the stables. No horses had been boarded there in twenty-two years, since Jennifer's death, because horses had been her love, not her husband's. The fencing was well maintained and so white that it was only dimly visible against the frosted fields.

The bare driveway was flanked by waist-high walls of snow that had been pushed there by a plow. Its course was serpentine.

At Steven Ackblom's request, the driver stopped at the house rather than proceeding directly to the barn.

Roy put up the window while Fordyce removed the shackles from the artist's ankles. Then the handcuffs. Roy did not want his guest to suffer the further indignity of those bonds.

In their journey across the mountains, he and the artist had achieved a rapport deeper than he would have thought possible in such a short acquaintance. More than handcuffs and shackles, the mutual respect between them was certain to guarantee Ackblom's fullest cooperation.

He and the artist got out of the limousine, leaving Rink and Fordyce and the driver to wait for them. No wind carved the night, but the air was frigid.

As the fenced fields had been, the lawns were white and softly luminous in the platinum light of the partial moon. The evergreen shrubs were encrusted with snow. Its limbs jacketed in ice, a winter-shorn maple cast a faint moonshadow upon the yard.

The two-story Victorian farmhouse was white with green shutters. A deep front porch extended from corner to corner, and the embracing balustrade had white balusters under a green handrail. A gingerbread cornice marked the transition from the walls to the dormered roof, and a fringe of small icicles overhung the eaves.

The windows were all dark. The Dresmunds had cooperated with Duvall. For the night, they were staying in Vail, perhaps curious about events at the ranch but selling their forgetfulness for the price of dinner in a four-star restaurant, champagne, hot-house strawberries dipped in chocolate, and a restful night in a luxury hotel suite. Later, with Grant dead and no caretaker job to be filled, they would regret making such a bad bargain.

Duvall and the twelve men under his supervision were scattered with utmost discretion across the property. Roy couldn't discern where a single man was concealed.

"It's lovely here in the spring," said Steven Ackblom, speaking not with audible regret but as if remembering May mornings full of sun, mild evenings full of stars and cricket songs.

"It's lovely now too," Roy said.

"Yes, isn't it?" With a smile that might have been melancholy, Ackblom turned to survey the entire property. "I was happy here."

"It's easy to see why," Roy said.

The artist sighed. " 'Pleasure is oft a visitant, but pain clings cruelly to us.' "

"Excuse me?"

"Keats," Ackblom explained.

"Ah. I'm sorry if being here depresses you."

"No, no. Don't trouble yourself about that. It doesn't in the least depress me. By nature, I'm depression-proof. And seeing this place again . . . it's a sweet pain, one well worth experiencing."

They got into the limousine and were driven to the barn behind the house.

§

In the small town of Eagle, west of Vail, they stopped for gasoline. In a minimart adjacent to the service station, Ellie was able to purchase two tubes of Super Glue, the store's entire supply.

"Why Super Glue?" Spencer asked when she returned to the pumps, where he was counting out cash to the attendant.

"Because it's a lot harder to find welding tools and supplies."

"Well, of course, it is," he said, as though he knew what she was talking about.

She remained solemn. Her fund of smiles had been depleted. "I hope it's not too cold for this stuff to bond."

"What're you going to do with your Super Glue, if I may ask?"

"Glue something."

"Well, of course, you are."

Ellie got into the backseat with Rocky.

At her direction, Spencer drove the pickup past the service bays of the repair garage to the edge of the station property. He parked beside a ten-foot-high ridge of plowed snow.

Fending off the mutt's friendly tongue, Ellie unlatched the small sliding window between the cab and the cargo bed. She slid the movable half open only an inch.

From the canvas duffel bag, she removed the last of the major items that she had chosen to salvage when the signal trace-back from Earthguard had made it necessary to abandon the Range Rover. A long orange utility cord. An adapter that transformed any car or truck cigarette lighter into two electrical sockets from which current could be drawn when the engine was running. Finally, there was the compact satellite up-link with automated tracking arm and collapsible Frisbee-like receiving dish.

Outside again, Spencer put down the tailgate, and they climbed into the empty bed of the pickup. Ellie used most of the Super Glue to fix the microwave transceiver to the painted-metal cargo bed.

"You know," he said, "a drop or two usually does the trick."

"Got to be sure it doesn't pop loose at the worst moment and start sliding around. It has to remain stationary."

"After that much glue, you'll probably need a small nuclear device to get it off."

Head cocked in curiosity, Rocky watched them through the back window of the cab.

The adhesive required longer than usual to bond, either because Ellie used too much or because of the cold. In ten minutes, however, the microwave transceiver was fixed securely to the truck bed.

She opened the collapsible receiving dish to its full eighteen-inch extension. She plugged one end of the utility cord into the base of the transceiver. Then she hooked her fingers into the narrow gap that she had left in the rear window of the cab, slid the pane farther open, and fed the electrical cord into the backseat.

Rocky pushed his snout through the window and licked Ellie's hands as she worked.

When the cord between the transceiver and the window was taut but not stretched tight, she pushed Rocky's snout out of the way and slid the window as tightly shut as the cord would allow.

"We're going to track somebody by satellite?" Spencer asked as they jumped off the back of the truck.

"Information is power," she said.

Putting up the tailgate, he said, "Well, of course, it is."

"And I have some heavy-duty knowledge."

"I wouldn't dispute that for a moment."

They returned to the cab of the pickup.

She pulled the utility cord from the backseat and plugged it into one of the two sockets in the cigarette-lighter adapter. She plugged the laptop into the second socket.

"All right," she said grimly, "next stop—Vail."

He started the engine.

⌒

Almost too excited to drive, Eve Jammer cruised the Vegas night, searching for an opportunity to become the completely fulfilled woman that Roy had shown her how to be.

Cruising past a seedy bar where flashing neon signs advertised topless dancers, Eve saw a sorry-looking, middle-aged guy step out the front door. He was bald, maybe forty pounds overweight, with facial skin folds to rival those of any Shar-Pei. His shoulders were slumped under a yoke of weariness. Hands in his coat pockets, head hung low, he schlepped toward the half-full parking lot beside the bar.

She drove past him into the lot and parked in an empty stall. Through her side window, she watched him approaching. He shuffled as if too beaten down by the world to fight gravity any more than he absolutely had to.

She could imagine how it was for him. Too old, too unattractive, too fat, too socially awkward, too poor to win the favors of a girl like those he so much desired. He was on his way home after a few beers, bound for a lonely bed, having passed a few hours watching gorgeous, big-breasted, long-legged, firm-bodied young women whom he could never possess. Frustrated, depressed. Achingly lonely.

Eve felt so sorry for that man, to whom life had been grossly unfair.

She got out of her car and approached him as he reached his ten-year-old, unwashed Pontiac. "Excuse me," she said.

He turned, and his eyes widened at the sight of her.

"You were here the other night," she guessed, making it sound like a statement.

"Well . . . yeah, last week," he said. He couldn't restrain himself from looking her over. He was probably unaware of licking his lips.

"I saw you then," she said, pretending shyness. "I . . . I didn't have the nerve to say hello."

He gaped at her in disbelief. And he was slightly wary, unable to believe a woman like her would be coming on to him.

"The thing is," she said, "you look exactly like my dad." Which was a lie.

"I do?"

He was less wary now that she had mentioned her dad, but there was also less pathetic hope in his eyes.

"Oh, exactly like him," she said. "And . . . and the thing is . . . the thing is that . . . I hope you won't think I'm weird . . . but the thing is . . . the only men I can do it with, go to bed with and be really wild with . . . are men who look like my father."

As he realized that he had stumbled into a bed of good fortune more exciting than any in his most testosterone-flooded fantasies, the jowled and dewlapped Romeo straightened his shoulders. His chest lifted. A smile of sheer delight made him look ten years younger, though no less like a Shar-Pei.

In that transcendent moment, when the poor man no doubt felt more alive and happier than he'd been in weeks, months, perhaps even years, Eve drew the silencer-fitted Beretta from her big handbag and shot him three times.

She also had a Polaroid in the handbag. Although worried that a car might pull into the lot and that other patrons might leave the bar momentarily, she took three snapshots of the dead man as he lay on the blacktop beside his Pontiac.

Driving home, she thought about what a fine thing she had done: helping that dear man to find a way out of his imperfect life, giving him his freedom from rejection, depression, loneliness, and despair. Tears melted from her eyes. She didn't sob or become too emotional to be dangerous behind the wheel. She wept quietly, quietly, though the compassion in her heart was powerful and profound.

She wept all the way home, into the garage, through the house, into her bedroom, where she arranged the Polaroids on the nightstand for Roy to see when he returned from Colorado in a day or two—and then a funny thing happened. As deeply moved as she was by what she had done, as copious and genuine as her tears had been, nevertheless, she was abruptly dry-eyed and incredibly *horny*.

℘

At the window with the artist, Roy watched the limousine as it headed back to the county road and away. It would return for them after the drama of the night had been played out.

They were standing in the front room of the converted barn. The darkness was relieved only by the moonlight that sifted through the windows and by the green glow of the security-panel readout next to the front door. With numbers that Gary Duvall had obtained from the Dresmunds, Roy had disengaged the alarm when they'd come in, then had reset it. There were no motion detectors, only magnetic contacts at each door and window, so he and the artist could move about freely without triggering the system.

This large first-floor room had once been a private gallery where Steven had exhibited the paintings that he favored among all those that he had produced. Now the chamber was vacant, and every faint sound echoed hollowly off the cold walls. Sixteen years had passed since the great man's art had adorned the place.

Roy knew this was a moment he would remember with exceptional clarity for the rest of his life, as he would remember the *precise* expression of wonder on Eve's face when he had granted peace to that man and woman in the restaurant parking lot. Although the degree of humanity's imperfection ensured that the ongoing human drama would always be a tragedy, there were moments of transcendent experience, like this, that made life worth living.

Sadly, most people were too timid to seize the day and discover what such transcendence felt like. Timidity, however, had never been one of Roy's shortcomings.

Revelation of his compassionate crusade had earned Roy all the glories of Eve's bedroom, and he had decided that revelation was called for again. Journeying across the mountains, he had realized that Steven was perfect in some way few people ever were—although the nature of his perfection was more subtle than Eve's devastating beauty, more sensed than seen, intriguing, mysterious. Instinctively Roy knew that Steven and he were simpatico to an even greater extent than were he and Eve. True friendship might be forged between them if he revealed himself to the artist as forthrightly as he'd revealed himself to the dear heart in Las Vegas.

Standing by the moonlit window, in the dark and empty gallery, Roy Miro began to explain, with tasteful humility, how he had put his ideals into practice in ways that even the agency, for all its willingness to be bold, would have been too timid to endorse. As the artist listened, Roy almost hoped that the fugitives would not come that night or the next, not until he and Steven were granted sufficient time together to build a foundation for the friendship that surely was destined to enrich their lives.

∽

Outside Hamlet Gardens in Westwood, the uniformed valet brought Darius's VW Microbus from the narrow lot beside the building, drove it into the street, and swung it to the curb at the front entrance, where the two Descoteaux families waited, fresh from dinner.

Harris was at the rear of their group, and as he was about to step into the Microbus, a woman touched his shoulder. "Sir, may I give you something to think about?"

He wasn't surprised. He didn't back off, as he had done in the men's room at the theater. Turning, he saw an attractive redhead in high heels, an ankle-length coat in a shade of green complementary to her complexion, and a stylishly wide-brimmed hat worn at a rakish angle. She appeared to be on her way to a party or a nightclub.

"If the new world order turns out to be peace, prosperity, and democracy, how wonderful for us all," she said. "But perhaps it will be less appealing, more like the Dark Ages if the Dark Ages had had all these wonderful new forms of high-tech entertainment to make them tolerable. But I think you'd agree . . . being able to get the latest movies on video doesn't fully compensate for enslavement."

"What do you want from me?"

"To help you," she said. "But you have to want the help, have to know you need it, and have to be ready to do what needs done."

From inside the Microbus, his family was staring at him with curiosity and concern.

"I'm no bomb-throwing revolutionary," he told the woman in the green coat.

"Nor are we," she said. "Bombs and guns are the instruments of last resort. Knowledge should be the first and foremost weapon in any resistance."

"What knowledge do I have that you could want?"

"To begin with," she said, "the knowledge of how fragile your freedom is in the current scheme of things. That gives you a degree of commitment that we value."

The valet, though standing just out of earshot, was staring at them oddly.

From a coat pocket, the woman extracted a piece of paper and showed it to Harris. He saw a telephone number and three words.

When he tried to take the paper from her, she held it tightly. "No, Mr. Descoteaux. I would prefer that you memorize it."

The number was designed to be memorable, and the three words gave him no difficulty, either.

As Harris stared at the paper, the woman said, "The man who has done this to you is named Roy Miro."

He remembered the name but not where he had heard it before.

"He came to you pretending to be an FBI agent," she said.

"The guy asking about Spence!" he said, looking up from the paper. He was suddenly furious, now that he had a face to put on the enemy who had thus far been faceless. "But what in the hell did I do to him? We had the mildest disagreement over an officer who once served under me. That's all!" Then he heard the other part of what she had said, and he frowned. "*Pretended* to be with the FBI? But he was. I checked him out between the time he made the appointment and when he came to the office."

"They are seldom what they seem to be," the redhead said.

"They? Who are *they?*"

"Who they have always been, through the ages," she said, and smiled. "Sorry. No time to be other than inscrutable."

"I'm going to get my house back," he said adamantly, although he did not feel as confident as he sounded.

"But you won't. And even if the public outcry was loud enough to have these laws rescinded, they'd just pass new laws giving them other ways to ruin people they want to ruin. The problem's not one law. These are power fanatics who want to tell everyone how they should live, what they should think, read, say, feel."

"How do I get at Miro?"

"You can't. He's too deep-cover to be easily exposed."

"But—"

"I'm not here to tell you how to get Roy Miro. I'm here to warn you that you must not go back to your brother's tonight."

A chill shimmered through the chambers of fluid in his spine, working up his back to the base of his neck with a queer, methodical progression like no chill he had ever felt before.

He said, "What's going to happen now?"

"Your ordeal isn't over. It isn't ever going to be over if you let them have their way. You'll be arrested for the murder of two drug dealers, the wife of one, the girlfriend of the other, and three young children. Your fingerprints have been found on objects in the house where they were shot to death."

"I never killed anyone!"

The valet heard enough of that exclamation to scowl.

Darius was getting out of the Microbus to see what was wrong.

"The objects with your prints on them were taken from your home and planted at the scene of the murders. The story will probably be that you disposed of two competitors who tried to muscle in on your territory, and you wiped out the wife, girlfriend, and kids just to teach other dealers a hard lesson."

Harris's heart was pounding so fiercely that he would not have been surprised to see his breast shuddering visibly with each hard beat. Instead of pumping warm blood, it seemed to be circulating liquid Freon through his body. He was colder than a dead man.

Fear regressed him to the vulnerability and helplessness of childhood. He heard himself seeking solace in the faith of his beloved, gospel-singing mother, a faith from which he had slipped away through the years but to which he now suddenly reached out with a sincerity that surprised him: "Jesus, dear sweet Jesus, help me."

"Perhaps He will," the woman said as Darius approached them. "But in the meantime, we're ready to help as well. If you're smart, you'll call that number, use those passwords, and get on with your life—instead of getting on with your death."

As Darius joined them, he said, "What's up, Harris?"

The redhead returned the slip of paper to her coat pocket.

Harris said, "But that's just it. How can I ever get on with my life after what's happened to me?"

"You can," she said, "though you won't be Harris Descoteaux any more."

She smiled and nodded at Darius, and she walked away.

Harris watched her go, overcome by that here-we-are-in-the-magic-kingdom-of-Oz feeling again.

∽

Long ago those acres had been beautiful. As a boy with another name, Spencer had been especially fond of the ranch in wintertime, swaddled in white. By day, it was a bright empire of snow forts, tunnels, and sled runs that had been tamped down with great care and patience. On clear nights, the Rocky Mountain sky was deeper than eternity, deeper even than the mind could imagine, and starlight sparkled in the icicles.

Returning after his own eternity in exile, he found nothing that was pleasing to the eye. Each slope and curve of land, each building, each tree was the same as it had been in that distant age, but for the fact that the pines and maples and birches were taller than before. Changeless though it might be, the ranch now impressed him as the ugliest place that he had ever seen, even when flattered by its winter dress. They were harsh acres, and the stark geometry of those fields and hills was designed, at every turn, to offend the eye, like the architecture of Hell. The trees were only ordinary specimens, but they looked to him as though they were mal-formed and gnarled by disease, nurtured on horrors that had leeched into the soil and into their roots from the nearby catacombs. The buildings—stables, house, barn—were all graceless hulks, looming and haunted, the windows as black and menacing as open graves.

Spencer parked at the house. His heart was pounding. His mouth was so dry and his throat was so tight that he could hardly swallow. The door of the pickup opened with the resistance of a massive portal on a bank vault.

Ellie remained in the truck, with the computer on her lap. If trouble came, she was on-line and ready for whatever strange purpose she had prepared. Through the microwave transceiver, she had linked to a satellite and from there into a computer system that she hadn't identified to Spencer and that could be anywhere on the surface of the earth. Information might be power, as she had said, but Spencer couldn't imagine how information would shield them from bullets, if the agency was nearby and lying in wait for them.

As though he were a deep-sea diver, encased in a cumbersome pressure suit and steel helmet, burdened by an incalculable tonnage of water, he walked to the front steps, crossed the porch, and stood at the door. He rang the bell.

He heard the chimes inside, the same five notes that had marked a visitor's arrival when he'd lived there as a boy, and even as they rang out, he had to struggle against an urge to turn and run. He was a grown man, and the hobgoblins that terrorized children should have had no power over him. Irrationally, however, he was afraid that the chimes would be answered by his mother, dead but walking, as naked as she'd been found in that ditch, all her wounds revealed.

He found the willpower to censor the mental image of the corpse. He rang the bell again.

The night was so hushed that he felt as though he would be able to hear the earthworms deep in the ground, below the frost line, if only he could clear his mind and listen for their telltale writhing.

When no one responded to the bell the second time, Spencer retrieved the spare key from the hiding place atop the door head. The Dresmunds had been instructed to leave it there, in the event that it was ever needed by the owner. The dead-bolt locks of the house and barn were keyed the same. With that freezing bit of brass half sticking to his fingers, he hurried back to the black pickup.

The driveway forked. One lane led past the front of the barn and the other behind it. He took the second route.

"I should go inside the same way I went that night," he told Ellie. "By the back door. Re-create the moment."

They parked where the van with the rainbow mural had stood in a long-ago darkness. That vehicle had been his father's. He'd seen it for the first time that night because it had always been garaged off the property and registered under a false name. It was the hunting wagon in which Steven Ackblom had traveled to various distant places to stalk and capture the women and the girls who were destined to become permanent residents of his catacombs. For the most part, he'd driven it onto the property only when his wife and son had been away, visiting her parents or at horse shows—though also on rare occasions when his darker desires became stronger than his caution.

Ellie wanted to stay in the pickup truck, leave the engine running, and keep the computer on her lap, with her fingers poised over the keys, ready to respond to any provocation.

Spencer couldn't imagine anything that she could possibly do, while actually under attack, to force a call-back of the agency thugs. But she was dead serious, and he knew her well enough to trust that her plan, however peculiar, was not frivolous.

"They're not here," he told her. "No one's waiting for us. If they were here, they'd have been all over us by now."

"I don't know. . . ."

"To remember what happened in those missing minutes, I'm going to have to go down . . . into that place. Rocky isn't company enough. I don't have the courage to go alone, and I'm not ashamed to say so."

Ellie nodded. "You shouldn't be. If I were you, I'd never have been able to come this far. I'd have driven by, never looked back." She surveyed the moon-dappled fields and hills behind the barn.

"No one," he said.

"All right." Her fingers tapped across the laptop keyboard, and she pulled back from whatever computer she had invaded. The display screen went dark. "Let's go."

Spencer doused the headlights. He switched off the engine.

He took the pistol. Ellie had the Micro Uzi.

When they got out of the truck, Rocky insisted on scrambling out with them. He was shaking, saturated by his master's mood, afraid to go with them but equally afraid to stay behind.

Shivering more violently than the dog, Spencer peered into the sky. It was as clear and star-spattered as it had been on that July night. This time, however, the cataracts of moonlight revealed neither an owl nor an angel.

∽

In the dark gallery, where Roy had spoken of many things and the artist had listened with increasing interest and gratifying respect, the grumble of the approaching truck brought a temporary halt to the sharing of intimacies.

To avoid the risk of being seen, they took one step back from the window. They still had a view of the driveway.

Instead of stopping in front of the barn, the pickup continued around to the back of the building.

"I brought you here," Roy said, "because I have to know how your son's involved with this woman. He's a wild card. We can't figure him. There's a feeling of organization about his involvement. That disturbs us. For some time, we've suspected there may be a loosely woven organization out to undo our work or, failing that, cause us as many headaches as it can. He might be involved with such a group. If it exists. Maybe they're assisting the woman. Anyway, considering Spencer's . . . I'm sorry. Considering *Michael's* military training and his obvious Spartan mind-set, I don't think he'll crack under the usual methods of interrogation, no matter how much pain is involved."

"He's a strong-willed boy," Steven acknowledged.

"But if *you* interrogate him, he'll break wide open."

"You might be right," Steven said. "Quite perceptive."

"And this also gives me a chance to help right a wrong."

"What wrong would that be?"

"Well, of course, it's wrong for a son to betray his father."

"Ah. And in addition to being able to avenge that betrayal, may I have the woman?" Steven asked.

Roy thought of those lovely eyes, so direct and challenging. He had coveted them for fourteen months. He would be willing to relinquish his claim, however, in return for the opportunity to witness what a creative genius of Steven Ackblom's stature could achieve when permitted to work in the medium of living flesh.

In anticipation of visitors, they now spoke in whispers:

"Yes, that seems only fair," Roy said. "But I want to watch."

"You understand that what I'll do to her will be . . . extreme."

"The timid never know transcendence."

"That's very true," Steven agreed.

" 'They were all so beautiful in their pain, and all like angels when they died,' " Roy quoted.

"And you want to see that brief, perfect beauty," Ackblom said.

"Yes."

From the far end of the building came the scrape and clack of a lock bolt. A hesitation. Then the faint creak of door hinges.

∽

Darius braked at the stop sign. He was traveling east, and he lived two and a half blocks north of where he had stopped, but he didn't put on the turn signal.

Facing the Microbus from across the intersection were four television-news vans with elaborate microwave dishes on the roofs. Two were parked to the left, two to the right, bathed in the sodium-yellow light-fall from the streetlamps. One was from KNBC, the local affiliate of the national network, and another was marked KTLA, which was Channel 5, the independent station with the highest news ratings in the Los Angeles market. Harris couldn't make out the call letters on the other vans, but he figured they would be from the ABC and CBS affiliate stations in Los Angeles. Behind them were a few cars, and in addition to the people in all those vehicles, half a dozen others were milling around, talking.

Darius's voice was colored by both heavy sarcasm and anger: "Must be a breaking story."

"Not quite yet," Harris said grimly. "Best to drive straight through, right by them, and not so fast that they pay any attention to us."

Instead of turning left, toward home, Darius did as his brother asked.

Passing the media, Harris leaned forward, as if fiddling with the radio, averting his face from the windows. "They've been tipped off, asked to stay a few blocks away until it goes down. Somebody wants to ensure there'll be plenty of film of me being taken out of the house in handcuffs. If they go as far as using a SWAT team, then just before the bastards break down the door, these TV vans will get the word to come on up."

Behind Harris, from the middle of three rows of seats, Ondine leaned forward. "Daddy, you mean they're all here to film *you?*"

"I'd bet on it, honey."

"The bastards," she fumed.

"Just newsmen doing their job."

Willa, more emotionally fragile than her sister, began to cry again.

"Ondine's right," Bonnie agreed. "Stinking bastards."

From the very back of the Microbus, Martin said, "Man, this is wild. Uncle Harris, they're going after you like you were Michael Jackson or someone."

"Okay, we're past them," Darius said, so Harris could sit up straight again.

Bonnie said, "The police must think we're home, 'cause of the way the security system handles the lights when no one's there."

"It's programmed with a dozen scenarios," Darius explained. "It cycles through a different one every night no one's there, switching off lamps in one room, on in another, switching radios and TVs on and off, imitating realistic patterns of activity. Supposed to convince burglars. Never expected I'd be happy about it convincing cops."

Bonnie asked, "What now?"

"Let's just drive for a while." Harris put his hands in front of the heater vents, in the jets of hot air. He couldn't get warm. "Just drive while I think about this."

Already they had spent fifteen minutes cruising through Bel Air while he'd told them about the man who had approached him during his walk, the second stranger in the theater men's room, and the redhead in the green coat. Even before seeing the TV-news vans, they had all regarded the woman's warning as seriously as the events of the past few days argued that they should. But it had seemed feasible to drive by the house, quickly leave off Bonnie and Martin, then return ten minutes later and pick them up, along with the clothes that Ondine and Willa had gotten at the mall and with the pathetically few belongings that Jessica and the girls had been able to remove from their own home during the eviction on Saturday. However, their aimless cruising had resulted in an indirect approach to the house, a chance encounter with the TV-news vans, and the realization that the warning had been even more urgent than they had thought.

Darius drove to Wilshire Boulevard and headed west, toward Santa Monica and the sea.

"When I'm charged with the premeditated murder of seven people, including three children," Harris thought aloud, "the prosecutor is going to go for 'first-degree murder, special circumstances,' sure as God made little green apples."

Darius said, "Bail's out of the question. Won't be any. They'll say you're a flight risk."

From her seat at the back, beside Martin, Jessica said, "Even if there was bail, we have no way to raise the money to post it."

"Court calendars are clogged," Darius noted. "So many laws these days, seventy thousand pages out of Congress last year. All those defendants, all those appeals. Most cases move like glaciers. Jesus, Harris, you'll be in jail a year, maybe two, just waiting for a day in court, getting through the trial—"

"That's time lost forever," Jessica said angrily, "even if the jury finds him innocent."

Ondine began to cry again, with Willa.

Harris vividly recalled each of his incapacitating attacks of jailhouse claustrophobia. "I'd never make it six months, not a chance, maybe not even a month."

Circling through the city, where the millions of bright lights were inadequate to hold back the darkness, they discussed options. In the end, they realized that there *were* no options. He had no choice but to run. Yet without money or ID, he wouldn't get far before he was chased down and apprehended. His only hope, therefore, was the mysterious group to which the redhead in the green coat and the other two strangers belonged, although Harris knew too little about them to feel comfortable putting his future in their hands.

Jessica, Ondine, and Willa were adamantly opposed to being separated from him. They feared that any separation was going to be permanent, so they ruled out the option of his going on the run alone. He was sure they were right. Besides, he didn't want to be apart from them, because he suspected that they would remain targets in his absence.

Looking back through the shadow-filled Microbus, past the dark faces of his children and his sister-in-law, Harris met the eyes of his wife, where she sat next to Martin. "It can't have come to this."

"All that matters is that we're together."

"Everything we've worked so hard for—"

"Gone already."

"—to start over at forty-four—"

"Better than dying at forty-four," said Jessica.

"You're a trooper," he said lovingly.

Jessica smiled. "Well, it could've been an earthquake, the house gone, and all of us besides."

Harris turned his attention to Ondine and Willa. They were done with tears, shaky but with a new light of defiance in their eyes.

He said, "All the friends you've made in school—"

"Oh, they're just kids." Ondine strove to be airy about losing all her pals and confidants, which to a teenager would be the hardest thing about such an abrupt change. "Just a bunch of kids, silly kids, that's all."

"And," Willa said, "you're our dad."

For the first time since the nightmare had begun, Harris was moved to quiet tears of his own.

"It's settled then," Jessica announced. "Darius, start looking for a pay phone."

They found one at the end of a strip shopping center, in front of a pizza parlor.

Harris had to ask Darius for change. Then he got out of the Microbus and went to the telephone alone.

Through the windows of the pizza parlor, he saw people eating, drinking beer, talking. A group at one large table was having an especially good time; he could hear their laughter above the music from the jukebox. None of them seemed to be aware that the world had recently turned upside down and inside out.

Harris was gripped by an envy so intense that he wanted to smash the windows, burst into the restaurant, overturn the tables, knock the food and the mugs of beer out of those people's hands, shout at them and shake them until their illusions of safety and normalcy were shattered into as many pieces as his own had been. He was so bitter that he might have done it—*would* have done it—if he hadn't had a wife and two daughters to think about, if he had been facing his frightening new life alone. It wasn't even their happiness that he envied; it was their blessed ignorance that he longed to regain for himself, though he knew that no knowledge could ever be unlearned.

He lifted the handset from the pay phone and deposited coins. For a blood-freezing moment, he listened to the dial tone, unable to remember the number that had been on the paper in the redhead's hand. Then it came to him, and he punched the buttons on the keypad, his hand shaking so badly that he half expected to discover that he had not entered the number correctly.

On the third ring, a man answered with a simple, "Hello?"

"I need help," Harris said, and realized that he hadn't even identified himself. "I'm sorry. I'm . . . my name is . . . Descoteaux. Harris Descoteaux. One of your people, whoever you are, she said to call this number, that you could help me, that you were ready to help."

After a hesitation, the man at the other end of the line said, "If you had this number, and if you got it legitimately, then you must be aware there's a certain protocol."

"Protocol?"

There was no response.

For a moment, Harris panicked that the man was going to hang up and walk away from that phone and be forever thereafter unreachable. He couldn't understand what was expected of him—until he remembered the three passwords that had been printed on the piece of paper below the telephone number. The redhead had told him that he must memorize those too. He said, "Pheasants and dragons."

∽

At the security keypad, in the short hallway at the back of the barn, Spencer entered the series of numbers that disarmed the alarm. The Dresmunds had been instructed not to alter the codes, in order to make access easy for the owner if he ever returned when they were gone. When Spencer punched in the last digit, the luminous readout changed from ARMED AND SECURE to the less bright READY TO ARM.

He had brought a flashlight from the pickup. He directed the beam along the left-hand wall. "Half bath, just a toilet and sink," he told Ellie.

Beyond the first door, a second: "That's a small storage room." At the end of the hall, the light found a third door. "He had a gallery that way, open only to the wealthiest collectors. And from the gallery, there's a staircase up to what used to be his studio on the second floor." He swung the beam to the right side of the corridor, where only one door waited. It was ajar. "That used to be the file room."

He could have switched on the overhead fluorescent panels. Sixteen years ago, however, he had entered in gloom, guided only by the radiance of the green letters on the security-system readout. Intuitively, he knew that his best hope of remembering what he had repressed for so long was to re-create the circumstances of that night insofar as he was able. The barn had been air-conditioned then, and now the heat was turned low, so the February chill in the air was nearly right. The harsh glare of overhead fluorescent bulbs would too drastically alter the mood. If he were striving for a roughly authentic re-creation, even a flashlight was too reassuring, but he didn't have the nerve to proceed in the same depth of darkness into which he had gone when he was fourteen.

Rocky whined and scratched at the back door, which Ellie had closed behind them. He was shivering and miserable.

For the most part and for reasons that Spencer would never be able to determine, Rocky's argument with darkness was limited to that in the outside world. He usually functioned well enough indoors, in the dark, although sometimes he required a night-light to banish an especially bad case of the willies.

"Poor thing," Ellie said.

The flashlight was brighter than any night-light. Rocky should have been sufficiently comforted by it. Instead, he quaked so hard that it seemed as if his ribs ought to make xylophone music against one another.

"It's okay, pal," Spencer told the dog. "What you sense is something in the past, over and done with a long time ago. Nothing here and now is worth being scared of."

The dog scratched at the door, unconvinced.

"Should I let him out?" Ellie wondered.

"No. He'll just realize it's night outside and start scratching to get back in."

Again directing the flashlight at the file-room door, Spencer knew that his own inner turmoil must be the source of the dog's fear. Rocky was always acutely sensitive to his moods. Spencer strove to calm himself. After all, what he had said to the dog was true: The aura of evil that clung to these walls was the residue of a horror from the past, and there was nothing here and now to fear.

On the other hand, what was true for the dog was not as true for Spencer. He still *lived* partly in the past, held fast by the dark asphalt of memory. In fact, he was gripped even more fiercely by what he could not quite remember than by what he could recall so clearly; his self-denied recollections formed the deepest tar pit of all. The events of sixteen years ago could not harm Rocky, but for Spencer, they had the real potential to snare, engulf, and destroy him.

He began to tell Ellie about the night of the owl, the rainbow, and the knife. The sound of his own voice scared him. Each word seemed like a link in one of those chain drives by which any roller coaster was hauled inexorably up the first hill on its track and by which a gondola with a gargoyle masthead was pulled into the ghost-filled darkness of a fun house. Chain drives worked only in one direction, and once the journey had begun, even if a section of track had collapsed ahead or an all-consuming fire had broken out in the deepest chamber of the fun house, there was no backing up.

"That summer, and for many summers before it, I slept without air-conditioning in my bedroom. The house had a hot-water, radiant-heat system that was quiet in the winter, and that was okay. But I was bothered by the hiss and whistle of cold air being forced through the vanes in the vent grille, the hum of the compressor echoing along the duct-work. . . . No, 'bothered' isn't the word. It scared me. I was afraid that the noise of the air conditioner would mask some sound in the night . . . a sound that I'd better be able to hear and respond to . . . or die."

"What sound?" Ellie asked.

"I didn't know. It was just a fear, a childish thing. Or so I thought at the time. I was embarrassed by it. But that's why my window was open, why I heard the cry. I tried to tell myself it was only an owl or an owl's prey, far off in the night. But . . . it was so desperate, so thin and full of fear . . . so human. . . ."

More swiftly than when he had been confessing to strangers in barrooms and to the dog, he recounted his journey on that July night: out of the silent house, across the summer lawn with its faux frost of moonlight, to the corner of the barn and the visitation of the owl, to the van where the stench of urine rose from the open back door, and into the hall where they now stood together.

"And then I opened the door to the file room," he said.

He opened it once more and crossed the threshold.

Ellie followed him.

In the dark hallway from which the two of them had come, Rocky still whined and scratched at the back door, trying to get out.

Spencer played the beam of the flashlight around the file room. The long worktable was gone, as were the two chairs. The row of file cabinets had been removed as well.

The knotty-pine cupboards still filled the far end of the room from floor to ceiling and corner to corner. They featured three pairs of tall, narrow doors.

He pointed the beam of light at the center doors and said, "They were standing open, and a strange faint light was coming out of them from inside the cabinet, where there weren't any lights." He heard a new note of strain in his voice. "My heart was knocking so hard it shook my arms. I fisted my hands and held them at my sides, struggling to control myself. I wanted to run, just turn and run back to bed and forget it all."

He was talking about how he had felt then, in the long ago, but he could as easily have been speaking of the present.

He opened the center pair of knotty-pine doors. The unused hinges squeaked. He shone the light into the cabinet and panned it across empty shelves.

"Four latches hold the back wall in place," he told her.

His father had concealed the latches behind clever strips of flip-up molding. Spencer found all four: one to the left at the back of the bottom shelf, one to the right; one to the left at the back of the second-highest shelf, one to the right.

Behind him, Rocky padded into the file room, claws ticking on the polished-pine floor.

Ellie said, "That's right, pooch, you stay with us."

After handing the flashlight to Ellie, Spencer pushed on the shelves. The guts of the cabinet rolled backward into darkness. Small wheels creaked along old metal tracks.

He stepped over the base frame of the unit, into the space that had been vacated by the shelves. Standing inside the cupboard, he pushed the back wall all the way into the hidden vestibule beyond.

His palms were damp. He blotted them on his jeans.

Retrieving the flashlight from Ellie, he went into the six-foot-square room behind the cupboard. A chain dangled from the bare bulb in the ceiling socket. He tugged on it and was rewarded with light as sulfurous as he remembered it from that night.

Concrete floor. Concrete-block walls. As in his dreams.

After Ellie shut the knotty-pine doors, closing herself in the cabinet, she and Rocky followed him into the cramped room beyond.

"That night, I stood out there in the file room, looking in through the back of the cupboard, toward this yellow light, and I wanted to run away so badly. I thought I *had* started to run . . . but the next thing I knew, I was in the cupboard. I said to myself, 'Run, run, get the hell out of here.' But then I was all the way through the cupboard and in this vestibule, without any awareness of having taken a step. It was like . . . like I was drawn . . . in a trance . . . couldn't go back no matter how much I wanted to."

"It's a yellow bug light," she said, "like you use outdoors during the summer." She seemed to find that curious.

"Sure. To keep mosquitoes away. They never work that well. And I don't know why he used it here, instead of an ordinary bulb."

"Well, maybe it was the only one handy at the time."

"No. Never. Not him. He must have felt there was something more aesthetic about the yellow light, more suited to his purpose. He lived a carefully considered life. Everything he did was done with the aesthetics well worked out in his mind. From the clothes he wore to the way he prepared a sandwich. That's one thing that makes what he did under this place so horrible . . . the long and careful consideration."

He realized that he was tracing his scar with the fingertips of his right hand while holding the flashlight in his left. He lowered his hand to the SIG 9mm pistol that was still jammed under his belt, against his belly, but he didn't draw it.

"How could your mother not know about this place?" Ellie asked, gazing up and around at the vestibule.

"He owned the ranch before they were married. Remodeled the barn before she saw it. This used to be part of the area that became the file room. He added those pine cabinets out there himself, to close off this space, after the contractors left, so they wouldn't know he'd concealed the access to the basement. Last of all, he brought in a guy to lay pine floors through the rest of the place."

The Micro Uzi was equipped with a carrying strap. Ellie slung it over her shoulder, apparently so she could hug herself with both arms. "He was planning what he did . . . planning it before he even married your mother, before you were born?"

Her disgust was as heavy as the chill in the air. Spencer only hoped that she was able to absorb all the revelations that lay ahead without letting her repulsion transfer in any degree from the father to the son. He desperately prayed that he would remain clean in her eyes, untainted.

In his own eyes he regarded himself with disgust every time he saw even an innocent aspect of his father in himself. Sometimes, meeting his reflection in a mirror, Spencer would remember his father's equally dark eyes, and he would look away, shuddering and sick to his stomach.

He said, "Maybe he didn't know exactly why he wanted a secret place then. I hope that's true. I hope he married my mother and conceived me with her before he'd ever had any desires like . . . like those he satisfied here. However, I suspect he knew why he needed the rooms below. He just wasn't ready to use them. Like when he was struck by an idea for a painting, sometimes he'd think about it for years before the work began."

She looked yellow in the glow of the bug light, but he sensed that she was as pale as bleached bone. She stared at the closed door that led from the vestibule to the basement stairs. Nodding at it, she said, "He considered that, down there, to be part of his work?"

"Nobody knows for sure. That's what he seemed to imply. But he might have been playing games with the cops, the psychiatrists, just having his fun. He was an extremely intelligent man. He was able to manipulate people so easily. He enjoyed doing that. Who knows what was going through his mind . . . really?"

"But when did he start this . . . this work?"

"Five years after they married. When I was only four years old. And it was another four years before she discovered it . . . and had to die. The police figured it out by identifying the . . . remains of the earliest victims."

Rocky had slipped around them to the basement entrance. He was sniffing pensively and unhappily along the narrow crack between the door and the threshold.

"Sometimes," Spencer said, "in the middle of the night, when I can't sleep, I think of how he held me on his lap, wrestled with me on the floor when I was five or six, smoothed my hair. . . ." His voice choked with emotion. He took a deep breath and forced himself to continue, for he had come here to continue to the end, to be finished with it at last. "Touching me . . . with those hands, those hands, after those same hands had . . . under the barn . . . doing those terrible things."

"Oh," Ellie said softly, as if stricken by a small stab of pain.

Spencer hoped that what he saw in her eyes was an understanding of what he'd carried with him all these years and a compassion for him—not a deepening of her revulsion.

He said, "Makes me sick . . . that my own father ever touched me. Worse . . . I think about how he might have left a fresh corpse down in the darkness, a dead woman, how he might have come out of his catacombs with the scent of her blood still in his memory, up from that place and into the house . . . upstairs into my mother's bed . . . into her arms . . . touching her. . . ."

"Oh, my God," Ellie said.

She closed her eyes as though she couldn't bear to look at him.

He knew he was part of the horror, even if he had been innocent. He was so inextricably associated with the monstrous brutality of his father that others couldn't know his name and look at him without seeing, in their mind's eye, young Michael himself standing in the corruption of the slaughterhouse. Through the chambers of his heart, despair and blood were pumped in equal measure.

Then she opened her eyes. Tears glimmered in her lashes. She put her hand to his scar, touching him as tenderly as he had ever been touched. With five words she made clear to him that in her eyes he was free of all stain: "Oh, God, I'm so sorry."

Even if he were to live one hundred years, Spencer knew he could never love her more than he loved her then. Her caring touch, at that moment of all moments, was the greatest act of kindness that he had ever known.

He only wished that he was as sure of his utter innocence as Ellie was. He must recapture the missing moments of memory that he had come there again to find. But he prayed to God and to his own lost mother for mercy, because he was afraid he would discover that he was, in all ways, the son of his father.

Ellie had given him the strength for whatever waited ahead. Before that courage could fade, he turned to the basement door.

Rocky looked up at him and whimpered. He reached down, stroked the dog's head.

The door was streaked with more grime than it had been when last he'd seen it. Paint had peeled off in places.

"It was closed, but it was different from this," he said, going back to that far July. "Someone must have scrubbed away the stains, the hands."

"Hands?"

He raised his hand from the dog to the door. "Arcing from the knob across the upper part . . . ten or twelve overlapping prints made by a woman's hands, fingers spread . . . like the wings of birds . . . in fresh blood, still wet, so red."

As Spencer moved his own hand across the cold wood, he saw the bloody prints reappear, glistening. They seemed as real as they had been on the long-ago night, but he knew that they were only birds of memory taking flight again in his own mind, visible to him but not to Ellie.

"I'm hypnotized by them, can't take my eyes off them, because they convey an unbearable sense of the woman's terror . . . desperation . . . frantic resistance to being forced out of this vestibule and into the secret . . . the secret world below."

He realized that he had placed his hand on the doorknob. It was cold against his palm.

A tremor shook years off his voice, until he sounded younger to himself: "Staring at the blood . . . knowing that she needs help . . . needs my help . . . but I can't go forward. Can't. Jesus. Won't. I'm just a boy, for God's sake. Barefoot, unarmed, afraid, not ready for the truth. But somehow, standing here as scared as I am . . . somehow I finally open the red door. . . ."

Ellie gasped. "Spencer."

Her sound of surprise and the weight she gave to his name caused Spencer to pull back from the past and turn to her, alarmed, but they were still alone.

"Last Tuesday night," she said, "when you were looking for a bar . . . why did you happen to stop in the place where I worked?"

"It was the first one I noticed."

"That's all?"

"And I'd never been there before. It always has to be a new place."

"But the name."

He stared at her, uncomprehending.

She said, "The Red Door."

"Good God."

The connection had escaped him until she made it.

"You called this the red door," she said.

"Because . . . all the blood, the bloody handprints."

For sixteen years, he had been seeking the courage to return to the living nightmare beyond the red door. When he had seen the cocktail lounge on that rainy night in Santa Monica, with the red-painted entrance and the name spelled out above it in neon—THE RED DOOR—he could not possibly have driven past. The opportunity to open a symbolic door, at a time when he had not yet found the strength to return to Colorado and open the other—and only important—red door, had been irresistible to his subconscious mind even while he remained safely oblivious to the implications on a conscious level. And by passing through that symbolic door, he'd arrived in this vestibule behind the pine cabinet, where he must turn the cold brass knob that remained unwarmed by his hand, open the real door, and descend into the catacombs, where he had left a part of himself more than sixteen years ago.

His life was a speeding train on parallel rails of free choice and destiny. Though destiny seemed to have bent the rail of choice to bring him to this place at this time, he needed to believe that choice would bend the rail of destiny tonight and carry him off to a future not in a rigorous line with his past. Otherwise, he would discover that he was fundamentally the son of his father. And that was a fate with which he could not live: end of the line.

He turned the knob.

Rocky edged back, out of the way.

Spencer opened the door.

The yellow light from the vestibule revealed the first few treads of concrete stairs that led down into darkness.

Reaching through the doorway and to the right, he found the switch and clicked on the cellar light. It was blue. He didn't know why blue had been chosen. His inability to think in harmony with his father and to understand such curious details seemed to confirm that he was not like that hateful man in any way that mattered.

Going down the steep stairs to the cellar, he switched off the flashlight. From now on, the way would be lighted as it had been on a certain July and in all the July-spawned dreams that he had since endured.

Rocky followed, then Ellie.

That subterranean chamber was not the full size of the barn above, only about twelve by twenty feet. The furnace and hot-water heater were in a closet upstairs, and the room was utterly vacant. In the blue light, the concrete walls and floor looked strangely like steel.

"Here?" Ellie asked.

"No. Here he kept files of photographs and videotapes."

"Not . . ."

"Yes. Of them . . . of the way they died. Of what he did to them, step by step."

"Dear God."

Spencer moved around the cellar, seeing it as he had seen it on that night of the red door. "The files and a compact photographer's development lab were behind a black curtain at that end of the room. There was a TV set on a plain black metal stand. And a VCR. Facing the television was a single chair. Right here. Not comfortable. All straight lines, wood, painted sour-apple green, unpadded. And a small round table stood beside the chair, where he could put a glass of whatever he was drinking. Table was painted purple. The chair was a flat green, but the table was glossy, highly lacquered. The glass that he drank from was actually a piece of fine cut-crystal, and the blue light sparkled in all its bevels."

"Where did he . . ." Ellie spotted the door, which was flush with the wall and painted to match. It reflected the blue light precisely as the concrete reflected it, becoming all but invisible. "There?"

"Yes." His voice was even softer and more distant than the cry that had awakened him from July sleep.

Half a minute didn't so much pass as crumble away like unstable ground beneath him.

Ellie came to his side. She took his right hand and held it tightly. "Let's do what you've come to do, then get the hell out of this place."

He nodded. He didn't trust himself to speak.

He let go of her hand and opened the heavy gray door. There was no lock on their side of it, only on the far side.

That July night, when Spencer had reached this point, his father had not yet returned from chaining the woman in the abattoir, so the door had been unlocked. No doubt, once the victim had been secured, the artist would have retraced his path to the vestibule above, to close the knotty-pine doors from within the cabinet; then from the secret vestibule, he would have rolled the back of the cupboard into place; he would have locked the upper door from the cellar stairs, would have locked this gray door from inside. Then he would have returned to his captive in the abattoir, confident that no screams, regardless of how piercing, could penetrate to the barn above or to the world beyond.

Spencer crossed the raised concrete sill. An exposed switch box was fixed to the rough masonry of a brick-and-plaster wall. A length of flexible metal conduit rose from it into shadows. He snapped the switch, and a series of small lights winked on. They were suspended from a looped cord along the center of the ceiling, leading out of sight around a curved passageway.

Ellie whispered, "*Spencer, wait!*"

When he looked back into the first basement, he saw that Rocky had returned to the foot of the stairs. The dog trembled visibly, gazing up toward the vestibule behind the file-room cupboards. One ear drooped, as always, but the other stood straight up. His tail was not tucked between his legs, but held low to the floor, and it wasn't wagging.

Spencer stepped back into the cellar. He pulled the pistol from under his belt.

Shrugging the Micro Uzi off her shoulder, taking a two-hand grip on the weapon, Ellie eased past the dog, onto the steep stairs. She climbed slowly, listening.

Spencer moved with equal care to Rocky's side.

$\wp$

In the vestibule, the artist had stood to the side of the open door, and Roy had stood next to him, both with their backs pressed to the wall, listening to the couple in the cellar below. The stairwell added a hollow note to the voices as it funneled them upward, but the words were nonetheless clear.

Roy had hoped to hear something that would explain the man's connection with the woman, at least a crumb of information about the suspected conspiracy against the agency and the shadowy organization that he had mentioned to Steven in the gallery a few minutes ago. But they spoke only of the famous night sixteen years in the past.

Steven seemed amused to be eavesdropping on that of all possible conversations. He turned his head twice to smile at Roy, and once he raised one finger to his lips as if warning Roy to be quiet.

There was something of an imp in the artist, a playfulness that made him a good companion. Roy wished he didn't have to return Steven to prison. But he could think of no way, in the currently delicate political climate of the country, to free the artist either openly or clandestinely. Dr. Sabrina Palma would again have her benefactor. The best Roy could hope for was that he would find other credible reasons to visit Steven from time to time or even to obtain temporary custody again for consultation in other field operations.

When the woman had whispered urgently to Grant—"*Spencer, wait!*"—Roy had known that the dog must have sensed their presence. They had made no telltale noise, so it could only be the damned dog.

Roy considered easing past the artist to the edge of the open door. He could try a shot to the head of the first person who came out of the stairwell.

But it might be Grant. He didn't want to waste Grant until he had some answers from him. And if it was the woman who was shot dead on the spot, Steven wouldn't be as motivated to help extract information from his son as he would be if he knew that he could look forward to bringing her to a state of angelic beauty.

Peach in. Green out.

Worse: Assuming that the pair below were still armed with the submachine gun they had used to destroy the stabilizer of the chopper in Cedar City, and assuming that the first one across the threshold would be armed with that piece, the risk of a confrontation at this juncture was too great. If Roy missed with his attempted head shot, the burst of return fire from the Micro Uzi would chop him and Steven to pieces.

Discretion seemed wise.

Roy touched the artist on the shoulder and gestured for him to follow. They could not quickly reach the open back of the cupboard and then slip through the pine cabinet doors into the room beyond, because to get there they would have to cross in front of the cellar stairs. Even if neither of the pair below was far enough up the stairs to see them, their passage through the center of the room, directly under the yellow light, would ensure that their darting shadows betrayed them. Instead, staying flat against the concrete blocks to avoid casting shadows into the room, they sidled away from the door to the wall directly opposite the entrance from the cupboard. They squeezed into the narrow space behind the displaced back wall of the cupboard, which Grant or the woman had rolled into the vestibule on a set of sliding-door tracks. That movable section was seven feet high and more than four feet wide. There was an eighteen-inch-wide hiding space between it and the concrete wall. Standing at an angle between them and the cellar door, it provided just enough cover.

If Grant or the woman or both of them came into the vestibule and crept to the gaping hole in the back wall of the cupboard, Roy could lean out from concealment and shoot one or both of them in the back, disabling rather than killing them.

If they came instead to look into the narrow space behind the dislocated guts of the cabinet, he would still have to try for a head shot before they opened fire.

Peach in. Green out.

He listened intently. Pistol in his right hand. Muzzle aimed at the ceiling.

He heard the stealthy scrape of a shoe on concrete. Someone had reached the top of the stairs.

∽

Spencer remained at the bottom of the stairs. He wished that Ellie had given him a chance to go up there in her place.

Three steps from the top, she paused for perhaps half a minute, listening, then proceeded to the landing at the head of the stairs. She stood for a moment, silhouetted in the rectangle of yellow light from the upper room, framed in the blue light of the lower room, like a stark figure in a modernistic painting.

Spencer realized that Rocky had lost interest in the room above and had slipped away from his side. The dog was at the other side of the cellar, at the open gray door.

Above, Ellie crossed the threshold and stopped just inside the vestibule. She looked left and right, listening.

In the cellar, Spencer glanced at Rocky again. One ear pricked, head cocked, trembling, the dog peered warily into the passageway that led to the catacombs and on to the heart of the horror.

Speaking to Ellie, Spencer said, "Looks like fur face is just having a bad case of the heebie-jeebies."

From the vestibule, she glanced down at him.

Behind him, Rocky whined.

"Now he's at the other door, ready to make a puddle if I don't keep looking at him."

"Seems to be okay up here," she said, and she descended the stairs again.

"The whole place spooks him, that's all," Spencer said. "My friend here is easily frightened by most new places. This time, of course, it's with damned good reason."

He engaged the safety on the pistol and again tucked it under the waistband of his jeans.

"He's not the only one spooked," Ellie said, shouldering the Uzi. "Let's finish this."

Spencer crossed the threshold again, from the cellar into the world beyond. With each step forward, he moved backward in time.

∽

They left the VW Microbus on the street to which the man on the phone had directed Harris. Darius, Bonnie, and Martin walked with Harris, Jessica, and the girls across the adjacent park toward the beach a hundred and fifty yards away.

No one could be seen within the discs of light beneath the tall lampposts, but bursts of eerie laughter issued from the surrounding darkness. Above the rumble and slosh of the surf, Harris heard voices, fragmentary and strange, on all sides, near and far. A woman who sounded blitzed on something: "You're a real catman, baby, really a catman, you are." A man's high-pitched laughter trilled through the night, from a place far to the north of the unseen woman. To the south, another man, old by the sound of him, sobbed with grief. Yet another unspottable man, with a pure young voice, kept repeating the same three words, as if chanting a mantra: "Eyes in tongues, eyes in tongues, eyes in tongues . . ." It seemed to Harris that he was shepherding his family across an open-air Bedlam, through a madhouse with no roof other than palm fronds and night sky.

Homeless winos and crackheads lived in some of the lusher stands of shrubbery, in concealed cardboard boxes insulated with newspapers and old blankets. In the sunlight, the beach crowd moved in and the day was filled with well-tanned skaters and surfers and seekers of false dreams. Then the true residents wandered to the streets to make the rounds of trash bins, to panhandle, and to shamble on quests that only they could understand. But at night, the park belonged to them again, and the green lawns and the benches and the handball courts were as dangerous as any places on earth. In darkness, the deranged souls then ventured forth from the undergrowth to prey on one another. They were likely to prey, as well, on unwary visitors who incorrectly assumed that a park was public domain at any hour of the day.

It was no place for women and girls—unsafe for armed men, in fact—but it was the only quick route to the sand and to the foot of the old pier. At the pier stairs, they were to be met by someone who would take them on from there to the new life that they were so blindly embracing.

They had expected to wait. But even as they approached the dark structure, a man walked out of the shadows between those pilings that were still above the tide line. He joined them at the foot of the stairs.

Even with no lamppost nearby, with only the ambient light of the great city that hugged the shoreline, Harris recognized the man who had come for them. It was the Asian in the reindeer sweater, whom he had first encountered in the theater men's room in Westwood earlier in the evening.

"Pheasants and dragons," the man said, as though he was not sure that Harris could tell one Asian from another.

"Yes, I know you," Harris said.

"You were told to come alone," the contact admonished, but not angrily.

"We wanted to say good-bye," Darius told him. "And we didn't know . . . We wanted to know—how will we contact them where they're going?"

"You won't," said the man in the reindeer sweater. "Hard as it may be, you've got to accept that you will probably never see them again."

In the Microbus, both before Harris had made the phone call from the pizza parlor and after, as they had found their way to the park, they had discussed the likelihood of a permanent separation. For a moment, no one could speak. They stared at one another, in a state of denial that approached paralysis.

The man in the reindeer sweater backed off a few yards to give them privacy, but he said, "We have little time."

Although Harris had lost his house, his bank accounts, his job, and everything but the clothes on his back, those losses now seemed inconsequential. Property rights, he had learned from bitter experience, were the essence of all civil rights, but the theft of every dime of his property did not have one tenth—not one *hundredth*—the impact of losing these beloved people. The theft of their home and savings was a blow, but this loss was an inner wound, as if a piece of his heart had been cut out. The pain was of an immeasurably greater magnitude and of a quality inexpressible.

They said good-bye with fewer words than Harris would ever have imagined possible—because no words were adequate. They hugged one another fiercely, acknowledging that they were most likely parting until they met again on whatever shore lay beyond the grave. Their mother had believed in that far and better shore. Since childhood they had drifted away from the belief that she had instilled in them, but they were for this terrible moment, in this place, fully in the faith again. Harris held Bonnie tightly, then Martin, and came at last to his brother, who was separating tearfully from Jessica. He hugged Darius and kissed his cheek. He had not kissed his brother for more years than he could recall, because for so long they had both been too adult for that. Now he wondered at the silly rules that had constituted his sense of mature behavior, for in a single kiss, all was said that needed to be said.

The incoming waves crashed through the pier pilings behind them with a roar hardly louder than the pounding of Harris's own heart, as at last he stepped back from Darius. Wishing there were more light in the gloom, he studied his brother's face for the last time in this life, desperate to freeze it in memory, for he was leaving without even a photograph.

"Must go," said the man in the reindeer sweater.

"Maybe everything won't fall over the brink," Darius said.

"We can hope."

"Maybe the world will come to its senses."

"You be careful going back through that park," Harris said.

"We're safe," Darius said. "Nobody back there's more dangerous than me. I'm an attorney, remember?"

Harris's laugh was perilously close to a sob.

Instead of good-bye, he simply said, "Little brother."

Darius nodded. For a moment it seemed that he wouldn't be able to say anything more. But then: "Big brother."

Jessica and Bonnie turned away from each other, both of them with Kleenex pressed to their eyes.

The girls and Martin parted.

The man in the reindeer sweater led one Descoteaux family south along the beach while the other Descoteaux family stood by the foot of the pier, watching. The sward was as pale as a path in a dream. The phosphorescent foam from the breakers dissolved on the sand with a whispery sizzle like urgent voices delivering incomprehensible warnings from out of the shadows in a nightmare.

Three times, Harris glanced at the other Descoteaux family over his shoulder, but then he could not bear to look back again.

They continued south on the beach, even after they reached the end of the park. They passed a few restaurants, all closed on that Monday night, then a hotel, a few condominiums, and warmly lighted beachfront houses in which lives were still lived without awareness of the hovering darkness.

After a mile and a half, perhaps even two miles, they came to another restaurant. Lights were on in that establishment, but the big windows were too high above the beach for Harris to see any diners at the view tables. The man in the reindeer sweater led them off the sward, alongside the restaurant, into the parking lot in front of the place. They went to a green-and-white motor home that dwarfed the cars around it.

"Why couldn't my brother have brought us directly here?" Harris asked.

Their escort said, "It wouldn't be a good idea for him to know this vehicle or its license number. For his own sake."

They followed the stranger into the motor home through a side door, just aft of the open cockpit, and into the kitchen. He stepped aside and directed them farther back into the vehicle.

An Asian woman in her early or middle fifties, in a black pants suit and a Chinese-red blouse, was standing at the dining table, beyond the kitchen, waiting for them. Her face was uncommonly gentle, and her smile was warm.

"So pleased that you could come," she said, as if they were paying her a social visit. "The dining nook seats seven altogether, plenty of room for the five of us. We'll be able to talk on the way, and we've so much to discuss."

They slid around the horseshoe-shaped booth, until the five of them encircled the table.

The man in the reindeer sweater had gotten behind the steering wheel. He started the engine.

"You may call me Mary," said the Asian woman, "because it's best that you don't know my name."

Harris considered keeping his silence, but he had no talent for deception. "I'm afraid that I recognize you, and I'm sure that my wife does as well."

"Yes," Jessica confirmed.

"We've eaten in your restaurant several times," Harris said, "up in West Hollywood. On most of those occasions, either you or your husband was greeting guests at the front door."

She nodded and smiled. "I'm flattered that you would recognize me out of . . . shall we say, out of context."

"You and your husband are so charming," Jessica said. "Not easy to forget."

"How was dinner when you had it with us?"

"Always wonderful."

"Thank you. So kind of you to say so. We do try. But now I haven't had the pleasure of meeting your lovely daughters," said the restaurateur, "although I know their names." She reached across the table to take each girl's hand. "Ondine, Willa, my name is Mae Lee. It's a pleasure to meet you both, and I want you to be unafraid. You are in good hands now."

The motor home pulled out of the restaurant parking lot, into the street, and away.

"Where are we going?" Willa asked.

"First, out of California," said Mae Lee. "To Las Vegas. Many motor homes crowd the highway between here and Vegas. We're just one more. At that point, I leave you, and you go on with someone else. Your father's picture will be all over the news for a time, and while they're telling their lies about him, you will all be in a safe and quiet place. You will change your looks as much as possible and learn what you will be able to do to help others like yourselves. You will have new names, first and middle and last. New hairstyles. Mr. Descoteaux, you might grow a beard, and you will certainly work with a good voice coach to lose your Caribbean accent, pleasant as it is to the ear. Oh, there will be many changes, and more fun than you imagine there could be now. And meaningful work. The world has not ended, Ondine. It has not ended, Willa. It's only passing through one edge of a dark cloud. There are things to be done to be sure that the cloud does not swallow us entirely. Which, I promise you, it will not. Now, before we begin, may I serve anyone tea, coffee, wine, beer, or a soft drink perhaps?"

∽

. . . bare-chested and barefoot, colder even than I was in the hot July night, I stand in the room of blue light, past the green chair and purple table, before the open door, determined to abandon this strange quest and race back up into the summer night, where a boy might become a boy again, where the truth which I don't know that I know can remain unknown forever.

Between one blink and another, however, as though transported by the power of a magical incantation, I've left the blue room and have arrived in what must be the basement of an earlier barn that stood on a site adjacent to that which the current barn occupies. While the old barn aboveground was torn down and the land was smoothed over and planted with grass, the cellars were left intact and were connected to the deepest chamber of the new barn.

I'm again being drawn forward against my will. Or think that I am. But although I shudder in fear of some dark force that draws me, it's my own deeper need to know, my true will, that draws me. I've repressed it since the night my mother died.

I'm in a curving corridor, six feet wide. A looping electrical cord runs along the center of the rounded ceiling. Low-wattage bulbs, like those on a Christmas tree, are spaced a foot apart. The walls are rough red-black brick, sloppily mortared. The bricks are overlaid in places with patches and veins of stained white plaster as smooth and greasy as the marbling fat in a slab of meat.

I pause in the curved passage, listening to my rampaging heart, listening to the unseen rooms ahead for a clue as to what might lie in wait for me, listening to the rooms behind for a voice to call me back to the safe world above. But there's no sound ahead or behind, only my heart, and even though I don't want to listen to the things it tells me, I sense that my heart has all the answers. In my heart I know that the truth about my precious mother lies ahead and that what lies behind is a world which will never be the same for me again, a world which changed forever and for the worse when I walked out of it.

The floor is stone. It might as well be ice beneath my feet. It slopes steeply but in a wide loop that would make it possible to push a wheelbarrow up without becoming exhausted or roll one down without losing control of it.

Across that icy stone, I walk barefoot and afraid, around the curve and into a room that's thirty feet long and twelve wide. The floor is flat here, the descent complete. A low, flat ceiling. The frosted-white, low-wattage Christmas bulbs on the looping cord continue to provide the only light. This might have been a fruit cellar in the days before electrical service was brought to the ranch, stacked full of August potatoes and September apples, deep enough to be cool in summer and above freezing in winter. There might have been shelves of home-canned fruits and vegetables stored here as well, enough to last three seasons, although the shelves are long gone.

Whatever the room might once have been, it is something very different now, and I am suddenly frozen to the floor, unable to move. One entire long wall and half the other are occupied by tableaux of life-size human figures carved in white plaster and surrounded by plaster, forming out of a plaster background, as if trying to force their way out of the wall. Grown women but also girls as young as ten or twelve. Twenty, thirty, maybe even forty of them. All naked. Some in their own niches, others in groups of two and three, face beside face, here and there with arms overlapping. He has mockingly arranged a few so they are holding hands for comfort in their terror. Their expressions are unbearable to look upon. Screaming, pleading, agonized, wrenched and suffering, warped by fear beyond measure and by unimaginable pain. Without exception, their bodies are humbled. Often their hands are raised defensively or extended beseechingly or crossed over breasts, over genitals. Here a woman peers between the spread fingers of hands that she's clasped defensively across her face. Imploring, praying, they *would be a horror unendurable if they were only what they seem to be at first glance, only sculpture, only the twisted expression of a deranged mind. But they're worse, and even in the cloistering shadows, their blank white stares transfix me, freeze me to the stone floor. The face of the Medusa was so hideous it transformed those who saw it to stone, but these faces aren't like that. These are petrifying because they are all women who might have been mothers like my mother, young girls who might have been my sisters if I'd been fortunate enough to have sisters, all people who were loved by someone and who loved, who had felt the sun on their faces and the coolness of rain, who'd laughed and dreamed of the future and worried and hoped. They turn me to stone because of the common humanity that I share with them, because I can feel their terror and be moved by it. Their tortured expressions are so poignant that their pain is my pain, their deaths my death. And their sense of being abandoned and fearfully alone in their final hours is the abandonment and isolation that I feel now.*

The sight of them is unendurable. Yet I'm compelled to look, because even though I am only fourteen, only fourteen, I know that what they've suffered demands witnessing and pity and anger, these mothers who might have been mine, these sisters who might have been my sisters, these victims like me.

The medium appears to be molded, sculpted plaster. But the plaster is only the preserving material that records their tormented expressions and beseeching postures—which aren't their true postures and expressions at death but cruel arrangements he made after. Even in the merciful shadows and cold arcs of frosty light, I see places where the plaster has been discolored by unthinkable substances seeping from within: gray and rust and yellowish green, a biological patina by which it's possible to date the figures in the tableaux.

The smell is indescribable, less because of its vileness than because of its complexity, though it is repulsive enough to make me ill. Later, it became known that he had used a sorcerer's brew of chemicals in an attempt to preserve the bodies within the plaster sarcophaguses. To a considerable extent he had been successful, though some decomposition occurred. The underlying stink is that of the world below cemetery lawns. The ghastliness of caskets long after living people have looked into them and closed the lids. But it is masked by scents as pungent as that of ammonia and as fresh as that of lemons. It is bitter and sour and sweet—and so strange that the cloying stench alone, without the ghostly figures, could make my heart pound and my blood run as icy as January rivers.

In the unfinished wall, there's a niche already prepared for a new body. He has chiseled out the bricks and stacked them to one side of the hole. He has scooped out a cavity in the earth beyond the wall and has carried that soil away. Lined up near the cavity are fifty-pound bags of dry plaster mix, a long wooden mixing trough lined with steel, two cans of tar-based sealant, both the tools of a mason and those of a sculptor, a stack of wooden pegs, coils of wire, and other items that I can't quite see.

He is ready. He needs only the woman who will become the next figure in the tableau. But he has her too, of course, for it is she who lost control of her bladder in the back of the rainbow van. Her hands have made the flock of bloody birds across the vestibule door.

Something moves, quick and furtive, out of the new hole in the wall, among the tools and supplies, through shadows and patches of light as pale as snow. It freezes at the sight of me as I have frozen before the martyred women in the walls. It's a rat, but no rat like any other. Its skull is deformed, one eye lower than the other, mouth twisted in a permanent lopsided grin. Another scurries after the first and also goes rigid when it sees me, though not before it rises on hind feet. It too is a creature like no other, encumbered by strange excrescences of bone or cartilage different from anything the first rat exhibits, and with a nose that spreads too wide across its narrow face. These are members of the small family of vermin that survives within the catacombs, tunneling behind the tableaux, nourished in part on that which has been saturated with toxic chemical preservatives. Each year a new generation of their kind produces more mutant forms than was produced the year before. Now they break their paralysis, as I can't yet break mine, and they scurry back into the hole from which they came.

Sixteen years later, that long chamber was not entirely as it had been on the night of owls and rats. The plaster had been torn down and hauled away. The victims had been removed from the niches in the walls. Between the columns of red-black brick that Spencer's father had left as supports, the dark earth was exposed. Police and forensic pathologists, who labored for weeks within that room, had added vertical four-by-four beams between some brick columns, as if they hadn't trusted solely to the supports that Steven Ackblom had thought sufficient.

The cool, dry air now smelled faintly of stone and earth, but it was a clean smell. The pungent miasma of chemicals and the stink of biological decay were gone.

Standing in that low-ceilinged space again, with Ellie and the dog, Spencer vividly recalled the fright that had nearly crippled him when he was fourteen. However, fear was the least of what he felt—which surprised him. Horror and disgust were part of it, but not as great as a diamond-hard anger. Sorrow for the dead. Compassion for those who had loved them. Guilt for having failed to save anyone.

He knew regret, as well, for the life he might have had but had never known. And now never could.

Above all, what overcame him was an unexpected reverence, as he might have felt at any place where the innocent had perished: from Calvary to Dachau, to Babi Yar, to the unnamed fields where Stalin buried millions, to rooms where Jeffrey Dahmer dwelt, to the torture chambers of the Inquisition.

The soil of any killing ground isn't sanctified by the murderers who practice there. Though they often think themselves exalted, they are as the maggots that live in dung, and no maggots can transform one square centimeter of earth into holy ground.

Sacred, instead, are the victims, for each dies in the place of someone whom fate allows to live. And though many may unwittingly or unwillingly die in the place of others, the sacrifice is no less sacred for the fact that fate chose those who would make it.

If there had been votive candles in those cleansed catacombs, Spencer would have wanted to light them and gaze into their flames until they blinded him. Had there been an altar, he would have prayed at the foot of it. If by offering his own life he could have brought back the forty-one and his mother, or any one of them, he would not have hesitated to rid himself of this world in hope of waking in another.

All he could do, however, was quietly honor the dead by never forgetting the details of their final passage through this place. His duty was to be witness. By shunning memory, he would dishonor those who had died here in his place. The price of forgetfulness would be his soul.

Describing those catacombs as they had been in that long-ago time, coming at last to the woman's cry that had roused him from his paralytic terror, he was suddenly unable to go on. He continued to speak, or thought he did, but then he realized that no more words would come. His mouth worked, but his voice was only a silence that he cast into the silence of the room.

Finally a thin, high, brief, childlike cry of anguish came from him. It was not unlike the one cry that had jolted him from his bed on that July night or the one that, later, had broken his paralysis. He buried his face in his hands and stood, shaking with grief too intense for tears or sobbing, waiting for the seizure to pass.

Ellie was aware that no word or touch could console him.

In glorious canine innocence, Rocky believed any sadness could be relieved by a wagging tail, a cuddle, an affectionate warm lick. He rubbed his flank against his master's legs and swished his tail—and padded away in confusion when none of his tricks worked.

Spencer found himself speaking again almost as unexpectedly as he had found himself *unable* to speak a minute or two ago. "I heard the woman's cry again. From down there at the end of the catacombs. Hardly loud enough to be a scream. More a wail to God."

He started toward the last door, at the end of the catacombs. Ellie and Rocky stayed with him.

"Even as I moved past the dead women in these walls, I was remembering something from six years before, when I'd been eight years old—another cry. My mother's. That spring night, I woke hungry, got out of bed for a snack. There were fresh chocolate-chip cookies in the kitchen jar. I'd been dreaming about them. Went downstairs. The lights were on in some rooms. I thought I'd find my mom or dad along the way. But I didn't see them."

Spencer stopped at the painted black door at the end of the catacombs. Catacombs they were and always would be to him, even with the bodies all disinterred and taken away.

Ellie and Rocky stopped at his side.

"The kitchen was dark. I was going to take as many cookies as I could carry, more than I would ever be allowed to have at one time. I was opening the jar when I heard a scream. Outside. Behind the house. Went to the window by the table. Parted the curtain. My mom was on the lawn. Running back to the house from the barn. He . . . he was behind her. He caught her on the patio. Beside the pool. Swung her around. Hit her. In the face. She screamed again. He hit her. Hit and hit. And again. So fast. My mom. Hitting her with his fist. She fell. He kicked her in the head. He kicked my mom in the head. She was quiet. So fast. All over so fast. He looked toward the house. He couldn't see me in the dark kitchen, at the narrow gap in the curtains. He picked her up. Carried her to the barn. I stood at the window awhile. Then I put the cookies back in the jar. Put the lid on. Went back upstairs. Got into bed. Pulled up the covers."

"And didn't remember any of it for six years?" Ellie asked.

Spencer shook his head. "Buried it. That's why I couldn't sleep with the air conditioner running. Deep down where I didn't realize it, I was afraid he would come for me in the night, and I wouldn't hear him because of the air conditioner."

"And then that night, all those years later, your window open, another cry—"

"It reached me deeper than I could understand, drew me out of bed, out to the barn, down here. And when I was walking toward this black door, toward the scream . . ."

Ellie reached to the lever-action knob on the door, to open it, but he stayed her hand.

"Not yet," he said. "I'm not ready to go in there again yet."

. . . barefoot on icy stone, I approach the black door, filled with the fear of what I have seen tonight but also with the fear of what I saw on that spring night

when I was eight, which has been repressed since then but all at once comes bursting up from within me. I'm in a state beyond mere terror. No word is adequate for what I feel. I'm at the black door, touching the black door, so black, glossy, like a moonless night sky reflected in the blind face of a pond. I'm nearly as confused as I am terrified, for it seems to me that I'm both eight and fourteen, that I'm opening the door to save not merely the woman who made bloody birds on the vestibule door but to save my mother as well. Time past and time present melt together, and all is one, and I enter the slaughterhouse.

I step into deep space, infinite night around me. The ceiling is ink-black to match the walls, the walls to match the floor, the floor like a chute to Hell. A naked woman, half conscious, lips split and bleeding, rolling her head in listless denial, is manacled to a burnished-steel slab, which seems to float in blackness because its supports also are black. A single light. Directly over the table. In a black fixture. It floats in the void, pin-spotting the steel, like a celestial object or the cruel beam of a godlike inquisitor. My father's wearing black. Only his face and hands are visible, as if severed but alive in their own right, as if he's an apparition struggling toward completion. He's extracting a gleaming hypodermic syringe from thin air—actually from a drawer beneath the steel slab, a drawer invisible in its blackness-upon-blackness.

I shout, "No, no, no," as I plunge at him, surprising him, so the syringe drops back into the thin air from which it came, and I drive him backward, backward, past the table, out of the focused light, into blackest infinity, until we crash into the wall at the end of the universe. I'm screaming, punching, but I'm fourteen and slender, and he's in his prime, muscular, powerful. I kick him, but I'm barefoot. He lifts me effortlessly, turns with me, floating in space, slams me back-first into the hard blackness, knocking the wind out of me, slams me again. Pain along my spine. Another blackness rises inside me, deeper than the abyss all around. But the woman cries out again, and her voice helps me resist the inner darkness, even if I can't resist my father's far greater strength.

Then he presses me to the wall with his body, holding me off the floor with his hands, his face looming before mine, locks of black hair falling across his forehead, eyes so dark that they seem to be holes through which I'm seeing the blackness behind him. "Don't be afraid, don't, don't be afraid, boy. Baby boy, I won't hurt you. You're my blood, my seed, my creation, my baby. I'd never hurt you. Okay? You understand? You hear me, son, sweet boy, my sweet little Mikey, you hear me? I'm glad you're here. It had to happen sooner or later. Sooner the better. Sweet boy, my boy. I know why you're here, I know why you've come."

I'm dazed and disoriented because of the perfect blackness of that room, because of the horrors in the catacombs, because of being lifted bodily and pounded against the wall. In my condition, his voice is as lulling as fearsome, strangely seductive, and I'm nearly convinced he won't harm me. Somehow I must have misunderstood the things I've seen. He continues speaking in that hypnotic way, words pouring out, giving me no chance to think, Jesus, my mind spinning, him pressing me to the wall, face like a great moon over me.

"I know why you've come. I know what you are. I know why you're here. You're my blood, my seed, my son, no different from me than my reflection in a mirror. Do you hear me, Mikey, sweet baby boy, hear me? I know what you are, why you've come, why you're here, what you need. What you need. I know, I know. You know it too. You knew it when you came through the door and saw her on the table, saw her breasts, saw between her spread legs. You knew, oh, yes, oh, you knew, you wanted it, you knew, you knew what you wanted, what you need, what you are. And it's all right, Mikey, it's all right, baby boy. It's all right what you are, what I am. It's how we were born, each of us, it's what we were meant to be."

Then we're standing at the table, and I'm not sure how we got there, the woman lying in front of me and my father pressing against my back, pinning me to the table. He has a vicious grip on my right wrist, pushes my hand onto her breasts, slides it along her naked body. She's half conscious. Opens her eyes. I'm staring into her eyes, begging her to understand, as he forces my hand everywhere, all the time talking, talking, telling me that I can do anything to her I want, it's right, it's what I was born to do, she's only here to be what I need her to be.

I come far enough out of a daze to struggle briefly, fiercely. Too brief, not fierce enough. His arm's around my throat, choking me, jamming me against the table with his body, choking with his left arm, choking, the taste of blood in my mouth, until I'm weak again. He knows when to release the pressure, before I pass out, because he doesn't want me to pass out. He has other plans. I sag against him, crying now, tears dropping onto the bare skin of the manacled woman.

He lets go of my right hand. I hardly have strength to lift it from the woman. Clink and rattle. Down at my side. I look. One of his disembodied hands. Sorting through the silvery instruments that are floating in the void. He plucks a scalpel from the weightless array of clamps and forceps and needles and blades. Seizes my hand, presses the scalpel into it, folds his hand over mine, grinding my knuckles, forcing me to grip the blade. Below us the woman sees our hands and the shining steel, and she begs us not to hurt her.

"I know what you are," he says, "I know what you are, sweet boy, my baby boy. Just be what you are, just let go and be what you are. You think she's beautiful now? You think she's the most beautiful thing you've ever seen? Oh, just wait until we've shown her how to be more beautiful. Let Daddy show you what you are, what you need, what you like. Let me show you what fun it is to be what you are. Listen, Mikey, listen now, the same dark river runs through your heart and mine. Listen, and you can hear it, that deep dark river, roaring along, swift and powerful, roaring along. With me now, with me, just let the river carry you

along. Be with me now and lift the blade high. See how it shines? Let her see it, see how she sees it, how she has eyes for nothing else. Shining and high in your hand and mine. Feel the power we have over her, over all the weak and foolish ones who can never understand. Be with me, lift it high—"

He has one arm loosely around my throat, my right hand gripped by his, so my left arm is free. Instead of reaching back for him or trying to jam my elbow into him, which won't work, I plant my hand against the stainless steel. Unendurable horror and desperation empower me. With that hand and my whole body, I shove away from the table. Then with my legs. Then my feet. Kicking against the table with both feet. Raging backward into the bastard, unbalancing him. He stumbles, still grinding the hand in which I've got the scalpel, trying to tighten the arm at my throat. But then he falls backward, me atop him. The scalpel clinks away in darkness. My falling weight drives the breath out of him. I'm free. Free. Scramble across the black floor. The door. My right hand aching. No hope of helping the woman. But I can bring help. Police. Someone. She can still be saved. Through the door, onto my feet, tottering, flailing to keep my balance, out into the catacombs, running, running past all the frozen white women, trying to shout. Throat bleeding inside. Raw and raspy. Voice a whisper. No one on the ranch to hear me anyway. Just me, him, the naked woman. But I'm running, running, screaming in a whisper when there's no one to hear.

The expression on Ellie's face cut through Spencer's heart.

He said, "I shouldn't have brought you here, shouldn't have put you through this."

She was gray in the light of the frost-white bulbs. "No, it's what you had to do. If I had any doubts, I have none now. You can't have gone on forever . . . with all of this."

"But that's what I'll have to do. Go on forever with it. And I don't know now why I thought I could find a life. I don't have any right to make you carry this weight with me."

"You can go on with it and have a life . . . as long as you remember it all. And I think now I know what it is you can't remember, where those lost minutes come in."

Spencer couldn't bear to meet her eyes. He looked at Rocky, where the dog sat in deep despondency: head lowered, ears drooping, shivering.

Then he turned his eyes to the black door. Whatever he found beyond it would decide whether he had a future with or without Ellie. He might have neither.

"I didn't try to run back to the house," he said, returning in his mind to that distant night. "He would have caught me before I'd gotten there, before I could use a telephone. Instead, I went up to the vestibule, out of the cupboard, through the file room, and turned right toward the front of the building, into the gallery. By the time I was on the stairs to his studio, I could hear him coming through the darkness behind me. I knew he kept a gun in the lower left-hand drawer of his desk. I'd seen it once when he'd sent me there to get something. Entering the studio, I hit the light switch, ran past his easels, supply cabinets, to the far corner. The desk was L-shaped. I vaulted over it, crashed into the chair, clawed at the drawer, got it open. The gun was there. I didn't know how to use it, whether it had a safety. My right hand was throbbing. I could hardly hold the damn thing, even in both hands. He was off the stairs, into the studio, coming for me, so I pointed and pulled the trigger. It was a revolver. No safety. The recoil about knocked me on my ass."

"And you shot him."

"Not yet. I must've pulled up hard on it when I squeezed the trigger, pulled off target, so the bullet took a chunk out of the ceiling. But I held on to the gun, and he stopped coming. At least he didn't come as fast, not pell-mell any more. But he was so calm, Ellie, so calm. As if nothing had happened, just my dad, good old dad, a little perturbed with me, you know, but telling me everything was going to be all right, romancing me with that sweet talk like in the black room. So sincere. So hypnotic. And so *sure* that he could make it work if I only gave him time."

Ellie said, "But he didn't know that you'd seen him beat your mother and carry her back to the barn six years before. He might have thought you would put together her death and his secret rooms when you came down from your panic—but until then he thought he had time to bring you around."

Spencer stared at the black door.

"Yeah, maybe that's what he thought. I don't know. He told me that to be like him was to know what life was all about, the true fullness of life without limits or rules. He said I'd enjoy what he could show me how to do. He said I'd already started to enjoy it back in that black room, that I'd been afraid of enjoying it, but that I'd learn it was all right to have that kind of fun."

"But you didn't enjoy it. You were repulsed."

"He said that I did, that he could see I did. His genes ran through me like a river, he said again, through my heart just like a river. Our shared river of destiny, the dark river of our hearts. When he got to the desk, so close I couldn't miss again, I shot him. He *flew* backward from the impact. The spray of blood was horrible. It seemed for sure that I'd killed him, but then I hadn't seen much blood until that night, and a little looked like a lot. He hit the floor, rolled facedown, and lay there, very still. I ran out of the studio, back down here. . . ."

The black door waited.

She didn't speak for a while. He couldn't.

Then Ellie said, "And in that room with the woman . . . those are the minutes you can't remember."

The door. He should have had the old cellars collapsed with explosives. Filled in with dirt. Sealed forever. He shouldn't have left that black door to be opened again.

"Coming back here," he said with difficulty, "I had to carry the revolver in my left hand because of how he'd clenched my right so hard in his, grinding my knuckles together. It was throbbing, full of pain. But the thing is . . . it wasn't just pain I felt in it."

He looked at that hand now. He could see it smaller, younger, the hand of a fourteen-year-old boy.

"I could still feel . . . the smoothness of the woman's skin, from when he'd forced my hand over her body. Feel the roundness of her breasts. The resiliency and fullness of them. The flatness of her belly. The crispness of pubic hair . . . the heat of her. All those feelings were in my hand, *still* in my hand, as real as the pain."

"You were only a boy," she said without any evidence of disgust. "It was the first time you'd ever seen a woman undressed, the first time you'd ever touched a woman. My God, Spencer, in supercharged circumstances like that, not just terrifying but so emotional in every way, so confusing, such a damned *primal* moment—touching her was bound to reach you on every level, all at the same time. Your father knew that. He was a clever sonofabitch. He tried to use your turmoil to manipulate you. But it didn't *mean* anything."

She was too understanding and forgiving. In this blighted world, those who were too forgiving paid a cruel price for a Christian bent.

"So, I came back through the catacombs, with the dead all around me in the walls, with the memory of my father's blood, and *still* with the feel of her breasts in my hand. The vivid memory of how rubbery her nipples had felt against my palm—"

"Don't do this to yourself."

"Never lie to the dog," Spencer said, with no humor this time, but with a bitterness and rage that frightened him.

A fury welled in his heart, blacker than the door before him. He was no more able to shake it off than he had been able, that July, to shake from his hand the remembered warmth and shapes and sensuous textures of the naked woman. His rage was undirected, and that was why it had been intensifying in his deep unconscious for sixteen years. He'd never been sure if it should be turned against his father or against himself. Lacking a target, he had denied the existence of that rage, repressed it. Now, condensed into a distillate of purest wrath, it was eating through him as corrosively as any acid.

". . . with the vivid memory of how her nipples had felt against my palm," he continued, but in a voice that shook equally with anger and with fear, "I came back here. To this door. Opened it. Went into the black room. . . . And the next thing I remember is walking *away* from here, the door falling shut behind me. . . ."

. . . barefoot, walking back through the catacombs, with a void in my memory more perfectly black than the room behind me, not sure where I've just been, what's just happened. Passing the women in the walls. Women. Girls. Mothers. Sisters. Their silent screams. Perpetual screams. Where is God? What does God care? Why has He abandoned them all here? Why has He abandoned me? A magnified spider shadow scurries across their plaster faces, along the looping shadow of the light cord. As I'm passing the new niche in the wall, the niche prepared for the woman in the black room, my father comes out of that hole, out of the dark earth, splattered with blood, staggering, wheezing in agony, but so fast, so fast, as fast as the spider. The hot flash of steel out of shadows. Knife. He sometimes paints still lifes of knives, making them glow as if they were holy relics. Flashing steel, flashing pain across my face. Drop the gun. Hands to my face. Flap of cheek hanging off my chin. My bare teeth against my fingers, a grin of teeth exposed along the whole side of my face. Tongue leaping against my fingers in the open side of my face. And he slashes again. Misses. Falls. He's too weak to get up. Backing away from him, I pull my cheek in place, blood streaming between my fingers, running down my throat. I'm trying to hold my face together. Oh, God, trying to hold my face together and running, running. Behind me, he's too weak to get off the floor but not too weak to call after me: "Did you kill her, did you kill her, baby boy, did you like it, did you kill her?"

Spencer still could not look directly at Ellie and might never be able to look directly at her again, not eye-to-eye. He could see her peripherally, and he knew that she was crying quietly. Crying for him, eyes flooded, face glistening.

He couldn't cry for himself. He had never been able to let go and fully purge his pain, because he didn't know if he was worthy of tears, of hers or his own or anyone's tears.

All he could feel now was that rage, which was still without a target.

"The police found the woman dead in the black room," he said.

"Spencer, *he* killed her." Her voice trembled. "It must have been him. The police said it was him. You were the boy hero."

Staring at the black door, he shook his head. "When did he kill her, Ellie? *When?* He dropped the scalpel when we both fell to the floor. Then I ran, and he ran after me."

"But there were other scalpels, other sharp instruments in the drawer. You said so yourself. He grabbed one and killed her. It would only have taken seconds. Only a few seconds, Spencer. The bastard knew you couldn't get far, that he'd catch up with you. And he was so *excited* after his struggle with you that he couldn't wait, *shaking* with excitement, so he had to kill her then, hard and fast and brutally."

"Later, he's on the floor, after he slashed me, and I'm running away, and he's calling after me, asking if I killed her, if I liked killing her."

"Oh, he knew. He *knew* she was dead before you ever came back here to free her. Maybe he was insane and maybe he wasn't, but he was sure as hell the purest evil that ever walked. Don't you see? He hadn't converted you to his way, and he hadn't been able to kill you, either, so all that was left for him was to ruin your life if he could, to plant that seed of doubt in your mind. You were a boy, half blind with panic and terror, confused, and he knew your turmoil. He understood, and he used it against you, just for the sheer, sick *fun* of it."

For more than half his lifetime, Spencer had tried to convince himself of the scenario that she had just painted for him. But the void in his memory remained. The continued amnesia seemed to argue that the truth was different from what he desperately wished had happened.

"Go," he said thickly. "Run for the truck, drive away from here, go to Denver. I shouldn't have brought you here. I can't ask you to come any farther with me."

"I'm here. I'm not leaving."

"I mean it. Get out."

"No way."

"Get out. Take the dog."

"No."

Rocky was whining, shaking, huddling against a column of blood-dark brick, in torment as racking as any Spencer had ever seen.

"Take him. He likes you."

"I'm not going." Through tears, she said, "This is *my* decision, damn it, and you can't make it for me!"

He turned on her, seized handfuls of her leather jacket, all but lifted her off the floor, frantically trying to force her to understand. In his rage and fear and self-loathing, he had managed, after all, to look her in the eyes one more time. "For Christ's sake, after all you've seen and heard, don't you get it? I left part of myself in that room, that abattoir where he did his butchering, left something there I couldn't live with. What in the name of God could that be, huh? Something *worse* than the catacombs, *worse* than all the rest of it. It has to be worse because I remembered all the rest of it! If I go back in there and remember what I did to her, there'll be no forgetting ever again, no hiding from it any more. And this is a memory . . . like fire. It's going to burn through me. Whatever's left, whatever isn't burned away, it won't be *me* any more, Ellie, not after I know what I did to her. And then who're you going to be down here with, down here in this godforsaken place *alone* with?"

She raised one hand to his face and traced the line of his scar, though he tried to flinch away from her. She said, "If I was blind, if I'd never seen your face, I already know you well enough that you could still break my heart."

"Oh, Ellie, don't."

"I'm not leaving."

"Ellie, please."

"No."

He couldn't direct his rage at her, either, especially not at her. He let go of her. Stood with his hands at his sides. Fourteen again. Weak with his outrage. Afraid. Lost.

She put her hand on the lever-action door handle.

"Wait." He withdrew the SIG 9mm pistol from under the waistband of his blue jeans, disengaged the safety, jacked a bullet into the chamber, and held the piece out to her. "You should have both guns." She started to object, but he cut her off. "Keep the pistol in your hand. Don't get too close to me in there."

"Spencer, whatever you remember, it's not going to turn you into your father, not in an instant, no matter how terrible it is."

"How do you know that? I've spent sixteen years picking at it, prying and poking, trying to dig it out of the darkness, but it won't come. Now if it comes . . ."

She engaged the safety on the pistol.

"Ellie—"

"I don't want it to go off accidentally."

"My father wrestled on the floor with me and tickled me and made funny faces for me when I was little. Played ball with me. And when I wanted to develop my drawing ability, he patiently taught technique to me. But before and after . . . he came down here, that same man, and he tortured women, girls, hour after hour, for days in some cases. He moved with ease between this world and the one above."

"I'm not going to keep a gun ready, point a gun at you, like I'm afraid you're some kind of monster, when I know you're not. Please, Spencer. Please don't ask me to do that. Let's just finish this."

In the deep quiet at the end of the catacombs, he took a moment to prepare himself. Nothing moved anywhere in that long room. No rats, misshapen or otherwise, dwelt there any more. The Dresmunds had been instructed to eradicate them with poison.

Spencer opened the black door.

He switched on the light.

He hesitated on the threshold, then went inside.

Miserable though the dog was, he padded into that room as well. Maybe he was afraid to be alone in the catacombs. Or maybe this time his misery *was* entirely a reaction to his master's state of mind, in which case he knew that his company was needed. He stayed close to Spencer.

Ellie entered last, and the weighted door closed behind her.

The abattoir was nearly as disorienting now as it had been on that night of scalpels and knives. The stainless steel table was gone. The chamber was empty. The unrelieved blackness allowed no point of reference, so one moment the room appeared to be hardly larger than a casket, but in the next moment it seemed infinitely larger than it actually was. The only light was still the tightly focused bulb in the black ceiling fixture.

The Dresmunds had been instructed to keep all lights functional. They had not been told to clean the abattoir, yet only the thinnest film of dust veiled the walls, no doubt because the room was not ventilated and was always shut up tight.

It was a time capsule, sealed for sixteen years, containing not the memorabilia of bygone days but lost memories.

The place affected Spencer even more powerfully than he had expected. He could see the glimmer of the scalpel as if it hung in the air even now.

. . . barefoot, carrying the revolver in my left hand, I hurry down from the studio where I shot my father, through the back of the cupboard into a world not anything like the one behind the wardrobe in those books by C. S. Lewis, through the catacombs, not daring to look left or right, because those dead women seem to be straining to break out of their plaster. I have the crazy fear that they might pull loose as if the plaster is still wet, come for me, take me into one of the walls with them. I'm my father's son and I deserve to choke on cold wet plaster, have it squeezed into my nostrils and poured down my throat, until I'm as one with the figures in the tableaux, unbreathing, a harbor for the rats. My heart's knocking so hard that each beat makes my vision darken slightly, briefly, as if the surges in blood pressure will burst vessels in my eyes. I feel each beat in my right hand too. The pain in my knuckles throbs, lub-dub, three small hearts in every finger. But I love the pain. I want more pain. Back in the vestibule and descending the stairs into the room of blue light, I repeatedly rapped the swollen knuckles of that

hand with the revolver that I held in the other. Now I rap them hard again in the catacombs, to drive out all feeling but pain. Because . . . because equal to the pain, dear Jesus God Almighty, I still have it on my hand, like a stain on my hand: the smoothness of the woman's skin. The full curves and warm resiliency of her breasts, turgid nipples rubbing my palm. The flatness of belly, the tautness of muscles as she strains against the manacles. The lubricious heat into which he forces my fingers against all my resistance, against her terrible half-dazed protest. Her eyes were locked with mine. Pleading with her eyes. The misery of her eyes. But the traitor hand has its own sense memory, unshakable, and it makes me sick. All the feelings in my hand make me sick, and some of the feelings in my heart. I have such disgust, loathing, such fear of myself. But other feelings too—unclean emotions in harmony with the excitement of the hateful hand. And at the door to the black room I stop, lean against the wall, and vomit. Sweating. Shuddering with chills. When I turn away from the mess, with only my stomach purged, I force myself to grab the lever-action handle with my injured hand, making pain shoot up my forearm as I violently jerk open the door. And then I'm inside, into the black room again.

Don't look at her. Don't. Don't! Don't look at her naked. No right to look at her naked. This can be done with my eyes averted, edging to the table, aware of her only as a flesh-colored form out of the corner of my eye, floating in the darkness over there. "It's okay," I tell her, my voice so hoarse from the choking, "it's okay, lady, he's dead, lady, I shot him. I'll let you loose, get you out of here, don't be afraid." And then I realize I haven't any idea where to find the keys to the manacles. "Lady, I don't have a key, no key, got to go for help, call the cops. But it's okay, he's dead." No sound from her there, out of the corner of my eye. She'd been dazed from the blows to her head, only half conscious, and now she's passed out. But I don't want her to wake up after I've gone and be alone and afraid. I remember the look in her eyes—was it the same look in my mother's eyes at the very end?—and I don't want her to be so afraid when she wakes and thinks he's coming back for her. That's all, that's all. I just don't want her to be afraid, so I'm going to have to bring her around, shake her, wake her up, make her understand that he's dead and that I'll be back with help. I edge to the table, trying not to look at her body, going to look only at her face. A smell hits me. Terrible. Nauseating. The blackness is dizzying again. I put one hand out. Against the table. To steady myself. It's the right hand, still remembering the curve of her breasts, and I put it down in a warm, viscous, slippery mass that wasn't there before. I look at her face. Mouth open. Eyes. Dead blank eyes. He's been at her. Two slashes. Vicious. Brutal. All of his great strength behind the blade. Her throat. Her abdomen. I spin away from the table, away from the woman, collide with the wall. Wiping my right hand on the black wall, calling for Jesus and for my mother, and saying "lady please lady please," as if she could mend herself by an act of will if only she'd listen to my pleas. Wiping wiping wiping the hand, front and back, on the wall, not only wiping off what I've pressed it into but wiping off the way she felt when she was alive, wiping hard, harder, angrily, furiously, until my hand seems on fire, until there's nothing in my hand but pain. And then I stand there awhile. Not quite sure where I am any longer. I know there's a door. I go to it. Through it. Oh, yes. The catacombs.

Spencer stood in the center of the black room, his right hand in front of his face, staring at it in the hard projected light, as though it was not at all the same hand that had been at the end of his wrist for the past sixteen years.

Almost wonderingly, he said, "I would've saved her."

"I know that," Ellie said.

"But I couldn't save anyone."

"And that's not your fault, either."

For the first time since that ancient July, he thought he might have the capacity to accept, not soon but eventually, that he had no greater weight of guilt to carry than any other man. Darker memories, a more intimate experience of the human capacity for evil, knowledge that other people would never want forced on them as it had been forced on him—all of that, yes, but not a greater weight of guilt.

Rocky barked. Twice. Loud.

Startled, Spencer said, "He never barks."

Slipping off the safety on the SIG, Ellie swung toward the door as it flew open. She wasn't quick enough.

The genial-looking man—the same who had broken into the Malibu cabin—burst into the black room. He had a silencer-fitted Beretta in his right hand, and he was smiling and squeezing off a shot as he came.

Ellie took the round in her right shoulder, squealed in pain. Her hand spasmed and released the pistol, and she was slammed into the wall. She sagged against the blackness, gasping with the shock of being shot, realized the Micro Uzi was sliding off her shoulder, and made a grab for it with her left hand. It slipped through her fingers, hit the floor, and spun away from her.

The pistol was gone, clattering beyond reach across the floor toward the man with the Beretta. But Spencer went for the Uzi even as it was falling.

The smiling man fired again. The bullet sparked off the stone inches from Spencer's reaching hand, forcing him to pull back, and it ricocheted around the room.

The shooter seemed unfazed by the whine of the bouncing slug, as if he led such a charmed life that his safety was a foregone conclusion.

"I'd prefer not to shoot you," he said. "I didn't want to shoot Ellie, either. I've other plans for both of you. But one more wrong move—and you'll take away all my choices. Now kick the Uzi over here."

Instead of doing what he had been told, Spencer went to Ellie. He touched her face and looked at her shoulder. "How bad?"

She was clutching her wound, trying not to reveal the extent of her pain, but the truth was in her eyes. "Okay, I'm okay, it's nothing," she said, yet Spencer saw her glance at the whimpering dog when she lied.

The heavy door to the abattoir hadn't fallen shut. Someone was holding it open. The shooter stepped aside to let him enter. The second man was Steven Ackblom.

◆

Roy was certain that this would be one of the most interesting nights of his life. It might even be as singular as the first night that he had spent with Eve, although he wouldn't betray her even by hoping that it might be better. This was an incredible confluence of events: the capture of the woman at last; the chance to learn what Grant might know about any organized opposition to the agency, then the pleasure of putting that troubled man out of his misery; a unique opportunity to be with one of the great artists of the century as he turned his hand to the medium that had made him famous; and when it was done, perhaps even Eleanor's perfect eyes would be salvageable. Cosmic forces were at work in the design of such a night.

When Steven entered the room, the expression on Spencer Grant's face was worth the loss of at least two helicopters and a satellite. Anger darkened his face, twisted his features. It was a rage so pure that it possessed a fascinating beauty all its own. Enraged, Grant nonetheless shrank back with the woman.

"Hello, Mikey," Steven said. "How've you been?"

The son—once Mikey, now Spencer—was unable to speak.

"I've been well but . . . in boring circumstances," said the artist.

Spencer Grant remained silent. Roy was chilled by the expression in the ex-cop's eyes.

Steven looked around at the black ceiling, walls, floor. "They blamed me for the woman you did here that night. I took the fall on that one too. For you, baby boy."

"He never touched her," Ellie Summerton said.

"Didn't he?" the artist asked.

"We know he didn't."

Steven sighed with regret. "Well, no, he didn't. But he was *that* close to doing her." He held up his thumb and forefinger, only a quarter of an inch apart. "That close."

"He was never close at all," she said, but Grant remained unable to speak.

"Wasn't he?" Steven said. "Well, I think he was. I think if I'd been a little smarter, if I'd encouraged him to drop his pants and climb on top of her first, then he would have been happy to take the scalpel afterward. He'd have been more in the spirit of things then, you see."

"You're not my father," Grant said emptily.

"You're wrong about that, my sweet boy. Your mother was a firm believer in marital vows. There was only ever me with her. I'm sure of that. In the end, here in this room, she was able to keep not the slightest secret from me."

Roy thought that Grant was going to come across the room with all the fury of a bull, heedless of bullets.

"What a pathetic little dog," Steven said. "Look at him shaking, hanging his head. Perfect pet for you, Mikey. He reminds me of the way you acted here that night. When I gave you the chance to transcend, you were too much of a pussy to seize it."

The woman appeared to be furious too, perhaps even angrier than she was afraid, though both. Her eyes had never been more beautiful.

"How long ago that was, Mikey, and what a new world this is," Steven said, taking a couple of steps toward his son and the woman, forcing them to shrink back farther. "I was so ahead of my time, so much deeper into the avant-garde than I ever fully realized. The newspapers called me insane. I ought to demand a retraction, don't you think? Now, the streets are crawling with men more violent than I ever was. Gangs have gunfights anywhere they please, and babies get shot down on kindergarten playgrounds—and nobody does anything about it. The enlightened are too busy worrying that you're going to eat a food additive that'll shave three and a half days off your lifespan. Did you read about the FBI agents up in Idaho, where they shot an unarmed woman while she was *holding* her baby, and shot her fourteen-year-old son in the back when he tried to run from them. Killed them both. You see that in the papers, Mikey? And now men like Roy here hold very responsible positions in government. Why, I could be a fabulously successful politician these days. I've got everything it takes. I'm not insane, Mikey. Daddy's not insane and never was. Evil, yes. I embrace that. From earliest childhood, I had it all in that regard. I've always liked to have fun. But I'm not crazy, baby boy. Roy here, guardian of public safety, protector of the republic—why, Mikey, *he's* a raving lunatic."

Roy smiled at Steven, wondering what joke he was setting up. The artist was endlessly amusing. But Steven had moved so far into the room that Roy couldn't see his face, only the back of his head.

"Mikey, you should hear Roy rant on about compassion, about the poor quality of life that so many people live and shouldn't have to, about reducing population by ninety percent to save the environment. He loves everybody. He understands their suffering. He weeps for them. And when he has a chance, he'll blow them to kingdom come to make society a little nicer. It's a hoot, Mikey. And they give him helicopters and limousines and all the cash he needs and flunkies with big guns in shoulder holsters. They let him run around making a better world. And this man, Mikey, I'm telling you, he's got worms in his brain."

Playing along with it, Roy said, "Worms in my brain, big old slimy worms in my brain."

"See," Steven said. "He's a funny guy, Roy is. Only wants to be liked. Most people do like him too. Don't they, Roy?"

Roy sensed that they were coming to the punch line. "Well, now, Steven, I don't want to be bragging about myself—"

"See!" Steven said. "He's a modest man too. Modest and kind and compassionate. Doesn't everybody like you, Roy? Come on. Don't be so bashful."

"Well, yeah, most people like me," Roy admitted, "but that's because I treat everyone with respect."

"That's right!" Steven said. He laughed. "Roy treats everyone with the same solemn respect. Why, he's an equal-opportunity killer. Evenhanded treatment for everyone from a presidential aide wasted in a Washington park and then made to look like a suicide . . . to an ordinary paraplegic shot down to spare him the daily struggle. Roy doesn't understand that these things have to be done for *fun*. Only for fun. Otherwise, it's insane, it really is, to do it for some noble *purpose*. He's so solemn about it, thinks of himself as a dreamer, a man of ideals. But he does uphold his ideals—I'll give him that much. He plays no favorites. He's the least prejudiced, most egalitarian, foaming-at-the-mouth lunatic who ever lived. Don't you agree, Mr. Rink?"

Rink? Roy didn't want Rink or Fordyce hearing any of this, for God's sake, seeing any of this. They were muscle, not true insiders. He turned to the door, wondering why he hadn't heard it open—and saw that no one was there. Then he heard the scrape of the Micro Uzi against concrete as Steven Ackblom plucked it off the floor, and he knew what was happening.

Too late.

The Uzi chattered in Steven's hands. Bullets tore into Roy. He fell, rolled, and tried to fire back. Though he was still holding the gun, he couldn't make his finger squeeze the trigger. Paralyzed. He was paralyzed.

Over the zinging-whining ricochets, something snarled viciously: a sound out of a horror movie, echoing off the black walls with more blood-curdling effect than the bullets. For a second Roy couldn't understand what it was, where it was coming from. He almost thought that it was Grant because of the fury in the scarred man's face, but then he saw the beast exploding through the air toward Steven. The artist tried to swing around, away from Roy, and cut down the attack dog. But the hellish thing was already on him, driving him backward into the wall. It tore at his hands. He dropped the Uzi. Then it was climbing him, snapping at his face, at his throat.

Steven was screaming.

Roy wanted to tell him that the most dangerous people of all—and evidently the most dangerous dogs as well—were those who had been beaten down the hardest. When even their pride and hope had been taken from them, when they were driven into the last of all corners, then they had nothing to lose. To avoid producing such desperate men, applying compassion to the suffering as early as possible was the right thing to do for them, the moral thing to do—but also the *wisest* thing to do. He couldn't tell the artist any of that, however, because in addition to being paralyzed, he found that he couldn't speak either.

∽

"Rocky, no! Off! Rocky, off!"

Spencer pulled the dog by the collar and struggled with him until at last Rocky obeyed.

The artist was sitting on the floor. His legs were drawn up defensively. His arms crossed over his face, and he was bleeding from his hands.

Ellie had picked up the Uzi. Spencer took it from her.

He saw that her left ear was bleeding. "You've been hit again."

"Ricochet. Grazed," she said, and this time she could have met the dog's eyes forthrightly.

Spencer looked down at the thing that was his father.

The murderous bastard had lowered his arms from his face. He was infuriatingly calm. "They've got men posted from one end of the property to the other. Nobody here in the building, but once you step outside, you won't get far. You can't get away. Mikey."

Ellie said, "They won't have heard the gunfire. Not if no one aboveground ever heard the screams from this place. We still have a chance."

The wife-killer shook his head. "Not unless you take me and the amazing Mr. Miro here."

"He's dead," Ellie said.

"Doesn't matter. He's more useful dead. Never know what a man like him might do, so I'd be edgy if we had to carry him out of here while he was alive. We take him between us, baby boy, you and me. They'll see he's hurt, but they won't know how badly. Maybe they value him highly enough to hold back."

"I don't want your help," Spencer said.

"Of course, you don't, but you need it," his father said. "They won't have moved your truck. Their instructions were to stay back, at a distance, just maintain surveillance, until they heard from Roy. So we can move him to the truck, between us, and they won't be sure what's going on." He rose painfully to his feet.

Spencer backed away from him, as he would have backed away from something that had appeared in a chalk pentagram in response to the summons of a sorcerer. Rocky retreated as well, growling.

Ellie was in the doorway, leaning against the jamb. She was out of the way, reasonably safe.

Spencer had the dog—what a dog!—and he had the gun. His father had no weapon, and he was hampered by his bitten hands. Yet Spencer was as afraid of him as he had ever been on that July night or since.

"Do we need him?" he asked Ellie.

"Hell, no."

"You're sure whatever you were doing with the computer, it's going to work?"

"More sure of that than we could ever be sure of him."

To his father, Spencer said, "What happens to you if I leave you to them?"

The artist examined his bitten hands with interest, studying the punctures not as though concerned about the damage but as though inspecting a flower or another beautiful object that he had never seen before. "What happens to me, Mikey? You mean when I go back to prison? I do a little reading to pass the time. I still paint some—did you know? I think I'll paint a portrait of your little bitch there in the doorway, as I imagine she'd look with no clothes, and as I *know* she'd look if I'd ever had the chance to put her on a table here and make her realize her true potential. I see that disgusts you, baby boy. But really, it's such a small pleasure to allow me, considering she'll never have been more beautiful than on my canvas. My way of sharing in her with you." He sighed and looked up from his hands, as if unperturbed by the pain. "What happens if you leave me to them, Mikey? You'll be condemning me to a life that's a waste of my talent and my joie de vivre, a barren and tiny existence behind gray walls. That's what happens to me, you ungrateful little snot."

"You said they were worse than you."

"Well, I know what I am."

"What's that mean?"

"Self-awareness is a virtue in which they're lacking."

"They let you out."

"Temporarily. A consultation."

"They'll let you out again, won't they?"

"Let's hope it doesn't take another sixteen years." He smiled, as if his bleeding hands had suffered only paper cuts. "But, yes, we're in an age that's giving birth to a new breed of fascists, and I would hope that from time to time they might find my expertise useful to them."

"You're figuring you won't even go back," Spencer said. "You think you'll get away from them tonight, don't you?"

"Too many of them, Mikey. Big men with big guns in shoulder holsters. Big black Chrysler limousines. Helicopters whenever they want them. No, no, I'll probably have to bide my time until another consultation."

"Lying, mother-killing sonofabitch," Spencer said.

"Oh, don't try to frighten me," his father said. "I remember sixteen years ago, this room. You were a little pussy then, Mikey, and you're a little pussy now. That's some scar you've got there, baby boy. How long did you have to recuperate before you could eat solid foods?"

"I saw you beat her to the ground by the swimming pool."

"If confession makes you feel good, go right ahead."

"I was in the kitchen for cookies, heard her scream."

"Did you get your cookies?"

"When she was down, you kicked her in the head."

"Don't be tedious, Mikey. You were never the son I might have wished to have, but you were never tedious before."

The man was unshakably calm, self-possessed. He had an aura of power that was daunting—but no look of madness whatsoever in his eyes. He could preach a sermon and be thought a priest. He claimed that he wasn't mad, but evil.

Spencer wondered if that could be true.

"Mikey, you really owe me, you know. Without me, you wouldn't exist. No matter what you think of me, I *am* your father."

"Without you, I wouldn't exist. Yeah. And that would be okay. That would be fine. But without my mother—I might have been exactly like you. It's her I owe. Only her. She's the one who gave me whatever salvation I can ever have."

"Mikey, Mikey, you simply can't make me feel guilty. You want me to put on a big sad face? Okay, I'll put on a big sad face. But your mother was nothing to me. Nothing but useful cover for a while, a helpful deceit with nice knockers. But she was too curious. And when I had to bring her down here, she was just like all the others—although less exciting than most."

"Well, just the same," Spencer said, "this is for her." He fired a short burst from the Uzi, blowing his father to Hell.

There were no ricochets to worry about. Every bullet found its mark, and the dead man carried them down to the floor with him, in a pool of the darkest blood that Spencer had ever seen.

Rocky leaped in surprise at the gunfire, then cocked his head and studied Steven Ackblom. He sniffed him as if the scent was far different from any he had encountered before. As Spencer stared down at his dead father, he was aware of Rocky gazing up curiously at him. Then the dog joined Ellie at the door.

When at last he went to the door too, Spencer was afraid to look at Ellie.

"I wondered if you would actually be able to do it," she said. "If you hadn't, I'd have had to, and the recoil would have hurt like hell with this arm."

He met her eyes. She wasn't trying to make him feel better about what he had done. She had meant what she'd said.

"I didn't enjoy it," he said.

"I would have."

"I don't think so."

"Immensely."

"I didn't hate doing it, either."

"Why should you? You have to stomp a cockroach when you get a chance."

"How's your shoulder?"

"Hurts like hell, but it's not bleeding all that much." She flexed her right hand, wincing. "I'll still be able to work the computer keyboard with both hands. I just hope to God I can work it fast enough."

The three of them hurried through the depopulated catacombs, toward the blue room, the yellow vestibule, and the strange world above.

✑

Roy had no pain. In fact, he could feel nothing at all. Which made it easier for him to play dead. He feared that they would finish him off if they realized he was alive. Spencer Grant, aka Michael Ackblom, was indisputably as insane as his father and capable of any atrocity. Therefore, Roy closed his eyes and used his paralysis to his advantage.

After the singular opportunity that he had given the artist, Roy was disappointed in the man. Such blithe treachery.

More to the point, Roy was disappointed in himself. He had badly misjudged Steven Ackblom. The brilliance and sensitivity that he had perceived in the artist had been no illusion; however, he had allowed himself to be deceived into believing that what he saw was the whole story. He had never glimpsed the dark side.

Of course he was always so quick to *like* people, just as the artist had said. And he was acutely aware of everyone's suffering, within moments of having met them. That was one of his virtues, and he would not have wanted to be a less tenderhearted person. He had been deeply moved by Ackblom's plight: such a witty and talented man, locked in a cell for the rest of his life. Compassion had blinded Roy to the full truth.

He still had hope of coming out of this alive and seeing Eve again. He didn't *feel* as though he were dying. Of course, he was unable to feel much of anything at all, below the neck.

He took comfort from the knowledge that if he were to die, he would go to the great cosmic party and be welcomed by so many friends whom he'd sent ahead of him with great tenderness. For Eve's sake, he wanted to live, but to some extent he longed for that higher plane where there was a single sex, where everyone had the same radiant-blue skin color, where every person was perfectly beautiful in an androgynous blue way, where no one was dumb, no one too smart, where everyone had identical living quarters and wardrobes and footwear, where there was high-quality mineral water and fresh fruit for the asking. He would have to be introduced to everyone he had known in this world, because he wouldn't recognize them in their new perfect, identical blue bodies. That seemed sad: not to see people as they had been. On the other hand, he wouldn't want to spend eternity with his dear mother if he had to look at her face all bashed in as it had been just after he had sent her on to that better place.

He tried speaking and found that his voice had returned. "Are you dead, Steven, or are you faking?"

Across the black room, slumped against a black wall, the artist didn't answer.

"I think they're gone and won't be coming back. So if you're faking, it's all clear now."

No reply.

"Well, then you've gone over, and all the bad in you was left here. I'm sure you're full of remorse now and wish you'd been more compassionate toward me. So if you could exert a little of your cosmic power, reach through the veil, and work a little miracle so I can walk again, I believe that would be appropriate."

The room remained silent.

He still couldn't feel anything below his neck.

"I hope I don't need the services of a spirit channeler to get your attention," Roy said. "That would be inconvenient."

Silence. Stillness. Cold white light in a tight cone, blazing down through the center of that encapsulating blackness.

"I'll just wait. I'm sure that reaching through the veil takes a lot of effort."

Any moment now, a miracle.

∽

Opening the driver's door of the pickup, Spencer was suddenly afraid that he had lost the keys. They were in his jacket pocket.

By the time Spencer got behind the wheel and started the engine, Rocky was in the backseat, and Ellie was already in the other front seat. The motel pillow was across her thighs, the laptop was on the pillow, and she was waiting to power up the computer.

When the engine turned over and Ellie switched on the laptop, she said, "Don't go anywhere yet."

"We're sitting ducks here."

"I've got to get back into Godzilla."

"Godzilla."

"The system I was in before we got out of the truck."

"What's Godzilla?"

"As long as we're just sitting here, they probably won't do anything except watch us and wait. But as soon as we start to move, they'll have to act, and I don't want them coming at us until we're ready for them."

"What's Godzilla?"

"Ssshhh. I have to concentrate."

Spencer looked out his side window at the fields and hills. The snow didn't glow as brightly as it had earlier, because the moon was waning. He had been trained to spot clandestine surveillance in both urban and rural settings, but he could see no signs of the agency observers, though he knew they were out there.

Ellie's fingers were busy. Keys clicked. Data and diagrams played across the screen.

Focusing on the winterscape once more, Spencer remembered snow forts, castles, tunnels, carefully tamped sled runs. More important: In addition to the physical details of old playgrounds in the snow, he faintly recalled the joy of laboring on those projects and of setting out on those boyhood adventures. Recollections of innocent times. Childhood fantasies. Happiness. They were faint memories. Faint but perhaps recoverable with practice. For a long time, he hadn't been able to remember even a single moment of his childhood with fondness. The events in that July not only had changed his life forever thereafter but had changed his perception of what his life had been like before the owl, the rats, the scalpel, and the knife.

Sometimes his mother had helped him build castles of snow. He remembered times when she'd gone sledding with him. They especially enjoyed going out after dusk. The night was so crisp, the world so mysterious in black and white. With billions of stars above, you could pretend that the sled was a rocket and you were off to other worlds.

He thought of his mother's grave in Denver, and he suddenly wanted to go there for the first time since his grandparents had moved him to San Francisco. He wanted to sit on the ground beside her and reminisce about nights when they had gone sledding under a billion stars, when her laughter had carried like music across the white fields.

Rocky stood on the floor in back, paws planted on the front seat, and craned his head forward to lick affectionately at the side of Spencer's face.

He turned and stroked the dog's head and neck. "Mr. Rocky Dog, more powerful than a locomotive, faster than a speeding bullet, able to leap tall buildings in a single bound, terror of all cats and Dobermans. Where did *that* come from, hmmm?" He scratched behind the dog's ears. Then with his fingertips, he gently explored the crushed cartilage that ensured the left ear would always droop. "Way back in the bad old days, did the person who did this to you look anything like the man back there in the black room? Or did you recognize a scent? Do the evil ones smell alike, pal?" Rocky luxuriated in the attention. "Mr. Rocky Dog, furry hero, ought to have his own comic book. Show us some teeth, give us a thrill." Rocky just panted. "Come on, show us some teeth," Spencer said, growling and skinning his lips back from his own teeth. Rocky liked the game, bared his own teeth, and they went *grrrrrr* at each other, muzzle to muzzle.

"Ready," Ellie said.

"Thank God," he said, "I just ran out of things to do to keep from going nuts."

"You've got to help me spot them," she said. "I'll be looking too, but I might not see one of them."

Indicating the screen, he said, "That's Godzilla?"

"No. This is the gameboard that Godzilla and I are both going to play with. It's a grid of the five acres immediately around the house and barn. Each of these tiny grid blocks is six meters on a side. I just hope to God my entry data, those property maps and county records, were accurate enough. I know they're not dead-on, not by a long shot, but let's pray they're close. See this green shape? That's the house. See this? The barn. Here are the stables down toward the end of the driveway. This blinking dot—that's us. See this line—that's the county road, where we want to be."

"Is this based on one of the video games you invented?"

"No, this is nasty reality," she said. "And whatever happens, Spencer . . . I love you. I can't imagine anything better than spending the rest of my life with you. I just hope it's going to be more than five minutes."

He had started to put the truck in gear. Her frank expression of her feelings made him hesitate, because he wanted to kiss her now, here, for the first time, in case it was the last time too.

Then he froze and stared at her in amazement as comprehension came. "Godzilla's looking straight down at us right now, isn't he?"

"Yeah."

"It's a satellite? And you've hijacked it?"

"Been saving these codes for a day when I was in a really tight corner, no other way out, because I'll never get a chance to use them again. When we're out of here, when I let go of Godzilla, they'll shut it down and reprogram."

"What does it do besides look down?"

"Remember the movies?"

"Godzilla movies?"

"His white-hot, glowing breath?"

"You're making this up."

"He had halitosis that melted tanks."

"Oh, my God."

"Now or never," she said.

"Now," he said, putting the truck into reverse, wanting to get it over with before he had any more time to think about it.

He switched on the headlights, backed away from the barn, and headed around the building, retracing the route that they had taken from the county road.

"Not too fast," she said. "It'll pay to tiptoe out of here, believe me."

Spencer let up on the accelerator.

Drifting along now. Easing past the front of the barn. The other branch of the driveway over there. The backyard to the right. The swimming pool.

A brilliant white searchlight fixed them from an open second-floor window of the house, sixty yards to their right and forty yards ahead. Spencer was blinded when he looked in that direction, and he could not see whether there were sharpshooters with rifles at any of the other windows.

Ellie's fingers rattled the keys.

He glanced over and saw a yellow indicator line on the display screen. It represented a swath about two meters wide and twenty-four meters long, between them and the house.

Ellie pressed ENTER.

"Squint!" she said, and in the same moment Spencer shouted, "Rocky, down!"

Out of the stars came a blue-white incandescence. It was not as fierce as he had expected, marginally brighter than the spotlight from the house, but it was infinitely stranger than anything he had ever seen—above-ground. The beam was crisply defined along the edges, and it seemed not to be radiating light as much as *containing* it, holding an atomic fire within a skin as thin as the surface tension on a pond. A bone-vibrating hum accompanied it, like electronic feedback from huge stadium speakers, and a sudden turbulence of air. As the light moved on a course that Ellie had laid out for it (two meters wide, twenty-four meters long, between them and the house but approaching neither), a roar arose similar to the subterranean grumble of the few grinding-type earthquakes that Spencer had ridden out over the years, although this was far louder. The earth shook hard enough to rock the truck. In that two-meter-wide swath, the snow and the ground beneath it leaped into flames, turned molten in an instant, to what depth he didn't know. The beam moved along, and the center of a big sycamore vanished in a flash; it didn't merely burst into flame but *disappeared* as if it had never existed. The tree was instantly converted into light and into heat that was detectable even inside the truck with the windows closed, almost thirty yards from the beam itself. Numerous splintered branches, which had hung beyond the sharply defined edge of the beam, fell to the ground on both sides of the light, and they were on fire at the points of severance. The blue-white blade burned past the pickup, across the backyard, diagonally between them and the house, across one edge of the patio, vaporizing concrete, all the way to the end of the path that Ellie had set it upon—and then it winked out.

A two-meter-wide, twenty-four-meter length of earth glowed white-hot, boiling like a lava flow at its freshest, on the high slopes of a volcano. The magma churned brightly in the trench that contained it, bubbling and popping and spitting showers of red and white sparks into the air, casting a glow that reached even to the truck and colored the surviving snow red-orange.

During the event, if they had not been too stunned to speak, they would have had to shout at each other to be heard. Now the silence seemed as profound as that in the vacuum of deep space.

At the house, the agency men switched off the searchlight.

"Keep moving," Ellie said urgently.

Spencer hadn't realized that he'd braked to a complete stop.

They drifted forward again. Easy. Moving cautiously through the lion's den. Easy. He risked a little more speed than before, because the lions had to be scared shitless right now.

"God bless America," Spencer said shakily.

"Oh, Godzilla isn't one of ours."

"It isn't?"

"Japanese."

"The Japanese have a death-ray satellite?"

"Enhanced-laser technology. And they have eight satellites in the system."

"I thought they were busy making better televisions."

She was working diligently on the keyboard again, getting ready for the worst. "Damn it, my right hand's cramping."

He saw that she had targeted the house.

She said, "The U.S. has something similar, but I don't have any codes that'll get me into our system. The fools on our side call it the Hyperspace Hammer, which has nothing to do with what it is. It's just a name they liked from a video game."

"You invent the game?"

"Actually, yes."

"They make an amusement park ride out of it?"

"Yes."

"I saw one."

Moving past the house now. Not even looking up at the windows. Not tempting fate.

"You can commandeer a secret Japanese defense satellite?"

"Through the DOD," she said.

"Department of Defense."

"The Japanese don't know it, but the DOD can grab Godzilla's brain any time they want. I'm just using the doorways that the DOD has already installed."

He remembered something that she had said in the desert only that morning, when he had expressed surprise about the possibility of satellite surveillance. He quoted it back to her: " 'You'd be surprised what's up there. "Surprised" is one word.' "

"The Israelis have their own system."

"The *Israelis!*"

"Yeah, little Israel. They worry me less than anyone else who's got it. Chinese. Think about that. Maybe the French. No more jokes about Paris cabdrivers. God knows who else has it."

They were almost past the house.

A small round hole was punched through the side window behind Ellie, even as the sound of the shot cracked the night, and Spencer felt the round thud into the back of his seat. The velocity of the bullet was so great that the tempered glass crazed slightly but did not collapse inward. Thank God, Rocky was barking energetically instead of squealing in agony.

"Stupid bastards," Ellie said as she pressed ENTER again.

Out of airless space, a lambent column of blue-white light shot down into the two-story Victorian farmhouse, instantly vaporizing a core two meters in diameter. The rest of the structure exploded. Flames filled the night. If anyone was left alive in that crumbling house, they would have to get out too fast to worry about holding on to their weapons and taking additional potshots at the pickup.

Ellie was shaken. "I couldn't risk them hitting the up-link behind us. If that goes, we're in deep trouble."

"The Russians have this?"

"This and weirder stuff."

"Weirder stuff?"

"That's why most everyone else is desperate to get their version of Godzilla. Zhirinovsky. Heard of him?"

"Russian politician."

Bending her head again to the VDT, entering new instructions, she said, "Him and the people associated with him, the whole network of them even after he's gone—they're old-fashioned communists who want to rule the world. Except this time they're actually willing to blow it up if they don't get their way. No more graceful defeats. And even if someone's smart enough to wipe out the Zhirinovsky faction, there's always some new power freak, somewhere, calling himself a politician."

Forty yards ahead, on the right, a Ford Bronco erupted from concealment in a stand of trees and bushes. It pulled across the driveway, blocking their escape.

Spencer halted the pickup.

Though the driver of the Bronco stayed behind the wheel, two men with high-power rifles jumped out of the back and dropped into sharpshooter positions. They raised their weapons.

"Down!" Spencer said, and pushed Ellie's head below window level even as he slid down in his seat.

"They aren't," she said in disbelief.

"They are."

"Blocking the driveway?"

"Two sharpshooters and a Bronco."

"Haven't they been paying attention?"

"Stay down, Rocky," he said.

The dog was standing again with his forepaws on the front seat, bobbing his head excitedly.

"Rocky, *down!*" Spencer said fiercely.

The dog whimpered as though his feelings had been hurt, but he dropped to the floor in back.

Ellie said, "How far are they?"

Spencer risked a quick peek, slid down again, and a bullet rang off the window post without shattering the windshield. "I'd say forty yards."

She typed. On the screen appeared a yellow line to the right of the driveway. It was twelve meters long, angling over an open field toward the Bronco, but it stopped a meter or two from the edge of the pavement.

"Don't want to score the driveway," she said. "Tires would dissolve when we tried to get across the molten ground."

"Can I press ENTER?" he asked.

"Be my guest."

He pressed it and sat up, squinting, as the breath of Godzilla streamed down through the night again, scoring the land. The ground shook, and an apocalyptic thunder rose under them as if the planet was coming apart. The night air hummed deafeningly, and the merciless beam dazzled along the course that she'd assigned to it.

Before Godzilla had turned the earth into white-hot sludge along even half those twelve meters, the pair of sharpshooters dropped their weapons and leaped for the vehicle behind them. As they hung on to the sides of the Bronco, the driver careened off the blacktop, churned across a frozen field beyond, smashed through a white board fence, crossed a paddock, rammed through another fence, and passed the first of the stables. When Godzilla stopped short of the driveway and the night was suddenly dark and quiet again, the Bronco was still going, fast dwindling into the gloom, as though the driver might head overland until he ran out of gasoline.

Spencer drove to the county road. He stopped and looked both ways. No traffic. He turned right, toward Denver.

For a few miles, neither of them spoke.

Rocky stood with his forepaws on the back of the front seat, gazing ahead at the highway. In the two years that Spencer had known him, the dog had never liked to look back.

Ellie sat with her hand clamped to her wound. Spencer hoped that the people she knew in Denver could get her medical attention. The medications that she had finessed, by computer, out of various drug companies had been lost with the Range Rover.

Eventually, she said, "We'd better stop in Copper Mountain, see if we can find new wheels. This truck's too recognizable."

"Okay."

She switched off the computer. Unplugged it.

The mountains were dark with evergreens and pale with snow.

The moon was setting behind the truck, and the night sky ahead was ablaze with stars.

15

E VE JAMMER HATED Washington, D.C., in August. Actually, she hated Washington through all seasons with equal passion. Admittedly, the city was pleasant for a short while, when the cherry blossoms were in bloom; during the rest of the year it sucked. Humid, crowded, noisy, dirty, crime-ridden. Full of boring, stupid, greedy politicians whose ideals were either in their pants or in their pants pockets. It was an inconvenient place for a capital, and sometimes she dreamed about moving the government elsewhere, when the time was right. Maybe to Las Vegas.

As she drove through the sweltering August heat, she had the air conditioner in her Chrysler Town Car turned nearly to its highest setting, with the fans on maximum blow. Freezing air blasted across her face and body and up her skirt, but she was still hot. Part of the heat, of course, had nothing to do with the day: She was so horny she could have won a head-butting duel with a ram.

She hated the Chrysler almost as much as she hated Washington. With all her money and position, she ought to have been able to drive a Mercedes, if not a Rolls-Royce. But a politician's wife had to be careful of appearances—at least for a while yet. It was impolitic to drive a foreign made car.

Eighteen months had passed since Eve Jammer had met Roy Miro and had learned the nature of her true destiny. For sixteen months, she had been married to the widely admired Senator E. Jackson Haynes, who would head the party's national ticket in next year's election. That wasn't speculation. It had already been arranged, and all his rivals would screw up one way or another in the primaries, leaving him standing alone, a giant of a man on the world scene.

Personally, she loathed E. Jackson Haynes and wouldn't let him touch her, except in public. Even then, there were several pages of rules that he'd been required to memorize, defining the acceptable limits relating to affectionate hugs, kisses on the cheek, and hand holding. The recordings that she had of him in his Vegas hideaway, engaged in sex with several different little girls and boys below the age of twelve, had ensured his prompt acceptance of her proposal of marriage and the strict terms of convenience under which their relationship would be conducted.

Jackson didn't pout too much or too often about the arrangement. He was keen on the idea of being president. And without the library of recordings that Eve possessed, which incriminated all of his most serious political rivals, he wouldn't have had a chance in hell of getting close to the White House.

For a while, she had worried that a few of the politicians and power brokers whose enmity she had earned would be too thickheaded to realize that the boxes in which she'd put them were inescapable. If they terminated her, they would all fall in the biggest, dirtiest series of political scandals in history. More than scandals. Many of these servants of the people had committed outrages appalling enough to cause riots in the streets, even if federal agents were dispatched with machine guns to quell them.

Some of the worst hard-asses hadn't been convinced that she'd secreted copies of her recordings all over the world or that the contents of those laser discs were destined for the airwaves within hours of her death, from multiple—and, in many cases, automated—sources. The last of them had come around, however, when she had accessed their home television sets through satellite and cable facilities—while blocking all other customers—and had played for them, one by one, fragments of their recorded crimes. Sitting in their own bedrooms and dens, they had listened with astonishment, terrified that she was broadcasting those fragments to the world.

Computer technology was wonderful.

Many of the hard-asses had been with wives or mistresses when those unexpected, intensely personal broadcasts had appeared on their television screens. In most cases, their significant others were as guilty or as power mad as they were themselves, and eager to keep their mouths shut. However, one influential senator and a member of the president's cabinet had been married to women who exhibited bizarre moral codes and who refused to keep secret what they had learned. Before divorce proceedings and public revelations could begin, both had been shot to death at different automatic-teller machines on the same night. That tragedy resulted in the lowering of the nation's flag at all government buildings, citywide, for twenty-four hours—and in the introduction of a bill in Congress to require the posting of health warnings on all automated tellers.

Eve turned the air conditioner control to the highest setting. Just thinking about those women's expressions when she'd put the gun to their heads made her hotter than ever.

She was still two miles from Cloverfield, and the Washington traffic was terrible. She wanted to blow her horn and flip a stiff finger at some of the insufferable morons who were causing the snarls at the intersections, but she had to be discreet. The next First Lady of the United States could not be seen flipping off anyone. Besides, she had learned from Roy that anger was a weakness. Anger should be controlled and transformed into that only truly ennobling emotion—compassion. These bad drivers didn't *want* to tie up traffic; they were simply lacking in sufficient intellect to drive well. Their lives were probably blighted in many ways. They deserved not anger but compassionate release to a better world, whenever that release could be privately given.

She considered jotting down license numbers, to make it possible to find some of these poor souls later and, at her leisure, give them that gift of gifts. She was in too great a hurry, however, to be as compassionate as she would have liked.

She couldn't wait to get to Cloverfield and share the good news about Daddy's generosity. Through a complex chain of international trusts and corporations, her father—Thomas Summerton, First Deputy Attorney General of the United States—had transferred three hundred million dollars of his holdings to her, which provided her with as much freedom as did the laser-disc recordings from two years in that spider-infested Vegas bunker.

The smartest thing she had ever done, in a life of smart moves, was not to squeeze Daddy for money years ago, when she'd first gotten the goods on him. She had asked, instead, for a job with the agency. Daddy had believed that she'd wanted the bunker job because it was so easy: nothing to do down there but sit, read magazines, and collect a hundred thousand a year in salary. He'd made the mistake of thinking that she was a not-too-bright, small-time hustler.

Some men never seemed to stop thinking with their pants long enough to get wise. Tom Summerton was one of them.

Ages ago, when Eve's mother had been Daddy's mistress, he would have been wise to treat her better. But when she got pregnant and refused to abort the baby, he had dumped her. Hard. Even in those days, Daddy had been a rich young man and heir to even more, and although he hadn't achieved much political power yet, he'd had great ambition. He easily could have afforded to treat Mama well. When she threatened to go public and ruin his reputation, however, he'd sent a couple of goons to beat her up, and she'd nearly had a miscarriage. Thereafter, poor Mama had been a bitter, frightened woman until the day she died.

Daddy had been thinking with his pants when he'd been stupid enough to keep a fifteen-year-old mistress like Mama. And later he'd been thinking with his pants *pockets* when he should have been thinking with his head or his heart.

He was thinking with his pants again when he'd allowed Eve to seduce him—though, of course, he hadn't ever seen her before and hadn't known that she was his daughter. By then, he had forgotten poor Mama as if she'd been a one-night stand, although he had been putting it to her for two years before he dumped her. And if Mama barely existed in his memory, the possibility of having fathered a child had been wiped off his mental slate completely.

Eve had not simply seduced him but had *reduced* him to a state of animal lust that, over a period of weeks, made him the easiest of marks. When she eventually suggested a little fantasy role-playing, wherein they would act like father and violated daughter in bed, he had been excited. Her pretend-resistance and pitiful cries of rape excited him to new feats of endurance. Preserved on high-resolution videotape. From four angles. Recorded on the finest audio equipment. She'd saved some of his ejaculate in order to have a genetic match done with a sample of her own blood, to convince him that she was, indeed, his darling child. The tape of their role-playing would unquestionably be viewed by authorities as nothing less than forcible incest.

Upon being presented with that package, Daddy had for once in his life thought with his brain. He was convinced that killing her would not save him, so he had been willing to pay whatever was necessary to buy her silence. He'd been surprised and pleased when she'd asked not for any of his money but for a secure, well-paid government job. He'd been less pleased when she'd wanted to know a lot more about the agency and the secret derring-do about which he'd bragged once or twice in bed. After a few difficult days, however, he had seen the wisdom of bringing her into the agency fold.

"You're a cunning little bitch," he said when they had reached agreement. He'd put an arm around her with genuine affection.

He had been disappointed, after giving her the job, to learn that they would not continue sleeping together, but he had gotten over that loss in time. He really had thought that "cunning" was the best word to describe her. Her ability to use her position in the bunker for her own ends didn't become clear to him until he learned that she had married E. Jackson Haynes, after a whirlwind courtship of two days, and had managed to put most of the powerful politicians in the city under her thumb. *Then* she had gone to him to begin discussions regarding an inheritance—and Daddy had discovered that "cunning" might not be a sufficiently descriptive word.

Now she reached the end of the entrance drive to Cloverfield and parked at a red curb near the front door, beside a sign that stated NO PARK-ING ANYTIME. She put one of Jackson's "Member of Congress" cards on the dashboard, relished the icy air of the Chrysler for one more moment, then stepped out into the August heat and humidity.

Cloverfield—all white columns and stately walls—was one of the finest institutions of its kind in the continental United States. A liveried doorman greeted her. The concierge at the main desk in the lounge was a distinguished-looking British gentleman named Danfield, though she didn't know if that was his first or last name.

After Danfield signed her in and chatted pleasantly with her, Eve walked the familiar route through the hushed halls. Original paintings by famous American artists of previous centuries were well complemented by antique Persian runners on wine-dark mahogany floors polished to a watery sheen.

When she entered Roy's suite, she found the dear man shuffling around in his walker, getting some exercise. With the attention of the finest specialists and therapists in the world, he had regained full use of his arms. Increasingly, he seemed certain to be able to walk on his own again within a few months—though with a limp.

She gave him a dry kiss on the cheek. He favored her with one even dryer.

"You're more beautiful every time you visit," he said.

"Well, men's heads still turn," she said, "but not like they used to, not when I have to wear clothes like these."

A future First Lady of the United States couldn't dress as would a former Las Vegas showgirl who'd gotten a thrill out of driving men insane. These days she even wore a bra that spread her breasts out and restrained them, to make her appear less amply endowed than she really was.

She had never been a showgirl anyway, and her surname had not been Jammer but Lincoln, as in Abraham. She had attended school in five different states and West Germany, because her father had been a career military man who'd been transferred from base to base. She had graduated from the Sorbonne in Paris and had spent a number of years teaching poor children in the Kingdom of Tonga, in the South Pacific. At least, that was what every data record would reveal to even the most industrious reporter armed with the most powerful computer and the cleverest mind.

She and Roy sat side by side on a settee. Pots of hot tea, an array of pastries, clotted cream, and jam had been provided on a charming little Chippendale table.

While they sipped and munched, she told him about the three hundred million that her father had transferred to her. Roy was so happy for her that tears came to his eyes. He was a dear man.

They talked about the future.

The time when they could be together again, every night, without any subterfuge, seemed depressingly distant. E. Jackson Haynes would assume the office of president on January twentieth, seventeen months hence. He and the vice-president would be assassinated the following year—though Jackson was unaware of that detail. With the approval of constitutional scholars and the advice of the Supreme Court of the United States, both houses of Congress would take the unprecedented step of calling for a special election. Eve Marie Lincoln Haynes, widow of the martyred president, would run for the office, be elected by a landslide, and begin serving her first term.

"A year after *that*, I'll have mourned a decent length of time," she told Roy. "Don't you think a year?"

"More than decent. Especially as the public will love you so much and want happiness for you."

"And then I can marry the heroic FBI agent who tracked down and killed that escaped maniac, Steven Ackblom."

"Four years until we're together forever," Roy said. "Not so long, really. I promise you, Eve, I'll make you happy and do honor to my position as First Gentleman."

"I know you will, darling," she said.

"And by then, anyone who doesn't like *anything* you do—"

"—we shall treat with utmost compassion."

"Exactly."

"Now let's not talk any more about how long we have to wait. Let's discuss more of your wonderful ideas. Let's make *plans*."

For a long time they talked about uniforms for a variety of new federal organizations they wished to create, with a special focus on whether metal snaps and zippers were more exciting than traditional bone buttons.

16

I N THE BROILING SUN, hard-bodied young men and legions of strikingly attractive women in the briefest of bikinis soaked up the rays and casually struck poses for one another. Children built sand castles. Retirees sat under umbrellas, wearing straw hats, soaking up the shade. They were all happily oblivious of eyes in the sky and of the possibility that they could be instantaneously vaporized at the whim of politicians of various nationalities—or even by a demented-genius computer hacker, living in a cyberpunk fantasy, in Cleveland or London or Cape Town or Pittsburgh.

As he walked along the shore, near the tide line, with the huge hotels piled one beside the other to his right, he rubbed lightly at his face. His beard itched. He'd had it for six months, and it wasn't a scruffy-looking beard. On the contrary, it was soft and full, and Ellie insisted that he was even more handsome with it than without it. Nevertheless, on a hot August day in Miami Beach, it itched as if he had fleas, and he longed to be clean-shaven.

Besides, he liked the appearance of his beardless face. During the eighteen months since the night on which Godzilla had attacked the ranch in Vail, a superb plastic surgeon in the private-pay sector of the British medical establishment had performed three separate procedures on the cicatrix. It had been reduced to a hairline scar that was virtually invisible even when he was tanned. Additional work had been done on his nose and chin.

He used scores of names these days, but neither Spencer Grant nor Michael Ackblom was one of them. Among his closest friends in the resistance, he was known as Phil Richards. Ellie had chosen to keep her first name and adopt Richards as her last. Rocky responded as well to "Killer" as he had to his previous name.

Phil turned his back to the ocean, made his way between the ranks of sunbathers, and entered the lushly landscaped grounds of one of the newer hotels. In sandals, white shorts, and a flamboyant Hawaiian shirt, he resembled countless other tourists.

The hotel swimming pool was bigger than a football field and as freeform as any tropical lagoon. Artificial-rock perimeter. Artificial-rock sunning islands in the center. A two-story waterfall spilling into one palm-shaded end.

In a grotto behind the cascading water, the poolside bar could be reached either on foot or by swimmers. It was a Polynesian-style pavilion with plenty of bamboo, dry palm fronds, and conch shells. The cocktail waitresses wore thongs, wraparound skirts made from a bright orchid-patterned fabric, and matching bikini tops; each had a fresh flower pinned in her hair.

The Padrakian family—Bob, Jean, and their eight-year-old son, Mark—were sitting at a small table near the grotto wall. Bob was drinking rum and Coke, Mark was having a root beer, and Jean was nervously shredding a cocktail napkin and chewing on her lower lip.

Phil approached the table and startled Jean—to whom he was a stranger—by loudly saying, "Hey, Sally, you look fabulous," and by giving her a hug and a kiss on the cheek. He ruffled Mark's hair: "How you doing, Pete? I'm going to take you snorkeling later—what do you think of that?" Vigorously shaking hands with Bob, he said, "Better watch that gut, buddy, or you're going to wind up looking like Uncle Morty." Then he sat down with them and quietly said, "Pheasants and dragons."

A few minutes later, after he had finished a piña colada and surreptitiously studied the other customers in the bar to be sure that none of them was unusually interested in the Padrakians, Phil paid for all their drinks with cash. He walked with them into the hotel, chatting about nonexistent mutual relatives. Through the frigid lobby. Out under the porte cochere, into the stifling heat and humidity. As far as he could tell, no one was trailing or watching them.

The Padrakians had followed telephone instructions well. They were dressed as sun-worshiping tourists from New Jersey, although Bob was pushing the disguise too far by wearing black loafers and black socks with Bermuda shorts.

A sightseeing van with large windows along the sides approached on the hotel entrance drive and stopped at the curb in front of them, under the porte cochere. The current magnetic-mat signs on each of its front doors declared CAPTAIN BLACKBEARD'S WATER ADVENTURES. Under that, above a picture of a grinning pirate, less bold letters explained GUIDED SCUBA TOURS, JET-SKI RENTALS, WATER-SKIING, DEEP-SEA FISHING.

The driver got out and came around the front of the van to open the sliding side door for them. He wore a stylishly wrinkled white linen shirt, lightweight white ducks, and bright pink canvas shoes with green laces. Even with dreadlocks and one silver earring, he managed to look as intellectual and dignified as he had ever been in a three-piece suit or in a police captain's uniform, in the days when Phil had served under him in the West Los Angeles Division of the LAPD. His ink-black skin seemed even darker and glossier in the tropical heat of Miami than it had been in Los Angeles.

The Padrakians climbed into the back of the van, and Phil sat up front with the driver, who was now known to his friends as Ronald—Ron, for short—Truman. "Love the shoes," Phil said.

"My daughters picked them out for me."

"Yeah, but you like 'em."

"Can't lie. They're cool gear."

"You were half dancing, the way you came around the van, showing them off."

Flashing a grin as he drove away from the hotel, Ron said, "You white men always envy our moves."

Ron was speaking with a British accent so convincing that Phil could close his eyes and see Big Ben. In the course of losing his Caribbean lilt, Ron had discovered a talent for accents and dialects. He was now their man of a thousand voices.

"I gotta tell you," Bob Padrakian said nervously from the seat behind them, "we're scared out of our wits about this."

"You're all right now," Phil said. He turned around in his seat to smile reassuringly at the three refugees.

"Nobody following us, unless it's a look-down," Ron said, though the Padrakians probably didn't know what he meant. "And that's not very likely."

"I mean," Padrakian said, "we don't even know who the hell you people are."

"We're your friends," Phil assured him. "In fact, if things work out for you folks anything like the way they worked out for me and for Ron and his family, then we're going to be the best friends you've ever had."

"More than friends, really," Ron said. "Family."

Bob and Jean looked dubious and scared. Mark was young enough to be unconcerned.

"Just sit tight for a little while and don't worry," Phil told them. "Everything'll be explained real soon."

At a huge shopping mall, they parked and went inside. They passed dozens of stores, entered one of the less busy wings, went through a door marked with international symbols for rest rooms and telephones, and were in a long service hallway. They passed the phones and the public facilities. A stairway at the end of the corridor led down to one of the mall's big communal shipping rooms, where some smaller shops, without exterior truck docks, received incoming merchandise.

Two of the four roll-up, truck-bay doors were open, and delivery ve-hicles were backed up to them. Three uniformed employees from a store that sold cheese, cured meats, and gourmet foods were rapidly unloading the truck at bay number four. As they stacked cartons on handcarts and wheeled them to a freight elevator, they showed no interest in Phil, Ron, and the Padrakians. Many of the boxes were labeled PERISHABLE, KEEP RE-FRIGERATED, and time was of the essence.

At the truck in bay number one—a small model compared with the eighteen-wheeler in bay four—the driver appeared from out of the dark, sixteen-foot-deep cargo hold. As they approached, he jumped down to the floor. The five of them climbed inside, as though going for a ride in the back of a delivery truck was unremarkable. The driver closed the door after them, and a moment later they were on the road.

The cargo hold was empty except for piles of quilted shipping pads of the kind used by furniture movers. They sat on the pads in pitch black-ness. They were unable to talk because of the engine noise and the hol-low rattle of the metal walls around them.

Twenty minutes later, the truck stopped. The engine died. After five minutes, the rear door opened. The driver appeared in dazzling sunshine. "Quickly. Nobody's in sight right now."

When they disembarked from the truck, they were in a corner of a parking lot at a public beach. Sunlight flared off the windshields and chrome trim of the parked cars, and white gulls kited through the sky. Phil could smell sea salt in the air.

"Only a short walk now," Ron told the Padrakians.

The campgrounds were less than a quarter of a mile from where they left the truck. The tan-and-black Road King motor home was large, but it was only one of many its size that were parked at utility hookups among the palms.

The trees lazily stirred in the humid on-shore breeze. A hundred yards away, at the edge of the breaking surf, two pelicans stalked stiffly back and forth through the fringe of foaming water, as if engaged in an ancient Egyptian dance.

Inside the Road King, Ellie was one of three people working at video-display terminals in the living room. She rose, smiling, to receive Phil's embrace and kiss.

Rubbing her belly affectionately, he said, "Ron has new shoes."

"I saw them earlier."

"Tell him he really has nice moves in those shoes. Makes him feel good."

"It does, huh?"

"Makes him feel black."

"He is black."

"Well, of course, he is."

She and Phil joined Ron and the Padrakians in the horseshoe-shaped dining nook that seated seven.

Sitting beside Jean Padrakian, welcoming her to this new life, Ellie took the woman's hand and held it, as if Jean were a sister whom she hadn't seen for a while and whose touch was a comfort to her. She had a singular warmth that quickly put new people at ease.

Phil watched her with pride and love—and with not a little envy of her easy sociability.

Eventually, still clinging to a dim hope that he could someday return to his old life, unable to fully accept the new one that they were offering him, Bob Padrakian said, "But we've lost everything. Everything. Fine, okay, I get a new name and brand-new ID, a past history that no one can shake. But where do we go from here? How do I make a living?"

"We'd like you to work with us," Phil said. "If you don't want that . . . then we can set you up in a new place, with start-up capital to get you back on your feet. You can live entirely outside of the resistance. We can even see that you get a decent job."

"But you'll never know peace again," Ron said, "because now you're aware that no one's safe in this brave new world order."

"It was your—and Jean's—terrific computer skills that got you into trouble with them," Phil said. "And skills like yours are what we can never get enough of."

Bob frowned. "What would we be doing—exactly?"

"Harassing them at every turn. Infiltrating their computers to learn who's on their hit lists. Pull those targeted people out of harm's way *before* the axe falls, whenever possible. Destroy illegal police files on innocent citizens who're guilty of nothing more than having strong opinions. There's a lot to do."

Bob glanced around at the motor home, at the two people working at VDTs in the living room. "You seem to be well organized and well financed. Is foreign money involved here?" He looked meaningfully at Ron Truman. "No matter what's happening in this country right now or for the foreseeable future, I still think of myself as an American, and I always will."

Dropping the British accent in favor of a Louisiana bayou drawl, Ron said, "I'm as American as crawfish pie, Bob." He switched to a heart-of-Virginia accent, "I can quote you any passage from the writings of Thomas Jefferson. I've memorized them all. A year and a half ago, I couldn't have quoted one sentence. Now his collected works are my bible."

"We get our financing by stealing from the thieves," Ellie told Bob. "Manipulate their computer records, transfer funds from them to us in a lot of ways you'll probably find ingenious. There's so much unaccounted slush in their bookkeeping that half the time they aren't even aware anything's been stolen from them."

"Stealing from thieves," Bob said. "What thieves?"

"Politicians. Government agencies with 'black funds' that they spend on secret projects."

The quick patter of four small feet signaled Killer's arrival from the back bedroom, where he had been napping. He squirmed under the table, startling Jean Padrakian, lashing everyone's legs with his tail. He pushed between the table and the booth, planting his forepaws on young Mark's lap.

The boy giggled delightedly as he was subjected to a vigorous face licking. "What's his name?"

"Killer," Ellie said.

Jean was worried. "He's not dangerous, is he?"

Phil and Ellie exchanged glances and smiles. He said, "Killer's our ambassador of goodwill. We've never had a diplomatic crisis since he graciously accepted the post."

For the past eighteen months, Killer had not looked himself. He wasn't tan and brown and white and black, as in the days when he had been Rocky, but entirely black. An incognito canine. Rover on the run. A mutt in masquerade. Fugitive furball. Phil had already decided that when he shaved off his beard (soon), they would also allow Killer's coat to change gradually back to its natural colors.

"Bob," Ron said, returning to the issue at hand, "we're living in a time when the highest of high technology makes it possible for a relative handful of totalitarians to subvert a democratic society and control large sections of its government, economy, and culture—with great subtlety. If they control too much of it for too long, unopposed, they'll get bolder. They'll want to control it all, every aspect of people's lives. And by the time the general public wakes up to what's happened, their ability to resist will have been leeched away. The forces marshaled against them will be unchallengeable."

"Then subtle control might be traded for the blatant exercise of raw power," Ellie said. "That's when they open the 'reeducation' camps to help us wayward souls learn the right path."

Bob stared at her in shock. "You don't really think it could ever happen here, something that extreme."

Instead of replying, Ellie met his eyes, until he had time to think about what outrageous injustices had already been committed against him and his family to bring them to this place at this time in their lives.

"Jesus," he whispered, and he gazed down thoughtfully at his folded hands on the table.

Jean looked at her son as the boy happily petted and scratched Killer, then glanced at Ellie's swollen stomach. "Bob, this is where we belong. This is our future. It's right. These people have hope, and we need hope badly." She turned to Ellie. "When's the baby due?"

"Two months."

"Boy or girl?"

"We're having a little girl."

"You picked a name for her yet?"

"Jennifer Corrine."

"That's pretty," Jean said.

Ellie smiled. "For Phil's mother and mine."

To Bob Padrakian, Phil said, "We *do* have hope. More than enough hope to have children and to get on with life even in the resistance. Because modern technology has its good side too. You know that. You love high technology as much as we do. The benefits to humanity far outweigh the problems. But there are always would-be Hitlers. So it's fallen to us to fight a new kind of war, one that more often uses knowledge than guns to fight battles."

"Though guns," Ron said, "sometimes have their place."

Bob considered Ellie's swollen belly, then turned to his wife. "You're sure?"

"They have hope," Jean said simply.

Her husband nodded. "Then this is the future."

∽

Later, on the brink of twilight, Phil and Ellie and Killer went for a walk on the beach.

The sun was huge, low, and red. It quickly sank out of sight beyond the western horizon.

To the east, over the Atlantic, the sky became deep and vast and purple-black, and the stars came out to allow sailors to chart courses on the otherwise strange sea.

Phil and Ellie talked of Jennifer Corrine and of all the hopes that they had for her, of shoes and ships and sealing wax, of cabbages and kings. They took turns throwing a ball, but Killer allowed no one to take turns chasing it.

Phil, who once had been Michael and the son of evil, who once had been Spencer and for so long imprisoned in one moment of a July night, put his arm around his wife's shoulders. Staring at the ever-shining stars, he knew that human lives were free of the chains of fate except in one regard: It was the human destiny to be free.

It darkles, (tinct, tint) all this our funanimal world.

—James Joyce, *Finnegans Wake*

AFTERWORD

No First Deputy Attorney General of the United States exists. I created Thomas Summerton's position in order not to embarrass any particular federal appointee.

The high-tech surveillance techniques in this story are real, not fictional. Enhancement of a highly magnified image shot from orbit would take longer than I allow for, but technology is swiftly catching up with fiction in that regard as well.

The technology exists to create a nuclear-powered laser weapon and to place it in orbit. It is purely speculation, however, that any world power has developed and deployed something like Godzilla.

The manipulation of data and the invasions of computer systems depicted in this story are all possible. For readability, however, I have simplified the technical details.

The asset-forfeiture laws under which Harris Descoteaux suffers are real. They are increasingly used against law-abiding citizens. For purposes of the story, slight liberties were taken with the manner in which the law applied to Harris and the pace at which his disaster unfolded. A recent decision by the Supreme Court, requiring a hearing prior to property seizure, is inadequate protection in a democracy. The hearing will take place before a judge who, if past practice is an indicator, will favor the government. Worse, there is still no requirement that proof be provided against the property owner or that he be charged with the commission of a crime.

The Branch Davidian compound in Waco, Texas, was a real place. It is fact that David Koresh regularly left the compound and could have been arrested in a conventional manner. Following the federal assault, cult members were found to have been armed, per capita, only half as heavily as the Texas population in general. It is also fact that before the assault, Texas Child Protective Services investigated claims of child abuse in the cult and found them baseless. However, it is speculation that the government hoped to use the Davidians as a test case to apply asset-forfeiture laws to religious groups.

Personally, I find the beliefs of the Branch Davidians peculiar and in some instances even repulsive. But I fail to see why their *beliefs* were all that was required to justify targeting them.

The type of criminal behavior by government agencies depicted in this novel does not spring entirely from my imagination. Paramilitary assaults against private citizens are a reality in our time.

One real-life event referred to in the story: Randy and Vicki Weaver, with son Sammy, moved to an isolated twenty-acre property in Idaho to escape the rat race and to practice a loosely held belief in white separatism. As separatists, they did *not* believe that people of any race should be persecuted or subjugated—but that the races should live apart from one another. Similar beliefs are held by some black religious sects as well. Though I believe people of such narrow views are woefully ignorant, the U.S. Constitution gives them the right to live separately as surely as it gives the Amish the right to live unto themselves, as long as they obey the law. The ATF and the FBI mistakenly concluded (for reasons still unclear) that Mr. Weaver was a white *supremacist* and dangerous. Agents repeatedly tried to entrap him, and ultimately he was charged with a technical violation of the gun laws. His order to appear for trial cited the date of March 20, although the trial was set for February 20. Federal prosecutors acknowledge that Mr. Weaver was improperly informed, yet when he was not in court on February 20, he was indicted for failure to appear.

In August 1992, federal agents armed with M16 machine guns, with laser scopes, laid siege to the Weaver property. Fourteen-year-old Sammy was shot in the back and killed by federal agents. Mrs. Weaver, standing in the doorway of her own home, holding ten-month-old Elisheba, was shot in the head and killed. The family dog was shot in the backside and killed as it tried to flee. Later, agents repeatedly ran over the dog's dead body with tanklike vehicles.

In July 1993, an Idaho jury found Mr. Weaver innocent of the murder of a U.S. Marshal (who died in the confrontation), innocent of conspiracy to provoke a confrontation with the government, and innocent of aiding and abetting murder. The jury was especially offended by the government's attempt to demonize the Weaver family as neo-Nazis, when in fact it was clear they held no such beliefs.

Gerry Spence, the defense attorney, later said: "A jury today has said that you can't kill somebody just because you wear a badge, and then cover up those homicides by prosecuting the innocent. What are we now going to do about the deaths of Vicki Weaver, a mother who was killed with a baby in her arms, and Sammy Weaver, a boy who was shot in the back? Somebody has to answer for those deaths."

As I write this, the federal government has avoided seeking real justice. If justice is ever served in this case, it will evidently be through the actions of the Boundary County Prosecutor in Idaho.

To preserve democracy, three things need to be done: (1) We must revoke all asset-forfeiture laws in their entirety. (2) The Congress must cease exempting its members from laws passed to govern the rest of us. (3) Congress must stop enacting laws that criminalize beliefs that are politically incorrect or unusual but that harm no one, for these are what George Orwell termed "thought crimes."

—Dean Koontz, April 1994

A NOTE ON THE TYPE

This book was set in Janson, a typeface long thought to have been made by the Dutchman Anton Janson, who was a practicing type-founder in Leipzig during the years 1668 to 1687. However, it has been conclusively demonstrated that these types are actually the work of Nicholas Kis (1650–1702), a Hungarian, who most proba-bly learned his trade from the master Dutch typefounder Dirk Voskens. The type is an excellent example of the influential and sturdy Dutch types that prevailed in England up to the time William Caslon (1692–1766) developed his own incomparable designs from them.

Composed by North Market Street Graphics,
Lancaster, Pennsylvania
Printed and bound by The Haddon Craftsmen,
Scranton, Pennsylvania
Designed by Virginia Tan